ALSO BY RICHARD LEIGH

Erceldoune & Other Stories

The Holy Blood and the Holy Grail
(with Henry Lincoln and Michael Baigent)

The Dead Sea Scrolls Deception
(with Michael Baigent)

The Messianic Legacy
(with Michael Baigent)

The Temple and the Lodge
(with Michael Baigent)

Secret Germany
(with Michael Baigent)

The Elixir and the Stone
(with Michael Baigent)

The Inquisition
(with Michael Baigent)

GREY MAGIC

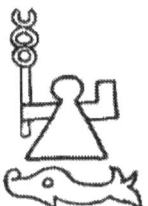

GREY MAGIC

RICHARD LEIGH

eGoetia Press

GREY MAGIC

Published in the United States of America
and the United Kingdom by eGoetia Press.
www.egoetia.com

FIRST PAPERBACK EDITION

ISBN: 978-0-6151-5937-9

Acknowledgement:
To Michael Maiden for single-handedly assuming the logistical burden of ushering this work into print.

Loin de cette douce val du lys,
La vanité s'évanouit.
Entre Déité et l'Homme,
Toi, Bergère,
La voie dévoile.

Il vit les longues tresses rubigineuses,
Chanter à faire pitié.
Qui ne veux pas qu'on
Sache ameuter
Les jeunes au jeûne.

-- Jehan l'Ascuiz (c.1418-c.1485)

for Roz
who launched me in 'this craft or sullen art',

and

for Sacha
whose luminous inspiration has sustained both me and my work during the last thirty years.

TETRAGRAMMATON
ANAPHAXETON

PREFACE

I first met Conor when he caught me one night spreading a carpet in the road for my lady to park on. He couldn't, of course, have divined either the chivalric or the pragmatic purpose of my action, and clearly assumed I was perpetrating a prank. I wasn't sure, without explaining more than I wished, how to disabuse him.

I'd discovered the principles of carpet-parking some years before, when I was teaching university in a Boston suburb. I occupied a ground-floor apartment about two hundred yards from the main campus and its parking facilities. In the States at that time, prior to the first traumatic drought of Arab oil and the advent of 55 mile per hour speed limits, one didn't walk two hundred yards when it was possible to drive, especially if one had a new car. I did – a sleek arctic-white German-made Capri, soon to become as banal in America as it already was in Britain, but, for the moment at least, an exotic novelty. Accordingly, I'd leave my parking space in the alley alongside my lodgings, speed the two hundred yards to campus in a minute or so and spend a quarter of an hour embroiled in the usual cutthroat struggle for the few available spaces in the departmental car park. In the meanwhile, some presumptuous interloper from further afield would usurp the space I'd vacated in the alley. When I returned, it'd prove impossible to find a berth. Irate at being thus dispossessed, I left ominous, official-sounding notes on windscreens, asserting the alley to be a private lane, reserved for occupants of the adjacent premises. Sometimes, this would work, but, with increasing frequency, some poacher would call my bluff. On one occasion, finding a trespassing vehicle unlocked, I pushed it out of the way, into the middle of the road, where it caused a tailback of half a mile and a pandemonium of braying horns sufficient to announce the Last Judgement. When the owner returned, he advanced on my car with a tyre-iron. I intercepted him, and only the ranks of gaping bystanders prevented the iron from being directed at me.

It was at this point that an overly domestic graduate student intervened, a recent divorcée with whom I was conducting a torpid flirtation. On her first visit to my apartment, some sort of misplaced maternal instinct was galvanised by – well, let's avoid the first word that comes to mind, 'squalor', and say the 'Spartan austerity' of my abode. I explained that I was only fastidious about seven things in the world - books, boots, cars, dogs, liquor, women and fountain pens, not necessarily in that order. I'd never been fastidious about my lodgings. Other people, I elaborated, chose to project their personalities into their homes. I didn't. My car, I said, indicating the white Capri visible through the window, was sufficient receptacle for such personality as I cared to project. Undeterred, she gave me a carpet.

It wasn't much of a gesture. The carpet in question, having filtered through various declensions of ownership, was redolent of cat piss and suggested the discarded toupée of a Frankenstein's monster. It was a tatty, ratty affair, disintegrating at the edges, patterned in buff and livid frostbite-blue except for a few ovoid discolorations which I ascribed to an incontinent pet, or perhaps someone's grievous misdeposit of vomit at a party. I didn't know what to do with the blasted thing. I certainly couldn't spread it on my floor without having it cleaned, and that seemed a consummately pointless waste of time, labour and money. I had no idea how or where carpets could be rehabilitated, assuming they could; and even if such a place existed, I'd have to trundle my ragged rug round to it in the car, thereby getting dust, grit, fibres and feline effluvia all over the maroon leather upholstery.

For a week, the carpet lay furled against the wall in the hall, unobtrusive except in the morning, when I'd invariably stumble over it en route to the bathroom. But then its donor, on an unsolicited visit, complained in chagrin at the continued nudity of the floor; and because I'm not always as ruthless as I'd like to be, I felt obliged to make a token show of enterprise. That night, when the alley was deserted, I spread the carpet out on the tarmac, immediately in front of my car. If anyone asked, I decided, I'd say I was 'airing it'. Not that that would've made any difference, but it would've attested, if only theoretically, to worthy intentions on my part.

The following day, I drove to campus as usual. It was raining with zest, and the sodden carpet, when I left, was more disgusting than before. At least, I reflected, the downpour might purge the cat piss. If I was lucky, the whole thing might liquefy, dissolve, flow quietly and painlessly away, fibre by fibre, down the streaming gutters. When I returned, my parking space had, of course, been hijacked. No one, however, had parked on the carpet in front of it. I had no hesitation about doing so myself, left the car there overnight and drove to campus again the next morning. On my return, the space occupied by the carpet was again vacant. I realised that I'd stumbled on a deep-rooted and largely undiscovered taboo in American society. One does not park on carpets.

For the duration of the term, until it finally and irrevocably disintegrated under my tyres, the carpet reserved my parking space. Alien cars would clog the road, the drive entrances, the alley, every available niche. Intruders would violate every parking prohibition in the Massachusetts book; but some unwritten rule, guaranteeing the sanctity of carpets, was scrupulously respected. Albeit ruefully, even the woman who'd inflicted the thing on me admitted it was better employed where it was than it would've been indoors. Other friends and colleagues agreed, and the white Capri on the carpet became enshrined in local folklore. Only one person ever confronted me about it directly, a lymphatic blonde exchange student from Sweden who'd tried to seduce me with a demented Marxist misinterpretation of 'The Lake Isle of Innisfree' as presage of Castro's Cuba. Plodding through the alley one morning with a green bookbag slung over her shoulder, she encountered me as I was leaving for campus.

"Would you mind if I asked you something?" she ventured. "Why do you park your car on a carpet?"

"Keeps my tyres clean," I replied.

As I drove away, I saw her in the rear-view mirror shaking her head mournfully - despairing, apparently, of ever fathoming the mysteries governing the American male's relationship to his car.

****

By the time I met Conor, I'd graduated from a seedy Boston suburb to a posh residential road in Hampstead's leafy purlieus, and - as a result of some lucrative hack work - from white Capri to black BMW. My new vehicle, however, didn't elicit the deference it should've done from drivers of lesser cars. My flat was around the corner from a major hospital and just north of London's regulated parking zones. From eight in the morning, a plague of commuters would descend like locusts, commandeering most of the available parking space, then catching the underground into the city. Visitors to the hospital, doctors, interns, student nurses in decrepit old bangers would wedge themselves into whatever interstices remained, ramming bumpers fore and aft, mashing grilles and pulverising taillights. Invariably, too, there were three or four skips along the road -- marking where the squats and mixed flats in some of the older, elegant but dilapidated Edwardian homes were being cobbled into 'townhouses' by buccaneering developers with limited companies in the Cayman Islands. Amidst the prevailing congestion, drivers seeking an unencumbered strip of kerb would circle like aircraft in a holding pattern. To move one's car during the day was tantamount to self-imposed exile. Seeking a berth on one's return fostered new frontiers in frustration and a morbid empathy with the Flying Dutchman.

There was, of course, no prospect of deploying a carpet. This wasn't a sequestered lane ending in a cul-de-sac, but a well-travelled thoroughfare overlooked by galleries of windows and voyeuristic eyes. Any carpet-laying on my part would've been witnessed by numerous nosy parkers both in and out of vehicles, and the ploy quickly sprung for what it was. A rug in the road was also bound to fall prey to the workmen in one of the houses, who would've plundered it, in a spasm of synthetic zeal, if only to make a skip look fuller. And inevitably, sooner or later, I would've had to deal with the police, whose local outpost was virtually around the corner and who patrolled the sidewalks at regular intervals, discernible from my windows like mobile inkpots sauntering beneath the festooned foliage. I sometimes wondered what the charge would be. Littering? Causing an obstruction? The penalties certainly wouldn't be severe, but I could hardly expect the carpet to be left unmolested.

I learned to adjust my schedule to the situation, contriving, if I had to go out during the day, to do so late in the afternoon. I'd time my return for five o'clock onwards. By that time, the hospital would be disgorging its personnel, the commuters would be draining homewards in their cavalcades towards *Brookside, Coronation Street* and Albert Square, and the patrons of the nearby pubs - who comprised the congestion's evening shift - wouldn't yet have begun to arrive. Once one adapted to the organic rhythm of the road, it became tolerable, if only just.

Unfortunately, such adaptation wasn't possible when my lady's daytime visits were involved. These weren't frequent. On the average of once a fortnight, she shunted between the 'official' residence on the outskirts of Belfast and a slightly more modest house in Holland Park. When at all possible, we'd rendezvous in the evening, and parking, whether we met at her premises or mine, wouldn't pose any major problems. Most of our daylight meetings were in her part of the city - at restaurants around Knightsbridge or Kensington if her husband were in town, at the Holland Park flat if he wasn't. I'd usually leave my car behind, endure the press and swelter of the underground and stop at one or another West End shop to add to my collection of fountain pens.

Once in a while, however - perhaps half a dozen times a year - the vicissitudes of my lady's schedule would dictate a daytime assignation at my place. She might, for example, just prior to gracing my dingy garret, have had a meeting, a conference or some other function in some outlying quarter of the city. She might be returning from a visit with her son, then at school in north London. She might have had business of some other kind that brought her into or near my vicinity. On such occasions, it would only have wasted time for both of us to make our respective ways back south of Hyde Park; and time - every incandescent minute we could filch from her fraught routines - would be as warming, as intoxicating and as precious as, say, a two-hundred-year-old cognac. But if time couldn't be wasted in travelling, neither could I let it be wasted in parking. Were I a demonic torture-master appointed to devise my own infernal sentence, it couldn't be worse than having to watch helplessly from my window while my lady circled the premises in quest of a parking space - slipping tantalisingly past on each orbit of the road, gliding within virtual touching distance for an instant, then vanishing again. Nor, on grounds of basic chivalry, as well as expediency, could I allow her to walk half a mile. She might, for instance, have been ambushed by Hampstead's notorious trick paving-stone, which, when one trod on the corner of it, tilted abruptly, catapulting the puddle it'd collected into one's shoe. To preclude such mishaps and indignities, and to maximise our moments together, drastic measures were required. I responded to the exigencies of the situation with, among other things, a carpet. Unlike its American predecessor, this one was fairly new, a furry black and golden-yellow, rather like the pelt of a Volkswagon-sized bumblebee.

Its effective deployment was a complicated manoeuvre, entailing intricate logistics, precise orchestration, meticulously calibrated choreography. The operation would commence a day and a half before my lady's expected arrival. Taking advantage of the road's nocturnal emptiness, I'd reserve the space immediately beneath my windows by moving my car onto it. That night, around midnight, after the pubs' clientele had reeled off into the darkness, I'd slink downstairs with the carpet, which, when off duty, reclined, furled and upended, against a wall in an alcove. I'd move my car from its space into the middle of the road, where it would wait with hazard lights flashing. Having spread the carpet in the space I'd just vacated, I'd then move the car to a new one nearby. As a further precaution, I'd anchor the carpet in position with a couple of flamboyant orange and white bollards, kept in my boot specifically for the purpose. As a final aesthetic flourish, I'd affix a large 'Wet Paint!' sign with luminous letters to one of them. (I'd thought of 'Quarantine!', or perhaps '*Achtung! Minen*!' with a skull and crossbones, then sternly curbed myself from such frivolity.)

Thus would my lady's parking space be reserved. I could retire complacently to the late-night antics of Kojak or Magnum on the box, secure in my provision for the morrow. Commuters arriving the following morning would find a segment of kerb effectively blockaded. The taboo proved as puissant in England as it had in the States. From my window, I'd see intruding cars accelerate down the long curve of the road, slow with screeching brakes, veer eagerly towards the apparent aperture, then swerve out again, the driver sometimes punching his dashboard in exasperation. (Even my lady, who should've been above such things, seemed to share the Western world's inhibition about parking on carpets. If, by some miracle, there *was* another opening available, she'd make for it, constricted though it might be. She'd stop, reverse, angle in, wrestle with the steering wheel, wrench her arms in their sockets, develop biceps, rather than avail herself of the preparations I'd devised in her honour.)

The whole apparatus - carpet, bollards, 'Wet Paint!' sign - also provoked some consternation among pedestrians. From my window, I'd watch them pause, stare, walk in perplexity all the way round the rug, look nervously at the housefronts, the workmen, the skips, the gutter, sometimes the trees, as if the wet paint in question might suddenly descend in a shower from the foliage.

****

I was, then, in process of mounting my ensemble one mid-May midnight when Conor happened upon me. He'd probably witnessed the whole mystifying (or antic) performance, from the moment I'd appeared at the door with the furled carpet under my arm. He might, at first, have taken me for a burglar. Who stole carpets? I was unaware of his presence until I'd moved the car from the all-strategic parking space, laid the carpet, relocated the car across the road, placed the bollards and was affixing the 'Wet Paint!' sign. Only then did I sense him watching me. Or perhaps, having stood motionless until then, he moved, shuffled, coughed, made some other sound or gesture that troubled the silence or the shadows. In any case, I turned to find him studying me with absorbed interest, no more than ten feet away, shrouded by a penumbra of overhanging boughs and the garden wall of the house next door. I promptly adopted my haughtiest demeanour - the demeanour of an eighteenth century aristocrat who catches a footman pilfering his linen - and glared back with a gaze calculated to wither the leaves from a tree. Responding to the challenge of my stare, he stepped forward into the urine-yellow efflorescence of the streetlamp. My initial impression was of a small, lithe, almost simian youth, twenty years old or so, with a triangular fox-shaped face and a floppy mop of tawny hair tumbling over his brow. The Belfast accent, too deep and gruff for his frail frame, was discernible even in the first words, as gutturally rough-hewn as if chiselled in coarse granite:

"It's a prank, is it? I like pranks."

Fleeting as the flicker of an eyelid, paranoia twitched at my mind. Something to do with Northern Ireland? With my lady? My lady's husband? A Provisional IRA operation of some kind? The *frisson* passed, leaving only an intensified alertness in its wake - an accentuated sensitivity to nuance, a preparedness to move instantly, as circumstances dictated, to sympathy or hostility. Ordinarily, I would've resented the intrusion, answered brusquely and curtailed any further dialogue. The accent, however, held my attention. I finished affixing the 'Wet Paint!' sign, stepped back to assess my handiwork, lit a cigarette and glanced round. No, I replied, it wasn't a prank. It had a practical purpose.

"It's as good as a prank, though," the youth observed. "I mean if ye're goin' to save a parkin' space, you might as well do it with a sense of humour. I like that."

"I'm gratified by your approval. You're a prankster, are you?"

"Well . . . " He looked a little disarmed, a little embarrassed, then grinned - a lopsided grin that tugged down one corner of his mouth. "Ye might say. Actually, I'm an artist. I paint. Pictures, ye know. But I've played some pranks in my time."

I was going to invoke Felix Krull, then guessed the allusion would be wasted.

"That augurs well for you," I drawled with offhand irony. "The artist and the criminal may be brothers under the skin, but so're the artist and the practical joker."

Conor beamed.

"D'ye think so?" he asked eagerly, his foxy face positively effulgent. "I like that! Christ, I like that! How exactly d'ye mean?"

"It'd take too long to explain now."

"Maybe we could have a drink some time and talk about it?"

"Yes, maybe."

"I just moved into a flat up the road. Last house but one from the end. Well, not a flat, really. A room. It's sort of a squat, ye know."

Again, a tremor - not exactly of suspicion, more of wariness -- crossed my mind. It might, I suppose, have crossed most people's. Only recently, a projected Provisional IRA bombing campaign in London had been thwarted, amidst a cascade of publicity. Police officers on television had urged the populace to remain vigilant, to note all transients or newcomers in their neighbourhoods, to report any untended packages, to keep alert for any 'unusual activity', whatever that might mean. By virtue of my lady's connections with the place, I had more of an interest in Northern Ireland than most people in mainland Britain, who preferred, generally, to imagine the Irish Sea merging into the Atlantic, with nothing in between. In consequence, I was more prone than most to images of IRA sleepers in squats, clandestine bomb factories, caches of concealed explosives and detonators.

"I thought they were renovating that place."

"They are. Not till September, though. Maybe not even then. Gives me a place for a few months, anyway. What d'ye do?"

"About what?"

"For a livin', I mean."

"I'm a writer."

"What d'ye write?"

"Books."

"What kind of books? Novels, I mean? Or other stuff?"

"Novels and other stuff."

"What kind of novels d'you write?"

A familiar question. I invariably found it irritating, but I'd long ago formulated a response, which I'd produce, like a rabbit conjured from a top hat, with combined sadistic and Socratic satisfaction:

"What kinds are there?"

"Well, there's science fiction . . . "

"No, I don't write science fiction."

"Crime stories? Detective stories?"

"No."

"Spy stories? Thrillers?"

Although perplexed, he was, I could see, enjoying the sparring, entering the game with zest.

"No."

"Not westerns?"

"Not westerns."

"Ghost stories?"

"No."

"Historical stuff!" he exclaimed triumphantly, one finger raised in the air.

"Not usually. If at all, only incidentally."

He looked crestfallen.

"Shit!" he muttered. "What's left?"

"Yes. Precisely."

"What?"

"What's left. My fiction probably comes into the category of what's left."

"What the fuck *is* left?" he asked, frowning, addressing the question more to the sidewalk than to me. Then some sort of penny dropped at he looked up with an awe so candid it disarmed me. "Ye mean . . . Literature?"

"Well, I'd like to think so," I replied, trying to keep a straight face.

"Ye mean you believe in . . . in Art?"

"I'm not sure you're supposed to believe in it or disbelieve in it. It's there. Either it matters to you or it doesn't. It does to me. You can ignore it if you want to, though. At your peril."

"That's what I meant!" Conor's head was nodding eagerly, his whole body quivering with excitement. He was shifting rapidly from one foot to the other, like a small boy needing to pee. "That's just what I meant! Especially the peril part of it!" He calmed down. Something occurred to him, and he flicked a furtive glance across the road at my car. "So ye make your livin' writin' Literature?"

"No," I replied dryly. "Literature's what makes me go tick-tick-tick. I have to write other things to make my living. To maintain my automotive standards, too."

"I hate that!" Conor snapped, suddenly rigid with indignation. "I hate the way people expect ye to be an artist in your spare time. They don't expect ye to be a brain surgeon in your spare time. Or a nuclear scientist. Or a dentist. Or even a fuckin' bank teller!"

I agreed perfunctorily, without sharing the emotional intensity of his *Weltschmerz*. Having known it myself at his age, I could now wax wearily and complacently cynical, and acknowledge – if not quite embrace – the way of the world with aplomb. By this time, too, I was anxious to get back inside. The conversation was veering in the direction of a prolonged session, the kind ideally lubricated by alcohol, and I had still to clean the flat for my lady's arrival. Between her visits, I'd allow it to fester peacefully. Then, in anticipation of her presence, it would undergo a transformation comparable to that of Clark Kent in a telephone booth. That transformation had last occurred some five weeks before. The rugs, since then, had become flecked with lint, grit, ground-in ashes, crumbs of spilled cereal that snapped, crackled and popped underfoot, shirt buttons gone AWOL, safety pins, toothpicks and assorted other débris, much of it too tenacious for my antediluvian Hoover. Most surfaces were furred with a fine mouse-grey film of dust. Baroque architectural edifices of tawny cigarette butts – pyramids, ziggurats, surrealistic cathedrals – reared themselves from the ashtrays. The mirror in the bathroom had somehow got spattered with toothpaste, and half a dozen bulging black rubbish sacks diffused a rancid effluvium through the kitchen. I had yet to minister to all this dereliction. The finishing touch would come tomorrow, when my ancient, jaded and fraying quilts were banished to the limbo of a wardrobe, and supplanted on the bed by a filmy valanced coverlet of flame-bright scarlet that might've done duty in the Hellfire Club.

Ostentatiously, I checked my watch, claimed to be expecting a telephone call from the States. With a vague non-committal promise to join him some time for a drink, I then disengaged myself from Conor. For the next three hours – I wouldn't normally retire to bed until four – I addressed myself to the task of civilising my premises. By the following day, I'd forgotten about the nocturnal encounter. It could, after all, hardly compete for precedence with my lady's imminent arrival.

****

During the ensuing fortnight, Conor no more than grazed my mind. Then, at the beginning of June, he hailed me in the road as I was returning from my daily sortie to the shops.

"What about that drink? Ye wouldn't be free this evenin', would ye?"

I had no particular desire for youthful protégés, and the discrepancy in our ages, as well, probably, as in our experience, didn't augur well for friendship. On the other hand, summer ennui was looming, and lethargy with it. My lady was away. I wasn't engaged in any specific literary projects. Most of my friends were either preparing for holidays or busily murdering their marriages. Why not? Yes, I was free, I replied, and we agreed to meet at eight in the pub around the corner.

In the course of that evening's progressively more besotted conversation, I learned something of Conor's background. Perhaps surprisingly, he was an only child. His parents – both lapsed Catholics and veterans of the moribund mid-seventies Peace Movement – lived in the Falls, where his father ran a chemist's shop. Conor himself dispelled any residual suspicions I might've harboured about his political allegiances. He displayed a virulent scorn towards any and all politics – an attitude I could only find sane, healthy and congenial. In vocation and orientation, he was precisely what he'd declared himself to be - an artist, if only in embryo, and a practical joker. He was also, it transpired, a grievously smitten swain, devoted with near-idolatrous adoration to a girl named Moira. Contrary to the usual pattern in such cases, his ardour, apparently, was reciprocated. They were, it seemed, lovers, if just on weekends. She'd studied medicine at university, he told me proudly, and was now working as an intern at the hospital. Tonight, she was on the late shift, which left him free to go tippling with me. Ordinarily, she'd join him when she finished work and they'd have dinner together, after which she'd retire to the flat she shared with two other girls, a few miles away in Bloomsbury.

"She supports you while you paint?" I asked.

Conor went rigid with outrage, his eyes flashing. He would *not* take money from the woman he loved, he stated stiffly, haughtily. On the other hand, he added, relaxing again and chuckling mischievously, he didn't mind collecting dole and moonlighting on the side - the odd layout for a small advertising agency, the odd poster or graphic design. He had hopes of a lucrative commission shortly, to devise and produce the signboard for a pub. If it came out well, it could lead to other such jobs. Most importantly, however, someone - a 'certain person', he said cryptically - had bought one of his paintings. This had financed his transplantation to London and kept him afloat until now.

Guessing from my accent that I'd migrated from the States, he asked how long I'd lived in London, and I told him. Apart from that, I said as little as possible, letting him talk, allowing him to feed my interest in everything pertaining to Northern Ireland. Eventually, however, he began to probe me on the relationship I'd mentioned between the artist and the practical joker. I expatiated briefly, citing some cultural examples and dictated a reading list that culminated with *Pale Fire* and *62: A Model Kit*. He transcribed it conscientiously (using a cheap ballpoint) and slipped it carefully into his wallet, then proceeded to regale me with some of his own more successful pranks. There were, for example, the pats of butter.

"Ye know the kind. Wrapped in foil. Ye get 'em at crappy restaurants and places like that. They used to dish 'em out in the refectory at school. And there was also, in the refectory, these long thin lights in the ceilin'. Neon tubes. I forget what ye call 'em . . . "

"Fluorescent lights, in the States."

"Maybe. Whatever. Anyways, what ye had to do was wait until ye'd just about finished your meal. Until ye were just about to leave the table. And then the trick was to take a pat or two of butter, and flip it up - this was where the skill came in - flip it up so's it stuck to the light in the ceilin'. And then ye'd just get up and go away, like any ordinary decent person. And someone else'd come and take your seat. And he'd be sittin' there only a minute or two before the butter'd start to melt and drip down on him, as if the ceilin', ye know, was pissin' . . ."

There were also the Polo mints.

"Or any other round hard sweet like that. Ye'd use them in school assemblies, when some big cheese - a bishop or somethin' - would come to bore the shit out of everyone. It was a long hall with a slopin' floor and a stage with a lectern at the front, and ye'd make sure to sit way at the back. And then, just when the silence was getting' all solemn and respectful and the speaker was hittin' his stride, ye'd set the mint rollin' down the aisle. Ye wouldn't hear it at first, but then it'd get louder and louder and faster and faster until it smashed into the stage at his feet. Ye know - whirr, whirr, Whirr, Whirr, WHIRR, WHIRR, WHIRR, CLACK!"

In his imitation of a runaway Polo mint, Conor was now yelling. He didn't realise it until the couple at the next table looked round in frumpy disapprobation. Unembarrassed, he grinned at them, raised his glass in tipsy salute and turned back to me. There were also, he went on, the coins he'd epoxied to the pavement and watched passersby scrabble to pick up.

"Only trouble was, ye'd have to stand around with your foot on the thing, waitin' for the epoxy to dry. A couple of times, when it was cold, I near froze my balls off. And once an RUC patrol stopped and asked me what I was doin'. They thought I was loiterin'. Or maybe worse. What was I supposed to say to them? 'No sir, I'm not loiterin'. I'm just waitin' for the epoxy to dry on this coin under my foot'? They grilled me for maybe fifteen minutes before they moved on. In the meantime, some of the epoxy'd squished out from under the coin and stuck my shoe to the sidewalk. When I pulled it, the whole fuckin' sole came away."

Having listened patiently until now, I decided to confer on him the benefit of my copious experience in such matters.

"You cover the coin with a plastic dog turd. The kind you get in joke shops. You could even use a real turd, I suppose, if you were desperate enough. It wouldn't necessarily have to be canine either."

Conor's mouth fell open on its hinges and his eyes widened in dawning recognition of soul-kinship.

"Ye've done this kind of thing, too, haven't ye?"

I confessed that, yes, I, too, had a certain propensity for antic mischief. Before he could reply, I held up one finger, enjoining patience and silence, then pointed to the salt cellar and the pepper shaker still left on the table from lunch. Conor looked at them enquiringly, then at me.

"Give me the serviette on the floor behind you."

Conor did so and watched, fascinated, while I tore a ragged circle, about two inches in diameter, out of the serviette. I unscrewed the cap of the salt cellar, spread the fragment of serviette over the open neck, poured an anthill of pepper onto the flat paper surface and screwed the cap back on. I then trimmed away any white fringes of paper that protruded. Conor picked up what appeared to be a perfectly innocent salt cellar, but when he turned it over and sprinkled it into his hand, it rained pepper.

"Holy Christ!" he exclaimed in a reverently hushed whisper, as impressed as if I'd performed an alchemical transmutation before his eyes. "That's amazin'! That's fuckin' amazin'! D'ye have any more?"

We were falling, I realised, into a weird species of master-disciple relationship. Did I want to become his mentor and guru in practical jokes? Ordinarily, I'd probably have recoiled from such a rôle, but we'd both, by then, drunk enough for it not to matter. Besides, practical joking had always been one sphere in which I'd welcomed protégés. I'd already corrupted the son of some old friends in the States, and would happily have drilled an élite cadre - a kind of SAS - of pranksters. The world would be none the poorer for having some of its more bowel-gripping solemnities injected with a serum of fun, some of its more pompous self-important conventions unsprocketed. If dyspeptic grouches such as Cromwell, Robespierre and Lenin had had a sense of humour, we might all be a bit more sane.

I therefore produced for Conor a few piquant selections from my own repertoire. I told him, for example, of the British Columbia Foundation for Lycanthropic Children, which, while living in Vancouver some fifteen years before, I'd managed to get featured on the six o'clock television news - Canadian television's reply to the BBC's famous spaghetti harvest. I also told him of a *jeu d'esprit* which had assumed quasi-legendary status in the publishing business - Phil Trillop's first trip to London.

Phil and I were old friends, having been undergraduates together in the Boston area. Subsequently, he'd risen from dogsbody to a senior position with a prestigious American publishing firm - and was all the more in need, therefore, of someone to take the mickey out of him. For twenty years, he'd been the patient, tolerant, ruefully resigned, long-suffering butt of my japes and insults. Indeed, he naïvely fancied himself inured to them until his company despatched him to London some five years before. He'd never previously been abroad, and would, I knew, epitomise the archetypal gauche and gullible American.

The day before Phil's scheduled arrival, I had a woman I knew prepare a salad. It was a noxious-looking concoction - segments of raw potato cut like sectioned apple, leaves of brown-stained lettuce, shreds of anaemic cabbage, shavings of desiccated carrot, a few pebbly beans, a rancid radish in the middle, all of it on a paper plate and covered with clear plastic food wrap. We then drove round to the hotel in which Phil was booked for the following morning. Here, my co-conspirator, dressed to look exceedingly prim and secretarial, brought her vegetable collage to the desk. She was, she explained, from Mr Trillop's London office. The gentleman liked his salads. Might the staff arrange to have this one waiting in his room for him when he arrived? The staff were happy to comply.

The next morning, I drove round to the hotel again. I found Phil - woozy and grumpy with jet-lag - poking perplexedly at a wedge of peeled potato. He licked it warily, then grimaced. What the hell was this all about? he wanted to know. I explained that it was a long-standing tradition in British hotels, one of those quaint national eccentricities - a British equivalent, so to speak, of 'Have a nice day'. Wherever one booked a room in England, one would find a salad waiting. It was pretty much *de rigeur* to eat the thing and compliment the staff afterwards. If one didn't, one would find them just a little less gracious in dispensing the amenities that alleviated the strain of travel - providing room service, obtaining the newspapers one desired, shining shoes, making prompt alarm calls, procuring taxis and clap-free prostitutes.

I poured myself a drink from Phil's liquor cabinet while he spent five minutes patiently flushing the foul fare, item by item, down the loo. On our way through the lobby, his mouth in a rictus of a smile, he commended the ovoid-shaped porter on the hotel's superb salads. The porter blinked, twitched his head as if to shake water out of his ear and nodded gravely. I could feel his stare boring into our backs. Out in the road, I confessed and Phil launched into a miniature tantrum.

"You bastard! That's why they've been giving these weird looks every time I pass. They must think I'm some kind of vegetarian kook or something!"

"Vegetarian cook?"

"Vegetarian kook! Vegetarian nut! Crank! You prick!"

I'd effectively established a leitmotif for the duration of Phil's sojourn. When he visited my publisher in Bedford Square, a petite secretary popped briskly out of a broom closet, like a cuckoo out of a clock, and presented him with a salad. He'd braced himself for a salad when he visited my agent, but didn't receive one initially and believed, with touching credulity, that he'd escaped. As he emerged from her premises, however, which were being repainted at the time, an inordinately large black workman swung down from the scaffolding, Tarzan-like, and presented him with another vegetal aberration. I arranged for Phil's wife to have a salad ready for him on his return to Boston. She, for her part, ensured that one was placed in his office as well.

But salads were only one component of the blitz that assailed him in London. I gleefully glutted his paranoia and staged so many additional happenings that I was soon credited with those I'd *not* staged. One afternoon, for example, a demented virago swanned into the hotel lobby, buttonholed Phil and half a dozen other hapless bysitters, proclaimed herself the reincarnation of Anne Boleyn and embarked on a twenty-minute harangue about Henry VIII's connubial turpitudes. She had nothing to do with me. I knew nothing about her, but there was no way of convincing Phil that she wasn't one of my agents. Had he been in town for much longer, I probably could've claimed responsibility for late cabs, traffic jams, the shock he got from a maverick electric razor, perhaps even the weather. It conduced to a feeling of omnipotence. Thus does one attain a semblance of godhood.

My *pièce de résistance* - and *coup de grâce* - was enacted at a French restaurant off Oxford Street, where Phil and I had gone for a lavish dinner on his expense account. Just as the waiter handed us our menus, two chic, elegant young *grandes dames* entered, deep in conversation, and glided to a table in the rear. In accordance with his wont, Phil ogled them and dropped some characteristically salacious remark, then immersed himself in the menu. Just after the waiter had brought our appetisers, the two ladies, apparently having changed their minds about the place, got up from their seats and drifted back towards the door, still conversing volubly. As they passed our table, one of them paused and asked, in a languid drawl, if I had a light for her cigar. Phil looked up quizzically but dared not say anything - cigars, for all he knew, might be the current fashion among London's more stylish women, and he couldn't risk betraying himself as a bumpkin. I produced my lighter. Cigar extended, the lady leaned over the table and, as she did so, contrived to drop her pearl bracelet with a splash into Phil's vichyssoise. Unperturbed, she exhaled a puff of smoke, shrugged disdainfully and glanced down at the soup-soaked pearls and publisher.

"Oh, do keep them," she drawled and, along with her companion, glided out of the restaurant.

By the time Phil's slack tongue and jaw regained mobility, the two women had gone and the waiters, clustered around the cash register, were gibbering away hysterically. It was, one of them confided, the most dramatic event to have occurred all month. In the meantime, comprehension had slowly suffused Phil's face. He glowered at me and said evenly, through clenched teeth:

"You set that up!

****

At the climax of my narrative, Conor spluttered into his beer and began to choke, turning an apoplectic red. At first, I thought it was mere histrionic effect, then realised he was indeed asphyxiating. It took half a dozen solid thumps on the back to restore him, after which he slumped limply in his chair, gasps and wheezes alternating with renewed spasms of laughter.

As we emerged into the June night, however, he turned thoughtful, even sombre.

"Ye never really hurt anyone with your pranks, do ye?"

No, I replied. Part of the art lay in making my pranks conform to my own chivalric code. I would readily embarrass my victims, but not humiliate them, still less hurt them.

"It'd be so easy to hurt someone, ye know," Conor mused.

Of course, I replied. The mechanism and dynamics of the practical joke could only too easily be turned to more serious, even sinister, purposes. I was about to cite some of the tactics whereby the Provisional IRA, in the early seventies, had systematically alienated the Catholic population of Northern Ireland from the British soldiers sent specifically to protect them. Then I curbed myself, at least until I knew somewhat more precisely where Conor stood on such matters. It was sobering to reflect that he, in those days, could hardly have been much more than an infant. Given his background, did he even know there was a time when British troops were welcomed in the Falls as saviours - and that only an ingenious campaign of psychological manipulation and deadly 'practical jokes' had transformed them into enemies?

"Could ye imagine yourself usin' a prank to hurt someone?"

Yes, I replied. Certainly. If someone genuinely crossed me. If someone harmed or affronted my lady. Were I required to fight a 'war' in any sort of earnest, I'd much prefer to fight it by so-called 'dirty tricks', even downright filthy tricks, than by violence. I could also accommodate myself to the possibility that a 'dirty trick' might lead to violence - preferably directed, of course, against my adversary.

Conor nodded approvingly.

"I hurt someone once with a prank," he said grimly. "Well, sort of a prank. I didn't think of it as a prank at the time. It was just my only way of fightin' back. Mind you, the bastard I hurt had it comin' to him."

I didn't hear the story then, however. It was only in the course of three subsequent meetings during the next five weeks that the drama unfolded for me.

"Ye might want to write about it sometime," Conor offered on one occasion, obviously relishing the prospect of being immortalised in print.

"It was your experience. Why don't you write it?"

Conor shook his head.

"I'm a painter. I don't have the words. Ye do. Ye could tell it like it was a novel or somethin'. An' besides, it sort of got me involved in politics. I don't think artists should be involved in politics.'

'Neither do I,' I replied.

I had, I added, expended a good deal of effort over the years trying to remain disengaged from politics. I'd tried to maintain that art was above politics. I'd tried to straddle a fence that enabled me to see and assess all points of view; and whoever attempted to knock me off my fence became, automatically, the enemy. Needless to say, my self-arrogated stance hadn't always been sustainable. Despite my wishes, there'd been certain occasions on which I'd been knocked off my fence; and what had previously been detached opinion on my part had become *engagé* commitment - commitment that prompted me no longer to observe and bear witness, but to *act*. Conor, not surprisingly, wanted me to recount something of these instances. During the weeks that followed, I proceeded to do so. In the meantime, I devoted a number of vacant evenings to brooding over my endeavours to hold politics at bay, and the periodic failures, sometimes ignominious, of these endeavours.

Yes, there had been at least three occasions on which, usually through ulterior motives, I'd been converted from opinion to commitment, from passivity to action. When I'd acted, however, I'd always attempted to do so in my own specific fashion. I'd attempted to act in a fashion that circumvented violence in favour of the practical joke, of the political dirty trick, of the action itself as an artistic 'happening', of dexterous psychological manipulation - all of which amounted for me to forms of magic.

I

Humanity in general consists of a few black magicians, a few white magicians and a great many victims. So I explained to Conor, a youth from Belfast, whom I'd met in London one evening. I was speaking of magic, I went on, in its broadest sense - as a metaphor for the manipulation of reality. Or, at least, of so-called reality. Black magicians attempt to control reality from a vantage point ostensibly outside it - from a vantage point confined entirely to their own psyches. They endeavour to handle reality as if with tongs. White magicians attempt to guide reality from within - becoming so intrinsically part of the moment, the situation, the relationship or whatever else is being manipulated that when they move, it moves with them. Victims remain passive, at the mercy of reality.

If church leaders and other public figures were asked, they'd probably reply, with brazen hypocrisy, that Western civilisation encouraged one to a Kempisesque imitation of Christ. I refused to partake of such hypocrisy. From the time I became sentient and then literate, I'd aspired to an imitation of Faust. And there was at least one occasion when, in my aspiration to Fausthood, I'd invoked 'black magic' of a more traditional kind.

In the mid-'60s, I was nominally enrolled in the M.A. programme at the University of Chicago, enclave of cloned dreaming spires like a medieval walled town, located improbably at the very centre of a black ghetto. Around the campus, a circular road, the Midway, pointlessly mimicked a moat. I found the place - both the school and the city - inimical. The school, in its orientation towards literature at any rate, was rabidly Aristotelian. Even more perversely, it was proud of being so. Within a week of my arrival, I was accused of Platonism, the most grievously heretical aberration in the department's jargon-ridden critical lexicon; and for the duration of my tenure there, we - the department and I - jousted with each other from diametrically antithetical poles of Greek philosophy. Not that I accepted the label they sought to foist on me. Goaded to cheerful iconoclasm, I declared myself an 'antinomian hermetic numinist', and derived, until the rôle became boring, a measure of fiendish glee from playing *enfant terrible*. Linear minds are easily flummoxed by the discourse of mystical paradox. On my papers and in classes, I revelled in such paradox, discreetly seasoned with technical terms from Vedantic metaphysics and Buddhist epistemology.

'You do this deliberately, don't you?' one harried professor complained to me querulously. 'You keep all this stuff up your sleeve and then you spring it on us. You know we're not equipped to assess it.'

As for the city, it seemed to me a species of sinister impersonal dynamo, a mechanised Moloch gorging with routinised insentience on human lives. Most of the world's great cities are washed by rivers or the sea. Chicago, with symbolic appropriateness, is situated on a stagnant body of water. Most of the world's great cities have some sort of aesthetic *raison d'être*. One visits London, Paris, Florence, Munich, Vienna, Petersburg - one even visits New York, Boston, New Orleans, San Francisco, Montreal - in order simply to *be* there, to imbibe a unique quality of culture and atmosphere, to experience the pleasures of a particular ambience. I can't imagine anyone in command of his faculties wanting to visit Chicago for any reason at all, except perhaps to make money or escape the monochrome hinterlands of Iowa, Kansas and Nebraska. Certainly the place wouldn't spontaneously leap to mind as one of the globe's - or even America's - more festive, scintillating or picturesque tourist attractions. Walt Disney wouldn't have chosen it as the site for a theme park. In London, blue plaques on house fronts denote the former residences of illustrious figures in politics, the sciences and the arts. Chicago's most famous celebrity is probably Capone.

Although supposedly a graduate student, I was in reality a sort of semi-housebroken bohemian, denizen of a somewhat equivocal and ill-defined class sandwiched somewhere between the upper derelict, or upper wastrel, and the lower sub-reputable. As a native of America's East Coast, I'd previously frequented the quasi-artistic underworlds of Boston and New York. Both had been essentially gentle, essentially civilised domains, slovenly perhaps, yet still cultivated. An orientation towards aestheticism prevailed. Education enjoyed a degree of currency rare in American society. Poetry, films, folk music, the coffee house circuit imparted a modicum of sensitivity; and whatever destructiveness lurked beneath the surface was usually self-directed. Marijuana and hashish fostered a dreamy narcoleptic ineffectuality, but no one particularly cared to be effectual anyway.

The sub-culture amid which I found myself in Chicago was appreciably different. It was a loutish and brutish milieu, violent, ruthless, oblivious to the arts, scornful of education. It was also eminently practical. With a brisk callous-souled efficiency, people got things done, made things happen. Unlike the cocooned and insulated underworlds of the East Coast, Chicago's, by an intricate cat's-cradle of relationships, was linked to the Black Power movement, to organised crime, to the municipal administration and the police. Routine exchanges of cash or favours readily purchased the protection of professional hit-men or the city's boys in blue - a horde of maniacally trigger-happy oafs who, between bribes, immured themselves in fantasies of Dodge City, Deadwood and Tombstone, swaggering about with a regulation .38 on one hip and a pearl-handled .45 reversed, Wild Bill Hickok-fashion, on the other. In the Boston and New York bars I'd patronised, drugs changed hands over the counter. In Chicago, the box or package sliding furtively between bartender and customer was more likely to contain a Beretta, a Walther PPK or some other such precision-crafted toy. In Boston and New York, the faces reflected in the mirror above the bar usually belonged to university drop-outs with dope-gutted delusions of artistic grandeur - poets *manqués* or *maudits* or both, aspiring absurdist dramatists, would-be song writers, escapee characters from Pirandello in search of a play, a diluted Baez or Dylan clone torturing a guitar in a corner. In Chicago, the faces were those of pimps, enforcers, syndicate soldiers, ex-convicts and parolees, latter day bootleggers in every conceivable contraband commodity, cash-and-carry killers. With what I'd previously spent on the East Coast for a three-month supply of cannabis, one could, in a casual over-the-table Chicago transaction, contract to have a person tastefully murdered and eternalised as a pillar of saltlike cement under the Dan Ryan Expressway.

In these picturesque subterranean realms, there was, needless to say, a primitive sense of humour and none whatever of irony. At my local - a pseudo-English pub called Reggie's - one of the bartenders was an impish youth named Willy. For some time, Willy had nursed a grudge against his brother-in-law - a baby-faced Transit Authority patrolman, Horst Wessel lookalike and psychopath named Al Hollis, with whom I myself was then contending for the affections of a particular woman. One evening, before polluting the bar with his presence, Hollis was seen depositing his wash at the laundramat across the road. By prearranged plan, someone at Reggie's then got him talking about the hazards of keeping the trains safe for democracy - or perhaps running on time. While he was thus engaged, Willy stole out to the laundramat and emptied a large bag of popcorn into his machine. On discovering the mess, Hollis wasn't amused, stormed back into the bar, swung at Willy, missed and cracked a mirror. Returning to the laundramat, he then transferred his clothes, complete with soggy popcorn, to a drier - into which Willy, stealing across the road again, poured a five-pound sack of ice-cubes.

There ensued a Keystone Cop chase, Willy dashing through the front door, along the central aisle, up the rear stairs and out the fire exit, with Hollis in rubicund-faced pursuit. Amidst the general hilarity of the clientele, they made three circuits of the premises. At last, Hollis, doubling back on his tracks, entered the south end of the alley beside the bar just as Willy entered it from the north. For a moment, the two of them stood there, breathless, face to face, across a distance of some twenty yards. Gasping and laughing, Willy tried to apologise. Hollis yanked out his pearl-butted .45 and started blasting away as if at the OK Corral. He managed to loose off four rounds before someone, tragically wasting good cognac, pulverised a Courvoisier bottle over his skull. In the bar half an hour later, reeking of brandy and still leaking blood from the gash in his cropped scalp, he protested indignantly that he'd been aiming well above Willy's head. In fact, as several of us ascertained, Willy owed his escape, and probably his life, not to any such magnanimity, but simply to inept marksmanship. The bullet holes in the wooden fence behind him were too far to the left of their intended target, but all at stomach, chest or head level.

By the time that incident occurred, I'd been in Chicago for a year and a half; I'd learned basic survival techniques, had improved on some of them, had acquired my own repertoire of reckless escapades and could find my way around like a veteran, moving with at least a show of confidence and impunity. I'd also pretty much mastered the often grotesque macho codes of etiquette that obtained - the nuances of slang, diction, address, demeanour and comportment that distinguished the prospective victim or muggee from the stud, dude, cat or other genus with whom it was imprudent to mess. During the two years I spent in the city, it was rather as if my life's itinerary, by virtue of a landslide or washed-out bridge somewhere on the planned main route, had been diverted through a swamp or a quagmire. There was no point in panicking, backtracking or trying to scramble to supposed safety, but neither could one afford to let oneself be sucked down into the quicksand below. The trick was to keep moving with one's head above the surface of the bog, while savouring the exotic Baudelairesque splendour of the local fauna and flora. They offered a signally more stimulating education than graduate school.

In the beginning, however, fresh from the very different sub-cultures of the East Coast, I felt painfully disoriented and vulnerable. My vulnerability was accentuated by the tenuousness of my contact with the university. I participated in the M.A. programme only insofar as the requirements for my degree dictated; I made few friends among my arid, desiccated, overly cerebral fellow students and professors; I found their rarefied and sanitised reality a sham compared to the one amidst which I found myself. For the most part, my existence orbited around the bar, whose habitués might have been unsavoury, but couldn't, at any rate, be described as Aristotelian. Some of them, indeed, were not only more antinomian, but also more hermetic and numinist than they themselves would ever know.

This was particularly true of Nina, the bar's svelte head waitress, my affair with whom brought me into progressively abrasive contact with the morally handicapped Al Hollis. In many respects, it was a classical, even archetypal, liaison between aspiring young writer and seasoned, mature older woman. I was twenty-two at the time, Nina ten years older - blonde and willowy, with a fragile masklike cover-girl face that belied her brusque, tough, no-nonsense, unromantic manner and gritty gangster's moll accent. She lived above Reggie's, with three children and two ageing parents, her mother suffering from arthritis, her father from some unspecified illness that bore a suspicious resemblance to delirium tremens. Her husband, whom she'd married at sixteen, had caromed in and out of jail and finally disappeared over the Wisconsin border some six years before, with State Police in hot pursuit. For some reason, she was evasive about the precise nature of his crimes; I never learned what they were. In fact, there were a number of things I never learned about her, whole spheres of unexplained reticence pertaining to her past. Today, I sometimes realise with bewilderment how few factual details of her background I actually knew. She still, however, occupies a luminous niche in my memory, something like an icon. Beneath her hard-boiled exterior - a prerequisite for survival - she was one of the most generous, most sensitive, most truly extraordinary women I've ever met. She was also one of the most courageous, most gifted and most tragic. Compared to Nina, the girls at the university were vapid - typical academic bimbettes, the contents of whose heads could've been exchanged for the contents of a pie with no discernible difference. Far more than they, Nina deserved the alleged benefits of American 'higher education' - the freedom, the mobility, the prospects, the opportunities and possibilities it theoretically confers. Instead, she'd been confined, with no hope of remission or parole, to the Chicago slums in which she'd been born and raised. She'd never travelled, never seen the mountains or the sea, never been granted a respite from the degrading, gruelling and soul-stifling task of providing for her dependents. Her life was effectively a cage, its bars formed by the shafts of soot-soiled sunlight sifting down through the tracks and girders of the elevated railway. When I think of her now, her existence seems to me a poignant wisp of muted music woven mysteriously into the bleak fabric of an icy Chicago day.

In the first weeks of our relationship, however, her streetwise shrewdness and savvy put me to shame. For Nina to shepherd me around the city, prompt me, teach me the ropes and thus expose my greenness was a galling affront to my male ego. In the past, on the East Coast, I'd habitually play (or try to play) knight errant, paladin and protector to my women; I'd even revelled in the rôle, eagerly seeking some persecutor - dragon, sinister sorcerer or husband - to quell. I can recall only one occasion when Nina was ever cast as a damsel in distress requiring rescue. She rescued herself with a panache and finesse I couldn't have equalled, and my attempt to help proved not just superfluous, but ignominious as well.

For a fortnight or so previously, she'd been pestered by a seemingly lobotomised would-be beau named Alfredo - squat, surly, with sleekly lubricated hair and jowls grizzled a perpetual dingy blue-grey. When Hollis or I happened to be around, Alfredo kept his distance, like a mangy cur. One night, however, Hollis was riding the rails, probably seeking some black youth, reluctant briber or potentially subversive stray dog to bludgeon or shoot. Suffering from an embryonic flu, I'd taken myself and my virus-in-residence home early, leaving Nina at the bar alone to finish her night shift. At two in the morning, she was climbing the stairs to my apartment when Alfredo ambushed her on the landing and waxed alcoholically importunate. In the slugfest that ensued, she fought back like a rabid Valkyrie. By the time the noise had dredged me out of bed, Alfredo was in full flight with a minced nose, two teeth left on the carpet in his wake. Mortified by my missed opportunity, I plunged down the stairwell in pursuit, clad at full gallop in unzipped jeans, contortedly misbuttoned shirt and one boot on the wrong foot. I attained the ground floor at a squalidly inglorious tumble, only to find Alfredo gone and the door to the cellar ajar. Stalking my quarry there, I descended into the darkness, hunting-knife brandished in one hand, lighter flaring in the other and casting a flickering flame-haze over the damp, uninhabited dungeon - uninhabited save for a traumatised-looking rat, which skittered into the shadows at my approach. I surfaced from the depths, knife still poised, to find the lobby swarming with police, who arrested me and confiscated my weapon.

'If you'd stabbed him, you could've been in trouble,' one officer stated superfluously, when I'd finally convinced them of my lofty intentions and persuaded them to release me.

'Love is a many-splendoured thing,' I grumbled, with what I realised was imperfect relevance.

Love, or what passed for it, was, in fact, so many-splendoured that it prompted me, one night, to drag Nina to a university demonstration. I had, needless to say, an ulterior motive, of which I was more or less aware. It was, of course, a juvenile but typically masculine need to overcompensate - to initiate my paramour into *my* world, to show her there were realms wider and deeper and vaster than her own, realms in which I presided with magisterial authority, functioned as Thoth-like gatekeeper and psychopomp. Unfortunately, I wasn't sure how to get to those realms from Chicago, especially with Nina in tow. It wasn't a city that offered much direct access to the sublime. I could, I suppose, have dragooned her into attending one or another class with me. There, for her pleasure, edification or (more likely) mystification, I could've demolished the Aristotelian wimps and swots around me. That seemed pretty puerile, however; and Nina, in any case, through no fault of her own, couldn't have appreciated the fine points of the aesthetic tourneys I'd tilt in her honour. Somewhere in Chicago at the time, there must've been at least one bohemian coffeehouse, one haunt of folk singers and musicians, one venue where literature was read and discussed by people who enjoyed Yeats for his poetry rather than for his use of the caesura. But if such places existed, I had no idea how to locate them, and neither, naturally, did Nina. In the absence of anything better, a demonstration would have to do.

I hadn't often attended demonstrations on the East Coast. If anything I was somewhat scornful of them. My vanity inhibited me from becoming just another body on a march or picket line, from doing something any yokel could do as effectively as I could. If I participated at all, it was, as a rule, in some highly individualised capacity - some administrative or organisational rôle which only I could perform, which depended on my resources of imagination, prose or oratory. I was prepared to contribute, but insisted, egocentrically, that my contribution somehow be unique, somehow distinctively my own. For all my aloofness, however, I wasn't wholly immune to the psychic contagion generated by the mass protests of those days. On occasion, I'd allowed myself to be infected by it and hitched a ride on the *Zeitgeist*. It was, after all, a stirring time. The events of Selma were less than a year in the past. In Boston, I'd helped organise demonstrations at the Federal Building, exhorting the government to protect the marchers by dispatching troops to Alabama. Like everyone else, I'd been outraged by the shooting of a woman transporting civil rights workers in her car, by the beating to death of a Massachusetts clergyman. I'd been galvanised by the current of moral electricity running through the country; I'd been moved by both the poignancy and the exhilaration of the atmosphere, by the passionate camaraderie, the intoxicating emotional energy, the plaintive simplicity and power of the songs. I still cherished in memory the image of a glacial Boston night, snowflakes swooning silver through the haloes around the streetlamps, and the majesty of a huge whale-shaped black woman clad only in a light calico dress on the steps of the state Attorney-General's office, her voice booming sonorously out over the crowd singing in unison:

And before I'll be a slave,
I'll be buried in my grave,
And go home to my Lord

And be free...

It was to something of all this that I hoped to introduce Nina – something of all this that I myself hoped to recapture, in her company, at the Chicago protest. I wasn't, of course, so naïve as to expect anything comparable to Boston. Boston students, after all, were professionals at the business, seasoned veterans. In Chicago, they were bumptious amateurs, callow novices and apprentices. Demonstrations had never been endorsed, or even sanctioned, by Aristotle. I was therefore braced for something pallid and parochial by my East Coast connoisseur's standards; but there might still, I fancied, be sufficient flavour, spirit and inspiration to strike a chord in Nina, to penetrate her imperturbable unflappable air of having seen everything and believed none of it. I don't even remember now what the purpose of the demonstration was – probably the Draft, which wasn't yet an immediate threat, but had already begun to cast a premonitory shadow over the nation's student population.

The god of protests overseeing the affair at the university – it hardly warranted being dignified as a 'demonstration' – must've been feeble-minded, semi-comatose, dyspeptic, myopic, with flying dandruff and a club foot. Outside the administration block, some twenty or so students were assembled, more diffident and perplexed than rebellious, manifestly baffled by what the protocol of the situation demanded. The authorities had locked the front door, beyond which, in the lighted lobby, a mere dozen or so booted and be-denimed undergraduates – shaggy youths and lank-haired duffel-coated girls – lay slumped about like derelict furniture. A solitary campus security guard patrolled the perimeter of the premises, now and then exchanging quips with the crowd, wearing the expression of a tolerant, broad-minded keeper humouring the inmates of an asylum. Seized apparently by the wind, a placard had torn loose from its staves and now lay in the gutter, flapping like a large white beached fish, its slogan illegible. Some fool with no sense of occasion kept revving a motorcycle, drowning out the tepid efforts of the protesters on the steps to synchronise their singing with those inside.

The whole business began to collapse when the latter discovered that, of the building they claimed to have 'occupied', they in fact occupied only the lobby, and were sealed off from the corridors and the lavatories. Crisis loomed. Everyone had brought a guitar, most had brought sleeping-bags, but no one had had the foresight to bring two of the most basic prerequisites for any self-respecting sittee of a sit-in – toilet paper and some species of receptacle. Whatever lofty political objectives might've been involved, they were soon eclipsed by a debate about whether it was legitimate, let alone modest, to relieve oneself in the space available, which fluorescent light had turned into a veritable aquarium. Rancour erupted in the ranks, pro- and anti-defecation factions became polarised, and I decided to lead Nina home before the idiocy became any more compromising than it was. The night's experience didn't appear to have afforded her any very great edification. I had, however, managed to breach her customary marmoreal impassivity: I'd never seen her look more mystified.

Apart from a few spurious excuses on my part, we walked in silence, I sullen and morose, she still bewildered but also, I sensed, wryly amused. By what? I wondered grumpily. By me? By the bunglers who'd perpetrated the farce we'd left behind? By all of us? There were two routes home. The longer one was a major thoroughfare, well-lighted, thronged with people, bars, late-night diners and other shops. The other, much more direct, ran through a nocturnal no-go zone, notoriously nasty, tenebrous, desolate and gloomy. That was the way I chose, prompted less by bravado than by impatience and preoccupation. Nina, I noticed, flicked me a glance – not so much nervous as simply questioning – but said nothing. Our itinerary led past a block of gutted tenements with graffiti-smeared walls, rubble-strewn forecourts, cavernously gaping windows and doors. Other edifices were studded with amber or honey-coloured lights. These radiated only darkness, rearing like sepulchral escarpments, projecting solid slabs of sombre brooding shadow over the road. Between them stretched denuded expanses of dusty weed-grown lots and waste ground littered with rubbish and débris. Here and there, fragments of broken glass glittered like chips of mica. Most of the streetlamps had either burned out or been smashed by local youths with stones or pellet guns.

We'd got perhaps a third of the way through this eerily quiet, pocked and pitted moonscape when I heard the footsteps behind us. Or, more accurately, the clink of metal heel-taps on the sidewalk. At least three pairs of them. Instinctively, without having to formulate it,

I guessed to whom they belonged. So, too, apparently, did Nina, whose arm I felt go tense in mine. Both of us kept walking, observing the established Orpheus-and-Eurydice code not to look back. In confirmation of my foreboding, I heard snatches of whistled tune, ostensibly casual, carefree, threaded like the piping of some demonic flute through the frost-bound darkness. Unless there were some newly coined American version, I couldn't believe the individuals doing the whistling actually knew the words. My mind, however, silently supplied them:

Die Fahne hoch! Die Reihen dicht geschlossen!
SA marschiert mit ruhig festem Schritt,
Kam'raden, die Rotfront und Reaktion erschossen,
Marschieren im Geist in unsern Reihen mit.

In those heady days, when the Civil Rights Movement had begun to overlap resistance to the imbecility in Vietnam, there were more certifiable lunacies than usual abroad in the land. One of the most purulent was the self-styled American Nazi Party of a bumpkin named George Lincoln Rockwell. Subsequently, in one of the less lamentable assassinations of the decade, he was messily dispatched to his own Disneyfied variant of Valhalla. (I can't imagine Wotan suffering his presence in the real one.) At the time, however, he'd established the Chicago suburbs as the command bunker and national headquarters for his Horst Wessel-wassailing windbags with warped *Weltanschauungen.* I sometimes suspected Al Hollis of clandestine membership in Rockwell's demented organisation, but Hollis could hardly have confessed to it without compromising his status, laughable though that was, as public servant. Certainly the shit-brown tunic, the leather harness, the swastika armband and the jackboots would've suited his mentality, or lack of it, more than his transit policeman's gear. '*Hauptsturmführer* Hollis' had a certain apposite, if not quite Wagnerian, ring - and among that lot, even he might've attained the rank of captain. There were, in fact, a number of Hollis types in Rockwell's entourage, *soi-disant* officers. But the would-be *Führer* of Illinois recruited most of his myrmidons from the steel, construction and other blue-collar workers in such neighbourhoods as Capone's old township of Cicero. Many of them were from Eastern Europe. Driven from their homelands by Soviet tanks, these exiles -

ill-educated, bigoted, messianically right-wing and prone to confuse intolerance with patriotism - were only too ready to flock to the standard of any tin-pot buffoon who bellowed the appropriate anti-Communist slogans. The younger ones - those in their late teens and early twenties - had, in recent months, evolved a new after-hours recreation, piling into cars of an evening, cruising around university campuses and ferreting out supposedly left-wing students to maim, cripple or concuss. There'd been several such incidents of late. Nina and I realised we might imminently participate in another one.

The clink of heel-taps grew more rapid behind us, drew quickly closer. Nina looked quite calm, almost pedagogically curious. About what might happen? What I might do? How I might acquit myself? She was in danger, too, yet her expression was that of a professor invigilating an exam. As if posing a final test question, she asked whether I thought we should run. I shook my head, knowing it would be futile. Her grip tightened on my arm. In anxiety? Approbation? The heel-taps broke into a sudden flurry of clinks, like metallic rain; I was jostled as someone surged past my shoulder and we abruptly found ourselves surrounded. Two figures, whom I couldn't see at first, pressed close behind us. The third - a youth of eighteen perhaps, in a leather motorcycle jacket, with squarish face and a blond brush of hair like Hollis' - positioned himself directly ahead, barring our path, looking me up and down with swaggering insolence. My long hair, the beard I sported in those days and the dark glasses I wore even at night must've conformed perfectly to some sort of 'Know Your Enemy' poster on his bedroom wall. To his mind, I might as well have been Che Guevara in person. He'd no doubt practised shooting at an approximate likeness during so-called 'weapons training' with his air rifle.

'Hey!' he exclaimed in mock astonishment. 'This guy looks like a Commie.'

There followed some dismally predictable banter, intended to goad me into a response - which, of course, whatever it was, would inevitably have been wrong.

'Ya think he's a Commie?'

'Sure looks like one to me.'

'Me, too.'

'Hey, Jan, whaddaya think?'

Heel-taps scraping the sidewalk, one of the figures behind slouched lazily round to join his companion in front. He was taller, long-faced, high-cheekboned, with straight plastered hair and the eyes - narrowed to what he must've fancied the appropriate steely slits - of a fledgling Reinhard Heydrich. On the collar of his nylon windcheater, he flaunted a button, the size of a coaster for a beer glass, with the so-called *Sig*-rune - two jagged stylised silver lightning bolts in the form of a double letter 'S'. I knew what it signified, of course, but not until some years later, in retrospect, did I fully appreciate the grotesque and disquieting incongruity of the situation - the fact that through some surreal slippage of time, I'd actually found myself here, on the streets of an American city in the mid-sixties, confronted by an aspiring SS officer.

'Yeah, he's a Commie, all right. Gotta be.'

'Whaddaya think we should do?'

'You think maybe we should kick some Commie ass?'

'Yeah, why not? Shit, we ain't had no fun all night.'

Had I been alone, I might indeed have bolted and run. I'd set sprinting records in my secondary school and - until I developed synthetic asthma to con my way out of Physical Education - at university. Even in my boots, I could probably have outdistanced my prospective assailants; but I could hardly hope to do so with Nina in tow, and I could hardly abandon her. Had I been alone, I might also have tried to fight my way out. As a hoodlum in secondary school, at the gang 'rumbles' that occurred every Friday afternoon outside the YMCA, I'd learned to wield a garrison belt to fairly gruesome effect; and I could've slipped that weapon from my waist in seconds. An adolescent obsession with British military history had, furthermore, acquainted me with a few supposedly lethal Commando moves; and I'd learned, too, though never employed in earnest, a species of scurrilous back-alley karate, not the honourable kind, with its ritual kow-tows and bows, but the kind intended to paralyse or kill - the single sharp-angled knuckle directed at windpipe or breastbone, the heel of the palm brought down like a hinge to ram the nosebone up into the brain.

But did the circumstances yet warrant anything so drastic? If I waited for confirmation that they did, it would be too late. If I moved first with all the resources at my disposal, I might, I realised, despite the tension of the moment, find myself facing a manslaughter charge.

And even if I did manage to inflict serious, possibly fatal, damage on one, perhaps two of my adversaries, I'd eventually, of course, be overwhelmed or worse. The vicious tricks I knew were aggressive, not defensive, and I'd not be able to fend off three attackers for long. It wasn't so much the risk of physical pain that deterred me as the humiliating prospect of Nina scraping me up from the pavement - assuming she were left in peace to do so. I briefly considered employing a rhetorical device we'd all occasionally used on the East Coast: '*I'm required by law to inform you that my hands are registered in the state of New York as deadly weapons.*' It'd been so overworked by now as to have become a running joke - even Woody Allen used it - but it still might've intimidated the brown-shirtlings who menaced us. One of them, the shorter youth in the motorcycle jacket, had just turned his attention to Nina, reaching up to finger her hair. With practised efficiency, she parried his arm, slapped it brusquely aside. The instant of crisis had come. He'd try again, she'd react accordingly and the situation would careen out of control. I prepared to recite my little formula, which would, at least, buy time. Before I could do so, however, something else supervened - another script, unplanned, unpremeditated, unrehearsed.

As an undergraduate, I'd learned in the university theatre to widen and glaze my eyes in a fixed, wild, unblinking, demoniac stare - the stare of a card-carrying maniac and axe-murderer, or perhaps a zombie in a horror film. It never failed to produce uneasy sniggers and giggles at parties, and I occasionally used it to terrorise neighbourhood urchins, wherever I happened to be living, when they become too noisy under my window. Prompted by some autonomous stage-manager in my psyche, I now, in impressively dramatic slow motion, doffed my dark glasses and assumed my Rasputinesque glower. Its effect was probably intensified by my unkempt werewolf's beard. At the same time, the words started to form themselves on my lips, entirely improvised, utterly spontaneous, issuing not from any calculated design on my part but from some more quick-witted self or sub-personality within me. I'd lapsed automatically into my theatrical voice, the voice I sometimes used to intone Yeats' more eerily evocative poetry - hollow, sepulchral, incantatory, seeming to emanate from an echo chamber. I heard it as if from a distance. It sounded ridiculous enough, but also appropriately uncanny, appropriately doom-laden:

'You may not know it, but you are in danger. In great danger. I am a magician. A sorcerer. I can harm you far more than you can harm me. I have powers you've never dreamed of. Powers that can drive you insane. Powers that will haunt you in nightmares. You may attack me tonight. You may even try to kill me. You may even succeed. But I give you my word, if any of you lays a hand on this woman or myself, all three of you will die. I promise you that. I guarantee it. I'll be more precise, if you like. I guarantee that all three of you will be dead by the end of this month. I guarantee it by this sign...'

I pulled my fountain pen out of my shirt pocket, uncapped it, snatched the hand of the tall youth with the SS button and inscribed a rough hourglass shape, or perhaps a dented and lopsided figure 8, on the flesh of his left wrist, just over the vein. He jerked his hand back as if he'd been stung and stared, affronted and alarmed, at my sloppy impromptu draughtsmanship.

'Lemme see,' the shorter youth breathed eagerly, craning his neck to pore over my handiwork as well.

There ensued a silence save for the city's indefatigable murmur, the quonk of a horn two or three streets away, the shrill but faint skirl of a distant siren. Then the figure behind me, whom I still hadn't seen face to face, guffawed nervously.

'Shit!' he muttered. 'Looks like we got us a real weirdo here...!'

The youth with the SS button licked his forefinger and began rubbing furiously at the Rorschach design on his wrist.

'It'll come off,' I continued, my voice dropping now to a whisper of insidious milky menace. 'But the curse won't. I can't tell you precisely how it'll happen. That's not up to me. That's up to the forces I've called into play. They work in their own fashion. But it *will* happen, I promise you. A car crash, maybe. A fire. Freak accidents occur all the time. Somebody's got to make up the statistics. Why not you? But in your case, the accident won't really be freak, will it? If you lay a hand on this woman or on me, you'll have set it in motion yourselves...'

Another pause, during which I regained my own lucidity. For the first time, I became fully conscious of the more subliminal awareness that'd prompted my extravagant routine. Yes, I had, of course, invoked something archetypal, something 'universal'; I'd elicited a *frisson* from a realm that exists in every psyche - the realm of superstition, nightmare, primitive childhood dread whose power turns archaic folklore and legend into box-office success, drawing even the most sophisticated viewers to cinematic monsters, vampires and wolfmen, for the paradoxical ecstasy of being terrified. But these self-styled storm troopers were particularly vulnerable. They were undoubtedly Catholic, whether practising or lapsed. They couldn't be more than two or three generations removed from their simpler, very likely peasant, ancestors in the old country. At virtual infancy, they must've been introduced to a domain of magic and miracle, where the evil eye was to be shunned and averted, where curses came to ineluctable dire fruition, where omen, portent and fatidic sign tolled like a knell through the quotidian, where the supernatural intruded regularly on the mundane. That domain remained dormant but intact within them, veiled but scarcely protected by the brittle façade of American culture, by local accents and contemporary dress. It was precisely in that domain that their prejudices were rooted, and the talismanic import of such devices as the *Sig*-rune. I'd tapped the same reservoir as their self-appointed *Führer*. Indeed, I'd dredged up from it echoes and resonances even more atavistic, more chthonic - which, usurping the foreground of consciousness, had transformed them into little boys again, children cowering in the dark. It only remained to administer to these brats a suitable *coup de grâce*.

'Yes, I know,' I said, lapsing into a slightly less orphic, slightly more conversational tone. 'You think I'm bullshitting. Or crazy, perhaps. You want to laugh in my face, don't you? Instead, you only snigger nervously. Why? Because there's a little voice in your head, isn't there, nagging and niggling away? '*What if he's not bluffing*?' that voice is asking you. '*What if he's telling the truth? What if these things can happen? What if...?*' You'd do well to listen to that voice. I'm not bluffing. But even if I were, it'd be a dangerous bluff to call, wouldn't it? If you don't call it, you stand to lose some face. If you do call it, you stand to lose more than that. You stand to lose your lives. Which is more important to you? You don't really want to raise the ante. You can't afford the stakes. Only a fool bets against a curse. Go home and get drunk or something. It'll be a lot healthier. And a lot less costly.'

I'd broken the mantic tone, I realised. Had I also broken the spell? In certain contexts, and with certain people, common sense can be a liability. The stillness held, however. The figure behind me had stepped back a pace or two. Very furtively, as if scratching a quadrilateral-shaped itch, the youth in the motorcycle jacket crossed himself. The youth with the SS button, and with my scrawl on his wrist to complement it, wore a sulky petulant look and refused to meet my gaze. Replacing my dark glasses, I took Nina by the elbow and pushed a path between the two in front of us, who shuffled deferentially aside. She was about to look back, but I warned her in a whisper not to do so. Behind us, there was a silence for some moments, then a muted murmur of voices. We'd walked perhaps twenty paces when we heard the clink of heel-taps again - not brisk now, but moving at a chastened shamble, and receding.

'You see?' I said to Nina, rather lamely and with strained insouciance. 'The pen *is* mightier than the sword.'

'That was quite some bluff,' she replied, glancing at me a little warily - as if she, too, were unnerved by the persona into whom (or into which) I'd metamorphosed. 'I mean it! Quite some bluff.'

'If that's what it was,' I mused aloud.

'You had me believing you.'

'I had me believing me, too.'

That, in fact, now that the threat had subsided, was probably the most disconcerting aspect of the night's adventure. Whom had I become? While I was speaking, I now realised, I'd not had the slightest doubt about my words. While I'd been waxing oracular, I'd been absolutely and utterly convinced of my own prophecies. In those moments, I felt, I'd actually possessed the power to pronounce a curse. And for the next month or so, I continued to wonder whether I'd possessed that power during those moments.

****

'Do that again, will ye?' Conor, my self-appointed protégé from Belfast begged eagerly, like a small boy pleading for another piggy-back ride. 'With your eyes, I mean.'

Patient and avuncular, I complied, resignedly dilating my pupils to a berserk glare. Conor snorted with amusement. He may actually have felt a genuine *frisson*, but transformed it into a farcically exaggerated shudder.

'Christ! It's no wonder ye scared the shit out of those fuckers.'

I may have produced a similar laxative effect on the trim collegiate couple across the aisle. In offering Conor an abridged account of my encounter with the Chicago *Sturmabteilung,* I'd dramatised the climax by doffing my dark glasses, glazing my eyes and making my voice resonate from my diaphragm: '*I am a magician...*'. The sonority, piercing tangled skeins of music and talk, had carried to the next table, where a crisp, well-tailored, obviously professional young woman and her dapper bespectacled consort, seemingly half-strangled by his tie, were poring over an open Filofax. They'd jerked their heads up in alarm and gaped speechlessly while I finished my recitation, then began to exchange anxious whispers - she with her nose in his ear, he flicking furtively anxious glances in my direction. Gradually, they'd returned to their own conversation - I'd overheard something about the planned décor of a new kitchen - but when, at Conor's insistence, I again impersonated a maniac, the girl jabbed an elbow into her companion's ribs. The two of them rose from their seats and, as hastily as deportment allowed, sidled away.

Conor, in the meantime, oblivious to our unnerved audience, had become serious.

'D'ye really think it would've worked?'

'Do I think what would've worked?'

'The curse...'

'How do you mean?'

'D'ye really believe they'd've died if they'd tried to beat up on ye? D'ye really believe it would've killed 'em?'

'Qui sait?' I replied, with an agnostic shrug. 'I've no idea.'

'But d'ye believe it?'

'I try not to believe or disbelieve in anything. 'Belief' is a dangerous word. People kill each other for beliefs, most of which are unwarranted. I distrust belief of any kind. Either I *know* something or I don't. If I know it, I don't have to believe. Belief is irrelevant. Superfluous. If I don't know it, the only honest thing I can say is 'I don't know'.'

'But how can ye know? For sure, I mean?'

'You can't. Not always. Not usually. Not so far as the 'big questions' are concerned. In the case of smaller questions, you sometimes can. If you accidentally burn your hand, you don't ask yourself if you believe in pain. You *know* pain directly. If you stick your finger into a light socket, you don't ask yourself if you believe in electricity. You experience it directly, and you can call it whatever you like afterwards - electricity, or magnetic current, or even the energy of the gods themselves. You can construct an entire theology around it. Afterwards. At the moment, however, all you know is the immediate sensation of being zapped. Being zapped fills the whole of your consciousness. You don't have any consciousness left over with which to wonder whether it's 'real' or not. All right - at that moment, in Chicago, I '*knew*' the curse would fulfil itself. Or thought I knew. Or felt I knew. Afterwards, of course, I wasn't sure. I'm not sure now.'

'But what about the notion ye'd planted in their heads? Wouldn't that...?'

'Ah, yes. But that's something different. Once the notion was planted in their heads, it wouldn't've had anything further to do with me. It would've had a life and a momentum of its own. It would've worked like a form of voodoo - the power of suggestion acting on their suggestibility. *They* might've turned my curse into a self-fulfilling prophecy. But that's not the same thing as attributing intrinsic power to the curse...'

Conor wasn't altogether satisfied - he'd sensed a fallacy in my argument, but didn't know how to pursue the matter further. In order to discourage any excessively Celtic credence in curses, I had, of course, been playing rationalist - intellectually splitting hairs in the name of scepticism. As Conor had intuited, the distinction I'd made was ultimately spurious, an artificial cerebral exercise in logical analysis. Reality, he instinctively divined, didn't reside in such distinctions, but in a combination of interrelated factors. The words I'd uttered in Chicago that night. The intensity of the conviction behind them, which 'energised' them, so to speak, with the puissance of a potential self-fulfilling prophecy. The susceptibility of my victims' minds. The latent actualisation of the prophecy in their minds. All of these elements, originating in my psyche and culminating in theirs, comprised a single integrated multi-faceted totality, and one couldn't attribute 'power' to any specific facet of it - no more to the facet I'd emphasised than to the facet Conor had. As in all transactions of consciousness, 'power' wasn't inherent in any one component, but something generated by the interaction of all of them. So, too, is it generated in the aesthetic experience - a dynamic infallibly misunderstood by Aristotelian professors and their disciples, for whom the alleged 'study' of a book amounts to little more than an autopsy.

On the other hand, as I tried to explain to Conor, I'd learned something profoundly important from that night in Chicago. In my encounter with George Lincoln Rockwell's American Nazikins, I'd glimpsed the underlying mechanism of what's generally called 'magic'—and become, at least to that extent, the magician I'd tried to impersonate. The mechanism in question consisted not in effects wrought on others, but in my own state of mind. During those moments of incipient nocturnal nastiness, I'd achieved a concentration of mental resources that precluded every alternative to the one that actually occurred. It wasn't an application of cold abstract will, a clench-fisted coercion of circumstance. It was a kind of *'focus of intentionality,'* analogous to the manner in which a magnifying glass focuses and concentrates the sun's rays - a laser-like fixity of purpose that allowed for only one possible outcome by the simple expedient of precluding all others. Other possible outcomes had ceased to exist, ceased even to be conceivable in my consciousness. I'd no longer entertained contingencies; I'd abdicated both my intellect and my will in order to achieve the result I desired, and I'd done whatever that result required to actualise itself.

During my undergraduate forays in theatre, I'd known a limp-wristed actor who, before each performance, would sit in front of a mirror in the 'green room', making faces at himself - twisting his rubbery features into facsimiles of comic or tragic Greek masks, breathing orgasmically, emoting his way into his character with as much anguish and apparent agony as if he were being physically neutered. His pig-pink face would incandesce scarlet, sweat would pearl his temples and one would expect him at any moment to levitate, or perhaps explode. A devotee of Stanislavski, he dignified the ordeal through which he put himself as 'The Method'. It wasn't a method that appealed to me. In my own cavortings on stage, I favoured my own style of so-called 'Technique' acting, calculating and memorising every line, every inflection, every gesture, every expression - programming myself, in short, then proceeding mechanically, as if on auto-pilot. During my nocturnal encounter in Chicago, however, I'd stumbled on something far beyond 'Technique', even beyond 'Method'. It amounted, in effect, to a form of 'possession' – 'possession' not by any external or occult agency, but by something within myself.

Within another six months, I'd have occasion to become 'possessed' again – to activate a state of 'focused intentionality' and sustain it not for the span of a transient encounter, but for a period of weeks. For a period of weeks, I had to let a state of 'focused intentionality' transform me into a species of alter ego, or *Doppelgänger*, who could manage a critical situation more efficiently than I could myself. The situation was induced by the vagaries of the Selective Service system, and the object of my deception was the vast, ponderous, humourless, culturally retarded and irascibly grouchy edifice of the United States Army.

II

The summer before my arrival in Chicago, Lyndon Johnson, formerly a decent, sympathetic and well-intentioned enough old machiavel, had taken scurrilous advantage of Congress' congenital astigmatism. With a conjuror's sleight-of-tongue, he'd whisked into effect the Gulf of Tonkin Resolution. The following spring, I found myself peering down the open and voracious maw of my local Draft Board.

It shouldn't have happened quite so precipitately. Other people at the university had no trouble obtaining deferments, which were still, at that time, cheerfully conferred on undergraduates and graduate students alike. I, however, came from the proudly self-styled 'colonial' town of Crestfall, New Jersey, a community so besotted with its star-spangled heritage that all public buildings - including petrol stations and supermarkets - were obliged, by municipal ordinance, to conform in architecture to the 18th century. In mentality, often, as well. The town council, the school board, every church, every civic and social organisation, the sanctimonious squib that passed for a newspaper, were all dominated by the DAR, the VFW and the American Legion. If there'd been any room for additional monuments on the main square, they'd no doubt have been erected in commemoration of Joseph McCarthy and George Armstrong Custer. Well, on second thought, perhaps not Custer. His long hair would probably have made him appear a hippie and rendered him disreputable.

There was little enough justification for the status the place arrogated to itself. During the War for Independence, Sir William Howe had stationed a battalion or so of Hessians at Trenton, far to the southwest; but he, his subordinates and all other British forces had had sufficient taste to come nowhere near Crestfall, which may not even have existed at the time anyway. Perhaps the town now hoped to overcompensate. In upholding the alleged honour of its milieu, my local Draft Board proved more frenetically energetic than most, performing its duties with an officious zest that would've made doddering old General Hershey hawk his phlegm with pride. The director, by an unhappy but not unpredictable coincidence, was also an American Legionnaire, who practised patriotism with the frigid fervour of an archangel. Deeming graduate study superfluous to the national welfare, he embarked on a systematic campaign to keep the level of education down to that of the government and his own. Acting with what he must've fancied to be inspired initiative, he abolished graduate student deferments for Crestfall a year and a half before the rest of the country followed suit.

When I applied for the 2-S deferment I assumed to be routine, I was informed that - except in Engineering, Physics and Medicine - such deferments were no longer being dispensed. A month later, two acquaintances at the university - former high school classmates registered with the same Draft Board as I was - received notice to report for their pre-induction physicals. Back in Crestfall, my relations with them had been glacial. Along with other pariahs, I'd regarded them scornfully as members of the so-called 'Rah-Rah Crowd' - football and basketball players, cheerleaders, officers of the Student Council, conscientious conformists, future lance-corporals of industry. They, for their part, had regarded me with edgy hostility, intimidated and righteously affronted by my ducktail haircut, motorcycle jacket and motorcycle boots. When, after four years of separation as undergraduates, we'd first encountered each other in Chicago, they'd been conciliatory, pleased to see that I'd ostensibly 'made good'. I was cordial but distant, feeling no closer to them than I did to anyone else at the school. Confronted by the Draft, however, I began to close ranks with them against what even they perceived to be a mutual threat. Their names came only a few letters before mine in the alphabet, and I knew that my call-up notice had to be imminent. I watched my former classmates wriggling and thrashing like hooked fish, and tried to learn what I could from their experience.

One of them promptly impregnated, then married, his girlfriend, paternity at that time still being a viable escape route. The second, not having a girlfriend to impregnate, embarked on a crash diet, hoping to lose forty pounds in three weeks, starve himself to debilitation and squirm under the Army's minimum weight requirements. When this regimen proved impossible to sustain, he consulted one of the university psychiatrists, an intern not much older than himself, and requested an official letter recommending exemption. Unfortunately, he made the mistake of being honest. Visibly trembling, he confessed to the doctor that the prospect of induction had produced tension, confusion, anxiety, insomnia, loss of appetite and possibly an incipient ulcer. Cavalierly consoling, the doctor assured him that things would somehow work themselves out, supplied him with a bottle of fat purple tranquillisers and, with a pat on the back, sent him home. At his physical a fortnight later, calmly rather than frantically desperate, the poor sod tried to feign hardness of hearing, assuming - and it seemed reasonable - that a deaf soldier would be a liability on the battlefield. The military physicians subjected him to nine gruelling hours of tests with batteries of humming, beeping, buzzing, burbling and burping machines, then brought him back again the following morning. After five more hours of examination, he was classified 1-A and a fraud to boot. Not being sympathetic to frauds below the rank of NCO, the Army inducted him a month later and exported him to Vietnam. Early the next year, he was reported killed in action.

As I watched his futile charade unfold, I'd attempted to erect some bulwarks of my own. My first stratagem - to enlist the sympathy and cooperation of my family physician back in Crestfall - had led simply to a waste of good prose. A former marine himself, Doctor Holbenburger wrote in reply that the Army would probably do me good. Besides, he added with hackneyed fatuousness, I *did* owe something to my country. Provoked, I wrote back, no longer expecting to accomplish anything:

> You've known me for twelve years. You know my psychological make-up. You know my aversion to authority. You know I was suspended three times from high school because of my so-called 'authority problem'. How can you say the Army would 'do me good'? Forgive me, but I can't help questioning your motivation. It seems to me you're promulgating an abstract dictum and ignoring the specifics involved.

The response I received a few days later was written in such manifest fury that the pen nib, at several points, had torn its way through the page. In huge, wild, wrathfully sprawling script, Doctor Holbenburger proclaimed:

> I deal with facts! There are no facts in your case to justify exemption from military service. It's not for you to question my decisions, and my motivations are none of your business.

I replied accordingly:

> I beg to differ. Your motivations are indeed my business. As a doctor, it's your responsibility to probe and diagnose physical maladies. As an artist, it's my responsibility to probe and diagnose moral embolisms, varicose values and lesions of character.

I felt only slightly catharsed, and my cause was no further advanced. Yet if nothing else, Doctor Holbenburger's xenophobic tetchiness confirmed me in my determination not to become transmogrified into cannon-fodder. Periodic inspections of my soul had failed to reveal a single star, a single remote spangle of anything that might be construed as patriotism. I wasn't in any sense a pacifist. On the contrary, I had to acknowledge in myself a slight, admittedly suspect, streak of romantic militarism. Had I been alive, sentient and of age in 1940, I'd not have waited for America to enter the war; I'd undoubtedly have presented myself as a postulant to the RAF's Eagle Squadron, or some similar, glamorously gallant confraternity. For the United States of the 1960s, however, I couldn't mobilise any such enthusiasm; and the cause could hardly claim a comparable urgency. I'd not previously been actively opposed to the country's involvement in Vietnam; I'd simply dismissed it as irrelevant, irresponsible and protuberantly stupid. It didn't become morally heinous until it threatened to engulf me, and to interfere with the various more important things I had to do.

I contemplated my meagre array of options. They were diminishing almost weekly, as Draft Boards around the country became increasingly sophisticated, increasingly conversant with the spectrum of dodges devised to elude their clutches. Two years before, escape had been a simple enough matter. At that time, a friend of mine, a university drop-out involved in the off-Broadway theatre, had responded to his call-up notice by donning cavalier's suede knee-boots, a scarlet-fringed blue cloak and an extravagantly plumed Cyrano de Bergerac-style slouch hat. In this swashbuckling attire, he'd stalked into his Draft Board, vaulted up on to the table in front of his examiners, swept off his hat with a flourish and performed an elaborate courtier's bow. 'You called,' he announced to the stunned faces before him. 'I am here.'

Cloaks and slouch hats evoked no particular echoes in New York. In rural Alabama and Mississippi, however, they conjured up cherished images of Bedford Forrest, Wade Hampton, J.E.B. Stuart and John Singleton Mosby. At the Draft Boards of such places in those days, there were separate queues for blacks and whites, and any white civil rights worker who joined the black queue would be summarily rejected as undesirable. Southern recruiting officers, stirred by memories of dashing Confederate cavalry commanders, wanted no 'nigger-lovers' in their army.

Now, lamentably, such techniques were becoming ever less effective as Draft Boards became ever more jadedly familiar with them, as well as with other standardised ploys - alien substances in the urine, for example, alleged bed-wetting, ostensibly ostentatious homosexuality, a crazed leer coupled with a loudly proclaimed voracity to kill. I'd have to contrive something more subtle and more original, and I couldn't afford to gamble - I'd have one chance only, and there'd be no margin for miscalculation, no latitude for trial and error. I cast vainly about for a suitable disability which could be sloughed, cured or repaired when the need for it had passed.

Pyromania perhaps? As an undergraduate, I'd attained a certain notoriety for fighting duels with fire in the dormitory. Two friends and I would take turns issuing challenges, standing off at ten paces and flicking flaming matchsticks at one another. Prompted by garish rumours, the Dean appeared in my room one morning to investigate. He found the cubicle littered with a welter of spent matches and the débris of a party from the night before - a girl's black bra flapping in the window like an epileptic albatross, gutted candle ends stuck to assorted surfaces, beer and wine bottles growing out of the floor, crunchy dunes of pulverised Rice Krispies with which someone had waggishly filled someone else's boots. There was also a charred-looking crater in the mattress, like a miniaturised bomb site. Accused of pyromania, I pleaded Prometheanism, which didn't prevent my eviction from the premises. Now, I was quite prepared to be a pyromaniac if it served to keep me out of uniform. Unfortunately, I suspected, it wouldn't. In the Army, pyromania would probably have qualified me for a commission.

Here in Chicago, it was too late to cultivate an appropriate medical history for the synthetic asthma which, during my undergraduate career, had exempted me from Physical Education. I tried to procure a testimonial from the university in Boston where I'd spent the previous four years. The requisite negotiations were conducted for me by an ex-muse, still enrolled there as a student. After prolonged arguments, appeals and the transfer of fifty dollars, she managed to extract a note from the school health service. It stated, under the official seal, that I'd established a campus record by appearing at the infirmary with acute asthma seizures no less than sixty-three times. I hadn't realised I'd employed the ploy so frequently. Perhaps I hadn't, and the doctors were now exacting revenge for having been conned. In any case, the note's frivolous tone, coupled with its extravagance, undermined its efficacy. Two weeks after forwarding it to my Draft Board, I received a brief acknowledgement, according to which the 'information submitted' had been included in my file. The following Friday, I received notice to report, on the 17th of the next month, for my pre-induction physical.

'If you marry a divorcée with three kids,' a confidant observed, referring to Nina, 'you'd be safe for the next five or six wars.'

Perhaps, but Nina wasn't a divorcée. She was still technically yoked in wedlock to the fugitive who'd absconded a few years before. On my precarious graduate student's fellowship, I couldn't afford a trip to Reno. Still less could I assume responsibility for my paramour, her parents and three children. In any case, I could no more see myself as a surrogate father than I could as a natural one. On the scale of imaginable misfortunes, paternity ranked for me at that time pretty much on a par with leprosy. Possibly lower, for one could, in a fit of pique, at least transmit leprosy to one's enemies.

I considered flight to Canada, but found it acceptable solely as a last resort. Only the Army and Vietnam would've caused a more grievous disruption of my life. I thought, too, of getting myself convicted on a minor drugs charge, marijuana or hashish. It'd be my first known offence, and I'd receive no more than probation or a suspended sentence, while the Army - unaware at that date that most of its personnel in Southeast Asia were perpetually stoned - wanted no felonious dope fiends in its ranks. But that, too, would've entailed repercussions - a criminal record, the probable loss of my fellowship, assorted other unforeseeable consequences. At one point, I toyed with the idea of a faked suicide attempt - an immobilising but (hopefully) not lethal dose of alcohol and barbiturates, a carefully synchronised arrival by a friend who'd 'discover' me in the nick of time, a resigned, brave, cheerful, even scintillating farewell note. Such enterprises, however, are liable to embarrassing, sometimes incommodiously fatal, backfires. I was (and still am) too much an egoist to relish self-destruction of any kind, least of all by a blunder. I recoiled, as well, from the prospect of the public display, of stretchers, ambulances, hospitals and stomach pumps.

For the moment, I was stymied; yet I remember being surprised at my own calm. I remember, too, an intensified alertness, which enabled me to discern, with a sharply etched lucidity, the precise contours of the impasse; and having thus discerned its contours, I could at least hope to see beyond them. I came awake with the mental equivalent of a jolt. During the whole of the conflict in Vietnam, I knew no one who, being genuinely resolved to avoid military service, had failed to do so. For such people, however, an abrupt awakening had invariably occurred. They'd suddenly realised, often with some shock, exactly what was at risk; they'd recognised that the matter was, quite literally, a matter of life an death - a game in which stakes weren't just one's comfort, or one's plans, or one's career, or one's nebulous idea of a future, but nothing less than one's very survival, one's continued existence in the world. They'd understood that they were faced with a full-fledged and certifiable *emergency*. One doesn't deal with an emergency by dithering, by relying on luck, by wishing it miraculously to pass. One *acts,* with the urgency and imaginative resourcefulness dictated by the circumstances. Those who got caught were those for whom the dilemma remained in some sense unreal. They never entirely awakened to it, never took it wholly seriously; they complacently assumed things would somehow be sorted out; they worked trustingly through available channels and remained somnambulistically passive. In certain instances, of course, such channels did provide an escape route. J. Danforth Quayle served in the National Guard, which didn't travel twelve thousand miles to kill people, but shot them down on the campus of Kent State University, or in the ghettos of Newark and Detroit. Yet if Quayle, through string-pulling and family influence, could thus sleepwalk his way to safety, there were many more – my ex-classmate, for example, with his pathetically feigned deafness – whose sleepwalking carried them over the precipice of their own lives.

I, fortunately, awoke in time to the magnitude of what was involved. And in so doing, I slipped spontaneously into a state of 'focused intentionality'. I knew suddenly what the internal dynamics of the situation dictated and knew how to fulfil their demands – knew what I had to do and knew, with a certainty like a rush of blood to the head, that it would work. The design crystallised in my mind not in piecemeal fashion, but in its totality, similar to the conception for a story or a novel – a conception with a unique density, texture and coloration, as precise as the density, texture and coloration of a dream. The only difficulty lay in steeling myself to lunge beyond my own personal pale. I remember the word 'drastic' flashing on and off in my consciousness, rather like the sign above the pharmacy down the road. I'd have to do something 'drastic'; I'd have to be *outré* by my own standards, embark on a course of conduct alien to my own nature and, in the process, become someone else; I'd have to let the required action, in short, shape and determine the personality of the actor.

Like my hapless ex-classmate, I'd resolved to deposit my problem on the desk of the university shrink. Unlike my hapless ex-classmate, however, I'd parade no marshmallow-centred vulnerability, no symptoms of a psyche and character in advanced stages of jellification. If I claimed to be confused, uncertain, insomniac and devoid of appetite, I, too, would be patronisingly reassured, given a bottle of fat purple pills and sent home, whence the Army could trawl me, stupefied, into its net. I'd therefore have to confront the university health service with something less malleable, something that couldn't be tranquillised away – a madness attained by pursuing a line of impeccably perfect reason from a deranged premise. I conceived of it as a kind of 'armoured madness', a lunacy protected by a logic as intricately knit and woven as a suit of chainmail. I imagined a solidly entrenched, coldly lucid and utterly unassailable intellectual position, an attitude congealed into the fanaticism of a theology – a veritable fortress of spurious, but icy and impregnable rationality.

High within these ramparts, a cackling and demented self would lurk, but no shrink could get to it without scaling the walls. When he attempted to do so, I'd be able to knock away his ladder, douse him in polemical boiling oil. He'd be reduced to catapulting syllogisms at me from a distance, and perhaps once things came to that, my rate of fire would decisively exceed his.

That afternoon, I filed a request to take my physical in Chicago. This would not only save me a safari back to Crestfall, but would also, I hoped, procure me a hearing before more sympathetic, less gung-ho examiners. At very least, it'd purchase me a few days grace at each stage of the proceedings while my papers were transferred to and fro. In the evening, I composed a letter - a model of *fin-de-siècle* aestheticism, laced with Proust and Mann at their most morbid, liberally seasoned with Schopenhauer and Villiers de l'Isle-Adam. Having retained the drafts, I can still reconstruct it:

> Gentlemen:
>
> I am a twenty-two-year-old graduate student whom you have just ordered to report for his pre- induction physical examination. Some months ago, you refused me a standard 2-S exemption. I should now - presumptuous though it sound - like to request what I've taken the liberty of calling a cultural deferment.
>
> Permit me to explain myself. I consider myself to be an artist, and, as such, believe I have a major contribution to make to culture - American culture, world culture, the life of the spirit, call it what you will. I believe further that to make this contribution is neither a luxury, as it were, with which one dabbles if he has time, nor a mere privilege. Rather, it is an obligation, both to myself and my society - an obligation of immense import, as painful and burdensome as it may be exalted, which must take precedence over any other.

I feel there is one point I should clarify. I refer above to my 'belief', but that word is hardly adequate to convey what I mean. Even 'conviction' will not truly suffice. I prefer to think of it as a 'sense of mission', a concept which, I realise, is difficult to explain. Two centuries or so ago, I suppose I would have seen myself as an 'agent' of God or Destiny. Now, however, as I deplore conventional Western notions of God and Destiny, that phrase, too, is inadequate and misleading. All I can say, really, is that this 'sense of mission' is neither an ideology nor a belief as such, but a perpetually present intuitive certainly which suffuses and determines every aspect of my life, every impulse, every thought, every action. It is not something I either 'think' or 'feel', but something which, in some indefinable way, I profoundly know. It is hardly anything pleasant. On the contrary, it is probably more a curse than a blessing, but the kind of curse one feels obliged to accept with something akin to gratitude.

I hold what many would no doubt consider a morbid view of human existence. I have no sense of humour. I do not 'enjoy life' in any conventional sense, but feel that life, in and for itself, is meaningless, purposeless, futile and quite without justification. My existence is more a burden to me than it is anything else, and were it not for my 'sense of mission', I should have no reason to live. I do not believe there is any point, or anything to be gained, in living, unless one can justify it, and there are not many ways of doing so. Art is one of the few there are. It may, perhaps, be the only one ultimately – to create something meaningful, beautiful and permanent, which subsists on a level above the petty endeavours and absurdities of human beings, and, in so doing, elevates and redeems them. To that extent, I see myself as a redeemer.

> So far as I personally am concerned, then, it is absolutely essential that I be allowed to create. Anything that threatens to inhibit or curtail my doing so is necessarily inimical to me. Should I be drafted, I would not merely lose two years, for those two years, I know, would permanently impair my creativity. I have seen this happen before to some of the most gifted individuals I know, and I am certain that after two years in the military, I would never be able to write again.
>
> What all this signifies - as you've no doubt anticipated - is that if I am drafted, I must kill myself. Please do not misunderstand me: I am not trying to threaten you, nor coerce you with the suggestion that my death might be on your heads. After all the others you've incurred, mine, I realise, would carry little enough weight. I am rather asking you to consider the loss you are risking - the loss both to yourselves and to the civilisation you claim so zealously to defend.

On re-reading my concoction, I allowed myself a smirk of grim complacency. It would be a daunting bluff for any conscience-ridden doctor or psychiatrist to call. He'd feel - so I hoped - crucified to his professional ethics. Were I in a position of comparable authority, and were someone to try such a routine on me, I'd undoubtedly want to murder him, preferably very slowly, by some excruciating Chinese torture.

It was late Friday night by the time I'd revised and polished the warped text to my satisfaction. I got to the bar just before it closed, then returned with Nina. When she left the following morning, I typed five copies of my letter and posted one each to my local Draft Board, the State Board, the National Board and the President. With the remaining copy in an unsealed and unaddressed white envelope, I walked to Billings Hospital, the university's health centre. Half an hour before, I'd taken a Dexedrine. When I arrived, my whole metabolism was appropriately hyper-functioning - palate furred, blood racing, pulse pounding, ears singing, nerves whining like high-tension wires. At the door to the waiting room, I paused at a drinking fountain and liberally daubed my face. Then, temples shining with a film of instantly synthesised sweat, I glazed my eyes, entered and approached the pudgy, bucolic-looking nurse at the reception desk.

'I'd like to see a psychiatrist,' I intoned in a sepulchral voice, hollow and devoid of all inflection.

The nurse glanced up at me, then away, then back again, furtive and a little nervous.

'I'm sorry...' she faltered. 'The psychiatrist isn't in on Saturdays, I'm afraid. Would you like to see the doctor...?' She paused, staring at me intently now, with quailing brown eyes. 'If it's urgent,' she added, her voice hushed, 'the doctor can call for a psychiatrist...'

'Let me see a doctor,' I muttered, injecting a tremor into my monotone, defying the 'NO SMOKING' sign and lighting a cigarette with fingers the amphetamine had already set trembling. I should've waited until Monday, I realised with exasperation. But I was keyed up for my performance now, and a weekend of waiting would've been the kind of ordeal to which only masochists submitted.

The nurse vanished down the corridor, from the bowels of which I could hear two voices engaged in hurried whispered conversation, tense with leashed urgency. A moment later, the doctor appeared - a scrawny red-headed man with protuberant Adam's-apple, wobbly bags under his eyes and a bulbous alcoholic nose. When he'd ushered me into his office, I handed him my ominous white envelope.

'You'll find the contents self-explanatory. I've sent copies to all relevant offices.'

The doctor studied me for a moment, the pouches under his eyes quivering. When I continued to meet his gaze, he looked away, opened the envelope, extracted the letter and began to read, holding the typed pages up to his face as if to sniff them. From time to time, he glanced at me briefly, then immersed himself again, frowning, in my convoluted prose. When he'd finished, he said nothing for a time, keeping his head lowered. At last, he nodded.

'Yes,' he said mournfully, 'I think you ought to see a psychiatrist. I'll call one for you.'

The man he tried to call proved to be inconveniently away – fishing, it transpired, in Wisconsin. A colleague had therefore to be contacted, whose office lay across town. It would take him, I was told, an hour to arrive. When I said I'd wait, the doctor looked manifestly relieved, obviously having feared the necessity of detaining me by force.

I was escorted down two flights of stairs, a nurse attending me at each shoulder, no doubt to ensure I did nothing unseemly or hazardous en route. In the emergency ward, I was led and locked into a tiny sterile white room, the traditional size of a prison cell. Apart from a solitary metal chair bolted to the floor in one corner, the cubicle was empty, denuded of all furniture and ornament – an hermetic container in which, short of holding my breath until I turned blue, I couldn't possibly damage myself. The light fixture was located in the corner opposite the anchored chair, presumably to discourage hanging. The only glass was a ridged and opaque blue pane recessed deep in the door, so thick it looked bullet-proof.

Here I waited, not for one hour, but for three, while the requisitioned psychiatrist navigated his way through the city's Saturday traffic. Now and again, a face pressed itself to the pane in the door, the glass turned from blue in colour to liverish and a blurred eye could be discerned, magnified to cyclopean proportions. This meant, I concluded, that I was 'under observation'. What did they expect to see? I wasn't prepared to flash for them. To demonstrate anxiety, I paced and smoked. To demonstrate psychological *deshabillé* and disorder, or perhaps petulance at the absence of an ashtray, I flicked my ashes about at random. To demonstrate compulsiveness, I lined my spent cigarette butts, on end, in a neat little file along one wall. To demonstrate generally erratic behaviour, I lay down on the floor between cigarettes and crossed my arms over my chest, like a chivalric effigy on a tomb. I would've liked to sleep, but the Dexedrine made that impossible. An invisible hand somewhere switched on a ventilator, and the blue haze of smoke filling the room began to dissipate.

The psychiatrist, when he arrived, proved to be a plump little man with a high, bald and greasily shining forehead, tufts of wiry hair like black pads of steel wool about his ears and horn-rimmed spectacles that gave him an owlish appearance. He introduced himself with a mumble that failed to convey his name. I seated myself on the chair and he in turn began to pace, wondering apparently where to begin. In his second circuit of the room, he inadvertently kicked down my tidy file of cigarette butts. Compulsively, he squatted and began to right them, then, feeling my eyes upon him, grew self-conscious and flushed. Sticking his head out of the door, he called for a second chair and an ashtray. At last, seated opposite me, he drew my letter from his jacket pocket and began to read, while I again reflected how deeply I would've resented being placed in his position. When he looked at me over the rims of his glasses, there was already a flicker of anxiety in his gaze, a harried quality, an incipient panic at the responsibility foisted upon him

'You seem to be serious about this,' he ventured tentatively.

I gave him a fleeting cold smile.

'As opposed to what? Frivolous? It's not a situation that encourages frivolity.'

'No,' the psychiatrist agreed, looking down again with a brisk but grave nod. After a pause, he tapped my letter with his forefinger. 'You speak here about your 'sense of mission'. In other words, you seem to be approaching the situation in highly personal terms...'

I stared at him. Was he trying to draw me out? Was he simply thick? Or was he hampered by his own toy vocabulary? How had this individual ever contrived to qualify as a shrink?

'You're suggesting I be impersonal about the prospect of my own death?'

'No,' he said judiciously. 'That's not quite what I mean. I mean you seem to be somewhat...well, shall we say "self-centred". . . in your perspective.'

'I can't think of a more appropriate centre in the circumstances. It's my self, after all, that's at risk. You're implying I'm egocentric. Or just simply selfish. But as I've stated in my letter, I'm not writing for myself; I'm not trying to gratify my own egotism. Art is a gift one makes to one's civilisation. There's nothing selfish about it. It involves as much self-sacrifice, as much martyrdom, as any other mission. Or vocation, if you prefer that term. You wouldn't call a doctor selfish, would you? Or a teacher? Or a priest? Or a psychiatrist? Each of these people supposedly gives something of himself. Do you think an artist gives anything less? And can you blame him if a loutish society fails to appreciate his gift? Or misuses it? It's my business, like yours, to treat maladies, but the maladies I treat lie in a sphere that's inaccessible to you - the mind's eye, the soul, the moral consciousness, whatever you choose to call it. To teach people how to *see* - see literally, in a visionary or clairvoyant sense, with their whole psyches, not just their eyes...'

'I understand, I understand,' the psychiatrist muttered with a brisk placating nod. 'Your argument's a very sound one. That's not quite what I was getting at, however...What I wanted to determine was...well, how you regard larger issues, things outside yourself. Your country, for example, What exactly does the United States mean to you? How do you feel about your country?'

'In a very profound sense, I think of myself more as a European writer. It's with European figures, particularly German and Austrian, that I feel the greatest kinship.'

'I see,' my interrogator murmured, scrutinising me suspiciously. 'Do you find this in any way...well, abnormal?'

I was appalled. From my reading, as well as from numerous students I knew and a number of friends in the business, I was familiar with the procedures of psychotherapy, psychoanalysis and analytical psychology. Granted, the increasingly flustered specimen before me was only a lowly shrink. Even shrinks, however, need some rudimentary qualifications, of which there was no trace in this fool's maladroit, protuberantly inept questions. Very well, I decided - I might as well have some fun and go exuberantly over the top.

'Not at all,' I replied. 'My mother's family was Austrian, my father's British. My heritage is a European heritage. Why shouldn't I be influenced by European literature? I might also, I suppose, invoke Jung. My mind at times seems to house a memory that transcends my own personal experience. Whenever I read something set in Vienna between, say, 1880 and 1914, I have a sense of *déjà-vu*, even a sense of homecoming. The old Habsburg double eagle invariably stirs me down in the archetypes. When I was a child, everyone said I was the image of my maternal grandfather. More recently, an occultist I know told me I was the reincarnation of Robert Musil. He died the year before I was born - Musil, I mean, not the occultist - so if you subscribe to metempsychosis, the whole thing can sound fairly plausible. Or maybe I'm his spiritual son. Musil's, I mean. But then again, Musil bore an uncanny resemblance to my maternal grandfather...'

'Who's this...er, Musil...?'

There may well have been others, of course, but I knew of no one in the States at that time, apart from Bernard McCabe and myself, who'd even heard of Musil, much less read him. Nevertheless, I contrived to look aghast, taken aback, assuming an expression of shocked astonishment and incredulity. My voice was an accusation:

'*You don't know Robert Musil*?'

'Well,...I...er, *do* faintly recall the name from...er, somewhere,' the psychiatrist faltered, thrown off guard, his large myopic eyes swimming nervous and ashamed behind his glasses. 'Perhaps you'd...er, refresh my memory...?'

'Presumably you've heard of Joyce?' I drawled, my words dripping with sarcastic scorn. 'Or Proust? Or Thomas Mann? Musil's stature is comparable to theirs. He's generally acknowledged to be one of the half-dozen or so greatest novelists of the century.'

The psychiatrist flushed slightly and lowered his eyes.

'Leaving the question of writing aside for the moment,...'

'I can't leave it aside. Not even for a moment. It's as basic to me as eating, drinking or breathing, pissing, shitting or making love. It's intimately bound up with all those things...'

'I understand,' the psychiatrist replied, a certain rigidity of exasperation suffusing his voice. 'I notice in your letter you don't express much of an opinion about the...er, situation...in Vietnam. How exactly do you feel about that?'

'I can't give you a simple answer. I respond to everything on two levels - as an artist, and as a quotidian human being like everyone else. As a human being, I suppose I regard the war with profound outrage. In the backbone of my soul, so to speak, I feel it's immoral, illegal, criminal, pointless and insane. When it threatened to suck me into its vortex, it became all the more so. As an artist, on the other hand, I'm somewhat calmer about it. Somewhat more detached. My predominant attitude, I guess, would be a kind of bottomless cynicism...'

'Cynicism?'

'What else?' I replied with a shrug of disdain. 'How could I not be cynical, watching millions of people swallowing the pabulum of incompetent bureaucrats who blither about learning the lessons of history and know so much less about history than I do? I see them as a gaggle of obstreperous brats playing roughhouse games. At first, it's all very polite, with diplomats and ambassadors and high-level conferences. Then someone turns out to be a sore loser, throws a tantrum, knocks all the pieces off the board and starts a new game, this time with helicopter gunships and napalm.'

'And that's all it is to you? Just a game?'

'Of course. It's deadly, and it forces people to play who don't want to, but it's still a game. Look at all the states, the empires, the civilisations that've come and gone throughout history. Isn't it naïve to assume that America's destined to endure longer than Egypt, or Rome, or the British Empire? Yet that's what we're expected to assume. Everyone more or less takes it for granted. As if, in another two centuries or so, America might not be a second- or third-rate power, the way Holland is now. Or Sweden. Or Spain. All of them were once major players. It's not just naïve. It's downright silly to presume that our culture is somehow above the misadventures of Carthage, or Rome, or the imperium of the Habsburgs. It's like declaring war against the phenomena of time and change. In order to justify my fighting for the United States, for an abstract notion and a peppermint-striped flag, I'd have to be convinced that Lyndon Johnson and the current administration represented the be-all and end-all of human civilisation, the absolute zenith of our development. If I were convinced of that, I'd feel obliged to kill myself on the spot...'

'An interesting point of view,' the psychiatrist mused, nodding thoughtfully.

'Do you still see it as personal? Or selfish?'

'Well, I wouldn't say...'

'I think it reflects a laudable breadth of vision. The kind that's lacking in the corridors of power. Don't misunderstand me. I admit I'm a product of my society, at least to some extent, and that saddles me, I suppose, with a certain obligation. I say this with reluctance, but, for better or worse, I'm indebted to this country. I acknowledge that I owe her something. But I know what I owe her better than my Draft Board does. I don't owe her a wasteful meaningless death, and my obligation doesn't consist of trooping off into the jungle and getting myself blown to hamburger in a rice paddy. With all respect to our honoured dead, any dolt with a two-candlepower brain can manage that, and whether I do it or not hasn't much bearing on the national welfare. I may be a megalomaniac, but not enough of one to think my presence in Vietnam would affect the course of the war. The point is that if I got myself killed over there, you and the United States and culture in general would be losing something more - and something even more irreplaceable - than just another soldier.'

For a moment, the psychiatrist said nothing, sitting with lowered eyes and tented fingers. At last, he looked up at me cautiously over the rims of his glasses.

'Has anyone ever accused you of the sin of pride?'

'That's cant. Besides, we're supposed to be talking psychologically. Sin's a theological concept.'

'Kant...?'

'Cant. With a 'C', I mean.' Was this the cultural equivalent of toilet training? Or had I perhaps induced a wholly new variety of paranoia - a compulsive defensiveness which fancies it sees erudite allusions everywhere? 'Of course I'm proud. But I'm also realistic. I'm not saying anything that isn't flagrantly self-evident. Let me repeat it in slow motion. There are certain things, certain human or spiritual values, which transcend petty questions of statehood or nationality or ideology. Time itself resolves those questions in its own way. Who gives a flying fuck now about who did what to whom in ancient Greece, or Rome, or Florence, or Weimar? It's what's survived that matters - Homer, Virgil, Dante, Goethe - and what such men have given us is above the politics of their time. Yes, I admit I have an obligation to what we call 'my country', but it's an obligation of a very unique kind. Anyone can fire a rifle and get himself punctured in return. But not everyone can do what I have to. That's why I have to do it, even if General Hershey and the members of my local Draft Board don't know how to read...'

'Everyone has some individual responsibility. To families, children, jobs. What would happen if everyone felt the way you do about their country?'

I was delighted. All through our conversation, I'd been waiting for that question - waiting for my interrogator to walk down that particular manhole.

'What would happen if everyone felt the way you do about art?'

The question knocked his face expressionless. It had, obviously, never occurred to him before, and he was groping for its relevance now. A pause, while he pondered. When he looked up at me again, his eyes held the uncertain look of a man who knows he's missed a point somewhere, but can't quite put his finger on it. *'What indeed?'* he probably wanted to say, but that wouldn't have sufficed.

'Suppose they'd drafted Shakespeare,' I continued, allowing him no time to regain his balance. 'Suppose Shakespeare'd been conscripted as a rank-and-file pikeman or arquebusier under the Earl of Essex, or Mountjoy? And suppose, during the 'limited war' in Ireland, he got himself impaled between the eyes by some bellicose Celt or Gael? Who, like General Hershey, didn't know how to read. Don't you think our civilisation would be the poorer for the 'accident'? Can you honestly say it wouldn't've made any difference?'

To judge from his expression, my interlocutor honestly could. As an allegedly educated man, however, he was patently unprepared to admit it. At the same time, he was clearly aware that the conversation had careened disastrously out of control – that he was out of his element and foundering. Almost desperately, he tried to return to basics:

'Tell me something about your past. About your childhood. Would you say you had a happy childhood?'

I teetered on the brink of temptation, flirting with possibilities. Lurid accounts of fabricated traumas skittered vertiginously through my mind. It was only with difficulty that I resisted them, reminding myself that I mustn't get lured into my interrogator's territory, mustn't give him anything potentially familiar to work with, mustn't allow myself to be diverted from my central premise.

'My childhood's irrelevant,' I replied. 'As Nabokov says, the only relevant biography for an artist is his work. I'll happily tell you about the evolution of my work. I'll happily expatiate on the creative process as I experience it.'

A pause.

'You don't really want to kill yourself, do you?'

'Of course not. I thought I'd made that apparent in my letter. I find the idea of suicide extremely distasteful. The only thing I find more distasteful is being drafted.'

'What would you like me to do?'

'Write to my Draft Board.'

'What would you like me to say?'

'I don't care, really. Tell them I'm mad. Tell them I'm manic depressive. Tell them I suffer from delusions of grandeur. Tell them I'm not suitable cannon-fodder. Tell them I'd undermine morale. Do you honestly believe I'd be an asset to the Army?'

The psychiatrist flashed me a brief hostile glance but said nothing. For some moments, he remained silent, meditating, his chin in his hand, his knee raised, his leg braced on the rung of the chair – a gargoyle travesty of Rodin's sculpture. At last, he pulled a handkerchief from his pocket, unfurled it and daubed his glistening forehead.

'I can't write your Draft Board, I'm afraid. I'm not the regular doctor here, you see, and I'm not authorised to take responsibility for you as a patient. They called me today because it appeared to be an emergency. They felt you might try...well, something drastic...unless you spoke to someone immediately. . . '

'So what happens now?' I asked gloomily, with a sudden incipient sense of despair.

'When they called me about you, my initial reaction was to have you...er, detained here. For the rest of the weekend, at least. Now that I've talked to you, though...Well, it seems that things aren't yet that critical, are they? If I understand you correctly, there's still some time before you...before you...er, attempt anything...?'.

'I wasn't planning to kill myself this weekend.'

'Good. Can we come to an arrangement, then? Will you give me your word, man to man, that you won't...er, kill yourself...before Monday? If you give me your word, I'll let you go. I'll trust you. In the meantime, I'll make a full report to the regular doctor here and schedule an appointment for you with him first thing Monday morning. And I'll include my recommendation. Is that agreed?'

'You have my word. Man to man, I won't kill myself before Monday. I swear on the works of William Shakespeare. Those of Goethe, too. And Pushkin. And Robert Musil...'

I returned home, drained by my effort, by the day's nervous tension and by the effects of the Dexedrine wearing off. I slept until evening and woke in a state of ambivalence – pleased by the qualified success of the morning's performance, depressed by the prospect of having to repeat it on Monday. Most of all, though, I was intrigued by my own mental processes during the three hours I'd spent sequestered in that sterile suicide-proof cubicle. I'd not consciously rehearsed my presentation; I'd known that I'd have to improvise, and that any prearranged speech would inevitably ring false. At the same time, however, I'd instinctively been creating, or releasing, or transforming myself into, the persona who, when the psychiatrist arrived, would begin to expostulate in my stead. That endeavour had been accompanied by an odd sense of familiarity, of doing something I'd often done before. It was, I now realised, precisely that of literary composition - the means whereby, in the past, I'd developed and projected an alter ego, a variant of myself through whom I expressed my values and attitudes on the page. In retrospect, I could see myself writing - or even conjuring - a fictitious personage into being. I could even see the spectral *Doppelgänger* rising like an astral double beside me, gradually assuming shape and form, displacing my own identity. I remembered the endless and tedious undergraduate debates: *Is* Stephen Dedalus actually Joyce? *Is* Tonio Kröger actually Mann? I now recognised how fatuous such questions were. The character I'd created - the replica or surrogate self crystallising beside me and wearing my name - was so eminently me, yet so eminently *not* me, that he defied all rational analysis. It was as if I'd taken a single mood, a transient fluctuation of the mind, and turned it into a trait - had intensified and amplified it in space and duration until, ceasing to be a mood, it became a constant state of being. Or as if, by some spontaneous alchemical experiment, I'd taken the basic components, elements or ingredients of my personality - so many grams of megalomania, so many of self-diminution, so many of certainty, so many of doubt - and simply shifted the proportions, adding a grain of morbidity here, removing one of irony or humour there.

I pondered Rimbaud's proclamation, *'Je est un autre'*. I pondered Flaubert's assertion that he 'was' Emma Bovary - meaning, of course, not that he'd endowed her with his personality or that she was a self-portrait, but that he'd forced himself to become her in order to actualise her as a literary character. I pondered Keats' principle of 'Negative Capability', which takes as much delight in creating an Iago as an Imogen. And then, with a slowly creeping chill, I began to wonder...I'd taken delight in creating a morbid, incipiently deranged, misanthropic and self-destructive aesthete. I'd allowed myself to become him in order to bring him to life and render him convincing. But if his performance had misfired, might *he* perhaps have tried to act on his threat? And would I have had the power to stop him? Had I perhaps stumbled on the mechanism whereby certain suicides occur?

As for the joust with my Draft Board, the rest was to prove anticlimax. On Monday, re-Dexedrined, I returned to Billings Hospital, prepared to give my encore. The psychiatrist awaiting me proved to be a younger man, not much older than myself, accustomed to ministering to students and their array of bizarre ills. He made no secret of his antipathy towards the country's involvement in Vietnam, gloated over some of the phrases in my letter and seemed to wish only that I had more of a 'political consciousness'. Later, I learned he was a veteran of SNCC, the Student Non-Violent Coordinating Committee, and had mass-produced exemptions for Civil Rights campaigners in the South. I don't know whether I genuinely conned him, as I'd conned his predecessor on Saturday, or whether he chose to play along out of sympathy. Whatever the reason, he promptly applied for a postponement of my pre-induction physical, pending 'formulation of a diagnosis', and requested that I see him twice a week for the next fortnight.

'You know,' he ventured at one of these sessions, despite my efforts to consolidate my maladjustment, 'I sometimes wonder whether you're really in as bad shape as my colleague thought. Or maybe as you might think.'

I hurled myself at once into a vertiginous relapse. Improvising furiously, I told him that, at age six, I'd consistently imagined myself a werewolf, and tried on one occasion to chew up my uncle. (In fact, I'd tried to decapitate him with a baseball bat.) In Vancouver, half a decade later, this seed was to bear fruit as the British Columbia Foundation for Lycanthropic Children. How it affected the shrink in Chicago I was unable to gauge. Neither have I any idea what it was precisely that he wrote to my Draft Board - what data he provided, what maladies he ascribed to me, what recommendations he submitted to help them make up their minds. Three weeks later, however, I received an official letter informing me that I'd been classified 1-Y - 'not draftable except in case of national emergency'. It wasn't quite the 4-F I'd coveted - 'not draftable in any circumstances' - but it would certainly do. I'd be safe at least until the Viet Cong invaded California. Had I in fact been deferred for cultural reasons, for lycanthropic reasons or for some sort of general, all-purpose and all-encompassing pottiness?

There was to be one postscript to my exercise in self-impersonation. It was more than a year later, after I'd received my M.A. and was preparing to leave Chicago for a more congenially anarchic academic milieu. I was on one of my increasingly rare visits to the campus when a voice hailed me from across the Gothic quadrangle. I paused - more or less on the spot where, early that spring, three trigger-happy policemen had grazed two students by banging away with their revolvers at an allegedly rabid squirrel - and waited for the strange figure to approach. Only when he'd drawn up to me did I recognise, under a wildly frizzed Afro and the foliage of an exuberant beard, the shrink who'd procured me my exemption.

'I've been hoping I might run into you,' he said, proffering his hand and pumping mine. 'I wasn't sure you were still enrolled here. I see they didn't draft you.'

I thanked him for his intervention on my behalf, and we exchanged a few ritualised amenities. He then asked me if I remembered Joe Samsa.

'Who?'

'Joseph Samsa. Doctor Samsa. My colleague. The man you saw the Saturday before you first saw me.'

Yes, I replied warily, I remembered Doctor Samsa.

'He died some three months ago, I'm afraid.'

'I'm sorry to hear that,' I said, mildly surprised, perhaps even a little shocked, but unable to muster any very dramatic display of grief.

'He took his own life. Prescribed himself an overdose, so to speak. I shouldn't really be telling you this - professional ethics, you know - but it can't make any difference now.'

'Why *are* you telling me? I met him only once. We didn't exactly become fast friends.'

'You may've underestimated his opinion of you. Anyway, I thought you might, just possibly, be able to clarify something. I saw Joe two or three times in the weeks before his death. He wasn't a very happy man in those days. I know he was reading something which...well, disturbed him in some way. And he mentioned you once or twice. He left a somewhat singular request in his will. He wanted a particular inscription on his tombstone: *'Here Lies a Man Without Qualities'...'*

'He missed the point,' I said. 'Musil's point, at any rate. He was probably trying to make one of his own.

III

In retrospect, my two fabricated self-mutations - into sorcerer and into suicidal aesthete - can be deemed to have had political implications, or, at any rate, to have reflected a political position of some kind. In both instances, I was on what most of my peers - indeed, most intelligent people - would regard as the 'side of the angels'. In both instances, my adversaries embodied the more philistine, if not Neanderthal, aspects of American society. In both instances, my stance could be defined, albeit loosely, as 'liberal' - a word of debased currency in the United States subsequently, but one which, in the days before Ronald Reagan's Disneyfication of the country, was legitimate coin of the realm, at least among those with a modicum of education and lucidity. Granted, my behaviour, in both instances, may have been somewhat unorthodox and extreme. Unlike that of J. Danforth Quayle or George W. Bush, for example, it wouldn't, I suspect, have qualified me for public office. But to have faced down a trio of neo-Nazi dunderheads, and to have outsmarted my Draft Board, were, in the circles amid which I moved, a commendable track record, and constituted impeccable political credentials.

Such assessments obtain, however, only in retrospect. At the time, I had no sense of doing anything in any sense political. I harboured opinions, of course, about American stupidity in Vietnam, about the self-styled National Socialist Party of Illinois; but those opinions were really pretty tepid, and rested on moral rather than political premises. Nor had they contributed in any respect to my actions. My actions, that evening in the Chicago streets, that Saturday in Billings Hospital, had been prompted by nothing more ideological than elementary self-preservation.

All the same, I wasn't quite as politically insulate as I sometimes pretended - and sometimes wished - to be. In fact, so-called political realities had first impinged on my world, as they did on many other people's, some two and a half years earlier, in the autumn of 1963. Unlike many other people, however, I endeavoured assiduously to ignore such realities, and, when that wasn't feasible, to hold them at bay. Or to handle them with tongs.

Until then - the beginning of my third year at university - I had indeed been politically insulate. So, too, had many, if not most, of those in my circle. We were precocious in a number of other respects. We were precocious in our literary insight and erudition, for example. We were precocious in matters of psychology and sexuality. So far as the sub-cultures of the East Coast were concerned, we were eminently streetwise. But the domain of politics seemed to us irrelevant, remote and boring to boot. I was engaged at the time in an energetic quest for Fausthood - and, as I'd been throughout my post-pubescent life, for a suitably qualified *Ewigweibliche* to lead me, Gretchen-fashion, *hinan*. *Hinan* lay - and, as far as I'm concerned, still lies - not amid abstract ideological principles, not amid dreary social reforms or squalid political programmes with their attendant jockeying for power, but amid the constellations of inner space. On one of my frequent romantically-motivated drives between Boston and New York, I was stopped by a bumptious Connecticut highway patrolman, ostensibly for speeding, in fact for looking subversively scruffy. What, he demanded, was my profession? Was I a student?

'I'm an alchemist,' I replied.

He blinked, struggled to remain impassive, then allowed himself a puzzled frown. At last, overcoming his intellectual inferiority complex, he asked, rather as if he were swallowing a pill:

'What's that?'

'What's what?'

'What you said...'

'What'd I say?'

'What you said you were.'

'Oh. An alchemist. A kind of metal-worker, I guess.'

He was reassured, presumably through some implicit association with blue-collar labour. No doubt he believed I'd eventually assume a responsible, productive and civic-minded place in American society. My definition had, of course, been frivolous, and insolent as well. Paradoxically, however, it'd also been quite serious, albeit in an oblique metaphorical fashion. The artist, I'd read somewhere during my formative years, must 'transcend his ego'. I'd adopted this maxim, along with my own codicil - that there's no point in transcending one's ego unless one has an ego worth transcending. Thus sanctioned epistemologically in vanity and arrogance, I'd set about cultivating an ego of the requisite specifications, while at the same time exploring techniques for transcending it.

Inevitably, I was led - some three years or so before an entire generation of youth with inferior egos - to mystical tradition, Eastern thought and Western esoterica. Seeking to twitch the numinous by the hem of its cloak, I plunged headlong into Vedanta, into Tantra, into Zen, into Sunyavada and Vinyavada Buddhism. I cavorted around the Zodiac and, with the simian dexterity of the White Ape who governs such activities, swung about in the branches of the Sephirothic Tree. I probed correspondences and the Gnostic gnooks of the Pleroma; I bounced up and down between Microcosm and Macrocosm; I charted the psychic location, not marked on any map, of Goetia; I finger-painted with assorted hues from the palette of magic - white, black, grey, mostly mottled, piebald and plaid. Of all the arcana through which I safaried, alchemy and Hermetic tradition had proved the most personally congenial - and the most aesthetically apt. Alchemy, as I understood it, used art to symbolise sexuality, sexuality to symbolise art and both to symbolise the process of self-transformation. As every adept knows, the alchemist himself is always the true subject of his own experiment.

For the most part, I wandered through this territory alone, except for the occasional muse-of-the-moment, who usually failed to keep pace and was ruthlessly abandoned en route. But there were other paths apparently leading to transcendence of the ego on which I was joined by a cadre of kindred spirits - three, to be precise, who, along with myself, were known on campus as the 'Fearsome Foursome'. One was owlishly bespectacled Bennett Patterson - suave, poised, urbane and given to dryly ironic understatement, an apostate of the Church and of snooty Scarsdale, who demonstrated conspicuous histrionic talent as Edmund in a production of *Lear*, then dropped out of school, became a bartender in Greenwich Village and, after sundry other vicissitudes, ended up running some sort of dog ranch in Montana.

Another was Kurt Radetzky, a product, like myself, of suburban New Jersey, but descended, at least according to his own personal mythology, from millennium-old Hungarian aristocracy. Volatile, mercurial, unpredictably temperamental, Radetzky self-consciously cultivated the supposed vagaries of genius, caromed between fits of manic gloom and spasms of pantheistic rapture, tyrannised his women and finally settled down as a behavioural psychologist, gleefully goading rats through mazes and seeking the point in the brain that induced non-manual do-it-yourself orgasms.

The fourth member of our quaternity was J.T. Swift, a native of South Dakota, who'd grown up riding range and rodeo, then mis-transplanted himself to Boston. Married to a German *Lorelei* with whom I subsequently became infatuated, A.C. - we never learned what, if anything, the initials stood for - attained celebrity status by serving as local avatar of the Marlboro Man. Like Patterson, he, too, dropped out of school, becoming, in a sequence of metamorphoses that would've flummoxed Ovid, a Civil Rights campaigner, a film-maker, a steel worker, a veterinarian, a lumberjack, a schoolteacher, a biker, a trimmer of trees for the City of Palo Alto, a guiding spirit behind *Whole Earth Catalogue*-style environmental publications and, eventually, a poet - or so he'd decided to style himself, 'because I can't any longer maintain a coherent thread of thought for more than two or three sentences, and no one's ever heard of a paragrapher'. According to a subsequent postcard, he'd become, in his own words, an underseer for a prostitutes' union in Sausalito and the foreman of a dude ranch, whose duties consisted of standing at the corral with thumbs hitched in his belt, saying 'yep' and 'nope' frequently enough to convince greenhorns he was a cowboy.

With these three co-Faustlings, I embarked on an ambitious programme of audacious exploration and experimentation. The way up and the way down, we constantly reminded ourselves, are one and the same - or, at any rate, lead to the same point, somewhere beyond the ego's barbed-wire perimeter of rationality. Here, in theory, lay '*l'Inconnu*' of Rimbaud, attainable, he'd declared, by a 'systematic derangement of the senses'. In seeking to emulate him, we systematically deranged our neural systems by inducing some sort of ersatz epilepsy through hyperventilation, our respiratory and digestive systems by the ingestion or inhalation of diverse chemical, if not alchemical, substances. We tried the heady bouquets of sundry glues, epoxies and other fixatives; we tried paint fumes and turpentine; we tried ether in aerosol tins of the kind used to gas somnolent carburettors awake. We tried mace. (Severe stomach upset.) We tried nutmeg. (Exquisite taste, but the worst gastric upheaval I've ever experienced, save for a case of ptomaine poisoning some years later in California, which J.T. Swift dubbed 'Rocky Mountain Scrowtch'.) We tried banana skins. (No effect.) We tried morning glory seeds. (No effect except on Radetzky, who claimed to feel a 'floating sensation', possibly because he'd ingested them in the bath.)

At the same time, of course, there were the more orthodox proscribed substances, the gamut of which we ran with the pedantic zest of professional gourmets. Having learned, in the jargon later made fashionable, to 'go with the flow', I never underwent the nightmare of the proverbial 'bad trip'. Nevertheless, as I admitted to myself even then, I didn't genuinely enjoy my drug experiences; I submitted to them primarily from a sense of Promethean duty. I suspected that many of my contemporaries felt the same and only pretended otherwise. There were, granted, intermittent moments that almost convinced me of the validity of the pretence. For the most part, however, I approached drugs with an underlying solemnity, a determination to 'bring back' from each 'trip' something of value - some image, some insight, some dimension of understanding. Eventually, when I concluded that drugs no longer had anything to teach me, I lost interest in them.

Thus cocaine and the various amphetamines, though readily available, held little appeal for me or for my colleagues - they took us to no place we hadn't been before. We were all endowed with a sufficiently developed sense of self-preservation to stay away from heroin, but we did, on half a dozen occasions, laboriously boil paregoric down to a white tincture of opium. (Only later did I realise we'd been fabricating laudanum, but the process required too much paregoric to be cost-effective.) By exploiting minor ailments, injuries and, in one instance, Radetzky's dislocated shoulder, we obtained codeine and morphine from the infirmary, but found them more soporific than illuminating. Through a network of obliging contacts, we procured 'trial samples', in generous abundance, of the first batches of LSD, then being dispensed by Alpert and Leary at Harvard. We devoted weekends to magic carpet rides on the stuff, as well as on psilocybin and, in the form of nauseating peyote buttons, mescaline. Cannabis, naturally, as both hashish and marijuana, were as prevalent as the oily purple-hued vinegar labelled Chianti which we guzzled literally by the gallon in those days.

One spring evening, J.T. Swift, returning from Harvard Square to his apartment in the nether reaches of Cambridge, was accosted by an elderly, surprisingly lyrical, black derelict - who, for the bargain price of five dollars, offered to show him 'the Elysian Fields'. A.C. was initially wary of what appeared to be a pathetic, if grotesquely novel, homosexual overture. His petitioner, however - whom he could obviously, if necessary, pulverise - convinced him to the contrary, and guaranteed complete satisfaction or his money back. The money accordingly changed hands, and the derelict led A.C. to a patch of waste ground, a vacant lot between two soot-smeared, untenanted, leprously dilapidated buildings. There, bucolically Arcadian, rippling green-silver in the windy moonlight, grew an acre and a half of pristine marijuana - an oasis of narcoleptic euphoria amidst the desolate squalor of the slums.

It took us the whole of that night to harvest and an entire alcove of A.C.'s apartment to stash. Jam jars, coffee and biscuit tins, assorted other receptacles, were commandeered for the purpose. The yield, when processed, proved to be pretty foul - coarse, harsh, acrid, with a propensity to leave throat and lungs feeling raked long afterwards. Someone - whether practical joker or fool, I never knew - convinced A.C. it could be rendered smoother by simmering in wine. Gullible alchemists, we poured nearly a quarter of the hoard into an assembled armoury of saucepans, soused it in some fairly expensive vintage and spent hours watching, stirring, occasionally tasting as the marinating mess burbled, gurgled, hissed and sizzled on the stove. In the end, we squandered half a dozen bottles of good wine and got marijuana no smoother or more mellow than before, only sodden and virtually impossible to light. The saucepans were ineradicably stained - left with permanent stigmata.

On one occasion, too, A.C., his wife and I were nearly killed by the stuff -- though that, it must be said in all fairness, might just as easily have occurred with even the best imported varieties of the weed. As all but the stodgiest veterans of the sixties must know, cannabis dehydrates, leaving the mouth dry, furred, desiccated, prickly with a clammy nap denuded of saliva. It also tends to make one voraciously hungry. Having got stoned in the small hours one morning, we found the fridge and cupboards depressingly empty - nothing save some stale bread and a jar of peanut butter. In theory, peanut butter had never looked so enticing. In practice, the glutinous ochre gunk glued itself to our palates, our gullets, our gums, our tongues. Our very jaw muscles seemed to have congealed, and we came closer to dying from combined laughter and asphyxia than I like now to contemplate.

Despite such mishaps, the harvest of that spring evening lasted for more than two years. It lasted long after A.C. and his wife bequeathed it to me, having left Boston themselves for the voter registration campaign in Mississippi. It lasted, in fact, until my graduation, the summer just before my departure for Chicago. Unable to confront the commencement ceremony unstoned, I equipped myself with a supply of 'cocktails' - cigarettes with half their tobacco removed and replaced by marijuana. Unfortunately, amid the flurry of preparation, the tussle with recalcitrant cap and gown, the rounds of drinks and fatuous convivialities, I got the 'cocktails' mixed up with my more quotidian cigarettes - and smoked more of them than was strictly necessary for the precise octave of anaesthetic trance I desired.

One result was a familiar adjunct of cannabis inhalation, a celestially vapid grin - a 'shit-eating grin', in the terminology of the epoch - which I found impossible to wipe from my face. In flapping gown and precariously perched mortarboard cap, I took my grinning place in the formal procession and filed ceremoniously across the quadrangle, between ranks of my colleagues' congregated parents, siblings, aunts, uncles, cousins, girl- and boyfriends, family pets and other intrusive spectators - all of whose eyes seemed focused unanimously on my grin. I was enraged, but couldn't stop grinning at them. They responded to my grin with asinine grins of their own, all the more irritating for being controllable and not drug-induced. The more I grinned, the angrier I grew, with them and with myself. The angrier I grew, the more hopelessly stuck my grin became. I had alarming hallucinatory visions of some new medical phenomenon, pre-mortem rigor mortis. Moreover, my mouth was desperately dry, and the fanatical June sun was stewing me in my robes. Possibly to stave off total liquefaction, possibly to pummel the grin from my face, I jerked my arm upwards. The movement was too abrupt, I misjudged distances and my elbow nicked my mortarboard, which toppled from my head, plummeted downwards in an aerodynamic spin and embedded itself, point-first, in the turf. I tripped over it, bent and, in fumbling slow-motion, groped to retrieve it. The person at my heels bumbled into me and stumbled. The person in his wake collided with him in turn, and the whole procession lurched juddering to a halt in staggering disarray, like a derailed train.

At the end of the gauntlet of eyes and spectators, before the neo-Howard Johnsonesque façade of the main dormitory, awaited the stage-set for the commencement address - tiered semicircles of wooden chairs aligned on the grass around an improvised platform or daïs. By the time we reached the site, I was thoroughly exasperated, half-delirious with thirst and far too stoned to know or care who the distinguished guest speaker might be. His sole interest for me resided in the overwhelming and passionate urge I suddenly felt to send my mortarboard scaling up, frisbee-fashion, over his imposing silver-maned head. A typical effect of psychedelic drugs is a blurring of the distinction, and of the transition, between idle fancy, intention and act, between imagination and actualisation. One wonders whether one really said what one contemplated saying, or whether it remained, confined and echoing, in one's skull. One fantasises the exhilaration of flight, ponders its dynamics and, with no discernible activation of the muscles, proceeds to fly. One isn't altogether sure if one is flying in one's mind or in actuality until one finds oneself in parachuteless free-fall from the summit of a skyscraper to the street below. Before I realised I'd removed my mortarboard, it was poised in my hand. The student on my immediate left -- a classmate and reasonably close friend who'd more or less diagnosed my condition and its cause - stared at me aghast. For better or worse, I confided to him in a whisper what I was about to do, or planning to do, or thinking of doing, or perhaps already in process of doing. Stretching across my torso, he clamped himself frantically to my right arm and restrained me; and thus we stood, entangled like homosexual lovers, beneath the pointed, then progressively more distracted stare of the speaker exhorting us to good citizenship.

Gradually, the impulse to fly my mortarboard subsided and I became conscious of a burgeoning headache. When my companion released my arm, I scrabbled under my gown, producing from my pocket the aspirins I'd kept there for just such an eventuality. Knowing very little about drugs, and assuming the white tablets were a second helping of whatever had deranged me, my companion clamped himself to my arm again, and a furious struggle ensued for possession of the aspirins - the kind of close-quarters tussle which, in films, invariably leads to a gun going off. Both of us ended up scuffling on the grass, with two chairs upset, a buzz of mortified murmur and shocked remonstrance rising around us, and the voice of the speaker droning on, in ludicrous pretence that nothing was amiss. The aspirins disappeared, probably ground into the turf, which was just as well - my mouth, by then, was far too dry to have swallowed them without water. To asphyxiate on a taste of aspirin would've been signally more gruesome than doing so on a taste of peanut butter. Unstaunched by analgesic, my headache punctually blossomed - a miniature Thor banging clamorously away with his hammer, hurling lightning bolts of multi-coloured torment through my skull. My chief consolation was that I'd embarrassed to near catalepsy the Dean, who, two and a half years before, had evicted me from the dormitories for fighting match-duels with Patterson and Radetzky.

****

In the autumn of 1963, my graduation, and the slapstick attending it, were still a good eighteen or nineteen months in the future. My third year of university - the 'junior' year, as it's called in the States - had just begun. Denied access to the dormitories, which I no longer wanted anyway, I'd rented a monkishly ascetic room, next door to Patterson's, in a rickety boarding house - diagonally opposite the Student Union, across a leafy but heavily trafficked avenue from the main campus. Whatever the austerities of the place, it was infinitely preferable to the dorms, with their Boy-Scout-prim bunk-beds. Granted, the bed in the boarding house wasn't much better - a fiendish contraption apparently designed for stunted nuns. But at least one could have women visitors at all hours, including overnight, without subterfuge, enquiry or repercussion. This in itself made for an exhilarating sense of freedom and precocious maturity, which spurred my Faustian quest *hinan* with intensified momentum.

The fad of the moment was amyl nitrate, which Patterson, prowling around New York's East Village during the summer, had discovered at an insalubrious bar-cum-bordello quaintly named Slug's Saloon. Though already in vogue in Manhattan, amyls, as we called them, were virtually unknown in Boston. In consequence, we could buy them over the counter at any gullible or mercenary chemist's, for a price even we could afford without scrimping. They were potently noxious little things resembling suppositories for an android - bright yellow cylinders about the size of a .45 calibre cartridge, made of some brittle crackling substance like thin fibreglass and sold by the dozen in toxic-looking yellow tins. Officially, they were supposed to be dispensed as a remedy for angina. We were told, though I don't know how accurately, that the military also used them as an antidote for blood gas, whatever blood gas was. Apparently, too, during the first two or three decades of the century, there'd be decorative bowls of amyls scattered like *hors d'oeuvres* on tabletops and mantelpieces in funeral parlours, for queasy ladies to use as a smelling salt. If this were true, more than one such matron must've rocketed into an orbit that left the memorial service far below.

The instructions for use, printed on every tin, were simple enough. One was advised to place the amyl between two fingers, snap it open and briefly inhale the released fumes. We, of course, improved on this technique. We wouldn't inhale briefly, but deeply and at length. Pressing one nostril shut, we'd inhale through the other, then change nostrils and thereby receive a double blast. The fumes seared the nasal membranes and sinuses more savagely than cocaine. One's entire metabolism would accelerate violently, like a Porsche kicked down a gear and floored. One would feel something akin to whiplash through the whole of one's system. A roaring would commence in the ears, as of an inner sea. The pulse would race vertiginously. The temples would pound. The heartbeat would surge alarmingly against the ribcage. The veins would become gorged and the face turn a fiery apoplectic scarlet, the colour of a bloated poppy. One would then be hurled, as by a turbocharged catapult, into some other dimension of consciousness or reality. If one kept one's eyes open, the world became resonantly visible, limning itself to the retinas. If one lowered one's eyelids and pressed them with the fingertips, one might hallucinate - briefly, but with incandescent vividness. The whole experience lasted some forty-five seconds, during which time one felt jolted and buffeted by some tumultuous seismic upheaval within. It'd take another minute or so to 'come down' - often with an embryonic headache, a faint ripple of nausea and a redolence in the nose of the most foul smell I've ever known. Of all the drugs we sampled during those years, amyls were among the most unpleasant. Nevertheless, we persisted in using them until our nostrils were seared raw. I had a handful of mildly impressive visions under their influence. One was of a thunderbird - not the vulgar dreadnought of a car, but a proper Indian thunderbird, the kind seen on totem poles, blankets, rugs and shawls. It was opalescent black, with plumage of molten gold, and hung splayed against a backdrop of quivering, diamond-bright, electrically radiant cerulean blue. Like many such visions, it was exquisitely beautiful and conspicuously irrelevant to everything - a consummate epistemological *non-sequitur*.

Orbiting around my three colleagues and myself, there were at the time concentric circles of satellites - friends and acquaintances of greater or lesser intimacy, disciples, acolytes, protégés, hangers-on, groupies, aspiring bohemians, aspiring writers, the rebellious and disgruntled of diverse ilk. We were, in effect, the nucleus of a mini-solar system, which careened erratically through the more fixed social galaxies on campus. Amongst the student body, we were unofficially acknowledged as supreme aesthetic potentates, but our influence periodically encroached on other spheres as well - on philosophy, on psychology, on religious studies, on history, on sociology and anthropology, on the theatre. In the course of such oscillations, we'd often acquire new satellites, sometimes lose older ones. Insofar as possible, I wanted the new satellites to be feminine and qualified as prospective muses, with at least the potential of a future *Ewigweibliche*. Inevitably, however, there were some males among the newcomers, and some dead - or, more accurately, inert - stars. The most prominent of these was Cletis Caffey.

Most social cliques require a scapegoat, a clown, a buffoon - a comic figure who becomes the butt of everyone else's japes and therein finds not just his *raison d'être*, but also a certain squalid apotheosis. During most of the 1980s, Ronald Reagan performed this function on a global scale, like the fool of the medieval carnival, who, for the duration of festivities, was proclaimed king. In our clique, the rôle was discharged by Cletis - a fat youth with lurid carrot-coloured hair, craggy gargoyle features, a hoarse raucous whining adenoidal voice and, invariably, two or three folds of livid white belly jelly-jiggling beneath a too-short tee-shirt. Unlike Ronald Reagan, however, Cletis recognised his limitations, and had few desires beyond being accepted. We liked him immensely. We trusted him more than we did others for whom we felt greater respect. But this didn't prevent us from exploiting his querulously docile good nature, and being, on the odd shameful occasion, genuinely cruel.

Having discovered amyls, we kept them at first to ourselves; we mantled them in an aura of mystery, referred to them by oblique portentous designations and certainly didn't admit they could be obtained from the pharmacy down the road. Eventually, however, sore of nostril and jaded by ennui, we decided to introduce them to the rest of our entourage. We chose Cletis as our trial initiate.

Taking him aside at a party one evening, Radetzky and I, with pregnant whispers and exaggerated exhortations to secrecy, showed him one of the sinister yellow ampoules. It was, we declared impressively, the most potent substance of all, never to be disseminated to the great unwashed. Mesmerised by mingled fascination and fear, Cletis pleaded to sample. We made a show of doubt, of reluctance, of hesitation, of uncertainty and misgiving, then relented. But, we added, he'd have to prepare himself properly for the experience. These ampoules weren't to be taken lightly, as mere facile diversion. They were too powerful to be employed as anything other than instruments of valid psychological and epistemological enquiry.

As it happened, Cletis, just then, had grounds for precisely such enquiry. In an attempt to resolve some sort of identity crisis, he'd tried to convince himself he was a poet, boring us and everyone else to near murder with copious verses which suggested Allen Ginsberg percolated through McGonagallese. He was also enrolled in a Modern Poetry seminar, which was at that point addressing itself to Robert Graves. *The White Goddess* was too long, too opaque and too erudite a book for him actually to read, but distillations of it in class had had an incendiary effect on his fancy. Hostage to his own suggestibility, he reviewed the frequent occasions on which, aslosh with rancid Chianti, he'd passed out. Insofar as he could recall, he thought he'd glimpsed, just before consciousness was eclipsed, a dim enigmatic puissant feminine presence hovering at the outermost frontiers of awareness, looming like...

'The Statue of Liberty?' Radetzky helpfully suggested.

'Like Alyosha. You know. In that book by some guy named Haggard or something?'

'Fyodor Haggard, you mean?'

Might this, Cletis wondered, ignoring the question, perhaps be the White Goddess? Or, at least, his personal White Goddess, she who governed his own creative activity, dispensed to him the spiritual manna of inspiration? Wasn't it the poet's duty to confront his muse face to face, with all veils torn aside? And might the yellow ampoules, dormant but instinct with explosive force as midget sticks of dynamite, provide a means of doing so? I paraphrase Cletis' own imagery and maladroit, if not mixed, metaphor. At the time, I pointed out that dynamite, as a rule, was better for clearing logjams, dislodging boulders, demolishing bridges than for piercing numinous veils and facilitating trysts with mystic muses. But yes, Radetzky and I replied - to all Cletis' questions, the answer was yes. He would, however, have to prepare himself.

We subjected him to an improvised *rite de passage* commencing the following morning. We made him fast for the day, a more arduous ordeal for Cletis, given his appetite, than for most people. We insisted that he go through at least the motions - or, more accurately, non-motions - of meditation. We advised him, superfluously, to empty his mind. We ordered him to bathe, first in intolerably hot, then in intolerably cold water. We forbade him to smoke, or to drink anything other than buttermilk. For each aspect of his regimen, we provided an elaborate casuistic rationale. We then left him to his day of self-mortification. That evening, he was instructed to rendezvous with us at A.C.'s apartment. Here, we stretched him out on the sofa, handed him an ampoule and explained how to use it to maximum visionary benefit.

Cletis' inaugural flight on amyls never quite got airborne. A fortnight or so before, bucolicised by the last lyrical efflorescence of Indian summer, he'd gone to the beach. It was too cold to swim, but he'd sprawled on the shingle in his bathing trunks, fallen asleep and got painfully sunburned. Now, under the influence of amyl nitrate, the sunburn manifested itself as thousands of microscopic little men on tricycles pedalling furiously up and down his legs. Not even Cletis could construe this as an ultimate confrontation with the Feminine.

There followed, of course, an obligatory inquest to determine what'd gone wrong. Cletis dared to query the efficacy of the ampoule. We counterattacked by interrogating him rigorously on his adherence - or more probable lack thereof - to the regimen we'd imposed. Gestapo-fashion, we even turned a lamp into his face. Under the ferocity of our inquisition, Cletis capitulated, confessing that, in a frenzy of hunger, he'd allowed himself a chocolate bar. Only one? Well, two actually. No, three, to tell the truth, and some cold spaghetti as well. And? And some Kool-Aid to wash it all down. We turned away in disgust, castigating him as unworthy, rinsing our hands of him. Adenoids querulously vibrant, he pleaded for a second chance. We punished him by making him wait for a week, then subjected him to another day of preparation. On the appointed evening, we again assembled at A.C.'s apartment.

In accordance with instructions, a genuinely emaciated Cletis lay back on the sofa, snapped the amyl ampoule between his fingers, inhaled first through one nostril, then the other, closed his eyes and pressed his eyelids with his fingertips. In the voice of a tranced medium, he began to recount what transpired as it revealed itself to his mental gaze, becoming, as he did so, progressively more rapturously excited. There appeared at first, apparently, the customary kaleidoscopic swirl of patterns and colours - fans, peacock tails, arabesques, mandalas of incandescent intensity coalescing, dissolving, re-forming in new and ever more dazzling permutations. Gradually, this display resolved itself into a molten sunset, engulfed in turn, and suddenly, by darkness. Out of the darkness, there emerged a breathtakingly beautiful vista of nocturnal firmament - vast stellar spaces of midnight blue, the remote sequinned sash of the Milky Way, a luminous nail-paring of moon, a silvery spume of drifting cloud-wrack. Against this backdrop, there slowly materialised an immense white wrist and hand, which Cletis instinctively recognised as feminine.

'It's her! It's her!' he was yelling, heaving to and fro on the sofa as though in the throes of fever, or of some weird phenomenological orgasm.

In the hand, there appeared a torch.

'I told you it was the Statue of Liberty,' Radetzky whispered.

And with the torch, the hand began to write, in letters of dripping red-gold flame across the firmament:

'*DRINK PEPSI-COLA*!'

****

At least one of my own drug-induced visions was somewhat more edifying, somewhat more symbolically resonant - or so, at any rate, it seemed at the time. Having ingested a brew of boiled peyote button, I was some two hours into a mescaline trip; I was slumped in a comfortably-cushioned old-fashioned rocking chair in Patterson's room, my pen poised in my hand, my notebook open in my lap. I'd been trying to monitor and record my mental processes with a pretence to clinical precision. In fact, I'd got mesmerised by the rich, lustrous, viscous flow of ink from the pen's nib, and my initially fastidious notes had given way to arbitrary lines, circles, zigzags, squiggles and Rorschach-shaped blobs. On the bed, Patterson lay reading, resignedly performing the rôle of 'straight man'. As a matter of policy, one of us would always assume this rôle whenever any of the others lifted off on a more powerful hallucinogen. It seemed a rudimentary precaution; and it was reassuring to know one would be restrained from any precipitate impulse to drink ink, walk through a mirror, stick one's finger in a light socket, saunter out of an upstairs window or immerse an electric fire in the bath to heat the water.

We hadn't actually been expecting Radetzky, but he dropped by frequently enough, and it wasn't surprising when he did so now. Apparently, he'd just emerged from a squabble with someone, professor or fellow student, and was buoyantly enraged. Scarcely glancing at Patterson and me, he vehemently slammed his books down on the desk.

'The world is full of pricks!' he snapped and began to pace, smouldering away.

Patterson stared at him in ironic amusement. From the depths of my stoned euphoria, I watched him, his wrath like a palpable halo around him, a sulphurous aura. And suddenly, his assertion, echoing and re-echoing in my skull, detonated with all the shattering impact of transcendent revelation. Son of a bitch! He was right! It was true! It was profoundly true! It was literally true! It was truer than Radetzky himself ever imagined! *There were, literally, millions and millions of penises in the world!*

'Everything one says,' I proclaimed, in a prophet's mantic monotone, 'is in some sense true. Therefore, it doesn't matter what one says.'

Patterson turned his stare of ironic amusement on me and shrugged phlegmatically. Unflappable anyway, he was also, like the rest of us, inured to the oracular pronouncements of drug-induced sagehood. Radetzky, unaware of my condition, began tortuously to argue, but I'd already left such logical quibbles far behind, or below, or in some other, irrelevant, dimension.

'Everything one says is in some sense true,' I intoned from the empyrean in which I was cruising, 'simply because one says it.'

Love, Musil observes in his major novel, can be a feather dropped from the wing of an angel, or of a goose. This applies, equally, to mystical and visionary experiences. One may glimpse, through prismatic depths, the flickering gold and silver sparkle of some fabulous treasure. On trawling for it, one may find in one's net nothing but the scales of dead fish. Today, I suspect, I'd maintain just the opposite of what I did that night - I'd probably maintain that everything one says is in some sense *untrue* simply because one says it. At that moment, however, my utterance seemed unimpugnable (and all the more so for my having just uttered it). In my mind's eye - the only eye in any kind of focus at the time - I suddenly found myself climbing some sky-high skeletal structure, something like a power pylon, or the derrick of a celestial oil rig. It was composed not of steel, but of some amber-gold substance that resembled immense luminous stalks of raw spaghetti, and I was pulling myself upwards, hand over hand, from one radiant girder to the next. As I ascended, I felt myself buffeted by bracing gusts of fresh spice-clean wind, redolent of fir forests and the sea. The heavens above me were a crystalline azure, but the light - gold at first, then bleaching to fierce white - was becoming ever more intense, ever more blinding. Well-versed in *The Tibetan Book of the Dead*, I endeavoured, as long as possible, to stare into it. Eventually, it became too excruciating, and I was forced to avert my eyes. Gazing down through diaphanous space, I saw the earth far below, spinning dreamily away in the surrounding emptiness, like a jewel-encrusted beachball, or an exquisitely wrought Fabergé egg, sapphire and emerald and topaz. When I peered at it more attentively, however, I could see it was cracked, riven by an intricate network of fissures less reminiscent of Fabergé than of Humpty-Dumpty. All that prevented it from splintering into fragments was some sort of honey-hued glue, or epoxy, trowelled like mortar into the jagged interstices. This adhesive, I suddenly understood, was language.

I was ecstatic. I felt I'd been vouchsafed the kind of numinous truth towards which the puny intellect, unaided, can aspire in vain for a lifetime. The next day, Patterson and Radetzky told me I'd sat there for some two hours, oblivious to them, gazing off into the distance with a seraphically smug and supercilious smirk, looking as I'd attained Buddhahood. In my notebook, after the first few clinical entries, my calligraphy'd rapidly deteriorated, becoming progressively larger and more illegible. '*I can't write as fast*,' I'd complained at one point, '*as my consciousness streams*.' I'd then expatiated at some length on the concept of a motorised pen. By some slippage of association, this had apparently prompted ideas for other inventions, because there followed something about registering a patent for socks with toes. '*The world is full of pricks*,' I'd transcribed, and added an aphorism of JT Swift's: '*The trouble with always keeping your feet firmly on the ground is that you can never get your pants off* .' From here, I'd attempted to describe, in garbled shorthand, my climb up a '*tower of luminous spaghetti*' and the vista of enlightenment it afforded. After a signally inept drawing of a cracked Rand-McNally globe, I'd proclaimed, in a wildly sprawling hand: '*I AM A SEER!*'

* * * * * * *

I couldn't know it at the time, but a week or so after I'd earned my self-conferred seer's certificate, the world was to be fractured along fault lines I'd not seen in my vision, and no adhesive has yet served to repair the damage. '*What were you doing when you first heard the news*?' That question has now become frivolous, jokey, something like a party game, but also a device whereby we orient our own pasts, establish our sense of personal continuity and locate ourselves in a larger chronology. When I first head the news, shortly after one o'clock on the afternoon of 22 November, 1963, I was again slumped in Patterson's rocking chair, reading - or, rather, re-reading - *Ulysses*.

I'd read it initially during the summer holidays of the previous year, some fifteen months previous. During the last few days, I'd been working my way through it again, lip-reading this time, whispering the text to myself so as to register every cadence, every nuance - for Joyce wrote, after all, to be read aloud. The night before, I'd got mildly stoned on marijuana. Now I was in what I'd come to regard as my customary cannabis hangover - a mellow state of achingly poignant well-being, a state akin to a sustained *presque-vu*, everything around me suffused with incipient radiance, seeming about to brim over with richness and burgeoning significance. It was an ideal state in which to read. To do so when fully stoned was virtually impossible, the mind's capacity for synthesis being unsprocketed. One would become arrested, mesmerised, by a particular image, a particular turn of phrase, but one would have trouble placing it in context, relating it to what preceded and followed. In the hangover, however - or, as I preferred to think of it, the afterglow - the capacity for synthesis was unimpaired, while images and turns of phrase retained their vividness, their intensity, their immediacy. To read then was a process akin to guided daydream or guided fantasy, an experience of total immersion and participation.

I was nearing the end of the seventh chapter, 'Aeolus'. Amidst a bevy of scampering newsboys, Leopold Bloom had just accosted Myles Crawford and J.J. O'Molloy outside the offices of the *Irish Catholic* and *Dublin Penny Journal* - when the door to my left opened, dispelling Joyce's spell, and Patterson stood there motionless, silhouetted against the light from the corridor.

'Kennedy's been shot,' he stated, eerily casual.

Caught between two realities, 1904 Dublin and 1963 Boston, I was dislocated for a moment, unable to orient myself, to make sense of what I'd heard. Kennedy? Which Kennedy? I couldn't recall any Kennedy in the novel, certainly not in the present chapter. The bevy of scampering newsboys were shouting about something else, weren't they? I must've blinked and there must've been a pause.

'In Dallas,' Patterson said.

Dallas? What had Dallas to do with Dublin? Dallas couldn't have been more than a hick town in 1904. Only gradually did comprehension cohere, like a photograph emerging from developing fluid. I don't remember feeling shaken or shocked; I don't, in fact, remember feeling anything whatever. I seemed to have switched onto some sort of auto-pilot, mechanically asking routine questions, holding the event itself at bay until I could assimilate it.

'Is he dead?'

'Apparently. Hasn't been officially confirmed yet, but everyone's saying he is.'

'And Jackie...?'

'Don't know. Don't think so. She was there, I think, but no one's said anything about her being hit.'

'Did they catch whoever did it?'

'Don't think so. Not yet, anyway.'

There seemed, for the moment, nothing more to say. Another pause ensued, slightly constrained. Patterson then asked me if I were coming to lunch at the Student Union. I replied I'd be along in half an hour or so, after I'd finished the chapter I was reading, and he left, closing the door quietly behind him. Later, we both wondered why I'd asked the questions I did, and in precisely that sequence, that phraseology. Why, for example, didn't I ask who'd done it, or even if they knew who'd done it, rather than whether they'd caught him. Why didn't I ask why?

Alone in the room, I paced to the window, trying, insofar as possible, to confront the event head-on. It proved curiously elusive, seeming to exist somehow on a rounded and slippery surface, its implications curving away and out of sight. In any case, it still failed to make much conscious impact. My life at the time was varied and full, thronged with activities, people, books, adventures, romantic escapades. So far as public affairs were concerned, however, I might've been living in a cloister. I read no newspapers, had no access to television and little to radio. The Kennedys had been only shadowy figures in the background of my existence, glimpsed occasionally in grainy photographs at the newsstands. They'd never, in any way, impinged directly on my reality. Like most of my contemporaries, I'd had occasional vague twinges of remote-control lust for Jackie; but with so many nubile nymphs in my immediate proximity, I couldn't sustain such interest in a woman more distant from me even than a film goddess. As for her husband, I felt nothing, one way or the other. I simply took him for granted, rather as I took the Queen for granted - both just happened to be 'there', as irrelevant as statues, and I felt no closer to him than I did to the Queen. I certainly didn't think of him as 'my' President - though that, I suspect, says less about my attitude towards him than towards the United States, which, given my family's European roots, I'd never really felt to be 'my' country. So complete was my insulation that I'd had no awareness, when it occurred, of the Cuban Missile Crisis, apart from the hysteria it induced in a girl at the theatre - a candidate for museship, subsequently rejected. When she waxed wildly apocalyptic, I'd mantled myself in a serene fatalism. I'd no idea whatever of the issues involved, but I couldn't believe anyone, even a politician, would be so thick as to precipitate nuclear war. If such war were indeed imminent, however, there was hardly anything we undergraduates in Boston could do about it, any more than we could do anything about the weather; and if we did indeed have only a few days or hours left, I refused to waste them in pointless panic.

I continued staring out of the window, peering through autumnally skeletal branches to the street below, where cars passed as usual, their tyres lagged with fallen leaves. '*Kennedy's been shot.*' Repeatedly, I conjured Patterson's words back to mind. My only reaction was the mental equivalent of a shrug. It seemed, simply, another of the crazy things that were prone to occur in the wider world out there, a world beyond my personal horizons, a world in which I had no interest, of which I wanted no part. Presumably, the Vice-President - my attempts to evoke an image of him proved futile - would take over, and everything would proceed more or less as before. Lincoln, after all, had been assassinated. So had Garfield. So had McKinley. I couldn't imagine how my life would be in any way affected by the death of another President. And yet it seemed odd, somehow, that cars were still passing through the fallen leaves below, as if on an ordinary day, as if nothing unaccustomed had happened. It seemed odd that off to the left, where the railroad embankment gaped raw behind lawns and gardens and the field used for football practice, a train passed, as it did every afternoon at this time, dragging its carriages along with their metallically hiccoughing clatter. In some obscure manner, the sheer obliviousness of things struck me as insensitive, unseemly, slightly indecent. There was something inappropriate about such apathy, such indifference.

I checked my watch, remembered I wanted to finish 'Aeolus' before joining Patterson at the Student Union. Settling myself in the rocking-chair again, I re-immersed myself in Joyce's Dublin. On the streets of that city, Stephen Dedalus, conversing with Professor MacHugh, had just emerged from a newspaper office, followed, amid a bevy of scampering newsboys hawking the latest edition, by Myles Crawford and J.J. O'Molloy. Hailed by Leopold Bloom, Crawford had just fallen back a pace. Before Bloom could speak, however, a passing newsboy yelled in his face: '*Terrible tragedy in Rathmines! A child bit by a bellows!*'

Something was disturbingly askew. I felt a weird sense of dislocation. A slippage of dimensions had occurred, opening fissures like those of an earthquake, and I'd tumbled into one of them. It seemed inconceivable that those men on the streets of Dublin could be unaware of what'd just happened. It seemed extraordinary that the whirl of wild newsboys weren't shouting about Kennedy's death. That, certainly, would've been a better story than a child bitten by a bellows in Rathmines; and Kennedy was, after all, Irish in heritage. Could Dublin, even in 1904, really have been so parochial, or was Joyce exaggerating? I was irritated, but not sure by what. By the blinkered provinciality of those Dubliners of sixty years before? Or by the brutishness of current events, which had polluted the atmosphere of a great novel?

I closed the book, got up and paced to the window again. And suddenly, at a remote distance, as though through the wrong end of a telescope, I glimpsed with my mind's eye a dilapidated garret room, and a figure - a university student - slumped in a rocking-chair, reading. But the room wasn't quite the room in which I stood, and I wasn't quite the figure in the rocking-chair. Both the room and its occupant existed in the future. Sometime in the future, I realised - in five years, fifty years, a hundred years, two hundred - another President would be shot, another head of state, another charismatic leader. More than one, probably. And somewhere, at each such traumatic moment, a young man like myself would be sitting in a garret, reading *Ulysses*. And he, too, having heard the news, would return to the book, and find between the covers that it was still 16 June, 1904, that it had never ceased to be 16 June, 1904. And he, too, would be disoriented, bewildered by Stephen and Bloom, MacHugh and O'Molloy and Crawford - by the serene obliviousness of those Dubliners, those individuals miraculously conjured to life not from clay but from ink, pursuing their allotted courses with the immutable imperturbability of the stars.

At the Student Union, shock and its attendant numbness hadn't yet set in. Nothing, of course, had as yet appeared in the newspapers. Here and there, small groups of people were congregated around transistor radios, but information was still sketchy and the mood of the place was that of a wasps' nest disturbed - rumour, gossip, speculation, bizarre theories and scenarios caromed about like the ping-pong balls in the adjacent room. I didn't stay long, though

I've no recollection what I did for the rest of the afternoon. I know I had no classes to attend, and Patterson had wandered off somewhere. Probably I returned to the boarding house and *Ulysses*.

In the evening, I considered dropping round to A.C.'s apartment, where at least there was a television. By that autumn, however, he and his wife were already busy dismantling their marriage. Not wanting to intrude unannounced on some turgid domestic tiff, I thought it best to telephone first. I therefore returned to the Student Union, only to find queues at the telephones stretching out of the door and half a block down the road. By now, the reality of the day's events was beginning to seep into people's consciousness. One consequence was that half the students on campus had felt impelled to call home - as if, reverting to nameless childhood terrors, they needed the reassuring sound of parental voices.

The campus the following morning, Saturday, was more than just subdued, more than just withdrawn into itself. It seemed to be cowering, cringing, as if before some threatening upraised hand. A flag twitched at half-mast against the grey sky, fluttered spasmodically, dropped limp again. Raw streaks of winter in the air accentuated the stricken atmosphere. The few students in sight seemed to be avoiding the main paths, preferring to move furtively against walls, in the protective shadow of the buildings - seemingly fearful of snipers. An eerie hush prevailed, like that of a sudden snowfall, muting everything. I still felt detached, but had a sombre subliminal sense of something portentous looming invisibly over the scene, something whose full significance I'd not comprehended. I was pervasively conscious that I'd always remember these two days, opaque though their immediate relevance might be, and that they'd assume in time a meaning not yet apparent. This, in itself, seemed ominous.

I made my way to my customary Saturday morning class, the same one Cletis attended, in Modern Poetry. The professor was himself a poet of some local celebrity - a large lumbering ebullient man, bald before his time, with bulging eyes, the face of an alcoholic cherub and the bouncy manner of an over-enthusiastic little boy. He arrived late and flagrantly drunk, but that scarcely mattered, there being no more than four or five of us present. Class would be cancelled, he announced, unwontedly brusque. There wasn't much to say today. What there was could be said better by someone other than himself. He therefore proposed to read, aloud, Yeats' 'Lapis Lazuli':

I have heard that hysterical women say
They are sick of the palette and fiddle-bow,
Of poets that are always gay,
For everybody knows or else should know
That if nothing drastic is done
Aeroplane and Zeppelin will come out,
Pitch like King Billy bomb-balls in
Until the town lie beaten flat.

All perform their tragic play,
There struts Hamlet, there is Lear,
That's Ophelia, that Cordelia;
Yet they, should the last scene be there,
The great stage curtain about to drop,
If worthy their prominent part in the play,
Do not break up their lines to weep.
They know that Hamlet and Lear are gay;
Gaiety transfiguring all that dread.
All men have aimed at, found and lost;
Black out; Heaven blazing into the head:
Tragedy wrought to its uttermost.
Though Hamlet rambles and Lear rages,
And all the drop-scenes drop at once
Upon a hundred thousand stages,
It cannot grow by an inch or an ounce.

On their own feet they came, or on shipboard,
Camel-back, horse-back, ass-back, mule-back,
Old civilisations put to the sword.
Then they and their wisdom went to rack:
No handiwork of Callimachus,
Who handled marble as if it were bronze,
Made draperies that seemed to rise
When sea-wind swept the corner, stands;
His long lamp-chimney shaped like the stem
Of a slender palm, stood but a day;

All things fall and are built again,
And those that build them again are gay.

Two Chinamen, behind them a third,
Are carved in lapis lazuli,
Over them flies a long-legged bird,
A symbol of longevity;
The third, doubtless a serving-man,
Carries a musical instrument.

Every discoloration of the stone,
Every accidental crack or dent,
Seems a water-course or an avalanche,
Or lofty slope where it still snows
Though doubtless plum or cherry-branch
Sweetens the little half-way house
Those Chinamen climb towards, and I
Delight to imagine them seated there;
There, on the mountain and the sky,
On all the tragic scene they stare.
One asks for mournful melodies;
Accomplished fingers begin to play.
Their eyes mid many wrinkles, their eyes,
Their ancient, glittering eyes, are gay.

The professor himself was unable to sustain the serene Olympian aloofness of those Oriental sages, composed of lapis lazuli, but also of the same substance, or essence, as Hamlet and Lear, Stephen Dedalus and Leopold Bloom. By the last stanza, his shoulders were heaving, his voice was wavering, cracking, breaking. He finished on a strangled sob.

'I'm sorry,' he choked, turned so abruptly on his ponderous bulk that he seemed about to topple, and, like a tottering tower, lurched out of the room.

Most of the students around me were rigid with confusion or embarrassment. One girl, however, was snuffling convulsively in the corner. Another sat in a more statuesque ecstasy of grief, tears and mascara streaming down her lifted face, her eyes widened on the distance, seeming to hold eternity in the fixity of their gaze. I, for my part, have never forgotten that agonised recitation. Even today, I refuse to employ the word 'gay' according to its current usage. I resent the way in which a perfectly valid word has been hi-jacked, its richness drained to a single circumscribed meaning. I resent the way in which that meaning sullies my memory of 1963 - and, by forcing upon it a grotesque *double-entendre,* reduces one of the finest poems in the English language to an object for giggles and sniggers.

Emerging from the classroom, I walked down the steeply sloping hill of the campus towards the main road, across which lay the Student Union. I saw J.T. Swift, bearded, booted and bedenimed, standing just outside the door, talking to someone. He saw me, too, waved in his desultory fashion, broke off his conversation and ambled in my direction, pausing at the kerb as the traffic light turned red. I continued my descent towards him.

The traffic light changed to amber, and a massively finned and chromed white Chrysler convertible, its top up, juddered to a halt at the crossing, swaying on its soggy springs. At a distance of perhaps fifty feet, A.C. passed diagonally in front of it. As he did so, there was a frenzied squeal of tyres and the car lunged forward, rear wheels spinning, rear end shimmying from side to side. I yelled a warning, but was too far away to be heard above the noise. Other people, closer by, yelled as well. And suddenly, as everything unscrolled in dreamlike slow motion, I knew this was no accident, no slipped gear or slither of foot on brake - the car was being *aimed* deliberately at A.C., was hurtling towards him like some immense arctic beast in wild stampede. It missed by inches. With the agility he'd learned riding rodeo in his teens, A.C. performed something like a half-pirouette and dived headlong, landing on the grassy verge. I heard a brutal thump, but that, I learned later, was only his boot, which had caught the car's door as it swept by. The car slewed past him, jounced sickeningly up the kerb and, with a crunch of mangled metal, slammed bumper-first into a fire hydrant. The hydrant burst and a geyser of water gushed upwards, hissing, blossoming open in petals of grey spray.

By the time I reached the road, half a dozen people were congregated around A.C., who sat, wet and somewhat puzzled, under the hydrant's freezing spume. Seeing he was unscathed, I joined two other students tearing at the car's door handle. I was personally bent on violence. Those around me, I think, were also possessed by the spirit of a lynch mob. When, after a brief struggle, we managed to wrench the door open, however, we stopped.

I'm not quite sure what, if anything, we expected - an oaf, a lout, a redneck, a joy-rider perhaps, a teenaged punk in his father's prestigious status symbol. Slumped at the wheel, enclosed by red velour upholstery and carpets more appropriate to a bordello, sat a tall, angular, silver-haired gentleman, dapper and distinguished-looking in an immaculate oyster-grey suit. Both he and the car's interior were rank with alcohol. He remained motionless for a moment, staring blindly through the windscreen rendered opaque by sheets of water from the hydrant. Then he turned, revealing a face haggard and slick with tears, through which his eyes flashed at us balefully.

'Ye long-haired Communist bastards!' he croaked in a thick brogue. 'Ye fuckin' Communist bastards! It's the likes of youse shot my President...!'

He tried to say something more but collapsed in sobs, his whole body wracked by them, his breath catching in his throat and wheezing like a death rattle. By this time, A.C. was standing beside me, peering through the car door. He and I exchanged glances. Behind us, voices were clamouring for the police to be called.

'Forget it,' A.C. drawled, straightening up.

Slowly, sullenly, the crowd began to disperse. Again, we stared at the man in the car, his face now buried in his hands, his shoulders still jerking convulsively. We closed the door on him quietly, leaving him to his weeping, and turned away.

Thus did politics first encroach on my reality.

IV

I resented the crass intrusion of politics. I endeavoured to hold them at bay. I regarded them as one might a drunken boor at a party, who attaches himself to one's sleeve, insists on recounting another tediously unfunny story and prevents one from crossing the room to the woman one wants to meet. Whenever I catch flu, I feel not just rotten, but indignant - indignant at finding my privacy invaded by a horde of imperialistic microbes. In the aftermath of Kennedy's death, the importunities of politics affected me as a comparable act of unprovoked aggression.

At the same time, I was prey to a gnawing disquiet. In the way *Ulysses* had been temporarily polluted, there seemed some species of vague yet ominous augury - as if the purity of my own aestheticism were liable to be similarly tainted. Certainly changes were occurring in the world around me. Among my entourage of associates, acolytes and disciples, more and more of the younger ones - those behind me by a year or more - were becoming politicised, enrolling in the proliferating organisations whose initials spilled like alphabet soup across every campus. One friend, until then a dedicated literary dilettante, founded a local chapter of SDS, Students for a Democratic Society. Rapidly rising in the hierarchy, he eventually became a guiding - or misguiding - spirit of the more manically militant Weathermen.

'We're a transitional generation,' Radetzky observed mournfully. 'Before us, except for the occasional beatnik, there were only jocks and grey flannel suits. After us, there'll only be demonstrators, agitators, organisers and would-be revolutionaries. America can't stand more than a couple of years of culture at a time.'

During the following spring, I paid scant attention to the election campaign's gathering momentum. I possessed only the most generalised awareness that Johnson - not yet the certified villain he later became - was preferable to Goldwater, whom informed opinion classified as a lunatic, liable to play Wild Bill Hickok with the country's nuclear arsenal. Anticipating nothing less than Armageddon, most of my contemporaries were more closely attentive to the issues than I was, and more concerned. Large numbers of them were scared into action.

In 1864, the American South had been invaded by the vindictive and ill-disciplined army of William Tecumseh Sherman, for whom war, if it was hell, was also exhilarating. On their acclaimed march to the sea, Sherman's troops had cheerfully implemented a calculated 'scorched earth' policy, had razed Atlanta, devastated Georgia and the Carolinas, ruined the region's economy for decades, displayed a general bestiality unique in the American military until Vietnam, and left a legacy of rancour, hatred and bitterness comparable to Cromwell's in Ireland. Exactly a century later, Dixie was again invaded, by another, very different but no less terrifying army - students and teachers from primary schools up to universities, drop-outs, wastrels, beatniks, housewives, film stars, folk singers, writers, journalists, lawyers, clergymen, nuns and assorted other manifestations of decadent or subversive tendencies, bred, it was claimed, by seditious un-American elements among the gullible intelligentsia of the abolitionist Northeast. To the average peace-loving bigot south of the Mason-Dixon line, this motley host was anarchy incarnate, all the demons of chaos and the void unleashed, the forces of darkness on the march. They swarmed down in their thousands, inundating Alabama, Louisiana, Mississippi. The objective was to register the black population of the old Confederacy - to bring millions of new voters into the electoral rolls and wrest the balance of Southern political power from white conservatives, who comprised one of Goldwater's staunchest bastions of support. Whether the crusade ultimately made much difference to the election, I don't know. Probably not. With the twenty-twenty vision of hindsight, it seems unlikely that Goldwater would've had much chance anyway. At the time, however, his prospects seemed much more tangible, and downright alarming. To that extent, they provided a concrete focus and impetus for the already active Civil Rights Movement, whose ranks were now swollen by an influx of fresh recruits.

The stories that filtered back to us up north were often, it seemed, unreal, or surreal, or mere figments of literature. In the Mississippi Delta, people I knew would detour haphazardly from the main road, pass through something akin to a time warp and find themselves in the heart of Yoknapatawpha County. Mournful vistas of grey-green cotton fields, flecked as if with dandruff. An occasional patrician house on the horizon, lapsed from its former grandeur but still flaunting a dingy white columned portico, like a classical temple. Nearer by, squalid, half-collapsed, tin-roofed or thatch-roofed or unroofed cabins with weed-choked kitchen gardens and aprons of brown dirt where a few emaciated chickens scratched, a pig wallowed in the dust, a spavined nag or mule drowsed under a cloud of flies, a plough or some other unidentifiable metal contraption rusted quietly away. Over everything, a miasma of brooding exhaustion, a torpor like an incessant buzzing of insects which only just masked a lazy smouldering violence and the sour smell of fear. Here subsisted, if only barely, somnolent enervated human beings whose standard of living, and mentality, dated from a century before. Never having seen vehicles of such size and shape before, many of them were baffled by the ubiquitous Volkswagons of the voter registration workers. '*Car looks like some kinda bug. Some kinda beetle, mebbe.*'

Patiently, step by step, my friends would explain the intricacies of the registration process. Most of the locals, even when they grasped the principle, dared not act on it, cowed by possible reprisals from the Klan. Most of them, at one time or another, had seen the notorious flaming cross luridly outlined against the night sky. On occasion, however, it wasn't the Klan that constituted the obstacle so much as sheer benightedness.

'Now remember, Johnson's the man you want to vote for. He's the Democrat.'

'But I cain't do that. If I'se gonna vote, I'se gotta vote for the Republican.'

'The Republican?'

'Yassuh. Abram Lincoln, he was a Republican, wasn't he? An' it was Abram Lincoln who done freed the slaves.'

For most of those who thronged south that spring and summer, the primary motives were, I think, laudably idealistic. Many, however, also had ulterior motives, not always conscious. Some were in search of something - adventure, vengeance either real or imagined, a sense of family and camaraderie, sexual opportunities of a kind precluded by the inhibiting constraints of accustomed milieux. Others were in flight from something - parents, stultifying or ruptured marriages, academic or professional routine, often themselves. Among those in this latter category was Ilona, JT Swift's German wife, a wistful and willowy woman with long gypsy-jet hair parted Madonna-like in the middle, immense brown eyes brimming with

Weltschmerz, features of a pure haunted saintliness and the lofty somnambulism, verging on hysteria, of an Iphigenia being led to sacrifice.

At the outbreak of the Second World War, her mother had been married to a Jew, who'd soon disappeared into the camps. She herself would've been deported in turn, had she not caught the fancy of an influential *Wehrmacht* officer. This man, subsequently killed on the Russian front, had become her protector, and Ilona's father. Ten years later, the widow, now remarried, had emigrated with her second husband and her daughter to Canada. Here, six thousand or so miles from bomb-gutted Darmstadt, Ilona had grown up, burdened with a self-imposed case of 'German war guilt' which - were that portmanteau label not handy to contain it - probably would've been classified an incipient psychosis. The American South offered more than just a refuge from her disintegrating relationship with JT. It also offered a superb opportunity for displaced or sublimated expiation. In April, she volunteered her services to the Student Non-Violent Coordinating Committee and fled to Mississippi. She was assigned to a compound of voter registration workers in the small town of Ashwood, just above the Louisiana border.

When I'd first come to know her a year and a half before, she was the single most erudite woman I'd ever met, with a love and understanding of literature that transcended mere aestheticism. It amounted almost to a form of religious ecstasy. In the privacy of her dreams, waking as well as sleeping, she'd churn herself into a state of intensely spiritualised eroticism, communing passionately with Lawrence and Rilke, Goethe and Thomas Mann, Hölderlin and Novalis. I'd been influenced by the same figures, disdaining my banal contemporaries who sought to emulate Hemingway, Fitzgerald and Kerouac. Ilona alone had any comprehension, not to say appreciation, of what I was trying to do with my prose; and our rapport, therefore, at least initially, derived from artistic *Wahlverwandschaften*. By the time of Kennedy's death, she'd begun increasingly to emerge as the *Ewigweibliche* I'd been seeking; but my respect for JT prohibited any liberties on my part. Even when his marriage began to buckle, my bond with Ilona remained etherealised, sublimated into a lofty literary mysticism. Once she was in Ashwood, however, my scruples evaporated, perhaps because they'd apparently been rendered superfluous. In any case, the letters that began to fly to and fro between us - as often as three or four a week - became both explicit and intimate. Our turbocharged prose didn't always attain the sublime.

'Don't hurt the warm little furry thing inside,' she wrote me on one occasion, from the troughs of a somewhat melodramatic depression. *'It's all we have.'*

'What'd you do?' Radetzky, never much of a romantic, asked, when I committed the solecism of quoting her. 'Take a mutual vow by each swallowing a squirrel?'

Such cynicism only made me feel more Faustian. It was, after all, in similar tones that Mephistopheles had introduced himself to Goethe's protagonist: *'Ich bin der Geist, der stets verneint.'*

Despite my most assiduous efforts, I couldn't imagine myself in Mississippi, slogging through cotton fields to register prospective voters. Neither could I imagine passion torridly blossoming in the incestuously claustrophobic confines of the Ashwood compound. Nevertheless, I began seriously to contemplate driving south that summer, joining Ilona, at least creating an opportunity for whatever'd failed to actualise itself in Boston. Before I could make up my mind, JT pre-empted me and headed south himself, in the forlorn - and, as it transpired, futile - hope of salvaging his marriage.

I did, in fact, later make the drive myself. I did so twice, in mid-August and then again in mid-September, shortly before my last year at university began. I didn't expect to 'claim' Ilona, only to renew my contact with her, to see her and her husband and assess the condition of their relationship - which proved hopeless enough to give me hope. I used a rented car provided by SNCC. As a precaution, I procured a press card which identified me, improbably, as a reporter for the Boston *Globe*. I timed my trips so that most of the journey through the South was by night. And I carried with me sundry vital supplies, which Mississippi shops wouldn't sell to voter registration workers or didn't sell at all. Newspapers, for example, with a somewhat less parochial perspective than those published locally. Volumes of Faulkner, who, perversely, was banned from the Ashwood library. Marvel Comics, just then coming into vogue on campuses of the Northeast. Mississippi was a 'dry' state, liquor being available only to 'authorised' customers through specially licensed outlets. I therefore brought bottles of bourbon disguised as a speciality for New Englanders nostalgic about maple syrup. And, in various crevices, crannies and interstices of the car, where no one in those naïve days thought to search, I brought cannabis – from the harvest garnered that evening in Cambridge a year before.

My recollections of these sorties are hazy, blurred by darkness, heat, boredom and fatigue. I remember the road unspooling hypnotically before me, lapped up by the front tyres. I remember a deer impaled by the stiff luminous lances of the headlamps, standing paralysed and quivering, its eyes glazed and widened in a stare subsequently associated with J. Danforth Quayle. I remember the sheer desolate emptiness of the nocturnal highway, the preternatural rural darkness to every side and, save for a shrill of crickets that seemed to ring the horizon, the smothering silence – so eerie a contrast to the lights, the noise, the congested bumper-to-bumper traffic of Boston and New York. I remember the split-banjo twang of a country-and-western singer on the radio, lamenting how he'd traced his lost love's little footsteps through the snow.

Few things seemed more remote than snow in the malarial Mississippi night, but the dreaded police, usually ubiquitous as vermin, were almost as scarce. On one occasion, I was stopped for a routine check by a typical 'peace officer' of the period – a swarthy swaggering deputy wearing Confederate grey uniform, Stetson, steel-rimmed spectacles and the squint-eyed, chronically suspicious look of his kind. He was dapper and slim, almost tubular. Obesity was no doubt a prerogative of seniority, and the mountainous paunch traditionally associated with the region's lawmen probably adorned his superior, the full-fledged sheriff. I considered recycling my 'I'm an alchemist' routine, then thought better of it and flaunted my press card instead. Instructed, I gathered, to display proverbial Southern hospitality to the media, he waved me on with a grudging air.

Of Ashwood itself, I recall little apart from a pervasive reek of manure, an odd juxtaposition of antediluvian pick-up truck with garishly chromed modern hotrods, typical small-town streets where prim offices – a solicitor's, a funeral parlour, a bank – alternated with modest shops and dingy cafés. Traditional clapboard architecture, now dilapidated and leprously flaking, was interrupted only occasionally by plate glass. An incongruously graceful white courthouse reared its pillared façade over one end of the dusty square, at the centre of which, amid rows of lurid flowers, stood the inevitable monument - an emaciated Confederate infantryman on his plinth, musket and bayonet raised in defiant futility. In the general store, an exhausted air-conditioner puffed and wheezed laboriously, manufacturing gusts of glacial clamminess. Elsewhere, the desultory rotation of ceiling fans spun cartwheels of light and shadow across rooms sizzling with flies.

The compound stood in the black section of town, a large, more or less rectangular block of a building which rose above the surrounding hovels like a hen amidst a brood of chicks. It'd once, I gathered, been the offices, workshops and warehouse of a small tannery, and the walls still oozed a redolence of carbolic, of hides and leather. A warren of makeshift cubicles and plywood partitions provided living quarters and common-rooms. In the rear, there was a cavernous, invariably smoke-filled, kitchen, where Ilona prepared meals for the dozen or so staff. It wasn't a milieu conducive to mending a marriage. On my first visit, husband and wife were scarcely on speaking terms. On my second, Ilona wasn't there at all, having driven with another worker to the FBI offices in Baton Rouge, across the Louisiana border, with a file of legal documents - affidavits and depositions from local people, testifying to harassment and intimidation.

On both of my visits, I was received effusively, not just by the people I knew, but by the entire compound. I was hailed as a co-worker, a colleague and, in a sobriquet that made me wince, a comrade. I might've been a one-man relief column bringing provisions to a besieged garrison - which, in a very real sense, the enclave at Ashwood was. For my part, I was too hot, too tired, too absorbed by my own amorous preoccupations to partake of the general conviviality, or to wear comfortably the rôle imposed upon me.

Neither could I take much interest in the various landmarks my hosts were eager to display. The graveyard where a murdered black youth was buried, the yard where the Klan recently burned a cross, the rutted unpaved roads, the cabins out in the cotton fields, the majesty of the river rolling its tons of mud down the length of a continent - all left me surly and morose. On grounds not altogether clear to myself, I felt guilty. For having abrogated my own aesthetic detachment, my own Olympian aloofness, and sullied my hands with political action? Or for not being as fervently *engagé* as those around me, who imagined me as committed as themselves?

Yes, I approved of the cause, but my approbation was cerebral - a matter of intellectual opinion rather than anything visceral. It was ultimately incidental to my infatuation for Ilona; and to that extent, I was in Ashwood under false pretences. At the same time, I'd compromised, as I saw it, my artistic integrity. Stephen Dedalus, after all, had refused to sign political petitions, had shunned mass movements in which creative individuality was subsumed. But then again, I tried to tell myself, my behaviour was only ostensibly political. In reality, it was something else - a kind of high chivalric enterprise, the noble service of a knight-errant performing deeds of derring-do for his lady's greater glory. I shrank from the status of crusader, but I was quite prepared to be a mercenary for love. That could be reconciled with art in a way that politics couldn't. *Das Ewigweibliche zieht uns hinan.* Later, back in Boston, I joked about having cards printed for myself with a chess knight emblazoned on them, like Paladin's in *Have Gun, Will Travel.*

In the planning of them, I'd approached both trips as something of a lark, with reckless insouciance, with a sense of romantic adventure, with a certain aesthetic curiosity - and with a tourist's fatuous propensity for 'collecting' places, as if peregrinations through the South at the time were no different from a visit to the Grand Canyon, or the top of the Empire State Building. This mentality gave way to boredom, fatigue, physical and emotional discomfort, then to frustration and a measure of depression. What I find interesting now, and more than a little naïve, is that I had no real appreciation of danger - no awareness, such as my Draft Board was later to spawn in me, of my life being on the line. What I was doing seemed to me scarcely more hazardous than, say, stealing apples - or smoking dope, or duelling with matches in the dormitory. I was cocking a snook at a particularly despicable manifestation of authority; but I was doing so with impunity, with a conviction of immunity, with no consciousness of personal risk.

In fact, the risk was real enough, even if my besottedness with Ilona reduced it to the status of a vaporous and easily outmanoeuvred dragon, which allowed me to play, if not knight-errant, at least toreador. Early that spring, three voter registration workers - two of them white and from the North – had been arrested, on a trumped-up charge, in a small town not far from Ashwood. On some puerile excuse – 'inadequate facilities', or something of the sort – the authorities had transferred them to another jail ten miles or so distant, in a town called Wisteria. At dusk the next day, after twenty-four hours of incarceration, they were released. There was, of course, no transport, public or otherwise, and the three youths were obliged to make their way back from Wisteria, along ominously lightless and empty rural roads. They set off on foot into the gathering darkness and simply disappeared. For the next two months, extensive searches of the area revealed nothing. At last, acting on an alleged tip-off – perhaps an agent had infiltrated the Klan, perhaps some guilt-stricken Klan member had turned informer – the FBI located and exhumed the three bodies. All three had been gruesomely tortured, then shot through the head and buried in the earthworks of a local dam.

After the barrage of publicity surrounding these grisly events, they seemed unlikely to recur. On my own trips south, I'd contrived to render myself more or less amnesiac of them. Some six or seven weeks after my second journey, however, the spectres of those three youths were to return and haunt the whole of metropolitan Boston.

It must've been around the middle of October. The academic year had already begun, and I'd moved into a proper apartment, which I shared with a graduate student, half a mile from campus. Radetzky occupied a similar apartment a further half mile away. Patterson, by then, had dropped out and was tending bar in New York's East Village.

I still lacked a telephone, and communication was cumbersome. Shortly after ten one Thursday evening, there was a banging on the door. Cletis, in more of a lather than he'd displayed since his amyl nitrate initiation, confronted me with the news. It'd been rung through, on reversed charges, to Brandeis University, to someone she knew there, by a black girl associated with the voter registration workers in Ashwood. Brandeis, in turn, had contacted our circle. That afternoon, JT, Ilona and all the other members of the Ashwood compound had been arrested. Nothing else was yet known, not even the charges.

Cletis and I caught a cab to JT's old apartment in Cambridge – which had been sub-let to friends and, with its two telephones, had now been transformed into an impromptu command post. Eight or nine people were already assembled there, others still arriving. In Radetzky's and my absence, authority had been assumed, or misassumed, by Donald Carlsmith, my sometime associate and disciple, subsequently to become field-marshal, or generalissimo, or whatever the rank was, of SDS. With the kamikaze zeal that would come to characterise all his activities, he'd rung the Ashwood jail direct. Adopting the magisterial and misplaced hauteur of his Brahmin upbringing, he'd first insulted and abused the sheriff, then *demanded* to speak to the prisoners.

'I'll tell you what, boy,' a lazy Mississippi voice had drawled at the end of his harangue. 'You come on down here from Yankeeland an' I jus' might let you kiss my ass.'

For an instant, as Carlsmith debriefed to me, I had an odd sense of *déjà-vu*. Something fleetingly reminded me of *Ulysses*, of the assassination nearly a year before. Then I lost my temper.

'What the fuck're you trying to do? Help JT and Ilona, or martyr them to the cause?'

Chastened, Carlsmith still started feebly to argue, to exonerate himself, to parry with slogans and stale rhetoric. I told him succinctly to shut up and he drifted off into a corner, to sulk and re-stoke his revolutionary flame. Having effectively browbeaten my colleague, I was wondering what to do next, about the real adversary, when the telephone rang. Radetzky, who'd just arrived, answered. It proved to be our contact at Brandeis. The charges against the Ashwood workers had now been specified. They were accused of running a boarding house and - because of Ilona's cooking, presumably - a restaurant without a licence. That, of course, was silly enough. Not even Mississippi prosecutors could milk a serious sentence out of it. But there was something more alarming. According to the latest reports, the prisoners, at dawn, were to be transferred to another jail, about fifteen miles away.

'Where?'

'Wisteria. Just over the county line, so there'll be all sorts of vagueness about jurisdiction.'

A chill descended on the room, as though at the passage of some ghostly presence. Surely they wouldn't be so stupid as to try the trick again? But these, after all, weren't cunning secret agents or Mafia machiavels, only bumptious slobs and yokels whose imaginations were as sluggish as their law enforcement, and whose individual IQs probably didn't exceed the temperature. If Ilona, JT and the others were transferred to Wisteria, their situation would be identical to that of the youths murdered six months before. They'd be released, no doubt at nightfall, and left to make their own way back to Ashwood. Granted, there were more of them this time, and someone associated with the Ashwood compound might manage to organise transport. En route, however, they'd still be at the mercy of the Klan, and anything could happen on the desolate nocturnal roads. Whatever did could be dismissed by the sheriffs in Ashwood and Wisteria as falling within the other's jurisdiction; and both, of course, would disclaim responsibility for the Klan's activities.

Radetzky and I tried to formulate a plan. We fell back on one of my basic principles in chess - when things become critical, muddle them up, precipitate chaos and hope to create options out of the confusion. At this hour, the FBI's various offices would be on night shift - minimal staff, only a few woozy personnel around to deal with emergencies. That, perhaps, could be turned to advantage. Accordingly, I rang the Bureau's Boston office, identified myself and explained the circumstances.

'I've been speaking to your Jackson office,' I said, lying like a psychopath. 'They told me to notify you...'

'Why'd they do that?' a voice asked, irked apparently at having been disturbed. 'It's not our jurisdiction.'

'Damned if I know. Possibly because some of the prisoners are Massachusetts residents? Or students in this state? In any case, Jackson seemed as concerned as some of the people here in Boston about the prisoners being transferred to Wisteria. If they're released and have to get back to Ashwood themselves, they'll be vulnerable. Jackson said the whole thing smelled of a set-up for an ambush. Like the one last spring.'

Not surprisingly, the FBI in Boston couldn't have cared less about events in Mississippi. Neither, however, could they admit that, and they remained mystified about Jackson instructing me to contact them. They were also disgruntled. It was as if some virus of information had been released into the system. They'd now been infected with it and could no longer plead ignorance. There was nothing officially they could do, I was told, but they would, at any rate, 'keep an eye on the situation'.

I then rang the FBI's Mississippi office in Jackson. I worked, I said, for the Boston *Globe*; I covered 'Southern affairs' for the newspaper. My 'desk' had just received a report from the FBI in Boston - something about Massachusetts students being arrested in Ashwood and transferred to Wisteria. The Boston office had advised me to liaise with Jackson, since Jackson was sure to be abreast of developments and have further details.

'First we've heard of anything,' the sleepy Mississippi voice protested in bewildered consternation. 'Boston told you to contact us?'

'Yes. They said you'd probably have agents on the scene already. Or on their way to the scene, at any rate. I got the impression Boston'd been in touch with Washington. Washington, I gathered, was worried about a possible repetition of what happened last spring.'

'We'll look into it straightaway. Can I get back to you?'

I gave them the home number of a *Globe* reporter we knew, a literate friend who'd graduated the year before. I rang him, briefed him and told him to expect a call from the Jackson office of the FBI. He said he'd try to get a story into the newspaper the next day, asked if we could provide biographical data on JT and Ilona and, if possible, photographs. I assigned Carlsmith to deal with this task, thereby restoring to him some justification for his existence, and discussed the next move with Radetzky. When the telephone was free, I telephoned the Ashwood jail myself. Adopting a courteous, impersonal and professionally brisk voice, I again identified myself as a reporter for the *Globe*. I had, I said, just received a routine briefing from the FBI in Boston...

'From who?' the surly Mississippi voice asked, suddenly awake and alarmed.

From the FBI in Boston, I repeated. They'd apparently been in touch with their Jackson office about the arrest and intended transfer to Wisteria of voter registration workers in Ashwood. Could Ashwood provide me with any further details?

Traditional Southern politeness promptly asserted itself. The circumstances of the arrests, or some tenuously plausible variant of them, were deferentially explained to me. The charge was fairly minor, I was told, a mere misdemeanour, and the prisoners would be released within the next thirty-six hours, as soon as the paperwork was completed. Why the transfer to Wisteria? Simply because the cells in Ashwood were overcrowded and lacked sufficient washbasins. In the meantime, the prisoners were being made as comfortable as possible. Did I wish to speak to one or another of them and reassure myself? I declined the offer. It wouldn't've accomplished anything, and JT or Ilona, on hearing my voice, might've exclaimed my name or something, thereby 'blowing my cover'. I didn't credit the Ashwood jail with anything so sophisticated as telephone taps or bugging devices, but there was bound to be someone listening in on an extension.

'What about transportation back from Wisteria?'

A pause, during which I could hear two or three voices in muted but still discernibly grumpy conversation.

'We...er...plan to provide that,' I was informed, grudgingly.

Everything that urgently needed to be done, I realised as I rang off, had been done. JT and Ilona were as safe as one could reasonably expect - perhaps safer, even, than before their arrest. Not even the vindictive louts of Wisteria and Ashwood would misbehave under the scrutiny, real or imagined, of the FBI and the Northern media. But all of us by then were high, intoxicated by the situation, by our triumph, by the pitch of intensity we'd attained. It was now past midnight and we were wide awake, heady on adrenaline, mobilised for further action. None of us could've wound down and relaxed. Nor, to be honest, did any of us want to. If we kept going, we recognised, there'd probably be an element of overkill; but overkill wouldn't be altogether superfluous or misplaced in Mississippi. And besides, we managed to convince ourselves, there remained a degree of risk.

Contrary to our own derisory depictions of them, the FBI didn't consist entirely of blundering dunderheads and buffoons. None of us underestimated their capacity for mischief. In the present circumstances, they weren't the most reliable of allies, especially if they discovered they'd been used. The Bureau was, after all, J. Edgar Hoover's plaything; and Hoover, then well into a baroque neurotic dotage, saw the world through a lurid miasma of misanthropy, misogyny, paranoia, incipient hysteria, sexual maladjustment, obsessive Puritanism and a garish array of other phobias, rampant and couchant. The Mafia, he maintained stubbornly, didn't exist. There was no organised crime in the United States, but Martin Luther King was a Communist dupe or worse. Northern liberals were witting or unwitting subversives. Anyone with originality or imagination or creative intelligence was a probable agent of one or another perfidious conspiracy dedicated to the overthrow of Truth, Justice and the American Way. It was common knowledge, moreover, that Hoover was then engaged in an increasingly bitter feud with Bobby Kennedy, the Attorney-General. Civil rights was Kennedy's *cause célèbre*, not Hoover's. From Hoover, anything associated with civil rights was more likely to elicit senile spite and mulish obstructiveness than it was sympathy or co-operation. By dint of my telephone calls, the FBI might've become involved in our campaign, but only under duress; and if they acted at all, it'd be with no loftier motive than to save face. Our real support would have to come not from the Bureau, but from Bobby Kennedy's Justice Department. Unfortunately, however, one couldn't galvanise the Justice Department with a telephone call.

This was the problem we were debating when Cletis - until then engaged primarily in aimless flurry - offered what appeared to be a raging *non-sequitur*:

'Hey, you guys! Remember Mindy Dunque? What you did to her, I mean. Maybe the same principle...'

Everyone stared at him in irritated perplexity, and his raucous voice tapered into abashed silence. Then the penny dropped, and Radetzky and I turned to each other with amazement, with delight, with exuberance, with widening grins of gleeful euphoria.

'Out of the mouths of babes, fools and court jesters...' Radetzky murmured appreciatively.

Mindy Dunque was a fashionably trendy debutante who, during my first two years of university, had swanned through several of my classes, balancing, like some ornately glazed native pot on her head, a sleekly coiffured beehive. Oozing an exaggerated, treacle-thick, syrupy sexuality, she'd flirted occasionally with both Patterson and myself, finding us, so she claimed, 'interesting'. It was the feminine equivalent of priapic curiosity. She might, I gathered, have found a convicted sex-murderer, a gypsy fortune teller, a circus acrobat or even a gorilla 'interesting' with pretty much the same mentality. The previous autumn, shortly before the assassination, she'd announced her engagement - to the dapper and pebble-brained scion of some patrician dynasty in New Hampshire. Patterson and I were invited to the wedding. Presumably, we were expected to constitute a species of rare social appetiser, comparable to exotic caviare or sturgeon, of which the other guests might partake. The invitations, when they arrived, weren't from Mindy herself, but from her mother: *'Mrs. Alethea Dunque requests the pleasure of your company at the nuptials of her daughter...'*

Both Patterson and I had, of course, received such invitations before. Neither of us had thought much about the etiquette or protocol involved. On this occasion, however, we were both provoked by the tone of regal command, and by the sheer impertinence of maternal proprietorship. It was, after all, Mindy whom we knew, not her mother. Why should it be the officious old harridan who invited us - especially when our appearance on the scene would probably scandalise her? And on what basis did she blithely assume our company would necessarily be pleasurable?

We accordingly devised what's remained one of my favourite and most memorable pranks - a prank I was to recycle in London, some fifteen years later, at the wedding of Juliet Sharman-Burke. We Xeroxed the invitation. We handed out copies to all our friends. We told them to make additional copies to distribute to *their* friends. Everyone was urged to RSVP. Mrs. Dunque, it later transpired, had sent out some 150 invitations. She received upwards of 350 acceptances, from places as far afield in some instances as Wyoming, Oregon, Puerto Rico, the Virgin Islands and Alaska. Among them was a collective response from the entire University of Toronto ice hockey team, and one from the madam of a bordello in Tijuana - where, it was implied, Mindy had displayed an impressively precocious aptitude and expertise. Three days were apparently required to sort through the replies and separate the legitimate from the spurious.

For the Justice Department, we initiated a similar chain reaction, on a much more ambitious scale. We began in the small hours of that morning and continued all through the hours of darkness. At daybreak, we commandeered the university's newspaper offices, where there were banks of telephones. Other available offices were also requisitioned, and many faculty members donated their own. By noon, every college and university in the Boston area had joined us, as had a number of schools in Connecticut and New York.

Throughout that Friday, we compiled and telephoned lists of parents, siblings, aunts, uncles, cousins, friends, friends of friends, ex-friends, prospective friends, lovers, ex-lovers, prospective lovers and anyone else who came to mind. One zealot among us began working his way systematically through the Boston telephone directory. Someone else, less methodical, would open the book at random, close his eyes, stab his finger at the page and ring the name chosen by chance. We urged everyone to contact as many additional people as he or she knew. Letters to the Justice Department, we explained, would take too long to arrive and wouldn't therefore be of much use. Calls would only clog the switchboards. In consequence, everyone was exhorted to send at least one telegram. We dictated a basic minimum-word economy text: *'EXPRESSING CONCERN STUDENTS ARRESTED IN ASHWOOD MISSISSIPPI TRANSFERRED TO WISTERIA STOP RISK OF AMBUSH ON ROAD BACK STOP.'* Variations were, of course, acceptable, and anyone who desired to spend further money on elaboration was encouraged to do so.

To my knowledge, this was the first concerted attempt to activate the vast interlocking network of the country's student population. Later, during the war in Vietnam, similar techniques were to be employed repeatedly and all too frequently, eventually losing whatever impact they had. On this inaugural exercise, however, the impact was both startling and considerable. Novelty and solidarity created an alluring bandwagon, and few hesitated to clamber aboard. One pedant among us - a fanatical statistician working on premises I never fully understood - computed that by Friday evening we'd swamped the Justice Department with an estimated 37,000 telegrams.

Around midday, I telephoned Ashwood again, then the jail at Wisteria, and repeated my masquerade as *Globe* 'Southern Affairs Correspondent'. The transfer of the prisoners, I was told, had occurred without incident. Their release was scheduled for the following afternoon. In the meantime, unknown to the hapless peace officers of those torpid Mississippi towns, a ferocious squall of publicity was gathering to descend upon them. That evening, the *Globe* ran its feature on the front page, complete with outdated photographs of JT and Ilona - he beardless and relatively kempt, she mirroring the whole world's anguished suffering in her eyes, both looking appropriately wholesome, winsome and vulnerable. By noon, rival Boston newspapers had pounced on the story, and it spread rapidly across the country, making early editions in California. By evening, JT and Ilona were national celebrities, poignant avatars of the nation's idealistic young. This image was accentuated by television, which had, of course, hastened to get in on the act. Each of the networks and various local stations around New England dispatched teams to the campus.

'They want to interview us,' Radetzky reported, stalking me into the inner office where I'd gone to ground.

'What the hell for?'

'We're being hailed as the masterminds of the thing.'

'What the fuck am I supposed to say to them? 'Actually, guys, I'm an apolitical aesthete. I did it all because JT's one of my best friends and I just happen to be smitten with his wife'? You want the whole business reduced to a single as-yet unconsummated adultery? Tell them they're better employed in Wisteria.'

Some teams were, in fact, flown down. Others, closer by, were ordered to the scene. Representatives from every relevant and sometimes irrelevant organisation - SNCC, CORE, the NAACP, the ACLU and assorted others we'd never heard of - began flocking into Wisteria and Ashwood, as did voter registration workers from all over the South. And on Saturday morning, a few hours before the prisoners' scheduled release, Bobby Kennedy, to his everlasting credit, called a special emergency meeting of the Justice Department. It was, we were told later, the first such meeting ever to have been convened on a Saturday morning - though I'm not sure whether this testifies to our achievement or to the Department's previous idleness.

In the meantime, Secret Service agents had already been assigned to Wisteria. By then, however, the town was already so awash with strangers that one couldn't distinguish between Justice Department personnel, FBI, media, curiosity seekers, voyeurs and, for all anyone knew, MI6 and the KGB to boot. To all intents and purposes, Wisteria's dinky little jail might've been the Bastille. When JT and Ilona were released, they told me later, they emerged into streets reminiscent of New Orleans at Mardi Gras. To the horror of the traumatised locals, Wisteria became the venue for an impromptu carnival, which, like some satanic magnet, drew every conceivable species of undesirable out of the woodwork. Makeshift stalls were erected, flogging soft drinks and forbidden beer. Television cameras whirred, flashbulbs popped, a helicopter from somewhere stuttered overhead. A cavalcade was formed, composed of everything from monster Mack sixteen-wheelers down to mule-drawn wagons; and JT,

Ilona and their colleagues were transported in triumphal procession back to the compound in Ashwood.

****

I'd performed my self-appointed mission; I'd helped to rescue my damsel-in-distress, my princess from Mississippi's approximation of dungeon or tower. My victory, however, quickly proved pyrrhic. What seemed at first an impressive exercise in power was revealed, for me personally at least, as a sickening revelation of helplessness.

On the telephone with JT and Ilona a day or so later, I learned additional details of their arrest. Ashwood's sheriff and his deputies had swooped at dawn on what they called the 'unlicensed boarding house and restaurant'. Handcuffed and on foot, the occupants had been paraded through the town's streets, from the compound to the jail. En route, they'd run the inevitable gauntlet - vicious jeers from the locals, insults, abuse, a pelting of rotten fruit and vegetables, the occasional turd and gob of spittle. Just around the corner from the main square, an unknown woman had leaned over a balcony and poured a kettle of scalding water down over Ilona.

It wasn't as dire as it sounded to me at the time. She'd not been disfigured, not required more than the most basic medical treatment and a change of clothes. For two hours or so, she'd been in severe pain, but that'd gradually subsided. When she told me about it, she'd already pretty much dismissed the matter, but I couldn't. For weeks, for months afterwards, I was to be haunted by the image of that harpy on the balcony. I invoked curses on the bitch, called imprecations and maledictions down upon her. Had I known her identity, I probably would've embarked on a sustained campaign of vengeful terror - mysteriously menacing telephone calls, poison pen letters, even a voodoo doll. Ultimately, however, my fury was too immediately physical to be satisfied by vicarious expedients - I longed to pulverise her to jelly with my bare hands.

In a numb and futile rage, I tried to fathom the mind capable of that malevolence. I was unable to comprehend how a human being, a woman, could do such a thing to another woman. In its bestiality, in its sadism, in what had to be its premeditation, it left me baffled and confounded. When I attempted to project myself into that alien psyche, my imagination balked, stopped dead, came up against an impenetrable wall. The mentality of that cruelty remained inexplicable, except by some temporary eclipse of consciousness, some monstrous failure of all sensitivity, all intelligent faculties. Only in some insentient and insensate darkness could such an act have originated.

Abstract formulations of this kind did little to assuage my own mortifying sense of helplessness. It was a compounded helplessness. I'd been rendered helpless by not knowing of the atrocity at the time. But even if I'd known, I'd've been rendered helpless by my absence. And even if I'd been present, I'd've been rendered helpless by...by the degrading impotence imposed by circumstance. That humiliation would've been intolerable. Had I been there, I realised with sudden shock, I'd've tried to kill that woman. Unlike hers, mine wouldn't've been a calculated or premeditated act. I'd simply have gone berserk. I'd've charged her balcony single-handedly, quixotically, insanely; I'd've tried to vault up to it, scale it or, like Samson in his wrath, drag it down upon me. I would, of course, have been clubbed to the ground, or shot, before I'd taken more than a few steps, but the oblivion would've been welcome.

The realisation both unnerved and matured me. I'd been in numerous fights before, but they'd always, even at their most ferocious, had an element of sport about them, a measure of restraint, an awareness of context and consequences. Now, for the first time in my life, I discovered no such inhibiting factors. I discovered in myself the capacity, and the desire, to kill - violently, brutally, in a single-minded intensity of hatred that eclipsed everything else. It wasn't a comfortable discovery. But it was with all this, I understood suddenly - the helplessness, the humiliation, the rage, the hatred - that the black population of the South lived incessantly. For them, it wasn't a unique phenomenon, but a premise of daily existence.

Carlsmith and his gauchist colleagues would no doubt have hailed my recognition as 'the birth of political consciousness', or some such drivel. For me, it was nothing of the sort. It was simply a revelation of outrage - of the meaning and nature of outrage. And outrage, I'd now maintain, is probably the single purest passion one can know. It has nothing to do with oneself. It's utterly unselfish, utterly impersonal, utterly devoid of ulterior motive. It stems ultimately from the obverse of itself - compassion.

V

The following spring - the spring of my last year as an undergraduate - Ilona returned north alone, without JT, arriving in time to witness the farce of my commencement ceremony, my stoned grin and public scuffle over aspirin. Until the end of that summer, we were more or less idyllically together in Boston. Albeit briefly, we were subsequently to see each other in assorted other cities - Chicago, San Francisco, New Orleans. For the next six years, we were to meet and part, meet again and again wrench ourselves asunder - or be driven so by circumstance. Our bond became increasingly elasticised, accommodating a sequence of prolonged separations punctuated by fleeting reunions of wild rhapsodic intensity that seemed to clamour from some Wagnerian orchestral accompaniment. In retrospect, I think not of a single relationship so much as a series of relationships, each divorced from the others by gaps in time, space, growth, maturation and experience. These relationships were to form brackets, so to speak, within which a number of parenthetical affairs were contained - some pointlessly ephemeral, some marginally more durable, and at least two, including my liaison with Nina, genuinely important to my development. For six years, Ilona's and my itineraries - like, for that matter, Patterson's, Radetzky's and JT's - were to trace patterns across the United States, Canada, Mexico and Western Europe as intricate and apparently random as those of flies buzzing around a room, arabesques of pilgrimage.

Eventually, harbouring some idiotic fancy of 'settling down' with my still *Angst*-ridden Rhine maiden, I transplanted myself to Vancouver in order to be with her, and there our paths converged for the last time. The bond that'd withstood the loftiest, most rarefied and operatic tests and stresses shrivelled - not surprisingly perhaps - at the prospect of domesticity. If required to do so, we might've contrived an exquisite *Liebstod* together, but we couldn't adjust to the quotidian; and our parting, on this occasion, was definitive. It was also, for me, particularly lacerating. Indeed, Ilona, like an amputated limb, continued to haunt me for six years after our final rupture, projecting her shadow over another sequence of relationships. Sublimated into some fairly bizarre forms, she manifested herself as an incipiently unhealthy obsession with all things German - from the medieval *Deutschritter*, through Scharnhorst, Gneisenau and the Prussian General Staff, to Marlene Dietrich. It took nothing less than the magic of my present lady to exorcise her.

All of that, however, to coin a cliché, is another story. The point is that after her return from Ashwood, my attachment to her was never again to involve me in political activity, never again to make me compromise the purity of my aestheticism. Other women were to do that; and Ilona, during those years, functioned for me as a species of refuge, a symbolic haven. Through her, I could wash myself clean.

I was in Boston for some ten months after the drama in Ashwood, six after Ilona's return north. During that time, I remained sporadically active in the Civil Rights Movement. Having become involved to the extent I had, it proved virtually impossible to disengage. I couldn't, for Ilona's and JT's sakes. Besides, the path back to my ivory tower was now cluttered with too many new acquaintances, whose petitions I wasn't callous enough to spurn. They importuned me to edit pamphlets and manifestos, to aid in the preparation of press releases and other documents requiring some command of prose. They consulted me as tactician, as strategist, as public relations advisor, as campaign manager, as high-level staff planner, as liaison between SNCC and sundry university bodies.

It was in a variety of such nebulous, unspecified and unofficial capacities that I helped to organise the demonstrations at the Federal Building during the march on Selma. But with Ilona removed from the theatre of operations, and with JT under no immediate threat, my own impetus was vitiated, becoming increasingly abstract and mechanical, less an emotional commitment than an intellectual exercise, something akin to a chess game. It also included elements of what in those days we called an 'ego trip' - a propensity, which I confess with shame, to revel in the manipulation of people and power. And while I couldn't get my hands around the neck of that woman on the balcony in Ashwood, I could at least deploy an icy calculation to exact vicarious retribution on others of her ilk.

With Lyndon Johnson's victory in the previous November's election, voter registration in the South had become superfluous, and the organisations comprising the Civil Rights Movement were turning their attention to other priorities. JT, who'd remained around the Mississippi Delta, kept me apprised of these, some of which were never made public. There was, for example, a secret edict whereby the Student Non-Violent Coordinating Committee, which had long ceased to be composed chiefly of students, now ceased also to be non-violent. SNCC began to arm, and handguns - pocket-sized Berettas, even heavyweight Colt and Browning automatics - were replacing booze and dope as statutory gifts. I remember JT, on a trip north, displaying the Walther PPK someone had just given him for his birthday. I stared suspiciously at the noxious little nickel-plated weapon in my palm. I tested it in a desolate patch of woods off the Massachusetts Expressway, was surprised by the petulant energy of its recoil, yet still found it oddly puny. I had forcibly to remind myself that this ostensible toy could wreak as much carnage as the hefty blued long-barrelled Smith and Wesson .38 conferred on me by my father, with which I'd grown up target-shooting.

Accompanied by the Walther, JT returned south and assigned himself to another compound, just over the Louisiana border, at a place called Bogaloosa. Here, every Saturday night for some weeks, fledgling members of the Klan would blood themselves by piling into a caravan of cars, driving past the post and discharging shotguns through the windows. It'd become an established, even ritualised, routine. Everyone accepted it. No one was ever hurt. And then, one June evening, to the shock of the marauders and the local newspapers, the compound returned fire - a well-disciplined, almost military, volley, which almost certainly included shells from JT's Walther. I can't believe there was any actual intention of hitting anything, but JT's familiarity with guns wasn't matched by that of his colleagues. In consequence, one misplaced bullet perforated a car's tyre, the vehicle careened off the road into a ditch and two of the churls inside splintered the windscreen with their skulls, suffering lacerations and contusions to faces and pride.

In itself, the subsequently vaunted 'showdown', or 'shootout', at Bogaloosa was a minor enough affair, as piddling in its way as, say, the skirmishes at Lexington and Concord; but the shots of that Louisiana night were heard, if not around the world, at least around the country. They marked a turning point in the attitudes and orientation of the Civil Rights Movement, and were soon to be echoed, downright reverberatively, elsewhere. With those shots, SNCC moved dramatically on to the offensive. Only now did it become apparent that voter registration hadn't been the sole activity of the last few months. Other, more clandestine forms of mobilisation had also been afoot. As if conjured out of nothingness, armed black secret societies began to appear across the rural South, paramilitary formations prepared to meet the Klan on its own terms. Through his aptitude for inspiring trust, JT persuaded one such cadre to let themselves be filmed. Their sophistication, their organisational effectiveness and their state of readiness blanched many a red neck a whiter shade of pale.

In fact, however, such rednecks had less grounds for panic than other people, who, in their complacency, suspected nothing. For it wasn't only in the South that militant cadres began to arm and organise. Unknown to outsiders at the time, there'd been another secret directive, succinct and chilling, which was to impinge more immediately on my own reality: '*Carry the war to the North.*'

I can't vouch for the actual causal connection, if any; but that summer, within two months of the directive being promulgated, Watts, the black ghetto of Los Angeles, erupted in frenzied self-immolating conflagration, and every American metropolis became a powder keg. Within two years, the Black Panthers had established themselves in cities across the country, 'Black Power' had become a nationwide mantra and the urban life of New York, Washington, Philadelphia, Newark, Boston, Detroit, Cleveland, Chicago, St. Louis, San Francisco and most other such centres had been transformed. Prior to Watts, my friends and I, long-haired, bearded, scruffy, booted and jeaned, could move with impunity through the swarming wastelands of Harlem, Georgetown, Roxbury and Dorchester. When challenged, we'd flash the SNCC buttons under our lapels, and the conclaves of young blacks milling ominously at the street corners would greet us effusively, hail us as soul-brothers, cheerfully make way for us to pass. Two years later, all that had changed. We were white, and the no-go areas obtained for us as much as for anyone else, regardless of our appearance. Not even SNCC could control the genie released from the bottled existence of the Northern slums.

I was more aware than most of the impending storm when, at the end of that summer, I prised myself away from Ilona and embarked for the first year of my M.A. programme in Chicago. But Chicago, in the developments to which I was privy, then lagged temporarily behind the East and West Coasts, and seemed merely a vicious backwater. Tensions were certainly detectable, but the storm, during that first year, didn't break, and I immersed myself in the life of the bar, in my attachment (after two false starts with lesser muses) to Nina, in reading, writing and general dissipation. I drank copiously, repairing to Reggie's every evening at eight or nine and remaining, usually, until closing time at two. I lived in a once-posh hotel, a relic of Capone's era, now converted into a domicile for graduate students; but the plush crimson velvets and velours, so divorced from my customary squalor, soon came to feel artificial and oppressive. Even the 'Murphy' bed which folded out of the wall, after Nina and I had mischievously imprisoned each other in it a few times, began to lose its novelty.

In January, there was a particularly vehement cold snap, the temperature remaining at ten below zero Fahrenheit for a fortnight. I'd raise the bonnet of my moribund Volvo to squirt starting ether into the carburettor and find my fingers sticking to the metal, leaving behind a thin film of skin. Apart from that, and my duel of wits with the Selective Service system, it was a torpidly uneventful period - and felt all the more so compared to the pace of Boston and New York. At the university, I desultorily played Platonic *enfant terrible* and antinomian Hermetic numinist. In the nocturnal streets, I played Rasputin with youthful Storm Troopers freshly poached from the hatching chamber. I made no new friends in the city, and missed my old entourage - their dynamism, their devil-may-care abandonment and week-long parties. Despite Nina's attempts to divert me, I was often restless, nostalgic and lonely. On one occasion, I went for ten days without speaking to a soul, save Nina and the shopkeepers and waitresses from whom I ordered cigarettes and food. By the end of the academic year, I was consummately bored. I resolved not to face another such year without the companionship of kindred spirits. On my return east for the summer holidays, I set about conning them into joining me.

While I'd been festering in Chicago, Patterson had been working in Slug's Saloon and one or two other comparably prestigious East Village establishments. Extolling Chicago bars, and Reggie's in particular, I had scant trouble convincing him he needed a change of scene. Radetzky, in the meantime, after wandering around Heidelberg, had gravitated to Dublin, where, for a few months, he'd lived in a Martello tower. He claimed, in fact, that it was *the* Martello tower, and assumed it would conduce to inspiration. It didn't. He wrote nothing during those months, apart from a handful of fatuous postcards, and returned shamefacedly, with a hang-dog look and a plethora of creaky excuses. Given his grades, I argued, he'd have little difficulty getting into Chicago's M.A. programme. I said nothing, of course, about its Aristotelian aridity. If anything, I contrived, with some poetic licence and a few flamboyant lies, to make it sound like *fin-de-siècle* Paris.

****

In September, the three of us puttered and wheezed west in my more-moribund-than-ever Volvo, all our belongings jammed into the boot and heaped high on the back seat, obstructing the view through the rear window and making the vehicle - it sounded like an asthmatic octogenarian gambler trying to shuffle cards - sag soddenly on its springs. The shimmering absinthe-green haze through which my gulled friends viewed the journey was quickly dispelled by soot, grime, concrete, brick and the chronic Western-Front glare of the blast furnaces across the river in Gary. Images of the *belle époque* and Mallarmé's Tuesday night *soirées* withered on contact with a city where sensibilities rasped like ground glass. Instead of languid courtesans in slinky feather boas, there were hard-boiled harpy-fierce hookers with hair tinted a steely gun-metal blue.

'It's not quite as I remembered it,' I said in perfunctory apology to my friends, and led them to Reggie's for alcoholic restitution and consolation.

If the city was less alluring than I recalled, or pretended to, Nina was more so. She welcomed me back in tight maroon stretch pants, white go-go boots and a fleecy white sweater - a jarring combination of seductive vulgarity and virginal girlishness. She'd had her hair cut during the summer, her fluffy blonde bouffant now replaced by a pert page-boy that made her look less sophisticated but startlingly younger. I'd not previously liked the style on other women, but it became her fetchingly. Appraising her through the eyes of my friends, I'd never found her more bewitching.

Radetzky and I obtained temporary accommodation at a hostel reserved for graduate students. For two nights, Patterson, too, managed illicitly to stay there, bluffing his way past the porter, an inept Cerberus, at the door. On being unmasked and ejected, he was obliged, grumbling, to seek shelter at a YMCA, lying awake in the rancid darkness, standing by to repel epicene boarders from the bed. In the morning, we'd assemble at Reggie's, which opened at ten, and pore over the classified columns, seeking habitable premises at a price we could afford.

"Sno wonder we can't find a plaish,' Radetzky slurred at one point. 'We keep getting drunk before noon.'

It was Nina who suggested the apartment on the top floor above the bar, diagonally over hers. There were, in fact, three floors of flats surmounting Reggie's. On the first lived two part-time hookers, one with a fourteen-year-old daughter who was herself to be arrested five times during the ensuing months for shoplifting, thrice for prostitution, once for robbery and attempted murder of a client. Opposite dwelt a large genial black bartender, a milquetoast in the physique of a gladiator, whom we cajoled into poker games, feigning the inexperience of novices, and hustled out of some four hundred dollars.

On the next floor up was the flat Nina shared with her parents and three children. Across the landing hibernated Zeke, a gaunt, gangling, dementedly religious hillbilly from Kentucky or Tennessee, whom I don't think I saw on more than half a dozen occasions during the entire year. He dwelt alone, Nina told us, in two of his numerous rooms, the others being crammed with old newspapers, variegated débris, junk he'd collected packrat-fashion from dumps and rubbish bins all over the city for some unspecified, obscurely messianic purpose. Once every six weeks or so, a species of spirit would descend on him - perhaps the Holy Ghost, on behalf of birds in general, exacting revenge on felines - and he'd call traumatic attention to himself. At three or four in the morning, we'd all be galvanised bolt upright in our beds, eyes bulging, ears ringing, blood hammering. Zeke, leaning out of his window, was blasting away with a shotgun at caterwauling cats in the alley. After every such incident, the premises would be surrounded by police and the offending blunderbuss confiscated. Zeke was undeterred. He seemed to have an inexhaustible supply of shotguns. Perhaps he manufactured them out of the scrap metal he'd filched in his forays. In any case, six weeks or so later, there'd be another thunderous nocturnal detonation and, in the dawn's early light, another puréed cat.

The top-floor flat, directly above Nina, was occupied by two improbably naïve and dislocated university girls, who initially welcomed us as protectors, then decided we were no more redeemable than anyone else in the building. One of them was pallidly attractive in a *gamin* sort of way. The other wasn't, but had pretensions to both intelligence and chic, and got up my nose by offhandedly referring to Nina as 'the slut with the brats downstairs'. Had she been a man, I might've flicked her face with a glove and challenged her. Not knowing what protocol demanded with a woman, I reluctantly contented myself with a glacial rudeness calculated to induce frostbite. It mystified her until she wandered down the stairwell one insomniac night and happened upon Nina and me entwined on the stairs in mid-fondle. After that, for the duration of her tenancy, she comported herself towards me with the prim frumpy disapprobation of a goosed abbess. Her tenancy, in any event, lasted a mere five weeks. By then, she and her flatmate had suffered sufficient outrage to their sensibilities and decamped, leaving the premises vacant for the rest of the year.

In the apartment across the landing, Patterson, Radetzky and I proceeded to install ourselves. The place was scandalously huge. A bathroom and three adjoining bedrooms opened on to a long corridor which, with its bare plank floor, might've doubled as a bowling alley or a shooting gallery. At one end was a dysfunctional kitchen, with two smaller rooms - for storage or guests - beyond. At the other end, a palatial front room overlooked the street, affording a vista of small shops, a pizza parlour, a pharmacy, a shoe repair establishment and a laundromat - where, later that year, Willie, the bartender, was to pour popcorn and ice cubes into Al Hollis' wash and be reciprocated with a fusillade of .45 shells. Immediately opposite, dominating everything, there loomed the vast denuded husk of a 1930s-vintage cinema and music hall - the beached hulk of an ark, boarded up and condemned to supposedly imminent demolition which never in fact occurred. Some fifty yards beyond, the sleaziness of milieu gave way to a spiffy modern complex of grass, glass and concrete - a miniature moonbase-style mall on two levels, with boutiques, a bookshop, a few offices and three restaurants which no one in the neighbourhood could afford. At the centre of this ensemble stood a cement tub with a dribbling spigot in the middle of it – some trendy local architect's *avant-garde* misconception of a fountain.

What our new home offered in spaciousness it exceeded in decrepitude. The building in fact reflected a kind of inverted image of the 'medieval world picture' tirelessly expounded at the university. At ground level, a measure of order and harmony, even of tidiness, prevailed. As one ascended, this gave way to an anarchy rivalling that of unregenerate nature. In our flat, one out of every four windows was cracked or broken, the mouldings around all of them were disintegrating, draughts traversed every room like a crossfire of icy javelins. With each passage of the elevated train two blocks away, the glass rattled in its sashes and a fine shower of dust sifted down from above. Plaster crumbled, paint peeled and flaked, and the walls, splotched with damp, looked as if they were about to sprout mushrooms. In the front room, sheets of yellowed newspaper were gummed to the splintery floor, dried brushes and empty cans of enamel stuck to the newspaper. Amidst this litter languished a large coffin-sized box of white styrofoam, intended for repairs to the bathroom ceiling but never used.

We had ambitious plans for the place initially. We couldn't afford proper furniture, of course, but we spun elaborate fantasies about repainting extensively, scrounging pillows and cushions for the front room, contriving a cosy Oriental décor. What happened in practice was that each of us cleaned up, refurbished and semi-civilised his own bedroom and retired into it, while the rest of the flat continued to marinate in pristine and unsullied disorder.

If the disorder rivalled that of unregenerate nature, there were also moments when unregenerate nature herself intruded. On our third day of occupancy, for example, we returned upstairs from the bar to find a neat, intricately sculpted mound of excrement rising from the precise geometrical centre of our doormat. We must've spent a good five minutes tipsily pondering it, examining it, discussing it, before we concluded it to be feline in origin.

'Here we are,' I observed, 'the three finest minds in Chicago, lost in contemplation of a pile of catshit.'

'You think it might've been put there deliberately?' Radetzky wondered in a sudden spasm of paranoia.

'Why would anyone do that?'

'I don't know. Maybe someone doesn't want us here or something. It could've been put there deliberately.'

'You mean,' Patterson drawled, 'that someone came up here and squeezed a cat?'

The catshit proved, in fact, to have issued from Thutmose, a large, aristocratic and effete Manx with an impressive *ancien régime*-style pedigree, who belonged to one of the girls next door. She hadn't squeezed him, and if his choice of our doormat was deliberate, it couldn't, at any rate, be ascribed to premeditated malice. In the few weeks before his owner alienated me, I established a congenial enough rapport with Thutmose, whom we let wander around our apartment at will. He was the first Manx I'd ever encountered. His taillessness, I discovered, deranged his sense of balance, causing him to do things no self-respecting cat would. An affectionate beast, he'd often, for instance, clamber into my lap while I was reading, then attempt to spring on to the bookshelf behind me - a six-foot-high kitchen cabinet plundered to house part of my library. Invariably, he'd miss, dragging the shelves and their contents down on both of us. Frequently, too, he'd pad into the bathroom when I or one of my flatmates was in the tub, hoist his paunchy body up and mince gingerly along the rim. Sooner or later, he'd slip on the slick surface. There'd be a frantic scrabbling of claws on porcelain, a desperate slithering, a strangled squawk, a prodigious splash - and Thutmose, bedraggled and indignant, would flail out of the water to flop on the floor like a fat furry seal.

Nor was lack of balance his only ignominiously uncatlike deficiency. I borrowed him one night for what I imagined the ordained purpose and *raison d'être* of his species, the mice that infested our premises. They were brazenly impudent creatures, emerging from their holes at dusk, even when the lights were on, even when two or three of us were present in the room. We'd shout, we'd hiss, we'd stamp our feet. They'd remain unperturbed, calmly staring at us until we lunged or threw a boot at them. Fancying Thutmose the solution to the problem, I bundled him into my bedroom one night, switched off the light and closed the door. Within minutes, two mice appeared, discernible in the leprous blue luminescence from the window. Thutmose started, went rigid and, fur bristling, backed away in what appeared to be horror. When he realised *they* weren't about to attack *him,* he turned phlegmatic, lapsing into an indolence worthy of godhood. At last, after a sustained pause, some atavistic impulse stirred sluggishly to life, some long-dormant tiger lulled to sleep by successive generations of coddling, and Thutmose, lumbering rather clumsily, pounced. To my amazement, he actually caught one of the vermin, surfacing from under the bureau with his prey in his teeth, and strutted triumphantly towards the door. I opened it for him and he disappeared into the front room. Moments later, he returned, waddled back into my room and vomited.

But if Thutmose, with his lack of toilet-training and incompetence as a cat, inaugurated our residence in the building, the squalor of the year we spent there was best epitomised by a canine rival - the German shepherd owned by Beryl, a part-time waitress with whom Radetzky was soon to become involved. I was in my room one afternoon, reading. Out in the corridor, Radetzky was entering as Patterson was leaving, or perhaps vice versa, and I heard a classic fragment of conversation:

'Beryl was looking for you. She was here with the dog yesterday.'

'Oh. That must be why there's dogshit in the front room.'

'There's dogshit in the front room?'

'Yeah, but I covered it with newspaper so no one can see it.'

And there it remained until dust blanketed it, the winter wind petrified it, mouse droppings surrounded it and it merged tastefully with the rest of the décor.

We rationalised domestic delinquency as preoccupation with loftier things, but our indifference to the flat was dictated primarily by the warmer, more vibrant, more colourful and congenial atmosphere of the bar below. It seduced us from the dereliction upstairs and became, in effect, our true home. The place was owned by a typically vulgar *nouveau riche* couple from prosperous Lake Shore Drive - an oily entrepreneur named Melvin Bloss and Babs, his luridly brass-haired wife. Her silky furs, flittering lashes, mincing manner and garish pretensions to style failed to conceal the tough, blunted or cauterised sensibilities of the ex-hooker. We saw little of the Blosses, however. Once a month, usually on a Sunday afternoon when the neighbourhood was safe, they'd purl round to collect receipts, gliding down the road in their creamy Lincoln Continental, pausing only for a brief drink and chat with the staff. Apart from that, they were strangers, and enthusiastically loathed by the clientèle.

The clientèle themselves were almost exclusively black, and their comportment, or lack of it, had established Reggie's as the wildest, raunchiest, most notoriously dangerous watering hole in the vicinity. Something of this reputation was fabricated, an exercise in obverse public relations. By now, however, SNCC's secret edict of the year before had begun to actualise itself, the 'war' was indeed being carried to the North, racial tensions rippled electrically just beneath the surface of things and the bar became increasingly a focus for organisations dedicated to 'Black Power'. Apart from certain of the staff - Nina, Beryl, Willie, one of the other bartenders and the bouncer, Terence Mulligan, an ex-Irishman who in everything but colour resembled the Incredible Hulk - white faces were rare on the premises. Patterson, Radetzky and I were among the few 'honkies' made to feel welcome, eventually accepted as 'blood brothers' by most of the habitués. In addition to us, there were perhaps half a dozen pale-skinned regulars, occasional sporadic visitors. Al Hollis was despised but - if only in deference to his guns - tolerated on provisional sufferance. And there'd be, of an evening, the wonted quota of two or three blue-haired hookers, whose *métier* circumvented or transcended race.

Anti-white hostility was directed chiefly at the suavely urbane, dapper and tweedy graduate students, attended by immaculately tailored girlfriends, who'd come round usually on weekends - patronising, condescending, with the air of tourists at a zoo. Many of them seemed to be collecting data for dissertations in sociology. They'd survey their surroundings with a clinical scientific curiosity, as one might scrutinise bacteria in a culture medium. On occasion, one of them would wax tentatively or gregariously affable, like an explorer trying to learn the customs of some undiscovered lost tribe. Resentment towards such interlopers was not only genuine and profound, but accentuated by loyalty to the bar, whose reputation for nastiness had, at all costs, to be upheld. As far as I know, none of the intruders was ever actually robbed, mugged, beaten, roughed up or subjected to any form of physical violence. Not on the premises, at least. They were, however, made to feel downright uncomfortable -

were often taunted, goaded, hectored, intimidated, humiliated, targeted for abuse which could sometimes turn ugly.

One Saturday, there was a greater influx of newcomers than usual, and the situation became particularly abrasive, particularly volatile. To deflect it into antic anarchy, Patterson and I switched the signs surmounting the lintels of the lavatories. The regulars, of course, didn't notice, not bothering to look up and barging through the accustomed door. The newcomers naturally checked the signs and followed them accordingly. The result was a night-long *opéra bouffe* of screams, squeals, apologies, drunken explanations, confusion, consternation and hilarity. The regulars so enjoyed themselves that our juvenile prank became an established Saturday evening routine - which did, in fact, defuse tension.

On a more civilised note, we introduced chess to Reggie's. And Radetzky, on some inspired whim, one day produced a box of pick-up sticks. Weirdly enough, they caught on, and became, for some six weeks, not just a fad, but an obsession. During that time, a spell seemed to have descended. Except for the jukebox, silence prevailed, while hulking massive-muscled blacks hunched over brightly-coloured plastic, trying, with bleared eyes and fingers alcoholically atremble, to manipulate the slender slivers.

With Nina's recommendation, and with the likes of Slug's Saloon on his CV, Patterson had no trouble obtaining a job as bartender. Being Promethean, he rose quickly in the hierarchy, first to head bartender, then to manager. One by-product of this was that we drank, for most of the year, on the house. According to Radetzky's calculations, each of us imbibed just under a thousand dollars of free liquor - a substantial sum at that time, and a substantial quantity of booze at any. In the process, we acquired fastidiously cultivated, spoiled, even snobbish, palates. Spurning tepid domestic brews, all fizz and water, we ordered rich full-bodied German and Scandinavian beers. We made Reggie's the first premises in Chicago to serve Bass and Guinness on tap. And with an industry and conscientiousness that I withheld from graduate studies, we embarked on a general alcoholic education.

We initiated ourselves into a (literally) dizzying array of intoxicating beverages, from fiery pisco and tequila to raki, arak and diverse flavoured vodkas - concoctions which no one in the bar, perhaps in the city, had ever heard of, still less tasted. Having seen 007 order calvados on film, we'd long wanted to try the stuff ourselves. Now, each of us had his own bottle. We never succeeded in obtaining absinthe, banned for half a century even in France, but there were periodic binges on ouzo and Pernod. Over the space of a fortnight, we conducted a series of elaborate cognac-sampling contests. I began by extolling Rémy Martin; Patterson endorsed Martell, while Radetzky insisted on Hennessey. Thoroughly soused, we concurred unanimously on Courvoiser. I designed my own connoisseur's training programme in brandy and - after some trial and error and a few seismic hangovers - attained a fair expertise. By the end of the year, I had my private stock of calvados, kirsch, slivovitz, Poire William, Asbach, Armagnac, Marc de Bourgogne, Metaxa and a selection of Special Reserve cognacs. On one occasion, a good-natured multi-megaton ex-boxer - a sort of black equivalent of the Jolly Green Giant - paused beside me, dubiously inspected the bottle of extra-proof kirsch beside my glass and wrinkled his battered brow over the label.

'Cherry brandy,' I explained.

'Shit, man!' he snorted. 'That's chicks' hooch. What you wanna drink that for?'

With a resigned shrug, I proffered the bottle. He guzzled half of it in two voracious swigs and, twenty minutes later, lay slumped unconscious over the bar, his head in a popcorn bowl. It took four cohorts to carry him out and home. When he reappeared the following evening, he grinned at me sheepishly, but the incident was never mentioned again.

As an essential adjunct of our studies, we experimented with techniques for obviating and alleviating hangover - milk, cream, butter, even olive oil before a binge, still more bizarre countermeasures afterwards. The most consistently efficacious remedy, we discovered, was also the most disgusting, but we learned to adapt to it. We wouldn't even necessarily wait for the room to start cartwheeling. At a signal from some internal monitoring apparatus, one or other of us would casually excuse himself from bar or table, lurch to the loo and, with the aplomb of a practised Petronius, stick his finger down his throat. It was unpleasant enough at first, but gradually became routine, rather like having a pee. One would emerged catharsed, refresh oneself with a squirt of breath spray and embark, capacity renewed, on the next round. My only mishap occurred when, in my drunkenness one night, I fumbled through Nina's handbag for what I thought would be the breath spray, extracted the wrong metallic cylinder and fumigated my gullet with some down-market imitation of Chanel.

Through Patterson's position of authority, we all became privy to the Byzantine sub-currents and cross-currents, social, political and economic, on which the bar drifted, tacked and often came near to foundering. It comprised, in effect, a microcosm of the city as a whole, and the city in those days, under the mayorship of frog-faced Richard Daley, was a model to which every would-be corrupt municipal machine in the country aspired. Granted, black limousines no longer careened around corners on squealing tyres, mobsters no longer unlimbered Thompsons from violin cases to spray the streets with chattering volleys. But the Mob's presence, if more discreet now, was no less pervasive.

They still exercised a stranglehold, for example, on alcohol distribution, all orders and purchases being made through their conduits and intermediaries. They exercised a similar control over that most lucrative of contraptions, the jukebox. Each of Reggie's three cash registers contained a roll of so-called 'red nickels' - nickels marked discreetly with a smudge of lipstick on the rim. All staff, immediately on taking up employment, were initiated into the mysteries of these coins. Whenever the jukebox fell silent, and at regular intervals between the clientèle's selections, a 'red nickel' was to be inserted and the songs of a certain Italian-American crooner repeatedly played. When the box was emptied - a gunsel in shark-grey suit and pointed shoes came round weekly to disgorge the thing - the 'red nickels' would be returned to the cash registers and recycled. For every record played by the clientèle, those stipulated by the Mob would thus be played three or four times, scoring themselves into the mind, polluting one's stream of consciousness. I assume - though I'm not sufficiently conversant with the music business to state definitively - that royalties must also have accrued from each playing. In any case, the more frequently a tune was played on jukeboxes, the higher it climbed in the charts. The higher it climbed in the charts, the more frequently it was played by disc jockeys and the better it sold.

Ordering specific brands of alcohol through specifically designated 'outlets' cost the bar relatively little. Recycling 'red nickels' was also fiscally painless. It was the pay-offs that bit most deeply into Reggie's revenue. There were pay-offs everywhere, in every conceivable direction. There were pay-offs to the Mob. There were pay-offs to the Blackstone Rangers, a particularly aggressive street gang who dominated the neighbourhood and, for an agreed remuneration, guaranteed the 'protection' of the premises, especially against fire. There were pay-offs to health inspectors, safety inspectors and sundry other municipal authorities. And, of course, there were pay-offs to the Vice Squad - between seven hundred and a thousand dollars a week, as I recall.

If this tribute happened to be tardy, an excuse would be found, or manufactured, to close the place down - for a night, for two nights, for a week, for however long the 'lesson', and the financial loss it entailed, were deemed necessary and appropriate. Usually, an officer in plainclothes - from another precinct and therefore unknown locally - would wander in, accompanied by a suspiciously youthful-looking girl. At the door, Terence Mulligan would, of course, check their identification, but the girl, despite her appearance, would prove to be over twenty-one. Accordingly, she and her companion would be admitted and served. Within a few minutes of drinks being brought to their table, there'd be an ostensibly random raid, a 'routine inspection' by Vice Squad personnel; and the girl, when queried, would produce alternative identification, revealing herself to be eighteen or nineteen. Immediately, the bar would be charged with purveying alcohol to a minor. An official police voice would commandeer the public address system, declaring the premises to be shut down and all patrons evacuated. On most such occasions, Patterson, Mulligan or someone else would make a hasty emergency call to Melvin Bloss, whose emissary, bearing apologies and an envelope of cash, would arrive within the hour. The charges would then be summarily dropped and Reggie's would reopen.

Such were the covert mechanisms whereby the bar sustained itself. Oblivious to those mechanisms, as an individual is oblivious to the working of digestive and respiratory systems, the surface life of the place bubbled merrily or tumultuously along, perpetually promising new dramas, new variations on immemorial themes, new amalgams of possibility - and occasionally even delivering on its promises. By virtue of Patterson's authority, as well as my liaison with

Nina and Radetzky's with Beryl, we enjoyed a uniquely privileged status. At the table specially reserved for us in a congenial corner, we'd sluice away the hours from early evening until two, savouring snifters from our private stock, surveying the surrounding pageant of derelicts, wastrels, misfits, outcasts and pariahs - the indigestible elements of American society, regurgitated into the wood-panelled room around us, illumined by the lamps burning in the alcoves behind jewel-bright panes of imitation stained glass. Amongst these orphaned, displaced and homeless souls, I myself felt more cosily at home than I've usually felt elsewhere.

Among the diverse components in the ongoing carnival, the hookers, of course, were a source of perennial entertainment. We knew most of them personally, chatted with them, listened to their ribald anecdotes, watched them parry advances, haggle, negotiate prices, make 'arrangements' of sundry semi-licit kinds, wax catty with one another. We relished the brisk no-nonsense efficiency with which they conducted their transactions, squelching the customary displays of macho bombast and braggadocio. Confronted by their hard-bitten assertions of feminine sexuality, even the toughest, most boastful and swaggering louts would succumb to a species of primordial dread, becoming as timorous as boys on a first visit to a whorehouse. We witnessed the novice males - strangers to the bar, to prostitutes in general or to both - performing their weird spectrum of mating calls and dances. We noted how men, in their priapic overtures, would revert to the semblance of one or another animal - transformed by the spell of slum-bred Circes into swine, peacocks, lions, bulls, sharks and, most frequently, asses.

We were constantly astonished, in fact, by the zest, the energy, the sheer resourcefulness with which prospective clients were prepared to make asses of themselves. On one occasion, for example, Trish, a flint-eyed blue-haired hustler with the fierce grace of a lynx, was accosted by a visiting businessman from Detroit - a beefy brilliantined specimen, the shoulders of his debonair blue suit flecked with dandruff, who apparently had no better place to go on holiday than Chicago. He sidled up to her with the inane repertoire of smirks, sniggers, nudges and winks later to be enshrined by Monty Python. After some twenty minutes of clangorously inept verbal foreplay, he contrived a rubber-lipped leer and managed to articulate the relevant question:

'So tell me now – d'you fuck?'

'You think I'm here for your conversation?'

'You any good?'

She raked him with a talon-sharp sidelong glance.

'Whaddya want?' she drawled. 'Five references?'

But the most memorable impact of all was produced by a girl none of us knew, a frisky, fresh-faced, vibrantly beautiful dryad with undyed – or, at any rate, unblued – chestnut hair, who wafted into the bar one night as if on a gust of spring wind. She was wearing a radiantly exuberant smile and a miniskirt – the shortest any of us had ever seen – which reduced everyone to ogling silence. Over her left breast, pinned to the fabric of her see-through blouse, she sported a saucer-sized button which proclaimed, in day-glow pink letters: '*FUCK BUTTONS!*'

'Hi!' she exclaimed into the stillness with ringing ebullience, then turned, beaming joyously to Terence Mulligan at the door. 'You'll never guess who I am!'

Caught off guard, Mulligan stared at her as if she were simply not to be credited, not possible.

'Probably not,' he growled suspiciously. 'Who the hell are you?'

'I'm Buttons,' she called over her shoulder, twirling her handbag and sauntering down the hushed aisle.

VI

Like most of the bar's staff and patrons, we were, of course, walking a precarious tightrope; and it wasn't long before we ran - or, to be more precise, flew - flamboyantly afoul of the police. Ostensibly, the reason was drugs, specifically marijuana - but only ostensibly. In reality, drugs had little to do with the matter. They merely provided the kind of handy all-purpose excuse officials across the country were by then using for everything, from muzzling 'subversives' to settling personal scores.

Three years before, at the time of our most assiduous pharmacological experiments in Boston, drugs, for most of our contemporaries, were still taboo. They were almost universally perceived as derivatives of sulphur and brimstone; and if we ourselves spoke jokingly about Fausthood, our professors and fellow students failed to see the joke, and regarded our activities as undilutedly demonic. On one occasion, a prospective muse - a soggy-souled woman from Rhode Island with whom I'd been conducting a desultory flirtation - had blundered into the room where Radetzky and I were rolling joints. When she realised what we were doing, her shock, her tears, her general trauma and hysteria attained near operatic proportions. In a salvo of anguished recrimination, I was castigated as 'evil' and 'perverted'. I might've been a hitherto irreproachable husband whose fond wife had just caught him prowling the streets at night, sniffing little girls' bicycle seats.

Now, half the country's student population was more or less chronically stoned. Drugs addled perspectives on every campus, were already sifting down into secondary, even primary, schools. Respected cultural and intellectual figures debated and often extolled the merits of the forbidden substances. Rimbaud, Hesse, Huxley, Burroughs, the godfathers of Surrealism and other sonorous names were invoked in roll-calls, like litanies of saints. Doctors - psychological and physiological - were using hallucinogens as often valuable aids in therapy. Church leaders began seriously to wonder whether mescaline, psilocybin and lysergic acid might indeed provide a kind of jet-assisted take-off to the numinous; and one Biblical scholar, John Allegro, went so far as to argue that Jesus himself was actually a mushroom. Sir Patrick Mayhew, a future pillar of the British judiciary, ingested LSD on television, waxed eloquently incoherent and beamed at his flummoxed interviewer with an owlish smirk of celestial vapidity. Timothy Leary and Ken Kesey had become gurus for a generation, exhorting America's young to turn on, tune in and drop out. The tenor of pop music had changed accordingly, adapting itself to chemically induced neo-Dionysian mysteries, and Lucy in the Sky with Diamonds assumed, by virtue of her acronym, a portentous significance for initiates. In the past, a single acoustic guitar had accompanied Baez's plaintively crystalline timbre, Dylan's raucous croak and coruscating lyrics. Now, people were being moved to psychedelic ecstasy by an electronic pandemoniac din, a solid sheet of unmitigated noise, against which the human voice, if audible at all, was but a distant toneless baying.

Drugs had become, in effect, a new religion, and San Francisco's Haight-Ashbury a new strobe-lit day-glow Mecca, where 'love-ins' drove scandalised squirrels from Golden Gate Park and flower-children cross-pollinated to the orgiastic rhythms of Jefferson Airplane and Grateful Dead. In the city named for Christendom's most spaced-out and hippified flower-child, the Age of Aquarius was being midwifed. Seeking pre-packaged self-realisation, freeze-dried Nirvana and boil-in-the-bag white light, thousands trekked westwards on Hegira. Others, in quest of a speedier shortcut to the absolute, took a more vertical route, launching themselves from upstairs windows and attaining a literal, if messy, union with the earth or sidewalk below. There was, in fact, a minor epidemic of such untidy descents, which led the authorities to conclude that drugs induced dementia – though the Stock Exchange, in 1929, had fostered a far more severe epidemic of window-diving and never incurred official opprobrium.

As psychedelia became ever more voguish and ubiquitous, my friends and I, not surprisingly perhaps, began to weary of it. It'd all become too easy, too banal, too debased – '*das Leichte*', as Stefan George had called the spiritual equivalent of the plastic. If Fausthood of this kind were so accessible, so readily procured by so many incompetents so unworthy and ill-equipped, it was no longer a Fausthood we particularly cared to pursue. '*The problem,*' JT wrote me from California, assessing the phenomenon at spitting distance, '*is that when you've got a hundred thousand unimaginative people all doing their own thing, it amounts to a hundred thousand people all doing more or less the same thing. Not much of anything.'*

If only because drugs were now a norm of our sub-culture, we continued to use them in Chicago. We did so with generally diminishing enthusiasm, however, and we seldom bothered with anything more potent than cannabis. We usually kept a small stash of the stuff in the flat - nothing like the old horde in Boston, just a paltry 'nickel bag' for immediate needs, which were modest enough. We concealed our contraband above the false ceiling in the bathroom, long unrepaired, for which the box of styrofoam in the front room had been intended. On occasion, any or all of us might get stoned in the early evening, before going down to the bar, in the wistful hope that the weed, coupled with one or another exotic spirit, might generate some new illumination. It rarely generated anything more than nausea. The time for drug-induced revelation had passed. We'd pretty much outgrown that particularly phase of *Hinanstrebe,* and there wasn't much Faustian feeling left of it save jadedness. I remember few 'trips' of any interest in Chicago; and such meagre interest as there was resided more in humour than in anything of epistemological consequence.

Thus I recall one instance in particular not because of any profundity of insight or vision it vouchsafed, but because it remains in my memory as a supreme example of doped logic - of the way in which the enstoned mind, or my enstoned mind at any rate, was prone to function. The experience had to do with a coconut which I'd purchased one morning and, for reasons that now elude me, was eager to take down with me to the bar. Having just finished shaving, I emerged from the bathroom and was about to turn left, towards the kitchen, in order to fetch the coconut. Suddenly, I remembered I'd left a lit cigarette on the edge of the desk in my bedroom. By now, it would've burned dangerously low. If I fetched the coconut, I knew I'd forget the cigarette, which would slip from the desk into the wastepaper basket and, in all likelihood, set fire to the entire building. If I turned right, towards the bedroom and the smouldering cigarette, I knew I'd forget the coconut; I'd only remember it later, downstairs, and I'd have to trudge all the way back up to the flat again. *'Alles Vergängliche ist nur in Gleichnis...' 'Everything transitory is but a parable...'* The implications of the situation unfurled in panoramic amplitude through my consciousness, and I stood there, poised at the threshold of the bathroom, paralysed by the sheer enormity of the existential dilemma. It'd become a paradigm, a metaphor, an epiphany, embodying in microcosm the perning of Yeatsian gyres, the conflict of all eternally warring opposites. On the one hand, pleasure; on the other, duty. On the one hand, reckless abandon; on the other, onerous responsibility. On the one hand, untrammelled self-indulgence; on the other, self-abnegation for the sake of others. And I was the protagonist of this epic drama, my soul the arena for the clash between principles of downright Manichaean magnitude! I was both humbled and exalted by the awesome weight of the decision confronting me. Thus must Marlowe's Faustus himself have felt, exhorted by mutually antagonistic elementals at each shoulder.

How long I stood there, I don't know. Probably for no more than a minute or so, though it seemed a minute of purgatorial duration. At last, with stoic acquiescence, I did the honourable thing: I turned towards the bedroom to extinguish the cigarette. With each step I took - there must've been fifteen or twenty of them - I became more pleased with myself, prouder of my virtuous action. How many lives had I saved, I wondered, through the sacrifice I'd made? So noble had the sacrifice come to seem, by the time I reached my desk, that I felt it warranted transcription. I sat down, uncapped my fountain pen and started to scribble an account of my nobility. In doing so, I forgot the cigarette burning quietly away a few inches from my elbow. Only when I smelled smoke did I look round to see a tentative tongue of flame flickering upwards from the litter in the wastepaper basket. And yes, when I got down to the bar, I had, of course, forgotten the coconut as well. I have a hazy recollection of Radetzky, drunk and stoned the night following, banging away at the thing with a hammer, seething at its fuzzy recalcitrance and cursing furiously when he mashed his thumb.

The moral struggle between cigarette and coconut occurred on a Thursday. Three days later, my flatmates and I unwittingly embarked on a trajectory which would lead us, in a *Stuka*-style dive, to Cook County Jail. It was one of those desolate, empty, torpidly soporific Sabbaths so typical of urban America, a grey smelted October day with a vacancy seemingly endless as a life sentence, an ennui debilitating as flu - the kind of day Kristofferson, a short time later, was to evoke so tellingly in 'Sunday Morning Coming Down'.

We weren't drunk. We weren't stoned. We weren't hung over. We were just desperately bored - bored to depression, bored to anguish, bored to near frenzy. If there was any alteration of consciousness involved in what ensued, it derived not from drugs or alcohol, but from boredom. I'd counted my books. I'd gone through the inventory of my library, most of it in storage on the East Coast. I'd computed I'd need 287 years to work my way through the whole collection - a prospect that conduced to demoralising intimations of mortality. I don't know what Patterson and Radetzky had been doing, but it'd left them equally dispirited. At last, we assembled in Patterson's bedroom, which, given the uselessness of the front room, doubled as our lounge. We were playing some apathetic poker, marking time, counting the hours until evening, when proper drinking would begin and the world come to life again.

'I feel like some exercise,' Radetzky grumbled.

'I have feelings of that sort too, occasionally,' I said. 'Usually I lie down and wait for them to pass.'

'We need something to fill up weekends like this,' Patterson decided. 'Something exciting.'

'Parachuting?' Radetzky suggested ironically.

'Too strenuous. Bad for you, too, when you've got too much blood in your alcohol stream. I wouldn't mind learning to fly, though. In a plane, I mean. Mulligan was talking about taking lessons. They're not all that expensive...'

'We don't need lessons,' I announced. 'We could fly a plane right now.'

My friends' faces wore the blankly quizzical expressions of people who've missed the point of a joke. I wasn't joking. Not, at any rate, in the sense they'd imagined. I got up, traipsed down the corridor to the front room, returned with a sheet of white styrofoam from the coffin-sized box. I then explained my inspiration, such as it was, and we immersed ourselves in building a glider - a styrofoam equivalent of the simple balsa wood contraptions which, like every other American male of those days, we'd flown in boyhood. It was, of course, appreciably larger than the traditional juvenile toys, with a wingspan of perhaps four feet. We brought no undue fervour to its construction, but it emerged an impressive-looking thing all the same.

'Well,' Radetzky concluded, stepping back to assess it, 'that killed the better part of an hour. Now what?'

'Damned if I know. We fly it from the window, I suppose.'

Patterson insisted on telephoning downstairs to the bar, which had just opened its doors to a skeleton staff and the afternoon's first smattering of parched patrons. He instructed them to assemble at the door in five minutes, we synchronised our watches and carried our handiwork to the front room. We needed some finesse to manoeuvre the cumbersome thing through the window, one wingtip getting somewhat mangled in the process and delaying take-off. Not wanting to cause an accident, we waited a minute or two longer, until the street below was empty of traffic, then launched our first joint venture in aeronautical engineering.

In its modest way, this maiden flight was fairly spectacular. The glider wafted out towards the derelict cinema opposite, swanlike against the hulk of soot-smeared brick and the grey sky beyond. It banked, tilted, caught a wind current, looped and performed a perfect Immelmann turn. Down on the sidewalk, a few people stopped to gape upwards. A little boy, tugging excitedly at a woman's arm with one hand, pointed with the other and yelled 'Look, Mommy!" his voice piercing in the muffled Sunday stillness. A cheer issued from the bar. The glider performed another loop, dipped its nose, straightened into a long flat descent, skimmed the surface of the road and skittered under a parked van. The entire sortie had lasted less than a minute, a pretty transient gratification for the effort we'd invested - but one could say the same, I suppose, for skiing, sky-diving, sexual seduction and a number of other sports. For reasons we never quite fathomed, Reggie's clientèle were perversely thrilled. Willie retrieved the aircraft and, for the next few days, it hung from a string over the jukebox, where drunken customers adorned it with a patchwork of Black Power insignias.

During the week, several of the regulars asked us if we intended, next Sunday, to 'submit another design'. No, we replied, surprised at first - the thought hadn't even occurred to us. They urged us to consider it. The previous flight had enlivened their day as much as it had ours; and they wanted, besides, a second aircraft in the bar, in order to stage dogfights. We shrugged. Why not, after all? Styrofoam dogfights were probably preferable to the usual kind. And, in its anodyne fashion, the enterprise had been diverting enough. All right, we consented, next Sunday we'd submit a new design.

On Saturday afternoon, we convened a planning session and debated the possible advantages of a delta wing. And then one of us - I forget who - suddenly remembered that the balsa wood gliders of our youth had been rendered more aerodynamically stable by a nail in the nose. To test this, we built a prototype - a small craft, no more than a foot and a half in wingspan - and weighted the nose with a nail pressed into the styrofoam. We then took it to the window for an unscheduled flight.

The nail proved aerodynamically disastrous. The glider started to soar, wobbled in its trajectory, entered a vertiginous spin and promptly plummeted. En route to the street below, it struck Lieutenant Lloyd Boyle of the Vice Squad on the bridge of his nose, just above the crosspiece of his spectacles. So, at any rate, he was later to testify in court. Other, more reliable eyewitnesses reported the aircraft had simply buzzed him - had, before crashlanding in the gutter, skimmed past his ear, eliciting a startled yelp and a convulsive, less than dignified two-step, the dance of a man dodging an angry wasp. We ourselves couldn't judge, the plane's dive slanting inwards towards the building, where the jut of the window-ledge eclipsed our view. On probing our memories afterwards, we agreed we might, just possibly, have heard something, something that might've been a shout or a curse; but it was indecipherable against the generalised pulse of the city, and there was no reason, in any case, to associate it with our test programme.

Deciding to reject nails from all subsequent designs, we'd just pulled out another sheet of styrofoam when the door shuddered under a barrage of imperious Gestapo-brusque knocks. I opened it to find myself staring down the blued snub muzzle of a cocked and levelled .38. Behind the revolver loomed Boyle's features, familiar from a recent raid on the bar - eyes with a maniacal gleam behind stodgy spectacles, tussocks of waywardly bristly black hair, a pale pasty oblong face of an incongruous scholarly austerity. To one side stood another man - a sergeant, it transpired - who looked like a miniaturised clone of Boyle himself.

'You guys throw something at me?' the lieutenant demanded.

'No,' I replied in all innocence, as Patterson and Radetzky emerged from the front room to join me.

'You threw something from the window.'

'We flew an aeroplane.'

'Been smoking something, haven't you?'

'Yes, as a matter of fact,' I said, producing and proffering my cigarette package. 'Lark. Made by Liggett and Myers, Durham, North Carolina. 'Richly rewarding. Uncommonly smooth'.'

'Search this place,' Boyle snapped to the sergeant. 'These guys were flying toy planes from a fourth floor window. They'd have to be on dope to do a thing like that.'

'You *do* have a warrant, don't you?' Radetzky asked, probably because it was what people always asked in films.

'Don't need a warrant. I'm following up on a crime. That gives me the right to search for anything used in the crime or anything that might've contributed to it.'

'Contributed to what?'

'The crime I'm following up on.'

'What crime is that?'

'Assault.'

'With an aeroplane?'

Boyle didn't answer. For the next few minutes, he held us, still at gunpoint, in the corridor, while the sergeant proceeded to ferret through the premises - poking into closets and cabinets, rummaging under mattresses, turning out drawers.

'This place is a mess,' he called from the kitchen.

'You have to appreciate,' Patterson explained, 'the weeks of creative neglect we've put into it.'

There were, we learned later, various technical grounds on which we might've challenged the legality of the invasion. We could also have made some rudimentary noises of defiance - requesting the presence of an attorney, for example - which, if nothing else, would've compelled Boyle and his lackey to adhere more closely to the book. At the time, however, we were simply too dumbfounded and bemused to take the situation seriously. It was all too grotesque, too unreal or surreal or farcically absurd, something that might've been scripted by Ionesco. I personally kept expecting Boyle to holster his gun, clap one or another of us on the back and dissolve in avuncular laughter. '*Scared you, didn't I?*' he might say. '*Well, that'll teach you to violate my airspace.*' I can't now remember most of what was, in fact, said while the search progressed. Much of it, as I recall, was pleasant enough -

perfectly equable, even good-natured and jocose banter. At one point, though, Boyle gestured at Patterson, then turned to Radetzky and me.

'I know him. He's the manager downstairs. What about you two?'

'We're graduate students,' I replied, volunteering our names.

'At the university, eh?'

A smirk of unconcealed delight flickered across Boyle's face. At the time, not believing he actually intended to arrest us, we weren't sure how to interpret this smirk. In retrospect, we recognised it as a smirk of vindictive triumph. It was the smirk of a man relishing a long-awaited opportunity to exact revenge on those to whom he feels intellectually inferior – the smile of all the world's rednecks, philistines, storm troopers and Calibans.

'If you're in the graduate school here, you must be pretty well-heeled.'

'Hardly,' I laughed. 'We're staggering along on the most meagre of fellowships.'

Boyle looked momentarily chagrined. We suddenly realised he'd been fishing for a bribe. By then, of course, the chance to offer one had passed. In any case, we couldn't've managed more than a derisory sum. And in his sadistic glee at finding two university students in his clutches, Boyle would've been perfectly capable of pocketing our money, then adding bribery to the charges against us.

Emerging from Patterson's bedroom, the sergeant stood portentously at the opposite end of the corridor. Boyle turned to him and the two men faced each other for a moment, expressionless. The sergeant shook his head, almost imperceptibly, and Boyle responded with a discreet nod. The sergeant disappeared back into Patterson's bedroom. We, for our part, still weren't worried. We had, as usual, a 'nickel bag' of cannabis stashed above the false ceiling in the bathroom, but it was hardly likely to be discovered by the sergeant's apathetic and lackadaisical search. What we failed to anticipate was that the police, not finding our drugs, would brazenly plant their own. We were thus momentarily stunned when the sergeant again emerged from Patterson's bedroom, brandishing an all-too-obvious brown envelope which none of us had seen before.

'Found it in the bureau,' he said, not bothering to explain why he hadn't found it there on his first inspection.

It must've been some two or three years before the Supreme Court's Miranda formula became obligatory for all American law enforcement agencies. We were therefore spared the incantation now familiar to fans of cop films: '*You have the right to remain silent. You have the right to an attorney. Anything you say may be taken down and used against you in a court of law...*' On Lieutenant Boyle's instructions, the sergeant simply used our telephone to ring for a paddy wagon. When it arrived some twenty minutes later, we were ushered downstairs, still at gunpoint, and bundled inside. From the bar, an old Baez record was audible on the jukebox: '*Swing low, sweet chariot, comin' for to carry me home...*'

We were trundled off to a local precinct jail - the inaugural way-station, we learned later, of a journey which could easily have ended with the State Penitentiary at Joliet. In a small interrogation room of the 'city lock-up', as it was called, Boyle purported to 'interview' us, in fact doing little save taking down names, home addresses and other personal data. We were then escorted down a corridor and consigned for the next twelve hours to an aseptic, recently re-painted cell, where reflected splashes of fluorescent light swam like radiant oil patches in the grey sheen of ceiling and walls. There being only two bunks, we took turns lying on the grey tiled floor. From adjoining cubicles issued an uninterrupted babble and hubbub, angry, drunken, stoned, sometimes undilutedly demented, like a scaled-down replica of Bedlam. Next door to us, someone whose mind had congealed into a broken record kept muttering 'Aw shiiiit!' in the same monotone, at regular thirty second intervals, all night long. From elsewhere, there were shouts, curses, bursts of raucous laughter, catcalls, whistles, hoots, flurries of generalised abuse, an intermittent lycanthropic howling. From the opposite end of the corridor, a particularly sonorous black voice filled the entire span of darkness with a non-stop repertoire of hymns and spirituals. In this milieu, the prospect of grace was indeed amazing.

By the steely light of dawn, we were transferred, in another paddy wagon, to Cook County Jail. We were housed initially in a holding cell - an enclosure the size of a small barn, packed beyond all possibility of lying down, or even sitting comfortably, with the night's sweeping of drunks, pickpockets, muggers, flashers, brawlers and other public enemies. The precise sequence of what followed was blurred even then by sleeplessness, fatigue and the sheer unreality of the state we seemed to be inhabiting. It's since been further hazed by time. At some point, however, we were charged officially with possession of marijuana, disturbing the peace and assault with a deadly weapon - the weapon being the nail in the nose of the glider. At some point, our belts, wallets, lighters, pocket knives, coins and other such articles were confiscated and we were searched, fingerprinted, photographed - the best photographs I think I've ever had taken. At some point, we were arraigned and bail was posted at three hundred dollars apiece. It might as well have been three thousand, or thirty thousand. Instead of the telephone call to which each of us should've been entitled, we were allowed only one for the three of us.

We were streetwise, but not jailwise. Knowing nothing of professional bail bondsmen and the rococo machinery of American justice, I tried to reach an acquaintance at the university's law school. His line was engaged, and that was the sole access any of us obtained to a telephone. Before we could determine how, or with whom, to lodge a protest, we were shepherded into a queue and moved to the cell block which Boyle had no doubt imagined, if not earmarked, as our residence for the next year or so. Behind us, successive barred portals clanged shut with metallic echoing finality. There'd been a dreamlike Kafkaesque quality about the whole procedure. Had a handful of Reggie's regulars not chanced to see us being carted off in the paddy wagon, no one would've known where we were nor what'd happened to us, and we might well have disappeared into Cook County Jail forever. People would've come round to our flat, banged on the door, telephoned, written, and we'd simply have vanished, been expunged from the world, like chalk drawings erased from a blackboard. We might've fallen through some crack in the cosmos, some fissure in the very substance of reality.

The cell block was T-shaped. The longer, or vertical, axis consisted of a corridor onto which opened snug rows of cells apparently no longer than refrigerators, each with a single grating recessed into its steel door. The shorter, or horizontal, axis at the end of the corridor consisted of a large rectangular space which resembled a shabby student union or cafeteria - randomly scattered wooden tables with benches attached, a few chairs, a television set perched high on a shelf. This was the 'day room', where inmates, for most of their waking hours, were allowed to congregate, talk, eat, watch television, play cards, chess or other board games or - if the spirit so moved them and they weren't too noisy about it - beat one another up. Walls and floor were a deep maroon shading to brown - so bloodstains wouldn't show, we were told - with tawny wood wainscoting and fittings. Apart from the paint and the television set, nothing seemed to date from later than the 1930s. Were some of Capone's 'torpedoes' and trigger-men conjured back to life, they might've found the outside world alien, but these premises would've been familiar turf.

Along with eight or nine other new arrivals, we were marched into the corridor of cells and abandoned by the uniformed warder. A pause ensued, after which someone emerged from the 'day room' - a lithe, very pale, almost bronze-skinned black, clad only in slippers, green silk pyjama bottoms and an iridescent multi-hued cloth wound in a turban round his head. His colouring and apparel made him look like a Mongol warrior. He half-slouched, half-swaggered his way down to where we stood, passed slowly in front of us, appraised us with the insolent scrutiny of an officer inspecting troops on parade. He then positioned himself opposite our little rank, lounged back against the wall and introduced himself, speaking in a pseudo-Texas drawl which, for some weird reason, seemed actually to suit his pasha-posh appearance.

'Howdy. My name's Otis Buckley. Buck, for short. I'm your barn boss. That means I'm in charge here. I'm the head man. The honcho-in-chief. Yeah, I'm a prisoner like you all, but I been here in this cell block longer'n anyone else, an' it's my job to keep order, if you know what I mean. You behave yourselves an' I keep outa trouble, so you can't afford not to behave yourselves. There's three things you should know 'bout me. I'm tough, an' I'm fast, an' I'm smart, an' that means I'll be able to handle any problems you might happen to have...'

He gestured at two colleagues, one tall, one short, who, wearing red and yellow turbans respectively, had ambled to his side during his presentation.

'These here cats're my lieutenants. Big one's Ralph. Little one's Rusty. You call 'em both "Mr.".' '"Mr. Ralph' an' Mr. Rusty".'

'Any problems you have, you take 'em to Ralph an' Rusty. Anything they can't handle, I can...'

Obviously enjoying his well-rehearsed and oft-played performance, he went on to outline the prevailing rules, which seeped only vaguely through our somnolence. No more than two prisoners at a time in the latrine. No one allowed in the latrine during the night except in emergency and with permission. The 'day room' open to everyone from eight in the morning until ten in the evening. From ten o'clock on, everyone confined to his assigned cell. Cigarettes, chocolate and other amenities to be ordered through Ralph and Rusty, who'd pocket a modest commission. The litany of regulations and stipulations went on and on, as lengthy, confusing and impossible to absorb at first hearing as the British driving code. Having reduced us to near stupor with his recitation, Buck then skilfully recaptured our attention:

'An' by the way, there's one other thing you should probably know. Like I said before, come ten o'clock, you're gonna be in your cells. Doors ain't locked unless there's a riot or somethin', but you're gonna be in your cells. An' you're gonna *stay* in your cells. No matter what happens, you're gonna stay in your cells. Now durin' the night, sometimes, you might think you hear some noises comin' from out here in the corridor, or mebbe from the day room. You might think you hear some thuds, or some smacks, or some groans, or some yells. If you think you hear noises like that, you don't pay no attention. You act like you don't hear them noises at all. You stay in your cells. 'Cause if you stick your nose out, them noises is gonna be happenin' 'round your head.'

Cook County Jail in those days was a versatile place, performing a varied array of functions and catering to multifarious clientèle. It was a kind of mini-penitentiary for prisoners serving terms up to two years. It was an improvised transit camp for more serious offenders en route to longer sojourns in Joliet and other such facilities. It was a detention centre for those awaiting hearing or trial. It was a general depository for anyone trawled off the streets and held for more than a single night. More than half of our cell block's fifty or so inmates were members of the Blackstone Rangers. Apart from Patterson, Radetzky and myself, there were only three whites. One was a lumbering ox-necked brute who'd strangled his wife, had already done six months in Joliet and been transferred back here for an appeal based somehow on 'new evidence'. The second was a mousy little specimen, an investment broker or something of the sort, who'd run up five hundred parking tickets in five years and been ordered to serve sixty days. The third was a wiry, olive-skinned, short-fused man awaiting trial for armed robbery and murder. During an abortive liquor store hold-up, he'd imprudently got involved in a gun battle, had shot one policeman dead and permanently crippled another. He himself had also been hit, in leg and shoulder. He hobbled about on crutches, proudly unwrapping his bandages and displaying his bullet wounds to the morbidly curious. Measured against transgressions such as his, our own were rather puny - and rather embarrassing.

'Grass,' we'd reply when asked. 'And assault with an aeroplane.'

Our story, needless to say, became the talk, and the joke, of the cell block. In its sheer lunacy, it even redounded to our credit. Few of our fellow prisoners, however, were surprised. A number of them knew Boyle already, or knew of him, and we were regaled with copious accounts of his idiosyncrasies. He was regarded as a maniac, it seemed, even amongst his colleagues. He used the police not only for the standardised corrupt purposes, but also as a mandate for his own inimitable form of self-expression. His job afforded him a licence to wallow in power, inflate his already distended ego, indulge his propensity to bully, conduct personal vendettas and act out a deep-seated imaginative identification with Wild Bill Hickok.

Our sojourn in Cook County Jail proved anticlimactically placid. I shared a cramped cell with Radetzky. Patterson, with a cell luxuriously to himself, was placed directly opposite - we could see and call to each other through the gratings in our respective doors. The time, though vacant, passed with an eerie fluidity, perhaps because we still seemed to be sleepwalking. In retrospect, I find it astonishing that we spent the better part of five days inside. During mornings and afternoons, we played chess and poker, watched children's programmes and soap operas on television, swapped stories with other inmates. At night, Radetzky and I filled the empty hours pacing, philosophising, introspecting, comparing impressions, impatiently awaiting the kind of illumination that's traditionally supposed to descend on the incarcerated - the illumination that descended on Dostoyevsky, on Koestler, on numerous other authors

and protagonists of prison literature. If such illumination was denied us, we were also spared the nasty nocturnal noises about which Buck, in his admonition, had waxed so pungently eloquent.
There was a surprising - and, it transpired, uncharacteristic - absence of violence. We weren't privy to anything worse than an occasional scuffle, and we ourselves were never touched.

Not until later - much later - did I learn how lucky we'd been. Some nine or ten years afterwards , by which time I'd already settled in London, exposés of Cook County Jail began to appear - in the British as well as the American media. It was only with Mayor Daley's death, and the dismantling of his municipal machine, that the full catalogue of nightmare became public - the abuses by warders and other inmates, the bribes and rake-offs and illicit commissions, the beatings and knifings, the trafficking in alcohol and drugs, the pimping and prostitution and homosexual rape that occurred within those walls. And the alarming number of prisoners who never emerged at all, who died mysteriously from 'accidents' and 'natural causes' and alleged suicides, or who simply disappeared, along with all records pertaining to them. Neither I nor, I suspect, anyone else who'd been inside the place was shocked by the revelation of such trespasses. More appalling was the sheer scale on which they were routinely perpetrated. The jail was situated in the very heart of a metropolis, yet might've been as insulate, as remote, as divorced from civilisation as the penal camp and chain gang in *Cool Hand Luke.*

That we escaped unscathed was owing in large part to Buck, who effectively guaranteed our immunity. From the very beginning, he took a liking to us, decided we were 'cool dudes' and appointed himself our protector. He also, as it happened, knew Reggie's and a number of our associates there. During lengthy conversations in the 'day room', he told us his story. He'd been arrested for shoplifting - 'serious shoplifting', as he put it, several thousand dollars worth of jewellery from one of the poshest department stores downtown. He'd been in Cook County Jail now for more than a year and a half. He'd refused both an attorney and a public defender, choosing rather to conduct his own defence. In the course of a dozen court appearances, he'd personally confronted, cross-questioned and broken down, one by one, a troop of hostile witnesses. His next court appearance was scheduled for the coming Thursday.

By the time Thursday arrived, Buck's favouritism towards us was beginning to be of equivocal benefit. Petty jealousies and rivalries of the sort that surface in prison were starting to manifest themselves, and certain of the inmates, including Ralph and Rusty, resented us for the status we enjoyed. There was also, Buck confided to us, increasing rancour about the fact that Patterson and I sported moustaches. According to the prevailing logic, or sleight thereof, only blacks were entitled to such facial adornment. The situation became acute when Buck was ushered out of the cell block for another court appearance, another phalanx of witnesses to confront. He failed to return; and amidst the anxious speculation and galloping rumour, surly glances were flicked at us, whispered conversations were conducted, huddles of two or three in the 'day room' would lapse into conspiratorial silence at our approach. In the absence of our protector, we realised, we'd become fair game.

That evening, fortuitously, a title fight on television, by the then Cassius Clay, distracted everyone's attention. Before the second round ended, we were bailed out. A warder, without explanation, escorted us from the cell block, through an intestinal tangle of corridors, to a lobby, where we were asked to sign release forms. The property office was closed for the night, we were told; we'd have to return tomorrow for our belongings. The jail then disgorged us into a wind-whipped polar night, where gusts of exhilarating sleet slashed at our faces and a taxi stood idling with Nina and Beryl in the back seat.

A veritable *fête* awaited us at the bar. We might've been gone for years rather than a few days. We might've been returning war heroes, conquerors of Everest, astronauts safely landed from the moon. A number of people presented us with plastic model aeroplane kits. Nina, I learned, had borrowed money for my bail from Al Hollis - a piquant irony which, alas, he could never be allowed to know. Beryl had similarly raised a sum for Radetzky - from her parents, I seem to recall. Patterson had no such solicitous angel, not yet having met the woman who was later to become his Chicago consort. Nor, lest it imperil his job, could Melvin Bloss have been approached for funds. In consequence, Reggie's staff and patrons had taken up a collection on his behalf.

We were regaled with further pathological profiles of Boyle, further accounts of his manias and antics. According to one report, he'd pursued a particular vendetta to the point of bursting in on a couple in mid-copulation and arresting them for disturbing the peace. His behaviour in our case was the focus of much debate and possibly slanderous hypothesis. Melvin Bloss, someone alleged, had fallen behind on payments to a personage in the upper echelons of the municipal machine; and Boyle, ordered to administer an admonitory lesson, had targeted Patterson as the bar's manager. Someone else insisted the lieutenant had been egged on by Al Hollis, who'd hoped to remove me from the lists as a rival for Nina's favours. If so, it was all the more apt that Hollis be my unwitting benefactor. American justice might wobble, but poetic justice still reigned. In Goethe's dramatic poem, after all, das *Ewigweibliche* stands celestial bail for Faust.

We returned to the jail the following morning in order to reclaim our property. At a small barred cashier-style window, we presented our prisoners' identification cards and photographs and received our personal possessions in exchange. All three of us wanted to keep our cards and photographs as souvenirs. We were trying to get them back, arguing with the lackey behind the grille, when someone behind us gave Patterson a jovial shove.

'Small world, ain't it, man?'

We turned to find Buck standing there, grinning like a gargoyle. His turban was gone now, revealing sleekly oiled and elaborately quiffed hair. He was dressed in a spanking new tan leather trenchcoat and pointed shoes of a polished lustre that might've passed muster in the Guards.

'You're out...?'

The two witnesses confronting him the day before had proved to be the last. He'd broken them down as he had all the others, and promptly been released. He'd gone directly from the jail to a solicitor's office, where he'd learned he could sue the city for false arrest - and for the year and a half he'd spent inside. According to authoritative legal opinion, he stood to receive a sum of five figures, possibly even more.

'An' shit, man!' he chuckled. 'I was guilty as all hell!'

* * * * * * *

From sundry acquaintances at the university, we managed collectively to borrow another three hundred dollars. The only attorney we could obtain for this sum - a sleazy back-street shyster who bore an uncanny resemblance to Richard Nixon - might, for all practical purposes, have been clinically brain-dead. In the end, like Buck, we pretty much conducted our own defence.

If our arrest had been surreal or absurdist, our court appearances were unadulterated slapstick. Our preliminary hearing was scheduled for the week following our release. We approached it with a banter and bravado that didn't altogether mask our anxiety, and our wit was sometimes strained.

'What the fuck's in his briefcase?' Patterson whispered as our putative lawyer bustled into the courtroom carrying something the size of a valise. 'He only took half a page of notes. He could've carried that in his pocket.'

'Maybe it's an inflatable witness,' Radetzky guffawed.

'What we really need,' I observed, 'is a judge with a sense of humour.'

'I wonder how many times Boyle's been through this routine,' Patterson mused, looking round the room. 'We're probably just notches on his pistol butt. When he's brought a hundred people like us to justice, they probably give him a gold-plated criminal.'

At our first court appearance, the police had to ask for a continuance because part of the 'evidence' - the marijuana part - had been 'misplaced'. Presumably it was being recycled and planted on some other unsuspecting victims. At our second appearance, *we* had to ask for a continuance because our lawyer failed to show up. It transpired that he'd overslept. At our third appearance, Boyle failed to turn up - he, in turn, had overslept - and the police had to request another continuance. At our fourth appearance - three hours before I was scheduled to sit my M.A. written exam at the university - our case was finally heard. *'The State of Illinois versus...'*. It sounded intimidating. The whole bloody state? Fifteen or twenty million people, in close military ranks, shoulder to shoulder, shaking the earth with their tread, marching inexorably against our three hapless selves? On a table to the right of the judge's raised bench lay the 'evidence'. '*Exhibit A*' - a small brown envelope which, as far as anyone present could gauge, might contain mouse droppings. '*Exhibit B* ' - a small styrofoam aeroplane, strikingly white against the courtroom's dark wood and general dinginess.

Our case was heard by Judge Amos Bent. His name augured ill but proved, in fact, to be signally inappropriate. Judge Bent was a splendid old duffer already past retirement age, an Orson Wellesish figure in girth, in love of histrionics and propensity to ham. His face was that of an Old Testament prophet - a mane of spume-wild white hair, white eyebrows the size of caterpillars that met over his nose, the craggy rough-hewn features of a Mount Rushmore sculpture. He recognised the inequities and iniquities of the narcotics laws, understood only too well how they were exploited to harass any and all 'undesirables'. He also, we learned later, had a grandson at university in Ohio, was familiar with the prevalence of drugs on campus, knew that cannabis users weren't invariably hardened felons. In consequence, he was frequently merciless to the police, especially when he sensed any irregularities in their procedures. He'd interrupt their testimonies, ask sarcastic questions, make jokes at their expense, play to the spectators in the gallery like a ringmaster. His courtroom was notorious for its lack of decorum, solemnity and propriety. People would shout, cheer, applaud, heckle, engage in banter and repartée. The judge, beaming effulgently, would trade quips and revel in the unruly circus atmosphere.

'Lieutenant,' he asked at one point in the proceedings against us, his irascible gravel-voiced query resonating through the room, 'would you kindly tell me again where precisely it was that the...er, attacking aircraft...smote you?'

'On my nose, your honour,' Boyle replied, pointing to the spot allegedly smote. 'The bridge of my nose.'

'Just above the crosspiece of your glasses?'

'That's correct, your honour.'

'I see. Well, Lieutenant, I must confess I find this extraordinary. Would you explain to me why, if the aircraft in question struck you precisely there, you failed to see it coming? And why, if you *did* see it coming, you made no attempt to get out of its way?'

The judge listened to everyone's statements with increasing incredulity. When we'd all finished, he glanced at us with a crystalline gleam of irony in his ice-blue eyes, then turned again to Boyle, grimacing impatiently.

'Lieutenant, this is possibly the most ridiculous case I've ever had occasion to hear. How exactly would you describe the aircraft that...er, strafed...you? A fighter-bomber perhaps?'

By now, of course, Boyle, in his rage, was changing colour like a traffic signal, from Dracula-drained white to apoplectic red. The courtroom, needless to say, was in pandemonium, each new salvo from the bench being acknowledged by explosions of laughter, catcalls, whistles, jeers. We alone remained impassive. We naturally relished the lieutenant's discomfiture; but it was obvious, after so blistering a public humiliation, that he'd become a vindictive and dangerous enemy.

The marijuana charge was dismissed on grounds of illegal search and seizure. Because we'd confessed to the original 'crime' immediately - that of having flown the aeroplane - there'd been no sanction for ransacking the premises. Anything found after our admission of guilt was inadmissible as evidence. Had we been acquitted completely, however, we could've sued for false arrest; and the judge apparently felt some obligation to protect Chicago from our retribution. In consequence, we were each found guilty of littering and fined ten dollars.

Among those who swarmed forward to congratulate us was Buck. Two reporters - the kind of hacks who hang about courtrooms in quest of the lurid or, failing that, the oddball - asked us for interviews. We declined. It wouldn't've been the kind of celebrity that interested us, and we had no desire to exacerbate further our relations with the lieutenant. We debated briefly whether it might be politic to approach him and make peace. Hell, no! we decided unanimously. Fuck him!

By that time, in any case, he'd long vanished, scuttling away in his ignominy. Patterson and Radetzky then wandered off to get drunk. I caught a taxi direct from the courthouse to my M.A. exam, where, for the next four hours, I wrote on More's *Utopia* and its putative 'relevance to the modern world'.

VII

Save for some generally bile-sour memories, Patterson suffered no particular after-effects from our *contretemps*. For Radetzky and me, however, it conduced, during the next month or so, to rampant paranoia. I became edgy, skittish, around drugs. I felt a burgeoning disquiet when anyone used them in my presence. To use them myself was to incur a state of self-induced anxiety. My mind would accelerate, would begin to race, would adumbrate hectic feverish scenarios of discovery, arrest and prosecution. In my car, for example, I imagined myself stopped for the proverbial burned-out taillight - a taillight kicked in, that is, to ensure it was indeed burned out. On foot, at the rancid café where I'd experiment with my digestion, at my table in the bar, in any of innumerable places, I imagined myself pounced on for any of innumerable reasons, and frisked. Whatever the circumstances, whatever the milieu, another brown envelope might deftly be planted on me, and I'd be powerless to disown it. When I was 'straight', such possibilities seemed remote, no more menacing than in the past. When I was stoned, however, they'd usurp the foreground of my consciousness, drawing my nerves taut as guitar strings, producing an incipient shrill singing in my ears, a vibration just beyond the threshold of sound. If I'd inhaled more than a puff or so of cannabis, I couldn't venture outside the flat without sensing that everyone was watching me, everyone knew I was high.

I became affronted, indignant. It seemed to me an outrage, a monstrous and appalling invasion of privacy, that my mind had thus been manipulated and programmed - that I'd had implanted in my consciousness so alien, and so pathological, a mechanism. I felt mentally violated. It was as if a stranger had poked clammy fingers directly into my skull and wired an alarm bell there, which I couldn't control.

Losing patience, I discussed the matter with Radetzky, who confessed to similar symptoms. Determined to exorcise ourselves, we embarked on a rigorously disciplined regimen, a species of psychic enema. Every night, I'd smoke at least two joints of marijuana. I'd force myself to breathe deeply and regularly, curbing the propensity to hyperventilate. I'd then force myself outside - to the streets, to the cinema, to the shopping mall, to the bar, where every conversation, every encounter, every random exchange of glances was paranoia fodder. I'd force myself to suppress the panic welling like nausea within me. I'd force myself to confront the imagined stares, to sustain the fancied pressure of a myriad probing and knowledgeable eyes. It was often a thoroughly unpleasant ordeal, an arduous *rite de passage*. As I walked down the aisle in Reggie's, I'd feel as if I were running a gauntlet. There were moments when I seemed to be the only stoned person in the whole of Chicago, and everyone else - including Boyle and all the anonymous figures around me, any of whom might be his snitches or snouts - seemed to know it.

Wondering vaguely whether mind-warping constituted grounds for litigation, I persisted doggedly in my regimen. I persisted in it for some five weeks. Radetzky did likewise. And then, one evening, everything seemed to reverse itself, to turn inside out. Radetzky and I had each smoked three joints and attained a reasonably rarefied altitude. As we sat at our table in the bar, some focus within me, both mental and visual, abruptly shifted. I sensed that something was different, that something had inexplicably altered. I couldn't at first identify it precisely, but, whatever it was, Radetzky apparently felt it too. He blinked quizzically, shook his head as one might shake a watch that's stopped, blinked again.

'Look around you...' he said tentatively, more questioning than anything else.

'Yes, I know. It's sort of as if...'

'As if everyone else...' he interrupted, beginning suddenly to laugh.

'Yes, as if everyone else...' I exclaimed, laughing now as well.

'As if everyone else were stoned...!' we gasped together, collapsing, choking, dissolving with mirth; and on that wave of cathartic hilarity, our paranoia flooded out and away. It never returned. We were indeed purged.

Unfortunately, there were elements in the world around me less prepared than my psyche to re-establish equilibrium. According to a witticism of the time, even paranoids - or, in this case, ex-paranoids - have genuine enemies. We indubitably had ours, in the grim grumpy vengeance-bent guise of Lloyd Boyle. It wouldn't be long, we knew, before the lieutenant surfaced again - not in our infected imaginations, but, such as it was, in the flesh. When he did, however, it was with bigger game in his sights than ourselves. Initially, at least, we were to be hijacked and used as instruments in his pursuit of a more formidable quarry, the awesome and terrifying Teddy Bronson.

Teddy Bronson was a Godzilla-sized eighteen-stone hulk who'd been washed out of the Marine Corps with a dishonourable discharge and enough blots on his records to've drained an inkwell. He was something of a celebrity in the neighbourhood, a certified local 'character'. He was certifiable in other respects, too. Most of the time, he was agreeable enough - amiable, courteous, soft-spoken, with an almost winsome boyish charm, a stammering shyness, a touching eagerness to be accepted and liked. He'd be deferential, anxious to please and, in his clumsy inarticulate way, poignantly eloquent - eloquent as men of intense and tormented nature, trapped by their own muteness, frequently are.

Periodically, however, Teddy Bronson would go berserk. Clinically berserk. Dramatically berserk. Majestically berserk. Violently and dangerously berserk. On a rampage, Teddy assumed a frenzied and devastating momentum, wreaking blind tempestuous havoc against anything in his path - and incurring, with the anaesthetised imperviousness of the mad, a damage to himself that would've felled most others. On several occasions, we were told, his strength had enabled him to burst the straps and buckles of his straitjacket. At such moments, he'd be less a sentient creature than an ungovernable force of nature running amok, something like a cyclone or a typhoon. Nobody'd yet identified the trigger that actuated his fits of dementia; nobody'd established whether it was some chance external stimulus, or some mysterious detonating mechanism within. Whatever it was, Teddy's explosions, when they occurred, attained downright epic proportions - the proportions of Achilles in tantrum, of Lear on the blasted and storm-wracked heath. The Jekyll-to-Hyde transformation would happen without warning, often without provocation, and within a matter of seconds. Teddy might be walking down the road, riding a train, talking equably in restaurant or bar. Suddenly, his face would flush, his eyes grow ominously bloodshot, his features writhe as in the throes of some subterranean seismic upheaval. The veins in his bullock-thick neck would swell like cords, and he'd simply wig out. An earlier age would've seen in him a classic, even textbook, case of demonic possession. But the demon, in this instance, hadn't chosen the usual frail vessel of child, hysterical nun or malformed village idiot. In this instance, it'd chosen the kind of host, the kind of abode, that any demon with half a brain might've been expected to choose for its depredations - the body of a human Panzer.

I'd seen Teddy at intervals during the previous year, Nina having pointed him out and told me his story. On those occasions, he'd been docile enough. When my flatmates and I moved into the apartment above Reggie's, Teddy wasn't around. He was busy serving another of his more or less regular jail sentences - for assault, as usual, this time of a woman one afternoon on the nearby main thoroughfare. Not sexual assault. Not even sentient assault. More the kind of assault that might've been committed, *en passant*, by a stampeding buffalo. He'd just been rousted, apparently, by a brace of police officers. Fuming, he'd stalked off, barged through the crowd at the crossing and knocked some housewife's shopping bag out of her hand. She'd called him a slob and he, scarcely bothering to look round, had nearly decapitated her with an uppercut to the jaw which left her sprawled unconscious in the middle of the road and brought traffic to a squealing halt for half a mile. They'd packed him away, as they'd done on every previous such occasion; and it wasn't until his release, shortly after the new year, that I even remembered his existence. At the news that Teddy was out, Patterson and the rest of Reggie's staff were quietly briefed and put on alert. On his reappearance in the bar, the whole place fell portentously silent - as when the black-clad gunslinger saunters through the swinging doors of Dodge City's Long Branch Saloon.

On that first evening, he was disarmingly placid, hunkering modestly over successive bourbons with beer chasers. So forlorn was he in his pariah's solitude that several of the regulars, who'd initially kept their distance, gradually approached, bought drinks for him, welcomed him back, engaged him in conversation. His boyish gratitude thawed everyone. In the days that followed, his squarish brick-red face and tight ginger-coloured curls became a familiar spectacle on the premises. There was always something forbidding about his gargantuan, tensely poised and alert body. But his behaviour, for a fortnight or so, was impeccable.

Patterson established a rapport, even a degree of friendship, with him such as few had previously dared. Radetzky and I would chat with him sporadically, on a first-name basis. On one occasion, I remember him - incongruously, in the context of Chicago - proudly extolling the IRA. This, needless to say, predated the commencement of Northern Ireland's subsequent 'Troubles' - predated them by two or three years. Teddy may perhaps have thought he was alluding to the IRA of recent history - the more or less puerile organisation which, between 1956 and 1962, had conducted a desultory bombing campaign in the North. In fact, however, he'd never himself been to Ireland, and the images in his mind, implanted apparently by his father, were images of an earlier epoch - images of Michael Collins, of the young de Valera, of the 1920s-vintage IRA, who, during the Civil War, had exterminated more of their fellow Irishmen than the British Army, or even the Black and Tans, had previously. At the time, of course, I myself had little awareness of such nuances or distinctions. My frame of reference was essentially literary, and Teddy's rhetoric seemed to be issuing from the world of O'Connor, O'Casey and O'Flaherty.

Some two weeks after his return to the neighbourhood, I had my first glimpse of Teddy 'in action' - in the full spate, that is, of his derangement. He was seated at the bar, hunched over his habitual bourbon and beer, more moody than he'd tended to be of late; and the stools to either side of him were therefore prudently vacant. He'd been there for some twenty minutes when a squat, stocky, barrel-chested black man swaggered in - shorter than Teddy, but no less solid and, ostensibly at least, more dangerous-looking. Obviously a stranger, the newcomer took the stool to Teddy's left. Teddy offered to buy him a drink. The black man assented brusquely, as if it were his due, and the two mechanically clinked glasses. Teddy offered to buy another, and the ritual was repeated, then repeated again. At the fourth offer, the black man demurred. Teddy insisted. The black man glared at him, encountered something in his gaze, flinched and turned away. When Teddy ordered the drink anyway, the black man ignored it, brooding grimly into emptiness. At last, saying nothing, he rose, lurching slightly, and aimed himself at the door. As he passed behind Teddy, Teddy half-swivelled and - quite casually, almost playfully - rammed an elbow into his solar plexus. The black man whuffed hugely, doubling up like a folded jack-knife. Teddy half-swivelled again, seemingly preoccupied with something else, and, in a single brisk karate chop, brought the edge of one hand down across the back of the black man's neck. The black man hit the floor like a dropped bag of cement, lying face down in a puddle of beer. Teddy stood up, seized the nearest ashtray and hurled it with the velocity of a cannonball into the mirror behind the bar. The mirror shattered, glasses smashed, bottles toppled with a crash and a crystalline tinkling. Stepping over his victim's inert form, Teddy stormed furiously out of the premises, nearly wrenching the door from its hinges, cursing some invisible presence in the air at his shoulder. The whole incident had lasted no more than a few seconds, was over before most people knew anything had happened.

In the wake of his misconduct, Teddy was of course, and inevitably, 'eighty-sixed' - banned from the bar. For the next few days, we kept expecting his reappearance, which would've precipitated a confrontation with Terence Mulligan - a true clash of titans. He stayed away, however, and anticipation gradually subsided. It was soon eclipsed entirely by the weather's tempestuous behaviour, more spectacular even than Teddy's. In the second week of February, Chicago was visited by its All-Time Record Snowfall.

I no longer remember the precise statistics, trumpeted gleefully by the local media as if they represented some achievement deliberately performed by the city, some feat on which all residents had grounds for pride. I dimly recall something like thirty-eight, or perhaps forty-two, inches of snow in twenty-four hours. In any case, it started around mid-morning - huge furry flakes lazily sifting down the dead air, tumbling endlessly, end over end, out of a muffled metallic sky. It continued incessantly, forming gauzy white curtains through which vistas even a few yards distant flickered and receded. By evening, there were a good three and a half feet of it, a uniform waist-deep layer, and it persisted unabated through the night. Snow rounded and softened all projections, all contours, and the town, transformed into an immense wedding cake, came to a complete stop. Trains, buses, cars, police vehicles, even snowploughs, were utterly immobilised. An eerie, spectral and enchanted silence supplanted the customary mechanised din. The modern bustling automated metropolis was more stricken by nature's self-assertion than 18th century Berlin or Petersburg would've been. It assumed the semblance of a massive mummified corpse, wrapped in arctic white winding-sheets and bandages. Within its shrouded and frozen arteries, however, a maggot-like life was stirring, teeming, pullulating. Having relinquished its stony, hard-edged impersonality, the city reverted once again to the human beings who'd created it. Bands of exuberant revellers marched arm-in-arm, six, eight or twelve abreast, down the white-swathed snow-lit thoroughfares, singing, cheering, pushing one another into drifts, exchanging volleys of snowballs, plunging intoxicatedly back into a vanished childhood, when all the world was magical.

So paralysed was everything that the mayor, in one of the few laudable acts of his political career, requested all bars to remain open round the clock and provide shelter for those cut off from home. Reggie's attained a new and unprecedented pitch of conviviality, a warm, cosy, fraternal glow. All stranded strangers, even those who'd ordinarily have been ostracised, were welcomed - welcomed as if they'd just arrived from a trek across the Klondike. Knowing he could claim more than adequate compensation from the city, Melvin Bloss ordered gallons of hot buttered rum to be dispensed at half-price. Other drinking establishments offered similar amenities. In the two and a half days before the snow ceased and the ploughs started sluggishly to function, Chicago was to have the greatest ratio of drunks per capita in its history.

Not until the fourth day did things return to what passed in the city for normality. Most things, that is. Not my already moribund Volvo. It'd been parked in a narrow frigid cul-de-sac behind the apartment building, where the ploughs, even if they'd been able to reach it, wouldn't've bothered. Insulated from all sunlight, the snow covering it congealed to a slick glistening carapace of ice that encased the decrepit vehicle for the better part of a month. Doors and locks, needless to say, were frozen to a petrified immobility. When I finally managed to clamber back into it, it was, of course, extinct, beyond hope of even the most adept automotive necromancy. I let it rust placidly away for another month or so, then sold it for scrap. By that time, Teddy was in jail again and our feud with Lloyd Boyle had attained its climax.

Despite an inopportune onslaught of bronchitis, I'd frolicked in the blizzard like everyone else. It was too unique, too beautiful, too festive a phenomenon not to be taken advantage of; and Nina and I had gone for long walks, joined Reggie's staff in snowball fights with other bars, rented skates and glided out onto the frozen lake. Along with Patterson and Radetzky, I'd also made a few lunatic leaps from upstairs windows into snowdrifts, sinking chest-deep in white slush and having to be hauled out. By the third night, I was thoroughly debilitated, exhausted and suffering from a massive sleep deficit.

I'd retired early, shortly after midnight, only to be shaken awake around three. Ungumming my eyes, I saw Radetzky silhouetted in the dim oblong of the doorway. Patterson loomed at my bedside, one finger raised portentously to his lips, exhorting me to silence.

'We've got a slight problem,' he whispered. 'Teddy Bronson's in my bed.'

It took a moment for the words to make any kind of sense at all; but even when I'd attained a modicum of lucidity, they still sound bizarre.

'Congratulations,' I grumbled, rolling on to my back and pulling the pillow over my head, leaving only my mouth uncovered. 'He's probably an impressive catch, I suppose, if you're inclined that way. I wish the two of you long life, happiness and a horde of progeny. Now let me get back to sleep. I'll give you a proper blessing in the morning.'

'This is serious!' Patterson hissed, dragging the pillow from my face and clubbing me on the head with a book.

'Why isn't Nina here?'

'She came up with me at closing time, but I sent her back to her place when I discovered we had guests. This could be a long night. And if there's trouble, you don't want her around.'

Fuming, I dredged myself out of the blankets, dressed, followed my flatmates on tiptoe down the corridor to Patterson's room. I still assumed I'd probably misheard or misunderstood, still awaited clarification. By the snowlight scintillating through the window, however, Teddy Bronson was indeed discernible in the bed, his face on the pillow rendered more boyish, more vulnerable than ever, by slumber. Nestled against his was the face of a blue-haired hooker - Pearl, a recent arrival in the neighbourhood, noted for her generalised, indiscriminate and all-purpose bitchiness. She, too, looked weirdly virginal, her features washed clean of their habitual hardness.

As usual, I'd neglected to lock the front door. So had Radetzky. It was pointless to do so, what with the three of us constantly coming and going, and the decorative, rather than functional, character of the toy lock, which wouldn't've foiled an old-age pensioner, much less a burglar. We could afford to be cavalier about security. We had nothing of genuine value in the flat anyway, apart from our books, and nobody in the vicinity ever read anything save the sports pages of the newspapers. As for Teddy, he'd been housed at the city's expense when we'd moved into the place, and had no idea we lived there. On his previous respite from jail, it'd been uninhabited, and he'd used it occasionally for amorous trysts, or when he was too tired or drunk to make his way home to his own, comparably seedy, lodgings. Having no reason to suspect our occupancy, he'd staggered upstairs with his trophy of the evening to what he believed an accustomed *maison de rendezvous*. All this we learned, gleaned and pieced together afterwards. At the time, we were simply stunned and bewildered - as a farmer might be, making his morning sortie to the chicken coop and finding a pterodactyl egg about to hatch. Or some affluent suburbanite, padding out for a midnight paddle and meeting, as it emerged from the tiled pool, the Creature from the Black Lagoon.

'Why don't you let them sleep it off?' I suggested, only half-joking. 'They should be up by the crack of noon or thereabouts, and they'll go peacefully, of their own accord. In future, you can booby-trap the entrance or whatever else you think appropriate.'

'I want my bed back!' Patterson snapped. 'What the hell am I supposed to do tonight?'

'I don't know. Play solitaire? Build an aeroplane? Take your sleeping-bag into the kitchen and crash there? You could even make coffee for them in the morning. No, we don't have any coffee, do we?'

'I want my fucking room back!'

'It really has become a fucking room, hasn't it?' Radetzky guffawed. 'You should charge rent next time.'

Ignoring our jibes, Patterson switched on the overhead lamp. Pearl remained placidly, even beatifically, oblivious. Teddy's face winced slightly against the light while his snore interrupted itself, shifted in timbre and resumed on a new octave. Patterson approached the bed and began to poke, prod and cajole him awake, very carefully, very gingerly, like an explosives expert defusing a bomb. When Teddy at last surfaced from sleep, he was muzzy and tipsy, but still lucid enough to recognise Patterson, to listen and comprehend the nature and magnitude of his *faux pas.*

'Jesus...!' he babbled, hoisting himself into sitting position, blinking, gouging sleep from his eyes with the knuckles of one ponderous paw, running the other through his tousled hair. 'I didn't know, man. Really didn't know. Feel like a damn fuckin' ass! You gotta believe me, man. I didn't know. I'm really sorry...'

Almost abjectly, he tried to explain, looking with beseeching embarrassment from one of us to another, grinning sheepishly, like a schoolboy caught red-handed in some compromising prank. Still groggy, he clambered out of the bed, groped for his clothes, performed the one-legged jig of a man tugging on his trousers. His left arm flailed behind him as he fished for the sleeve of his shirt. My flatmates and I relaxed, fancying the problem painlessly resolved. We hadn't reckoned on Pearl. She'd apparently been awake for some time but hadn't stirred. Now she did. Out of some obscure and warped need of her own, she was determined to see blood spilled.

'Shit, Teddy!' she jeered. 'I wanna sleep! Why you lettin' these guys push you round? They ain't got no right to mess with us. They're treatin' you like dirt, roustin' you outa bed, an' you're lettin' 'em get away with it.'

Teddy abruptly went rigid, as if some electric current, surging from the floor into the soles of his feet, had galvanised him. His face froze for an instant, then began to twitch convulsively. An opaque haze - the unseeing fixity of a sleepwalker - darkened and filmed his eyes. Tensely alert, he backed into the nearest corner, panting, half-crouching, like a creature harried and brought to bay by nightmare. And then something erupted within him. He loosed an enraged Tarzan-wild bellow and charged the opposite wall, hurling himself across the room and ramming full-tilt against the flaking plaster. Stepping back a pace, he began to batter it with his fists - not aimlessly, but with long clean vicious punches, as if it were an adversary who refused to go down. To one side, half a dozen boards - seven-foot lengths of lumber intended for bookshelves - leaned tilted on end. Knocking against each other, they drew Teddy's attention and he turned on them, lunging into them, wrestling with them, flinging them furiously one after another to the floor, gasping over them triumphantly.

My flatmates and I stood paralysed. We'd encountered diverse forms of violence before and plumed ourselves on being able to cope with most of them. In theory, Teddy should've been manageable. There were, after all, three of us aligned against one of him. It would've been messy, would probably have demolished half the flat; but, with a concerted effort, we could've subdued him. Yet there was something so awesome, so electrifying, so chillingly *non-human* about his insane frenzy that we were stupefied, numbed to helpless immobility. Achilles flicked through my mind. So did Lear. But there was also something else archetypal as well, something of specifically Celtic resonance which I couldn't for the moment identify. Later, I realised what it was – Cuchulain, on Baile's Strand, contending with the waves.

As suddenly as it'd descended on him, the spell passed. Teddy straightened up slowly, stiffly, almost painfully, like a man suffering from cramp or rheumatism. He jerked his head, as though shaking his mind free from cobwebs, blinked, looked around, looked down at the lumber at his feet, looked up again. Ruefully, he rubbed his bruised and skinned knuckles. His face was abashed, even agonised, with guilt and self-deprecation.

'Happened to me again, didn't it? Shit, man, I'm so fuckin' sorry. Really sorry. Didn't mean for it to happen again. Thought I'd be all right tonight. Gettin' laid an' all, you know. Releases tension...' Plucking Pearl's skirt and blouse from the chair over which they were draped, he tossed them at her. 'C'mon. We gotta go. We caused enough hassle for these guys.'

'I ain't goin' nowhere,' Pearl muttered, turning her back on him, sulky and sullen. 'You go ahead. Let'em fuck you round if that's what you want. You ain't got no balls, that's your problem. I can stand up for myself.'

Again, Teddy's eyes grew harried, then hazy, suffused with something like storm-scud. Again, his face began to writhe, conflicting expressions struggling for supremacy on his features. Again, he dropped into his half-crouching posture and glared balefully – at us, at Pearl, at invisible presences closer to hand swarming upon him, hemming him in. On the wall, next to where the toppled lengths of lumber had stood, hung a small cabinet with glass panes painted over to resemble wood. Whirling abruptly, Teddy drove his fist into it. Glass and wood splintered and Teddy withdrew his hand, blood sluicing from his lacerated wrist, spattering his shirt and chest, pooling viscous and luridly red on the floor. He stared at it in bewilderment, as if at some alien substance - as if not he but the cabinet were bleeding, bleeding from some magically inflicted wound, and he repented the hurt he'd caused it. Tenderly, he reached out and stroked the damaged thing, the way one might beg forgiveness of a dog one has kicked.

Patterson slipped out into the corridor, returned with two towels from the bathroom. He tossed one to me and we approached Teddy from opposite directions, proffering the towels, mouthing mechanical formulae to calm him. He noticed us no more than he would've noticed a pair of coat-racks, but he accepted the towels, wrapped one around his wrist as a tourniquet and pulled it tight with his teeth. His attention was still focused on the pulverised cabinet and the puddle of blood on the floor. Behind us, Radetzky, in a furious whisper, was berating Pearl:

'You goddamn stupid bitch! You're really enjoying it all, aren't you? You like seeing blood flow? You think it's you he's fighting for? What the fuck is it you're trying to prove? You'll only land him back in jail...'

The whisper carried. The word 'jail' pierced the trance in which Teddy stood cocooned. His head jerked up intently, awareness snapped back into his eyes. Shoving past Patterson and me, he yanked the blankets from Pearl with one hand, punched her with the other - a brutal crippling punch in the kidneys. Pearl howled. Had Teddy's fist not been swaddled in the towel, she'd probably have suffered serious injury. Patterson and I gripped his arms, and this time he allowed himself to be restrained, going limp and docile.

'I'm sorry, man,' he muttered, shaking his head in some dismal, all-pervasive negation. 'Jesus, I'm sorry. It's okay. I'm all right now. You can let me go. Don't worry. I won't hurt her again. Just let me get her dressed and we'll split. I didn't mean to cause you so much hassle. Soon's I raise some money, I'll stop by the bar and pay for the damage...'

It seemed an apt moment for a token of chivalrous magnanimity. Patterson pointed the way through the kitchen to the rear entrance, which opened on to the fire escape. The three of us then retired to the front room, leaving Teddy and his companion to dress in privacy. We heard a rustle and slither of clothes, low bickering voices. Footsteps sounded in the corridor, receding through the kitchen. The rear door creaked quietly, closed again. We hastened to lock it. Fairly drained, Radetzky and I slumped at the wobbly kitchen table, passing a bottle of cognac to and fro between us and swigging from it. In his bedroom, Patterson was attempting to tidy up, mopping the blood from the floor, sweeping up fragments of broken glass and splinters of wood. A few minutes later, he joined us.

'You haven't seen the gun, have you?'

We shook our heads apathetically, irritated at so apparently trivial a concern. It wasn't, after all, a real gun, only an impressive-looking replica Patterson had purchased a fortnight before - a pellet-firing reproduction of a Browning automatic.

'Teddy must've lifted it.'

'So what? It was only a fake.'

'Not quite. It's still classified as a dangerous weapon. It could still kill a person at close range...'

'So close you could just as well use an umbrella...'

'And it was licensed in my name.'

****

Two days later, the gun had returned to haunt us. In Patterson's hands, it'd been essentially innocuous - useless unless employed to drill someone between the eyes at a range of six inches. In Lloyd Boyle's hands, however, it'd suddenly become nocuous indeed. It'd been transformed into a Damoclean sword, wielded clumsily but nonetheless potently as an instrument of blackmail.

The snow had melted just enough for the university to begin functioning again, and I'd made one of my increasingly infrequent forays to the campus. My presence there, now that I'd passed my exams, was even more superfluous than before; and apart from ennui, a desire for novelty or an impulse to make a nuisance of myself, I had few reasons to visit the place. On this occasion, I'd picked up some mail. I'd bought some books. Out of routine courtesy, I'd stopped by the office of the departmental secretary. It was she who effectively managed the M.A. programme, as well as most of the professors; and it was she, therefore, whom I formally notified that I'd not be pursuing my doctorate at the school, having received an offer to do so at a more congenially anarchic institution back east.

On my return to the flat, I encountered Boyle descending the stairs. I slowed, expecting the worst. We brushed past each other in surly silence, neither of us wanting to engage in conversation. Apparently, however, he felt obliged to say something and turned, as if in afterthought.

'Let me ask you a question. If you're not high on dope, why d'you wear those dark glasses all the time?'

Deliberately cryptic, I stared at him through the opaque lenses.

'They keep people with whom I don't want to be bothered at a distance. Usually, that is. Some people are too obstreperous, or obtuse, to be so easily deterred. Just planted another bag, have you?'

'No need. We're on the same side now. You guys'll be helping me.'

Determined not to give him any satisfaction, I betrayed nothing of my mystification.

'You mean you've started building styrofoam aeroplanes and want to draw on our expertise?'

He wasn't amused.

'Don't get wise with me,' he flung over his shoulder and continued down the stairs.

In the flat, I found Patterson and Radetzky embroiled in a moral dilemma, which also, needless to say, embroiled me. The evening before, Teddy'd again been arrested. It was a minor infraction - vandalism, or defacing public property, or something of that sort. He'd had another spasm of anti-social behaviour, had punched the entrails out of a police call-box, ripped it from its telephone pole and hurled it through a car's windscreen. On being wrestled to the ground by four officers, he was found to be in possession of a gun - an imitation gun, admittedly, but still a gun - which, of course, had promptly been traced to Patterson. Quick to pounce on any opportunity, Boyle had taken over the 'case', such as it was.

'If Bronson stole your gun,' he'd said, after hearing Patterson's and Radetzky's cursory account of the events two nights before, 'why didn't you file a complaint?'

'Didn't seem worth it,' Patterson had replied. 'The gun was only a fake.'

'It was still theft. Of an offensive weapon. With Bronson's record, that'd put him away for a while.'

'I know. That's why I didn't file a complaint.'

'You don't want to see him put away?'

'No. Not in jail, anyway. He needs psychiatric help. He should be institutionalised. Jail isn't any kind of answer.'

'I don't have time for bleeding-heart liberalism. I just want Teddy Bronson off the streets. I need an excuse to get him off the streets. If he stole a gun from you, that's all the excuse I need. I want you to file a complaint.'

'I'm not filing a complaint. Send the poor guy down for two years or so just because he stole a toy gun? No way, lieutenant.'

'It wasn't a toy gun. It was an offensive weapon. A pellet in the eye's all it'd take. You could blind a person with one of those things.'

'You could blind a person with an olive,' Radetzky had chimed in, unhelpfully.

'Let me put it like this,' Boyle had said, after a brief, exasperated pause. 'Teddy Bronson's an ex-con. He's been out on parole. If you don't file a complaint against him for theft, I can only assume you gave him the gun. It's a criminal offence to give a gun to an ex-con on parole.'

'Why didn't you nail us for that in the first place?'

'I was tempted, believe me. But I want him more than I want you. For now, anyway. You file a complaint and it means we understand each other. You might even find it's worth having me as a friend. You don't file a complaint, and I'll have to charge you.'

Confronted by so signal a dearth of options, there wasn't much to debate. Nevertheless, we debated the matter for a good two hours before deferring to the brute realities of the situation and agreeing to file a reluctant complaint. Having been released that morning, Teddy was back in jail by nightfall. We were notified of a court appearance scheduled for the following week, at which Patterson would be expected formally to press charges.

During the intervening time, we continued to discuss the problem, soliciting impromptu advice from friends and associates more legally *au fait* than ourselves. There was, it transpired, only one viable ploy whereby we could elude Boyle's ultimatum, extricate ourselves from the squeeze he'd applied to us. Having duly filed our complaint, we could no longer be held in breach of the law; and having thus covered ourselves, we could, at the last moment, decline to press charges. It wouldn't endear us very much to Boyle. If anything, we'd be making a fool of him anew, and rendering ourselves all the more liable to vindictive reprisals. But if Teddy did get himself packed away again, it wouldn't, at least, be on our consciences.

Except among masochists, certain foredoomed revolutionaries and certain strenuously self-righteous Christians, martyrdom has never been easily reconciled with egoism. My flatmates and I all being arch-egoists, the prospect of self-sacrifice for our fellow man prompted us to dither energetically. We weren't even sure to what extent Teddy qualified either for fellowship or humanity. We remained irresolute, in fact, until his day in court, continuing to juggle pros and cons, to rake over implications, repercussions and consequences with paranoid pedantry and embellishment. It was Teddy's appearance in the dock that decided us, definitively, beyond any further vacillation. One of his eyes was swollen shut, reduced to a narrow slit in a massive purplish-yellow bruise. A jagged fretwork of stitches marked a gash in his cheek. His head was swathed in bandages. His left arm was in a sling.

We had no need to consult with each other. An exchange of glances and a brief nod were sufficient. When the judge gave us our opportunity to speak, Patterson flatly stated that we wished to drop all charges. It wasn't a considered, calculated or rehearsed response, wasn't a lofty stand on political or any other kind of principle, wasn't a symbolic gesture of solidarity with the 'oppressed'. It stemmed simply from an access of sympathy for the battered titan slumped dejectedly between his warders - and from a renewed recognition of how contemptible a prick Boyle was.

Escorted, limping, from the dock, Teddy flung us a look of embarrassingly abject gratitude. As we made our way down the steps of the courthouse, he called to us, emerging from the side door through which he'd just been released. We paused, and he joined us in the diffuse wintry sunlight.

'Just wanted to thank you guys. Know I shouldn't've took that thing, but I didn't think it'd be too big a deal. Anyway, thanks. I mean it. People ain't usually so decent to me. Shit, man, I really couldn't've taken another stretch inside. I'd've gone crazy. I mean, really crazy. I'd've got out sometime, somehow, and I would've killed you. I know it. Wouldn't've wanted to, but I would've killed you. Can I buy you all a drink?'

'Why not?' Patterson drawled. 'Let's drink to our survival.'

We descended the steps slowly, keeping pace with Teddy's painful, half-blinded hobble. Out in the road, Lieutenant Boyle leaned against the door of a blue-and-white patrol car, watching us narrowly. As we passed him, he gave us a curt rueful nod - an unspoken promise for the future.

****

Our largesse towards Teddy might've warmed the cockles of his heart, but it accomplished little. Five days later, he was apprehended while allegedly robbing a liquor store. In process of 'resisting arrest', whatever that meant precisely, he was shot down. According to the newspapers, he'd survive, but probably with the loss of one leg, shattered just below the knee - an incapacity sufficient, if not to 'get him off the streets', at least to impede his movements there. Apart from this meagre information, details were sketchy. There were no witnesses, and our attempts to learn more proved fruitless. Along with everyone else in the bar, we had our doubts about the official account - robbery of liquor stores wasn't Teddy's style - but none of us by that time could disentangle valid suspicion from paranoia. In any case, Teddy'd now committed a major offence and, what with his past record, couldn't expect much leniency. When he eventually emerged, one-legged, from hospital, he was to be sentenced to a five-year term in Joliet.

So far as we ourselves were concerned, the situation had assumed new and alarming dimensions, was no longer in any sense a game. The threat now posed by Lieutenant Boyle was both genuine and urgent. Somewhere out there lurked a man quite as demented in his way as Teddy Bronson, and potentially more dangerous. Unlike Teddy, he acted deliberately, with malice aforethought and calculated premeditation. Unlike Teddy, he was moved by intensely personal vindictiveness and animosity. Unlike Teddy, he boasted a badge, was authorised to use a gun and had the entire ponderous weight of the municipal establishment behind him, providing him with a mandate, with sanction and support. And it was this man who'd embarked on a self-appointed mission to punish us. We weren't imagining it. He'd confided his intentions to Al Hollis, who'd incautiously blabbed them to Nina.

The most obvious risk, of course, was that Boyle would frame us for drugs again. There was no safeguard whatever against his invading our premises and brazenly planting another stash; but he could just as easily do so in my car, defunct though it was, or on our persons. Our word would then be pitted in court against his, but it'd be our second arrest and our chances of acquittal would be proportionately diminished. This time, moreover, Boyle wouldn't make any clumsy mistakes. Nor were his options confined just to fitting us up. Given the messianic fervour of his vendetta, there was no real limit to what he could do. Alone, or together with his colleagues, he could even contrive to shoot one of us and fabricate a plausible enough claim of self-defence or 'justifiable homicide'.

'You know what they say,' our friends and associates in the bar would insist, unwittingly parroting Frederick the Great. *'The best defence is...'*. Rarely, in my own experience, had Friedrich's by now clichéd wisdom been more apt. Out of sheer self-preservation, we'd have to act first, launch a pre-emptive strike, and we'd have to do so quickly. Boyle was unlikely to wait more than a month or two - just long enough for our public association with Teddy to recede from official view. After that, he'd move swiftly, leaving us neither time nor space in which to manoeuvre.

Nights formerly consecrated to carefree dissipation were now devoted to strategy conferences and councils of war. Certain of Reggie's rougher clientèle offered us an economy-priced contract on the lieutenant. We could've had him murdered for a mere five hundred dollars; and there were moments, I confess, when it seemed an attractive bargain.

'But then again,' Patterson wondered, 'could he possibly be worth much more?'

Other well-wishers volunteered their services for a set-up; and the bar's pimps, hookers, snitches, stooges and genuine pushers comprised an abundantly stocked manpower pool for any such scheme. In this respect, too, we were tempted. Boyle, after all, was pulling no punches with us, and it would've been fatuous, if not downright foolhardy and quixotic, to play by Marquess of Queensbury rules. Here, as in the clash with my Draft Board, the issue, in all its bald existential immediacy, was survival; and here, as in the previous clash, it would obviously be necessary to step beyond the accustomed pale.

Eventually, we decided against murder. In the throes of deranged range, I could've killed the woman on the balcony in Ashwood who'd poured scalding water over Ilona; but I couldn't bring myself, with icy premeditation, to endorse Boyle's dispatch. Neither could my flatmates.

'It'd be a public service,' Patterson concluded. 'Sort of like garbage removal. But I don't think we want it on our consciences.'

Radetzky shook his head reprovingly.

'When did we start acquiring this taste for luxury?'

We put a façade of cavalier bravado on what we secretly deemed an embarrassingly ethical weakness. Murder, we declared, would be somewhat too churlish, too devoid of style. Of our style, at any rate.

A set-up, on the other hand, was a different matter, altogether less onerous, more congenial. We preferred, however, to devise our own - ideally with some distinctive personal touch, perhaps an artistic flourish or two. The fewer people privy to it, therefore, the better. As Machiavelli'd pointed out five centuries before, mercenaries were notoriously unreliable. Involving outsiders would inevitably have entailed risk - someone talking too loquaciously, boasting, being bullied or bribed. We were grateful to many of those who offered aid, but loth to underestimate their venality. By that time, too, we'd come to trust poetic justice more than the kind dispensed by America's judiciary. We wanted to incorporate an aesthetic element in our design, to do something with panache, something worthy of our imaginative resources.

I was personally eager to exploit the assets of the university. Although I sneered at its propensity to calcify literature, I nevertheless endorsed what it theoretically or symbolically stood for - education, intelligence, culture, literacy. Boyle had arrested two of us - Radetzky and me - precisely because, to his circumscribed mind, we represented and embodied those qualities. It was by means of those qualities, therefore, that I wanted to bring him down.

In practice, the university was admirably suited to our purposes. After the mayor's office, it was perhaps the single most powerful institution in Chicago, a self-contained feudal fiefdom within the metropolis. It exercised many of the rights and prerogatives of the medieval principality it physically resembled. It owned enormous tracts of land throughout the urban sprawl, from which it collected rents raised or lowered at will. It conferred or withheld planning permission for business and industry. It bestowed respectability on otherwise dubious people by granting them honorary degrees. Its administrators and trustees had access to the most puissant individuals and offices, not only in the city, but in the county and the state as well. Its alumni were among the most influential figures in local affairs, commercial, financial and political. We had only to wind Boyle up and get him unwittingly pitted against this awesome monolithic edifice - to make him run conspicuously afoul of its august and rarefied interests. In order to accomplish this, of course, we'd have to sink to his level, if not, indeed, lower. Our plan would have to work like an unseen hand reaching up from a sewer grating and snagging his ankle. But if all went smoothly, he'd then be squashed like an insect by the very values he'd subjected to his petty spite. '*Alles Vergängliche ist nur ein Gleichnis...*'

We proceeded to exercise our ingenuity. We concocted a number of grandiose Byzantine schemes, some of which would've required the manpower, finance, resources and expertise of Paramount Studios. While our scenarios became more and more baroque, however, we remained convinced that the basic ingredients, the basic components for what we desired, were already inherent in the existing situation - already present amidst the fermenting broth in which we lived our daily lives. It was simply a question of applying traditional alchemical principles - of isolating the relevant elements, processing them in the crucible of creative imagination and causing them to precipitate out, transmuted into the requisite compound. And gradually, the elements we needed began to cohere, drawn magnetically into a pattern by their own intrinsic *Wahlverwandschaften*.

The first step in this process occurred one desultory afternoon when Trish - the hooker who'd squelched the businessman from

Detroit - complained to Nina about her pimp. Roscoe, she declared with succinct eloquence, was a prick. She longed to get him off her back. If people knew Roscoe for the vicious little bastard he really was, they'd understand and sympathise with her. In fact, none of us knew Roscoe. He didn't frequent the bar, preferring, as he'd apparently said to Trish, places 'with more class'. As things transpired, we were never to meet him, never to see him, never to learn his race, colour, creed, hat size or anything else. Only one thing about Roscoe was in any way relevant to us, which Trish, in her tirade against him, vouchsafed to Nina - Roscoe was one of Boyle's snitches. This conformed perfectly to our needs. With access to one of Boyle's snitches - particularly an indirect access of which Roscoe himself was unaware - we could proceed to contrive a trap. Roscoe, serenely unwitting and oblivious, would provide its trigger mechanism.

The bait for our trap, we decided, would consist of one Faye Flinders, a graduate student working for her doctorate in medieval French poetry. I'd met her three or four times at parties but we'd only been ritually introduced, exchanged routinised courtesies, stepped inadvertently on each other's toes and drifted asunder to talk to other people. Radetzky knew her slightly better, but still only as a casual acquaintance. He'd have coffee with her now and then in the cafeteria and swap meteorological commonplaces.

On the surface, Faye was reminiscent of Mindy Dunque, victim of our undergraduate mischief. Like Mindy, Faye was suave, sleek, glamorous, sophisticated, with all the polish of the debutante, the glossy patina of the cover-girl. Unlike Mindy, however, she was tolerably intelligent. It didn't require half a dozen drinks to get down to her mental level. On the contrary, she displayed an urbane professional briskness and competence, an elegant self-assurance, in her handling of literature. With a precocity on which her mentors plumed themselves, she'd already published a couple of articles - models, so it was said, of their kind. I'd skimmed them and found them overly ingenious, overly pompous, overly laden with scrupulous footnotes; but I tended in general to respect her critical judgement. To the extent that I'd encountered it, I respected her judgement in most things, apart from her choice of paramour - and that, I guessed, had been made with cheerfully ruthless cynicism and an eye to her future career.

In the incestuously closed world of the graduate programme, Faye's liaison was a more or less open secret. She herself, if coyly and obliquely, flaunted it, and it furnished others with copious grist for ribald gossip. Her paramour was the eminent Dr. Crispin Whelk, Senior Professor in French Studies and in the Committee for Social Thought, a high-powered interdisciplinary body offering courses on the history of culture and consciousness.

Dr. Whelk died in 1980, which allows me to cite him without fear of litigation. At the time of his affair with Faye, however, he was very much alive and reportedly practising a sexual athleticism tantamount to second puberty. He was also one of the university's most illustrious and hallowed names, a pillar of the scholastic community, a venerable ancient oak in this particular grove of academe. Like many of his ilk at schools across the country, he enjoyed a prestige which permitted him to come to campus at rare intervals, promulgate a few stale pontifical pronouncements and return home with a salary two or three times that of his more energetic, more enthusiastic, more creative and more overworked juniors. In fact, Dr. Whelk's status rested on the kind of dubious basis all too frequent in institutions of higher education. He was both a plagiarist and a bastard. He was known to have pilfered research, even entire papers, from pupils too intimidated to protest. He was noted, too, for the sexual sadism he vented in his classes, taking a smug perverse pleasure in humiliating students, especially women, and, whenever possible, reducing them to tears.

As a lecturer, he was massively boring. I'd verified this personally the year before when, drawn by the sonority of his name, I'd occasionally sat in on one of his exegeses. His publications were few in number, but accepted with the kind of reverence usually accorded Papal encyclicals. He'd written obsessively - some said 'definitively' - on Villon, but from the perspective of the so-called 'New Criticism', which those of us with a genuine love for literature, on grounds of aesthetic morality, felt obliged to repudiate. Some ten years before, he'd got embroiled in a squabble with Dr. Hugh Payne of Rutgers, the country's leading authority on the life and work of Villon's contemporary, Jehan l'Ascuiz. Whelk, in a prominent article, had aspersed Jehan's luminosity in the firmament of 15th century French poetry. Payne, indignant, had replied with vitriolic fury, and a tortuous academic controversy had ensued - like Nabokov's, following his translation of *Evgeny Onegin*, with Edmund Wilson. Vituperative mandarin missives had clogged the letters pages of learned journals, as well as the *Times Book Review*. Partisans of both antagonists had joined the fray, sniping at one another from as far away as *Times Literary Supplement*. More perhaps than anything else, this rumpus had consolidated Crispin Whelk's claim to celebrity, and he'd published virtually nothing during the subsequent decade.

Apart from what passed for his scholarship, Dr. Whelk, as a nominally young man, had made the equivalent of an important dynastic marriage. Until she'd absconded with her tango teacher some years before, he'd been, so it was said, loyally-spliced to the daughter of some exalted personage in the university's administrative history - some magisterial figure of the twenties, Dean or President or something of that sort, whose sententious portrait graced, or defaced, half a dozen corridors, offices and lecture halls. By virtue of this alliance, Dr. Whelk had come to wield immense influence on campus - not just in his pedagogical capacity, but in formulating the school's orientation and policies, in allocating funds, in establishing salary scales, in determining tenure and promotion. Since his wife's defection, he'd had frequent dalliances with students, usually nubile undergraduates, not all of whom recoiled from his importunities. His affair with Faye Flinders was allegedly more 'serious', more durable, and verged on respectability. She'd be his public companion at official functions, his hostess at receptions in his home. His divorce belatedly finalised, he was rumoured to have proposed to her, and those preoccupied with such matters prophesied an imminent betrothal. She, for her part, had apparently seen him as a kind of literary agent-cum-tutelary genius presiding over her academic career. Having bewitched him, she wasn't prepared to let him go, and he basked in his captivity. He was known to be an habitual visitor, a virtual part-time occupant, at her posh ground-floor flat on leafy Woodlawn Avenue.

If Faye Flinders served to bait our trap, Dr. Crispin Whelk would furnish its steel jaws. Assuming all went well, it'd be his wrath that snapped shut on Lloyd Boyle - his wrath and, by extension, that of the university administration as a whole. The critical factor would be timing. In order for the mechanism to work effectively, both Faye and her lover would have to be present in her apartment at the crucial moment - the moment designated as H-hour. There was, of course, no way of guaranteeing this. All we could do was proceed on probabilities and hope the wing-footed God of Tricksters smiled on our undertaking. We endeavoured to propitiate him with prolific toasts and libations.

We scheduled 'Operation Pnin' - so Radetzky and I had dubbed it in homage to a more endearing pedagogue than Dr. Whelk - for a Wednesday during the first week of March. In the days immediately preceding, Nina and Beryl had prepared a foul mixture of sugar, salt, flour and pulverised aspirin. The suspect-looking white powder was then decanted and sealed into half a dozen small clear plastic bags, containers originally of elastic bands. (Patterson had initially suggested condoms, but we dared not dilute our enterprise with frivolity.) The plastic bags had then been stuffed into a brown envelope. This was elaborately wrapped, glued and taped, and addressed to Professor Crispin Whelk, care of Miss Faye Flinders at her flat on Woodlawn Avenue.

At eleven that Wednesday morning, in one of the university cafeterias, Radetzky, quite casually, invited Faye to Reggie's for an early evening drink. Had she surprised us by accepting, we would've been obliged to shelve our plans, confide in her, tell her about our feud with Boyle and ask her, in all honesty, for support in enlisting Dr. Whelk's aid. As we'd hoped and expected, however, she gracefully declined Radetzky's invitation, explaining, with a meaningful flittering of lashes, that she had to prepare dinner for 'someone special' scheduled to arrive at seven. This gave us our go-ahead. Radetzky telephoned the bar, and 'Operation Pnin' juddered into motion.

At eleven-thirty, acting on information allegedly leaked by a loquacious client, Trish telephoned Roscoe. She'd learned, she reported, of an important dope drop scheduled for later in the day. She didn't yet know the precise time or place, but expected to obtain these details by early evening. In the meantime, Roscoe might want to put Lieutenant Boyle on alert.

We spent the next few hours waiting, the tension only slightly slackened by alcoholic lubrication. At five-thirty, as dusk was falling, I walked to the university. I checked my mail, bought a newspaper, poked around the library, flicked through the card catalogue and headed home again, arranging my itinerary so that it placed me on Woodlawn Avenue, within sight of Faye's flat, just before seven. Pausing under a streetlamp to scan my newspaper, I saw Dr. Whelk arrive in his sedate forest-green Buick. It was actually rather touching. He'd been involved with Faye for more than three academic terms, but he still brandished a bouquet of flowers.

As soon as her door had closed behind him, I saw the ten-year-old black urchin - commissioned by Nina for ten dollars - emerge from the cover of a hedge across the road. Wraithlike, he scooted up the steps to Faye's entrance, slipped the brown envelope through the letterbox and scampered off into the shadows. Hurrying to the public telephone at the service station around the corner, I rang the bar. I then resumed my leisurely walk home, while Trish rang Roscoe with the address to be passed on to Boyle.

To our disappointment, nothing appeared in the next day's newspapers. On Friday, however, Radetzky learned from Faye at least something of what'd happened. Boyle, apparently, had been standing by in a state of primed and charged combat readiness, with four cars, a veritable task force of detectives and uniformed officers. On receiving Roscoe's call, they'd launched themselves accordingly, with whirling and flashing lights but silenced sirens. Hearing the clatter of her letterbox, Faye had found the brown envelope and brought it into the kitchen. She and her lover had required some time to hack their way through the mummy wrappings of tape and glue. Having finally got it open, they'd stared at it in consternation, had just begun with horror to suspect what the white powder *might* conceivably be. At that moment, Boyle had erupted into their tranquil domestic idyll - not merely knocking or even banging on the door, but, with the single-minded intensity of a guided missile, crashing through it and reducing it to splinters in his wake. He'd entered, in effect, like a projectile, caromed off an abutment of wall and nearly disembowelled himself on the prong of the umbrella stand. After the initial shock, Dr. Whelk had taken a stand on dignity, bristling with glacially patrician hauteur. Boyle had almost been cowed, then seen the white powder on the kitchen table. Seizing it, he'd promptly placed Faye and the professor under arrest. The professor had responded with a tantrum, castigating the lieutenant in half a dozen tongues, including Chaucerian English and medieval Occitain.

'*I resist arrest*!' he'd bellowed apoplectically, refusing to leave the premises until officers of the university's own security force and been called to the scene. On their arrival, they, Boyle, the task force and the two detainees had proceeded in caravan to Cook County Jail. Within an hour, of course, Faye and Dr. Whelk were out on bail, and Boyle must already have begun to feel the first queasy misgivings.

During the fortnight or so that followed, we speculated gleefully on the befuddlement that must've prevailed in the police laboratory when they'd analysed the white powder and definitively determined its composition. Did they realise it was a hoax, or did they imagine it some new, bizarre species of high? In any event, the components were all perfectly legal, and the packets, tidily resealed, were obsequiously returned to Faye and her lover. Charges were dropped before the case came to court, an official apology was humbly extended and the damage to Faye's flat scrupulously repaired.

Dr. Whelk, however, was not prepared to let the matter rest. We never learned the precise details, but in some rarefied upper echelon, where the university's dark-suited trouble-shooters and power-brokers met with municipal functionaries, restitution was demanded and obtained. Boyle simply evaporated from the neighbourhood. It wasn't until some six weeks later that we learned on the grapevine he'd been demoted and transferred to another, safely remote, precinct of the city.

'And they never told us what the white powder was,' Faye reported subsequently to Radetzky. 'After they gave it back to us, I tried some. Tried it in hot water. Tried it in tea. It tasted pretty awful. Salty and sugary at the same time. It cured my headache, though.'

VIII

Long afterwards, Radetzky said that our experience of Chicago 'radicalised' him. I wasn't sure I understood precisely what he meant by that term, nor am I sure even now. During the years that followed, our paths took us in very different directions, and we saw each other only infrequently, hearing news and gossip through second and third parties more often than we actually met. To my knowledge, however, he never became one of the militants or *soi-disant* 'revolutionaries' so prominent during the second half of the decade - never joined the Symbionese Liberation Army, for example, the Weathermen or even SDS. As far as I know, he took no more active a part in politics than Patterson or I did.

And yet, in another sense, Chicago 'radicalised' all of us - by forcing upon us an awareness of political realities such as we'd never previously encountered. In the past, political involvement had been, for all of us, essentially voluntary, a matter of freely exercised choice. To some extent, politics had existed elsewhere, in spheres remote from our own - in the South, for instance, or in Washington. But even when they'd encroached more importunately, participation in them had still been optional. One could become politically *engagé* or not, as mood or inclination, personal loyalty, moral principle or ideological commitment dictated. Except for the occasional outrageous impertinence - like my Draft Board's attempt to shanghai me - politics had imposed no particularly intrusive demands, and one could, if one wished, ignore them.

In Chicago, for the first time, we experienced political realities as integral and inescapable aspects of our daily existence. We couldn't disown them; we couldn't repudiate them; we couldn't indulge ourselves in the luxury of non-involvement. Our status in the city, in the community, in the neighbourhood, in the bar, was, *de facto*, a political status. Our relations with the sub-strata of society, with local blacks, with Reggie's staff and patrons, with the university, with the police and the judiciary, entailed and implied a political position. Our very lifestyle, by its intrinsic and inherent values, came to constitute a political statement - not because we desired it to be so, but because others, those in authority, insisted on making it so. In attempting to pursue our own, private, essentially aesthetic, ambitions, we found ourselves cast as adversaries by what was then called 'The Establishment'. By dint of our apparel and the length of our hair, we were perceived as a threat; we were treated as a threat; and by defending ourselves, we became the very threat we were supposed to be.

Constant exposure to the political power impinging on us forced us to recognise the unworthiness, the incompetence and ineptitude of those who exercised it. Spawned by the 'baby boom' of the forties, my contemporaries and I comprised the best-educated generation America had ever known, the best equipped to express and deploy its resources - and we were pervasively aware of this. At the same time, we were daily confronted with political power wielded by people so shockingly less intelligent than ourselves, less imaginative, less creative, less responsible, less knowledgeable and informed, less conversant with the historical, cultural, psychological and religious foundations on which any such power rests. To this extent, authority, hitherto sacrosanct, inviolate and unimpugnable, became, for our generation, increasingly suspect. It was, of course, this cavalier contempt for authority - on such elementary grounds as intelligence, morality and vision - that characterised our generation and its era. When those in authority - acting out of prejudice, complacency, crass self-interest or sheer stupidity - imposed upon us their assumptions, their strictures, their codes, their taboos, their laws and their wars, we were provoked to scepticism, to cynicism, to resentment, to defiance, eventually to rebellion.

Among television evangelists and self-appointed custodians of public decency, among dour pundits and would-be preceptors, among stodgy governmental spokesmen and even heads of state, among assorted other old ladies of both sexes throughout Britain and America, it's become fashionable, during the last few years, to inveigh against the sixties. The sixties are currently held responsible for a substantial percentage of today's ills - broken marriages, proliferating divorces, fragmented or single-parent families, religious apathy, 'secular humanism', foul language, sexuality and violence on the screen, abortion, drugs, soaring crime rates and, in general, what Robert Musil described as 'a relativity of perspective verging on epistemological panic'. The da-glo decade is now roundly castigated for a calamitous inventory of transgressions and derelictions, paramount among them being that most dire knell of words in today's lexicon, *'permissiveness'*. Of all the charges levelled against the sixties, 'permissiveness' - pronounced in a tone of loftily sniffy opprobrium - rings most damningly for indictment.

I am a product of the sixties. I'm proud to regard myself as a product of the sixties. I challenge the facile judgement now routinely promulgated against the sixties. And I challenge particularly the logical, conceptual and moral legerdemain latent in the charge of 'permissiveness'. It implies that sexual, verbal, artistic or other forms of expression are indeed matters of 'permission' - matters in some sense *requiring* 'permission'. It implies that such things exist in a sphere where 'permission' can or should legitimately be granted or withheld. It implies that sleeping with the partner of one's choice, reading *Ulysses* or *Lady Chatterley's Lover* or *Lolita,* should *need* 'permission' from someone. And there's also the implication that if 'permissiveness' constitutes a vice, its antithesis must be a virtue. But what *is* the antithesis of 'permissiveness'? Lack of 'permissiveness'? Restriction? Repression? Prohibition? Are these virtues?

If the sixties were an era of 'permissiveness', the word itself must be redefined - or, at least, defined more precisely. For the sixties, albeit on a more modest scale, of course, were 'permissive' in essentially the same ways that the Renaissance was. Yes, the sixties were an age of licence - licence to flout existing sexual mores, for example, to experiment with drugs, to question established authority. But licence, too, to re-appraise, to test, to explore, to probe, to discover, to evolve new permutations of possibility.

'Permissiveness' obtained, for instance, in racial relations - in claiming, for America's blacks and other minorities, at least a prospect of the opportunities previously withheld from them. 'Permissiveness' obtained in re-asserting the status and rôle of women - in confronting the ways whereby women, as well as the feminine principle, *das Ewigweibliche,* had for twenty and more centuries been diminished, bullied, usurped, denied an integral identity. 'Permissiveness' obtained in determining patriotism - in transcending obsolete 19th century conceptions of nationalism, in learning that a war wasn't automatically 'just' simply because one's own country happened to have embarked on it. 'Permissiveness' obtained in religious affairs - in recognising the difference between 'religion' and 'spirituality', in acknowledging the sterility of ossified dogma, but accepting transfusions of other faiths and thereby regaining a sense of the sacred. 'Permissiveness' obtained in attitudes towards psychology and the mind - in learning that 'normality' wasn't the *ne plus ultra* of human aspiration, that other states of consciousness and cognition existed, that the frontiers between 'madness' and 'sanity' were more elusive than hitherto believed, that there were rich worlds within us demanding integration, that 'imagination' was no longer a pejorative word denoting some species of excess or imbalance. 'Permissiveness' obtained in the arts. The novel, for example, ceased to be merely a modest trivial 'mirror of society', unfettered itself from the dingy dreary conventions of post-war British and American fiction and generated new forms, new conduits for prose no longer shackled to the literal. 'Permissiveness' even obtained in such peripheral matters as dress - in allowing people to express their personalities through their attire, rather than being reduced to clonehood by a monochrome conformity. And perhaps most important of all, these manifestations of 'permissiveness' were accompanied by a love of colour, by an exuberant affirmation of life, its wonder and its mystery - by an ebulliently humane creative energy, a zest for experience, a passionate aspiration to joy. To condemn the sixties is to condemn all these things. I defy even the most frumpish critic of the era to do that.

If 'permissiveness' is thus a double-edged term, so, too, are many of the others whereby the sixties are indicted by today's kangaroo courts. Language, as we all know, is the slave of rhetorical whoremasters, a tribe best exemplified by journalists and politicians. One can play endless games with nomenclature and semantics - can make words, and nuances of words, behave like performing fleas. The ethos of the sixties can be described, and often is, as 'selfish', 'egocentric', intent on thoughtless, amoral and irresponsible 'self-gratification' - as if those phrases couldn't equally be applied to the ethos of the eighties, or of many other decades. But where, precisely, lies the distinction between those phrases and what might just as easily be described as, say, 'a renewed affirmation of the individual', of his uniqueness, of his ultimate importance, of the sanctity of his psyche and his quest for self-actualisation?

We of the sixties were the first generation to grow from infancy to maturity in the ominous tripartite shadow of nuclear holocaust, overpopulation and environmental destruction. Unlike our elders, who'd loosed the prospect of these cataclysms on us and the world, we knew something of history - we'd studied its mistakes and its recurring cycles, learned at least a little of the lessons it had to teach. We recognised the impasse in which calcified modes of thought had culminated. We recognised the bankruptcy to which all the grandiose systems and isms of our predecessors - the systems and isms that seemingly promised so much at the dawn of the century - had led. We recognised the cul-de-sac to which analysis, running amok, had brought our culture - the proliferation of specialisations, the lack of contact and context between them, the claims proffered by conflicting absolutes and the resulting fragmented reality. We recognised the need for re-orientation and re-integration - for a shift in emphasis from analysis to synthesis. We recognised the necessity of re-embedding man in the natural world of which he was intrinsically a part, of establishing channels of communication between disparate disciplines, of providing a matrix in which diverse forms of endeavour were incorporated and the various compartments of learning re-unified into some totality approximating wisdom - or, at very least, a sufficiently broad moral imperative. We understood the distinction between wisdom, knowledge and mere information - and the extent to which most of what passed for the first or the second was in fact the third.

As a generation, we found ourselves confronted by hitherto unprecedented questions, unprecedented problems - which, by virtue of their sheer uniqueness, required new answers, new solutions. In our attempts to formulate such answers and solutions, there was inevitably much idealism, sometimes lofty and laudable, sometimes flagrantly silly, sometimes both at once. Inevitably, too, there were casualties, as there are among every generation. There were those who, prompted by panic, sought too instant, too facile, too simplistic a conclusion, and paid the price of underestimating reality's complexity. There were those who, intoxicated by the mere concept of freedom, failed to discern its dependence on responsibility. There were those who, cowed or brutalised or denied expression by old tyrannies, knew what they wanted to be free *from*, but not what they wanted to be free *for* - and, as a consequence, squandered their gifts, committing the unpardonable sin of waste. There were those who plunged so deeply into the prevailing ethos as to lose all perspective on the past, all sense of roots, of tradition, of continuity. There were those who, constitutionally unable to keep pace with the *Zeitgeist*, fell, debilitated, by the wayside.

The sum total of such casualties, however, remained small, especially compared to those of previous generations - those of European Romanticism, for example, or the generation of 1789, of 1848, of 1870 and, of course, 1914. When it was marched off to war, our generation at least had sufficient lucidity not to fancy itself bound for a carnival - not to bellow songs of mindless jingoistic bravado, not to spin fatuous dreams of martial glory, not to delude itself with prospects of occupying an enemy capital by the end of a given year. And of the casualties suffered by our generation, most weren't a result of *our* values and attitudes. They were imposed on us by our elders, incurred through our elders' ineptitude. Whatever the tumult and upheaval we ourselves created, the most traumatic event of the decade wasn't of our making, but of other people's - people who presumed to lecture us on virtue, on duty, on responsibility. It was they who cost us our most severe casualties, not any aberration in our own ethic. In ten years of conflict, fifty thousand young Americans were to die in the jungles, river deltas and rice paddies of Southeast Asia. Between sixty and a hundred thousand were subsequently to take their own lives. Vietnam's was the first war in recorded history whose combat deaths were later to be exceeded by its veterans' suicides.

* * * * * * *

Vietnam had, of course, already impinged on me, albeit indirectly, through my Draft Board. My struggle then, however, hadn't been with the war itself, with its stupidity, its morality or lack thereof, so much as with the android-minded bureaucrats who'd tried to pack me off to it, tried to make me fight their quixotic battles for them. And when I'd measured psychiatric swords against poor, hapless, neurotic and now dead Doctor Samsa, I'd been too intent on my own localised tussle for survival to pay much attention to the broader issues involved. At that time, the body bags hadn't yet begun to return in quantity to middle America. In consequence, the broader issues seemed pretty remote to everyone. Framed by the television screen, they were safely contained, insulated, reduced to reassuringly manageable proportions, with no more immediacy than the average soap, horse or cop opera. Against this background, drained of all potentially disturbing colour, even blood was diluted to a matter of black on white. But not even the anaesthetic jargon of the official communiqués could altogether conceal what was happening. I remember one such communiqué as it appeared in a Chicago newspaper: '*A jeep carrying four Marines struck a mine two miles south of Da Nang. Casualties were moderately heavy.*' Such gibberish no longer served to mask the actuality, which leered through the meshes of language. And that actuality, even if only at second-hand, was soon to encroach on me more directly - well before it encroached on the country as a whole.

In appropriately symbolic fashion, our squalid but vibrant enclave of Chicago was bounded by two imposing bastions of established authority. To the west lay the majestic leafy parade of the Midway, its stately arrow-straight avenue of trees forming a moat around the Gothic ramparts, crenellations, towers and spires of the university. To the east, overlooking the lake, loomed an anonymous, multi-storied, myriad-windowed structure of red brick, with immaculate white facings and a forecourt of pristine concrete. To one side of the entrance - on a patch of grass kept fastidiously manicured and Peter Pan-green - a glistening white Nike missile pointed its needle-thin nose-cone at the sky. The noxious thing actually managed to look lyrical, graceful, supernally innocent - as if, were it ever to rocket heavenwards, it might frolic harmlessly in the azure, like a good-natured porpoise, then glide docilely downwards again to nuzzle its keeper's hand.

Here, behind this elegant instrument of death, was the administrative headquarters of the United States Sixth Army. It housed primarily clerical and bureaucratic staff, the base with its combat personnel being situated elsewhere. During the spring of the year I spent above Reggie's, however, the first sizeable contingents of troops began to return from tours of duty in Southeast Asia, and Sixth Army Headquarters was swarming with the government's spiffy, newly issued, forest-green uniforms. They quickly spilled out from their sequestered precincts to inundate the adjacent streets and, with nightfall, the bars.

The drama that ensued, here and across the country, has been abundantly chronicled in all its mercilessness, pathos and tragedy - has become, indeed, a paradigm for an entire era. Gullible young GIs, bundled off to a war they never understood, had been indoctrinated to believe they were fighting for the nation's survival - for Truth, Justice and the American Way, for God, Mother, Apple Pie. Half a world away, they'd blundered up against the fierce actuality of such confections as napalm and the drolly named Agent Orange. Some had been traumatically disillusioned. Some, unable to accept the pointlessness of the horror they'd experienced, had coerced themselves to believe yet more fervently in its necessity, its justness, its rectitude. All, however, had expected, on their return, to be welcomed - if not as conquering heroes, at least as martyrs to a cause. Instead, they were received, by their own contemporaries and former schoolmates, as bloodstained pariahs - were jeered at, spat upon, insulted, stigmatised as ogres, sadists, rapists, bestial murderers of women and children. Many were confused and disoriented. Many were definitively broken, their already sagging morale irreparably ruptured. Many, accepting the guilt imposed upon them, embarked on a lifelong pilgrimage of atonement. Many were furiously embittered and sought to overcompensate.

But the bravado that still, in those days, might've impressed the farmland and small towns of middle America met, amid Chicago's ghettos, a wall of sullen smouldering hostility. Brawls between returned veterans and local youths - especially Blackstone Rangers - became an increasingly frequent occurrence. Now and again, a zealous Green Beret might display his expertise in unarmed combat, kung-fooing some over-confident black swaggerer to chop suey. Usually, however, the soldiers had only the most rudimentary skills, and a misplaced sense of honour to boot - more handicap than anything else against switchblades, stilettos, broken bottles, baseball bats, coins filed down to a razor thinness and hurled like Ninja throwing-stars. Whenever possible, the gang members looked after their own, spiriting their injured away to their own tenements and the care of neighbourhood physicians - some of whom had, in fact, received medical training in Vietnam. One heard, therefore, little or nothing about their losses. The soldiers, on the other hand - cut, bruised, abraded, lacerated, with fractured limbs and often knife slashes - were decanted into the nearest hospitals, where their complaints became public and vociferous. Newspapers fulminated against the fate of gallant GIs, who'd escaped the diabolical wiles of a fiendish foe in the rice paddies, only to be felled by 'subversive elements' on American streets.

Reggie's, with its insalubrious reputation, was supposedly a no-go area, one of the places explicitly specified as off limits to military personnel. That, of course, didn't deter many of them. If anything, it posed an irresistible challenge. Non-combatants in particular - cooks, clerical workers, staff and liaison officers, bandsmen, numerous others whose functions had kept them from the war zones - could now flaunt their mettle and their manhood by invading a Chicago dive. Around mid-March of that year, the new forest-green uniforms began to seep into the premises, gradually becoming a familiar sight - half a dozen nightly, on the average. As a token gesture of good will, 'The Ballad of the Green Berets' was added to the selections on the jukebox, and sometimes even played - albeit to an invariable accompaniment of jeers.

At our reserved table, Radetzky and I usually had two or three vacant seats - for Patterson when he emerged from behind the bar, for Nina and Beryl, who'd join us between shifts of waitressing. Ours being among the few white faces discernible, the seats at our table became a magnet for the soldiers - drunken soldiers, traumatised soldiers, belligerent soldiers, numbed soldiers, vindictive soldiers, mourning soldiers, soldiers suffering from guilt, grief, shock or the frazzled nervous condition euphemistically dubbed 'combat fatigue'. They'd join us generally for a drink or two, regale us with their stories, their braggadocio, their recrimination or their anguish, then lurch off into the darkness and, frequently, one or another swift violent encounter in some dank alley, some shadowy crossroads - followed by the skirling of ambulance sirens. Their attitudes spanned the spectrum. There were, of course, the gung-ho trigger-happy psychopaths, the bloodthirsty maniacs with their grisly trophies of Viet Cong ears. There were also fervent converts to pacifism, with the missionary's loquacious eloquence. There were moodily brooding somnambules, trapped in a lurid, darkly flickering nightmare. There were shattered and gutted husks of human beings, with nervous tics in cheeks and eyelids, jittering heads and hands. In retrospect, the influx of green uniforms is embodied for me by two representative figures, from diametrically opposing poles.

The first announced himself one evening by an initially confused commotion at the door. We heard voices raised in anger, saw a muddled mêlée of bodies. Only gradually did the knot of jostling torsos disentangle itself to reveal Terence Mulligan, the bouncer, in grotesque confrontation with a diminutive truculent GI - a boy who looked little more than sixteen, sandy-haired, with a saddle of freckles across his nose. He was obviously under drinking age and, despite that, just as obviously drunk - perhaps having got served at some other bar, less threatened by the Vice Squad and less punctilious, therefore, in checking identification. Against Mulligan's hulking bulk, he might've been a terrier yapping around a patient, long-suffering ox. One hand around his throat, Mulligan was holding him at arm's length while he swung wildly and ineffectually with both fists, never getting close enough to land a blow.

'You bastard!' the boy was yelling hysterically. 'You fuckin' bastard! Just 'cause I'm eighteen, you think I can't drink? Shit, man! I could drink you under the table! Any day, man! Any fuckin' day! You just give me a chance an' I'll drink you under the goddamn fuckin' table...!'

Voice rigid with exasperation, Mulligan was attempting patiently to reply with the customary mechanical formula - it wasn't up to him personally, he didn't make the rules, he'd gladly serve the young man if he could, but he dared not risk crossing the police, who'd welcome the opportunity to shut down the bar.

'Bullshit!' the soldier yelled. 'That's bullshit! You just don't want me drinkin' here! That's what it comes down to, don't it? I ain't good enough to drink with you bastards! You can me send me off to 'Nam, but you can't serve me no booze? You can trust me with an M-16, but not with a glass of beer? If I ain't old enough to drink, how come I'm old enough to kill?'

His logic couldn't be faulted. At that point, he had all our sympathies, including Mulligan's - who, of course, was indeed helpless in the matter. Radetzky and I wondered briefly if we might somehow help the boy soldier find one or another means of circumventing the law's idiocy. But there was already something apparent in him that rubbed us the wrong way - he was too brash, too boisterous, too belligerent, too out of control. Besides, he was enjoying himself hugely, hurling himself into his rage with a zest that amounted to pleasure, even exuberance.

The rumpus continued for some time. We soon lost interest, only occasionally glancing round to monitor its progress, then returning to our own conversation. A sudden cessation of noise made us look up. Some agreement, it seemed, had been concluded. The soldier, it transpired, now wanted to take a pee. Mulligan consented to let him use the lavatory, after which, he promised, he'd leave the premises peaceably. En route to the men's room, he passed our table, weaving giddily. On his return, he aimed himself unsteadily at one of our vacant seats and flopped into it, glaring in Mulligan's direction.

'Fuckin' bastard pisses the shit out of me...!'

'You must have an unusual anatomy,' Radetzky observed, but the quip failed to register, and the youth continued in full and aggrieved spate:

'How can they tell me I ain't old enough to drink? Hell, I been boozed up every fuckin' day over in 'Nam. Not a day I ain't been bombed outa my skull. And then I come back home and they tell me I ain't old enough! After all I been through, too! Why in hell should I fight for a goddamn fuckin' country that screws a guy round like that? Christ, man, if you'd seen what it was like in 'Nam, you'd understand. If you'd seen me in combat situations, man...! You know how many rounds I can fire per minute with my M-16?'

We didn't, and I can't remember now how many rounds he said it was. It seemed a lot, as I recall, but we had in those days no idea of what an M-16's rate of fire might be, and no particular interest anyway. He went on at length about his prowess, his proficiency, the heroism of what sounded like various Homeric exploits, which he alluded to but never in fact described. Most of his tirade was rambling, disconnected, fragmented. He was too drunk, too resentful, too preoccupied with his grievance for us to coax any coherent narrative out of him.

'How many men've you killed?' Radetzky asked challengingly at one point.

'Eight,' the youth replied promptly – that tally, if nothing else, being fixed precisely in his mind. 'I killed eight of them slope-eyed bastards. Eight gooks! Eight, that is, credited to me personally. Me alone. Six of 'em my bullets, two finished off with my bayonet. An' then there was mebbe another dozen or so in firefights, when you couldn't tell my rounds from the other guys'. An' that's the kind of man I am! An' they don't let me drink in this fuckin' country! Let me tell you 'bout this fuckin' country, man. Like we come back from 'Nam, you know, from all the shit we been through over there. You know what I mean? An' we land in San Diego. An' you know the first thing we see when we disembark? We see a crowd of these long-haired peace freaks...not you guys, I don't mean you guys, you weren't in San Diego...we see a crowd of these long-haired peace freaks with their VC flags an' their banners an' everything, marchin' up an' down, singin' songs and yellin' their slogans at us. They don't welcome us back or nothin'. They treat us like we was...well, murderers, or criminals, or somethin'! You know what we did? Well, what would you've done? What would anyone do in a case like that? We kicked the shit out of them fuckers! I got one of 'em in the windpipe myself, with my elbow , you know, an' when he hit the sidewalk, he didn't get up again...'

By now, our garrulous guest had the ironic and contemptuous attention of all the adjacent tables, and Radetzky and I were beginning to feel soiled by his very presence. Glancing towards the door, I caught Mulligan's eye and indicated with a nod that we'd had enough – it was time to get rid of the intruder. Lumbering down the aisle, Mulligan descended on the soldier from behind, seized him by the back of the collar and hoisted him bodily into the air. Kicking, cursing, flailing, spitting and sputtering like a cat held by the scruff of its neck, he was carried aloft to the entrance, where, amid a salvo of taunting laughter, Mulligan perfunctorily dropped him. He landed on his arse, tried to clamber upright, slipped in a puddle of beer and fell flat again, at last hauled himself to his feet by clinging to the jukebox.

'You goddamn motherfuckin' son of a bitch!' he screamed, positively rabid now, frothing with rage. 'I just wish...! Son of a bitch! I just wish I had my M-16 with me now! If I had my M-16 with me now, I'd show you I was old enough to drink! You bet your fuckin' ass, man, I'd show you! You know how many rounds I can fire per minute with my M-16? You see all them bottles up there behind the bar?' He dropped into a crouch, training the finger of his left hand, swivelling an invisible weapon, juddering, mimicking the stutter of an automatic rifle. 'All them bottles in a single burst! All them bastards, too...! Shit, man, don't look at me that way! I know what I'm doin'. I wouldn't hit no innocent people! Wouldn't hit no white guys! Just the niggers...!'

The silence was like an explosion. For nearly a minute, the entire bar was deathly still, frozen to a fatal immobility - as if the soundtrack of the scene had suddenly broken, leaving only a noiseless pantomime or tableau. Amidst the stricken hush, I heard only, from outside, the sticky swish of tyres in the wet street, and, on the jukebox, seemingly very remote, Baez's plangent, crystalline, disincarnate voice: *'And it's all over now, Baby Blue...'*

The soldier himself seemed abashed, some intimation of his gaffe filtering through even his alcoholic stupor. He started to gabble something, but Mulligan gave him no opportunity, seizing his collar with one hand, his belt with the other, and flinging him bodily through the door which someone else held open. Although I thought nothing of it at the moment, I recalled in retrospect hearing a chair scrape back at one of the tables behind me. Cat-light footsteps padded up the stairs leading to the rear exit, the door creaked open, creaked shut again.

I'm not sure precisely what it was that roused me the following morning. Perhaps the skirl of sirens threaded through my dreams. Perhaps some somnolent awareness of bustle and hubbub in the world beyond my sleep. Perhaps simply the cold. I was conscious initially only of the absence of warmth - the absence of Nina's body beside me, the absence of the blanket as well. Suddenly alarmed, I sat up. Nina stood at the window, staring down into the alley below. She was wrapped in the hijacked blanket, using one corner of it to wipe mist from the frosted pane, which emitted a faint squeaking.

'What is it?'

'That soldier from last night.'

Shivering, I draped a coat over my shoulders and blundered to her side, my toes curling in recoil from the freezing floor. Through the streaky, moisture-slicked glass, everything was pretty much a blur. I hauled up the sash and a gust of glacial wind seared our faces and torsos, making us gasp. In the alley below, I saw at first only the stooped blue backs of policemen congregated in a circle, like a football huddle. Then some of them straightened up, and the huddle parted to reveal the soldier of the night before. He lay with arms splayed, as if crucified, one leg bent sharply inwards at a grotesque angle, reminiscent of the Hanged Man in the Tarot. Despite the height, I could see his face clearly, white as drained veal, and his eyes, wide and unwaveringly motionless, fixed sightless on the sky. There wasn't much blood visible. Most of it had soaked into the surrounding mud, sludge and puddles of rainwater, to which it imparted a slight tinge, pinkish or rusty according to the angle of the light. Across his pallid throat, however, there was a jagged red slash that resembled a ragged bandanna. When they tried to lift him, his head fell away like a pumpkin.

Thus Vietnam came to Chicago, with an immediacy no longer containable by the television screen, no longer diluted to black and white.

****

It must've been some three weeks after the death of the boy soldier that I made the acquaintance of Wes Tyler. For a week or so prior to our meeting, I'd seen him drifting aimlessly around the bar. A mournful, distracted, haggard-looking man, shortish, stocky, barrel-chested and bandy-legged. A pasty bloated face which must once have been full but had now sagged in upon itself. Deeply sunken eyes. Thin sandy hair sharply receding above a bulging expanse of furrowed forehead. He was dressed usually in jeans and an army combat jacket, and I didn't at first realise he was a soldier. I mistook him, in fact, for an abject homosexual on the make, and regarded him, accordingly, with distaste. When he asked if he could join me at my table – I happened to be there alone that night – I wasn't very eager to welcome him. I adopted what I always thought was simply a hostile glare, but Nina called my 'queer-deterrent look'. Wes, as his name proved to be, read the reservations in my expression.

'Don't turn me away, man. I ain't queer. Just want to talk. Got to talk. Need someone to talk to. I seen you an' your buddies talkin' to some of the other grunts that come in here. I was hopin' you might listen to me.'

I nodded to one of the empty chairs and Wes sagged into it, his body slumped with something more profound than mere physical fatigue.

'You're a soldier?'

'Yeah. Corporal. Medical Corps. An' I got my own stories to tell.'

'About Vietnam?'

He nodded grimly, gazing into the distance with hollow haunted eyes – the eyes of a sleepwalker staring back, aghast, over landscapes of nightmare.

'I lost my half my mind an' my whole soul over there.'

He came, he told me, from a small lumber town in Michigan, just below the Canadian border. He'd scarcely known his father, who'd died in a timbering accident when Wes was six. His family consisted of his mother and his two brothers, one of them two years younger than himself, the other four.

'My brothers're the most important thing in my life. They're what I live for. They're what keep me alive. An' over there, in 'Nam, I mean, I used to cry myself to sleep at night in my bunk. Couldn't bear it, the thought that in another year, another two years or three, my brothers'd be sent over to that shithole, to fight an' probably die in the same crazy meaningless fuckin' war.'

I signalled Nina to bring him a drink and began, tentatively, to draw him out. My tentativeness proved unnecessary. Now that he'd begun to talk, to articulate his rage and bitterness, it was as if a sluice gate had opened. For the rest of the evening, he regaled me with stories from the combat zones.

'We don't know what the fuck we're doin' over there. Don't know what we're fightin' for. Don't even know how to fight. We stomp through the jungle in these close-packed files, you know, like we was on parade or somethin', an' Charlie picks us off like we was ducks in a shootin' gallery. A ten-year-old kid with a rifle shoots the shit outa a whole platoon. South Vietnamese troops ain't worth spit. Just a bunch of sadistic bastards stuffed into uniforms and struttin' round like turkey cocks. No guts. No discipline. No tactics. Only people on our side who got a clue what they're doin' are the Aussies. They got these special units called SAS, copied from the British, an' they know how to fight that kinda war. Like the British did in Malaya, they told me. But there ain't enough of 'em to make a difference. An' their hearts ain't in it anyway. Still, though, you don't have no Aussie troops fraggin' their officers. Don't have no Aussie officers that need fraggin'...'

It was from Wes that I first heard that term which, during the next few years, was to become so painfully familiar to the American public – to those, at any rate, prepared to hear it, those unafraid to acknowledge that such things occurred.

'You don't know what fraggin' is? I'll tell you. They fragged the lieutenant of my outfit. I suppose I should say, actually, that *we* fragged him. I knew it was goin' to happen, an' I went along with it. This lieutenant, he was a real bastard. West Point type an' all that, but he was always scared shitless. Had the shakes the whole time. It made him even more of a prick, 'cause he knew we knew. Whenever there was some grunt he didn't like, usually a black guy, he'd send the poor kid out on point. Our point riders suffered ninety percent casualties. We got ambushed one day on a trail through the jungle, an' the lieutenant got pinned down. Bullets spittin' up dirt an' leaves an' roots all 'round him. Couldn't advance no further. Couldn't retreat neither. So what's he do? He reaches out an' grabs this corporal, a buddy of mine, and he drags the corporal - I mean, like, actually *drags* the guy - in front of him. Corporal gets hit, of course, gut-shot, an' the lieutenant uses his body for cover to duck back where it's safe. An' we had to watch the corporal die, screamin'. Well, that was the last straw. That night, some of the fellas held a meetin'. Next mornin', the lieutenant, he goes off for a crap at the end of his slit trench an' gets a fragmentation grenade dropped on him from the trees overhead. Wrote off as an enemy mine. That's fraggin'. Happens all the time over in 'Nam. An officer gives you shit, you frag him.'

He told me of Saigon, the glittering feverish decadence and nihilism of a war-torn capital, where people whose futures had all but run out frantically sought distractions of the moment, where everything could be bought or sold - vehicles, weapons, murder contracts, military contraband, medical supplies, alcohol and drugs, political favours, women's and boys' bodies. He told me of the bars, the opium dens, the bordellos and whorehouses where they played the games of Russian roulette subsequently depicted in *The Deer Hunter*.

'You get to like livin' on the edge. Some guys even get to need it. It becomes a kind of high, flirtin' with death. Almost as if death was a woman, one of my buddies used to say. But if you're gonna gamble with your life, you may's well be comfortable while you're doin' it. Sittin' back in your chair, you know. Glass of hooch in your hand. Thirteen-year-old hooker in your lap. Better to put the bullet in your brain yourself an' go out that way. I'm not talkin' 'bout myself, mind you. I couldn't ever get into that sort of thing. But I could understand the guys who did.'

I was impressed by Wes' lack of swagger, his disdain for broad political issues, his sensitivity to human needs, human reactions, human dreams. It was, of course, precisely this sensitivity that'd made his sojourn in Southeast Asia such an ordeal.

'Trouble is, we don't treat the people over there like they was people. We call 'em gooks and geeks and slopes - slopin' eyes, you know - and we treat 'em like they was shit. I was on furlough in Saigon once, standin' outside a bar, waitin' for a coupla buddies. 'Cross the street, there was this little Vietnamese kid, must've been eight or nine mebbe, with his shoeshine kit. He's callin' out his shoeshinin' in this high twitterin' voice they all have over there, sorta like a bird. These two Marines pass, real close. Kid reaches for the arm of one of 'em, asks if he can shine their boots. Marine just turns and kicks the kid in the face. Kid's face is like a mask of blood. Kid's teeth all over the road. Kid runs off screamin' at the top of his voice. I stood there starin' at the shoeshine kit he left behind him. It was just lyin' there. A shoeshine kit without a kid, lyin' there on the empty sidewalk. Made me so sad, my buddies come up and find me with tears streamin' down my face. They said I must be havin' some kinda breakdown or somethin'. But what I was thinkin' was, where's that kid gonna be in another year or so? You know where he's gonna be, don't you, man? He's gonna be on the other side. In black pyjamas. Out in the jungle. Aimin' his rifle at our guys. And seein' in every one of 'em that fuckin' Marine who kicked his face in. Hell, man, the VC don't have to recruit. We're such assholes, we send 'em all the manpower they need.'

The evening wore on and freshened towards midnight, Nina brought successive rounds of drinks, Wes grew more loquacious. He told me of the Army's notorious 'kill ratio' - how, as a matter of course, ten of the enemy were automatically assumed to have perished for each American serviceman, the actual losses then being added to this 'handicap'. He told me of spurious and falsified casualty lists - how those who died of wounds in the aftermath of combat, who died in accidents or blunders, who died through illness or drug overdose or suicide, were omitted from the official figures, as if they'd never existed at all. He told me of the ubiquitous cannabis and heroin smuggled from the Golden Triangle - and how certain individuals, certain entire units, wouldn't engage in action unless stoned. He told me of dope shipped home in body bags, even in embalmed corpses, and of search-and-destroy missions on the Laotian border which served merely to protect the opium trade. And he told me, needless to say, of atrocities.

My Lai, or 'Pinkville', was at that point a year in the future, its public disclosure longer still. But if Wes' narrative was of events less scandalous, they were only so in scale, not in their intrinsic ugliness. I heard from him, for the first time, of what was later to emerge as one of the nastier commonplaces of the war, the collection of enemy scalps and ears. I heard from him a grisly catalogue of rape, looting, indiscriminate murder and wanton sadism. And I heard the specific circumstances which had led to his being sent home.

He'd been attached to a Ranger battalion, operating on - and, illegally, across - the Cambodian border. Intelligence reports, or what passed for them, had named a village just over the frontier, a supposed depot for Viet Cong arms. Ordered to locate and destroy these weapons, Wes' company had embarked before dawn by helicopter, had landed in the drop zone at first light. In the ensuing search, no weapons whatever were found, nor, for that matter, any able-bodied men - only women, children, a few youths convalescing from disease, a few cripples and oldsters. They'd naturally denied all knowledge of concealed matériel. In reprisal for this ignorance, whether feigned or genuine, the GIs had razed the village and exterminated its inhabitants, some sixty or seventy in number. The troops had sustained one casualty - a white-bearded elder had tottered from a hut and stabbed a soldier in the arm with a wooden stake. Before he could do any further damage, he'd been scythed in two by a burst from an M-16.

'I just stood there an' watched. I was paralysed. It was like some kinda dream or somethin'. I kept shakin' my head an' tellin' myself this ain't happenin', this ain't happenin'. I seen this one girl, must've been 'bout ten...'

He stopped, his voice starting to break, his lower lip trembling, a tic suddenly appearing in the pouch below his left eye, making him seem to wink convulsively at two-second intervals. He'd obviously been about to recount specific details, specific images, then changed his mind. He jerked his head as if to shake them from memory, the way a drenched dog shakes itself free of water.

'Couldn't sleep that night when we got back to base camp. Couldn't stop shiverin' neither. Felt like I had jungle fever. Next mornin', I still couldn't stand it, so I went over the head of the lieutenant. Went to the captain. Asked him why we had to do that – had to do what we done. He just stared at me all stony-faced an' said it was orders. "But our orders were fucked up,' I says to him. "They told us the village was a depot for VC arms. An' we didn't find no arms." He just shrugs an' says we had no way of knowin' that, an' it ain't a soldier's business to question orders anyways. I reckon I must've lost my temper. I told him there were some things you got to question, no matter who or what you are. His faces goes even stiffer than before, an' he says I can take what he calls my 'problem' to the major next mornin'. Next mornin', I go to see the major. He don't even give me a chance to open my mouth. Just looks me up an' down like I was somethin' drug in by the cat an' says: "Corporal Tyler, it's clear you're sufferin' from emotional instability. I think it'd be best if you were sent home soon's possible." An' here I am. . . '

By closing time, Wes had talked himself virtually hoarse. We arranged to meet again the following evening, and I returned upstairs to the flat, where I spent the rest of the night transcribing as much as I could remember – I'd been reluctant to take notes in his presence lest it inhibit him. Nina entered to find me hunched over my desk. Accustomed to my occasional spasms of nocturnal inspiration, she made no comment, just readied herself for bed. When I continued writing, however, she became curious. I offered a cursory explanation. She wasn't particularly interested, but warned me to be careful – Wes, she said, had probably been labelled subversive and was very likely under FBI surveillance. If I became one of his 'known associates', they'd be watching me as well. I said nothing, dismissing her worry as another manifestation of the paranoia filling the air like ozone.

In the morning, feeling muzzy and brittle with lack of sleep, I debriefed to Patterson and Radetzky. Like mine, their sense of *Realpolitik* was then only marginally more capacious than Nina's, but both were eager to sit in on the evening's session. We decided, however, that new faces might, just possibly, have a dampening effect. Or prompt Wes simply to repeat himself. Since I'd already gained his trust, we agreed I should again meet him alone.

In our first dialogue, he'd seemed stricken, anguished but sane enough, and his revelations had been sufficiently disturbing in themselves. Our second night's dialogue produced different grounds for concern. This wasn't at once apparent. Initially, I was only aware of a simplistic but downright heroic attempt on Wes' part to generalise. Here was a man, or boy, rather, who, as he told me, had left school at the age of ten, who'd had virtually no education - no training in history or philosophy or logic, no experience in learning to conceptualise, to formulate abstract thought and draw consistent conclusions. Reality had previously consisted for him solely of the concrete and immediate, of what was tangible and palpable, accessible directly, at first hand, to fingers, eyes, ears, heart and head. He'd never had any reason to extrapolate upon it. Now, however, he was struggling desperately to ascribe some broader meaning and significance to the ordeal through which he'd passed. The endeavour was admirable, courageous and at the same time poignant, even pathetic, to witness - like hearing a child forced to articulate some all-encompassing exegesis on love, or on God.

Uncomplicated principles of a backwoods boyhood, primitive notions of service, duty, responsibility, patriotism, right and wrong. In contrast, a welter of complex, diverse, ambiguous and morally tainted phenomena encountered half a world away. How to reconcile the two? In order to do so, Wes had tried to evolve some sort of comprehensive diagnosis of America's ills - some explanation to accommodate the bewildering conflicts and contradictions with which Vietnam had confronted him. His efforts had led him to identify three focal points of culpability in the nation, three founts of depravity and corruption, three sources of 'evil' whereby the American ideal, as he understood it, had been betrayed. These were - predictably, perhaps - Washington, Hollywood and Wall Street. Here lay, he'd concluded, the vested interests which had plunged the country into iniquity. Here resided the men - the politicians, the film moguls and the financiers - who, in their rapacity, greed and lust for power, had abused the trust a people reposed in them.

'And what can you do with those bastards? How can you get through to 'em? You talk. You write books and articles in newspapers. You sign petitions. You organise protest marches and demonstrations.

And they don't listen. None of it does any good. They don't care. They don't give a fuck. I'm askin' you, what can you do?'

The question, I knew, was rhetorical, but he looked at me as if he actually expected an answer.

'I'm not sure,' I replied warily. 'You tell me. What do you have in mind?'

It was then, for the first time, that a manic glow, a turgid and murky conflagration, flared briefly in his eyes. Behind his filmed and opaque gaze, something blazed for an instant, subsided but continued to smoulder.

'There's only one thing left for *me* to do,' he said quietly, with a leashed but fierce urgency. '*I* have to smash 'em.'

'How do you propose to do that?'

'I seen a movie not too long ago. *Doctor Zhivago*. You know it? Based on a book by some Russian writer. Dostoyevsky, I think. That's what gave me the inspiration.'

His imagination kindled by the celluloid images he condemned, he'd begin to fancy himself a latterday Strelnikov, thundering in an armoured train across the steppes of the American Midwest. For the last six months, he said, he'd been working his way through every account available, including official Army manuals, on guerrilla warfare in diverse terrains. He'd read all there was to read on the tactics of Trotsky, Mao, Che, Ho Chi Minh. He'd addressed himself to the campaigns of T.E. Lawrence, of Wingate's Chindits in Burma. He'd studied the irregular or semi-irregular cavalry units of the American Civil War - Mosby, Morgan, Forrest. He'd also studied the great Indian leaders - Crazy Horse, Sitting Bull, Cochise, Geronimo.

With this accumulated knowledge, he told me, his voice dropping to a conspiratorial whisper, he planned to organise his own partisan army and embark on a guerrilla war across the cornfields and prairies of America's heartland. By the end of the year, he guaranteed me, he'd have between two and three hundred picked men 'in the field'. They'd be armed initially, he explained, with privately purchased under-over combinations - fearsome things that fired both rifle bullets and shotgun shells, not particularly well-known in the States in those days, but now much favoured by the SAS. Wes outlined in meticulous detail - even drawing a map on a serviette - how he and his 'troops' would take advantage of a snowstorm to launch a surprise attack on a vulnerable National Guard base in Nebraska.

'It'd be a quick raid. Straight hit an' run. Objective'd be to procure ordnance an' supplies. Nothin' too heavy, mind you. A stock of M-16s. A dozen or so BARs - Browning automatic rifles. Two or three mortars. Bazookas. Rocket launchers. Grenades. Ammo. An' some vehicles too, to make us mobile. Jeeps. Coupla APCs - armoured personnel carriers. Mebbe, if we can manage it, a self-propelled howitzer.'

Thus equipped, he intended to withdraw and go to ground in the north woods - Minnesota, Wisconsin, his native Michigan, the Canadian border and the fringe of the Great Lakes. From this refuge, he proposed to launch his next raid, against another, much more strategically significant target.

'Fort Benjamin Harrison in Indianapolis. The beauty of it's that Fort Ben's what they call an open fort. No special security because there ain't no weapons or anythin' there. Anybody can just walk right into the base. What's important about Fort Ben's that it's the Army's payroll centre. That's where they keep all the pay records. That's where they process the salaries for everyone in the whole fuckin' machine, from privates right up to five-star generals. I figger we could just waltz right into Fort Ben, shoot the place up, burn everything, plant some charges mebbe an' destroy all the pay records. Can you think of a better way to undermine morale? Hell, within a coupla months, morale's start collapsin' all the way from 'Nam to Germany.'

Having administered this blow, he'd retire to the north woods again. During the summer months, he'd lie low, distributing his force across the countryside where, in established guerrilla fashion, they'd blend with the local populace. They might emerge, two or three at a time, for an occasional bank raid to finance their activities, for an occasional attack on government installations - like Federal Buildings, Wes said. At the advent of winter, they'd resume their operations, pursuing their campaign amidst the fir forests, frozen lakes and snow.

There was a pause, during which Wes seemed to be groping for appropriate phraseology. I watched him testing various formulations in his mind. He resolved, at last, to be blunt.

'Don't suppose I could interest you in joinin' me, could I?'

I pretended to consider.

'No, I don't think so,' I said judiciously. 'Not my kind of war, really. I prefer to fight in my own way. A different sort of campaign.'

'How d'you mean? What is it you do?'

'I'm a writer. Whenever possible, I prefer the pen to the sword.'

Wes looked dubious.

'Writin' don't change nothin'.'

'No, not usually. Poetry makes nothing happen, as a distinguished poet once said. But it's not my business to change things. Only to testify. To bear witness. And to help people to *see*, in the clairvoyant sense of the word.'

Wes pondered this, frowning, wrestling with its implications. Then, understanding suffused his features, smoothing away their tense furrowed concentration. In his eyes, there was a momentary sparkle - a fleeting dream of immortality, of glory and sacrifice enshrined.

'If you came with me, you'd sure have plenty to testify to.'

'I don't have to come with you in order to testify to it.'

The light in his eyes went out and he nodded sadly.

'You're right. I know that. And you wouldn't live long enough to do much testifyin', would you? Because I won't live that long. I know that, too. I know, in my bones, nothin''ll come of it all. I know, in my bones, they'll track me down. Sooner or later, they'll corner me, an' I'll die up there in the north woods. Won't even be much consolation to've gone down fightin'. No one'll ever really understand what it was all for. No one'll want to. I won't go down in history or anythin' like that. I'll just be some kind of crazy fool, some poor screwed-up bastard who lost his marbles in a stupid war. That's how it'll be, I reckon. An' if you joined me, I wouldn't be able to con you 'bout it. I couldn't promise you victory. Couldn't promise you anythin' in that way. Only one thing I could promise you. That's that my two brothers - an' you know how much they mean to me - my two brothers'd be there fightin' right alongside you, an' dyin' there when the time came. I wouldn't ask anythin' of you I wouldn't ask of them.'

'I appreciate that thought,' I replied, clinking my glass to his. 'I'm grateful for your honesty. As I said, though, I've got my own path to follow.'

Wes stared into his drink for a moment, then looked up with beseeching eyes.

'Promise me one thing, will you? Promise me someday you'll write my story?'

'I'll try to do that.'

For the next fortnight or so, I continued to see him moping around the bar. We had no further conversations, however, only exchanged greetings, smiles, occasional nods or glances of tacit complicity. I watched him accost other clientèle, obviously seeking recruits for his crusade - and just as obviously failing to find them. On each successive night, he appeared more woebegone, more haggard, more hollowed out by despair. It was clear to me, to Nina, to Patterson and Radetzky, that his forlorn and foredoomed quest couldn't sustain itself much longer.

'I wonder what'll happen to him,' Nina mused aloud one evening as she sat beside me at my table, observing Wes drift mournfully down the length of the bar, seeking sympathetic faces he hadn't yet canvassed. She knew the answer as well as I did. It took no very piercing prescience to foresee.

'He'll keep trying to recruit for a while,' I prophesied, merely articulating her unvoiced thoughts. 'He'll get nowhere. He'll become increasingly frustrated. And then he'll do something apocalyptic. Walk into Sixth Army Headquarters with a shotgun or something.'

I was mistaken only about the shotgun. When Wes entered Sixth Army Headquarters one Thursday some ten days later, it was with a grenade. We actually heard the blast in the bar - a distant dull thump from the direction of the lake, a shock wave that jarred the windows, made glasses and bottles tinkle on the shelves. At the time, of course, we didn't know what it was. It might've been any of a number of things - a car backfiring, a road accident, a gas leak, perhaps one of the indeterminate shots that periodically troubled the Chicago twilights - and we took scant notice of it. Not until the following morning did we learn what'd happened from the newspapers.

According to the 'official' reports, a twenty-one-year-old Vietnam veteran, Corporal Wesley Tyler of Forest Falls, Michigan, had slipped into Sixth Army Headquarters just before six o'clock, armed with a live grenade. He'd apparently intended to take hostages, senior officers if he could find them. Alerted by his suspicious demeanour, a sentry had challenged him. I couldn't imagine Wes dissembling. He must've made no attempt to disguise his purpose - might even have tried to convert the sentry. In any case, shots had been fired in the corridors, Wes sought refuge in an empty office and there barricaded himself. When the sentry began shooting through the door, the grenade had been detonated - perhaps deliberately, perhaps by a stray round or ricochet.

Another anaesthetising statistic. Another addition to the roll of casualities from Southeast Asia. But one who'd never appear on any official list. Who'd never be granted a military funeral or buried with honours. Who'd have no plot in a cemetery reserved for martial heroes, no volley fired over his grave - and not enough left of him to ship back to Forest Falls. Who'd never, in all likelihood, be named among the suicides. Who'd earned no obituary save that report in the newspapers, which reduced him to what he'd expected it would - 'some kind of crazy fool, some poor screwed-up bastard who lost his marbles in a stupid war'.

IX

Had Wes gone out with a whimper, or at least with less of a bang, I might not just have written his story, but published it as well. To fictionalise him wouldn't, of course, have been feasible. Any attempt to do so would only have produced a seemingly implausible narrative, verging on propaganda, which - in those still war-happy and gung-ho days - would've been both unpalatable and unplaceable. But if he'd kept himself alive, I might conceivably have stooped to a piece of journalism, which, if nothing else, would've ensured that his voice - the authoritatively anguished voice of a genuine Vietnam veteran - be heard. By virtue of his death, however, he'd become a Vietnam veteran only incidentally and secondarily. He'd died primarily not as a frustrated, disillusioned and demoralised witness, but as something else - a criminal, perhaps a species of terrorist, at best a deranged husk of a man who, by his actions, had compromised the reliability of his testimony. Or so, at any rate, he'd be perceived.

Prompted by some obscure sense of obligation - to him, or to something else? - I 'wrote his story' all the same. When I showed it to Patterson, Radetzky and other literary friends, their opinions concurred with mine. There was no point in sending the piece out. To do so would've been like tossing a bottle with a message into the sea - or, more accurately perhaps, pissing into the wind. No 'mainstream' journal or magazine of those days would've been interested; and had my account appeared in some fringe publication, I'd only have been preaching to the converted. I'd also have got myself scrutinised, investigated and interrogated by the FBI; I had, after all, 'consorted' with a man who'd heinously plotted high treason, who'd died in what could be construed as a treasonable act. Not that I was particularly afraid of J. Edgar Hoover's shiny-shoed minions. If anything, I was sufficiently iconoclastic, and perhaps sufficiently naïve, to relish the prospect of some moral and intellectual sparring with them. But the process would've been distracting and time-consuming - too much so to justify embarking on it for the sake of an exercise in futility. Besides, other, more immediate things were starting to usurp the foreground of our lives.

Some of these, I admit, were pranks, shamelessly frivolous in themselves, all the more so in the wake of Wes' tragic drama. One night, for example, Patterson, Radetzky and I lifted a ripped, tattered, stained, scandalously dilapidated barstool from Reggie's. We packaged it in a huge, refrigerator-sized box and posted it anonymously to Bernard McCabe, our favourite ex-professor, back in Boston - posted it not to his home, but to his office at the university, where its ungainly arrival, effected by a squad of stumbling delivery men, attracted maximum attention. For some years thereafter, it remained as a rueful trophy beside his desk.

A fortnight or so later, Patterson - yoked by then to Sabina, a slinky woman who dressed like a *Vogue* model and haemorrhaged money with cheerfully profligate abandon - sped east for the Easter holidays in her E-Type Jaguar. Availing ourselves of his absence, Radetzky and I perpetrated one of my more memorable, and visually spectacular, practical jokes. We allowed ourselves two days, proceeding in a relaxed, leisurely, convivial fashion. Aided by shifts of volunteers from the bar, Radetzky, Beryl, Nina and I seated ourselves on the floor of the corridor with sheaves of discarded tabloids and copious supplies of alcohol. Chatting, tippling, idling, interrupting our work when the spirit moved us, we crumpled up sheets of superseded news and tossed them haphazardly into Patterson's bedroom. Gradually, of course, the sheets uncrumpled, unfurled, expanded. The litter level, initially knee-high, quickly rose like a soufflé - hip-high, then waist-high. We continued adding to it. When we'd finished, we were confronted, on opening the door, by some species of bizarre Cubist or Dadaist architecture - an apparently solid six-foot-tall wall of seething, rustling and crackling pages, jagged-edged, multi-planed, myriad-faceted. Thoroughly drunk by then, we frolicked in it for a while, burrowing through the stuff like moles, chasing and ambushing one another, playing hide-go-seek to the accompaniment of a deafening stereophonic crepitation. Someone from the bar came up to take photographs, and there must still exist somewhere, in some album or bureau drawer, a snapshot of me standing on my head amidst our handiwork, supported by the pressure of the paper, only my boots visible above the choppy rumpled sea of print.

Downstairs, in Reggie's, bets were taken and a contest was announced - a bottle of VSOP cognac for the person who correctly predicted Patterson's first words on his return. They proved, in fact, not to have a pithiness, or a sonority, worthy of enshrinement: '*Oh no!*

Oh no! Oh fuck! Oh no!' Accustomed as we were to somewhat more eloquence and urbanity, none of us won the cognac, which, in consolation for his trauma, we conferred on Patterson. In an operation that took all night, the newspaper was laboriously transferred to the front room, where it covered the petrified dogshit of the autumn and the notorious box of styrofoam.

To some extent, this and other such escapades reflected a burgeoning need to release tension, an instinctive reaction to events and developments around us. For some weeks - concurrent with Wes Tyler's quixotic recruitment drive - a sinister atmosphere had begun to envelope all of us in the bar. The dementia of Vietnam - the cult of weaponry, the zest for killing, the scores notched up on gun butts, the pathology now associated with the rabid antics of Rambo - had, in effect, polluted the very air we breathed. It added a new, even more volatile element to an already dangerously incendiary milieu.

I can't now recall how or where the whole business started. I'm not even sure we ever knew. No doubt it'd been latent in Chicago at least since Capone's era, a potentiality constantly seeking actualisation. By the time we became conscious of it, or conscious at any rate of its prevalence, it was already a *fait accompli*. But all at once, it seemed, guns were everywhere, sprouting like the dragon's teeth sown by Cadmus, proliferating around us with what might've been a spontaneous, perfectly natural and sane impetus to wax fruitful and multiply. Everybody we knew seemed suddenly to have obtained a gun, or to have possessed one all along. And we ourselves, I confess, weren't proof against the noxious contagion. Today, in retrospect, I find the phenomenon mind-boggling; I can't fathom precisely what our motivation was, can't imagine against whom, or in what circumstances, we thought we'd ever employ such ordnance. Perhaps we simply got infected by the prevailing mood, to which our aestheticism and romanticism rendered us susceptible anyway - some typically warped American assumption that a gun was a valid extension of one's personality, that it made one the proverbial 'bigger man'. In any case, to possess a gun now become, in our reprobate little sub-culture, *de rigeur*.

In a quiet transaction conducted across the bar - a modest sum slipped over in an envelope, a shoebox-sized parcel in plain brown paper furtively delivered a week later - Patterson obtained a sleek, elegant, state-of-the-art nickel-plated Beretta, not quite as prestigious as a Walther, but the next best thing. Radetzky, more slapdash and louche about the matter, purchased something altogether less impressive - I forget now what it was, have only a vague memory of a dinky low-budget little automatic, which the local *cognoscenti* dismissed sniffily as anodyne. I, for my part, disliked and distrusted automatics generally, on principle. I'm not sure now precisely why - why weapons apparently good enough for the likes of James Bond, Harry Palmer and a host of other celebrated spooks should've seemed inadequate for my decidedly questionable and probably nonexistent needs, whatever I fancied those to be. Less accuracy? Less range? Less reliability? A propensity to jam? I can't have been governed by such pragmatic considerations. Why did I prefer revolvers? Ultimately, I suspect, my reasons were purely - and anachronistically - stylistic. Or perhaps, by some spurious mental association, my prejudice against automatic transmissions in cars was projected on to firearms.

In any case, I had two perfectly functional guns at home, and there was little point in wasting money on a new one. When Patterson drove east for the spring holidays, I arranged for him to stop at my family's home in New Jersey, where he picked up my armoury - my rifle, a conventional .22, and my long-barrelled Smith and Wesson .38. He held them for ransom until I helped him bale the newspaper out of his bedroom. He might just as well have kept them indefinitely. I was never, fortunately, to use, or even brandish, either of them in anger. But I still find it unnerving to recall how ready I was to do so, and how close I eventually came.

Not that we had grounds for concern, with Lieutenant Boyle effectively out of our hair, but our arsenal was quite legal in Chicago at the time, provided we didn't carry any of it out on the streets. In the home, it was deemed as acceptable a household accoutrement as, say, a torch, or a hammer - or the various other aggressive implements, such as axe handles and hunting knives, with which our flat was stocked. There was even a municipal ordinance which allowed bartenders, in the event of a disturbance on the premises, to produce a gun from behind the bar and discharge it into ceiling or floor. A somewhat histrionic gesture perhaps, but it seldom failed to focus people's attention and brought many a brawl to an abruptly docile halt.

If my flatmates and I were vague in our reasons for stockpiling firearms, we were no more so than others. The entire neighbourhood was arming itself, without having any clear idea why. Not initially, at any rate. Gradually, however, a purpose began to coalesce, as if spawned by the guns themselves, by their very existence. They were there, in quantity, and demanded to be used, or at least justified, for something - demanded a *raison d'être*, a rationale. Such a rationale wasn't difficult to find - or to manufacture. It resulted from the convergence of several diverse factors.

Discontent with the Vietnamese conflict hadn't yet filtered down to 'Middle America', nor even - apart from those on the East and West Coasts - to the universities. It already obtained, however, in the nation's black enclaves, where resistance was gathering, was escalating inexorably. It was from these enclaves, of course, that a preponderance of cannon fodder was drawn. Here and there, in one or another maniacally zealous municipality, local Draft Boards had contracted the idiotic fervour of mine; but most were still dispensing deferments, and the majority of students were still immune. Radetzky, for example, had remained unthreatened - as did Patterson, who'd conned his Draft Board into thinking he'd never left school. Even the dim, the thick, the wobble-witted, the dunces with smudged or mediocre academic records - J. Danforth Quayle, for instance - could, if seriously pressed, find refuge in the National Guard.

Those most at risk were urban blacks, who enabled the country's policy-makers to display the wisdom of age by killing two birds with one stone - furnishing the military with manpower while removing thousands of young men from both the streets and the unemployment rolls. In consequence, the Draft swept through the ghettos like a medieval plague, harvesting its monthly quota, or crop, of victims. Its attrition left gaping holes in families, in whole communities. Most of the blacks in our neighbourhood already had relations - fathers, uncles, sons, brothers, cousins - serving in the Armed Forces. They knew it was only a matter of time before they, in turn, were called up, stuffed into uniform and - like the drunken boy soldier, like Wes Tyler, like their own relatives - packed off to the conflagration in Southeast Asia. They knew, too, that a sizeable percentage of them wouldn't return - or, if they did, would only do so in body bags. Not surprisingly, they were loth to sacrifice themselves in a war of no discernible relevance to them - loth to die for a country from which they felt alienated, to which they felt they owed nothing.

In the meantime, circulating insidiously through the bars, the pool halls, the gang headquarters and the derelict tenements, there was the secret SNCC injunction of two years before - to 'carry the war to the North'. Here was a war more immediate, more comprehensible, more congenial than the one in Vietnam. While the Panthers, the Black Muslims, the Blackstone Rangers and other such organisations were active in most northern cities, the war they claimed to be conducting had previously lacked focus, direction, clearly defined objectives and delineated goals. It'd also lacked a concrete central issue around which support could be rallied. The Draft now provided at least that much, just as the voter registration drive had for the Civil Rights Movement. Dodging conscription, young blacks swelled the ranks of hard-line paramilitary cadres - where, ironically, discipline and skills were taught by returned veterans, who'd themselves been trained by the Army. If one had to die with a gun in one's hand, so the rhetoric ran, it was preferable to do so on the streets of one's native city, fighting for one's own people, rather than twelve thousand miles away.

It must've been a fortnight or so after Easter - after Patterson's holiday and our stuffing of his room - that rumours first began to percolate through the bar. The riots of two summers before in Los Angeles were to be the prototype; but Watts, according to the grapevine, 'was only the beginning'. During the coming summer, a dozen other cities were scheduled to ignite. Conspiratorial voices whispered - erroneously, as it proved, in some cases - of upheavals in preparation for Detroit, for Cleveland, for Dayton, for St. Louis, for Boston, Newark, Washington and New York. Chicago, with the largest black population in the Midwest - perhaps in the country - couldn't allow itself to be outdone. It was almost as if civic pride were at stake. Within a fortnight, everything had become 'official' - Chicago was going to explode on the 1st of August.

A few of the more fanatic and deluded blithered volubly about full-fledged 'revolution', wove loopy fantasies about declaring the city an independent 'African' state, contrived to place themselves in a lineage running from Lenin and Mao to Castro and Che - with Malcolm X usually appended as an afterthought. Others, rather more cynical, or simply more realistic, spoke of confounding the authorities, disrupting public order, embarrassing America in the eyes of the world, calling attention to the plight of the nation's blacks, creating sufficient turmoil and anarchy to scare the government into action and reform. As usual, the action and reform demanded weren't specified, but abolition of the Selective Service system, or at least of its inequities, was always implicit. Poor Wes Tyler had died only a few weeks too soon. The guerrilla campaign he'd envisioned was now about to be launched - not in the plains and forests of the country's rural heartland, but in the urban ghettos. Had he lived to hear the plans assiduously being hatched, they'd nonetheless have pleased him. They amounted, indeed, to nothing short of open war. None of the strategists involved had any doubt that blood would be shed. That casualties would be heavy. That arms would be deployed on a hitherto unprecedented scale. That Chicago, in the aftermath, would resemble Berlin, Hamburg or Dresden in 1945.

In the wake of Lieutenant Boyle's disgrace, my flatmates and I, together with our abode, had come to enjoy an aura of immunity. This owed something to our own carefully orchestrated machinations. On three or four occasions, Radetzky had persuaded Faye Flinders to drop round to Reggie's for drinks, with the eminent Crispin Whelk in tow. Lying blithely through our teeth, we let it be known - and made sure Boyle's replacements in the precinct's Vice Squad heard - that we were Dr. Whelk's prize protégés. No one in the Police Department was unaware of the havoc the dreaded Whelk, when ruffled in feather, could wreak. We basked in his unwitting protection; and, had we felt so inclined, we probably could've flown all the styrofoam gliders we wished with impunity. Al Hollis glumly complained to Nina that only the most grievous provocation would cause the police to venture near our flat again. Word of this quickly spread through the bar, and it was therefore natural that our premises came to be regarded as an ideal arms depository. Numerous militant blacks of our acquaintance approached us, asking us to stash guns for them. We fended off most such petitioners; but there were some - our regular drinking companions and 'blood brothers', for example - whom it would've been difficult, even diplomatically rash, to refuse. At one point, towards the middle of May, we had nearly a dozen guns in our apartment, not counting our own.

We maintained a stance of studied - and, so it seems to me now, disingenuous - neutrality. We consented to hold weapons in 'safekeeping' provided they were legally registered - we insisted on having the certificates - and collected within a week or so. At the same time, we stressed repeatedly, we weren't ourselves prepared to participate in 'armed insurrection'. That, it transpired, wasn't expected of us anyway. Our involvement, we were told with what laboured to be tact and delicacy, would somehow have impaired the 'racial unity' of the enterprise. Whatever was planned for 1st August had to be implemented by blacks alone. We were already doing more than enough. But by the first week of June, scarcely a night passed without one or another of us receiving some sort of well-intentioned warning, often genuinely concerned, sometimes urgent, even passionate:

'You gotta get outa Chicago, man. I'm tellin' you this as your friend. Don't take it the wrong way. I wouldn't be tellin' you at all if I didn't like you. For God's sake, get outa Chicago before the first week of August. I know you're all right. I know you're cool. So do the other dudes 'round here. But come August, we ain't gonna be able to control things. Come August, all hell's gonna bust loose, an' there's gonna be all kinds of other dudes pourin' in here. Brothers from the North Side, from all over the fuckin' place. An' they ain't gonna know nothin' 'bout you 'cept that you's white.'

On one occasion, the ex-boxer - the man who'd sneered at my kirsch as 'chick's hooch', guzzled half the bottle in two swigs and passed out - intercepted me as I was approaching the bar. He beckoned me into the alley where, the most improbable-looking of Cassandras, he subjected me to an earnest lecture:

'I'm tellin' you for your own good, man. I don't wanna see you get hurt. You an' your buddies gotta get outa this town by August. Me an' the other cats, we ain't gonna be able to protect you. And this bar here's gonna be a prime target. A prime target, man. I mean, there's brothers from 'cross town who know all 'bout Melvin Bloss. He owns these blocks of tenements up on the North Side, see, an' he's been fuckin' people 'round there for years. Real fat-cat honkie landlord. Worst kind. There's lotsa dudes just waitin' for a chance to trash his property. Come August, this here bar ain't gonna be standin' no more...'

He clutched my arm with one hand, pointed with the other to the derelict cinema across the street.

'You see that place? Well, they's already designated that place the prime stronghold in this part of town. That place's gonna be a fuckin' fortress. Come August, there's gonna be sharpshooters with rifles behind every one of them boarded-up windows. Whole building's gonna be one big snipers' nest. An' them snipers ain't just gonna be shootin' into the bar. They's gonna be shootin' into the upstairs pads, too. They won't know who lives there. They ain't gonna say "Let's shoot at this window an' not at that one". Far's they's concerned, it's all gonna be the same thing. I tell you, man, this here building's gonna be so riddled with bullets you'll be able to see the lake through the holes. An' then they's gonna storm through the place an' ransack it. Ain't nothin' gonna be left in one piece. An' when they's finished with the place, they's gonna torch it.'

'What about Nina?' I asked.

'We done give her the same advice I'm givin' you.'

'I know that. But she's got her children and two sick parents. She's not as mobile as I am. Or Patterson. Or Radetzky.'

He shrugged helplessly, a gesture of self-absolution.

'She's gotta make up her mind, don't she? Same's you an' your buddies gotta do. Me an' the other cats 'round here, we don't want none of you to get hurt. Like I said, though, we ain't gonna be able to protect you...'

At moments, these doom-laden predictions sounded grotesque, as improbable as Wes Tyler's dementedly grandiose designs. At other moments, they were genuinely alarming. Not, of course, that they had much prospect of success. Chicago was hardly likely to become the 'captured city' many of the conspirators imagined. At the first shots, the police would be out in force, massively armed, only too zealous to shoot back. They'd be reinforced by equally trigger-happy units of National Guard - and, if necessary, of the Sixth Army. Before the merciless reality of the situation could be established, however, a bloodbath might well occur. It'd already done so once, in Los Angeles. Watts loomed as a precedent which no one could afford to ignore.

In theory, there was no reason why I shouldn't be out of the city by August. My plans for the autumn had already been finalised. My attitude was cheerfully mercenary. Provided it didn't interfere with my own priorities - my reading and writing - I was ready to go through the motions of working for my Ph.D. As long as academia continued to offer me a 'free ride', I'd be silly to relinquish its largesse. Here in Chicago, however, the Ph.D. programme would've imposed impertinent, even presumptuous, demands on my time and energy - demands I wasn't prepared to tolerate. I could afford to be snooty and high-handed about the matter, having the luxury of an option.

Earlier that spring, I'd been offered a unique position in another Ph.D. programme, far from Chicago's rancid wind, soot and stone. Come autumn, I was invited to be on the north shore of Long Island, forty-five miles east of Manhattan, at the freshly hatched darling and showpiece of New York's State University system. It was the first year of the doctoral programme there - a programme described, in brochures and other bumf, as 'unorthodox', 'experimental', 'innovative', 'radical'. To ensure a 'lively balance' in the department, recruitment was aimed not just at respectable scholarly drudges, but at others as well - at published and aspiring writers, at maverick bohemian types and rebels, who'd add, it was felt, a dash of informal vigour, a distinctive style and flair. I'm not sure which of the stipulated categories was supposed to include me. On the basis of my record at Chicago, no one with moderately intact wits could possibly have mistaken me for a scholar. In any case, the architects of the new programme had written to universities across the country, requesting recommendations for suitable candidates. Hoping no doubt to get rid of me, someone in Chicago had submitted my name and transcripts. I'd not even been required to make a formal application. The invitation had arrived unsolicited.

It would've been too attractive to refuse, even if I'd not been in need of just such an alternative. The university was situated not amidst the squalor of urban slums, but in a postcard-pretty expanse of bucolically green woods and scenically salty shoreline. Those of us entering the programme were to be dubbed 'Teaching Assistants'. We'd be free from traditional fetters, shackles and restrictions, at liberty to devise or design our own custom-tailored, idiosyncratic, even eccentric, degrees. We'd have only a bare minimum of course requirements; we'd be generously subsidised, enabled to live comfortably, if not quite extravagantly; we'd enjoy the status, rights and privileges of junior faculty. In exchange, we'd be expected to conduct at least two courses per term - to undergraduates or, as part of a community relations exercise, to local adults.

The objective, obviously, was to turn us not just into turbocharged professional scholars, but also into the vanguard of the country's higher education, a new breed of trendy university teachers - finely tuned and honed precision instruments calibrated to imbue taste, discrimination, uplift, moral and aesthetic judgement into subsequent generations. Within some three years, of course, under Nixon's administration, America came to decide that subsequent generations didn't really need taste, discrimination, uplift, moral or aesthetic judgement after all; and my colleagues and I, after having five-figure sums invested in each of us, found ourselves cast adrift in a glutted job market for which we were labelled - a new death-knell among words - 'overqualified'. We were to become, in short, a unique species of white elephant engendered by American society of the late sixties. During my last spring in Chicago, however, there was, needless to say, no way of foreseeing that.

I was twenty-four then, still revelling in unbridled fecklessness, in an utter lack of responsibility; I was accountable to no one, constrained by no obligations or commitments save those I chose voluntarily to incur. Yet had Nina been alone, I'd've tried to bring her with me. I plaited elaborate fantasies about doing so, conveniently neglecting to consider how misplaced she'd be in the milieu for which I was bound. In reality, however, I recognised how futile my scenarios were. Nina wasn't alone. She had her children and two decrepit parents to look after. Even if I'd wanted to do so, I couldn't possibly have supported that chaotic household, and I couldn't expect her to abandon it. I'd therefore resigned myself to a wrenching, poignant, operatic separation. Painful though parting would be, I'd ride - or drive - stalwartly off into the sunset. Or rather, since the sun's trajectory ran counter to my personal mythology, the sunrise. And at intervals, I told myself, I'd pelt westwards again, and we'd glory in wildly passionate reunions, and one day perhaps - when her parents died, or her children were grown enough to be packed off to school, or I'd somehow raised enough money to make it feasible - we'd be together again, on a more permanent basis.

All of that, however, lay in the future. My vista of it was now suddenly eclipsed by more immediate, more tangible concerns, beyond which I couldn't see. Before I could even begin to actualise my fantasies, there'd be the summer, and the impending 1st of August. I realised, of course, that if Chicago erupted in flames, I could hardly, single-handedly, ensure Nina's safety, still less that of her family. Not even my chivalric pretensions could accommodate such naïveté. But that didn't mean I could leave her alone, to the mercy of whatever upheaval might occur. I toyed with sundry contingency plans - renting a car, for example, and bundling her, as well as her domestic establishment, to some provisional refuge, some motel in the suburbs for a night or two. I lacked money, however, even for so modest an expedient; and she, in any case, when I tried to broach the subject, turned furiously adamant. She refused stubbornly to budge. She'd lived in the city all her life, she maintained stoutly. The flat above Reggie's was her home, and she wasn't going to let herself be bullied out of it - by me, by the police, by a horde of rioters, by anyone else.

There ensued for me one of the most anguished bouts of soul-searching I've had occasion to experience. I understood well enough - understood with a grim, metallically lustreless lucidity - what remaining in Chicago would entail. For the police, I harboured only antipathy and hostility. My loyalties - only incidentally political - should properly have aligned me with the blacks from the bar, my friends, my drinking companions, my 'blood brothers'. But my loyalty to Nina ran deeper still. I'd already begun to realise what I came to appreciate more fully in retrospect. Not only was I profoundly attached to my head waitress, I also owed her an immense debt. I might still, in some recess of my psyche, cherish Ilona's mummified image. I might still be capable of playing juvenile practical jokes. But in the course of my liaison with Nina, I'd learned more, grown more, matured more, come to understand more about the dynamics governing sexual relationships, than in the whole of my previous amorous career.

In the end, I realised, the decision wasn't mine to make. It'd already effectively been made for me - not by any conscious or voluntary process on my part, but by some unchallengeable inner imperative. Even though I might be elsewhere by the autumn, I'd have to be in Chicago during the first week of August.

It wasn't the most comforting of prospects, but I found it impossible to evade. I'd do whatever I could, of course, to avoid violence and keep Nina out of harm's way. If that wasn't manageable, however, and if the predicted holocaust occurred, I'd have no choice - I'd be in her flat, with my rifle and revolver, aligned with the police whom I despised, aligned with Al Hollis whom I despised even more, against my black friends and 'blood brothers'. If they peppered her windows from the derelict cinema opposite, I'd be crouching in those windows, shielded by barricades of mattresses, shooting back. And if they stormed the building, I'd be defending it - or defending Nina's premises, at least - with my weapons. In retrospect, of course, it all sounds garishly histrionic, melodramatic. At the time, however, it seemed to me the most savagely raw existential situation of my life.

For reasons of their own - part loyalty to me, part sense of adventure - Patterson and Radetzky also resolved to remain in Chicago, if only until the crisis, assuming there was one, had passed. Before the proverbial shit hit the fan, though, I'd have time for a holiday. In mid-June, therefore, leaving Patterson to hold down the flat, keep a general eye on things and continue as manager in the bar, Radetzky and I returned east. Borrowing against the autumn's anticipated income, I contrived the down-payment on something to replace my defunct Volvo.

I'd wanted, of course, a vehicle in keeping with my nominally fastidious automotive standards - a sleek and stylish European tourer ideally, a steel fist in a velvet glove, rather than the brute vulgarity of some American Panzer. Unfortunately, fiscal considerations inhibited the free exercise of my taste, dictating reluctant compromise. I test-drove assorted exemplars of senile, sometimes moribund, elegance - clapped-out Porsches, Mercedeses, Jaguars, even P.1800s. But anything second-hand would've entailed considerable risk, especially in cross-country jaunts. Outside metropolitan centres, service for foreign exotica was virtually unobtainable in those days, when gas-guzzling mastodons hogged the roads and anything not Detroit-made was viewed with squint-eyed suspicion as unpatriotic. To break down in such places as Iowa, Utah or the Dakotas was tantamount to being shipwrecked and marooned. I therefore capitulated to gross common sense and acted with ignominious practicality - I bought a new, metallic blue Mustang, which came with a warranty valid at Ford dealerships in even the most parochial of hick towns. It proved, in fact, a worthy enough machine. It was to serve me nobly, indeed heroically, enduring a martyrdom of three years and ninety thousand miles. When I finally got rid of it, it behaved like a faithful specimen of the beast whose name it bore, promptly dying - a sort of automotive embolism - on its new owner. But during the whole of our time together, I couldn't help resenting it, regarding it scornfully as 'a housewife's car'. I treated it callously and insensitively, never accorded it its due, never quite forgave it for not being at least a Datsun 240Z.

In the Mustang, Radetzky and I drove west, to California, to visit JT Swift. Ilona by then had absconded, was wafting around Yucatan and New Orleans, trying to gatecrash the numinous under the auspices of a particularly sinister cult. JT had a new paramour, with whom he shared a bungalow at Half Moon Bay, just south of San Francisco. With ironic detachment, we all attended the occasional 'be-in' at Golden Gate Park. We explored orgiastic, wildly pulsating, strobe-lit nightspots, where the apocalyptic decibels compelled me to wear cigarette filters as improvised earplugs. We wandered the warrens of Haight-Ashbury, a depressing wasteland inundated with spaced-out waifs and runaways, hysterical teeny-boppers and, it seemed, escaped troupes of medieval mummers teleported through some species of time warp. No collective enlightenment irradiated the air, no nimbus of Nirvana. There was only an all-pervasive lostness, a frenzied flight from selfhood, a ferocious conviction of having discovered something which, somehow, wasn't living up to expectations.

A week or so before our arrival, a new drug, supposedly more potent than acid, had made its début - something called STP, a designation previously used for a promiscuously advertised engine additive. The old variety of STP allegedly pepped up tired motors by scouring away deposits of sludge and carbon. In fact, it caused valves and pistons to burn themselves out more quickly. The new stuff had a similar effect on people's brainpans. Orbiting on it one night, some poor fool had free-fallen into a classic 'bad trip'. A second fool had administered the standard remedy for 'bad trips' on acid, the tranquilliser Thorizen, and the first fool had reacted traumatically - had gone into convulsions and, his 'trip' re-routed to oblivion, had died on the spot. In consequence, the shabby litter-strewn streets were awash with crazed-eyed, drunkenly weaving figures wearing T-shirts emblazoned in admonition: *'I'M ON STP. DO NOT GIVE ME THORIZEN.'*

By this time, our own interest in drugs had almost completely atrophied, and I found 'The Scene', as everyone called it, incipiently inimical. To become part of it, one had to relinquish form, in one's personal life and in art, to a degree that made me balk. My values had by then defined themselves as what might be called 'European aesthetic bohemian'. Form, tradition, cultural heritage, *Kultur* in the old Germanic sense, all figured prominently for me. In Haight-Ashbury, none of these things was, according to the fashionable word, 'relevant'. San Francisco comprised a world suspended precariously in an essentially seedy present overlaid with a brittle day-glow patina - a world devoid of past and future, as ultimately purposeless as a self-induced orgasm and decidedly less exhilarating. Like consciousness itself under the influence of acid, the milieu lacked all capacity for synthesis - all capacity for relating the moment it was living to the moment that preceded, the moment that would follow.

If only because there was so much cannabis around, I still occasionally got stoned. More frequently, I got drunk. Sometimes, I got both; and I spent one particularly luminous stoned and drunken night sprawled on the beach at Half Moon Bay, watching the moon-silvered Pacific roll in to lap my toes, talking at elaborate and bare-souled length to JT's dog, a golden Labrador - the most patient, attentive and, so it seemed at the time, understanding listener I'd ever had, a veritable therapist. My most dramatic alteration of consciousness resulted, however, from a near-lethal onslaught of food poisoning, induced by over-indulgence in toxic apricots. JT, also prostrated by the affliction, christened it the Rocky Mountain Scrowtch.

I was still Scrowtch-ridden - still shivering, still quaking, still rubber-kneed, still semi-delirious - when Radetzky loaded me into the Mustang and we drove headlong back to Chicago. My malady notwithstanding, I was determined to be there in time to embark with Nina on (*pace* Browning) our last binge together - and, if necessary, play my part in the impending confrontation. We arrived on 29th July. The city was tense, the general atmosphere as if a gunfight were scheduled. Thus must Tombstone have felt on the eve of the shootout at the OK Corral.

During the next two and a half days, the bar was uncharacteristically empty. None of the black militants who'd planned the 'insurrection' was present, but I assumed they were busy elsewhere, attending to last-minute details, adding the final touches, the culminating flourishes, to their design. Blue-and-white patrol cars were more in evidence than usual. At intervals, too, conspicuously inconspicuous unmarked vehicles crawled warily up and down the streets, clean-shaven white faces peering from the windows with stony watchfulness - the unmistakable deportment of the FBI conducting surveillance while aspiring to invisibility.

On the morning of the 1st, I checked and cleaned my guns, loaded the revolver. Around mid-afternoon, I joined Patterson and Radetzky in the bar. Apart from Nina, Terence Mulligan and the other staff, the place was utterly deserted - not a single patron, a single customer. Among the allies forced upon me by circumstance, I'd expected to find Al Hollis; I'd imagined him rallying to Nina's defence with the whole of his travelling-Wild-West-Show armoury. Not even Hollis was around, however, all police leave - that of Transit Police as well - having been cancelled. Tension burgeoned in the humid and clammy silence, a sense of latent smouldering violence that reminded me of pool halls and greasy-spoon diners in Mississippi. On the jukebox, Baez was singing - *'There but for fortune go you and I...'*. Outside, gusts of heat made the vista seem to waver and ripple like a tapestry, behind which something lurked, awaiting its cue to emerge. The blue-and-white patrol cars continued to prowl.

Chatting desultorily, swapping quips and anecdotes, playing endless games of poker and chess, drinking relatively little, we managed to while away the afternoon, the early evening. As dusk seeped into the air, Radetzky returned upstairs to our flat, wading through welters of wadded newspaper and positioning himself at the window of the front room, overlooking the street. I collected my guns and joined Nina in her premises one floor below, her parents and children having been banished to the rear of the apartment. Along with Terence Mulligan, Patterson remained in the bar. Thus we awaited the anticipated *Götterdämmerung*.

Nothing happened. Nothing whatever. Not, at any rate, for another year. During the course of that week, both Newark and Detroit exploded in convulsions of blood and flame. Death moved through the ghettos with the brisk efficiency of a census-taker, whole blocks were afire, martial law was declared, police and National Guard thronged the streets, cordoned off entire quarters, shot looters on sight. If I recall correctly, there were also serious disturbances in

Harlem and in Roxbury-Dorchester, the black sections of New York and Boston.

Ferment and sporadic flurries of carnage continued for the duration of the summer. Towards the end of August, I was back on the East Coast, driving through riot-scarred ruins of Plainfield, New Jersey, when I heard a resounding splang and the Mustang juddered. Guessing instinctively what'd happened, I hunched as low as visibility allowed, accelerated with squealing tyres. A mile or so away, I stopped, got out to inspect the car and found a dent in the roof directly above my head - a ricochet, to judge from its shallowness, or perhaps a spent round, but still potentially deadly. In Chicago, however, the night of the 1st of August proved a thunderous anticlimax.

During the fortnight that followed, we learned why. The explanation was ludicrously and outrageously simple - so much so that we didn't at first believe it. A discreet check, however, revealed the improbable rumours to be true. Throughout the city, meeting places for black militants - bars, pool halls, nightclubs, cafés and restaurants - had been bugged. With Melvin Bloss' assent and co-operation, so had Reggie's. In each alcove, in each corner and along each wall, there were recessed niches, covered by panes of imitation stained glass. Behind each such pane, a transmitter had been installed. During the last three nights of July, all known agitators and activists had quietly been picked up. They'd been charged with a diverse spectrum of delinquencies, real and fictitious, from piddling misdemeanours to conspiracy. Few of these charges were to stick, but they'd kept the ringleaders off the streets and rendered the 'insurrection' headless. Thus decapitated, it'd collapsed - leaving my flatmates and me feeling like asses, but relieved asses.

When I look back on that ignominious dénouement, I can see it, and much of my comportment during it, as laughable. I can adopt an attitude of detached irony, mixed with embarrassment, towards my own macho posturing, my own impetuous romanticism, my own zealous eagerness to play the rôle of knight-errant or hired gunslinger. And I confess myself abashed as well at my readiness to re-enact some fanciful heroic saga, to turn my quotidian milieu into the stuff of legend - Rourke's Drift, Lucknow, Mafeking, Tobruk, the Belogorsky Fortress commemorated by Pushkin in *The Captain's Daughter*. But thus, after all, were Troy and Derry transmuted into myth.

At the same time, I'm also pervasively aware of how those days, and the decisions imposed on me by those days, established a pattern that's obtained ever since - a pattern that's governed my attitude towards politics and all things political. For if Chicago had immersed me in politics, it'd also taught me that I personally possessed no politics. In future, I'd often take a stand on one or another specific political issue, but I'd refuse to enslave myself to the artificial, spuriously logical consistency demanded of its adherent by any comprehensive political programme, any comprehensive political orientation. My stand on a given political issue would be, ultimately, only a matter of opinion. Such an opinion might be tepidly or fervently held, might remain private or be forcefully, even passionately, expressed. But it'd remain a matter of opinion, an intellectual stance.

Beyond all opinions, all stances, I reserved the traditional artistic prerogative of straddling the fence - of placing myself above the political arena, assessing the entire vista displayed before me and, from this vantage point, bearing witness. I reserved the artistic right to Olympian aloofness, the right to take equal pleasure, as Keats says, in the creation of an Iago or an Imogen - and the right to speak with equal eloquence or sympathy for both. More than ever, that right seemed to me integral to the creative process.

And yet I'd also now come to recognise how easily I could be pushed, knocked or driven from my fence, or have it demolished under me. Once a political issue became personal, for example - once it harmed or threatened me as an individual, harmed or threatened people or things I loved - I'd be deposed, forcibly, from my neutrality. Once I were so deposed, I'd become, like it or not, *engagé*. My position would no longer be one of mere opinion, but of commitment. Commitment, in other words, would be determined not by political allegiances, but by personal loyalties, by moral and emotional imperatives more deeply rooted, more visceral, than any intellectual opinion. And commitment would demand action on my part such as no mere opinion ever could. The action dictated by commitment wouldn't stem from ideological principle, but from personal crusade or personal vendetta. And whoever provoked such action - whoever denied me the right to straddle my fence and tried to coerce me from it - would become, automatically, the enemy.

X

To exasperated New Yorkers who endured it regularly, the Long Island Expressway was known in those days as the L.I.E. - or, rather more trenchantly, as 'the Big Lie'. Its official designation, certainly, was a misnomer. At most daylight hours, the artery was congealed, if not sclerotic. Interminable tapeworming tailbacks, slowly oozing seepages of bumper-to-bumper traffic, a ubiquitous blatting of horns and a chronic fug of exhaust fumes rendered suggestions of 'express' travel downright laughable. Any such suggestion added insult if not to injury, at least to the likelihood thereof. When not constipated, the Expressway was at that time the most notoriously lethal road in the country, a Passchendaele of thoroughfares. I don't think there was a single foot of the central dividing rail whose rust-pitted glinting metal hadn't been banged, dented, crumpled, smashed, mangled or in some other fashion marked by the impact of delinquent cars. It provided a perpetual and sobering reminder of vulnerability, of mortality - more effective than any signs of billboards warning one to 'drive defensively' or reduce speed.

Forty-five miles from Manhattan, at what was then the Expressway's easternmost exit, one turned off and threaded a path north. Almost at once, the roads became denuded, winding placidly between flat swampland, small pastures and imposing tracts of unsullied woods. Through festooned foliage, one might glimpse a scimitar curve of coastline, flashing scintillas of sea unfurling across Long Island Sound towards Connecticut. Sedate white houses, often mansion-sized, stood embowered in greenery, insulated from passing vehicles by long aprons of hedge-fringed lawn. At intervals between forested expanses, there nestled self-consciously quaint little villages and hamlets, sometimes sporting pseudo-Indian names - Poquott, for example, or Setauket. Some overlooked the water, boasted toy harbours or marinas and catered, during the holiday season, to the more domesticated species of tourist, thriving on antique shops, on fresh fish stalls and restaurants acclaimed by gourmets. Some were less hospitable to visitors, remaining primly buttoned within themselves, looking newly swept, painted and polished each morning - neatly tidy scale-models intended more for display than for use or habitation. Some, with aspirations to historical pedigree, strained for a supposedly 'colonial' quality, but rarely attained more than a certain vulgarity, a certain gaucheness or protuberant kitsch. Above the entrance to the Post Office in one, an immense mechanical bald eagle laboured to emulate a clock cuckoo, wheezing every day at noon and creakily flapping its plaster and wire wings.

Amidst these bucolic surroundings sprawled the university. I've not seen the place for many years and dare not imagine how it looks now. At the time, much of it was still a construction site. One proceeded towards it for some two miles through a woodland-shagged wilderness rendered eerie, brooding and tenebrous at night by a total absence of streetlamps - an atmosphere worthy of the draculoid Carpathians. The road, wide and curved like a boomerang, conduced to drag races, timing of 0-60 figures and - until some frumpy bureaucratic killjoy installed traffic signals - a general Grand Prix mentality. Midway along it, a sneaky little entrance, veiled by leafage, led to a gatehouse and an unoccupied sentry box, then to a long drive that unravelled in loops and arabesques around a vast bowl-shaped amphitheatre hacked out of the enveloping trees.

One was here confronted by a vista of craters and excavations, raw red earth, mournful mud and pungent puddles. Yolk-yellow diggers and bulldozers lurched, lumbered and crawled about, grinding their gears, engaged apparently in weird mating rituals amidst steel scaffolding and skeletons, stumps of unfinished buildings, litters of pipes, paint drums, cables, girders, cinder blocks and other materials. No dreaming spires would rise here, no Gothic arches with florid embellishment, only something resembling a factory - which, of course, the place ultimately was. My department was housed in one of the few completed structures, an edifice of gruesome blood-coloured brick in a style that might be described as neo-penal - or, more accurately perhaps, late brutalist.

Here, I was to spend the next three years. Although physically an eyesore, the school was a typical 'country club university' of the era. Except for a desolate railway station half a mile distant, the place lacked all public transport, and this handicapped lowly bachelor degree candidates, who were forbidden cars. Faculty, however, and those of us in the graduate programme, revelled in a relaxed, enviable, even sybaritic, lifestyle. We barrelled at breakneck speed around the curling country lanes. We rented not apartments, but whole houses -

often opulent houses, which two, three or four of us would occupy for a year at a time before moving on. Whenever we wished, we had privileged access to the department's private Gatsby-vintage mansion overlooking the Sound, as well as to its exclusive beach - serenely remote both from boisterous undergraduates and from bumptious local philistines with squalling infants. We luxuriated in leisurely champagne breakfasts, in trendy 'brunches', in barbecues with games of badminton and lawn darts, in lazy afternoon parties spent lounging in garden chaises with coolly clinking iced drinks. On occasion, there'd be more raucous weekend-long debauches, with inebriates splayed on the grass, on the roofs, boots and bonnets of parked cars. It was all a hedonistic contrast to Chicago, though no less decadent.

Amongst those in the graduate programme, one divulged weakness or vulnerability at one's peril. I therefore perfected a haughty, inscrutable, authoritative, even autocratic, persona - the persona, in effect, of a magus. It was only a spurious semblance of Fausthood, but it stood me in reasonably good stead amid the unique variety of snobbery that prevailed. Contrary to what one might expect, this wasn't a conventional intellectual snobbery. My friends and I had been guilty of that as undergraduates in Boston - accepting or rejecting people, acknowledging or dismissing them, respecting or despising them on the basis of what they had or hadn't read. In Chicago, that snobbery had been dispelled and supplanted by a different kind, a snobbery rooted in streetwise efficiency, in one's capacity to comport oneself with the appropriate 'cool'. On Long Island, the standards of neither Boston nor Chicago obtained. Streetwise efficiency was incidental, if not irrelevant. As for erudition, everyone in the programme had, of course, read everything, or was tacitly assumed to have done so; and it would've been ungracious, even churlish, to expose gaps that gaped under the patina of learning. The snobbery of the place rested on other things. On style. On flair. On a patent *savoir-faire,* a patent urbanity and sophistication. Most important of all, perhaps on charisma, on panache, on a distinctive and colourful individualism, on a flashy flamboyance of personality, on traits that allowed one to be regarded as a 'character'. These were the prerequisites for being 'one of us'; and for not displaying them, some eminently decent and intelligent people were patronised, ostracised, shunned or spurned.

If only ostensibly, I satisfied the necessary criteria. Fresh from my escapades in Chicago (which I deftly romanticised and mythologised), I cut, apparently, a dashing and swashbuckling enough figure on the scene - and possessed, I found, an element of *cachet*. I qualified, it seemed, as a suitably flamboyant personality, who brought a heady whiff of danger, of abrasiveness, of jaded adventurism, of life-lived-on-on-a-needlepoint intensity to the rarefied, sanitised and domesticated milieu. I added spice to gatherings; I was an adept *raconteur*, with a fashionable ironic detachment, a sensitivity to nuance and an eye for the droll; and my erudition, as well as the authority with which I asserted it, brooked no challenge. (Musil aided me as effectively here as he had in my evasion of the Draft.) In consequence, my social and amorous agendas were full - at least until an adulterous affair provoked a minor scandal and prompted most of the husbands in the programme to see me as a sort of pestiferous contagion, liable, if not quarantined, to infect their wives. But while my circle of friends and associates was wider than it'd been in Chicago, wider even perhaps than in my undergraduate days, few of those relationships ran very deep - or, for that matter, survived very long. In retrospect, I find it significant that of the numerous people I dined with, drank with, visited and received, whose homes I frequented, whose parties I attended, I've retained contact with only a single couple. Except for them, and one or two others perhaps, I forged no bonds as tenacious as those which, in the past, had bound me to Patterson, Radetzky and JT, to Ilona and Nina.

On the surface, at any rate, I enjoyed the years I spent on Long Island, but the enjoyment was of a brittle kind. The reality there, as I appreciated even then, was a hollow one, and dangerously incestuous to boot. As in many such 'closed' communities, isolation forced people into an artificial hothouse proximity, an intimacy imposed and symbiotic. By dint of this, one came to know more about others than one particularly wanted to know, and than they themselves wanted known. The result was a knowledge unaccompanied by warmth or genuine solicitude, an unavoidable invasion of privacy that inevitably fostered friction. It also, of course, fostered a sometimes frantic quest for diversion.

Not surprisingly, romantic imbroglios proliferated - dalliances, betrayals, swapping of partners, a piquant palette of *liaisons dangereuses*. In this country club for the latterday Laclos, love was played as a game, a sport which required skill, cunning, ruthlessness and much cynical calculation. It resembled, in effect, a complicated hybrid of chess, fencing, wrestling and football; and one had to be psychologically, as well as physically, dextrous in ducking, dodging, twisting and parrying. Essentially the same principles applied to professional academic intrigues. Cabals and counter-cabals were formed to modify or unmodify curricula, to support or shaft colleagues, to obtain or deny somebody's tenure or promotion, to oust fat Herman Blimmer, the gargoyle-shaped and bran-brained departmental chairman. There were orgies of petty sniping, backbiting, asp-tongued squabblings, squirtings of verbal vitriol. Repartée was conducted like a duel, and words were used in a fashion reminiscent of blades and projectiles in Chicago - to inflict wounds. As far as I know, there was never any actual recourse to rapiers or pistols. If there had been, I suspect, a fair number of us, including in all likelihood I myself, would've gone the way of Pushkin and Lermontov. But the air resounded constantly with fustian and umbrage, with the clack of charging hobby-horses, the clangour of clashing egos, the crunch of splintering self-esteem, the pop and hiss of deflating swank.

Ultimately, and despite the solemnity with which some people pursued these activities, it was all immense fun. It was also intoxicating. But it required an expenditure of much hectic and feverish energy, and it wasted a great deal of time. And the more one immersed oneself in it, the more it assumed a disproportionate importance, becoming a species of surrogate reality, a vicarious alternative to 'real life'. This tendency, of course, is endemic to academia. It was one of the factors that'd estranged me from professional colleagues in Chicago, had made the university there seem so febrile, so pallid, compared to the raw vivacity of the bar. But here, on Long Island, the tendency was all the more persuasive for being less stodgy, and all the more pervasive for being largely unchallenged; and I, having no Reggie's to serve as a corrective, allowed myself to succumb to it. Within the cocooned mandarin realm of the graduate programme, I therefore flirted, courted, intrigued and machinated with zest; I acquiesced in at least certain rules of the game and revelled in my sense of mastery. It was only in fitfully lucid moments that I'd wax nostalgic for Nina, for the pithier, more substantial diet of experience I'd left behind on the shores of Lake Michigan, and ask myself what I was doing in my new surroundings. But the sheer effortlessness of my existence, and the tang of amusements it offered, quickly placated such spasms of integrity. Thus I made my facile Faust-pact with '*der Geist, der stets verneint*' – the principle of detached cynical mocking laughter, whose icy gusts leave nothing unwithered, unshrivelled.

One of the few forms whereby the wider world encroached on us was politics. Inevitably, of course, people here played at politics as they played at other things. Politics were yet another aspect of reality to be manipulated, as if with tongs, from the comfort of a *chaise longue*. But so severe by then were the schisms fissuring American society that politics didn't always submit to such treatment. They sometimes impinged with a rude and ill-bred insistence of their own on our loftily sequestered demesne – and sometimes became crassly importunate.

Thus, for example, the Draft now began to prey increasingly on graduate students, deemed superfluous to the national welfare by more and more local boards. A number of individuals in the programme, previously immune, suddenly found themselves in jeopardy. The situation was more alarming in that the authorities had learned to twig most ploys and dodges. The routine I'd employed two years before probably wouldn't've worked any longer. Certainly it would've been much more difficult to carry off, would've been subjected to far closer and far more sceptical scrutiny. In their intemperate and impetuous zeal, my local Draft Board had in fact done me a favour, compelling me to dupe the system when the system was still susceptible to being duped.

From the security of my coveted 1-Y status, I watched anxiety flare rampant among my colleagues. There were periodic suicide attempts. There were three or four nervous breakdowns. And flight to Canada began to assume the proportions of an exodus. Some of us lent our services to the 'underground railway' of the time, shunting fugitives over the border to Toronto or Montreal. I made the drive to Toronto on three occasions. On the first, my passengers were a couple, recently married, both of them working for M.A.s in Victorian poetry and prose. After passing his pre-induction physical, after submitting numerous fruitless appeals, the young man's resorts had run out, and he'd been ordered to report for basic training.

I transported him and his wife through the frost-bound darkness, and we bade each other farewell, amid soiled rags of snow, in the gun-metal light of a bleak Canadian dawn. Only then did it occur to me that this couple were actually going into *exile*. The word printed itself in my mind, like the black-bordered lettering of an obituary. It jarred me. '*Exile*', in those days, was something one associated with the Soviet Union and her Eastern European satellites, with Castro's Cuba, with Franco's Spain, with military dictatorships in Latin America, with assorted other bullying totalitarian régimes of left or right. To use it in connection with the United States seemed grotesquely melodramatic, hyperbolic. And yet it was the only appropriate word. This young couple - essentially gentle creatures, who wanted nothing more presumptuous than to have children, raise a family, read and teach Trollope - were indeed being forced into *exile*.

The Draft displayed itself at its most barbarously obstreperous when it threatened Sidney and Vanessa, a British couple, exchange students working for their M.A. and Ph.D. respectively, and two of my closest friends in the programme. On arriving in the States with his student visa, Sidney'd been obliged to register with a local Draft Board. Six months later, he received notice to report for his pre-induction physical. All of us at first imagined there must've been some mistake. How could the military forcibly pressgang a foreign national? They could, it transpired. For the benefits, such as they were, of American 'higher education', one was expected to pay, if necessary, with one's life. It seemed a rather extortionate rate of exchange. At least Sidney had a recourse - if things became genuinely desperate, he and Vanessa could abscond back to England. He therefore had little to lose by gambling on a stratagem.

Drawing on my own expertise in such matters, I coached him in the acquisition of synthetic asthma. So did a friendly physician, who ministered to some of the graduate students and sympathised with Draft-dodgers. Sidney augmented our instruction with a fabricated case history and tips gleaned from medical texts. Having worked on the stage before, he rehearsed conscientiously, applying himself to his rôle with the earnest concentration and empathy of the method actor. One might drop by his and Vanessa's house of an evening and watch him perfecting his wheeze, sounding like a perforated pibroch.

On the day scheduled for his premiere, I picked him and Vanessa up in the Mustang. We paused for coffee and a last-minute briefing, then launched into our melodrama. I floored the car. All lights ablaze, horn braying, we blistered at apocalyptic pace down the forest-lined road to the university, skidded round the turn at the entrance in tyre-smoking Le Mans fashion, belted on past the gatehouse and a swivel of startled faces. Juddering to a halt at the infirmary, Vanessa and I unloaded our gasping, panting, bagpiping charge and helped him up the steps, where a gaggle of previously bored nurses promptly swooped upon him.

Leaving Vanessa at the desk to deal with whatever paperwork might be involved, I made my way to the office we shared in our department's building. I'd no sooner sat down at my desk than the telephone rang. Something was grievously wrong, Vanessa reported. I returned to the infirmary, and she explained. Sidney's performance had been, if anything, too impressive. They thought he was having a heart attack. We were ushered to an upstairs room and struggled to remain decorously grave-faced while a grim doctor assured us it could only have been a 'minor seizure'. Behind the man's white-coated back, Sidney lay cocooned in an oxygen tent, manifestly spaced out on the purest air, giggling, grinning at us happily and wagging a hand in welcome. When he received his 4-F classification, no Oscar could've been more resourcefully earned.

American society was by then more bitterly divided than it'd been since the Civil War a century before. At moments, indeed, it appeared to be verging on a new civil war - a conflict that would cut through the entire fabric of the nation, pitting not just states against one another, but members of the same community, the same family. Advocating withdrawal from Southeast Asia, Eugene McCarthy, as well as Bobby Kennedy until his assassination, had splintered the Democratic Party. Lyndon Johnson, estranged from much of his formerly faithful constituency, moped and sulked and declared his intention of not seeking a second term of office.

'Must be something his speechwriter slipped in without him knowing it,' Vanessa drawled when he made his announcement on radio.

At ground level, gangs of construction workers - so-called 'hard hats', propelled by the inflammable vapour they called patriotism - were running amok in Wall Street, clubbing and crippling student demonstrators. Similar assaults followed elsewhere, becoming a fashionable alternative to bowling. The ghettos were now chronically asmoulder. Virtually every college and university across the country was in ferment. When more illustrious schools upstaged them in protesting against the war, our own undergraduates found other things about which to agitate - the mud miring the campus, for example.

The liberal intelligentsia, particularly on the East and West Coasts, were becoming more confident, more vociferous, more eloquently persuasive, more impossible to ignore. From behind façades of 'impartiality' and 'objective reporting', newspapers, radio stations and television networks sniped snidely among themselves. Even Hollywood was polarised, Hope and Heston and their ilk being aligned against Newman, Redford and Beatty. Leering and hectoring as always, playing cravenly to his audience, Johnny Carson invited Baez on to his self-styled chat show, determined publicly to humiliate her. With a mournfully sweet smile, she summarily demolished him. I can't now recall his precise words; but with his customary vulgar joviality, he tried to goad her, jeering at how little, through the centuries, non-violence had accomplished. '*Of course*,' she replied demurely. '*I don't deny it. I can't think of anything that's been more futile - except violence, maybe.*'

In the meantime, Saigon was still groggy from the hammering it'd suffered during the Tet offensive, a *contretemps* not even the propaganda machine could transmute into victory. And in the imaginative wastes of Long Island, a handful of us went to sneer at stalwart John Wayne intrepidly bashing celluloid gooks and slopes - gooks and sloped paid to play dead - in *The Green Berets*. Before the opening credits, a raspy phonograph, concealed somewhere in the projection booth, ground out the national anthem, and a cohort of drunken, flag-flapping sots lurched loyally to their feet. When we refused to follow suit, an incipient brawl ensued. It was averted only by the cinema's manager, who - gung-ho himself but more worried about blood spattering his recently refurbished décor - threatened to eject all of us and cancel the film.

This less-than-epic confrontation was symptomatic of rapidly deteriorating relations between the university and the adjacent community. The relations in question had attained, by now, a state of open hostility. Ensconced in their mock-colonial shops and houses, the local people were stolidly conservative anyway, stolidly behind what they regarded as Uncle Sam's divinely ordained anti-Communist crusade in Southeast Asia. From the very beginning, they'd objected to the institution being constructed in their previously tranquil midst. They'd been mollified by the promise of a sober William-and-Mary-style school on a sedate campus reminiscent of quaint Williamsburg. What they got was a sprawling, unruly, loud-mouthed Berkeley-style school on a campus reminiscent of tacky Levitown, and the betrayal rankled. Luridly fantastic images of the place circulated unchecked throughout the surrounding towns and villages. It was perceived as a proverbial den of iniquity, where spoiled, depraved and degenerate wastrels smoked dope, popped pills, wallowed in obscene saturnalia, studied pornographic books, plotted sedition and behaved generally in a scandalously un-American fashion. Not surprisingly, therefore, the incumbent District Attorney, standing for re-election, sought to score points with his constituency by targeting the citadel of sin. In doing so, he projected the citadel on to the front page of every major newspaper in the country, and the television screen as well.

Conscious of its parvenu status, the university had been trying assiduously to place itself on the academic map – to establish itself as a respected centre of learning, to earn a prestige comparable to that of other and older institutions. To this end, it'd recruited one of the most nominally illustrious faculties in the country, a staff star-studded with luminaries, with august personages of the Crispin Whelk variety. Like Whelk in Chicago, these figures seldom contributed more than the lustre and sonority of their names. They'd swan out from Manhattan once or twice a week, deliver themselves of a perfunctory pontification, then return home – and receive, for their token endeavour, staggering *prima donna* salaries. The lavish expenditure produced negligible results. Despite the glamorous reputations associated with it, the school continued to languish in obscurity. The 'Big Bust', however, as it came to be known, obtained for the place a celebrity – or notoriety – that no academic achievement ever did. It was the first of what, during the next few years, was to be a series of paramilitary raids on university campuses.

On a spring night towards the end of my first year there, a veritable task force was assembled, armed with secret indictments from a local Grand Jury. At three in the morning, crammed into sixty vehicles, some three hundred police mobilised with masked headlamps on the approach road. At a pre-arranged signal, they swooped. To all appearances, the operation might've been modelled on an SS or Gestapo raid in films - the Night of the Long Knives, for example, as depicted by Visconti in *The Damned*. Slumber was ripped asunder by skirling sirens, the crackling static of official radios, the strobing pulsations of blue and red lights. Shadowy figures surged onto the campus, fanned out through the darkness, swarmed into lounges and dormitories. Ponderous feet pounded reverberatively along corridors, clumped clangorously up stairs. Doors quaked under brusque peremptory knocks, and those that remained shut were burst violently open, smashed in, kicked down. If much of this was dramatically spectacular, so, too, was the scale of the overkill. In the end, some two dozen students were arrested, charged with using or selling marijuana and led away in handcuffs.

None of us in the graduate programme resided on campus. I lived, I suppose, as close as anybody, sharing a house with two colleagues some four or five miles distant. I knew nothing of what'd happened, therefore, until the telephone drilled into my sleep. Like other teaching assistants, I received several calls from panic-stricken or outraged undergraduates, students in my classes. By the time my companions and I reached the scene, the police were already leaving and made no attempt to interfere with our arrival. The backlash, however, was already setting in, with electrifying energy and rapidity.

By morning, the vote-hungry District Attorney must already have had some inkling of the genie he'd released from its bottle. The university had erupted in riot. There being nothing else accessible, expendable and combustible, the gatehouse had been set aflame. A 'general strike' had been called, and barricades were being erected in anticipation of a second police assault - which, needless to say, never came. Instead, the media turned up *en masse*, with proffered microphones, sound equipment, whirring and clicking cameras, even a helicopter stuttering overhead to film the spectacle in aerial perspective. There followed caravans of vehicles, carloads and chartered busloads of sympathisers converging from distances of fifty, even a hundred, miles. All day, they continued to arrive, inundating the site, churning the mud into more of a quagmire than usual - students from Columbia, NYU and other schools, rock and folk singers, film and television personalities, poets and novelists, hippies, yippies, professional agitators, Black Panthers and militants of diverse other hues. Slinking amongst them, of course, there were the customary undercover operatives and *agents provocateurs*. A chaos compounded of outrage and the spirit of carnival prevailed for the better part of a fortnight. The community's collective blood pressure rocketed.

In the aftermath of the fuss, the university's administration, duly intimidated, abjectly endeavoured to appease the irate authorities. To preclude any further crackdowns, a sop was offered to the apoplectic District Attorney. A private 'security force' would be recruited from the neighbourhood, volunteers specially trained in sniffing out drugs. They consisted, for the most part, of the local unemployed - ex-cops, retired night watchmen, jobless construction workers, former bus conductors, taxi drivers and railway guards, a few younger yokels fresh out of secondary school. They were uniformed, so to speak, in spiffy maroon blazers of collegiate cut with yellow insignia on the biceps, and they sniffed quite literally and in earnest - much of their instruction entailed learning to detect, with the naked nose, the bouquet of cannabis. Among their various tasks was that of keeping strangers off the campus at night - unauthorised visitors who might be hard-core rabble-rousers. But their primary brief was to patrol, with finely tuned nostrils, the dormitories, the lounges, libraries and lavatories, the paths between the buildings, the mud, most of all the surrounding woods, where amorous couples went to tryst, court, cavort, copulate and get stoned.

The 'Sniffer Squad', as it was called in derision, initially made little impact and accomplished nothing. On several occasions, its members were mischievously duped by oregano and accordingly embarrassed. Within a month, however, the bumbling cadre had been re-christened the 'Goon Squad', and complaints about it began to proliferate. Goons were accused of bullying, of ogling offensively, of harassing couples in the woods, of conducting searches in which girls were groped, of punching one youth in the stomach and generally comporting themselves in a fashion only to be expected of their kind. Seeking redress of such grievances, upset and indignant students appealed primarily to my colleagues and me. They invoked us because we wielded authority, while being closer to them in age and attitudes than more senior faculty.

With a vigour stimulated by ennui, we turned the issue into a *cause célèbre,* devising a scheme of blatant provocation and entrapment. Mustered into an *ad hoc* commando squad, a dozen of us assembled, on an appointed night, at a mutually convenient tavern. We'd contrived (with minimal effort on my part) to make ourselves appear as sleazy, as dishevelled, as unsavoury, as sinister and suspicious-looking as possible. In a cavalcade of cars, we proceeded to the university's approach road, parked and began to fumble our way through the woods. Beyond reared the buildings of the campus, squat hulks shaped out of the darkness by the glow of their windows. Mist ghosted eerily between the trees, draped itself from branches like filaments of uncongealed ectoplasm; and our phalanx, in its progress, became fragmented into several smaller units.

As was usually the case when I participated in 'political' activity of this kind, I'd had an ulterior motive for my involvement. To be more precise, I harboured designs on a specific woman, one of our number, and welcomed the prospect of co-blundering with her through a nocturnal forest. Unfortunately, there was a logistic cock-up, she got separated from me in the gloom and was dragged off by her husband with another section of our strike force. Clawing through the undergrowth, I found myself attended only by Roland, one of the two colleagues with whom I shared a house, and Thelma, a murderably maternal woman with the muscular equipment of a sphinx. She, at the time, was incubating a doctoral dissertation on the Brontës, had muddled my image in her mind with Heathcliff's and evolved an incommodious infatuation for me.

There must've been paths, but we failed to find them in the enveloping murk. Instead, we had to thread a precarious passage between treacherous low-lurking boughs, pick our steps over malevolently jutting roots, disengage ourselves from the briers and brambles that snagged our clothes. We were roughly halfway to where the lights of the campus winked and beckoned when we heard something thrashing and flailing towards us through the undergrowth. We stopped, screened by foliage, and waited.

Out of the gloom loomed a goon - a runt of a goon, in fact, diminutive, balding of pate, one hand raised to keep the spectacles straddling his nose from falling off. He seemed to have a fertile fantasy life. Thinking himself alone and unobserved, he was practising Western-style fast draws - assuming a gunfighter's poised crouch, whipping his electric torch out of his pocket and making explosive fart sounds with puckered lips, like those of a pistol with a silencer.

Potty though he might be, however, his appearance placed me in a quandary. Was I to be righteously and responsibly political, or simply antic? To be righteously and responsibly political would've entailed something like, say, clasping Thelma in a feigned (for me, at any rate) embrace and hoping the intruder would pester us. With unimpeachable evidence of harassment, we could then proceed to call him and his entire cadre to account. But Thelma was too unpalatable and too uncuddlesome for the conscientious exercise required. Politics didn't justify so drastic a martyrdom on my part. And my romantic interests were too emphatically, too single-mindedly, directed elsewhere. Might Thelma embrace Roland? Or he her? Not a hope. She was already clamping herself to my arm with what seemed some sort of lethal glue.

I hesitated, therefore, only until the goon had virtually stumbled over us. I then jack-in-the-boxed up in front of him. He jerked back with a semi-strangled yelp which defies orthographic transcription and with a sharp intake of breath. I glazed my eyes, as I'd done with the three neo-Nazi louts in Chicago, raised one finger in the air like a candle and began, in a sepulchral voice, to intone

Yeats at his most weirdly uncanny:

> I saw a staring virgin stand
> Where holy Dionysus died,
> And tear the heart out of his side,
> And lay the heart upon her hand
> And bear that beating heart away;
> And then did all the Muses sing
> Of Magnus Annus at the spring,
> As though God's death were but a play.

As goon and loon, we faced each other for a frozen moment. He gaped, slack-jawed. I've no idea who or what he thought I was – perhaps the officiant of some infernal coven about to perform a ritual sacrifice. In any case, he made a rather wobbly sign of the cross, edged slowly backwards, half-tripped over a root, turned and scuttled away.

'You shouldn't've done that!' Thelma hissed, then rounded with perplexed dismay on Roland, who was cackling maniacally behind us.

Before I could reply, the underbrush seethed again, and the goon reappeared, with a larger comrade in tow.

'What da hell d'ya tink you're doin'?' he demanded in a querulous voice, only slightly emboldened by reinforcements.

'Reciting Yeats,' I said scornfully. 'You didn't imagine it was Wordsworth, did you? I might also be able to offer you a bargain on some Rilke. *"Wer, wenn ich shriee, hörte mich denn aus der Engel Ordnungen...?"'*

A pause, broken only by Roland's sniggering. The goon flicked a nervous glance at his comrade, who remained lugubriously silent, then faced me again, shining his electric torch into my eyes. I countered it by donning my dark glasses.

'Ya tink you'se some kinda wise guy?'

'It's my business to be wise,' I stated, trying also to be as insolent as possible.

'Ya betta come along wid us.'

'Where?'

'Backta da dormitories.'

'I don't live in the dormitories.'

'Ya don't live on da campus here?'

'No. Why would I want to do that?'

He grinned with unconcealed triumph. If I had no affiliation with the university – if I were an outsider, a visitor, say, from Columbia or NYU – he'd be subject to even fewer constraints than if I were an undergraduate.

'In dat case, you'se is comin' wid us,' he repeated, more menacingly this time. 'An' I mean right now! We got percedures for dealin' wid people who ain't got no business here.'

We might, I suppose, have played along – let them lead us to the dormitories, let them start to interrogate us or worse, then confront them with the enormity of their *faux pas*. But by baiting them, I'd cost us the moral high ground. If they'd molested us without cause, we'd've had them hoisted, maroon blazers flagrantly flapping, on their own petards. Now, however, as I had to admit, they were acting under severe and somewhat unusual provocation. The hell with it, I decided, tiring of the game.

'As a matter of fact,' I said, producing my identity card and holding it under the goon's nose while he focused his torch on it, 'I *do* have business here. More constructive than yours, I expect. I'm faculty. You have no authority over me.'

He squinted at my identity card again, then blinked, palpably wilting with chagrin.

'Oh,' he muttered. 'Jeez, I'm sorry 'bout dat, sir. We...er, . . didn't know. Ya shoulda tol' us. Yeah, ya shoulda tol' us. But it's awright. Ya jus' go on wid...wid your poetry readin' was it?'

I stepped back and Thelma, as if on cue, delivered a sententious hectoring lecture - how serious complaints had been lodged, how we'd undertaken to investigate the matter, how there'd be dire consequences should any further untoward incidents occur. Chastened and badly henpecked, the two goons slunk away to carry the word to their fellows. Roland, Thelma and I continued through the woods, emerged onto the campus and rejoined the rest of our party in one of the dormitory lounges. By that time, of course, every goon on duty was aware of our presence and our identity. Most of them kept studiously at a distance, or out of sight. The few we encountered were abjectly obsequious.

Thus did I scupper the operation. Roland succinctly summed up the night's endeavour:

'Seldom in the course of human conflict have so many Don Quixotes assembled in one place to attack one small windmill.'

Despite Thelma's querulous recriminations, however, I was unrepentant. If I were prepared to become politically *engagé* for romantic reasons, I was equally prepared to disengage for reasons inimical to romance. My politics, such as they were - or weren't - might be inconsistent, but not my amorous allegiances. And our foray, in any case, accomplished its purpose. During the fortnight that followed, complaints about the 'Goon Squad' grew markedly fewer, then ceased. The goons reverted to their original laughing-stock status and, shortly thereafter, were quietly disbanded.

Not so certain marginally more competent organisations which appeared on campus in the aftermath of the 'Big Bust'. One of my classes that spring, though composed primarily of undergraduates, was open to a sprinkling of adults from the community. Their attendance was fluid, often erratic, and I therefore paid scant attention to them, making small effort to know them by name. Those who spoke gregariously, intelligently or obtusely registered, of course, in my consciousness, as did three or four others who made themselves conspicuous - and, needless to say, two or three attractive women. But I had no reason to notice one well-groomed, casually dressed man - an accountant, perhaps, on a bank cashier in his mid-thirties - who seemed so tenuously sketched against the backdrop of reality he might've disappeared at any moment. What little he said was banal and innocuous; and as I realised later, his face hadn't impressed itself on me because he'd always kept it lowered, bent over the notebook in which he scribbled assiduously. Until one day, as he sat down at his desk, a mishap occurred. I'm not sure precisely what caused it. Perhaps he stabbed himself on a pencil, or a key, or something in his trouser pocket. Perhaps he was simply trying to pull something out - a handkerchief or comb or writing implement. At any rate, he half rose from his seat, and the contents of his pocket tumbled out on to the floor, and amidst the chink and clink and clatter of coins and keys and other metal objects I heard a splat, and there in the aisle - like some mortifying issue of slackened continence - lay a brown leather wallet open to disclose a gold badge.

Heads craned over it as though it were some loathsome living creature - a giant spider, a cockroach, a rodent loose among the chair legs. A deathly hush detonated in the room, spreading ever-widening ripples of silence. Having hastily collected his compromising débris, the 'nark', or whatever he was, sat rigid, turning white, then red, then white again, as though communicating with his head office by some bizarre species of epidermal semaphore. It wasn't just embarrassment. He looked downright terrified. Possibly he expected to be lynched.

Pacing to and fro before the blackboard, I pretended I'd seen nothing unusual. For the last two or three sessions, I'd been expatiating on *A Portrait of the Artist as a Young Man*. I didn't customarily assign written work in class; but now I told my students I wanted them to write for twenty minutes on what Joyce meant by the term 'epiphany', citing at least one specific example. Most of them appeared flummoxed. A few of the more astute chuckled and applied themselves to the task with relish. The erstwhile secret agent hadn't a clue what I was talking about, but sensed that he was somehow being 'got at'. Flustered, he asked to be excused, like a schoolboy requesting permission to go to the lavatory. Needless to say, he didn't return.

What kind of dope-related, subversive, seditious or otherwise un-American propaganda had he fancied he was culling from my disquisitions on pre-First World War European *Bildungsromane* - from *Portrait*, from *Tonio Kröger*, from Musil's *Törless*, from Rilke's *Malte Laurids Brigge*? I longed to see the notebook in which he'd been scribbling so industriously. Perhaps I was suspect for not including any American works on my syllabus? Or perhaps such themes as self-discovery, maturation, coalescence of identity and art as a vocation were deemed inimical to the American ethos?

But apart from my ironic amusement, I was also mildly indignant. When I'd finished my lecture for the day, I conjured myself into a state of righteous wrath, stormed into the Dean's office on the ground floor, reported the incident and demanded an explanation. The Dean - a gentle sort of bureaucrat with frizzy iron-grey hair, incongruously boyish features and eyes too innocent for literature - assumed a dutifully chagrined expression. He apologised copiously and with zest. He didn't like it, he bleated, any more than I did. Unfortunately, he was helpless in the matter. The decision had been imposed on him from above - from Albany, he added in clarification, presumably lest I assume he meant God. But in fact there were, on campus at the moment, undercover operatives of seventeen different municipal, county, state and federal agencies.

'That man who dropped his badge - he must already be in trouble with his superiors. They probably had someone else in your class. Keeping tabs on him, as well as on you.'

Such was the climate at the university - a climate in which, amid the froth and wrath of that spring, suspicion filled the air like pollen and paranoia raged rampant as hay fever. On the whole, everyone rather enjoyed it. It offered a heady aromatic for dilettantes who dabbled with danger. This wasn't Chicago, after all. No one brandished knives here, still less guns. No one was threatened with anything as messy as death, nor even with physical injury. Nor, for that matter, with imprisonment either. The few who'd been arrested in the 'Big Bust' received only probation or suspended sentences. The anxiety, in consequence, was of a sort calculated to induce an exhilarating *frisson,* similar to that of a roller coaster ride, or a Hitchcock film. People whipped it up like a cocktail, to just as much intensity as they could accommodate without seriously inconveniencing themselves.

XI

Against the District Attorney and his minions, against the police, against goon squads and other pests, I would, of course, close ranks with my colleagues, present a united front, a façade of solidarity. Within the insulate sphere of our department, however, there were a number of individuals whose complacent smugness and aloof superiority implicitly begged to be punctured and deflated. I was irresistibly impelled to answer that appeal. Along with Roland, Sidney, Vanessa and a few others, my chief ally, in at least one such operation of correctional therapy, was to be Jim Harrison, subsequently an established wolf-breeder, novelist and scriptwriter, but then regarded primarily as a poet.

Harrison at the time was 'Assistant Director of Graduate Studies', and he had no more cogent a conception than we did of what his job description actually entailed. He chose to interpret it in his own idiosyncratic way. As significant as his own work was his octopus-armed network of contacts with other poets across the country. This network was to produce, the following summer, a lavishly touted 'International Poetry Conference', which brought together bards and versifiers not only from every quarter of the nation, but from abroad as well. The event culminated with an unseemly brawl between two illustrious laureates, while Alan Ginsberg tried to invoke peace by standing between them and chanting Buddhist mantras. '*C'mon, you guys! Cool it! You're supposed to be poets!*' he pleaded between '*Om Mani Padme Oms*'. Mantras and appeals to poetic honour both failed, and Ginsberg received a stray punch on the jaw in recompense for his efforts. A modernistically trendy glass coffee table became the next casualty when both combatants, locked in a grunting gasping embrace, stumbled and toppled on to it, smashing it to a futuristic collage of shards. A convention of poets, Vanessa concluded, wasn't significantly different from a convention of shoe salesmen.

During the period just before and after the 'Big Bust', however, poets hadn't yet debased their currency at the university, and Harrison turned his network of contacts conscientiously to account. At least once a fortnight, there'd appear in our letterboxes a standardised Xeroxed notice: '*To: All Faculty From: Jim Harrison.*' The accompanying memo urged us to announce to our classes that one or another distinguished troubadour would be on campus the following week, giving a reading from his work. A brief biography of the troubadour in question would follow, along with an opportunity to commandeer him for a talk to one's own class. On the appointed day, the guest of honour would appear, would address a few select classes, would read from his work in the evening. The event would be attended largely by starry-eyed undergraduates and doting matrons from the local community, 'culture vultures' voraciously intent on procuring autographs. On a table near the door, there'd be stacks of the guest's books, which he'd deign to sign after his performance. A party would then ensue, with caravans of cars wending their way through the night to the department's Gatsbyesque mansion on the shore. So established had this routine become that I was moved to unsprocket it. I did so by a pseudo-necromantic resuscitation of William McGonagall - undisputed master of English illiterature, whose deluded conviction of his own genius had never wobbled once.

At the time, McGonagall was entirely unknown in the States, except for a few initiates, a few professors of poetry and visiting or resident Britons. In Boston some three years before, I'd been introduced to his *oeuvre* by Bill Powell, a wandering British travel writer for the *Telegraph* and veteran of SNCC's compound in Mississippi, whom I'd met through JT and Ilona. On hearing Bill's memorised recitation of 'The Tay Bridge Disaster', I was immediately hooked:

> Beautiful Railway Bridge of the Silv'ry Tay!
> Alas! I am very sorry to say
> That ninety lives have been taken away
> On the last Sabbath day of 1879,
> Which will be remember'd for a very long time.

Even more edifying was the last stanza of the poem:

> Oh! ill-fated Bridge of the Silv'ry Tay.
> I must now conclude my lay
> By telling the world fearlessly without the least dismay
> That your central girders would not have given way
> At least many sensible men do say,

Had they been supported on each side by buttresses,
At least many sensible men confesses,
For the stronger we our houses do build,
The less chance we have of being killed.

Bill and I had managed to find a musty copy of McGonagall's *Poetic Gems* at the Cambridge Public Library. It inspired us further -- inspired us, in fact, to create the Greater Boston McGonagall Society. Unfortunately, we'd had no idea of what the society, once founded, was supposed to do, apart from running off some mimeographed flybills announcing its existence; and before the matter had clarified itself, I'd departed for my first year in Chicago. In the world I inhabited there, McGonagall would hardly've been appreciated as he deserved - though some of the people we knew, like Al Hollis or Lieutenant Boyle, might well have deemed him a major poet. But wasted though he would've been in Chicago, the university on Long Island offered a climate in which he could thrive.

There were some minor inconsistencies. According to the meagre biographical data we'd found in reference books, McGonagall was born in 1825. According to his own autobiography, however, he was born in 1830, and no one seemed able to account for the discrepancy. Whatever his true birthdate, his appearance at a poetry reading on Long Island in the late 1960s would've entailed a longevity commensurate with that of the Comte de Saint-Germain. On the other hand, no one save Sidney, Vanessa, myself and those we initiated could be expected to know that.

The British couple and I accordingly presented our scheme to Harrison, who enthusiastically welcomed it. To impersonate McGonagall, or function as McGonagall's avatar, I recruited Patterson, whose dramaturgical gifts were lying fallow while he ministered to customers and a docile boa constrictor at Slug's Saloon. There then appeared the customary memo in everyone's letterbox:

'To: All Faculty
From: Jim Harrison.
Please announce to all classes that noted Scottish poet William McGonagall will be on campus next Thursday to give a reading from his work. Those wishing him to address their classes please notify me.'

On the appointed Thursday, Patterson arrived by train from Manhattan and I met him at the station. He'd brought with him an anachronistic-looking tailcoat, rented from a theatrical costumers', and a gauche cravat that might've been produced equally by silkscreen or by accident. He'd also brought a supply of cognac in a hip flask, despite the fact that McGonagall wasn't just a teetotaller, but also a militant temperance evangelist, constantly inveighing against the 'Demon Drink'. Patterson expressed misgivings about what was, admittedly, a rather dodgy Scottish accent. Apart from Sidney and Vanessa, however, no one - least of all the gullible undergraduates and local matrons who'd be queuing for his autograph - was likely to detect its dodginess. Anyone who by some remote chance did would be too tactful, or too embarrassed, or simply too baffled, to challenge it.

That afternoon, I introduced him as guest speaker to my class, fulsomely praised his work, then retired to the back of the room. Patterson briefly expounded his improvised McGonagallese aesthetic, the hallmarks of which, he explained, were directness, simplicity and a doggedly dogmatic insistence on rhyme - rhyme at all costs. To illustrate these putative virtues, he opened at random the volume of *Poetic Gems* I'd located and began to read from 'The Battle of El-Teb':

> Ye sons of Great Britain, I think no shame
> To write in praise of brave General Graham!
> Whose name will be handed down to posterity without any
>   stigma,
> Because, at the Battle of El-Teb, he defeated Osman Digna. . .

A weedy, scrub-bearded youth in the second row flapped a hand aloft. Patterson nodded to him, welcoming his question.

'Who's Osman Digna?'

Patterson flicked me a glance of incipient alarm, then quickly recovered himself, albeit at some cost to his Scottish accent.

'Commander of the enemy forces. The forces defeated by General Graham.'

'Who's General Graham?'

'The hero of my poem. Why do you think I wanted to commemorate him?'

'I don't know,' the youth replied, shaking his head in genuine perplexity. 'What was this Battle of El-Tub . . . ? I never heard of it.'

'El-Teb. You're here at a university, aren't you? With a library? Now you've got a research project.'

Regaining his stride, Patterson resumed his recitation of the poem. The faces of his audience displayed a raddled spectrum of expressions - uncertainty, doubt, befuddlement. It was obvious to most of my students that something was very seriously wrong, very grievously askew, but no one dared acknowledge, even privately, what it was. To do so would've entailed the unthinkable - questioning my oracular authority. Having concluded his jangled account of Osman Digna's rout, Patterson pointed out how the piece he'd read illustrated the qualities he'd extolled - directness, simplicity and rhyme. To demonstrate how these qualities had been flouted by inferior poets, he then recited an opaque passage from 'Burnt Norton' (which I'm prevented from transcribing by the stroppiness of Eliot's estate in sanctioning quotes).

'You see what I mean?' he concluded. 'Can anyone here tell me what that was about?'

Silence burgeoned almost painfully in the room, accentuating the sizzle of a horsefly at the window. Outside, in the car park, a motorcycle revved irrelevantly, as though amplifying the horsefly's sizzle to throaty thunder. At last, an earnest-looking girl in the front row - oval-faced, with long straight Madonna-like hair, one of my more intelligent students, but timid - tentatively raised her hand.

'You know, Mr. McGonagall, I'm beginning to think there may...well, there may be something in what you've said. I wasn't sure at first. But now I can't help wondering if Eliot...if Eliot really is that great a poet...'

'*Shit*!' I heard my own voice castigate me in the privacy of my skull. '*What've we done*?'

'Who the fuck *was* Osman Digna?' Patterson muttered to me, *sotto voce*, as my class, at the end of the hour, filed, glazed-eyed, out of the room.

That evening, we assembled in the lounge requisitioned for the reading. Patterson took his place at the front of the room, where a table stood with a carafe of water and a glass. Harrison arrived a few minutes late, manifestly tipsy, his rolling gait that of a seaman trying to keep upright on a pitching deck. The only empty seat within easy access was next to Mildred Muffage, most ferociously predatory of the 'culture vultures' among the community's matrons, known for collecting poets' autographs with a hawk's rapacity and understanding the poetry itself with as much acumen as a hamster. I'd often considered pointing out to her that her blue-rinsed coiffure was identical to those worn by Chicago hookers, but refrained for fear of precipitating some sort of seizure. When Harrison wavered into the room, she promptly detected - or perhaps scented - his inebriation and fixed on him a long pointed look with a taloned hook on the end of it. When he took aim at the chair beside her and slumped into it, she glared at him balefully, desiring apparently to eviscerate him with her eyes.

Bobbing up and down eccentrically, struggling occasionally with a guttural Scottish glottal, Patterson recited his way through half a dozen poems. Here and there, two or three more knowing individuals allowed themselves tenuous smirks. For the most part, however, the faces of the audience were similar to those of my class a few hours before - bewildered, bemused, befuddled, betraying a burgeoning sense of something not quite right in the cosmos. Harrison proved unable to restrain a guffaw, which elicited another basilisk glare from Mildred Muffage. After some forty minutes, Patterson was showing some strain to keep from corpsing. Seated in my strategically chosen corner, I signalled that he might as well terminate his performance. He closed the book from which he'd been reading and invited questions or comments from the floor.

'Mr. McGonagall,' a lank-haired undergraduate ventured, politely, but with a glimmer of irony in his voice, 'I can't help noticing that you tend to rhyme a great deal. Sometimes at the cost of metre.'

This, of course, afforded Patterson a fresh opportunity to discourse on the virtues of directness, simplicity and rhyme. The audience listened quizzically. Mildred Muffage nodded silently in agreement. Harrison guffawed again, and got raked by Mildred's glaucous oyster eyes. A willowy blonde girl in a minuscule miniskirt fluttered her hand, and Patterson nodded to her.

'Mr. McGonagall, I notice that sheep tend to recur in many of your poems. At least half of those you recited talk about sheep. Do sheep have any special significance for you? Or are they just something...well, something of specific relevance to Scotland?'

Patterson paused to ponder. Despite having recited at least two militant temperance poems, he reached into his coat, extricated his flask, unscrewed the cap and took a thoughtful swig.

'It has to do with Scotland,' he stated judiciously. 'You have to understand that sheep...sheep enjoy a rather unique status in Scotland. Somewhat similar to that...that which...*mothers* enjoy here.'

Harrison, who'd just produced a flask of his own and gulped from it, promptly choked. Laughing and coughing uncontrollably, he slipped and slithered downwards from his seat, eventually lying coiled in a foetal position on the floor, red-faced and still gasping. Mildred Muffage refused to look at him, staring rigidly straight ahead, as though into the muzzles of a firing squad.

McGonagall being out of print in the States at the time, there were no books for Patterson to autograph when the event ended. We had, however, thoughtfully provided Xeroxed pages containing typed versions of selected poems, and these were snatched up eagerly by his newly acquired devotees. While he appended the Scottish bard's forged signature to the pages proffered him, I waited by the door. Having got her page signed, Mildred, en route out, paused to confer on me her assessment of the evening.

'I'm so ashamed of Jim Harrison!' she hissed indignantly. 'If he didn't like Mr. McGonagall's poetry, he could've left. He didn't have to sit there laughing!'

When Patterson had disengaged himself from the fans besieging him, we made our way out into the night, then drove to the mansion on the shore for the obligatory party. Mildred not being one of the elect who enjoyed access to the place, he was spared any further blandishments from her, and I any further complaints. There was, however, a fresh group of *soi-disant* poetry lovers queued up to pester him for an autograph. He looked at me despairingly. I retreated to the tables across the room on which the drinks were waiting. As I poured myself a cognac, a petite young woman named Patsy Farrell, a querulously belligerent proto-feminist in the M.A. programme, stalked diagonally from a corner to confront me. I'd antagonised her a month or so before by scoffing at her invitation to join an 'encounter group'. If I bared my soul to Mildred Muffage, I explained, and if she bared hers to me, she'd get much the better of the bargain. On the basis of this statement, Patsy had come to the conclusion that I was arrogant. Now, it transpired, she had a fresh grievance with which to indict me.

'You're a sadist!' she snapped, quivering with outrage.

'What leads you to assume that?' I asked blandly.

'That was unforgivable. It was just too cruel. I mean, like, here's this poor lunatic sitting in some garret in the city, writing this God-awful poetry, and you bring him all the way out here to make a fool of him...!'

****

In the meantime, the 'Big Bust' was continuing to produce fallout in the community, much of it silly but with an incipient ugliness. I experienced something of this one night towards the end of term. Depressed by a lesion in a liaison, made restless by the sultry evening, I'd driven to a tavern near the university. It wasn't the most congenial of our various drinking establishments. It was the only one in striking distance with a pool table, however, and, if only for that reason, my colleagues and I had periodic recourse to its otherwise meagre amenities.

Usually, I could expect to find two or three of my circle hanging around the place; but on this occasion, it was empty save for the bartender, polishing glasses in endless slow motion, and a solitary customer at the far end of the bar - a bear-shaped man, probably a construction worker, with grizzled hair surmounting a square skull and squat neck. Despite the clammy humidity, he was wearing a red-and-black plaid lumberjack's shirt. He was apparently a regular, on chummy terms with the bartender, who, in snatches of desultory conversation during the next twenty or so minutes, addressed him as Gil.

Leaving perhaps half a dozen stools between us, I sat down and ordered a bourbon and beer chaser. In the mirror behind the bar, Gil and I studied each other's reflections. My dark glasses prevented him from reading my eyes. His, I could see, were hostile, raking my image with a moody sulking melancholy. I half expected him to say something, but he remained sullenly silent. Perhaps I still exuded some after-reek of Chicago, some quality of comportment or demeanour too sinister for casual baiting. Nevertheless, the tension burgeoned between us, a pressure all the more insistent for being denied expression. Had this been Laredo, El Paso or some other such celluloid place a century before, there'd've been a pre-established ritual for the occasion. He'd've bought me a deliberately provocative drink, I'd've felt obliged on principle to refuse it and we'd've stepped outside with our six-guns to blast each other to hamburger.

The tension was dispelled, if only briefly, by the creak of the door and the advent of a newcomer - an undergraduate, to judge from his appearance, with a stipple of fledgling beard and dark hair in a frazzled post-electrocution 'Afro' style. Gil glanced at him over one shoulder with disgust - the kind of look one might cast a dog vomiting in the road. Ebulliently oblivious, the youth swaggered to the bar, seated himself on a stool midway between Gil and me and ordered a white wine. And then, apart from the clink of glasses, silence descended again, and the youth's jauntiness drained away, and our three gazes crossed, clashed, locked, parried, pursued their mute fencing match in the mirror. Until Gil lost patience and swivelled lazily, with a slow surly spite, to his neighbour.

'You from over there?' he asked, gesturing towards the university, its lights winking through the trees.

'That's right,' the youth replied, facing his interrogator, eager to be sociable. 'First year there. Be a great place, 'cept for the mud.'

'You must know something 'bout all the dope they use there,' Gil prodded - whether with calculated or inadvertent clumsiness I couldn't at first tell.

The youth, of course, promptly tensed, going rigid and averting his eyes. He flicked a glance into the mirror, then stared into his wine. Narcotics agents, after all, came in all shapes and guises.

'Don't know nothing about no dope, man,' he muttered into his glass. 'Never use the stuff.'

'Yeah,' Gil sneered sarcastically. 'I bet you don't. I bet you don't know nothing at all. I bet you wouldn't kid me 'bout a thing like that, would you?'

'I told you - I don't use the stuff. I prefer alcohol.'

'Alcohol my ass!' Gil drawled, looking disdainfully at the glass of pale wine. 'You call that alcohol? Stop bullshitting me, you puke-faced little snot!'

The youth flushed and refused to meet Gil's mocking eyes, staring fixedly, almost desperately, into the mirror. His voice, when he replied, rose an octave, becoming shrill with indignation:

'What the fuck difference does it make to you what I drink?'

Gil ignored the question.

'So you don't know nothing 'bout the drugs they use over there?'

'No. I told you, man, I don't use drugs. Tried them a few times. Didn't like them. Don't believe in them. Ain't my scene, man. Just ain't my bag.'

'Yeah. And I suppose protesting 'bout the war ain't your bag neither. I suppose you're a real red-blooded patriotic American. I suppose you don't have no truck with those freaks and misfits and degenerates who squeal like stuck pigs 'bout us bombing all the poor Commie women and children in Vietnam.'

'That's different,' the youth replied huffily. 'I *am* opposed to the war. We *don't* have any right to be in Vietnam.'

'You burned your draft card yet? What're you planning to do when they call you up? You don't look like you got the guts to go to jail. You planning to run off to Canada, or Sweden, or someplace like that? Or maybe you're just a faggot. That'll get you out, won't it? Ain't no room for faggots in the U.S. Army.'

'What's all this got to do with anything?' the youth snapped, his temper fraying. 'What I do's beside the point. The point is we don't have business being in Vietnam. Why should I fight in a war that's morally wrong?'

'Morally wrong? And smoking dope, and fucking girls before marriage, and turning your back on your country are all morally right, are they?'

And so it continued for some ten minutes, their voices becoming increasingly strident and enraged, each mouthing the same stale rhetoric, each hurling slogans at the other like buckets of paint, random and indiscriminate. Each remained entrenched behind the carapace of his own tortoise-shelled mentality, his own fiercely embunkered position, sandbagged and fixed in concrete. No actual communication of any sort was occurring. Neither was hearing the other. Neither was even seeing the other, except as some sort of symbolic effigy, some abstract embodiment of everything most despised and feared. It was a familiar enough squabble for those days, the kind that could be heard constantly all across the country, neither more nor less likely than most to spill over into violence.

'No wonder this country's fucked up!' the youth shouted at last, his voice almost hysterical, spitting and sputtering furiously. 'With an asshole in the White House, with shitheads like you allowed on the streets, it's no wonder...'

'You snot-nosed little prick!' Gil hissed, sieving the words between his teeth. 'You goddamn puke-faced little twerp...!'

It was obvious what would happen next - what had to happen next. Vocabulary was breaking down. Words no longer sufficed. In the lather of their wrath, both adversaries had run out of available insults. Each had had epithets and expletives plundered by the other. Phrases of abuse were become interchangeable, and each would soon hear something close to his own language issuing from the other's lips. Each would then find himself playing the clown, the ventriloquist's dummy, cast haplessly in a farcical double act - and this, of course, would be the worst humiliation of all. Neither would've formulated the situation to himself in quite those terms; but it was clear to both that only one recourse remained. With a sluggishness intended to catch his victim off guard, Gil swung round, then lunged. He moved with surprising agility for a man of his bulk, but the youth was still too quick for him, slithering off the stool, twisting free from the grasping paws, pivoting and scuttling towards the door.

'Come back here, you little shit!' Gil roared.

'Go fuck your mother!' the youth yelled, darting out into the night.

Gil lumbered after him as far as the threshold, panting as if from having run some immense distance. Pursuit, of course, was pointless. Seething, fuming, puffing and brick-red, the bear-shaped man trudged back to his seat. Silence accumulated again, broken only by his laboured breathing. And then, as I'd known he would, he turned to me.

'I suppose you're one of them, too,' he growled.

I faced him with what I tried to make seem a vague and quizzical bemusement - a bland 'are-you-talking-to-me?' expression.

'One of whom?' I asked mildly.

'One of them fucking student demonstrators - pro-Commie dope freaks and whatever the hell else they are.'

'No,' I said quietly. 'I teach them.'

He blinked, but his features remained stony, rigorously motionless.

'You teach them?'

'Yes. I'm a lecturer at the university.'

'You teach them to betray their country and shit like that?'

'Not exactly. I teach them - or try to teach them - to appreciate literature. And literature teaches them to *see*. "*See*", I mean, with a kind of X-ray vision. To understand things. To penetrate beneath the surface. Whatever conclusions they draw from what they see are their own. The best literature wouldn't address Vietnam at all. Not directly. But yes, I suppose it might help a person to understand why this country shouldn't have half a million troops in Southeast Asia.'

I'm not sure how much of my fastidious hair-splitting he really fathomed. For a moment, he looked disarmed, almost vulnerable, as if he were prepared to entertain something of what I'd said. Then, fearing perhaps to find himself out of his depth, he retreated again behind his fixed emplacements.

'In other words, you teach them crap!'

At that point, to my own surprise, the issue suddenly became personal. I'd thought I was detached, aloof, controlled beyond any possibility of tantrum. But to hear Joyce, Mann, Proust, Musil, Broch, Lawrence, Rilke and Yeats called 'crap' by this dolt triggered a spasm of black murderous fury. I was as affronted as if he'd aspersed a woman I loved; and I rose to the defence of literature as I might've done to that of a paramour. Not that I formulated or rehearsed anything mentally - as I did, for example, the carefully shaped sentences and paragraphs with which I addressed my classes. On this occasion, I was aware only that I had to seize the initiative with language - that I couldn't get into a mere slanging match, a muddled free-for-all in which Gil and I flailed at each other with our respective views. I'd already discovered with my students that one can't convey *what* one knows until one first establishes *that* one knows. As with my students, I now had quickly to establish my authority, and to do so by a species of pre-emptive strike. Everything that followed from this awareness formed itself spontaneously, organically, with a coherence and momentum of its own. I began speaking softly, then let myself be carried away by the flow of my rhetoric, borne along by its rhythms and cadences. At intervals in the course of my tirade, those rhythms and cadences produced a fleeting sense of *déjà-vu;* but caught up in them as I was, I had no opportunity to probe the sensation.

'You're not qualified,' I said bluntly, 'to judge what's crap and what isn't. You're not qualified to make judgements about literature, about history, about politics, about patriotism, about education, about the rightness or wrongness of the war in Vietnam. What do you know about such things? You don't know piss-all! You don't know what makes wars happen. You don't know the mistakes people and governments've made in the past. You don't know how fools obsessed with power or paranoia or both've plunged one nation after another, one culture after another, into crazy self-destructive conflicts. You don't know how or why we're repeating in Vietnam the same blunders that so many other countries have committed all through history. You don't know how such blunders have led those countries, as they'll lead this one, to tear themselves apart and compromise whatever claim they have to integrity. You're pitiful, really, in your spoon-fed second-hand judgements and your lazy thoughtless ignorance. You don't even know why American troops were sent to Vietnam in the first place. Yes, I can guess what you're about to say: "To stop the Communist menace". But what the fuck do you know about the Communist menace? Have you ever met a Communist? Have you ever spoken to a Communist? Have you ever even seen a Communist? I have as little love for Communism as you do, but at least I know why. You don't. Once upon a time, someone planted in the pudding you call your brain the notion that Communism was somehow threatening to the United States. And yes, it may indeed be so, but not for the reasons you imagine, assuming you imagine any reasons at all. If you can tell me what Communism is, if you can tell me why it threatens the United States, if you can tell me how despatching half a million troops to Southeast Asia obviates that threat, then I'll be prepared to listen to you. Then you'll've earned the right to be heard. Then you'll have the right to an opinion. But for the moment, you don't have any such right. Opinions require some element of responsibility - responsibility to be informed, to know the situation, to have some understanding of the facts involved. Until you can demonstrate such knowledge and understanding, don't presume to challenge me.'

Gil looked stunned. He sat there, sagging on his bar stool, with the expression of a man who's just been punched in the stomach. His mouth was like the gasping mouth of a fish out of water. He was obviously trying to shape his lips around words, but words wouldn't come. He gulped, took an eager sip of beer, then turned to me again in a renewed effort to speak. I didn't give him the chance. My harangue, when I resumed it, was quieter, more conciliatory, less orotund and histrionic, but no less outrageous:

'You're forgetting something very basic. So far as matters of this kind are concerned, I'm what people like you call an 'expert'. All of us live in a world of 'experts'. We survive by confiding in their expertise. Reality today is too complex for any one person to handle alone. We therefore entrust whole areas of our lives to 'professionals', who've made it their business to know those areas. We entrust our cars to expert mechanics - or mechanics whom we hope are experts. We rely on expert plumbers, carpenters, builders, electricians. We have expert doctors and dentists to treat our ills. We have expert lawyers to negotiate our divorces, or manage whatever other legal problems arise in our lives. We employ expert accountants to process our tax returns. We consult psychiatrists and psychoanalysts to help with mental or emotional problems. We commission expert architects to construct our houses and offices. You yourself probably have some professional expertise; and you expect people who know less about it than you do to respect your informed judgement. Don't you? All right - I'm an expert in the social, historical, political, philosophical and moral implications of our involvement in Vietnam. You, and thousands of taxpayers like you, have spent a great deal of money to train me - to turn me into a specialist, to equip me with an understanding of the broader principles that govern our lives. You've turned me into an expert on those principles, just as you might pay to have your children turned into expert lawyers, or doctors, or lab technicians, or engineers. You've turned me into an expert of the same kind, perhaps, as you yourself might be in whatever your profession is. It's my *professional* business to know why we're in Vietnam - and why we shouldn't be. It's my business to understand how we repeat the mistakes of history. It's my business to make people see when something's gone wrong with their attitudes and values. It's my business to diagnose, just as a doctor would, the psychological or social or political illnesses that infect a country or a people – the kind of sickness that poisons the Soviet Union, or that you yourself might've fought in Nazi Germany when you were the age of that kid you want to pulverise a few minutes ago. It's my business to diagnose those things, just as it's a doctor's business to diagnose physical maladies. That's what education entails. That's the whole point of education. And from the standpoint of my professional expertise, I'm telling you we don't belong in Vietnam. I'm not talking about personal preferences. I'm not talking about my feelings on the matter, or yours. I'm giving you a clinical assessment, formed on the basis of my professional expertise. How I feel about it is irrelevant. A doctor has no particular feelings when he tells you you're suffering from high blood pressure, or low blood sugar, or an incipient ulcer. He's not going to cheer, but he won't tear his hair either. He certainly won't waste time debating his diagnosis with you. All right – it's as a kind of doctor that I'm telling you our policy in Southeast Asia is screwed up.'

Another pause. My performance – for that was what it'd been – had left me as drained as it'd left Gil cowed. His whole body had slumped, his pose reflecting a collapse of all resistance, a dull and docile receptivity.

'How many returned veterans do you know?' I asked. 'How many've you spoken to? About what's really happening in Vietnam, I mean?'

Gil glanced at me with haunted eyes, then plunged his gaze back into his beer again.

'I got a boy in the Marines. Last I heard, he was up near Da Nang. My wife and I, we get letters, but you know how it is – he can't say a hell of a lot, and they censor things anyway. He ain't happy over there. I can read that much between the lines.'

I'd intended originally to invoke Wes Tyler and some of the other soldiers I'd met in Chicago, or at least something of what they'd told me. Now, however, seeing Gil reclaimed from androidhood and restored to humanity, I changed tack.

'And so you naturally resent that kid who was here a few minutes ago – who leads a slapdash carefree life, and isn't in any danger, and bitches about the war, and slurs everything you son's risking his life for in Da Nang.'

Gil nodded eagerly, with something like gratitude - gratitude that I'd expressed him to himself, had articulated his emotions and, by couching them in my emphatic language, validated them.

'Yeah,' he said appreciatively. 'You hit the nail right on the head.'

'But don't you see? It's my business to help you understand why your son shouldn't be in Vietnam at all. It's also my business to help that kid understand that your son isn't a psychopath, or a crazed rapist, or a bloodthirsty killer, but someone not very different from himself. Only more unfortunate. Someone who's got caught up by the insanity and become the pawn of incompetent men playing international power games they themselves don't understand and aren't intelligent enough to play responsibly.'

Gil faced me mutely, his formerly hard gaze now melting, liquefying, brimming with incipient tears. I, too, was unexpectedly moved. Fumbling for some appropriate gesture, I clinked my glass to his.

'To your son. May he return safely.'

Gil tried to croak his thanks in a strangled voice, swallowed hard, turned away to regain his composure. We drank in silence for some moments, with what I think was a genuine sense of fellowship. At last, he turned back to me again.

'You think maybe you could...well, give me the names of some books or something? Some stuff I could maybe read? So's I could...well, you know, learn a little more about things?'

There wasn't much in print at the time, at least in book form, that addressed the subject directly. I recommended *The Armies of the Night,* which had just appeared, a handful of articles, some indictments of older wars by Tolstoy, Zola, Stephen Crane, Remarque, Barbusse - as well, naturally, as some basic history texts. He asked, tentatively, if he might enrol in my class for the autumn. I discouraged that, doubtful whether the rarefied European works on my syllabus would have much apparent bearing on his immediate concerns. I steered him instead towards the class Roland intended to conduct, which would deal with more specifically American material and might've been subtitled 'The Intrinsic Maladjustment of American Culture'. With Roland to guide him, Gil could pick his way through

Lawrence (*Studies in Classic American Literature*) and William Carlos Williams (*In the American Grain*).

For the duration of the evening, we bought each other successive rounds of drinks. He told me how he'd just missed combat in the Second World War, having been called up a month too late. He'd always felt guilty about not re-enlisting for Korea.

'But they were a different kind of war, I guess,' he concluded. 'I never thought of that before.'

'Thought of what?'

'That you didn't have people protesting against them other wars. I suppose that says something, don't it?'

I left it to Roland to clarify precisely what. With the autumn, Gil enrolled in my colleague's class, and then, having discovered an appetite for reading, in two others. Roland, irate with me at first, described him as ignorant and argumentative, but eager, even obstreperous, to learn. To everyone's surprise, including his own, Gil found he preferred Fitzgerald to Hemingway. More than anything else perhaps, this prompted him to wonder, to ponder, to reassess.

During the next two years, I often encountered him in the corridors, on the footpaths, in the car park. We'd sometimes chat, perhaps have coffee together in one of the lounges or cafeterias. On two or three occasions, we went out for a drink. His son, he told me at one point, had returned from Vietnam - minus a foot lost to an anti-personnel mine, but alive and, before too long, reasonably mobile. I could guess the kind of stories the young Marine - soon actively involved in the newly founded Veterans Against the War - must've recounted to his father. When I next saw Gil, he was boarding a bus for one of the larger anti-war demonstrations in Washington.

In the years since my first encounter with him, however, I've often brooded about Gil and what I did at the tavern that night. Did for him? Or did *to* him? Had I 'educated' him, in the valid sense of that word? Had I performed a laudable job of salvage and reclamation? Or had I brainwashed him? Or subjected his brain, at any rate, to a quick rinse? But then isn't most so-called formal education - as it's generally understood and perpetrated - a species of brainwashing? Where, exactly, is the demarcation between the acceptable, morally admissible procedure and the one universally condemned?

If, by some process for the moment confined to the realms of science fiction - by some chemical in the water supply, for instance, some pulsation beamed down from a satellite, some emission emanating from television screens - one could *impose* something like, say, 'world peace', would it be legitimate to do so? I don't mean, of course, the kind of thing depicted by Orwell or Huxley. Nothing *à la* 1984 - which we've already left behind anyway, both chronologically and technologically. No brave new world. No manifest coercion. No forcible transmogrification of individuals into vegetables, automatons, zombies or clones. No monochrome and mechanistic uniformity. I mean, on the contrary, what 'education' is ultimately supposed to entail, but 'artificially induced'. If, by some process that involved chemicals or technology, one could 'educate' people, could activate in them a faculty for vision, a capacity for tenderness, an instinct for decency and all the other qualities alleged to reside inherently in humanity - if one could actualise such qualities so as to suppress or contain or neutralise man's more destructive propensities - would the process be morally justified? Is it ever valid to manipulate the psyche, unknown to the individual, perhaps against the individual's will, in the name of what one deems the individual's welfare or best interests? But if one lectures, or teaches, or writes, or makes films, or works in any sphere of what we call the media, is it possible *not* to manipulate psyches? Are all the subtlety, sophistry and casuistry associated with the Inquisition any more insidious than the techniques of modern advertising? Especially the advertising whereby power, vested interests, complacency, imbecility, dogmatism, greed, fear and sheer childishness mask themselves as politics?

I don't have answers to all these conundrums. I do know, however, that, despite the end result of my encounter with Gil, the means I employed were ultimately tainted - '*ein Haarbreit nur fehlt*', as Stefan George says of the miracles performed by Simon Magus, 'a hair's-breadth impure'. Not that I regretted or repented those means. If anything, I was prepared, even after I'd understood them, to employ them again. I'd readily employ them today - if doing so helped, say, to restore a modicum of sanity to Northern Ireland. But the techniques I'd utilised against Gil were nonetheless morally questionable - 'black' magic which, though deployed on behalf on 'white' objectives, must still leave the magician soiled. I'd practised, in effect, a form of spiritual or psychological violence, a spiritual or psychological bullying and brutality, a spiritual and psychological equivalent of what modern sloganeers call 'Fascism'. I'd *forced* Gil to see. I'd coerced him - by a shameless process of browbeating, by tyrannising and intimidating him, by imbuing him with a sense of his own 'inferiority' and my 'superiority' to him. In order to dominate, in order to assert my authority over him, I'd deliberately and systematically diminished him, cowed him to the requisite submission - and, by something akin to mesmerism, quelled any impulse to resist.

The morning after our encounter at the tavern, I realised why the rhythms and cadences of my tirade had produced a sensation of *déjà-vu*. In their drumbeat repetitiveness, in their incantatory and hypnotic character, in their sledgehammer impact on the mind, they were the rhythms and cadences of Adolf Hitler.

XII

While our local undergraduates waxed frenetic about the 'Big Bust', the 'Goon Squad' and the mud, Parisian students had been setting their own example to the world. In the months that followed, the university population of the States, arrogating ever greater grounds for grievance, sought to emulate their French contemporaries. That summer, a year behind schedule, Chicago erupted. Jean Genet, having revelled in his own country's upheavals, arrived to savour America's - a bullet-headed, porcine-faced, thuggish-looking connoisseur of chaos, gleefully inhaling the bouquet of anarchy as an experienced wine-taster might that of some choice vintage.

The earthquake that rocked Chicago wasn't along the fault lines demarcated the year before. The fissures by this time were primarily and unabashedly political, only incidentally racial. It wasn't just blacks now who spoke of 'revolution', but a substantial percentage of the nation's youth. Had he lived, Bobby Kennedy might possibly have channelled the fermenting energy - might've transformed the Democratic Party, wrested the nomination from Hubert Humphrey and gone on, in the November presidential contest, to trounce his adversary, shifty-eyed blue-jowled Richard Nixon. In the wake of Sirhan Sirhan's bullet, however, only Gene McCarthy remained to conduct a quixotic crusade against the Democrats' intractable dinosaur-ruffed old guard - the paunchy professional bosses, the cigar-chomping impresarios, the wheelers and dealers and power-brokers and king-makers who, from their smoke-hazed caucus and conference rooms, pulled the levers of the party's national machine. As a newcomer, an outsider and, worst of all, an idealist, McCarthy stood meagre chance against the bastions of vested interests and carapaced minds. I don't think anyone really expected him to succeed. But his campaign was imbued with the *élan vital*, the exaltation, the heady fervour of all such lost causes, which invariably magnetise, galvanise and glamorise illusions. When the Democrats convened in Chicago to nominate their candidate, America's young congregated in the streets to acclaim their apostle. If he was thwarted - as he'd inevitably be - disillusion with the electoral process would be vindicated, revolt and civil disobedience sanctioned as justified.

The ensuing *mêlée* scuppered not only McCarthy's prospects, but Humphrey's as well. Yet if the protestors inspired distaste and alarm, so, too, did the police, whose comportment fostered a new queasiness in the public mind. The evolution would prove slow, sluggish, gradual, scarcely perceptible at first; but the running street battles of that week marked the beginning of a general shift in American attitudes - towards the war, towards the law, towards the country's leaders and policy-makers. Across the Western world, television viewers were treated to pictures of Chicago cops going berserk, racing rabidly and rancidly amok, battering demonstrators, assaulting newsmen and photographers, conducting themselves in a fashion commensurate with the *Sturmabteilung* to whom their adversaries compared them. Mortified middle-class parents across the nation witnessed *their* progeny being clubbed and gassed on the screen, in living colour, and this imbued the issues with an unprecedented immediacy.

Having lived in the city for two years, having known the likes of Lieutenant Boyle and Al Hollis, I found nothing new or surprising in the bellicose behaviour. One can claim to've achieved wisdom when, instead of exclaiming '*Et tu, Brute!*', one shrugs and says 'Yeah, it figures'. In the convention hall, however, a number of delegates were shocked. One senator, a liberal Jew, presumed to condemn the intemperance of local law enforcement. He was called a 'dirty kike' by an embarrassed and indignant Mayor Richard Daley, whose multiple chins wobbled like turkey wattles. The epithet, of course, brought turmoil to the convention floor itself, which now mirrored, albeit in miniature, the furore outside.

On the embattled streets, coils of tear gas eddied and billowed, swathing the vista in opaque smog. Boxes of Kleenex soaked in lemon juice were distributed as an antidote. Blue-uniformed brutes continued on the warpath, wielding truncheons like tomahawks, braining young people on sight, even assailing non-militant, non-protesting bystanders in Grant Park. Organised resistance began to coalesce, to contest order with ordure. From upstairs windows and balconies, plastic bags filled with excrement and urine flew like Molotov cocktails. Besieged by sycophantic interviewers, Genet sniffed the air, assumed the expression of an *aficionado* and voiced approval in terms too obscene to be transmitted even in their original

French, without dubbing or sub-titles. Looking somewhat less enraptured by the situation, a breathless, malodorous and grievously bespattered Riot Squad officer appeared on screen, still weeping from his own gas. He blamed a mysterious cadre of 'hard core agitators', then hastened away to break more heads open, as if seeking evidence of a hard core inside. In the meantime, word spread that the authorities were studying television film, hoping to identify individual demonstrators. The demonstrators responded by lipsticking 'fuck', in diverse pungent amalgams and combinations, on placards, on T-shirts, on arms and faces - which, of course, prevented them from being televised. Some flashed penises, breasts, buttocks or exaggerated facsimiles thereof - from which the cameras, with demure maidenly modesty, averted their lenses. Shit-bombs began to detonate around photographers as well as police, staining brown the clouds of tear gas.

I took no part in these festivities. Many of my colleagues did, trekking to Chicago by air, by rail, by road, cadging rides with friends or with friends of friends, hitchhiking if necessary. Only Nina, however, could've lured me back to the city, and Nina, by that time, had vanished. We'd remained in contact for the first two months or so of my residence on Long Island. Then, as the separateness of our lives became an internalised *fait accompli,* our correspondence had grown more laboured and mechanical, more an obligation than a pleasure. As winter approached, her letters had ceased abruptly, without warning or explanation. Mine remained unanswered, and her telephone, when I occasionally tried to ring, was out of order or disconnected. So, too, was the bar's.

I shrugged, some part of me at least relieved to be absolved of the attenuated long-distance bond - which, by becoming an encumbrance, might've poisoned my memories. Nina'd always been more pragmatic, less romantically sentimental than I had. No doubt she'd adjusted herself to the reality of the situation, acknowledged to herself that our relationship was definitively over. She was, after all, no callow Gretchen; she'd recognised how much she'd done for me, understood she could do no more, appreciated that my Fausthood, such as it was, must lead me into realms where she could no longer follow. Lacking any more promising alternatives, she'd probably finalised her divorce and resigned herself to marrying Al Hollis. And

Reggie's, in all likelihood, had closed, the plans for renovating the old neighbourhood at last being implemented.

It'd been more than ten months since I'd heard from Nina when my colleagues began planning their pilgrimage to Chicago, eager for confrontation and the novelty of being tear gassed. By that time, any attempt to trace her was doomed to futility. Her telephone number, when I tried it again, plunged me into a garbled dialogue with a stranger - someone with what sounded like a parody of a Bela Lugosi accent, who'd never heard of Nina and lived some distance away. The operator reported no new listing for her. The city directory, which I consulted in the university library, disclosed a dismal column and a half of Hollises, some two dozen under 'A', eight under 'Albert', five under 'Alfred'; and as if that weren't discouraging enough, I suddenly recalled that 'Al' was an abbreviation not of his first, but of his middle name. In the circumstances, there seemed little point in joining my colleagues on their crusade westwards. And what could I have expected anyway? If Nina were indeed married to Hollis, my reappearance, transient though it might be, would only create difficulties for her. Our reunion, if it ever occurred, would be more awkward, constrained, frustrating, painful, than it would anything else.

Nevertheless, I delegated Janet, a girl with whom I'd conducted a tepid on-again-off-again affair, to play private detective - to reconnoitre my old neighbourhood, visit Reggie's or whatever was there in its place, learn what she could of Nina. If Nina could indeed be located, Janet was to ring me, and I'd perhaps drive out at the last minute. Janet pounced on the commission. It'd be 'fun', she said, to step thus into my personal mythology. What she didn't say, and probably couldn't've formulated, was that it would also gratify her masochism to confront the paragon by which, in our liaison, I'd tended consistently to measure her and find her sub-standard. But I received no beckoning call, and my inept sleuth found other, more physical means of gratifying her masochism. When she returned a week later, it was with one arm in a sling, bandaged head and face covered in roseate blotches - an allergic reaction, apparently, to tear gas. In a pause between poundings by the police, she had in fact made a foray to my former stamping-ground. Neither Reggie's nor the apartments above it any longer existed. There was only an immense hole in the ground, out of which the skeleton of some new structure had just begun to rise. Of Nina, there'd been no sign, nor had enquiries yielded any information.

If my attempt thus to seize a fragment of my past proved futile, so, too, did that of my colleagues to seize the future. His image tarnished beyond refurbishment, Hubert Humphrey won the now blighted prize of the nomination and embarked on the vertiginous piste towards defeat in the autumn's election. Our contempt was eclipsed by horror at television film of events far from Chicago - film of Soviet tanks grinding through the streets of Prague, of Russian soldiers training guns loaded not with tear gas canisters, but with live rounds. I remember in particular one especially hideous clip of a Volkswagon scuttling like a trapped cockroach in a vain effort to escape the blundering bulk of a T-34 - until finally, cornered in a cul-de-sac amid heaps of rubble, the little car was simply rolled over, crushed to a mangled and flattened mass beneath the leviathan's steel treads. I couldn't know, of course, that three years later, in Vancouver, I'd become involved with a Czech woman whose closest friends had perished in that vehicle.

But Czechoslovakia, after all, was far away, divorced from our immediate interests and experience. In those days, we lacked even the literary access to it subsequently afforded by Kundera and Skvorecky. For most of us, therefore, it seemed a remote fairy-tale place - it'd figured briefly in the prelude to the Second World War, but its real history had effectively ended with Kafka, or perhaps with Karel Capek. Confronted by film of Prague, we felt a helpless outrage, similar to that engendered in the world more recently by events in Tiananmen Square; and then, if only to anaesthetise our humiliating sense of impotence, we re-focused our attention on things closer to hand - things about which there was at least the illusion of being able to do something.

We all, of course, sneered at the tasteless and vulgar circus of the presidential campaign, the antics of politicians whose every utterance was an insult to one's intelligence. Nevertheless, several of my colleagues became active in the sordid business, sporting bumper stickers, conducting special lectures, presiding over meetings and rallies, organising committees. I remained haughtily and superciliously aloof from such puerile behaviour. I had no intention of voting. My attitude towards the charade had already attained a new nadir – from which, I confess, it's never since risen. Most people have a healthily jaundiced view of the process anyway, voting despairingly for what they deem the 'lesser of two evils'. But that still implies a modicum of affirmation. One is still voting *for* something. If I were to vote at all, I'd decided, it would be out of a deeper abyss of cynicism – I'd vote not *for* the lesser of two evils, but only *against* the greater. There'd be no implicit affirmation whatever in the act.

But in the circumstances that then prevailed, even so purely symbolic a gesture would've been humiliating in its futility; and my ego, as usual, shrank from the kind of anonymous effort that allowed me no latitude to do anything unique, that merely subsumed me in an amorphous mass. In consequence, I boycotted the polls. On election night, my friends and I sat before the television set, getting thoroughly, disgustedly and disgustingly soused, and – with plastic guns, cap pistols, blank firers, anything else that came to hand – shooting at the screen as the returns from each state were tediously intoned. A shamelessly juvenile thing to do, I acknowledge, but, in its perverse way, cathartic.

I viewed the newly hatched President with blistering and undiluted scorn. Lyndon Johnson had at least had the courage to make Vietnam *his* war, to assume some sort of personal responsibility for it. He'd had a stature deserving of genuine hatred, deserving of the esteem which genuine hatred necessarily implies or entails. He'd been, so to speak, a worthy adversary; and had we ever met face to face, I'd've felt tempted to punch him in his. He merited, that is, the respect latent in the closed fist. Richard Nixon, in contrast, merited only a backhanded slap – a gesture not of respect, but of disdain. Lacking the courage to make Vietnam his war, he foisted responsibility for it on to a new, hitherto fictitious entity – the so-called 'Great Silent Majority'. By thus naming and invoking it, he conjured that entity into being, and tried to make Vietnam its war, not his. The cravenness, the deviousness, the duplicity, were characteristic. I saw Nixon as a would-be machiavel, a would-be Borgia or Medici, a would-be Faust, who lacked the grandeur of his own ambitions. I imagined him conjuring up the Devil and, with all the style of a second-hand car dealer, wheedling for a pact. The Devil would've stared at him with ironic incredulity. '*What? You? Evil? Come off it! Surely you jest! But if you're interested, worm, I might offer you a bargain on some near-evil – the equivalent, more or less, of near-beer, denatured beer, low-alcohol lager.'*

Near-evil, of course, was to become the hallmark of the new administration. It manifested itself through creative tackiness and innovative stupidity – not to mention corruption, spite, recrimination, pettiness, ineptitude and the other sorry, watered down demonic qualities so sleazily exposed by the Watergate affair. Perhaps most flagrantly of all, near-evil manifested itself through mediocrity – as embodied and extolled, for example, by the wooden-tongued Vice-President, a man almost too dumb to be true. My memory is hazy about the precise circumstances; but if I recall correctly, Nixon had selected some like-minded dunce for appointment to the Supreme Court, and critics, not without justification, had stigmatised the nominee as mediocre. Not knowing the meaning of the word, thinking apparently that it meant 'normal' or 'conventional', Spiro Agnew had rushed in where even accredited fools feared to tread. There was nothing wrong, he blustered, with being mediocre. Perhaps the country's present problems stemmed from a lack of sufficient mediocrity. Perhaps America needed more good healthy mediocrity to regain her stability and sense of purpose. That Christmas, the best-selling book on the nation's campuses was *The Wit and Wisdom of Spiro Agnew*. It consisted of a sententiously learned and pompous introduction, aslosh with fulsome praise, followed by some fifty or sixty utterly blank pages. In its way, I suppose, it was a triumph of the entrepreneurial spirit. Somebody, somewhere, made a fortune by attaching a slick jacket and a clever preface to an empty notebook.

While Nixon and Agnew busied themselves bringing a new odium to the White House, the war continued tenaciously, with its novocain-numbing adumbration of kill ratios and other sterile statistics, its less publicised but ever-burgeoning casualty lists. And although the administration had promised a new 'rule of law', a new range of remedies for urban mildew, a new dawn of domestic well-being, the situation in the cities continued to deteriorate. I'd grown up around New York; I'd spent much of my teens there, many of my holidays and summers as an undergraduate; I considered the city to be, in some measure at least, 'my' city – I felt, that is, the sense of proprietorship that derives from knowing a place intimately. Once upon a time, I'd been able to move with heedless impunity through every quarter, every neighbourhood. Now, the entire metropolis was a 'combat zone', and the 'no-go' areas extended well beyond just the black and Puerto Rican precincts. People I knew were afraid to use the subway. My closest friends, a couple who lived on the Upper West Side, would venture out at night, even if just to shop, only together. On returning, they'd perform what, to an outsider, would've seemed a bizarre and melodramatic ritual. She'd insert the key in the lock. He'd assume a sentry's position behind her, guarding her, facing away from her, out towards the sidewalk. These weren't timid souls, novices, naïve bumpkins from the provinces. On the contrary, they were native New Yorkers, streetwise and experienced, more familiar with Manhattan than I was. They knew it was when one opened a door - when one fumbled with lock and keys and had one's back turned - that muggers would most frequently pounce.

On one of my visits to them, I pulled a chair to their sixth floor window and monitored the road below as we talked and drank. In the space of an hour or so, I witnessed half a dozen muggings. There was nothing very dramatic about them - no violence, no bloodshed. Certainly there wasn't time to do anything - to get down from the sixth floor, for example, and intervene. In each case, the incident lasted little more than a minute. A well-dressed, dapperly overcoated pedestrian might be hurrying along, carrying a briefcase and umbrella. As he passed through the pools of light from the streetlamps and the chasms of shadow between them, he'd slip in and out of visibility, in and out of definition. Suddenly, two or three furtive figures would materialise from an alley, an entrance hall, the gloom in the lee of a building. In a swift flurry of movement, they'd intercept their victim, hemming him in fore and aft, and a brief huddle would ensue. Seconds later, the furtive figures would scuttle off into the darkness, leaving the victim standing there, bereft of wallet, keys, briefcase, umbrella and anything else portable. Sometimes he'd bellow and gesticulate indignantly. More often, he'd look ruefully resigned.

Such was the city. Out on Long Island, forty-five miles to the east, friction intensified between university and community, but the surface of things remained, for the moment, relatively placid. In that brittle, artificially insulate atmosphere, I continued to play pedagogue. I'd relinquished my undergraduates, transferring my entire course load to adult education and what in Britain would mistakenly have been called 'mature students' from the environs. Ostensibly, my colleagues and I in the department addressed ourselves to literature, some 'classic', some contemporary. In reality, however, by accident or design, we'd find ourselves addressing the issues most prominent at the moment, the prevailing anxieties, the most recent developments or disturbances. And it reflected some measure of progress, perhaps, that the adult education programme was flourishing. Despite the abrasion between the school and its surroundings, our classes were swamped. People from the adjacent towns and villages - from all walks of life, all backgrounds, all levels of literacy or lack of it, many of them with children of their own from whom they'd become estranged - thronged to enrol *en masse*. And behind the assertions they'd make, behind the questions they'd ask, there constantly echoed, as though in chorus, a single, mute, incipiently panic-stricken appeal: *'Tell us what's happening! Tell us why everything's going wrong! Tell us why the things we've subscribed to, believed in, taken for granted, accepted as givens, are all collapsing around us, are all proving so terrifyingly fragile! Tell us why we've become alienated from our sons and daughters! Tell us why we feel guilty! Help us to understand!''*

In responding to this appeal, some of my colleagues were warm, patient, compassionate, sympathetic. Some, for all their worthy intentions, were wretchedly incompetent. I, for my part, systematically developed, perfected and deployed the techniques I'd used against Gil at the tavern the year before. I adopted a maxim which, ever since, has remained a basic educational premise for me - that one can't convey to people *what* one knows until one first establishes *that* one knows. Unless one establishes *that* one knows, one is simply offering another point of view, neither more nor less valid than their own, than anyone else's - just another opinion among a multitude of possible opinions proffering claims to supremacy, jostling to be vociferated, clamouring for a hearing. Once one establishes *that* one knows, however, one is dealing with a captive audience. Once one has established the requisite authority, people will be prepared to listen; and one can then communicate *what* one knows in an ambience of silence and attentiveness, free from static, from the interference and jamming apparatus of other voices, other minds.

Proceeding on this premise, I undertook to convince my students *that* I knew. I did so in part by erudition, by insight, by eloquence, by the spectrum of resources traditionally employed by anyone functioning in a pedagogical capacity. But I also did so by other means, which, in their brazenness, their outrageousness, their histrionic excess, now embarrass me. And yet, for all that, they were extraordinarily effective - as such devices have proved to be throughout history, as they continue to be today. Good teaching consists, at least in some measure, of good acting. The 'job' I'd done on Gil at the tavern that night had been, as I'd realised at the time, a performance. It was into just such virtuoso performances that I turned my classes.

My persona became, even by the standards of that flamboyant era, ridiculously exaggerated. Masked by my dark glasses, I'd consistently dress entirely in black, with silver accoutrements - my 'evil suit', as Patterson had once dubbed it. I'd appear before my students as some sinister hybrid compounded of Paladin from *Have Gun Will Travel*, Zorro, Nero and a *Hauptsturmführer* in the SS. I'd speak in a haughty, autocratic, definitive fashion, laying down the law with an unimpugnable, unchallengeable authority. I'd maintain a façade of disquietingly icy impersonality. I'd present myself as an uncannily penetrating oracle, whose human dimension, if there was one, remained mantled in mystery, shrouded in enigma. And at times I'd find it alarming how readily people deferred and submitted to the intimidating image I projected. And how hungry they were for such 'larger-than-life' images, how eager to be cowed and dominated.

Much of it had to do with what I can only call a matter of 'proximity' or 'immediacy'. For half a century, the United States had held at bay the 'disintegration of values' experienced by Western Europe - and charted by such visionaries as Hermann Broch - in the aftermath of the First World War. Now, that process had caught up with America as well, and with a vengeance all the more ferocious for being deferred. With previous bastions of certainty falling increasingly into disrepute, there was - and there remains today - a frantic yearning for authority figures, for gurus, for prophets, for ayatollahs, for messiahs. It was, of course, in response to this yearning that a dizzying spectrum of self-created saviours crawled out of the proverbial woodwork, or from under sundry stones - Charles Manson and Jim Jones, Jerry Falwell and Jimmy Swaggart, not to mention the new fundamentalists and all the other propagators of sects, cults, disciplines and therapies which promised, if not answers, at least absolution from the terror and responsibility of thinking for oneself.

The young seemed more vulnerable only because they were unabashed in their craving, made no secret of it, lusted for it openly and publicly. But their elders, though less flagrant perhaps, were no less desperate, no less susceptible.

Coached by machiavels more astute than himself, Richard Nixon exploited this situation. In a way that no President before him had ever done, he availed himself of television, appearing regularly and promiscuously on the screen. Still furtive-looking behind his caked makeup, still blue-jowled, still shifty-faced, he countered his unsavoury demeanour by familiarity - by constantly invading people's living-rooms and making himself a kind of self-appointed member of the family. He'd establish an ostensibly sincere eye contact with the viewer. He'd adopt a spuriously intimate tone of voice, a confiding and soulful expression - or, at least, as close to soulful as a vacuum could simulate. And by such devices, he'd convey the illusory impression of addressing each person in his audience individually. Unctuously informal, chummy, paternally concerned, he purported genuinely to care, to sympathise, to understand; and he thereby made the gullible *want* to believe in his solicitude, in his compassion, in his capacity to share their preoccupations, salve their anxieties. In one of the most grotesque miscastings of recent history, Richard Nixon managed to play the improbable rôle of avuncular protector, of reassuring and consoling paterfamilias, patting a child's head before packing it off to sleep - or, at any rate, off to a fuddlement of all critical faculties. For many, it was flattering and gratifying, thus to be coddled and adopted as confidant by the President of the United States, whose office imparted an aura even to his lacklustre personality. Every sentence he uttered was, needless to say, mere rhetorical massage; but his sheer *'presentness'*, actualised by the television screen, created a specious semblance of emotional warmth. It lulled one into quiescence, prompted one to forgive him his inanities, rather as one might those of one's parents.

But however close the television screen brought him, Nixon remained inevitably two-dimensional, a flat image, and truncated in mid-torso to boot. And however much he pretended to address each segment of the country, each individual specifically, he was nevertheless confined to generalities. Promises applicable to Texas or Iowa made little impact on the intelligentsia of East and West Coasts; and promises made to placate them were wasted on 'Middle America'.

I enjoyed an advantage over Nixon in that I could interpose myself between his image on the television screen and his audience. I was three-dimensional. I could address myself to local issues, local problems, local frictions. I could deal personally with each member of my class, call him or her by name, answer his or her questions directly. More precisely than Nixon, I could formulate, articulate, enunciate each person's most immediate and pressing concerns. I could venture into territory that Nixon couldn't on camera. I could explain, for example, patiently, without dogma or moral opprobrium, why my listeners' sons and daughters had revolted, had sought meaning outside traditional frameworks, had felt impelled to experiment with drugs. I could speak of changing sexual attitudes, of identity crises, of the complex psychological ordeals through which many of my students were passing. I could probe depths of whose existence Nixon himself hadn't a clue. I was thus able to *demonstrate* to my audience that I understood them, their predicaments, their dilemmas, their uncertainties. By expressing them to themselves, I placed them in my debt. And having verbalised their point of view more cogently than they could, I might then proceed to verbalise what was often its antithesis. Yes, it was, I suppose, a form of brainwashing, but no more insidious than that practised by the President himself. And when I washed people's brains, I at least used water distilled from the purest springs of the West's cultural heritage, not from the sewers running beneath the Watergate.

That, however, is only a qualified extenuation. The fact remains that the means I used were tainted, and I myself was soiled by using them, if only in some absolute moral or - to use a word then in vogue - 'karmic' sense. And there were times, too, when, losing perspective, I'd underestimate the impact of the rôle I'd assumed - or when I identified with that rôle too closely, grew into my mask and found I could no longer remove it without tearing away my face.

On one occasion, for example, we'd been discussing *Tonio Kröger*. By extension, I'd expatiated on some of Mann's other protagonists - on Goethe as portrayed in *Lotte in Weimar*, on Gustave von Aschenbach and Adrian Leverkühn - and waxed scathing about the artist. In previous weeks, my class had heard me snipe cynically not just at obvious and predictable targets, but also at graduate students, university professors, critics and intellectuals. To hear me now castigating the artist as well - his egoism, his cold aloofness and detachment, his amorality, his inhumanity, his ruthlessness - took them aback. With what must've seemed to her a reckless audacity, one woman at the rear of the room raised her hand and dared to confront me.

'Who are you?' she asked, her voice plaintive with perplexity. 'You're in the graduate programme, yet you attack graduate students. You teach in a university, yet you attack university teachers. You're a brilliant critic, yet you attack critics. You seem to be an intellectual, yet you attack intellectuals. You write, yet you attack writers. Who are you? What are you?'

I was, of course, amused. And there was, of course, an obvious, if flip, response. It tempted me. I framed it in my mind: '*Ich bin der Geist, der stets verneint.*' They wouldn't've understood, however, and if I'd explained, the matter would no longer have been frivolous - would've become, in fact, rather more sinister than I was prepared to condone. I therefore improvised.

'I'm a magus,' I said, allowing myself the mere flicker of an ironic smile.

Here and there in the room, a few people giggled or sniggered nervously, uneasily. The woman who'd posed the question, however, just nodded. So did a number of others. They weren't only quite satisfied with my answer, I realised, horrified. They were perfectly prepared to accept it.

In my smugness about my own self-awareness, I should've realised by then that my demagogic skills were going to my head; but it took a more dramatic incident to hoist me on my own petard, to make me appreciate the magnitude of the forces with which I'd been so cavalierly tampering. I was discussing a contemporary work. I'd been particularly eloquent in condemning a weedy anti-hero who, for all the usual reasons, shrank from the affections of a woman far worthier than himself. In impressive oratorical fashion, I'd used my voice as an instrument, intoning long evocative hypnotic sentences which accelerated in cadence, built orchestrally to a crescendo. At the appropriate climax, I shifted an octave, lowered my tone and dropped quietly, into the mesmerised silence, the punchline to which I'd been leading:

'But then again, how many of us have rejected the love of someone who's genuinely and validly loved us - because accepting it would've meant accepting ourselves?'

A trenchant aphorism perhaps, telling enough in its insight. But I'd recited it mechanically. For me, it was warmed-over wisdom. I'd conceived it a week or so before, had written it into the nouvelle on which I was working. When I uttered it in my class, I uttered it quite coldly, like a technique actor responding to cue. To all intents and purposes, I might've simply pressed a button, feeling nothing at the moment save satisfaction with my own performance. I'd expected to produce an essentially aesthetic impact. To my shock, however, a woman in the second row - a strikingly attractive woman, elegant, even haughty, with an exquisitely poised and stately demeanour - emitted something like a stricken squawk. For an instant, she stared at me, wide-eyed and accusing, as if I'd deliberately singled her out and stabbed her. Her face then crumpled and she began to sob - great wrenching convulsive sobs that jerked her shoulders, wracked her entire body.

I was startled at first, not realising her hysteria had any connection with what I'd said. Then I grew simultaneously embarrassed, disconcerted, affronted. How dare she disrupt my class with so extravagant an outburst? How dare she mar the mood I'd painstakingly created with such unseemly exhibitionism? Maintaining a façade of dispassionate but patient *sang-froid,* I asked her if she wished to be excused. She sniffed in the affirmative, thanked me, apologised tearfully for her loss of self-control, struggled from her seat and lurched drunkenly out of the room on her high heels, while I tried to restore some semblance of decorum to the proceedings.

Later, poring over a brandy in a nearby bar, I attempted to assess what'd happened. Only then did my own responsibility - if not quite guilt - become apparent to me. I'd known nothing about that woman, not even her name; I'd never had reason to wonder about her personal life. She'd been no more to me than a glamorous presence who'd added piquancy to my class, inspired me to greater fluency in my rhetoric. In other words, she'd been mere raw material, on whom - or on which - I'd heedlessly exercised and honed my skills. And yet, in practising those skills, I'd not just shamed her before her peers, not just mortified and humiliated her; I'd also extorted from her a moment of self-exposure, a moment of nakedness, to which I had no legitimate claim. I'd violated more than what the courts would've called her 'civil rights'; I'd violated rights far deeper, far more intimate. I'd made a public display of something only a confidant, a lover or a husband should've witnessed. And I'd done so carelessly, thoughtlessly, by a feckless revelling in my own power. Nor could I argue that this was the kind of effect every artist aspires to achieve, the kind of effect I myself sought to produce through my own work. I wasn't at all sure I wanted to produce such effects through my work - effects less aesthetic ultimately than emotional, perhaps just sentimental. And even if my work did produce them, it would produce them in private, as part of an intensely solitary artistic experience, not before a gallery of strangers' eyes.

I didn't expect to see the woman again; I assumed she'd absent herself in future, not daring to show her face. I wasn't to be so spared. No, she wasn't in class the next day; but when class adjourned, she was waiting in the corridor, hovering at the door as my other students jostled their way out. Intercepting me, she asked if I could spare her a moment. I couldn't very well refuse - she'd apparently regained all her former poise and was breathtakingly lovely. We walked together to a deserted alcove at the end of the hall, where a bleary window overlooked the car park. Here, she again apologised for her 'silliness', as she called it, of the previous afternoon. I dismissed the matter, told her not to worry about it.

'But I do,' she replied in a kind of muted wail. 'I've never lost control of myself like that before. I'm going through a difficult time just now, you see. My life's in something of an upheaval. It always seems to happen to me in my relationships. I've so often wished there was a person I could talk to, but I never met anyone I thought would understand. After some of the things you said yesterday, though, I'm beginning to think you might. I'd be ever so grateful for any advice you might have. Or any suggestions...'

'I'll be happy to do what I can,' I said, keeping my voice studiously neutral and non-committal, already feeling some misgiving, some foreboding.

'Well,' she began briskly, in a no-nonsense, businesslike fashion, as if she were talking about some automotive trouble, some difficulty, say, with a recalcitrant carburettor, 'I should probably start by telling you that I'm frigid...'

I stopped her there. With maximum phlegm, aplomb and every other deterrent resource I could muster, I told her gently that I wasn't either a sexologist or a psychotherapist - that there were specialists who ministered to malfunctions such as hers, that the problem no doubt stemmed from complex deep-rooted factors, that one couldn't hope to do justice to these through a casual conversation in a corridor, that it wouldn't in any case be appropriate for me to venture an opinion. In short, I scuttled away as fast as my tongue could carry me. She was astute enough to recognise my reluctance to get involved and made no effort to press the issue. She asked a few anodyne and routine questions. We exchanged a few ritualised cordialities and parted. Although she returned to my class a week later, she said little for the duration of the term, and we had no further personal contact.

I didn't neglect to learn from the episode, awkward though its dénouement had been. Among other things, it revealed to me, more clearly than I'd ever appreciated before, the insidious subterranean relationship between trust and power. With Gil, with those of my students prepared to accept me as a magus, with that woman whose psychic maidenhead my words had accidentally pierced, I'd used power to elicit trust. Indeed, I realised, the business of eliciting trust had been, all along, the single most important aspect of my pedagogical efforts. But trust is a volatile commodity, dangerously unstable. For the giving of trust isn't passive. It's active. It's a dynamic process, a *transaction*, whereby some sort of energy, so to speak, is transferred. And as though by some chemical or alchemical transmutation, what originates as trust in the donor becomes converted, in the recipient, to a form of power. Thus I'd been using power to elicit trust, and the trust I'd elicited had been transformed back into greater power. It wasn't a voluntary or deliberate procedure on my part; it was something inherent in the nature of things, in the laws governing the interaction of psyches. If fifty, a hundred, a thousand, a hundred thousand people conferred their trust on me, my power would increase proportionately.

In this energy of elicited and conferred trust, this vital electrifying current, lay the secret of so-called 'charisma'. It was in this energy that the fundamentalist preacher trafficked. It was on this energy that all the Hitlers and would-be Hitlers of the world - all the mystagogues and demagogues, self-appointed saviours and messiahs - fed like vampires and flourished. It was on this energy that Richard Nixon, in his furtive and mangy manner, sought similarly to trade. And it was by diverting this energy, if only on a modest local level, that I could neutralise his influence - at the cost, however, of sullying myself. To dabble with the chemistry of trust and power - especially if one does so impersonally - is a dodgy and ultimately demeaning affair. One can justify it only by a full consciousness of what one's doing, and a well-developed sense of responsibility. For the distinction is shifting and elusive between a guru or a magus on the one hand and a *Führer* on the other, between a disciple on the one hand and, on the other, a slave.

That year, at Altamont Speedway in California, Mick Jagger, on a much more ambitious scale and with much more catastrophic consequences, learned a similar lesson. Signatory of his own Faust pact, he, too, boasted sympathy for *der Geist der stets verneint*. By word, by sound and rhythm, by incantatory repetition, he, too, sought to conjure. From within the magic circle of the floodlit stage, he endeavoured, in his own way, to exorcise his audience. And like so many sorcerers before him, he lost control of the forces he'd invoked. The concert, billed as the West Coast's Woodstock, fostered no peace, no love, no reconciliation. It disintegrated instead into demoniac frenzy.

I was driving to a rendezvous with a prospective muse when I heard what'd happened on the car radio - a youth murdered, stabbed to death in a moment of insensate delirium. Later, at my prospective muse's house, we watched television film of the event. We saw hippies and Hell's Angels jostling and shoving one another, rupturing the fragile, motley and mismatched alliance imposed on them by an imprudent would-be thaumaturge. We saw tempers fraying and snapping, scuffles erupting. We saw the upraised arm. We saw the knife blade, seemingly in slow motion, trace its fatal arc across the screen, stark white as a meteor.

* * * * * * *

In front of my class, as well as with Gil in the tavern, I'd personally experienced the proximity of magus to *Führer*. Across America at the time, one could witness almost daily the mutation of disciples into slaves. I was to encounter that mutation on one particularly telling occasion in the autumn of my third year on Long Island. For non-political reasons, as usual, I'd broken my own rule and accompanied some of my colleagues to a demonstration in Washington, the largest such demonstration to date. In this instance, my ulterior motives weren't amorous. Not, at any rate, primarily so. Although I had designs on no specific woman at the moment, I was prepared to welcome whatever romantic opportunities might materialise – I was out of love and therefore out of sorts, out of inspiration, out of *joie de vivre*. Chiefly, however, I was bored, and impelled to Washington by aesthetic curiosity. The sheer scale of the protest promised an impressive spectacle, and a convivial outing as well. Most of my friends were planning to attend, were pestering me to join them, and I would've been a spoilsport to refuse. Ponderously, like a brontosaurus stirring in its sleep, public opinion was beginning to change. We all scented it in the air; and the mood, in consequence, though still laced with outrage, was ebullient – the mood of a carnival, a festival.

The mood was quickly dispelled. The capital, that day, was hot, clammy, muggy, humid, sweltering – Indian summer asserting itself on the perimeter of the old South. The weather was more tyrannically oppressive than anything the government could contrive. In the stifling heat, under a mercilessly incandescent sun, exuberance soon wilted, giving way to a very different quality of energy. We had to park some distance away, then make a veritable safari on foot to the designated site. There were more people than the space allotted could accommodate.

At a certain point, the march – or, rather, the shambles – got stalled. No doubt fully cognisant of what they were doing, the authorities had created a deliberate bottleneck – demonstrators were forced to filter through a narrow gate before funnelling out on to the grounds surrounding the Washington Monument. Delays ensued. The crowd began to back up on itself. Throats got parched, heels trodden on, rib cages elbowed, bottoms groped, pockets picked. Nerves became frazzled, tempers shredded. Impatience, frustration, exasperation and burgeoning belligerence began to spread like palpable currents through the stifling throng. One felt helplessly trapped in the crush, incapable of advancing, of withdrawing, of extricating oneself. Discomfort engendered claustrophobia and, here and there, nascent panic - the awareness that if, for any reason, a stampede occurred, bodies would be trampled, lives lost.

As things came increasingly and literally to a boil, a coven of a dozen militant demonstrators, brandishing a Viet Cong flag, clambered over one of the barriers. Cursing, shouting abuse at the white-armbanded marshals appointed to keep order, they invaded an expanse of open grass bristling with 'No Trespassing' signs. Dishevelled, mangy-looking, prancing about in what resembled an Indian war dance, they began to chant - '*Peace now*! *Peace now*! *Peace now*!'Their faces - sweating, sunburned, aggressive, angry-eyed, contorted with a demonic intensity verging on possession - were anything but peaceful. As they cavorted, they glared balefully at the crowd, challenging the docile herd to join them in their defiance, their loosing of pent-up emotion.

This, I realised, was the spirit that had broken free, run abroad and amok at Altamont. Few, however, made any effort to resist it. Gradually but inexorably, the crowd succumbed to its appeal, being carried along, taking up the invocation - '*Peace now*! *Peace now*! *Peace now*!' To bellow was an intoxicating release. People numbed themselves by the incantatory repetition of those two words. It dulled consciousness; it provided a species of oblivion, a respite from the misery of the heat, the congestion, the stultifying stench and press of other bodies. It channelled all the discomfort, the frustration, the exasperation, the hostility into a single rhythm, like a drumbeat, in which critical faculties faded, minds merged. The rhythm began to take precedence over the words. When the demonstrators on the grass accelerated the rhythm, the crowd at once followed suit, instinctively, automatically. The words, by then, had ceased to matter. The words could've been changed. Had I or anyone else chosen to change them, the crowd would've been swept along, unwitting. With no perceptible transition, '*Peace now*! *Peace now*! *Peace now*!' could've become '*Sieg heil*! *Sieg heil*! *Sieg heil*!' And most people would've repeated it perhaps half a dozen times before they realised what they were yelling.

No single faction had a monopoly on this kind of energy. It was perpetually in the air, like ozone after a thunderstorm; it was part of the *Zeitgeist*, and easily hijacked by the quickest and most adept manipulator. Measured against it, ideologies - rooted in the intellect alone, catering to the intellect alone - were puerile. Nevertheless, the ideologues, like panhandlers amidst a hurricane, continued to peddle their piddling wares, and their efforts sometimes provided comic relief.

Thus, for example, during that demonstration in Washington, two of my colleagues and I were accosted by a film crew, all hard-line members of the Italian Communist Party, who'd been making a television documentary on the 'new American Revolution'. They stumbled on us by chance; they could've stumbled on any number of other people; but finding us signally articulate - which we were, I suppose, compared to many of the rank-and-file undergraduate demonstrators - they asked us if we'd consent to appear in their programme, to act as representative spokesmen, to be interviewed at length. Arrangements were made accordingly, and a week later we convened in Manhattan, in their hotel room, where cameras and recording equipment had already been set up.

In the interview that followed, the Italians were flummoxed by what seemed to them our vagueness, our 'lack of ideological focus'. Again and again, they tried to extract from us some sort of 'revolutionary manifesto', some sort of definitive militant policy statement. Again and again, our evasiveness - the equivalent, so to speak, of a firm 'maybe' - confounded them. One of my colleagues was a self-avowed socialist. Even he, however, seemed to the Italians dreamy, mystical, nebulous, wishy-washy, devoid of the requisite 'rigour'. By the time they got to me, I'd become annoyed by their simplistic dogmatism. I decided to be perverse, to present myself as an irretrievably lost cause.

'If I am not mistaken,' the interviewer began, as the camera started whirring, 'you consider yourself a leftist...'

'A leftist?' I replied. 'I'm not sure what you mean by that. Presumably something derived from the French '*gauche*'? Do I consider myself a gauchist? No. Of course not. Why should I consider myself gauche?'

After a moment's consternation, the Italians apparently concluded the problem had to do with language. Perhaps they weren't making themselves clear. Perhaps their English wasn't as fluent as they'd imagined.

'Do you consider yourself,' the interviewer began again, patiently, 'a representative of the American left?'

I contrived to look baffled, feigning invincible obtuseness and naïveté.

'Left what?'

'The political left. The left wing of the American political...scene, as you would say.'

'The American political scene doesn't have wings. It doesn't fly. It's leaden. Ingloriously earthbound. Mired, even.'

'To the left of the political centre.'

'There's no political centre here. No more than there's any other kind of centre. It's all hollow. Weren't you aware of the hollowness?'

Two of the Italians - I couldn't determine which of them was the producer, which the director - exchanged glances of despair. The interviewer changed tack.

'How would you summarise the...how shall I say?...the central organising ideology of you and your contemporaries?'

'I can't speak for my contemporaries. As for myself, I repudiate all ideologies. Any *system* is inimical to me. What matters to me is vision, not systems or ideologies or philosophies. Least of all political systems, ideologies or philosophies.'

'But surely as an American intellectual...'

'Whether I'm American or not, I can't say. I certainly don't *feel* very American. In any case, I'm not an intellectual.'

'Oh, come now! Surely you are too modest! Surely you underestimate yourself!'

'Too *modest*? *Under*estimate myself? Shit, I'm being *im*modest! You think I find it flattering to be called an intellectual? I find it insulting.'

The interviewer looked suddenly anxious and defensive, as if I might challenge him to a duel.

'Forgive me, but I do not understand. Why do you find it insulting?'

'An intellectual's a fool who believes his intellect's the most valid or accurate monitoring apparatus of reality. He trusts in his intellect. I don't. I use it, certainly. I like to think I use it well. But I certainly don't trust it, and I try to keep it confined to its own proper domain - the domain of conveniences, as opposed to truths. Conveniences like clock time. Time as measured by the clock, in contrast to genuine time. To understand genuine time, or anything else genuine, I trust my intuition and my feelings far more than I do my intellect.'

'But this is...this is *mysticism*!'

'Of course it is. Though I personally prefer to use the term "numinism".'

'It is not reasonable!'

'I should hope not. Why should it be reasonable? To believe in reason or rationality's as irrational as believing in anything else. It's just another blind act of faith - as blind as any act of faith.'

'But how can you use this philosophy as...?'

'It's not a philosophy. As I told you, I'm not interested in philosophy, only in vision.'

'How can you use this...this "vision"...as a basis for revolution?'

'You can't. Not your kind of revolution, at any rate. But I never claimed to be conducting a revolution. I've no desire to conduct a revolution. You simply assumed I did.'

The Italians again exchanged glances, this time of irascible impatience. They'd wasted by now, on all of us, a substantial quantity of film and still not got the sort of statements they wanted.

'How, then, would you describe yourself?' the interviewer demanded, exhausted and bellicose.

'I prefer not to,' I replied, echoing Melville's Bartleby. 'But if you stuck a gun in my ribs and insisted on an answer - you know: "Your *Weltanschauung* or your life' - I suppose I'd say I was an antinomian Hermetic numinist.'

The interviewer shook his head hopelessly.

'Hermetic...?' he faltered, groping for a frame of reference. 'You mean as in the writers of our *Ermetismo*? Ungaretti...?'

'And Quasimodo. And Montale.'

'But they are mere aesthetes! They reduce politics to poetry!'

'Precisely. I certainly wouldn't want poetry reduced to mere politics.'

I've no idea whether the film was ever actually transmitted on Italian television - or even, for that matter, ever actually made. If my colleagues or I appeared in it at all, which I rather doubt, we can only have do so as adverse examples, warped specimens - embodiments of everything the doctrinally correct Marxist shouldn't be. We could hardly have provided much in the way of propaganda for the Italian Communist Party - except perhaps illustrations of how *not* to foment a Leninist or Maoist style revolution.

For those seeking revolutionary propaganda, however, events were soon to furnish enough raw material of their own. In the spring of my last year on Long Island, Bobby Seale - prominent Black Panther and one of the so-called 'Chicago Seven' - was brought to trial for murder. The case against him, which most people believed fabricated, became a *cause célèbre* on every campus in the country. But even this was upstaged by the escalating momentum of developments. Of those developments, the most important for me personally was the death of Alison Krause.

In the first part of Goethe's dramatic poem, Faust seduces Gretchen, impregnates her, then abandons her. Outcast and friendless, the girl, in a fit of hysteria, drowns her child and attempts to take her own life. Before she can do so, she's apprehended, imprisoned and sentenced to death for infanticide. When Faust, pausing for breath between more cosmic adventures, learns of her predicament, he resolves to rescue her from her cell. Mephistopheles endeavours to dissuade him. Faust waxes poignant about Gretchen's plight. The Devil remains unimpressed. '*She is not the first,*' he observes dryly, sardonically. Her dilemma, he implies, is trite, banal, contemptibly laughable, and as old as humanity itself. It's one of the clichés of mortal experience that silly peasant girls, serving maids and kitchen wenches should get themselves knocked up, bear illegitimate children and suffer the consequences. They've done so since the beginning of the human experiment, will continue to do so for as long as sexual chemistry works its magic. Faust has more momentous matters to preoccupy him, more important things to do than waste energy on so tiresome and hackneyed an affair.

Confronted by this implacably callous cynicism, Faust is affronted. For the first time, he loses his temper with the Devil. For the first time, he's seriously tempted to abrogate his demonic pact. Cursing and abusing Mephistopheles, he proclaims the death of any such young woman to be a crime that rends the very fabric of creation:

> Not the first! Misery and woe more profound than the human soul can fathom, that more than one poor being should be mired in this swamp of

> wretchedness...The anguish of this one creature pierces me to the marrow, while you smirk coldly at the fate of thousands!

That sequence in Goethe's poem has always possessed a profound resonance for me. In our society as a whole, the greatest tragedy is generally deemed to be the death of a child, the most monstrous crime that of child-murder. I'd certainly not presume to impute the magnitude, the enormity, of either. But not being a parent myself, and having had relatively little to do with children, the death of a child has seldom had more impact on me personally than most other deaths.

From earliest boyhood, on the other hand, even from before puberty, I'd always been most deeply moved, most painfully, poignantly and wrenchingly shaken, by the death of a young woman. The great literary tragedies for me haven't been Othello or Lear, Prince Andrey or Julien Sorel, but Faust's Gretchen, Emma Bovary, Anna Karenina, Effi Briest, Hardy's Tess - young women doomed for no more grievous a transgression than yearning and daring to love. No doubt some grumpy feminist somewhere, by some gnarled contortion of logic, will contrive to find my attitude one of outmoded chivalry, and therefore 'sexist'. If so, *tant pis*. I make no apology for it. I can't help it, just as I can't help being more aroused by female breasts and buttocks than by female elbows.

During the spring of my last year on Long Island, Richard Nixon, in violation of both national and international law, sent units of the American military across the Vietnamese border into Cambodian territory. Already in ferment over Bobby Seale, the campuses, inevitably, exploded anew. Ronald Reagan, who subsequently condemned the shooting of students in Tiananmen Square, had no compunction, as Governor of California, about dispatching the National Guard to Berkeley; and in the ensuing turmoil, one youth perished, another was permanently blinded. Guardsmen were despatched to other schools as well - including Kent State in Ohio.

To this day, lawsuits, investigations and enquiries have failed to establish the reasons for what followed - whether it resulted from deliberate malice, an excess of patriotic zeal or simply from naïveté, greenness and panic in callow Sunday soldiers of diminished capacity or intelligence, to whom loaded weapons should never have been entrusted in the first place. In any case, a contingent of Guardsmen found themselves confronted by a ragged column of protestors. The protestors were ordered to disperse. When they refused to do so, the Guardsmen opened fire - discharged a volley not over their heads, but directly into their ranks. Among those who died was Alison Krause. She'd not even been participating in the demonstration. She'd simply been walking to a class, making her way along a path some distance from the tumult. It was here that a Guardsman's bullet struck and killed her.

I never, of course, knew Alison Krause personally; I never met her, never even saw her in the flesh. Had we encountered one another, I might possibly have become infatuated by her; I might equally well have found her a bimbo - vapid, shallow, superficial, perhaps offensive or obnoxious. But I could never know her now, except through her photograph in the newspapers and on television - the photograph of an exquisite, achingly beautiful girl, with a radiance, a haunting and luminous loveliness that seemed actively to pulse at me from page or screen. Nor was mine the only such reaction. Most of my colleagues felt something similar. So, too, did Yevgeny Yevtushenko, who, stirred to outrage, memorialised her in a now-famous poem. In an intensely private, idiosyncratic and irrational way, she became for me, as she did for Yevtushenko, transmuted into symbol. Alison Krause was das *Ewigweibliche*, incarnate and trampled on, martyred by the blindness of incompetent men. Richard Nixon might not have been worthy of undiluted full-proof evil. But in his smallness, his pettiness, his evasion of responsibility, he'd attained something no less destructive. Her death reflected what the war, the country, the administration, the gang of bungling misfits in charge of things were doing to poetry, to magic, to sensitivity, to imagination, to wholeness and harmony, to everything embodied by the feminine principle. It wasn't evil, after all, that crushed Gretchen, Emma Bovary, Anna Karenina, Effi Briest and Tess. They were crushed by smugness, banality, mediocrity, moral myopia, sanctimonious self-righteousness and flannel-mouthed hypocrisy.

Scarcely had the news from Kent State broken than Nixon, obliged to extemporise to the press, castigated the dead, including Alison Krause, as 'troublemakers' and 'hoodlums'. No one on any campus in America - no graduate or undergraduate, no professor, no administrator, no person in any way associated with education - could be blind to the import and innuendo of the words. In effect, the President had implicitly declared open season on students. He'd pinned a facile label to the backs of those killed, and, by so doing, condoned what'd happened to them. It was acceptable to shoot down hoodlums and troublemakers.

Whatever upheavals the campuses had hitherto experienced paled against the inferno now unleashed. With the casual and obscene insolence of the thoughtless, the clod in the White House had indeed begun to reap a whirlwind. For a period of perhaps a week, violent insurrection, if not some species of full-fledged civil war, seemed to many people an imminent possibility. It was no longer the wild pipe dream of small militant cadres, but a prospect seriously entertained by much of the nation's college and university population. Incidents spread across the country like a conflagration leaping from tuft to tuft of brush. Rednecks assaulted students and raided schools, sometimes firebombing dormitories where hundreds slept. Gangs of marauding youths retaliated with forays into adjacent communities, smashing windows, vandalising Post Offices and other government installations, setting fires of their own. As in Chicago three years before, guns began to appear.

During those diaphanous blue-and-gold May afternoons and dusks, I found myself trapped in a bizarre, Janus-faced, almost schizoid existence. At five or six o'clock, I'd be addressing some of the adults from my classes, or perhaps a meeting of anxious local people organised by adults from my classes. I'd be explaining to them the general folly of the war, and why it wasn't altogether sporting for soldiers of a democratic government to shoot students on university campuses. By eight or nine o'clock, I'd be in one of the dormitories, where a mob mobilised by some of the loopier radicals was working itself up to burn down the computer centre and the library. I didn't particularly care about the computer centre. It was a singularly ugly structure anyway. Books, however, were a different matter. I'd therefore exhort the agitators to see how counter-productive their proposed action would be. To incinerate buildings in Bobby Seale's name, I'd argue, was hardly likely to inspire public sympathy for him.

'At least be honest with yourselves about what you're doing. Do you want to help Bobby Seale, or do you want to martyr him? If you torch the library on his behalf, you may martyr him, but you certainly won't help him. If martyrs are what you want, well and good. But don't try to con yourselves or anyone else into thinking you're doing Bobby Seale a favour. You're simply exploiting him. You're simply sacrificing him to your cause.'

By virtue of our age, our status and our values, my colleagues and I enjoyed a measure of credibility in most quarters - among adults from the community, among undergraduates, among more senior faculty and administrators. As a result, we were often caught in a vice between these diverse factions. We were expected to establish channels of communication, to act as liaison officers and interpreters, to negotiate truce terms between disputants, to provide leadership and sanity, to minister to a panoramic array of maladjustments, obsessions and paranoia. And at moments, amid the fury and frenzy of those days, we'd slip towards internecine strife amongst ourselves. One night, for example, I found myself, along with Roland, Sidney, Vanessa and a number of others, forming part of a protective cordon around our own department's office block, guarding it against a mob bent on arson - a mob composed of many undergraduates we knew and led by three of our associates in the graduate programme. As one of them, playing demagogue, endeavoured to galvanise the rabble, Vanessa turned to me in horror. I don't think she realised how tellingly her words pierced to the core of the situation:

'We've got to stop them. We've got to stop the barricades from going up in earnest. No one's ready for that. It'd be a form of mass suicide, and we'd all be drawn into it. If the barricades go up, there'd be no question which side we'd be on. We'd have no choice. And we'd all become martyrs to no purpose.'

Paradoxically, she was right and wrong in the same breath. In that instant, I discerned for the first time the nature of the mechanism confronting us - the insidious, inexorable and inhuman dynamic inherent in so-called 'revolutionary politics'. If the barricades did indeed go up, Vanessa, by her statement - an eminently sane, cogent, lucid and penetrating statement - would've automatically placed herself outside them, in a kind of no-man's land between the radicals and their adversaries. She'd've been, in effect, fair game for both, a sitting target. And if I tried to justify her - if I merely asserted that Vanessa was really 'one of us' - I'd place myself outside the barricades in turn, in the very position from which I'd sought to rescue her.

As in Chicago, circumstances were conspiring to polarise me against my will, to wrest my neutrality from me, to render untenable the fence I wished to straddle. To defend the library, to defend Vanessa, to defend my own independence and integrity, I might find myself perversely aligned with the forces that'd destroyed Alison Krause. I became all the more scathing towards those whose simple-minded zeal threatened me with so appalling a prospect - and, in the process, of course, placed myself all the more definitively outside the barricades. I would maintain, however, a stance of defiance. If I were going to be coerced into no-man's land, at least I'd occupy it properly and plant my flag there. It was probably where I belonged anyway.

The period of crisis lasted some five days. During that time, my colleagues and I remained, so to speak, on constant alert. We functioned as a sort of flying column of socio-political firefighters, moving on instant notice to quell whatever conflagration might erupt, from whatever quarter - from local pressure groups, from the university's more radical activists, from small enclaves of right-wing students, from various other vested interests seeking to hijack, exploit or capitalise on the situation. We curbed and thwarted sorties into the community. We stepped between demonstrators and 'hard hats' with mayhem in their eyes. We persuaded fanatics of opposing camps to shake hands - or, at any rate, to talk, before resorting to violence. Most important of all perhaps, we managed to keep the police and National Guard off campus. It was an exhausting task, sometimes infuriating, sometimes exhilarating. It wasn't, however, the sort of thing for which I felt myself cosmically ordained.

At the end of five days, tension had abated sufficiently for me to relax. I drove into Manhattan, intent on a cathartic binge with my friends there. But scarcely had I slumped down on their sofa with a cognac than the telephone rang. There were, in fact, two calls in quick succession, from colleagues out on Long Island. Both were distraught, one of them so much so his voice was breaking and tears were audible in his words. At the university, trouble had exploded anew. Cars had been set afire. The gatehouse, rebuilt after the 'Big Bust' three years before, had again been burned down. Another assault had been launched against the library, and my two colleagues had been on opposing sides. In the *mêlée* that ensued, amidst the darkness and confusion, they'd found themselves locked in a hand-to-hand struggle, and one had knocked the other down. Both at that point had awakened, as if from a bout of mania or delirium. Both were stricken with remorse.

During the same confrontation, I learned later, another friend had been felled by a blow from a wooden stave, had needed hospitalisation and stitches. The stave had been wielded by a shadowy figure whom he hadn't recognised in the murk and muddle, who hadn't recognised him but who'd proved to be his undergraduate girlfriend. He was rehabilitated within two days, albeit rather unsightly, sporting a black eye, a gash on his temple and a helmet of bandages. By that time, however, mortified by what she'd done, his girlfriend had taken a fatal overdose of sleeping pills.

XIII

When the last summer of the decade had seared itself away, I'd transplanted myself to Vancouver. For some months prior to my expatriation, I'd been in renewed touch, by letter and telephone, with Ilona. She, in her peregrinations, had caromed from Yucatan to New Orleans, thence to Los Angeles, to New York, to Germany, eventually to Canada - where, after pausing in Alberta, she'd pocketed herself in British Columbia. In transit, she'd suffered what might've been construed as a nervous breakdown, or, alternatively, a conversion to Catholicism. I'm not sure there was that much difference between the two, though conversion apparently gave her some rationale for regaining her virginity. At any rate, we'd not seen each other for four years. By means of our long-distance epistolary foreplay, we'd whipped ourselves into a fresh froth of passion, and the Pacific Northwest seemed an aptly picturesque milieu for the resumption of our operatic idyll.

I'd had my fill of the States and its lunacy anyway. Nor was there much to keep me in the country any longer. I'd completed all course and teaching requirements for my Ph.D. Invoking Stifter, Fontane, Musil, Broch, Bely and other figures unknown to my doctoral committee, I'd cruised insouciantly through my exams. I'd been offered a fourth year of subsidy on Long Island. Friends and patrons among senior faculty had also volunteered to help me find some lucrative professorial position, and enticing possibilities were dandled before my eyes. But my amorous aestheticism prevailed over such merely practical considerations. Ilona was more alluring than anything so quotidian as a job, and I welcomed the opportunity - or the excuse - to rid myself of all things American save the country's literature.

Accordingly, at the beginning of August, I'd sold my car, stored my books, burned my boats or bridges or whatever it is one metaphorically burns in such circumstances, abandoned all my prospects, flown out to Vancouver and, through improvisation and luck, landed a post as librarian at the most scenically imposing of mountaintop universities. To some of the colleagues I'd left behind on Long Island, it was a certifiably demented thing to've done, a deplorably soft-brained plunge into romantic extravagance. To others, it was heroic, chivalric, lyrical, poignantly poetic and sublime - something like Edward VIII's abdication, like Nelson's diversion of the entire British Mediterranean Fleet to rescue Lady Hamilton at Naples. Redeemed and transmuted by love, the local Faust-in-residence had repudiated the Devil, converted to pristine white magic, sacrificed everything and winged off into the sunset (yes, this time I was travelling in the right direction) to clasp his suitably Teutonic *Ewigweibliche* in a mystical alchemical conjunction. Never having shrunk from mythologising my own life, I saw it more or less in those terms myself.

I'd never previously experienced anything I could legitimately call love at first sight. Now, however, I experienced it for Canada. I'd grown up on the pestilential periphery of New York, generally recognised as the armpit of the country - if not, indeed, some even less savoury portion of the national anatomy. The vapid suburban commuter belt which included Crestfall. The derelict slumscapes of Newark and Bayonne. The grime and soot and bleakness and stench of Hoboken and Jersey City. The spindly black arches of the Pulaski Skyway looming like some sinister extraterrestrial spiderweb under a chemically yellow sky. The smog-bleared prospect of Manhattan beyond, jagged and spiny as an immense spectral sea-urchin perceived in a feverish mirage. None of this conduced to much sense of rootedness. Amidst the scabrous sprawl, gruesome as a spill of acid over the landscape, there was little to which one could attach oneself, with which one could establish any sort of identification - at least if one were sane.

However impressive some of them had been, most of the landscapes I'd subsequently come to know were essentially domesticated, or lethally infected by tourists. The Canadian West, even more than the American West, was still wild, untamed, majestic, awesome - inhuman, and with no concessions made to man. It re-established a sense of perspective, of proportion. In Canada, for the first time, I found myself in a place of which I longed passionately to say 'This is my home'.

Even today, Vancouver shimmers in memory as the most beautiful city I've known, the city for which I retain the most profound affection, suffer the most acute nostalgia. Its images continue to haunt my dreams. An amphitheatre of fir-forest-shagged slopes and heights, lapped by the sea. The stark and sombre stateliness of the evergreens, dark against the snow. Sentinel-stern trees across the inlet from my office window, climbing the crests and remaining, amid gale-force winds, perfectly, eerily and preternaturally still. A point at Horseshoe Bay to the north, where the road ended and there was nothing for four hundred miles up the coast save a vista of ice-sheathed summits, fang after diamond-bright fang of mountain reverberating away into the distance - the most palpable intimation of the infinite I've ever encountered. And the glory of the metropolis itself, as seen, for example, from the eminence of the university by night - lights filling the brimming bowl below like a welter of fallen constellations, a terrestrial mirror of the Milky Way. At the time of his death, Malcolm Lowry was engaged in an immense seven-part projected opus, his own modern version of Dante's *Divine Comedy*. Mexico, as depicted in *Under the Volcano,* corresponded to *Inferno*. According to Lowry's design, his *Paradiso* was to be set in Vancouver. At some of the pubs I frequented, Faulkner had sometimes travelled up to visit Lowry, and the two of them would challenge university students to drinking contests.

My apartment overlooked an inlet, at the foot of the mountain crowned by the university. When I woke, the morning would often be mantled in mist - long sinuous scarves of it seething everywhere, swathing the world in drifting gauze-veils. Driving uphill, I'd encounter, as though in a plane, an opaque grey broth of fog, a band or zone of vapour dense-packed as a cloud-bank. And then, seemingly by some magical transformation, I'd emerge above it, and the trees and peaks and sapphire-deep sky in all directions would be glowing, dazzlingly incised by the sunlight and burnished to lustrous radiance. Below, everything would've vanished. Nothing whatever would be visible save a billowing carpet of silver-white spume foaming away to the horizon.

Canada, at least as I found it then, was the sanest place I'd ever known. This sanity was almost instantly detectable, the moment one crossed the border. One inhaled it with the very air - an absence of the skittish insecurity inherent in the American mentality, an absence of the attendant latent violence, an intrinsic equilibrium and balance, most of all perhaps an instinctive respect, verging on reverence, for the land. A kind of Faulkneresque awareness pervaded the collective psyche - that man was effectively on probation, that he only held the land in trust, that he occupied it on a temporary and provisional sufferance, that any abuse on his part would cause the land to turn against him, repudiate him, exact retribution. Thus must the Indians have regarded the continent before it was plundered from them - as a vast feminine and maternal sentience whose mystery they sought to approach, to partake of, to experience as one experienced a woman's, but never to dominate or violate, never crassly to own.

In the States at that time, as in Britain today, Canada was deemed provincial. Provincial the small rural towns unquestionably were, but no more so than small rural towns in Iowa, or in Maine, in Devon or Dorset. Vancouver, however, like Montreal and Toronto, was, if anything, more cosmopolitan and sophisticated than most urban centres in the States. In the wake of the Second World War, Canada took in quantities of German refugees - including Ilona's family. Following the civil strife in their respective countries, she took in more Greek and Yugoslavian exiles than any nation in the world. In 1956, she took in the most Hungarians, in 1968 the most Czechs. She already possessed the second-largest Chinatown in North America, and the largest Japanese, Indian and Pakistani populations. She had a substantial Russian community, including a sect of Tolstoy's immediate disciples. During the two years I lived there, she was welcoming an influx of Portuguese, as well as people from the West Indies, from Vietnam and from elsewhere in Southeast Asia. Later, in the aftermath of the coup that toppled Allende, more Chileans found a haven in Canada than anywhere else, as did Argentines in flight from the military junta in their country.

None of these émigré communities had yet been subsumed by the melting pot, had yet lost its unique cultural identity. Many of them gravitated westwards, establishing roots in Vancouver. One could thus move from enclave to enclave of the city, from quarter to quarter, from neighbourhood to neighbourhood, and discover a different ethnic character, different restaurants and shops, different handicrafts and hand-made commodities for sale, different folk traditions, festivals and music. The result was an extraordinarily rich and fertile spectrum, more diverse than, say, San Francisco's, more flexible, less brittle, less shallow; and the surroundings were no less scenic.

Admission to Canada, whether on a work permit or as a so-called 'landed immigrant', was in those days determined by an elaborate points system. Having been duly and portentously summoned, one presented oneself for an interview with an immigration officer. During the inquisition that followed, one notched up points for various aptitudes, qualifications and accomplishments - years of occupational experience, years of formal education, degrees held, foreign languages spoken, professional expertise, specialised training and skills. The single most crucial factor, however, which often tipped the balance one way or the other, was slapdash, imprecise, subjective and wildly arbitrary - the general impression one made on one's interviewer.

In order to spare me the ordeal of a haircut, Ilona, before my interview, put my hair up in bobby-pins. As a result, I dared not turn my head, comporting myself as if robotised from the neck up. My interviewer proved to be a suave, debonair, alcoholically florid-faced man in his fifties, disarmingly informal, with an air of relaxed urbanity and louche, somewhat affectedly British mannerisms. When, in reply to his question, I said I knew French and German, he handed me a page of text in each and asked me to translate. The passages in question were pretty much on the level of 'This is a dog. His name is Spot. See Spot run'. '*Voici un chien . . .*' '*Hier is ein Hund...*'. I translated accordingly, allowing myself, whenever possible, some stylistic flourishes, some baroque embellishments. I no longer remember the sequence or development of the dialogue that followed; but my interview ended in a pub, with my interrogator and I engaged in a weightily sozzled consideration of whether it was Proust or Mann who posed a more daunting challenge to the English translator. We concurred, I seem to recall, on Mann. Such was my experience of Canadian bureaucracy. It was hardly the kind of experience one could expect in the States - or in Britain, for that matter - and it still reflects for me something of Canada's essential soundness, Canada's well-ordered priorities.

I felt, in Vancouver, serenely above the turmoil of the States, not just geographically, but psychologically and spiritually as well. Not that Canada was proof against political turmoil of her own. For a few months prior to my arrival, I gathered, an amateurish terrorist campaign had been conducted by the FLQ or Quebec Liberation Front, a militant Québecois separatist organisation. Most of it was nuisance-level activity - the bombing of defenceless letterboxes, for example. But shortly after I'd obtained my landed immigrant status, the situation in Quebec turned genuinely ugly. Two high-ranking functionaries, as I recall - the British Trade Commissioner and Quebec's own Minister of Labour and Immigration - were kidnapped, and one of them was murdered. In an overreaction uncharacteristic of him, Pierre Trudeau invoked the War Measures Act, the equivalent of martial law. For most Canadians, it was probably the most traumatic political occurrence since the Second World War. I, however, in my ignorance of Canadian affairs, failed to appreciate the import of what'd happened. For all I knew, martial law might've been imposed as routinely in Canada as it was in the States; and the events in Quebec, though distasteful enough, seemed muted by American standards.

In any case, few of the repercussions extended as far west as British Columbia, where there was scant French influence and scantier sympathy for the Québecois cause. At the university, a cadre of manically messianic Maoists, who knew nothing of the FLQ and cared less, disseminated lurid rumours. An 'attack' on the campus by the Mounties was said to be imminent. The words evoked impressively colourful images - squadrons of scarlet-clad horsemen clattering up the mountain, sparks flying from hooves, bugles blaring, guidons streaming in the wind. I quite relished the prospect; I'd wanted to be a Mountie myself at the age of seven or so.

In the event, two bored-looking officers turned up in sports jackets, driving an unmarked lymph-hued Chevrolet. Their wry good humour deflected every attempted provocation. Courteously, even somewhat apologetically, they confiscated a few sample tracts and broadsheets - shrilly pro-terrorist and therefore, by the statutes of the War Measures Act, technically seditious. The Maoists, of course, howled censorship, repression and police brutality. Having seen an abundance of such things in the States, I didn't feel particularly censored, repressed or brutalised. Neither did most other people. And then, as the Maoists re-directed their invective at the general apathy, the whole crisis, such as it was, blew over. Needless to say, the Maoist propaganda continued. It flowed across my desk at the library - and thence, immediately, into the wastebin. Among its more crassly dumb impertinences was the exhortation to repudiate Orwell, Silone, Koestler and Malraux as 'traitors to the class war', and to remove their works from the shelves.

My job at the library required a certain specialised knowledge. If one possessed that, which I did, one could've performed the job superbly and still been clinically brain-dead. Officially, I was charged with maintaining, superintending and developing the university's prized 'Special Collections', primarily the 'Contemporary Literature Collection', or 'CLC'. Jealously immured in an airless windowless fluorescent-lit cubicle to which I alone held the key, the CLC comprised a hoard of original manuscripts, preliminary drafts, proof copies, marginalia, first or limited editions and similar rare or unique items of the kind most coveted by bibliophiles, antiquarians, scholars, cultural ghouls and other such obsessives - as well, of course, as North American academic libraries.

Most of the material was more or less literary. We possessed, for example, all the embryonic longhand scrawls, working notes and revisions by the West Coast's most important third-rate poet. But there was also a cache of Aleister Crowley's texts in lavish leather bindings, kept under my protection ever since a coven of his erstwhile disciples had taken to pilfering them from the open stacks. And because there was no other place to sequester it from sundry imagined forms of misuse, the CLC bunker housed a meagre collection of pornography and erotica - donated, I was told, by the widow of some esteemed industrialist, who, on his death, had left it, instead of the expected stock certificates, in his office safe. The bulk of it was Victorian flagellation fiction of the sort then being re-issued, in cheap paperback format, by Grove Press.

Over this diverse and questionable treasure trove of paper, I presided as guardian dragon. Anyone desiring access to it had to petition and placate me with the requisite pink application form. Since most people didn't even know the stuff existed, I received few such applications, and my stewardship proved undemanding enough. So, too, was the task of augmenting a corpus of material which scarcely anyone ever used. On the average of once a fortnight, I'd sift through portentous catalogues from rare book dealers, private collectors and auction houses. I'd determine whether, and how much, to bid for such prizes as a get-well note personally penned and initialled by one or another Black Mountain poet, or the doodles on a typescript by some marinated Boston prosateuse, or the whiskey-spattered pages of some New York manic depressive's epic, or a series of spiteful postcards sent by some beat bard in Algiers to a jilted homosexual lover in San

Francisco, who'd put them on the market in a spasm of pouting petulance and pique. I was also authorised to decide whether the university should spend $5000 on a first edition of *The Sound and the Fury*, $20,000 on a first edition of *Ulysses*.

None of this, needless to say, imposed much strain on my time. Lacking anything more exciting to do, I undertook to build up the prose, poetry and drama in the open stacks. There were, of course, all the statutory British, Commonwealth and American texts, as well as a respectable, if not definitive, selection of Russian and Western European material - in translation and in the original language. Seeking gaps to fill, I embarked on less trodden paths - the literature of Latin America (just then beginning to impinge on the English-speaking world), of the Indian sub-continent, of Persia, China and Japan. I also addressed myself to neglected tributaries of the cultural mainstream - to Greece, for example, to Turkey, Poland, Hungary, Holland, Belgium, Scandinavia. Within some six months, I'd furnished the university with the most comprehensive collection of obscure work, from Baltic to Balkans, in North America. Most of it probably hasn't been touched since I placed it on the shelves.

In addition to my specialised activities, I was expected, along with most of the library's other staff, to do a regular stint - an hour or so per day - on the General Information and Reference Desk. Dominating an alcove at the rear of the reading room, flanked by blond wood catalogue cabinets and escarpments of shelves bulging with encyclopædia and dictionaries, the Reference Desk was designed to offer a sort of genial oracle service, dispensing chummy advice and guidance. This wasn't a function that became me, and I made no pretence to civility, still less to helpfulness-with-a-smile. Grumpy as a Nirvana-bound sage importuned by a pesky novice, I'd scarcely respond to the questions posed by fuddled students - questions I was usually no better equipped to answer than they were. I could, of course, direct them to the fiction, poetry or drama they desired. Had any of them been interested, I could even have pointed the way to Ivo Andric, author of The Great Bosnian Novel. But how was I supposed to know where to find a précis of some 1956-vintage doctoral dissertation - the fatuous phallic fallacies of some Freudian fraud at Fordham on, say, alleged anal retentiveness in Kafka? Or the screed of some Aristotelian scribe from Chicago on the use of the caesura in

Joyce Killer's poetry? I had only the most cursory understanding of how libraries worked, and none whatever of the scholarly and bibliographical apparatus they contained. In my own academic career, such as it was, I'd naturally written many papers, but prided myself on having only once used a footnote. That'd been to a pseudo-philosophical term coined one evening by JT Swift. I'd footnoted it solely because I'd used it before, on a previous paper, and a pretentious professor, parading erroneous erudition, had ascribed it to Kierkegaard.

To queries dumped on me at the Reference Desk, I'd reply usually with an airy wave of my hand in one or another vague direction - towards the stacks, towards the lavatories, towards the stairwell, towards the broom closet, the window, the sunset beyond. My questioner would wander off with a perplexed frown, head lifted and swivelling, as though sniffing the air for spoor - and sooner or later, with predictable consistency, would blunder into the broom closet. By that time, I'd naturally have absented myself - gone to the loo, to inspect the condition of a dust jacket in the CLC bunker, to deal with some other ostensibly pressing business such as counting the rails in the banister, the cars in the car park, the firs on the mountainside - and a more conscientious colleague would be manning the desk in my stead. For two years, I effectively purveyed the illusion that I knew what I was doing, that those failing to find material they wanted had only themselves to blame.

In the jargon then prevalent, I was deemed 'overqualified' for my job; and according to the accepted wisdom, 'overqualified' people were potentially dangerous. 'Overqualification', it was believed, led one to become bored, and boredom led one into mischief - agitating for higher wages or longer tea breaks, organising unions, fomenting discontent and other such diversions. In this instance, the accepted wisdom had a measure of validity to it that accepted wisdom usually doesn't. True to form, I did indeed become bored. I could perform my duties far more quickly than my working day was intended to accommodate, and thus found myself with time on my hands. I also had an office at my disposal, two secretaries, four electric typewriters and a photocopier, and these resources begged to be deployed. I wasn't prepared to sully myself with squalid labour squabbles or political activity, but I had no compunctions about other forms of mischief.

My mischief-making was further stimulated by the rupture of my relationship with Ilona. Our separation, whatever Vancouver's attractions, left me stranded and bereft. Having cut myself off from diverse roseate futures, I was marooned in a demeaning job three thousand miles away from the friends, the status, the cosy and comfortable world I'd left behind on Long Island. I couldn't really feel bitter, having duped myself with my own romanticism. I did, however, feel as if a practical joke had been played on me by the cosmos; and this justified me, I decided, in playing practical jokes on the rest of humanity. Thus disparate elements converged to engender the Vancouver Foundation for Lycanthropic Children. I'd originally thought of resurrecting the William McGonagall Society, stillborn in Boston six years before; but British Columbia, I discovered, retained enough of its Scottish heritage for McGonagall already to be established as a cult figure. Juvenile lycanthropes seemed a viable alternative.

It started as a casual whim, an insouciant by-product of idleness. I was between fictional projects and seeking something on which to exercise my prose. Accordingly, I drafted a letter on behalf of the Foundation, signed by its alleged director, one Virgil Frost. I couldn't solicit funds. That would've rendered me guilty of criminal fraud; and besides, few people have a sense of humour about money. I could, however, solicit moral support and prospective patrons. Never, of course - neither in my initial text nor in anything that followed - did I or anyone else explicitly use the word 'werewolf'. Lycanthropy was never defined. Instead, I waxed poignant about how remiss the modern world had become in seeking cures for it. I stressed, without actually specifying, the dire depredations of the dread disease. I extolled the worthy work of the Foundation, whose unique, specially adapted programmes of treatment varied from lycanthropic individual to lycanthropic individual, and boasted a 79.8 percent improvement in 87.9 percent of the cases entrusted to its care. Then, having run off some two hundred photocopies of my charitable missive, I instructed my dumbfounded secretaries to put it into circulation. Queasily, anxious lest they be doing something illicit, they placed sheaves of it around the library, the cafeterias, the student union and other strategic locations.

For a week, nothing happened. Then, without consulting me (or Virgil Frost), the library's Audio-Visual Department seized the initiative. Situated in the lower intestinal tract of the building, the Audio-Visual Department was obliged, every second fortnight or so, to mount some sort of eye-catching pictorial or graphic display in the front lobby, in a glass showcase facing the door - a public relations exercise, I suppose, to lure students inside and acquaint them with the mysteries of books. For someone in the A-V Department, the concept of the Foundation had obviously kindled inspiration.

I arrived one morning to find a lavish display in the glass showcase. Under bold, five-inch-high black letters - 'THE BRITISH COLUMBIA FOUNDATION FOR LYCANTHROPIC CHILDREN - there appeared an artistically arranged, fan-shaped spread of photographs. In one, the sinister, angular and wasted protagonist of *Nosferatu* stood superimposed against the backdrop of a grim Gothic façade - the façade, in fact, of British Columbia's provincial penitentiary. Below, there was a caption: 'Our Founder'. Another shot, which might've been a still from a Bergman film, showed a bleak vista of snowbound forest, captioned 'Rehabilitation Centre'. Over a third caption, 'Famous Lycanthropes of the Past', hung half a dozen distinguished, brooding, bushy-bearded faces - portraits of Nicholas II, Edward VII, George V and sundry other regal or imperial personages. And there was one famous (or notorious) photograph of a wild-eyed, bottle-brandishing Rasputin surrounded by a bevy of buxom beauties in gauzy gowns with extensive *décolletage*. 'Annual Christmas Party', the caption explained.

The display in the lobby launched an epidemic of lupine loopiness. Towards the end of that week, the university newspaper published a letter from one L. Talbot, who claimed to represent the Lycanthropic Liberation Front. '*You have nothing to lose but your muzzles,*' Mr. Talbot boldly proclaimed, urging all lycanthropes to unite in militant revolutionary action under the banner of the LLF, and dismissing the Foundation as a puerile, wishy-washy, vapidly liberal institution, patronising and 'crypto-racist'. I debated whether or not to squander prose on a reply. Before I could make up my mind, another scribe rallied to the Foundation's defence. For the next month, the letters column was dominated by an increasingly vituperative exchange between the LLF and the BCFLC. Graffiti began to appear in the loos, endorsing or castigating one or the other. Lycanthropy had properly 'arrived,' I realised, when I discovered an '*Up the LLF*!' slogan scrawled above the urinals in the men's room of a posh hotel lounge downtown. Shortly after that, the first LLF T-shirts made their début.

The Foundation was losing the propaganda war, but that hardly mattered. What gratified me was that the whole business had acquired a momentum of its own. It was developing into the kind of prank I most prefer - the kind of prank that enables me to play the rôle of magus-cum-architect, devising or designing the thing, then stepping back, washing my hands of it and letting it evolve according to its own internal laws and logic, its own inherent pattern, its own energy and dynamics. Thus does the practical joke attain its apotheosis. Thus does the hoax approach the status of art.

I couldn't remain altogether aloof, however. One afternoon, there appeared in my office a dapper spiffy little man with a precise pencil-line moustache and hair sleekly coifed above a trendy, wasp-waisted, oyster-grey suit. I asked if I could help him, vaguely feeling I'd seen him somewhere before. He said he was looking for Virgil Frost, Director of the British Columbia Foundation for Lycanthropic Children. Mountie Fraud Squad? Just in case, I replied that Mr. Frost was away for the month, on a fact-finding tour of the Carpathians. Chagrined, my visitor then introduced himself. Lest I compromise him in whatever position he now occupies, I should probably be discreet and refer to him only by his initials - A.G. But as soon as he'd proffered his name, I'd placed him. I'd seen his face, it transpired, almost every evening. He was the 'anchorman' and presenter for the local outlet of a national television network. He'd long envied, he explained, the BBC's celebrated spoof film on the annual spaghetti harvest in Italy, had long dreamed of producing something comparable. Lycanthropy offered a unique opportunity, and he'd hoped to do a feature on the Foundation for the six o'clock news. There was a film crew waiting down in the lobby. They could've been ready to shoot in ten minutes. At that point, confronted by so kindred a spirit, I confessed that I was Virgil Frost, and we got down to business.

There was, of course, no time to script or rehearse. Everything would have to be ad libbed. Improvising at a headlong pace, we half-recruited, half-dragooned, two volunteers. One was the head librarian of the Sciences Section, a woebegone mournful-looking man with haggard features and basset-hound bags under his eyes. The other was a young woman, an administrative assistant, who, when pressed, could also muster a plaintive, anguished, gauntly doom-harried expression. This couple became, for the next hour or so, Jakob and Rebecca Schlöss, the parents of little Ferdy, a three-year-old lycanthrope.

At the opposite end of the corridor, there was a lounge, empty save for two bewildered undergraduates. A.G., Jakob and Rebecca, the film crew and I summarily commandeered it. Lights were briskly and efficiently set up, cameras positioned, sound levels tested, and A.G. then proceeded to interview Jakob and Rebecca. Avoiding anything that might define lycanthropy too precisely, he asked conventional, even banal questions, in the muted and respectful voice with which one addresses extreme grief. How had little Ferdy's disease affected his parents' lives? How had coping with an infant lycanthrope disrupted their domestic establishment, their relations with their neighbours, their peace of mind, their sleep at night? What were their feelings about the affliction visited so cruelly upon them?

'He's still my child!' Rebecca choked. 'I still love him!'

Apart from that, she couldn't say a lot, having too much trouble suppressing her giggles. For the rest of the interview, she confined herself to nodding pathetically, looking stricken, sniffing promiscuously and dabbing her nose with successive wads of Kleenex, a box of which had been placed conveniently at her side. Jakob was more loquacious, extemporising with a resourcefulness that astonished us. He replied to A.G.'s queries in the stunned, numbed, traumatised, somnambulistic monotone of a man in a state of near shock, a man still reeling from the impact of some hideous and inexplicable tragedy. Had the Foundation afforded much solace? A.G. asked.

'The Foundation's been a godsend to us!' Jakob declared fervently. 'A godsend! I don't think we could've managed without the Foundation. Mr. Frost is a wonderful man! A truly wonderful man!'

'When,' A.G. enquired, 'did you first realise something was wrong with little Ferdy? They say it's often when hair appears in the palm of the hand.'

'No, before that,' Jakob replied, shaking his head as if to dispel clinging cobweb tendrils of nightmare. 'Very early. Very early indeed.

But we didn't know what it was at the time...The sounds...Yes, I think it was the sounds that first frightened me...At night, I mean, I'd *hear* the most dreadful...*sounds*...coming from Ferdy's room. They'd wake me. And I'd open the door, and see him lying there in his crib...He'd look so helpless, you know, so...*innocent*...in the light of the full moon coming through the window...And he'd be making these utterly dreadful noises...In his sleep, I mean...They weren't exactly cries...I'm not sure I know how to describe them...Except maybe as a sort of ...well, a sort of *howl*...'

A.G. nodded gravely, his eyes, his whole face exuding sympathy and solicitude.

'How was the disease finally diagnosed?'

'They didn't know what to make of it at first,' Jakob replied woefully. 'I mean, we took Ferdy to our paediatrician...and he performed all kinds of tests. But this was in daylight, you understand...So nothing could be detected. In the end...he advised us to take Ferdy to a psychiatrist...It all seemed very odd to me...very odd indeed...Because Ferdy, you see...Ferdy was only eleven months old at the time...'

The cameraman, who'd been struggling heroically to control himself, at this point succumbed. He collapsed in a fit of hysterics. The camera slipped from its tripod and crashed to the floor, shattering one of its lenses. Everyone else, of course, also disintegrated into laughter - except for Jakob and Rebecca, who continued to look wretchedly miserable, and the two undergraduate observers, who looked baffled, shocked, indignant and alarmed. Something, they realised, was manifestly, even grievously, wrong in what they'd witnessed. Something had been discordant, surreal. They weren't quite sure what it was, and lacked, in any case, the courage to challenge the august authority of television. When the filming was finished, however, they hovered uneasily in their corner, muttering in subdued voices and flicking frequent glances in our direction. At last, one of them mobilised himself for confrontation and strode up to where A.G. and I stood talking.

'Excuse me. Can I ask you a question?'

'Certainly,' I replied.

The student hesitated a moment, unsure of his footing.

'Were those two married?' he then blurted, fretful and implicitly accusing.

I assumed an expression of affronted surprise.

'Why should you suspect they weren't?'

The student shook his head, fumbling for words.

'Something wasn't right about all this,' he faltered. 'I don't understand what was happening here. I mean, there were things that just didn't make sense...'

'I would've thought it was all perfectly straightforward.'

'No. I mean...like here was this couple being interviewed. Because their kid has some weird disease or something. And they were really upset about it and all. I mean, they were really *suffering*, you know. And the rest of you guys were standing around *laughing*...!'

'It's a Canadian equivalent of French absurdism,' I said solemnly. 'There're are certain injustices in the cosmos - certain design faults in reality, so to speak - which can only be coped with by means of laughter. Otherwise one might go mad.'

He stared at me lengthily and very dubiously, then turned to A.G.

'You're supposed to give us the news. I mean, we rely on you. We rely on you to keep us informed about what's happening out there in the world. And now, all of a sudden, I'm not sure any more. I have doubts. I don't know whether I really can trust you after this. *Can* I trust you?'

'Of course not,' A.G. replied cheerfully. 'Anyone who trusts the media's crazy. There's no war in Vietnam either. They just have a bigger budget than we do.'

The feature on the Foundation appeared that evening, an 'Insight Special' appended to the six o'clock news. It ran for seven minutes of peak television time and was transmitted as far east as Toronto, as far south as Seattle and Portland. At a modest estimate, therefore, it would've been seen by a million or so people. A.G. and his team had added studio footage to the material filmed in the lounge. After the interview with Jakob and Rebecca, there was a cut, and the viewing audience then saw A.G. in what might've been a laboratory, white-coated and wielding a pointer. On a blackboard behind him, a tangled scrawl of equations formed a hedge around a large molecular diagram of sticks and balls, like those found in chemistry books. Flapping his pointer at the diagram, A.G. launched into a learned scientific disquisition on the 'Lycanthropin molecule', allegedly diagnosed as the disease's 'prime causal factor'. He then rubbed out one of the circles in the diagram, chalked up a triangle in its stead and waxed hopeful about a newly developed vaccine, to be called 'Anthropin'. Except for substituted words, his text had in fact been cribbed from Linus Pauling and pertained to the effects of Vitamin C on the common cold.

I waited for some ten minutes after the transmission, then rang the studio. Adopting a fake Germanic accent, I embarked on a gabbled appeal - I was a concerned father, I'd just seen a terrifying programme on the six o'clock news, I wanted additional information because my child was making strange sounds at night...I was interrupted by a wearily amused voice, which I recognised as that of the cameraman:

'It was a put-on, sir. I have to tell you that. It was a put-on.'

Dropping the fabricated accent, I revealed myself as Virgil Frost and asked if there'd been any feedback.

'Any feedback? Christ, "Virgil"! You wouldn't believe what's been happening here! It's incredible! How long's it been since the broadcast? Ten minutes, maybe? Our switchboards've been clogged non-stop. It's a wonder you got through. At last count, a couple of minutes ago, we were up to six hundred calls...'

So great was the volume of calls, in fact, and so distraught were the callers, that A.G., the next day, felt obliged to issue a retraction. At the end of the six o'clock news, he appeared on screen again, looking a bit sheepish perhaps, but unrepentant.

'Yesterday,' he began dryly, 'some of our audience saw a feature on the British Columbia Foundation for Lycanthropic Children. In view of the response we've received, I must in all conscience confess the feature was a hoax. I'd also like to reassure the population of Vancouver. To my knowledge, this city is not, I repeat, *not*, threatened by an epidemic of lycanthropy.'

Not everyone, of course, saw or heeded the retraction. For the rest of the week, calls and letters continued to swamp the studio. Of all those who wrote or telephoned, only one appeared to have twigged - an intern at the University of British Columbia's Dental School. In a formal, neatly typed, professionally polite page, he requested permission - if it wouldn't inconvenience Mr. and Mrs. Schlöss - to examine little Ferdy's teeth.

* * * * * * *

When I first joined Ilona in Vancouver, I'd allowed myself to be vulnerable. I'd eagerly disencumbered myself of the armour I'd worn on Long Island - an armour fashioned largely from images. I'd lowered the mask I'd sported for three years, abandoned the persona I'd cultivated, stepped out of the rôle I'd played. I'd also renounced my alchemical experiments in transmuting trust to power. When Ilona and I separated, I instinctively had recourse again to the implements, accoutrements and techniques of Fausthood. The Foundation, of course, was harmless enough, and, I'd like to think, charmingly zany. But I was pervasively conscious of how readily its governing mechanisms and dynamics could've been utilised for more sinister ends. That flummoxed undergraduate in the lounge - wondering plaintively whether he could trust the media, panicking on learning he couldn't - wasn't wholly a figure of fun.

By the time the Foundation attained its apotheosis on television, I'd reverted to Fausthood in other spheres as well. I was involved, for example, with another best friend's wife. And I was employing the same manipulative devices, the same deceptions and dissimulations, as I'd employed in my amorous affairs on Long Island. Thus, to keep my friend oblivious to his antlers, I had to do something about my own apparent celibacy; I had to allay, defuse and deflect suspicion by finding a woman to serve as decoy and thereby screen my primary liaison. Quite coldly, as if it were a mere tactical or logistic problem, I discussed the matter with my muse-of-the-moment. She entered gleefully into the spirit of the game, and we even invoked Laclos as a precedent, referring to each other ironically as 'Vicomte' and 'Marquise'.

We selected my decoy as one might a dish from a menu. She was a Czech woman named Magda, who'd fled Prague in the wake of the Soviet invasion three years before. It was her friends - one of them, if I recall, was her sister-in-law - whom I'd seen die in their Volkswagon on television, crushed by a Russian tank. Golden blonde, vivacious, with a broad Slavic face and slightly slanted eyes, Magda also worked in the library - a demeaningly menial job that imposed no excessive strain on her still teething English. She was yoked connubially to someone named Boris, whom I never met, never even saw. He functioned, I gathered, in some subterranean capacity for the city - fixed boilers, repaired electrical cables, declogged drains or something similarly vital and boring. I never ascertained the precise details, but there seemed only the most tenuous of bonds holding Magda to him. It was essentially a *mariage de convenance*, contracted to facilitate or expedite or legitimise their access to Canada.

Speaking sometimes in French or German, as well as English, I seduced Magda with what might be called a benevolent cynicism. I made no concessions to the then fashionable cult of 'honesty' for its own sake. My chief priority was to avoid inflicting superfluous pain, either on Magda or on my cuckolded friend; and that objective, I felt, justified whatever subterfuge might be required. On the whole, I daresay, I handled the situation adeptly, adroitly, skilfully, with tact and finesse. My friend never learned of his cuckoldom. And while the tepidness of my passion may have prompted Magda to divine a rival, I think she ascribed it more to general diffidence, or preoccupation with other things. Even at the time, however, I couldn't pride myself on my behaviour. My affection and respect for Magda were genuine enough. I even tried - fatuously, of course, and fruitlessly - to will myself into love with her. I endeavoured, perverse though it sounds, to conduct myself as honourably as the shabby circumstances allowed. But Magda was an extraordinary woman and an extraordinary human being - warm, courageous, generous, resourceful, with a reservoir of profound feminine wisdom. She deserved better - deserved more than I was able to give her. In my inventory of romantic transgressions, it's my treatment of her that inspires me today with the most guilt and shame.

Magda introduced me to the work of Skvorecky and Kundera, both of whom she'd known personally, both of whom had just appeared in English translation. She also familiarised me with some of the older, more established and enshrined names in her cultural heritage - Nemcová, Jirásek, Neumann and Vancura, as well, of course, as Hasek, Hrabal and Havel. I was thus able to augment appreciably the Czech literature section in the library. I learned, too, from Magda how to curse and toast in most of the Slavic languages. And she regaled me with copious tales of her adventures in

Czechoslovakia, especially among the torn and trampled blossoms of the Prague Spring.

She told me of how, in their youthful rebellion, she and her friends had darted furtively back and forth across the Austrian border, dodged military roadblocks, smuggled contraband books and booze, defied curfews, played pranks on visiting KGB officers, talked their way out of *contretemps* with dunderheaded bureaucrats and, on several occasions, been interrogated by the secret police. So rabid was the mistrust and paranoia among the inquisitors, she told me, that two of them insisted on being present throughout every interrogation, each watching the other. If one of them had to pee, the interrogation was suspended until the thug with the bloated bladder could return, or be replaced by a stand-in.

Magda may have been a surrogate paramour, but she was still a paramour on whose behalf I could've entered the political lists. There, in her harried history, was a political cause for the sake of which I might indeed have donned the mantle of chivalric crusader. Now, of course, it was too late. All of it was in another country, and besides, dissent was dead, not to be resurrected until some years later by Charter 77. It would've been quixotic, even for me, to campaign against an issue three years in the past and several thousand miles distant. But the drama of Magda's background cast a pall for me over our present relationship. I found my own rôle ignominious. In Czechoslovakia, with former lovers, she'd engaged in escapades and exploits worthy of James Bond films. With me, the hazards to be confronted, the obstacles to be overcome, were depressingly inglorious. There was always, naturally, some risk of Boris in the closet, jack-in-the-boxing out at an incommodious moment; but I'd acquired by then sufficient expertise in dealing with usurped husbands, and Boris wasn't very uxorious anyway. In contrast to the dungeons and dragons of yore, Magda had nothing more daunting to face with me than a suicidal Volvo and an artificially inseminated flu.

Having always been prone to flu, I naïvely welcomed the library's offer of free flu shots to all staff, and presented myself promptly at the infirmary. In my delusion, I'd assumed a flu shot would provide immunisation. It provided, in fact, just the opposite and, true literally to its definition, shot me full of flu - a particularly nasty flu, and all the more mortifying for being synthetically concocted. I was invaded, in short, not by a virus alone, but by a virus incubated in a test-tube of chicken lymph, with the whole edifice of Canadian socialised medicine aligned behind it. Outraged, I stormed back to the infirmary and accused the desperately defensive doctor of sabotaging my metabolism. He ferreted in his desk, produced the brochure dispensed to him with the vaccine and read the small print, then looked up at me with the quailed expression of all criminals caught red-handed. Apparently, two percent of all those vaccinated against the disease could be expected to contract it; and I, élitist as always, was one of the elect - Stendhal's happy sensitive few.

I adopted my usual policy towards flu - I rebuffed its attempts to impede my functioning, refused to acknowledge its existence, acted as if it were no more than a passing mood. As a result of this policy, I naturally transmitted my malady to both Magda and my best friend's wife. All three of us were soon debilitated and feverish. And when Magda and I kissed one evening, I had an appalling, semi-delirious vision of a myriad militaristic microbes rushing outwards from our mouths, breaking ranks, throwing down weapons and helmets, cheering and embracing in joyfully fraternal reunion, like Russian and Allied soldiers at the Elbe in 1945.

As for the Volvo, it was another in my sorry repertoire of reluctantly owned cars. Had I stayed on Long Island, I probably could've contrived a second-hand Porsche, but that, too, I'd renounced for Ilona. Given the destitution in which I'd come to Vancouver, the Volvo appeared the best I could manage. I should've known better, of course, having had a vehicle of similar ilk die on me in Chicago. Yet the Vancouver Volvo, in its dumpy way, seemed a bargain - no prodigy of style or performance, granted, but safe, sturdy, indestructible, economical and with an aura of Swedish reliability. That didn't prevent it, within a month, from entering on a vertiginous decline. Once I started drawing salary from the library, I could, I suppose, have afforded repairs. But I resented the car; I regarded it more or less as one might a spoiled brat, and refused to be blackmailed by its clamouring for attention.

For eight months, it miraculously survived. I'd drive with ears anxiously attuned to every alien sound, like a hypochondriac monitoring his symptoms. Choked by exhaust fumes, I'd coax the decrepit heap up and down the mountain, a shimmy in the left front wheel, the motor farting and sputtering as compression sighed away.

When the electrical system began to pack up, night became increasingly a problem – and rain, too, for it rained in Vancouver almost as frequently as it got dark. Grimly undeterred, I careered along in all weathers, with one headlamp (my side), one windscreen wiper (passenger's side) and burnt-out taillights (both sides), as well as an emergency brake which, without warning, would snap on of its own accord, bringing the vehicle to an abrupt neck-wrenching halt. When the second wiper expired, I ran a string through the blades and into the windows, and the car blundered through drizzle and downpour while my passenger – Magda or best friend's wife – pulled frantically back and forth with me in turn. Until, on a torrential evening, steering and trying to change gears, I found myself, at sixty, inextricably tangled with wheel and shift lever, right foot tied tight to the clutch. At that moment, fortunately, the emergency brake performed its trick. Across the windscreen, two severed strands of sodden string squirmed like amorous tapeworms.

I was bowling down the mountain with Magda one afternoon when the brakes failed. It was a chilling discovery. They didn't just strain or slacken. They'd somehow disengaged completely, and the pedal lay inert, limp and flaccid under my toes. The emergency brake, when I tried it, promptly snapped. I downshifted – to third, to second, to first. The car slowed slightly. The sound of the engine rose to the grinding whining scream of a jet. Then there was a ping, a splang, a metallic tinkle of gear teeth on the road behind, and the car resumed its precipitous descent, weaving, swaying, banking with squealing and smoking tyres. No, my life didn't flash before me. There was only a fleeting but vivid sense of how banal the situation was. I'd seen it countless times before on television and film, when nefarious villains drained the hero's brake fluid, cut his cables. I quipped something of the sort to Magda, but she appeared to have gone cataleptic. I resumed visual control of the car, which now, with cataclysmic velocity, was approaching the stop sign at the foot of the mountain. At the junction below, two other cars and a petrol tanker squatted patiently, waiting to nose into the stream of traffic.

The embankment to the left looked softer and less flammable – a shoulder of loose soil, beyond which lay a hedge and a pasture strewn with a few copses, with desultory clots of livestock. I wrenched the wheel sharply. The car veered violently leftwards, bumped hideously, banged Magda's and my heads concussively against the roof and soared up over the embankment like an aircraft catapulted from a carrier. For an instant, it hung suspended in mid-air. Then, with a sickening jolt, it landed and continued through the field, slashed by angry whips of foliage, jouncing and hiccoughing over ruts, decapitating dandelions, interrupting the coitus of rabbits, eliciting a meditative moo from a friendly uncowed cow.

The damage wasn't terminal. The vehicle still ran, albeit rheumatically and minus first gear. One wing, jammed up into the wheel well, precluded all possibility of a right turn, and it took seventeen left ones to get home, with assorted metal entrails dragged rasping over the road. A week later, I sold the wreck for scrap, having first plundered the front seats for my underfurnished apartment. Subsequently, in a fit of faulty judgement, I let myself be seduced by a new model Vauxhall - a flimsy thing with a fiercely oversized engine designed, according to the adverts, 'specifically for Canadian conditions', whatever those were supposed to be. Unlike the Volvo, the Vauxhall did nothing dramatic. For much of the time, in fact, it did nothing at all. Through most of the winter months, it simply went on strike. Its manufacturers, in determining 'Canadian conditions', had apparently neglected to include cold.

During those same winter months, the convulsions of the leviathan to the south attained new ferocity, new epileptic-scale proportions, as Nixon announced his candidacy for a second term and the burlesque show of another presidential campaign took to the boards. In the shadows, unknown to outsiders at the time, sleazy operatives of aptly-nicknamed CREEP - Committee to Re-elect the President - were gnawing away, termite-fashion, at the last vestiges of the country's political credibility. In the sunlight, opposition to the Vietnamese adventure grew ever more vociferous, ever more widespread. Even Johnny Carson, never one to let a bandwagon pass unclimbed on, was now sniping at American involvement in Southeast Asia. Demonstrations increased in frequency and numbers. So, too, did the body bags, returning no longer just to the urban ghettos, but also to the small towns and farms of 'Middle America', heartland of the 'Great Silent Majority' whom the administration had saddled with the war. Forming a separate clandestine army, draft dodgers poured across the border. They were welcomed by a spectrum of volunteer organisations dedicated to providing food, shelter and, whenever possible, jobs. Canadians - from the proverbial 'man in the street' up to Trudeau himself - made no secret of their distaste for the Vietnamese conflict. Anti-Americanism was rampant, but directed at the government, not at individuals fleeing its clutches. Gastown, Vancouver's hippie section, was awash with American exiles. So were the equivalent quarters of Toronto and Montreal.

But Vietnam wasn't the only political issue to impose itself on Canadian headlines and consciousness. Whatever Canada's geographical proximity to the States, she maintained, especially in the West, an almost mystical attachment to the British Crown. Like Australia and New Zealand, Canada had rallied to beleaguered Britannia through two world wars. Like Australia and New Zealand, she'd dispatched two generations of her youth, like idealistic knights-errant, to defend a mother country they'd never seen. Unlike Australia and New Zealand, however, Canada'd had no Gallipoli to embitter her; and the disillusion of her soldiers - at Ypres, for example, and the Somme - was a disillusion shared with those of other nations. Nor, except in Quebec, was there the kind of anti-British rancour fostered by Australia's large Irish-Catholic population and origins as a penal colony. In Canada, especially in the West, the prevailing influence was Scots Presbyterian. It was thus inevitable that Britain's problems should command Canadian attention and sympathy, and that Vietnam should often be eclipsed in the news by Northern Ireland.

The 'Troubles', or the most recent phase of them at least, were then entering their third year. I'd been, as it were, subliminally or peripherally aware of them before I left the States. Not that they'd impinged on my Long Island reality. I don't recall a single discussion on the subject there, not even with Sidney and Vanessa. But on my frequent trips to Boston, I'd patronise an Irish pub in Cambridge, *The Plough and the Stars,* and listen, bemused, to ferocious drunken disputations. I could muster, at most, only a desultory curiosity. The antics in Parliament of the then Bernadette Devlin inspired me with vague distaste, but more for stylistic than for political reasons. I knew virtually nothing of her political grievances; I simply recoiled from her hectoring raucousness. On the whole, Ulster's turmoil had seemed unreal and piddling compared to the larger issue of Vietnam. To the extent that it registered on me at all, it did so aesthetically and anachronistically, through the poetry, the poignancy, the power of the old Republican songs.

In Vancouver, Northern Ireland encroached more insistently. As much as Vietnam, the lunacy raging in Ulster dominated Canadian newspapers, Canadian television. Headlines and film clips confronted one incessantly with Bloody Sunday, Bloody Friday, Belfast and Londonderry gutted by explosions, rioters silhouetted against sheets of flame, deranged paramilitaries murdered by one another or blown up by their own bombs, soldiers and policemen shot, civilians slaughtered, youths kneecapped, pregnant women beaten, girls tarred and feathered for the crime of falling in love.

Irish Republicanism had few sympathisers in western Canada. With android mindlessness, the Maoist cliques, of course, zealously endorsed all terrorism, regardless of who perpetrated it; but their manifest incomprehension of the situation rendered their imbecile pronouncements more derisory than provocative. Their conception of the 'Troubles', insofar as they had one at all, was rooted in images of the 1916 Easter Rebellion, the Black and Tans, the Civil War of the early twenties. Yet few Canadians had conceptions much more sophisticated or up to date. The predominant attitude was one of outrage commingled with slack-jawed, utterly baffled perplexity. It all seemed, 'so unnecessary,' people said, 'so senseless'.

This bewilderment was echoed by Magda. She'd come, after all, from a country where the troops on the streets were quite literally and in grim fact an 'army of occupation', where soldiers opened fire without worrying about legal niceties or repercussions, where the authorities weren't accountable to anyone, where public opinion enjoyed no legitimacy and no voice, where even verbal protest was summarily muzzled. For Magda, it seemed incredible, inconceivable, that part of the United Kingdom - one of the Western democracies she'd admired from afar - could be transformed into so barbarous a killing ground.

'I do not understand!' she'd exclaim, impatient and exasperated, sitting with me in the library cafeteria, poring over each newly headlined atrocity and hopelessly shaking her head. 'I do not understand at all! I wish someone would explain to me!'

I tried, on one occasion, though my own grasp of the problem was simplistic and rudimentary enough. In retrospect, I can appreciate just how simplistic and rudimentary it was. I had no real awareness of the political subtleties involved, the tribal loyalties, the nature of the conflicting traditions. I think I divined obscurely that both religion and nationalism were incidental, mere excuses for something else, but I had no idea of what. And yet, despite its naïveté, I still find a kernel of validity in the analogy I offered, the parallel I drew.

'Let's take Texas as an example,' I suggested, improvising between sips of coffee - and forgetting that Magda probably knew as little about Texas as she did about Ulster. 'Suppose the Mexican government, or the Mexican constitution, still laid claim to Texas. In theory, anyway. And suppose a small group of hard-line militant Mexicans in Texas organise themselves into a paramilitary faction. They dub themselves the Texan Liberation Army. Or Texan Republican Army. Ultimately, of course, they're simply intent on power. Their own power. They're as hostile to the Mexican government as they are to the American. But they talk in poetic terms about reunifying Texas with Mexico. And they use public relations skilfully to portray themselves as representing the welfare of Texas' Latino population. They advocate equal opportunities, improved housing, education and job prospects - for which the need, in fact, is very real. They thereby contrive to depict themselves as benefactors, protectors, saviours. If they stage-manage their campaign effectively, they'll command considerable allegiance. So far, so good - and so quixotic. But what happens if they then move to terrorising Texas' white population, shooting cops and civilians as well, planting bombs in restaurants and saloons? Texas' white majority'll be scared shitless. They'll scuttle to their bunkers. And then all sorts of ugly reactions start setting in. The Klan takes to the warpath, boasting of a new mandate. Vigilante groups appear, posing as latterday Texas Rangers or something, yelling "Remember the Alamo!", purporting to safeguard the rights and freedoms for which Texans fought and died back in the 1830s. Rhetoric would quickly eclipse common sense. And yes, Dallas and Houston would soon become battlefields, like Londonderry and Belfast. *Voilà*.'

I'm not sure how closely Magda followed my scenario, how well she understood my allusions. But she gathered the gist of what I'd outlined. When I'd finished, she stared at me, her mouth open, her face frozen midway between laughter and horror.

'But that would be insane!' she protested. 'That would be...would be just crazy!'

'Of course,' I replied with offhand cynicism. 'Few people've ever suggested Ireland was anything else.'

I was less fluent, however, in coping with another of her queries.

'I remember...It was year after I escape from Prague. First anniversary of my freedom. These gangs...how would you call them?...Protestants? Loyalists?...they were beating up Catholic demonstrators, no? And the Catholics, they wanted English Army sent to protect them. Like you said happened in your country, in South, during time of Civil Rights and march to Selma, when you and your friends wanted soldiers to protect demonstrators. And English government sent soldiers to Ireland, to protect demonstrators. I saw on television. Was very moving. Little old ladies, you know, running out to serve tea to English. Girls standing to pose with them for pictures. Like in films you see of cities liberated at end of war against Nazis. And now Catholics riot at soldiers and shoot them. Here. Look. In today's newspaper. Eighteen-year-old English soldier, it says, wounded by bullet, lying in Falls Road. Stoned to death by mob of children. Not one of them over age of fourteen. Most of them seven or eight. I do not understand. Such hatred is sick. We would not even do that to Russians when they come in tanks...'

I had no answer. I don't remember what I replied. It couldn't've been anything very cogent or illuminating. The contradictions Magda had raised confounded not just her, not just me, but the media as well. None of us knew anything at that time of the cunning and carefully calculated policy whereby Northern Ireland's Catholic population was being systematically alienated from the British Army. The conversion of trust into power was being undone by the deliberate sowing of mistrust. And the mechanisms being employed in the process were, ironically, the mechanisms of the practical joke - mechanisms of the kind I'd recently used myself to promote a phoney foundation for juvenile werewolves. Some of them were even simpler, reminiscent of the pranks my friends and I had played in primary school.

Thus, for example, even as Magda and I were talking, an anonymous caller might've been on the telephone to a British Army compound in Belfast, or Lisburn, or Omagh. There was an arms cache, he might be reporting, upstairs, in Mrs. O'Malley's flat in the

Ardoyne. Mrs. O'Malley - a peaceable woman who only wanted to keep her sons out of trouble - would've been as tolerant and understanding as circumstances permitted when the troops banged on her door, invaded her premises, ransacked them and found nothing. She'd be less forgiving when - as the result of another anonymous 'tip-off' - the same thing happened again two or three nights later. After the fourth or fifth such occurrence, she'd have little love or patience left for the army, and her sons would've been recruited by the Provisional IRA.

There were many Mrs. O'Malleys. There were also many women and children coaxed, conned or coerced to march in the van of demonstrations - to shield the stone-throwers and the snipers, to be filmed and photographed afterwards as brutalised victims. But there were more ingenious stratagems as well, dextrously exploiting the media's inherent need to be exploited. A fake gunman, for instance, might be positioned, crouching or prone, among the toddlers on a playground - armed with a stick perhaps, or a length of piping, or a water pistol. As a British foot patrol passed, he or someone else might clap hands, pop a paper bag or even just shout 'Bang!'. The squaddies would spin round, weapons trained, and the shutters of hidden cameras would click - often of several cameras, showing different angles which would seem to show different locales. A day or a week later, there'd appear, in the local, national or international press, photographs of British soldiers ostensibly prepared to massacre infants.

A non-stop campaign of such techniques, after two years, had transformed the Army, in the eyes of the populace, from protectors into monsters. Both had been duped, pitted unwittingly against each other by unseen hands - just as my unseen hand, for very different reasons, had pitted Lieutenant Boyle in Chicago against Crispin Whelk. In Ulster, however, the success of these ploys was measurable in a wholesale shift of public opinion, and in blood. It was also measurable in the little old ladies whom Magda'd found so touching. When they served tea to the troops now, they added ground glass to the sugar.

Unaware of the dynamics at work behind events, I couldn't at the time dispel Magda's perplexities. As a result of those perplexities, however, my attention was drawn to Northern Ireland in a way it wouldn't otherwise have been. Not, of course, that Ulster became in any sense a pressing concern for me. Its reality hadn't yet registered. It remained remote, peripheral, devoid of immediacy or urgency. I would've scoffed had seer or soothsayer foretold otherwise - foretold that before the new decade was out, Ulster would dominate my personal agenda. And no scrying glass of my own, no Tarot spread, no I Ching, no runes could've predicted that before the new decade was out, Ulster, like the Civil Rights Movement in the South, like Vietnam, would've unseated me from the impartial fence I sought to straddle, and toppled me into another political commitment.

****

A year later, I was back in Boston, teaching, under Bernard McCabe's departmental chairmanship, at the university I'd attended as an undergraduate. I was conducting a course for which I couldn't devise a title and which Bernard, in the name of all *non-sequiturs*, had dubbed 'Through the Sahara With a Bone-Handled Umbrella'. I was parking my white Capri on a carpet outside my lodgings. And I was also, once a month or thereabouts, bolting up to Montreal, where my ex-best friend's ex-wife from Vancouver now lived.

Together, we'd plunge into the vibrant pulsating nocturnal pageant of Canada's largest and most cosmopolitan city. We'd patronise in particular the dim-lit small-hour-of-the-morning cafés, where folk singers performed for bohemian audiences and other indefatigable drinkers. At one such place, we came to know the resident troubadour, an expert guitarist with a copious, eclectic and ecumenical repertoire - from the Occitain lyrics of Jehan l'Ascuiz to the most contemporary anthems of protest. And with an insensitivity that now makes me wince, I'd blithely request 'Kevin Barry,' 'Roddy McCorley', 'The Rising of the Moon' and other such bitter or bellicose ballads. I assumed they were as innocuous as the songs of the American Civil War, safely immured by history. I was oblivious to their inflammatory significance in the context of Ulster's current 'Troubles'. I was indifferent to the surly mutters, grumbles and objections of the patrons around me, as well as to the constrained diffidence of the singer. On one occasion, I nearly got into a brawl. I wasn't, of course, prepared to fight for Irish Republicanism, only for my right to listen to its music without being politically pigeonholed.

But I refused to recognise how offensive, how painful, this music often was to many Canadian sensibilities. Or the way in which it used language and melody to celebrate violence and hatred.

XIV

When the Provisional IRA first interfered with me personally, they did so unbeknownst to themselves, and in an oblique fashion that threatened my fountain pen collection. I was conscious of the threat; but not even I, at the time, realised the extent of their responsibility.

My contract in Boston had only been for a year, the department lacked money to renew it and I was therefore cast adrift. I washed ashore, rudderless, in the place I most loathed, New Jersey. Here I found a stop-gap position, supposedly teaching rudimentary English composition, at a dinky community college. The job, if undemanding, was as dreary as the grimed industrial milieu; and I was chronically bored, chronically restless, chronically destitute, chronically lonely. Most of my friends were scattered like buckshot across the country, and I had few opportunities to make new ones. My only muse at the time, a woman who'd been in the graduate programme with me on Long Island, was purely and chastely platonic. In principle, or lack of it, I wouldn't've balked at another adulterous affair; but in this instance, I respected both her husband, and the validity of their marriage, too much to trespass on the prerogatives of either.

Lacking anything more stimulating or convivial to do, I spent many hours driving. I'd set off at random, with no particular destination in mind; I'd get off the main thoroughfare at some arbitrary point, find the nearest winding back road through wooded countryside and let it take me wherever it happened to be going. In this haphazard manner, I toured the pretentious plasticised towns of the suburban commuter belt, the farmland and rural communities beyond - places with such apt names as Flemington. Sometimes, my wanderings carried me as far as the Pennsylvania border to the west. On one foray, a state policeman, interpreting my aimlessness as incipient skulduggery, stopped me and asked what I was doing. I told him I was looking for a damsel in distress to rescue. Why else would I be driving a white car? I never found any such damsel. I did, however, find a good many fountain pens.

I'd always cherished fountain pens, ever since the cheap but sturdy Esterbrook with which I'd first learned to form letters, first drawn misshapen cars and six-guns on every flyleaf of my parents' books. There was a certain elegance, a certain satisfying definitiveness, in the way the ink flowed from nib to page - a liquid line of jewel-dark colour which dried, so I fancied, to something as immutable as a monument, as the Magna Carta. I never used washable ink. I found something reassuring in the mere words 'Permanent Black' on the bottle. Or 'Permanent Red', which evoked images of Faust pacts ratified in blood. With a fountain pen, moreover, one could scribble on one's hands, which it was trickier to do with other implements. At the age of nine or ten, I had the most lavishly decorated hands in my class. And fountain pens could also double as weapons. I'd flicked ink over more than one pest or foe in primary school. Later, during a gang fight in the ninth grade, I'd parried a bicycle chain with my garrison belt, then stabbed my assailant in the shoulder with my Esterbrook. It'd been filled with red ink at the time, he'd panicked, thinking he was haemorrhaging, and scuttled cravenly away.

Compared to the fountain pen's versatility, precision, individuality and aesthetic character, pencils, ballpoints, even the new felt-tipped markers then just making their début, were tacky, vulgar, crassly utilitarian - like a 'Saturday Night Special' compared to a Walther, a Ford or a Chevy compared to a Porsche, a bottle of rotgut compared to Jack Daniels or a decent malt. The sheer disposability of the modern junk diminished it, stamped it as a typically tatty product of a society based on planned obsolescence - a society in which neither people nor objects were appreciated for their own sakes, only used perfunctorily and discarded.

At the time, of course, fountain pens were deemed outmoded, dated, no longer fashionable. Stationers, too, for that matter, were a dying breed. To the extent that people in New Jersey used writing materials at all, they purchased what they needed at the appropriate aisle or counter in one of the supermarkets, hypermarkets, drugstores or megatstores spawning amidst aerodrome-sized shopping malls every few miles. In bedraggled little towns with names like Garwood and Scotch Plains, the dilapidated, thirty-year-old stationer's establishment couldn't compete with Korvette's cornucopia of kitsch. On my drives, I'd often pass such establishments sinking forlornly into neglect and oblivion, dwarfed by the bulk, just down the road, of some garish emporium with the bloated dimensions of an aircraft carrier. And in such mournful establishments, mummified in dust-furred display cases unopened for years, I'd find tiers of pristine fountain pens - hooded-nibbed Parkers with the sleek profile of jet fighters, rare bulbous-domed Eversharps in casings of ornate rolled gold, long torpedo-shaped Sheaffer Snorkels in rich-hued plastic, in precious or semi-precious metal. As a child in the early to mid-fifties, I'd seen such instruments advertised - in *National Geographic* particularly - for the then exorbitant sum of thirty, fifty or seventy dollars. Now, I could pick the unwanted things up for five.

I bought copiously, often in bulk. I'd no very clear idea in the beginning of what to do with my acquisitions. At that point, certainly, I didn't have a collection as such in mind, still less anything that might be called an 'investment'. But my aesthetic sense bridled at the prospect of these beautiful, fastidiously designed and crafted artefacts mouldering to scrap, being tossed in a rubbish bin, melted down, incinerated or pulverised to powder. I justified my purchase of them as a worthy enterprise of salvage, of reclamation, preservation, conservation. Some of my bounty I conferred as gifts, either by post or hand. My platonic muse, for example, received an especially elegant Snorkel, the colour and texture of coral. Descending from the platonically ethereal, she somehow contrived, a week later, to sit on the thing and bend it into a pitifully warped cripple of its former self. I was affronted. It seemed a disgracefully cavalier way to treat a veritable *objet d'art*, and an irresponsible misuse of her bottom.

Sulking, I began to hoard the pens myself, to take pleasure in the unique balance and distinctive workmanship of each, the idiosyncrasies of its ink flow and nib. Thus did my collection coalesce, more by default than by any deliberate plan. By that summer, it numbered some sixty genuine rarities, as well as another two dozen pedestrian or more recent items which I'd bought for the sake of comparison and contrast. I dismembered a few expendable specimens, studied their viscera, learned how to reassemble and repair them, how to replace or resuscitate desiccated bladders, refurbish finishes, restore damaged nibs. Before I realised what I was doing, it'd become a *fait accompli* - an idle whim had blossomed into a full-fledged hobby, and the hobby, in the vacancy of my existence during those days, quickly assumed obsessive proportions. On my drives now, I sallied forth in specific quest of fountain pens. When someone teased me about it, I invoked Nabokov, Montreux's magus-in-residence, cavorting up and down Alps in pursuit of lepidoptera.

Not even fountain pens, however, could fill the emptiness surrounding me at the time. I was paralysed by my inability to determine just where I wanted to be, and neither the cosmos nor my network of contacts was vouchsafing any very coherent signals. I'd never before encountered this particular problem. On three occasions in the past, the decision had effectively been made for me; I'd acquiesced in it, and circumstance, as well as other people, had smoothed my path. Thus, in a state of semi-somnambulism, I'd let myself be sent or drawn to Boston originally, thence to Chicago, thence to Long Island. On two subsequent occasions, I'd known, quite lucidly, by virtue of a woman, where I wished to go; I'd resolved, one way or another, to get there, contrived to do so and then proceeded to create a viable reality for myself. Thus I'd launched myself at Vancouver; thus I'd returned to Boston. Now, however, the principles that'd formerly sustained me no longer functioned. No muse beckoned from afar to provide incentive. No prospects presented themselves, to be acted on or transformed into adventure. Possibility might not've been wholly exhausted, but it'd certainly become jaded, lost its zest. The result was inertia, an all-pervasive apathy and a slough of despond.

It was at this juncture that my sister, warming to the rôle of *dea ex machina,* intervened. We'd seen one another twice during the previous ten years, for no more than a few hours on each occasion. On the first, en route to JT Swift's place in San Francisco, Radetzky and I'd stopped by her abode in the Hollywood Hills. We were knackered to near-debilitation, having driven straight through from the Grand Canyon and spent part of the journey jockeying with rednecks in a pickup, who'd tried to run us off the road all through the Mojave Desert. In my sister's house, a sort of makeshift commune, a dozen or so people were sprawled about, only dimly visible through a wavering gauze haze of cannabis smoke - on which the few words she and I exchanged wafted wispily away before reaching each other's ears. On the second occasion, she'd descended on me by surprise in Vancouver while honeymooning with a Mormon - a more bizarre and improbable trip than any likely to be induced by acid. The risk of scathing her husband's pious ears had kept our conversation to the level of inanity.

Now, having defenestrated the Mormon and two marriages, she'd settled in London with a new consort and proceeded to establish herself as high priestess of the city's esoteric sub-culture. Having learned of my impasse, she'd consulted my horoscope and begun to pelt me with letters, urging me to consider England as an option. I'd find the milieu congenial, she insisted; I'd be among kindred spirits; I could function on a shoestring more comfortably than I could in the States, could survive while maintaining a lifestyle of seedily genteel bohemianism.

That June, accordingly, I embarked for London to conduct my own reconnaissance. I spent the better part of a month in the capital, staying with my sister and her consort in South Kensington. For both of us, our reunion proved exhilarating. During the ten year lacuna in our rapport, we'd pursued radically different trajectories and arrived, at least so far as vision and hierarchy of value were concerned, at pretty much the same destination - a destination to which few other people, and least of all our despairing parents, could follow us.

Apart from the re-established contact with my sister, what impressed me most immediately about London was the Happy Hunting Ground it constituted for fountain pens. Thus must Mexico's riches first have appeared to Cortés, Peru's to Pizarro. I ran joyously amok, like a boy with his parents' credit cards in a toy shop. At Harrods, Selfridges and other West End Meccas, there were cases of foreign exotica - Montblancs, Lamys, the newly imported French Watermans, all unknown at that time in the States. At stationers in Hendon and Golders Green, there were ranges of recently discontinued models - English-made Watermans, Swans, Conway Stewarts, posh-looking Osmiroids with rolled gold caps and hooded nibs, produced before the company went down-market. At Brick Lane and Portobello Road, there were Aladdin's Caves of classical antiques, now bartered for extortionate sums by dealers, then obtainable for pennies. A further stimulus was that my mind hadn't yet adjusted to the exchange rate between British and American currency. Twenty was twenty, and I paid scant attention to the squiggle preceding the numerals - or reflexively projected a dollar sign instead of sterling. As a result, my month in London yielded a harvest of thirty-four fountain pens.

On the night before my scheduled return to the States, I suddenly became uneasy. I knew I didn't look respectable. I'd long since ceased trying to look respectable. I'd long since resigned myself to the impossibility of doing so. Whether I wore a suit or not, whether or not I asphyxiated myself with a tie, regardless of how I cut or combed my hair, I'd still, I recognised, appear suspect - a wastrel at best, more likely a thug or professional hit man. Then, too, I'd had ample experience, on my drives to and fro across the Canadian border, with the cranky fervour of American Customs officials. Invariably, they'd ransack my luggage, my laundry, my shaving kit, every conceivable seam, interstice, nook and cranny of my vehicle. There was one contortionist zealot, for example, who'd performed a display of downright simian acrobatics, slithering under the car, crawling in one door and out the other, sprawling on the floor and on the seats, clambering literally into the boot, draping himself upside down to forage under the carpets. His face, when he'd surfaced, was a boiled lobster colour from the blood that'd rushed to his head.

'All you had to do was ask me,' I'd said to him politely. 'I'd've told you I wasn't carrying any contraband, and you could've saved yourself all this exertion. It doesn't seem to've been very healthy for you.'

Unamused, he'd turned his back on me grumpily and paced in a suspicious circle around the car.

'You mean you wouldn't've trusted me?'

He'd only glowered, then embarked on another circuit - like a dog orbiting a tree before urinating.

'Look,' I'd said. 'If I really wanted to smuggle contraband - no, let's not mince words - if I really wanted to smuggle dope, do you think I'd carry it in the predictable places you've searched? You're insulting my intelligence. If I were smuggling dope, I'd carry it on the roof. Yes, up there. In an envelope. Taped to the metal. Concealed under the layer of snow.'

It'd struck him with all the impact of a revelation. For the next fifteen minutes, he'd busied himself scraping - and inspecting - every trace of snow from the car. When he'd finished, the vehicle was as immaculate as if it'd just been washed.

With fanatical commitment like this, I now had to reckon, as well as with my own dubious appearance. How, given such factors, was I to get thirty-four fountain pens through American Customs unscathed? How was I to prevent some overenthusiastic vandal from thinking me a dope smuggler, swooping on my new acquisitions and, with the single-minded brutality of his kind, disembowelling them, eviscerating them? I imagined an unbridled orgy of destruction and inkshed. But then again, what would I've done if I were a Customs officer and some surly-looking character - dark glasses, black leather jacket - tried to get thirty-four fountain pens past me?

I distributed half my hoard as widely and plausibly as I could amidst my luggage. I distributed the remainder as discreetly as possible about my person - two in each shirt pocket for symmetry and balance, four in my inside jacket pocket, three in my jacket's breast pocket, the others in the several pockets of my trenchcoat. Thus cuirassed in fountain pens, I embarked for the airport.

My sole anxiety was American Customs. I didn't anticipate difficulty at Heathrow, had no reason to assume there'd be any. What I didn't know, failed to remember or simply neglected to allow for was that the IRA, some six weeks earlier, had launched a bombing campaign against the British mainland. It hadn't been as nasty as some that'd preceded it, others that were to follow. There'd been no series injuries, as I recall, certainly no deaths. But the memory of bloodier incidents was still fresh, and the public had been exhorted to vigilance. Signs in tubes, pubs and shops warned of unattended parcels - and, needless to say, airport security had been intensified. When I strolled through the electronic gates, my fountain pens - gold, silver, plate, steel, chrome, lacquer on brass - must've triggered every metal detector in the terminal.

I've no idea how much less sophisticated the apparatus was in those days, but it was unquestionably noisier and more obtrusive. Bells, buzzers, sirens, klaxons erupted in cacophonous chorus from every quarter, eclipsing all other sounds with their din. In the three or four seconds at my disposal, I assumed there must be some sort of fire alarm. Like most of the other paralysed people, however, I couldn't determine the source of the disturbance. I certainly didn't realise *I* was the source of it until men in diverse shades of blue uniform materialised from half a dozen different directions, converged on me at a headlong run and surrounded me in a jostling huddle. Enclosed by a phalanx of blue, I was bundled off to a secluded alcove and ordered to empty my pockets. Only then did I begin to guess what'd happened, but explanations by that time would've been pointless. With a shrug, I complied. Coins, both British and American. A snuffbox-sized tin of aspirin. Keys, Pocket knife. Lighter, Spare lighter. And then, like an endless scarf being conjured and unfurled from a magician's waistcoat, a seemingly interminable succession of fountain pens. Two. Two more. Four. Three. Another two...The officer in front of me was having trouble controlling the débris in his cupped hands. A pen dropped, and I protested angrily. Another officer removed his cap and proffered it as a receptacle. I filled it with the remaining fountain pens. The officers exchanged glances of amused befuddlement.

'Excuse me, sir,' one of them asked, the merest flicker of irony in his politeness. 'If you don't mind me asking, why do you have so many fountain pens?'

What was there to say? Except the obvious.

'I'm a writer.'

'I see,' my interrogator drawled, raking me with a ruefully sardonic glance. 'Well, sir, if you don't mind me saying so, you might as well've been wearing a suit of armour.'

'No doubt. But isn't there an old adage of some sort? Something about the pen being mightier...?'

He didn't press the matter further. Writers, apparently, were expected to parade dementia, even at Heathrow. But when, divested of metallic accoutrements, I passed through the electronic gates again, all hell broke loose for the second time. Amidst the consternation caused by my pens, we'd forgotten the studs on my belt and the buckle.

'Most excitement we've had all bloody month!' I heard one officer enthuse to another as I was finally admitted to the boarding area.

And in New York, where I'd anticipated all manner of trouble, I encountered none whatever. One of the desks at Customs was manned by a pony-tailed bearded young man, probably a graduate student on a summer job, whom not even his prim uniform could wholly descruff. Trading on a tacitly acknowledged freemasonry of scruffiness, I made a beeline for his desk, and he waved me through without so much as a question.

During a party in London some three or four years later, I had occasion to recount my *contretemps* at the airport. Most of my audience were duly amused and laughed appreciatively. But one trendily bellicose Hampstead radical - the species of *chaise-longue* revolutionary who romanticised 'armed struggle' and boasted membership in silly organisations like 'Troops Out' and 'Time to Go' - objected, displaying the humourless pomposity of his kind. He'd apparently misheard or misconstrued. He apparently thought my pens had actually been damaged or confiscated or something. And he apparently believed that I genuinely, with all the intensity of heartfelt grievance, held the IRA responsible.

'You can't blame them for what happened,' he bleated huffily. 'It was airport security, not the IRA.'

Everyone, of course, stared at him, baffled, provoked or - in the case of his wife - embarrassed by his sententious literal-mindedness.

'I'm just using the kind of logic they themselves use,' I replied dryly. 'When some poor hapless sod gets shot or blown up by mistake, for example, and they express their "regrets" for the mishap, and then go on to claim it wasn't really the bomb or the bullet that killed him at all, but the presence of British troops on the streets of Belfast.'

****

My June reconnaissance more or less confirmed my sister's sanguine assessment. Even apart from the fountain pens with which it burgeoned, London did indeed appear a congenial milieu - more so, at any rate, than any I could imagine in the States. I hadn't fallen passionately in love with the place, as I had with Vancouver; I wasn't so desperate or deranged as to do that; but I could see myself finding some sort of habitable niche in London, testing my resources against the challenges it posed, forging a new, more flexible reality. The city also promised a generous circle of friends, a sub-culture in which the arts commanded some nominal respect and the possibility of independence from the brittle, artificial structures of academia.

On returning to the States, therefore, I spent July and August mobilising for definitive expatriation, paying farewell visits around New England, New Jersey and New York. I arranged for the storage of books and papers, the transatlantic shipment of my typewriter and other necessities. To finance my relocation, I braved pangs of ruptured comradeship and sold my white Capri - a sacrifice made more painful by the prospect, for the first time in a dozen years, of imminent carlessness. Then, in September, having tied up all loose ends, I again embarked for London, determined to make it my home for the foreseeable future, turbocharging my morale with thoughts of Henry James, Eliot and Pound.

For the next month and a half, I shunted between my sister's premises, the flats of new acquaintances, squalid ersatz hotels of the kind that prey on immigrants, then a prissified bed-sit in South Kensington, where my Italian landlady's absurd restrictions and prohibitions quickly embroiled us in a feud. It might easily have culminated either in litigation or murder, had not well-wishers found me alternative lodgings. Early in December, I moved into a spacious, dilapidated but once elegant and stately dwelling in Camden, on a sedately leafy residential crescent, just around the corner from the bustle of the high street, the gaudy pageantry of the outdoor markets, the dereliction of London's largest dosshouse.

My lodgings were owned by a woman more or less my own age, a neurotic retarded flower child from the sixties, who'd purchased the premises with a legacy some years before and now rented rooms to other lost or vaporously diffuse souls. I convinced her that I qualified as one such. In addition to displaced people, she collected cats. Five were installed as permanent residents, but the number increased at intervals, with broods of kittens, to as many as sixteen. Too niggardly to spend money on proper litter, my proprietess filled the beasts' boxes with earth dug up from the garden, which were then left to fester in the loo. In warm weather, the malodorous cubicle played host to a Luftwaffe of flies, engaged in a round-the-clock re-enactment of the Blitz. Other insects, earthbound and airborne, were equally intrusive. In mid-bath one afternoon, I was strafed by a belligerent bumblebee. I crash-dived and flooded half the adjoining kitchen.

I was to occupy my Camden accommodations for the next four years. The route to my garret led usually through a front room redolent of cat piss and marijuana smoke, where – on a stereo blasting at apocalyptic decibels – one or another gang of caterwaulers was strenuously murdering the very concept of music, contriving a tortuous electronic pandemonium comparable, in volume and cacophony, to the Battle of the Somme. In addition to the fluctuating quota of regular lodgers, there was generally a parade of transients, itinerants, visitors, fad-peddlers, paramours, friends of friends –

moulting ex-hippies, burnt-out druggies, would-be witches and warlocks, Nirvana-bound pilgrims chanting mantras and yantras, deserters from assorted European armies, wanderers returned from obscure corners of the globe where one got athlete's foot in one's armpits, unwed mothers by the coven, a California groupie who proudly claimed to've had the meridian of her sexual organs re-aligned, and hordes of verminous infants howling, yowling, babbling, cooing, vomiting, drooling and practising forms of self-asphyxia that exhausted the anatomical possibilities of the human body.

Insofar as feasible, I remained aloof from this bedlam, sequestered in my garret two floors above. Like the mirror, my window was smoked an opaque grey-brown by nicotine and paraffin fumes. To the extent that it offered any vista at all, I could see, blearily, the garden below, a narrow drive, a soot-bleakened electrical supplies depot where taxis came to get jaded batteries recharged, a defunct factory whose tall cylindrical chimney, glazed with pigeonshit, bisected the sky. Inside my room, teetering towers of books threatened to avalanche downwards at any moment. Ink and paint blots rorschached the surface of the antique rolltop desk, its patina stripped to expose expanses of dingy nude wood profligate of splinters. Welters of crumpled paper not only cascaded from the wastebasket, but effectively submerged it, while pyramids of tawny cigarette butts reared ceilingwards from the ashtrays. Coats lay heaped on the bed like corpses on a battlefield, stray boots lurked in ambush amidst the shadow. Only the gleaming and burnished ranks of my fountain pens, arrayed on the shelves of a glass-fronted cabinet, attested to any sort of order.

My relations with my co-denizens in the house were, for the most part, cordial but distant - not hostile nor even particularly frosty, just remote, disinterested, impersonal. The one exception to this was cranky Snidley Wusslet - not a co-denizen, strictly speaking, so much as a kind of resident troll banging metronomically away under the floorboards. Scrawny, emaciated, dishevelled, with long gingery hair and unpruned beard which made him resemble an undernourished yeti, Snidley in fact lived elsewhere, but rented part of the basement as a workshop. Here, for a time, he'd endeavoured, in wheedling manipulative fashion, to boss, bully, browbeat and tyrannise his cousin and petite assistant - until she'd rebelled, mobilised superior business acumen and, through a discreet palace *coup*, took over their joint enterprise, retaining him as her employee.

The joint enterprise in question entailed the manufacture of belts, wallets, keycases, handbags and assorted other leather goods to sell from a weekend stall at Camden Lock market. The stall also trafficked in various macrobiotic surrogates for food. Harbouring Napoleonic delusions of culinary grandeur, Snidley concocted watery tahini, congealed humus and lumps of pita bread that might've doubled as coshes. Despite experiments of near-alchemical complexity, however, he failed in his quest to produce the ideal peanut butter - or, for that matter, any peanut butter at all. It solidified, it liquefied, it hardened like papier-mâché, it dribbled like oily gruel, but never attained the consistency of anything spreadable. Snidley persisted undeterred, fabricating leathery food and food-stained leather while his mind free-floated through endless successions of ultimate get-rich-quick schemes, each more daft than the last. These crackbrained projects he'd then try to peddle to those who knew him, deploying all the subtlety, tact and finesse of a dropped drawer of silverware. Inevitably, of course, his grandiose projects would come unstuck. '*It's not fair,*' he'd bleat, when reality, simply being true to itself, outfoxed him anew.

Such revenue as he did manage to generate was often squandered on courses, programmes or intensives designed, in theory at least, to endow him with 'powers'. By inflicting sundry masochistic regimens on himself, he aspired, for example, to become invisible at will; and by trying to 'act invisible', whatever that entailed, he became predictably conspicuous. Other undertakings yielded comparably inglorious results. While he meditated-cum-dozed in a lotus position one night, intending thereby to fine-tune his body, his foot fell asleep - and caused him, when he eventually stood up, to sprain his ankle. When I told him I lusted after BMW's newly launched 635CSi, he promised to procure me one through the magic of visualisation. This involved clipping a photograph of the car from a newspaper, taping it to the wall above his workbench and concentrating on it while munching his nut cutlet. Five years later, I was indeed the proud owner of a 635 coupé, and Snidley smugly claimed credit for it. At the time, however, he'd neglected to tell me I had to supplement his mental exertions by writing a bestselling book.

For an individual in the vanguard, as he fancied, of 'human development and evolution', Snidley was fussily prim and prudish. He disapproved of pubs, only frequenting them when liable to be left behind by others. He disapproved of women using four-letter words, and used them sparingly himself in mixed company. He seldom drank, and when he did, being incapable of holding his liquor, his moderation would verge on fanaticism. Having flaked his way through thirty some years of life, he'd never once smoked, not even cigarettes, still less cannabis, and shunned drugs in every form - from hallucinogens, through antibiotics, down to headache remedies. Neither did he gamble, except for one occasion when, relinquishing my Faust rôle for that of Mephistopheles, I managed to tempt him.

Bound for a party on the Finchley Road, I was awaiting a bus in Camden one Saturday afternoon. As I paced there, fuming at my carlessness, Snidley approached, jack-in-the-boxing up and down as he pedalled along on the antediluvian bicycle he'd repainted and proudly dubbed his 'Silver Steed' - though it was, if anything, more a mechanical avatar of Rocinante. Despite the day's warmth, he was wearing, as usual, his mangy Astrakhan jacket, which might've served as toupée for a senile Frankenstein's monster. En route to the same party as I was, he paused to commiserate with my demeaning dependence on public transport. In his whining adenoidal voice, he boasted triumphally of the contraption he was riding, urging me to get one of kindred ilk. When I sneered at the suggestion, Snidley gloated at the prospect of having long since arrived on the Finchley Road while I was still waiting at the bus stop. Responding to his challenge, I proposed a wager of five pounds that I'd get there before him, using my own 'magical' resources. Snidley embarked on a sententiously pompous proclamation of how he never gambled, then - seduced by the lure of quick and seemingly guaranteed money - promptly tossed principle to the wind. We accordingly shook hands on the matter. As soon as he'd puffed and wheezed his way out of sight, I hailed a passing cab and, for less than a third the cost of our bet, reached our joint destination ten minutes ahead of him. My duplicity, he proclaimed querulously in outrage and mortification, vindicated his taboo against gambling.

On the whole, Snidley might've been a figment escaped from a Monty Python skit. But copious and baroque though his eccentricities were, I discovered in him a sense of humour approximate to my own - as well as a propensity and aptitude for practical jokes. He displayed a genuine originality in devising pranks, a quickness and zaniness of imagination that sometimes seemed perversely inspired, a competent tactical (if not strategic) grasp of antic operations. Some of his schemes would've required the resources of *Candid Camera,* if not of Paramount Studios, but there were others which worked impressively even with our limited budget and personnel. In the years that followed, we were to hatch an extensive repertoire of impish routines. They ranged from old favourites such as 'Dial-an-Apology', 'The Electric Head' and 'The Telephone Police', through fictitious transit camps at Heathrow, to fastidious tailor-made deviltries. Snidley became, in effect, my Chief of Staff for Pranks; and together we assembled what I liked to think of as a well-honed, expertly drilled, versatile and professional squad of madcap jokers - like an SAS or Commando unit, capable of being mobilised and deployed on almost instant notice.

Just before I'd left the States, pranks had begun to establish themselves there as a potentially lucrative business. This development owed much to a company registered under the name of 'Pie-Kill'. For surprisingly modest remuneration, 'Pie-Kill' would undertake special commissions - would undertake, that is, with custard pies, Mafia-style contracts or 'hits' on targets designated by its clients. The client, according to the arrangement, assumed responsibility for any fines or legal fees that ensued. Snidley and I toyed briefly with a British variant of 'Pie-Kill'. It would've been called 'Just Desserts', but wouldn't have confined itself solely to custard pies. On the contrary, it would've offered a broad range of custom-designed and personalised 'services', reminiscent of scenarios from *Mission Impossible.* In the end, of course, inertia triumphed and nothing came of the project. We rationalised this as integrity - a reluctance to sully the essential artistic purity of the practical joke for the sake of filthy lucre. The pranks we perpetrated, we told ourselves, were perpetrated for lofty aesthetic reasons alone - to afford pleasure, to entertain, to instruct and enlighten. That, needless to say, didn't prevent us from performing 'hits' requested by friends. Or conducting personal vendettas. Or succumbing to temptation when one or another particularly irresistible target - a gullible American, for example - blundered into range.

The halcyon days of my practical joking in London coincided with, and to some extent stemmed from, a period of creative sterility. I was museless at the time, and, in my muselessness, destitute of inspiration. I felt hollow, desiccated, written out, drained of verbal and imaginative resources. Still trying to exorcise Ilona's ghost, I embarked on, then abandoned, a fictionalised history of Germany narrated by Wotan. The few stories and nouvellen I tossed off were mere contrivances, mechanical exercises in style, in form, in imagery, in mood, but devoid of vision, devoid of anything worth saying, showing or illuminating. During this phase of inner drought, my pranks provided a conduit. Through them, a febrile inventiveness, too fitful for literary shape, sublimated itself and found expression. Conscious of the mechanism, I acquiesced - better to be an ingenious mischief-maker, piddling though that was, than lie completely fallow.

In the course of my mischief-making, I became pervasively aware of the relationship between the practical joke and the work of art - the degree to which a well-designed, well-orchestrated, well-choreographed prank incorporated an aesthetic dimension, became a species of artistic 'happening'. I pondered some of literature's great pranksters-cum-confidence men, such as Melville's trickster, Gide's Lafcadio, Mann's Felix Krull, Gaddis' cast of swindlers in *The Recognitions*. And I pondered the artist himself as practical joker - Queneau, for example, Joyce, Cabrera Infante, most obviously perhaps Nabokov in *Pale Fire*. It was in this direction that I began to seek renewal of inspiration, some egress from my cul-de-sac. I couldn't know that circumstances were already conspiring to unblock the impasse, to furnish both a muse and a focus for my creative energy. The muse was to be my lady, and the focus Northern Ireland.

XV

Nine weeks after I'd officially migrated to London, shortly before I moved into my Camden garret, the IRA had impinged on me again - still not in any sense directly or personally, but in a fashion that nevertheless shocked me as much as it did the public at large. On an evening towards the end of November, two pubs in Birmingham - not military installations or targets, not even hang-outs for soldiers, just ordinary taverns packed with civilians - were ripped apart by bombs. Twenty-one victims died in the explosions, nearly two hundred were injured - young people for the most part, having no connection whatever with Ulster's affairs.

A fortnight or so of acute tension followed. Everyone I knew, as well as I myself, became wary, suspicious, incipiently paranoid. One scrutinised strangers with hostility. One prickled at every trace of an Irish accent - common enough around Camden. One furtively studied the closed faces on the Underground, in shops and pubs. One edged tentatively around every parcel, package, briefcase or valise, as if it portended imminent doom. There must've been plenty of harassed publicans during those days, called to inspect obscure alcoves and crannies of their premises and defuse bags of mouldering sandwiches, abandoned pornography, neglected nappies, assorted domestic essentials forgotten by absent-minded tipplers en route home.

Inevitably, there was a backlash of sorts, and a few ugly incidents ensued. I seem to recall an incendiary device hurled at a church, a fire started in an Irish community centre, a punch-up between English and Irish workers at a factory. On the whole, however, I was struck by how different, how much more violent, the reaction would've been in the States. Americans would've shunned bars - as they later shunned flights to Europe in the wake of Reagan's air raid on Libya. And lynch law would've prevailed. Few Irish establishments would've escaped undamaged. No Irishman, assuming he were identifiable as such, would've been safe on the streets. I fully expected some eruption of collective hysteria, some vicious outburst of commingled vindictiveness and fear. I witnessed instead something dramatically different - something that must've been, I told myself (not shrinking from cliché), the vaunted 'spirit of the Blitz'. No raging and bloodthirsty mobs. No frenzy. No gruesome acts of reprisal. No self-appointed avengers. Only a quiet determination, a dogged refusal to be intimidated, a comportment as if nothing particularly untoward had happened, a phlegmatic getting on with business. I wasn't sure whether to be impressed or disgusted by such impassivity, such stoicism, such fanatical moderation. I found it as baffling as the infuriating patience with which people resigned themselves to waiting endlessly in queues.

Birmingham was a hundred or so miles away, but the bombs there were the closest I'd yet come to the reality of modern terrorism. It'd been, until then, a phenomenon alien to my experience. Other forms of violence had, of course, encroached in the States. There'd been the chaotic urban riots of the sixties. There'd been muggings, assaults, sporadic acts of kidnapping and sabotage. There'd been the depredations of organised crime and the occasional berserk gunman on a killing spree. To all of these, I'd become in some sense inured; but nothing had prepared me for the deliberate, calculated and wholesale slaughter of civilians in the name of a political ideology - and an unrealistic political ideology to boot. America's knowledge of such things was at that time only vicarious - the massacre of Israeli athletes, for example, at the Munich Olympics, which had indeed caused a sensation throughout the country. That, too, however, was different, involving as it did specific rather than random targets, in an insulated setting rather than in the heart of a city. And its impact on me had in any case been diminished by my general ignorance of it - I was travelling at the time, had no access to radio or television and only learned of the atrocity a week later, after its initial horror had subsided.

The Birmingham bombings thus confronted me with something I'd never encountered before, and rendered me rigid with revulsion. I was familiar, of course, with the theoretical foundations of terrorism, the programme adumbrated by Bakunin and his disciples. But such programmes had never imposed themselves on my reality, and seemed to me, in any case, too simplistic, too psychologically naïve, to warrant serious consideration. I couldn't condemn, as a matter of ironclad general principle, all acts of political assassination, especially when they were directed at precise noxious individuals. In certain circumstances - the bomb plot, for example, engineered by

Claus von Stauffenberg against Adolf Hitler - I was prepared to regard such acts as valid, even laudable. I had also to acknowledge, in certain circumstances, the validity of guerrilla operations conducted against an entrenched authority. In France during the Second World War, in Holland, in Greece, in Yugoslavia and other prostrate countries, an organised resistance had attacked targets of strategic significance, had sabotaged German military installations, killed German troops; and while I personally saw no parallel between occupied Europe and Northern Ireland, I recognised that others, by sleight of logic, might, and might justify themselves accordingly.

But neither Stauffenberg's bomb plot nor the Resistance in occupied Europe had involved the intentional, gratuitous and arbitrary murder of civilians. I couldn't imagine any cause, however lofty, however exalted, which sanctioned that sort or magnitude of atrocity; I couldn't imagine any cause which wouldn't be tainted thereby beyond any vestige of credibility, any claim to legitimacy, to rectitude or support. And yet I knew people in the States - otherwise intelligent people - who, insulated by three thousand miles of ocean, glamorised such lunacy as the deeds of heroic 'freedom fighters'.

In the initial flush of outrage, I rummaged for a frame of reference, for some precedent by which I might assess and interpret my feelings. Alison Krause and her fellow students, dead on the campus of Kent State in Ohio? Not really. Appalling though that was, it couldn't be ascribed to malice, to deliberation, to the premeditated intention of extinguishing lives - only to incompetence, ineptitude, inexperience, panic on the part of the National Guardsmen. The woman on that balcony in Mississippi - who'd poured scalding water over Ilona and revealed to me, for the first time, my own capacity to kill? Her act had unquestionably been an act of malice, but generated by fear and fuelled by the fury of the moment, not something coldly, clinically and scientifically devised. Nor had it been fatal. Nor had Ilona been an indiscriminate haphazard victim. On the contrary, she'd been marked out individually, targeted as a stranger, an invader, an enemy who threatened an established order.

I failed to find a precedent, a recognisable or familiar frame of reference. I was faced, I realised, with something altogether new. And the more I faced it - or it me - the more demonic appeared that combination of randomness and premeditated malice. And the more I realised how easily - had I lived in Birmingham, had the bombers struck in London – I myself might've been their victim. Or, worse still – since I, if I'd been their victim, wouldn't've felt much of anything – my sister or my friends. The sheer perversity of the act fostered a concurrent perversity in my mind, and I found myself, for the next fortnight or so, contemplating images of vengeance – the vengeance I knew I'd seek, had I been bereft by one of those blasts.

From the age of seven or so, I'd watched, on film and television, a seemingly endless reel of spy, crime and western adventures. I was still watching them, for that matter, when I went to the cinema or had access to a television set. And inevitably, at frequent if irregular intervals, a predictable hackneyed variation on the predictable hackneyed plots would recur. There'd be a hackneyed but sympathetic supernumerary – a decent bloke, an innocent bystander, a law-abiding citizen, an honest cop or newspaper editor, a beloved relative or, most tellingly for me personally, a beautiful young woman. For one reason or another, this individual – the beautiful young woman, say – would run afoul of the villain. Perhaps she'd be an unfortunate chance witness to a murder, or to some other crime. Perhaps, through no fault of her own, she'd be incommodiously in the way, an obstruction to the villain's nefarious designs. Perhaps she'd simply bumble into his line of fire as he was drawing a bead on his real target.

In any case, she'd be snuffed out like a candle, brushed aside like a fly. She'd be expendable; and whatever the specific details of the scenario, she'd become a haphazard sacrificial victim. Invariably, of course, the hero would soon surge on to the screen, to avenge her death and ensure that 'justice be done'. At the end of the story, there'd be some sort of statutory reckoning, usually in the form of a shootout. Guns would blaze. Walls, trees, cars would be pocked and peppered with shells. The villain would stick his head a little too far up or out from wherever he was skulking. The hero would take judicious aim. The morally sanctified bullet would strike unerringly home. The villain would fling out his arms, double up, perform a pirouette or some other balletic manoeuvre, then topple satisfyingly into the dust where, snake that he was, he belonged. The implications were always that justice had indeed been served, that cosmic accounts had been balanced, that order and equilibrium had been restored, that the world's workings could again proceed in accordance with some harmonious original plan. The disruptive speck of dirt or grit had been removed from the machinery, and that machinery could once more function smoothly, with well-oiled precision and equipoise.

I must've been ten or eleven when something about this formula first began to bother me, to seem somehow seriously wrong, seriously askew. It was another two or three years before I realised exactly what - and then the realisation struck me as if I'd stepped on a rake, with all the blatant impact of the overlooked self-evident. Justice *hadn't* been served, I realised. The scales *hadn't* attained equilibrium. Accounts *hadn't* been balanced. There remained a major deficit - simply because the eradication of some sleazy hoodlum or gunman or Mafioso goon couldn't possibly compensate for the death of a decent man or a beautiful young woman. There couldn't be a mere trade-off of a life for a life, because the lives, in this case, weren't equal. If that were so, however, could the ledgers be settled more fairly, the credit and debit columns brought more into accord? Probably not. I'd discerned even then, I think, that such bookkeeping was fatuous, doomed to futility; and I resented Hollywood's facile, hypocritical attempts to suggest otherwise. But given that some imbalance must inevitably obtain, what was the best one could expect? Or, more precisely, what form must vengeance take to confer some measure of satisfaction, some hope of catharsis? At the time, I had no answer to that question. Now, an answer suggested itself. It would have to encompass, I concluded, something of the theological concept of atonement.

I was familiar, of course, with conventional watered-down interpretations of the word. In some quarters, for example, 'atonement' was believed to derive from 'at-one-ment' - the yearning, after a fall from grace, to become 'at one' again with God and the divine order. I found this interpretation both etymologically and theologically suspect. It only worked, as far as I could gauge, in modern English. And 'at-one-ment', or 'at-one-ness', was something to which, as a matter of course, any self-respecting would-be saint or mystic routinely aspired. Atonement, with everything it implied of infraction and culpability, had to signify something else. It had to entail at least some element of remorse. And remorse, if genuine and valid, had to entail some awareness, some understanding, some comprehension and appreciation of the magnitude of one's transgression. Were I ever to seek vengeance in earnest, I realised, it wouldn't be sufficient to dispatch a villain to a neat and tidy oblivion. Or even to a messy oblivion. He'd have to be brought to some sort of empirical, visceral, emotional reckoning with the staggering enormity of what he'd done. He'd have to be so imbued, so infused, so inculcated with guilt, with self-recrimination and self-loathing that he'd *want* to die, if only to escape the lacerating harrow of his own conscience. And his real punishment would be the denial of the death he craved.

This process, needless to say, presupposed the existence and activation of a conscience. And a conscience couldn't be generated or activated by rope, electric chair, gas chamber or firing squad. Nor, even, for that matter, by imprisonment. At least not reliably so. Solitary confinement might, on occasion, do the job, but only by chance, coincidentally, as a by-product. The same applied to institutionalised religion. Conscience - the capacity for understanding and remorse - lay in the recesses of the psyche; and it was only through the psyche that conscience could be poked and prodded awake.

I had no interest in such tedious philosophical conundrums as whether conscience was acquired or innate. However they came by it, however 'real' or 'illusory' it might be, most people, for better or worse, were encumbered by it, and it could be stirred to tumult by deft psychological manipulation - manipulation of the kind practised by churches for centuries, of the kind often unconsciously practised by parents, of the kind I myself had practised as a lecturer on Long Island. Here again, the question was one of utilising 'black' magic on behalf of 'white'. Through knowledge of the psyche's dynamics, through a skilful pushing of key buttons, through an exploitation of mental or emotional pressure points, most villains could be reduced to shuddering husks.

But the terrorist, the fanatic or the ideologue posed a more complex problem, in that his indoctrination had cauterised the usual pressure points - had programmed out of him the established modes of access to conscience, to humanity, to sensitivity. By procedures akin to military training, he'd been rendered impervious, impermeable, immune. Thus, in evading the clutches of my Draft Board, I'd made myself invincible by hiding behind an armoured shell of logical concepts - though that shell, of course, had only been façade, a patchwork affair hastily devised for the occasion. For the terrorist, the fanatic or the ideologue, the shell was no temporary expedient, but a way of life, a mode of being, something he fervently believed in, adhered to; and the soft mollusc of sensibility inside it was all the more inaccessible.

How, then, could that mollusc be reached? How could the programmed mind, encased in its rigid structures, be 'de-programmed'? Only by a process as ruthless, as inhuman, as implacable as the original programming itself - a process that seared through the calluses and scar-tissue on the soul, the reopened the cauterised points of vulnerability. Or, alternatively, by a process that stole up on its target, so to speak, that seeped through unexpected apertures left unsealed, uncaulked, unguarded. A process that exploited religious susceptibility and suggestibility, for example. That created apparently meaningful coincidences to suggest the intervention of some 'supernatural' or some 'higher' agency. That actuated curses. That implanted voodoo-like mechanisms in the psyche and caused the individual to self-destruct. That tapped the reservoir of superstitious dread in, say, the Catholic imagination - as I'd tapped it in Chicago, playing sorcerer to three neo-Nazi hooligans. That fed ultimately on fear and constituted a kind of *internal* equivalent of terrorism - a terrorism of the soul.

These were some of my gentler conclusions. I also fantasised macabre, grisly, even fiendish scenarios, lurid and garish techniques in whose ingenuity I took no pride. Not torture. Not physical torture, at any rate. But things that would certainly have qualified as 'cruel and unusual punishment', to be visited on, say, the man who planted a bomb - assuming, of course, he could be captured and his guilt definitively confirmed. In my formulation of such ghoulish pantomimes, I had, needless to say, no particular quarrel with Irish Republicanism. My vindictiveness lacked all political bias, was wholly moral in character. It could, theoretically, have been directed at any of a number of organisations which trafficked in indiscriminate murder - at terrorist factions in the Middle East, in France, Germany, Italy, Spain and assorted other places. And there were also, of course, the so-called Loyalist paramilitaries in Ulster, who also shot people at random, who also planted bombs. But their bombs pre-dated my arrival in England. Their bombs hadn't exploded on the British mainland. Their bombs hadn't come as close to me, or to individuals I knew, as Birmingham. Those of the Provisional IRA had. It was therefore the Provisional IRA who came to embody for me everything most contemptible about terrorism; and it was the Provisional IRA who figured most prominently in my reveries of retribution.

Through such reveries, I endeavoured to contain, focus, channel and eventually purge my outrage. But the outrage also sought opportunities to externalise itself, to find expression in the world around me, as well as in my imagination - to be somehow objectified, if only through the paltry expedient of polemic. In the aftermath of the Birmingham bombs, however, such opportunities for polemic were few. I'd begun to lecture again by then, two part-time courses at a suburban polytechnic. I expected some of my more radical students to shoot their mouths off, say something stupidly provocative and thereby set themselves up for me as foils, as scapegoats. But they, too, to their credit, remained glumly silent about what'd happened - abased, ashamed, confused, struggling to reconcile their principles with their revulsion. My own bohemian and esoteric circles, though perhaps a little more blasé than I was, shared my feelings. In the month or two that followed, I had, as I recall, only one opportunity to exact some species of vicarious reprisal.

I was in a pub on the Finchley Road one frostbitten evening, with Snidley, Cassandra, two other London friends and a trio of itinerant Americans. All of us looked pretty scruffy, and it must've been our appearance, as well as the aggressively discordant accents, that drew the stranger to our table. He, too, it transpired, was American, though I gathered he'd lived in England for some time. He was long-haired, semi-shaven and wearing the uniform of his kind - tattered jeans, boots, an anorak with copious bulging pockets. Stuck to his chest there was a paper badge, green shamrock in white circle. In one hand, he brandished a cylindrical tin jangling with coins. He introduced himself with an Irish name - Kelly, if I remember correctly, or perhaps O'Kelly - and announced he was collecting for 'Troops Out'.

'I thought they already were,' I said, feigning American obtuseness.

'Were what?'

'Out. Hasn't Saigon just been evacuated? Or maybe it's about to be...'

'No, no, no. Not Vietnam. The Six Counties.'

'Which six counties?'

'Ireland, man. Northern Ireland. We want British troops out of Northern Ireland. We support Sinn Féin.'

'You mean the IRA?' one of the Londoners at the table queried.

'Well, yeah, I guess. It's all pretty much the same thing. We're opposed to the fascist British government. We want them to pull their army of occupation out of the Six Counties.'

'The IRA...,' I echoed thoughtfully, becoming more obtuse than before. 'They were active during the Second World War, weren't they? Lighting fires in places like Belfast? As markers for German bombers? Seems a funny way to oppose a fascist government.'

Kelly, or O'Kelly, or whatever his name was, looked confounded, slack-jawed with consternation for a moment. My statements were obviously news to him. Despite his residence in England, he was clearly as ignorant of Ulster's reality as Americans across the Atlantic.

'You sure about that, man?' he asked uncertainly.

'Fairly sure. I was reading a book about the Blitz recently.'

'That don't make sense,' Kelly, or O'Kelly, muttered. 'I mean, like the IRA, they're Marxist.'

'So was Stalin,' I replied with a shrug. 'That didn't prevent him from signing a pact with Hitler.'

'Yeah, but...I'm gonna have to check up on this. You wanna give some money?'

'No, I don't think so. Not for the moment. You go and check up. If I'm wrong, come back some other night and we'll see. But I wouldn't want to give money to a Nazi organisation. You might not want to collect money for them yourself. Or would you?'

'Hell, no, man!' Kelly, or O'Kelly, exclaimed, slipping his tin hurriedly into an anorak pocket, 'Like I said, let me do some checking. Friend of mine's got this book on the history of the IRA. Like going back, I mean, to the Fenians and the Famine in World War One and all that stuff. That oughta have the answers.'

****

My reaction to the Birmingham bombs was intense, almost obsessive at moments, but ultimately short-lived. It had, of course, been accentuated by my unaccustomedness; and if I wondered at British aplomb, I also tended to forget that the 'Troubles', for the people around me, had already entered their fifth year. What I found unwonted and unprecedented had already, for those around me, become something to which they were inured - had become just one more in an already copious catalogue of atrocities. Granted, this particular atrocity was more savage and produced a greater, if still temporary, impact. Granted, too, that any such barbarity on the British mainland caused more of a fuss than it did in Ireland - which seemed, to most Londoners, as remote and irrelevant as the moon. But even in Ireland, sensibilities were becoming dulled, blunted, anaesthetised, as American sensibilities had been by Vietnam. Horror was becoming part of a way of life, an accepted 'given' of existence. As I eased myself into the London scene, created a groove for myself and began to adapt to my surroundings, it was inevitable that I should come to share the prevailing apathy about Ulster. When a bomb exploded in a London shop or street, when IRA gunmen were besieged in a London apartment, my mind was fleetingly concentrated. Apart from that, however, I took only a fitful and desultory interest. I became as blasé as my friends, as habituated, as unruffled.

Few Londoners, it transpired, really cared. This indifference, I discovered, extended even to the pub I adopted as my local. Now, lying adjacent to a new-sprouted concrete mushroom of a television studio, the place has become trendy, fashionable, slickly yuppified, with a plethora of chrome and glass reflected in its freshly burnished wood. It caters to slick young hustlers in the media, who bargain with barracuda bonhomie and shed scruples as fast as they can climb. In the days when I brought it my custom, however, it was still a typical Camden pub - seedier, if anything, than most. I patronised it because it was the only establishment in the neighbourhood with a pool table. And its jukebox was then refreshingly free of the thunderous electronic din to be found elsewhere, playing only wistful and haunting Irish folk melodies. Its clientèle, at that time, were almost entirely Irish - hard-drinking garrulous oldsters for the most part, some of them derelicts from the nearby dosshouse, some of them veterans of the 1920s civil war or even, seemingly, of Ivy Day in the

Committee Room. I came to know many of them. I also eavesdropped on many conversations. And Ulster, I found, was a taboo subject. Kilburn, a few miles distant, was, I gathered, more militant; but in Camden, the current 'Troubles' generated only tedium at best, more often acute embarrassment. If the IRA were mentioned at all, they were mentioned reprovingly, scornfully, scathingly, often bitterly - as 'bastards who make a man ashamed to be Irish'.

'They're poison,' I heard a bleary-eyed old boozer complain one evening. 'Like the chemicals they're dumpin' in th'Irish Sea. Turnin' it the wrong shade o' green.'

Three or four years before, when I was reading about it in Vancouver's newspapers, Northern Ireland had undoubtedly been a burning issue in mainland Britain as well. Now, however, it'd receded to the status of 'white noise' in the background. Like crime in American cities, like accidents on American roads, it was incessantly there, incessantly taking its toll, but no longer newsworthy, unless something particularly horrific happened. Despairing of seeing the problem resolved, most people were content to see it contained - contained to a so-called 'acceptable level of violence'.

On the other hand, politics - routine day-to-day politics, the regular raucous debates in the Commons, the pronouncements of one or another government or shadow minister - seemed to figure more pervasively than such things ever had in the States. Politics seemed to dominate television, the newspapers, the campuses. If these were a gauge, one might assume the British psyche to be obsessed by politics, like a child by a new toy. Were British people's lives really so empty, so vacuous, that they had nothing better with which to preoccupy themselves? Was I merely paying more attention to public affairs than in the past? Was the emphasis in the media different? Or was Britain just so small compared to the States, where size and diversity constantly furnished the media with stimulating fare?

In any case, I found British politics stupefyingly, insufferably, infuriatingly boring. Worse than that, I found them juvenile, trivial, intrinsically inane. Granted, politics in America were more vulgar, more tasteless, more gauche. Granted, too, that British politicians were generally more intelligent, more literate, more articulate and better informed than their American counterparts. (One couldn't imagine a certified and card-carrying buffoon installed in Downing Street - although no one, in those days, ever imagined Ronald Reagan in the

White House either.) And granted, too, that political machinery functioned more smoothly, more quickly, more expeditiously in Britain than it did in the States. In Britain, for example, a Watergate-scale scandal would promptly have toppled a government. Indeed, British governments had fallen for far less, with no need for Hamletesque agonising about whether to institute the prolonged, unwieldy and cumbersome ordeal of impeachment proceedings.

In theory, the British system should've been more effective. In practice, however, it trivialised and diminished the allegedly lofty, hallowed and consecrated process it purported to enshrine. Behind the squabbling of Republicans and Democrats in the States, there remained a more or less general consensus about how the country should run, what kind of country it was supposed to be. The consensus was often a stupid one, but it could also foster partnership and goodwill, out of which more positive things occasionally grew. In Britain, there was no such underlying consensus. On the contrary, there was a chronic state of undeclared and non-violent civil war between irreconcilable factions, each entrenched behind ramparts of ideology and party allegiance, each with its own partisan concept of the nation. And because their antipathy never actually degenerated into armed conflict, it was perforce reduced to the level of puerile adolescent insult and abuse, carping and sniping.

Much of the so-called debate in the Commons was little more than a polite (if that) equivalent of 'Your mother wears combat boots!'. Nothing the government in power did could possibly, whatever the circumstances, be condoned, approved or endorsed by the opposition. Every statement, every measure, had necessarily to be condemned – on principle, as a knee-jerk response, though one's own credibility might thereby suffer. If the government acquiesced in some policy advocated by the opposition, such acquiescence was itself castigated as too little, too late, too much or too soon. Or it was gleefully, triumphantly, derided as a 'climb-down', rather than used as a basis for future co-operation. Tact, diplomacy and statesmanship consisted in large part of not rubbing an adversary's nose in the dirt, not chortling 'I told you so'. British politics often amounted to little more than jockeying for a position which enabled one to bellow 'I told you so', with an accompanying fanfare. Every issue, even tragic accidents and natural disasters, provided a potential opportunity to gloat, if it served to discredit an opponent - or just supplied ammunition for doing so. Instead of dialogue, intelligent criticism or a preparedness to work constructively together, there was only pettiness, spite, meanness, bickering and piddling recrimination - the rancorous eagerness of schoolboys anxious to score points at any cost. Through the political system, the 'childishness' so sternly reproved in children themselves was vouchsafed a wholesale and licensed mandate for expression.

Perhaps the chief culprit in the shoddy charade was a species, or sub-species, of humanity that'd never impinged on me before - the professional politician. He'd obviously existed previously, but I'd had no reason to notice him. By some process of inverse evolution, however, he *was* of relatively recent date. Once upon a time, and not a long time ago it was, politics had been conducted by men of broad and questing minds, original, imaginative, innovative, with curiosity and interest in a diverse spectrum of spheres. Once upon a time, politicians had also been poets, novelists, historians, philosophers, psychologists. Once upon a time, politics were the province of those fit for leadership, who'd established their qualifications and credentials in other fields of endeavour, who'd displayed some notable degree of knowledge and understanding, who'd proved themselves to their contemporaries. In its mania for specialisation, the 20th century had midwifed a new breed of misconceived political creature - an unimaginative, monochrome and pedantic individual of pygmy stature, qualified for nothing, absolutely nothing, except recycling rhetoric worn smooth by overuse, trowelling out promises no one believed and publicly making an ass of himself.

This creature, of course, was hardly unique to Britain. If anything, he was more indigenous to the States, where mediocrity (as Spiro Agnew instinctively divined) had long been synonymous with virtue. In the States, however, my experience had kept me insulated from such specimens. And American society, in any case, was already degenerating beyond them. For governmental office in the States, even the rudimentary qualifications of the professional politician would soon be superfluous. It would suffice to be a semi-senile third-rate actor with an addiction to jelly-beans, or a Robert Redford lookalike with a wealthy father and a pushy wife. But in Britain, the professional politician seemed to've attained some sort of apotheosis. I felt importuned daily by his intrusion on my life through newspapers and television; I felt affronted daily by his indefatigable zest for publicity, his paucity of insight, his desiccated language, his flannel, his waffle, his cliché; I felt personally insulted by his constant implicit aspersion of my intelligence - his assumption that I, or anyone else for that matter, could actually be conned by his guff.

No less offensive and patronising was television's perverse infatuation with such midgets and their activities. Again, there was an implicit condescension at which I found it impossible not to take umbrage. It seemed to be a basic premise that I and most other people actually *needed* to have the implications of each policy statement, each parliamentary debate, each by-election laboriously explained to us by politicos, commentators, pundits and self-styled 'experts' trundled into the studio for the occasion - that we actually required their tortuous analysis-cum-mastication, which invariably amounted to hemming, hawing, equivocating, prevaricating and coming to diametrically opposed conclusions. It seemed not to've occurred to programme makers that most people were more or less capable of thinking for themselves, and that those who *did* in fact need exegesis of the self-evident wouldn't bother to watch it anyway.

In consequence, all the best mindless escapism, all the most healthy sex and violence, was ruthlessly bumped off the air to make way for the same drearily predictable rota of faces being subjected to the same drearily predictable questions, and replying with the same drearily predictable drivel. ('*Well, Minister, what do you make of your party's showing in the Effing and Swiving by-election? Wouldn't you see that as a resounding defeat*?') Was the inquisitor with the bounty hunter's gleam in his eyes really so dumb as to expect an honest, or even a cogent, response? ('*Absolutely! No question about it! An unmitigated disaster! Our party's now irreparably fucked! I'm heading straight from this studio for Number 10 and handing in my portfolio.*') Imbeciles! Dunderheads! There's admittedly a certain *Schadenfreude*, a certain sadistic satisfaction, in seeing some pompous blusterer squirm to rationalise an electoral débâcle. But the ways, directions and formulae by which a man can squirm in such circumstances are finite. They're soon either exhausted or ritualised, and even the public squirm then becomes a tiresome spectacle. Yet British audiences - assuming British television reflected their taste - remained insatiable in their appetite for such squalid spectacles. Thus must decadent

Romans have enjoyed their circuses, but with no hypocritical sublimation of bloodlust.

If the preoccupation with politics and professional politicians constantly bewildered me, so, too, did the pathological, jubilantly masochistic relish with which Britain contemplated and castigated her past. Balanced, measured and judicious self-criticism would've been fair enough. This, however, was nothing of the sort, but a bizarre rite of self-abasement and self-denigration, performed amid ecstasies of guilt, in full regalia of sackcloth and ashes. Collective historical culpability - a kind of psychic breast-beating, hand-wringing and hair-tearing - seemed to have assumed the status of a national sport. At every opportunity, the country's conscience was eager to squeal a *Mea Culpa*. India, Africa, Australia and other far-flung outposts of the Empire weren't the only grounds for contrition, recrimination and reproach. Modern Britain was also prepared to mortify herself for what medieval barons had done to their peasants in the 12th century, what Saxon monarchs had done to their serfs. Every newly discovered blunder, every freshly uncovered oversight, every recently exhumed misdemeanour, provoked an almost audible 'Tally-ho!', as prosecutors peeled off like Spitfire pilots to swoop.

I found this orgy of exuberant penitence incomprehensible. With the so-called wisdom of hindsight, Britain's mercantile, colonial and imperial behaviour could, of course, be indicted for all manner of derelictions and delinquencies, miscalculations and misjudgements, sins of omission and commission - but only by the late 20th century mind, working on late 20th century assumptions rooted in late 20th century values and attitudes. In the context of their own epoch, the men who'd created the *Pax Britannica* had sometimes acted ineptly and incompetently, but often enough, too, with commendable enlightenment. Certainly the track records of other nations, other cultures, other peoples, were far shabbier. Certainly the most estimable governments and institutions of the Third World owed more to British influence than to anything else. And if Britain had treated the 'native Irish' as shamefully as many Famine-fleeing Irish-Americans treated the Apache, the Sioux and the Cheyenne, there probably wouldn't've been any subsequent 'Irish problem'.

On the whole, Britain's heritage was one in which she could take a modest and tempered pride - more so, at any rate, than most countries could in theirs. At very least, she'd earned the right to a quota of self-respect. Yet it was this that I found so conspicuously lacking. The implication, in books, in academic courses, in television documentaries, in media exposés, was that the whole of British history had been a single sorry millennium-long mistake - perpetrated by men to be damned forever by posterity merely because their foresight hadn't been twenty-twenty. It was as fatuous as damning Shakespeare as anti-Semitic for *The Merchant of Venice*, racist for *Othello*, jingoistic for *Henry V*, sexist for *The Taming of the Shrew*.

I joked, as did Monty Python, at the great superfluous British need to apologise. But there were other things, decidedly more ugly, at which I couldn't joke. In the bleak aftermath of the Great War, D.H. Lawrence, with his customary prescience, had prophesied the advent of a new phenomenon in British society. Lawrence was familiar enough with traditional caste distinctions, the traditional tensions and frictions they engendered. He'd long chafed at these, but now gloomily warned of their displacement by something more ominous, more soulless, more dehumanising and destructive - a brutish, nasty and vicious species of inverse snobbery and class antagonism rooted wholly in materialism, envy and greed.

Fifty years after Lawrence penned his prediction, I found its actualisation all around me. This wasn't even the 'class warfare' exhorted and extolled by Marx. Whatever its simplistic naïveté, that at least could pretend to be morally 'clean', pretend to reflect some striving for 'equality', pretend to rest on clear perceptions, a lucid assessment of social and economic realities. There were no clear perceptions in the resentment I witnessed, no lucid assessments. There was no striving for 'equality', except by denigration and tearing down. Least of all was there anything morally hygienic in the process. There was only prejudice of the most blind and mindless kind - prejudice as blind and mindless as the kind I'd encountered in the American South, and with the same surly, smouldering, incipiently violent edge to it. In this case, however, it was directed 'upwards', towards imagined 'betters', whose very 'betterness' constituted grounds for antipathy.

Cadillac owners in the States were generally ignored. At worst, they were regarded ironically, were teased or twitted, but with no real rancour. In Britain, Rolls and Bentley owners were actively despised and reviled. Anyone who 'spoke well', who enunciated precisely, who displayed a 'posh accent', was automatically derided and mocked - not good-naturedly, but with the jeering malice reserved for an enemy. People my own age who'd had the alleged benefit of education sought to disown and repudiate it, sought to assume a veneer of illiteracy and oafishness, sought to adopt - like some sort of weird pedigree - an abrasive diction and manner deemed fashionably 'working class'. Being ascribed to the 'working class', sloppiness and vulgarity in thought and language were assiduously cultivated. Through a laboriously fabricated uncouthness, would-be imitators demeaned the very 'working class' they claimed to represent - and uglified, rather than dignified, themselves. In the States, loutishness came naturally. In Britain, an entire generation was self-consciously aspiring to it and calling it 'political awareness'.

When probed on my own political allegiances, I replied with my now standardised formula - that I had no politics as such, merely opinions on certain political issues and none whatever on most. I doggedly refused to acknowledge any system as more than provisionally and temporarily valid - valid, that is, not as a permanent fixture, but only in specific circumstances, to cope with specific problems, for a specific and limited period of time. In her medical establishment, for example, America would probably benefit from more socialism. Britain, in many of her institutions, would probably benefit from less. But I saw no 'ism' as holding all the answers, as being definitively applicable or desirable across the board, as constituting a universal panacea. I thought it more important, I'd say blandly, to be adaptable - to retain the flexibility required to draw on whatever 'ism' happened to be appropriate at a given moment, then discard it when it'd served its purpose. Thus one avoided perhaps the worst 'ism' of all - dogmatism.

This attitude, as I saw it, involved no profound insight or clairvoyance, only rudimentary common sense. To many of those around me, however, it was, of course, appallingly louche, appallingly mercenary, appallingly 'cynical', appallingly 'opportunist'. I didn't particularly object to any of these adjectives - which rendered me, naturally, all the more reprehensible, especially among my more militant colleagues at the polytechnic. Some of them simply wrote me off as hopeless and ceased thereafter to bore me with their polemics. Others, however, were more persistent, and afflicted as well by a compulsive need to classify, categorise and pigeonhole - as if my heterodoxy somehow threatened their neatly structured and compartmentalised realities. They accused me of being 'evasive'. Even if I 'had no politics', they'd argue, the sum of my opinions on various political issues must amount to some sort of aggregate, must constitute a political position of some sort, must place me somewhere on the political spectrum.

I shrugged, while they, further goaded by my indifference, computed their sums. They added up my opinions, insofar as I had any, on assorted questions they rattled off. They multiplied or divided by whatever arcane factors they deemed relevant. To their frustration, the results could never be made to tally. In American politics, I'd constantly emerge 'slightly to the left of centre'. In British politics, I'd emerge 'slightly to the right'. Like manic bookkeepers chasing an elusive debit, they'd perform their calculations again, only to end up with the same inconsistency. Infuriated, they'd address themselves once more to the enigma, checking and double-checking each issue, checking and double-checking my opinion on it. What they'd overlooked, of course, was the so-called 'centre' itself, which wasn't the same 'centre' in Britain as it was in the States.

While others wallowed in this silliness, I recoiled with energetic apathy, tinged by disgust. Turning my back on all such matters, I concentrated on my fountain pen collection. I made occasional sorties to Brick Lane and Portobello Road, almost always returning with some booty. My most convenient, accessible and productive stalking ground, however, was Camden Lock, virtually around the corner from my lodgings. Here, overlooking a canal of Styx-black water, the booths and stalls of the outdoor market exhibited their weekend wares under ragged, faded, usually dripping awnings. Foraging through this accumulation of detritus became a regular feature of my Saturday and Sunday afternoons. I'd first visit the grotty stall where Snidley endeavoured to purvey his latest foul compôte or compost, his latest congealed or liquefied experiment with misprocessed peanuts. I'd pester him, embarrass him by complaining loudly about the indigestibility of his alleged food, make a general nuisance of myself. I'd then thread my way through the congested, jostling and empuddled aisles, scanning the array of junk on the weather-gnawed wood tables - old lighters, cigarette cards, dolls, watches, china, ashtrays, egg cups, penknives, toys, pipes, cutlery, rings and other jewellery, the welter of dismal débris from two or more centuries of superseded lives.

I soon became known to most of the stallkeepers, who - accustomed as they were to weird quirks and hobby-horses - put aside for me whatever fountain pens they'd picked up during the week's bartering. Within a year, my collection had burgeoned to some three hundred items and was threatening to swamp my garret. Except for my desk, every flat surface was covered by ranks and tiers of fountain pens. Additional flat surfaces had to be created. Books, boots, papers, clothes had constantly to be shunted into ever more remote and cluttered recesses to make room for my new acquisitions.

It must've been during my third year in London that complications began to arise. By that time, I'd established a sizeable network of friends and acquaintances, most of whom knew that fountain pens would be cheaper, less troublesome and more welcome than other gifts or tributes. At Christmas, therefore, and for a fortnight or so before my birthday, my circle would descend in a horde on Camden Lock. Since the weekly crop of pens had already been put aside for me, none would be out on the tables, and prospective purchasers would have to ask for them. Perplexed stallkeepers couldn't know, of course, that the numerous requests they received were all on behalf of one monomaniacal individual. They concluded, understandably enough, that fountain pens were becoming an 'in thing' - a new fad on which lucrative profits could be made.

Prices began to increase. Adverts began to appear in trade papers, in antique dealers' catalogues. Supply began to dry up. Two stallkeepers jettisoned their other bric-a-brac and devoted themselves exclusively to fountain pens, lavishly displayed in old-fashioned glass-fronted showcases. The prismatic iridescent colours, the burnished celluloid finishes, the intricate patterns of tortoiseshell, whorl, arabesque, ripple, scallop and diamond, soon attracted other customers. Before anyone really twigged what was happening, still less how or why, a new fad had indeed been born, and business wasn't just booming, but reverberating.

Today, fountain pens are back in vogue. At least two shops, located in London's West End, deal wholly in vintage specimens, and instruments for which I once paid a pound or two now go for upwards of a hundred. Fashionable and prestigious department stores all have large, prominent and elaborately arranged pen departments, some with sections devoted to antiques. Responding to demand, Parker, Sheaffer, Waterman, Pelikan, Montblanc and other manufacturers have brought out so-called 'Limited Editions' - costly instruments produced in restricted quantities, as well as reproductions of their own hefty and ornate classics dating from the first third of the 20th century. Designer houses - Dior, Cardin, Gucci, Cartier, Yves St. Laurent - market unique models of their own. So, too, do Porsche, Ferrari, Alfa Romeo. And new pen manufacturers début every few months.

Can I claim, single-handedly, to've resurrected the fountain pen? That would be immodest of me, and something of an exaggeration. But I can, I think, pride myself on having contributed signally to the fountain pen's renaissance - on the whole, a more laudable, more tasteful and civilised achievement than most professional politicians can boast of. Unfortunately, however, I never got around to perpetrating the hoax I occasionally discussed with Snidley - the discovery of a William Morris fountain pen, pre-dating the earliest known Waterman.

XVI

At a publishing party one night, I alluded in passing to 'my lady'. Resentful perhaps that I valued women for certain qualities she'd ruthlessly expunged in herself, a dour and sour feminist standing nearby promptly bristled. 'My lady', she declared officiously, as if promulgating a new piece of legislation, was a 'sexist phrase'. I was genuinely astonished, genuinely perplexed, but also defiant. If my lady, whose femininity far exceeded that of my termagant accuser, found nothing objectionable in the phrase, I saw no reason for amending it - or for ascribing any justness to the accusation.

Contrary to what many of my friends, acquaintances and associates may've believed, the phrase wasn't a mere twee affectation or conceit. It derived, in fact, from the least twee and least affected people I'd known, the black clientèle of the bar in Chicago. They'd talk frequently of their 'ladies'; they'd refer to Beryl as Radetzky's 'lady', to Nina as mine; and I adopted their terminology as part of our shared dialect, our shared shorthand communication. For it was indeed a species of shorthand, an abbreviated method of conveying something often complex.

Behind the phrase loomed a hierarchy of subtle connotations. There were important distinctions, for example, between one's 'lady' and one's 'woman'. To speak of 'my woman' implied ownership. It generally implied co-habitation and frequently, though not always, marriage. It also implied a person so insignificant as to be taken for granted. It implied a relationship based on rudimentary physicality and not too much more. And, not unusually, it implied brutality and abuse. One's 'woman', in short, was a pitifully abject creature whose rôle consisted primarily of punch-bag, erotic sponge and all-purpose drudge.

To speak of 'my lady', on the other hand, implied an entirely different kind of bond, an entirely different attitude. It seldom, if ever, implied marriage. It did, however, imply partnership, rather than possession of chattel. It implied separate domiciles. It implied not just a sexual contract, but an emotional attachment, an emotional investment. It implied, in contrast to a person taken for granted, a person of whom one was proud. It implied deference, respect and even - insofar as the milieu could accommodate such a thing -

courtliness or chivalry. It was used - especially in conjunction with such adjectives as, say, 'foxy' - not only as the supreme flattery, but also as a form of homage. It reflected an element of humility, an element of submission to the feminine principle, of which those who employed the phrase were themselves largely unaware.

By all these standards, Nina had indeed been 'my lady', and the phrase, with its attendant implications, had aptly defined our relationship. To varying degrees, it'd also been apt for my relationships with Ilona, with Magda, with perhaps half a dozen other women in Boston, New York, Long Island and Vancouver. It'd never been more apt, however, than it was for my relationship with Delphine in London.

Yes, it implied everything it'd implied in Chicago, but much more as well. And there was, ultimately, no other appropriate nomenclature. 'Mistress' was both demeaning and, in its patronising connotations, scandalously inaccurate. 'Lover' was similarly demeaning, suggesting an exclusively sexual rapport, the assignation conducted for no purpose other than lovemaking. 'Sweetheart' was gushy, tacky, vulgarly American and dated to boot, redolent of an insipid saccharine sentimentality; and I wasn't prepared to let Delphine, or my attachment to her, be Barbara Cartlandised. 'Friend' was altogether too bland, too casual and too undifferentiated - in gender, in magnitude of importance, in everything else. If Delphine were merely my 'friend', what distinguished her from the numerous others, of both sexes and diverse degrees of intimacy, who might also be so labelled? 'Ladyfriend' sounded arch, coy, superciliously ironic. 'Girlfriend' was insultingly juvenile; I'd not had a 'girlfriend' since I was sixteen or so; and Delphine, in any case, possessed too much stature, too much intrinsic dignity, too much significance for me personally to be trivialised by so puerile a term. There remained, of course, 'muse', the appellation I'd employed most often in the past. More emphatically than any of her predecessors, Delphine was indeed my 'muse', but she wasn't solely that, or even primarily that. I looked to her not just for transfusions of aesthetic inspiration, and her status, among my priorities, came ultimately to transcend even my own art. In reference to her, then, 'muse', too, would've been condescending, inadequate, inappropriate.

'My lady' was thus not just the most apposite, but the only apposite, designation for Delphine. It came naturally and spontaneously to mind when I thought of her. It suited her. It conveyed or connoted the respect and esteem in which I held her. It reflected something of the chivalric character of our relationship, the desire on my part 'to serve' in the old courtly sense - to achieve or attain something, to perform something through or for or on behalf of one's beloved, to prove oneself worthy of her trust. It embodied the aspiration and the capacity to make everything I did - driving her to or from the airport, helping her with a particular project, advising her on one or another personal or professional matter, providing spiritual and emotional support - as much a manifestation of love, as much an act of lovemaking, as coupling or a kiss.

I readily confess to something quaintly anachronistic in all this, something unfashionably and archaically poetic, something at odds with the state-of-the-art mating theories of the late 20th century - an echo of the troubadour's erotic mysticism, the *amour courteois* of, say, Jehan l'Ascuiz. But that wasn't inappropriate either. I'd always been unabashedly, even fiercely, romantic, perfectly prepared to let my attachments assume the sacred status of a cult. That didn't, of course, mean facile idealisation, idolatry, enshrinement, the proverbial installation of a woman on a pedestal. It meant seeing her quite clearly, recognising her as a unique and separate individual, while exalting one's bond to her - the mystery of the bond between a man and a woman - into something sacrosanct, something inviolable. It meant transmuting a relationship into the sort of thing Lawrence extols - a process of constant and incessant renewal, for both one's partner and oneself.

In my metaphysics (insofar as I embraced any), in my epistemology (which I did embrace), I naturally remained an 'antinomian Hermetic numinist'. By disposition, however, I was an aesthete and an amorist, my real 'religion' being a combination of art and my lady - or, more accurately, art and my commitment to my lady. If valid, I'd long ago concluded, loving - as opposed to the merely passive business of being 'in love' - was always, necessarily, active, a creative act. And any valid creative act was always, necessarily, an act of love. As always for me, the dynamics were essentially alchemical - art as a metaphor for love, love as a metaphor for art and both as a single complex metaphor for the alchemist's metamorphosis through his own experiment.

By all these criteria, Delphine was incontestably 'my lady'. Unfortunately - neutered indefinite articles notwithstanding, perhaps there's an inherent 'sexism' in the English language - I've no idea what the male equivalent might be. Certainly not 'my gentleman'. No one, not even my most virulent enemies, would ever accuse me of being a 'gentleman'. And even apart from misconceptions fostered by the silent 'k', Delphine could hardly, without sounding certifiably deranged, speak of me to others as 'my knight'. Someday, however, I might suggest 'paladin' to her.

****

'It wasn't enough to organise parties and lectures,' my sister observed wryly, shortly after Delphine and I became involved. 'We had to organise an international conference.'

To find 'the right woman' had always been for me a laborious and haphazard business, entailing much trial and error, demanding in perseverance what it lacked in precision. After two and a half years in London, I'd tried and erred repeatedly, and my perseverance was pretty much exhausted. There'd been a modest handful of 'one-night stands', which left me, and usually my co-debauchee, feeling soiled; I'd never had any particular zest for such encounters, and now seemed to have lost the appetite for them entirely. If the word were used very loosely, I could count two apathetically conducted 'relationships', one of which had actually managed to drag itself along, coughing, sputtering, stalling and being jump-started, for some five months. And there were several latent or potential affairs, mostly (as usual) with friends' wives - affairs which, if they emerged from the chrysalis stage at all, would do so more out of desperation than enthusiasm.

The situation was becoming alarming. I'd begun to wonder if it was possible to be 'loved out', so to speak, in the way that an author can be 'written out'. For a mystical amorist, this was indeed a dark night of the soul. And in the absence of any feminine influence, my pranks were growing less harmless, more barbed. During a weekend-long symposium at the University of Nottingham, for example, I slipped notes under the doors in the dormitories where I and other participants of my acquaintance had been assigned accommodation:

> Dear Lester,
> I'm really deeply upset. I think you misunderstood what I was trying to say earlier. If at all possible, I'd like very much to clarify the matter. Do you think you could come to my room around eleven?
> Virginia

And:

> Dear Virginia,
> I was intrigued by a number of the points you made over lunch this afternoon. Would you be interested in pursuing some of them further? If so, come to my room around eleven.
> Aleister

And:

> Dear Aleister,
> Nora and I are both rather worried about the way Virginia's been behaving lately. We think we know what the problem is and want to help. Could you and Phoebe meet me in Lester's room around eleven to discuss the situation? If you can, bring Teddy and Shirley as well.
> Nigel

That night, as a result, I managed to get some two dozen people blundering into each other's rooms. In mid-rut with his secretary, hapless Lester was barged in on by eight visitors. Other genuine trysts were incommodiously and embarrassingly interrupted as well. Perplexed Virginia became the object of universal solicitude. No anarchic Cupid in the throes of delirium tremens, no berserk computer at a dating bureau, could've precipitated greater chaos. Some of the victims still haven't forgiven me.

It was probably only a matter of time before something disastrous happened - before I turned my attention, say, to some target that bit back and got me seriously into trouble. I was already contemplating a campaign against the philistinism of W.H. Smith, that boa constrictor of bookshop chains with its stranglehold on the British reading public. By not stocking Nabokov, Patrick White, Fuentes, García Márquez or Michel Tournier, one of their branches - a branch near the polytechnic where I lectured - had incurred my especial displeasure. The manager - a beefy and bumptious bloke who'd been cowed by my complaints but woodenly insisted the authors I'd cited weren't sufficiently 'commercial' - seemed to warrant uniquely fiendish retribution.

According to the scheme we'd devised, Snidley and I would telephone the Soviet, Czech, West German, American and a dozen or so other embassies. '*The microdot you want,*' we'd say cryptically, '*is in W.H. Smith's Hendon shop. The top half of the last semi-colon on page 69 of Jeffrey Archer's latest novel. Third copy from the end of the shelf. But you'd better hurry, before someone else buys it or the copies get mixed up.*' I couldn't realistically expect a hundred percent turn-out; but I hoped to lure at least a few trenchcoated spooks forth to investigate - to throng the premises, jostle each other for the book, squabble for the opportunity of first rummage.

'There might even be some sort of international incident in the shop,' Snidley suggested optimistically. 'Think of the headlines! If they started shooting each other over the book, for instance.'

'I'd rather they shot the book,' I replied. 'A proper professional execution. Prose that maims, mangles, mutilates and murders the language deserves capital punishment.'

In such directions as these were my pranks tending. It was clear enough - not just to me, but to my sister and my friends as well - that the only antidote would be a woman. And people were duly assiduous in organising parties, lectures, outings and other hypothetically opportune occasions - transparently veiled auditions, deviously engineered to wedge me together with successive prospective Ideal Feminine Companions.

There was certainly no shortage of eligible candidates, some of them not even married. London positively abounded with plausibly potential paramours. But while many of those I met were attractive enough in theory, the crucial element was always missing in practice. I felt no magic, no intoxicating *frisson*, no electricity, none of the visceral magnetism that galvanises the psyche, the nervous system, the blood, the loins, when authentic *Wahlverwandschaften* come into play. I remained woefully ungalvanised, indifferent, torpid, capable only of an apathetic shrug. '*Why not?*' I might sometimes say to myself about one or another candidate, but it wasn't the most compelling of incentives.

I recognised part of the problem. I'd previously been involved with some genuinely extraordinary women. Now, unable to help myself, I'd invariably subject each provisional consort to the cruellest, most invidious and unfair of tests. I'd instinctively measure her against my glamorised, romanticised, mythologised mental images of Ilona, Nina and other important muses in my past. This process, of course, inevitably diminished those of the present. I required an individual of Delphine's stature and uniqueness to contend successfully against such figments, against spectres imbued with all the puissant witchery of nostalgia - to exorcise them, dispel them, banish them and, by the sheer wonder of her being, the miracle of her existence in the world, to establish her own luminous identity in their stead. But Delphine, at that point, was still below my horizon.

The conference was scheduled for the first weekend in April, at the campus of a teachers' training college north of London, in the remote fastnesses of Hertfordshire. It was a prestigious, high-powered and lavishly publicised affair, luring people from as far away as the continent, even from the States. Though incidental to my purposes, its theme was the relationship between esoterica, psychology and the arts. This territory was, of course, familiar turf to me, but I'd hardly have bothered to attend without an ulterior motive. Even with an ulterior motive, I winced at the thought of the thing - a swarm of amateurs, novices and dilettantes dipping their toes, paddling childishly about, perhaps floundering in waters too deep and murky for most of them. I hoped, however, that the prevailing atmosphere - the intensification of reality engendered by abrogated routine, by hermetic insulation, by the enforced proximity of a weekend in the country - might constitute an alchemical alembic, a retort in which my dormant *Wahlverwandschaften* might be goaded from stupor.

With that wistful objective in mind, I spent the last fortnight of March sitting in, as unexplained and enigmatic guest, on my sister's astrology classes and workshops. I made due note of possible candidates. I compiled a short list of five. Selene badgered and bullied them into attending the event in Hertfordshire, and we studied their horoscopes for points of compatibility with mine. The most promising prospect, we concluded, was androgynously called Sam, presumably an amputation of Samantha; but I didn't necessarily have to fall in love with her name. She was a divorcée, Selene'd ascertained, and taught literature at London University. She lived conveniently close to my abode in Camden, a mere two tube stops away. And she was, needless to say, attractive, if slightly inclined to dumpiness. On the basis of her astrological, psychological, physical and professional CV, no computer, it seemed, could've coughed up a more harmonious match. When I embarked for the conference, therefore, it was primarily with conquest of Sam in mind. I travelled by bus, accompanying Selene, whose own consort happened to be abroad at the time, Cassandra and three or four other people I knew. Snidley'd also planned to attend, but got diverted into spring-cleaning his aura, or some other such 'evolved' activity.

For so august an assembly, the venue was pretty tacky - a straggling complex of low brick buildings in a fashionably unidentifiable style, equally suitable for dairies, electrical component factories, minimum security prisons. Modernity was further manifest in a plethora of plastic, vinyl, opalescent tiles and stainless steel. There was also a prodigal, even promiscuous, deployment of glass, which concentrated the sunlight in the corridors to infernal intensity and led me, along with most other people, to blunder into windows I mistook for doors. Beneath the merciless glare of fluorescent lights, the cafeteria vaguely suggested an operating theatre.

For the sake of economy, as well as the numerous non-carnivores present, the menu consisted largely of indeterminate substances in varying states of viscidity - semi-liquefied potatoes, assorted lentil gruels, pies of vulcanised apricot, a rice stew or risotto of some sort which resembled maggots simmered in porridge and probably didn't taste significantly worse. Even Snidley couldn't've concocted fare much more noxious. Outside, across a patrician sweep of gravel drive, stood a few denuded trees. They looked flustered, as if caught in the act of escaping. Beyond them loomed another complex of buildings - Quonset huts disguised as would-be quaint but actually kitsch country cottages. With a misplaced access of optimism, these had been designated as our sleeping quarters. In fact, sleep would be effectively precluded by the flimsy, tissue-thin partitions, which amplified even the most dulcet snores to the sonorous drone of a Lancaster, which made each toilet flush reverberate through the silence like Niagara Falls. Not the most auspicious setting, I reflected sourly, for my proposed first night with Sam.

Despite my misgivings, I proceeded conscientiously, spent most of Friday evening chatting her up in the canteen. I found her congenial enough, even charming in a muted sort of way - not conducive to any tumultuous passion, but promising a cosy, pleasantly companionable liaison of a low-key kind, with little emotional wear and tear, minimal 'demands'. Feeling no impetus to haste, I decided to proceed patiently; I'd usher her back to her quarters, arrange to have lunch with her the next day and let things develop at their own pace. With a sense of responsibly discharged duty, I escorted her to the door.

As I pushed it open, I saw Selene watching from across the room, flashing me a conspiratorial smirk. She was seated with a mutual friend of ours - a man whose genteel demeanour concealed a ravening satyr - and another woman, whom I erroneously assumed to be his latest trophy. At that moment, she stood up, to reach for something across the table - a tall, svelte, willowy figure, fleecy white sweater, apparently new blue jeans, a sleekly swept-back helmet of wavy honey-hued hair. Such was my first glimpse of Delphine. Seen at this distance, across a dingy-lit expanse of eddying cigarette smoke, she appeared to be just another glossily patina-ed seductress among the many thronging the room - more striking than most, granted, more elegant, but no doubt only superficially, and, in any case, already taken.

At lunch the next day, I renewed my courtship of Sam, albeit desultorily. The effort now seemed laborious, as if I were slogging through deep snow. Not suspecting the onslaught of something much fiercer, I wondered vaguely if I were coming down with flu. Even today, I'm not sure how to account for that precognitive torpor, that attack of diffidence. Perhaps the shadow cast ahead of itself by impending passion.

In any event, hoping to resuscitate my enthusiasm, I suggested Sam join me for dinner. She said she'd promised to dine with two former schoolmates from Wolverhampton, whom she'd not seen for years and wanted me to meet. Their presence, I decided glumly, would hardly facilitate my suit. I therefore demurred, pleading an anti-social mood. Sam and I agreed, however, to rendezvous for drinks in the canteen at ten. I think we still both tacitly assumed we'd end the evening if not in bed together, at least vertically in each other's arms. We then separated for the afternoon, she to attend one or another abstruse lecture, I to ferret out my sister, whom I found in a nearby lounge with her friend and his unknown companion.

When I arrived at their table, they were discussing the awfulness of the food. That topic seemed to have deflected everyone's attention, usurping the conference's intended theme. I contributed a few snide comments of my own, but solely, as it were, on some sort of verbal auto-pilot. The foreground of my mind was suddenly and overwhelmingly dominated by the revelation of Delphine's beauty, the full impact of which had just begun to register on me. It was a beauty at once conventional and utterly distinctive, utterly unique - the beauty of an actress or a cover-girl, coupled with something else, a vivacity, an animation, a mercurial mobility issuing from a source too profound to be captured by any camera, too elusive to be fixed or frozen. I positively basked in that beauty, letting it seep into me, suffuse me, radiate through my consciousness with virtually tangible effect. It acted on me rather like some sort of spiritual liniment, a spiritual rubbing alcohol, warming, soothing and easing the cramp that'd clamped my psyche for longer even than I'd been in England.

My appreciation of the woman before me was still detached, impersonal, purely aesthetic - comparable to that with which I might contemplate, say, the Mona Lisa. So, at any rate, I tried to convince myself. But it was under the influence of her spell that I spontaneously proposed an alternative to whatever gastronomic masochism the evening held in store. If anyone had a car, I suggested, we might embark on a foraging expedition - might sortie into the nearest town for dinner, and there perhaps find palatable fare. Delphine, it transpired, had a car - a Lancia saloon, whose luminous sea-grey-tinged-with-azure colour almost matched her eyes.

'You're not inviting Sam?' Selene whispered to me as we sardined ourselves into the rear seat.

'She's busy with friends,' I replied contentedly.

For a Saturday evening, the town was perversely somnolent, and nearly as destitute of cuisine as the conference. Eventually, however, we found ourselves in the dining hall of the place's solitary hotel - an austerely dilapidated room with sepulchral light, a mortuary silence, an aroma of desuetude and stale cigar smoke exuded from faded velvet and musty plush. As she inserted herself into our booth, Selene's coat brushed a plate, which smashed to the parquet and shattered. Racketing through the stillness, the noise sounded loud enough to dislodge the cobwebs, to traumatise the bats one imagined sleeping in the shadowy rafters. I cavalierly slipped the fragments of cracked crockery under a menu on the next table - where, a few minutes later, a mystified waiter discovered them and stalked off to the kitchen to harangue an equally mystified colleague.

In the meantime, trying conscientiously to think of Sam and our scheduled assignation, I sat down beside Delphine and immersed myself anew in her beauty - her relaxed but fastidious manners, her elegantly arched neck, her profile against the dark drapery as regal as the image of a sovereign on a coin, the demure grace which, like a cuirass, at once became and encumbered her. She seemed slightly constrained among us, slightly lost, slightly disoriented - a water nymph out of her accustomed element. But her impeccable decorum failed to conceal her effervescent curiosity, her almost parched eagerness to learn. And the courage with which she displayed her inexperience of our arcane territory, her preparedness to plunge into it without pretension or preconception - the courage to be vulnerable, and not try to disguise her vulnerability.

She said very little, only asked a few tentative questions pertaining to subjects addressed at the conference. Feeling too emaciated at first to say much, I left most of the conversation to Selene. Gradually, however, a steak began to neutralise the effects of malnutrition, and I regained a measure of loquacity. Before too much longer, I was holding forth in my customary fashion, with all the autocratic authority of a pope in mufti. It was only then, eavesdropping on myself in mid-sentence, that I recognised the eloquence Delphine had elicited from me. I recognised, too, that while ostensibly speaking to the whole table, I was in fact addressing only her. And I was doing so with an energy, a lucidity, a charisma, an inspiration that hadn't informed my thoughts, my words, my speech or my prose for more than three years.

By nine o'clock, we were back at the conference and I felt bereft. In the canteen, I quickly downed four double cognacs to brace myself for the anticlimax of my appointed rendezvous. I still as yet had no very clear designs on Delphine, still assumed she was romantically attached to her escort, still couldn't envision how, once the weekend's conclave disbanded, I'd see her again. Neither, for that matter, did I yet know anything about her, not so much as her surname. But though I was loth to admit it, dared not admit it, couldn't afford to admit it, my tepid interest in Sam had now been scuppered beyond all prospect of salvage.

I tried gamely to pretend otherwise, to convince myself otherwise. I chatted with Sam. I drank more brandy. We conducted a sterile discussion about the complexities of teaching Blake. I listened hopefully for the new zest in my voice, but heard only the old familiar apathy. I drank more brandy still. Even while getting methodically pissed, I felt hung over - hung over from the intoxication of Delphine's presence. Outside, the great bestiary of the constellations tilted tipsily through the nocturnal sky, and the evening wore itself woefully away. Around me, the room began slowly, vertiginously, to cartwheel.

At last, despairingly, I ushered Sam back to her quarters. We paused on the manicured grass beside her hut. I had a sudden sickening sensation of descending precipitously in a very fast lift. Sam tipped towards me, presumably for some statutory caress or embrace. I remembered, with searing vividness and precision, the exquisitely incised slant of Delphine's cheekbones. Seeking refuge in a mock gallant gesture, I bade Sam a chivalrous goodnight, ludicrously clicked my heels, bowed to kiss her hand, misjudged the distance and stabbed my nose on her fingernail. It could've been disastrous, even fatal, I reflected soddenly as I lurched back, alone, to my assigned accommodations. I could've pierced myself in the eye, possibly in the jugular. Death by fingernail. Legal history might've been made. Would Sam have been charged with manslaughter or I with suicide?

The next morning - with furred palate and a *Götterdämmerung*-scale headache which the anaemic imposture of breakfast hadn't dispelled - I goaded myself early to the lecture hall. I wasn't altogether sure why. Possibly to avoid Sam? Certainly I had no interest in the lecture. The room was empty save for Delphine, who'd also, for some reason, arrived early. My initial impulse was to flee temptation, feeling too wretched either to resist it or to succumb to it in style. Alerted by the creak of the door, however, Delphine'd already seen me; and not even post-libational stupor allowed me to snub so lovely a woman. I therefore joined her and, for the first time, spoke to her alone.

Our conversation was brief enough - was truncated after only a few minutes by interlopers trooping into the hall. I later supplemented such information as Delphine vouchsafed by discreet interrogation of her escort. What I learned wasn't encouraging and did little to assuage my hangover. Inevitably, she was married, with two daughters and a son to boot, all still in primary school. In London, she occupied a *pied-à-terre* at Holland Park, but that was only when a particular project dictated her presence in town. For most of the year, she lived in the most awkwardly incommodious of places, Northern Ireland - in Belfast, on the Malone Road, an address which meant nothing to me at the time, but which I subsequently discovered to be the most prestigious of neighbourhoods. Her husband was a prominent and influential civil servant attached to the Northern Ireland Office - the kind of figure whose name rarely reaches the public ear, but whose imprint, to the savvy, is discernible in speeches, pronouncements, working papers, feasibility studies, 'initiatives' and sundry other forms of the improvisation usually dignified as 'policy'. Her uncle, a distinguished judge, was a more eminent personage still in Ulster's fraught affairs, noted for his humane, scrupulously non-partisan integrity, his emphasis on reconciliation and the healing of wounds. Even I'd heard of him. He was acknowledged to be one of the few voices of sanity in the province, and commanded respect from both sides of the so-called 'sectarian divide'. Delphine was particularly close to him - closer, it transpired, than to her father. She herself was Anglo-Irish, educated in England but born and raised in Fermanagh. Her family, of Huguenot descent, had been in Northern Ireland since the Revocation of the Edict of Nantes in 1685.

From nothing very definite - her tone perhaps when she spoke of her husband, a nuance, an inflection, the ghost of a grimace, a rueful purse of her lips - I gathered her marriage had passed, or was passing, through an unquiet phase. It was apparent in any case, that, after what must've entailed some struggle, she'd begun to assert her independence, to embark on a career of her own. For the last eighteen months, she'd been working as a researcher for Ulster Television, collecting and collating material for documentaries, meeting with 'experts', sometimes booking interviewees.

During the decade that followed, she was to earn her spurs in this world, rising eventually to the status of producer. Even then, however, and despite her increasing confidence, her ever more impressive track record and accumulated credits, she retained an excessive measure of self-effacing modesty. Years later, for example, having handled with consummate poise the most imposing and temperamental political pundits, poseurs and prima donnas, media personalities, athletes and other celebrities, she was still intimidated by the prospect of meeting Seamus Heaney - and surprised when he proved engagingly human, cordial, convivial, devoid of the inscrutable Olympian arrogance and aloofness she'd fancied a poet of his stature must possess. Despite the egalitarian thrust of television, she could also succumb to the mystique of a coronet, becoming unnerved before an interview with the Duchess of Abercorn. Again, to her surprise, the Duchess proved neither dragoness nor haughty frump. Delphine, in fact, found her not just 'gorgeous', as some newspaper diarist or gossip columnist had said, but gracious and charming as well, with an extraordinary, almost therapeutic, aptitude, for putting people at ease. A genuine rapport had apparently developed between the two women, each of whom recognised in the other something of herself.

'But she's got something like an aura around her,' Delphine reported to me afterwards, with a certain bemused wonder. 'That's the only way I can describe it. A kind of serenely *gentle* charisma, you might say. And she's almost as shy as I am.'

It was in her capacity as researcher that Delphine'd come to the conference - which, of course, explained her air of dislocation. Someone in the upper echelons of Ulster Television wanted, it seemed, to make a documentary on Yeats. He'd struggled for months to wrestle to the mat the meaning of some of the more recondite poems. He'd nearly unsprocketed his faculties on *A Vision*, plunging with a rationalist's smug self-assurance into the whirling blades of the book's cosmological milkshake-mixer, getting trapped amongst them and being unlikely ever to emerge with mind unminced. Yeats' 'system' had apparently assumed for him the proportions of a certifiable obsession. He'd ordered the construction of charts, diagrams, working models, concentric and superimposed circles of cardboard and perspex which rotated simultaneously in antithetical directions. He'd had recourse to animated film sequences and computer graphics. He'd consulted Yeats scholars at half a dozen universities. Despite his enterprise, he still couldn't get his gyres to perne correctly.

To salvage the programme, as well as its producer's sanity, Delphine'd been commissioned to map an itinerary through the maze, to provide an Ariadne's thread. She knew the poetry well enough, but had the courage to admit she needed help with the Hermetic principles underpinning it. Unlike professional academics - who repudiate what they can't comprehend and what doesn't fit their critical pigeonholes - she wasn't prepared to dismiss Yeats' esotericism as a mere embarrassing aberration.

'He was an intelligent man, after all. In many ways, he was very wise. And he took these things seriously. If you want to understand him, don't you have to understand the things that mattered to him? At least to try?'

Even if Delphine'd been short, squat, fubsy, pear-shaped and gargoyle-featured, this hesitant assertion would've endeared her to me. Much of my own academic career, such as it was, had been devoted precisely to that kind of heterodoxy - to insisting, despite the scandalised scepticism of my colleagues, that Yeats, Joyce, Mann and other such figures had to be approached through the Hermetic thought that comprised the core of their aesthetics. Then, too, I relished the image of an Ulster Television producer trapped forever, like an insect in amber, amid the spinning vortices of *A Vision*'s mystical prism. For Yeats' sake, as well as my own (since I didn't, after all, want to see him ludicrously misrepresented on thousands of screens), I offered Delphine my services - free-lance tour guide to Byzantium and ports of numinous call beyond.

My services, it transpired, had been rendered superfluous. Two days before the conference, the television project had been cancelled when its erstwhile producer was assailed by Yeats' dire 'Thirteenth Cone' - the eruption of the unlegislated-for contingency - in the form of a nervous breakdown. Officially, it'd been ascribed to executive stress and domestic difficulties, the fury and the mire of human veins. Not wishing to waste her booking, Delphine'd come to Hertfordshire simply to satisfy her personal curiosity. She was due back in Belfast the following morning.

I tried dutifully to feel relieved. After all, I kept reminding myself, I'd wanted nothing more than a relaxed, unmessy, unmuddled, trouble-free dalliance - a companionable woman on tap, readily accessible for the spur-of-the-moment party or pub crawl, the talked-about film, the sporadic spasm of loneliness or horniness. No tumultuous passions. No bowel-gripping operatic intensity. No undue strain. Above all, no baroque complications. Delphine embodied everything I'd sought to avoid. An elasticised bond stretched painfully across the Irish Sea. The subterfuge dictated not just by an ordinary clandestine adultery, but by the cuckolding of a public figure. An incessant threat of scandal dragged around like a ball and chain. Frequent and prolonged separations. Furtively filched trysts in frantically fraught circumstances, with all the attendant paranoia - tapped telephone lines, binoculars glinting from upstairs windows, private or Special Branch detectives masquerading as garden gnomes amidst the shrubbery. Worst of all, a liaison with no conceivable, no imaginable, future. Even if I prised Delphine loose from her husband, what then? Support her (and her children) in the style to which she was accustomed? I could scarcely support myself, in any style at all.

I neither wanted nor needed these complexities, these hindrances and encumbrances. To incur them seemed tantamount to insanity - a wilful plunge into unadulterated folly, into depths of hitherto unexplored frustration. And even if I *were* so idiotic as to get involved with this woman, could such an involvement feasibly survive more than, say, a month or two? Common sense, better judgement, prudence, caution, self-preservation, every other tribunal to which I submitted the question all emphatically said no. *Et voilà,* I decided, with pretensions to brisk and ruthless efficiency. I'd carapace myself in cynicism. I'd write the weekend off as a poignant but foredoomed possibility - an illusory opportunity never ordained to be acted on. I'd defer to the inimical exigencies of circumstance and revert to my original, more manageable designs. On my return to London, I'd exorcise Delphine from my mind, renew my courtship of Sam and try, by whatever artificial respiration necessary, to resuscitate such moribund prospects as it still offered. I'd let Delphine recede to the status of a luminous apparition, like some Queen of the Sidhe in a Celtic twilight - something perfect and unattainable glimpsed in a vision or a dream, never to be actualised.

I proved incapable, of course, of adhering to these eminently sensible resolutions. True, I invited Sam out to lunch a few days later, and we flirted desultorily at a seedy Camden café, and I felt as bored and slack and apathetic as if I were applying for a job taking a census of gulls in the Orkneys. She, no doubt, felt the same. The whole situation was intolerably false, a creakily constructed play in which Sam and I woodenly performed to the jaded and sceptical audience of ourselves - an audience too jaded and sceptical to be conned for a moment by the script's mechanical contrivances. And all through the performance, I remained searingly conscious of Delphine - searingly conscious that somewhere, however many hundred miles away across the Irish Sea, there lived a limpid-eyed slender-necked creature compared to whom Sam, and everyone else I knew in London, and Nina, and Ilona, and all the other women of my past were but shadows, watered-down surrogates, pallid and diluted reflections. Delphine was a reality of which her predecessors had been but symbols.

To this day, I find it difficult to define precisely what she elicited from me during that weekend in Hertfordshire. I reject the facile formula of 'love at first sight'. I find that formula, in fact, demeaning. Love being a creative act, it entails, as does any work of art, a measure of investment, a measure of commitment, a measure of resourcefulness, a measure of labour, a measure of time. It may stem from something akin to inspiration, but it doesn't simply 'happen'. It's the fruit of a process, and the harvest, rather than the seed.

But what, then, if not 'love at first sight'? Infatuation at first sight? The passive state, in other words, which most people mean when they speak sloppily of being or falling 'in love'? That's not adequate. Certainly I'd experienced infatuation at first sight before, was familiar enough with the symptoms. The chords Delphine'd struck within me, the response she'd evoked from them, lay deeper than anything that could be called infatuation. Deeper, too, than any of the other things I'd previously experienced at first sight - lust at first sight, priapic curiosity at first sight, fascination at first sight, sympathy, respect, even soul-kinship at first sight. What I felt no doubt involved elements of all these, but none in itself was sufficient to describe, much less explain, the magic that'd implanted in me a compass needle pointed unwaveringly in one direction.

The closest I eventually came to diagnosing my feeling was what I could only call 'tenderness at first sight'. A poignant life-quickening pain. A molten warmth that thawed and melted the ice floes clogging my amorous volition. A desire of almost anguished urgency somehow to give this woman something, console her for something, release her from something, help her to actualise something that had nothing necessarily to do with me. Seeing themselves as mystical gardeners, Renaissance alchemists compared their art not to chemistry, but to botany - the patient and sensitive husbandry whereby a rare plant or flower was nurtured to organic fruition. I, too, now longed to be an alchemical gardener, bringing some unique, some exquisite, some miraculous but hitherto stifled richness to blossom - and in the process, like any self-respecting alchemist, transforming myself. And Delphine, through the solicitude she evoked in me, the yearning to cherish and protect, midwifed my own psychic rebirth. She induced an intoxication of the kind claimed for their product by Dutch brewers - a capacity to refresh the parts other women (like other beers) failed to reach.

Humanised by Delphine, I was to discover a newer, or perhaps merely a truer, emotional and sexual identity - to discover that my attachment to a woman sought its primary expression through the medium of tenderness. Delphine inspired tenderness precisely because she had the courage to accept it as her due - to accept it simply and serenely, in utter nakedness and candour, without elaborate defence mechanisms, without coyness or coquetry, without attempts to disguise her own need, without embarrassment. And her lack of embarrassment in accepting my tenderness absolved me of embarrassment in conferring it.

At the time, of course, I couldn't articulate any of this. I only knew that Delphine'd become some sort of enigmatic imperative for me - a portent or avatar of some 'consummate appropriateness' which I could no longer dissemble or ignore. Common sense, better judgement, caution and all the other tribunals governed by crassly practical considerations seemed suddenly no longer sage, but craven. I'd hitherto plumed myself on my amorous audacity. Had I now become a coward, daunted by plodding logistic obstacles, deterred by the quotidian? Had the failure of my last grand romantic enterprise - my flight to Vancouver to claim Ilona - rendered me cowed and timid? I recoiled angrily from the possibility, felt compelled to defy it. After all, I told myself, I'd played abundant mythic rôles in the past. I'd played God. I'd played Prometheus. I'd played Odysseus. I'd played Parsifal. I'd played Faust. I'd played, in some sense, Don Juan - Byron's, as well as Mozart's and Tirso de Molina's. Why not now play Don Quixote?

To telephone Delphine in Ulster proved impossible. According to the operator, there were copious listings under her surname in the Belfast book, but none on the Malone Road. Presumably the number was ex-directory - a reasonable assumption, given her family's prominence in the province's affairs. Or perhaps, in her professional capacity, she used her maiden name, which, of course, I didn't know. In any case, a Belfast number in all likelihood would've connected me not with her, but with her husband, and I'd have little enough to say to him.

On the other hand, I readily found the number for the *pied-à-terre* in Holland Park. I tried it intermittently every two or three days, whenever restlessness spurred me to recklessness. On one inopportune occasion, a man answered - very likely her husband. Waxing glibly guttural, I asked, in Germanically accented gobble, for Herr Wolfram von Eschenbach, whom I was grumpily told didn't live there. Once, too, I got a strange woman with a foghorn voice of raucously nasal hauteur - a nanny-cum-sentry as I later discovered, probably an officer in the Pope's Swiss Guard during some previous incarnation. When I asked simply for Delphine, she seemed affronted by such offhand familiarity. Her mistress, she replied, as if dropping the words disdainfully from the heights of a castle's battlements, wasn't 'at home'.

It wasn't until some three weeks later that I finally established contact with Delphine. She made no attempt to conceal her pleasure at hearing from me. We arranged to meet the following evening and had dinner at a candle-lit, cavernous, semi-subterranean Greek restaurant in Camden, around the corner from my lodgings. Afterwards, in the empty nocturnal road, under sibilant festoons of young May foliage, what began as a ritual goodnight peck culminated in an embrace all the more seismic for being wholly unexpected and spontaneous. Two nights later, we dined alone at her Holland Park flat and officially became lovers.

To the triumphant discomfiture of common sense, better judgement, prudence, caution and all other such stodgy virtues, our relationship has continued ever since. And, in the process, we produced a tonic effect on each other professionally, both of our careers prospered and she was beleaguered by prestigious job offers. Not being pressed for funds, however, she preferred to remain with Ulster Television until her children had left Belfast for secondary school in England and eventually university. At last, some six months after I first met Conor, Delphine formally shed her husband, accepted a position with the BBC and assumed sole occupancy of the flat in Holland Park. Although the journey takes almost as long, our bond no longer spans the Irish Sea, only the breadth of Central London.

XVII

I'd long been accustomed to elaborate and often devious courtships, chessboard calculations and manoeuvres, the cut and thrust and parry of amorous duels. I was disarmed and rather dazed by the dizzying awareness, openness and intensity with which Delphine and I embarked on our liaison. In the throes of my addled euphoria, it was impossible not to relish the elegant aesthetics of what'd happened - the extent to which circumstance had begun to emulate art, to which I was in effect living a novel, or perhaps a fairy tale.

Despite my befuddlement, of course, I recognised that Delphine was an extraordinary woman - the most extraordinary woman with whom I'd ever been involved. I also recognised that I couldn't afford to cock things up, couldn't begin to take the miracle for granted, couldn't let myself, as so often in the past, grow bored, weary, jaded, blasé. I incessantly reminded myself that I had to prove adequate to the trust Delphine'd reposed in me, that I couldn't exploit or abuse her vulnerability - that, above all, I mustn't hurt her. I was pervasively conscious of being on trial myself, on probation - as if I were sitting some crucial exam. After my prolonged emotional drought, I'd been vouchsafed - by whatever gods or stars presided over such matters - a unique opportunity 'to love correctly', to exercise the understanding of sexual relations I preened myself on possessing. And I flinched from the sheer magnitude of the opportunity. If I bungled it, I sensed, I'd never be granted its like again.

Such doubts as haunted me pertained, in short, not to Delphine's worthiness, but to my own. Other people, in idle moments, might doodle - might draw boxes, grids, squiggles, arabesques, mazes, cartoon figures, obscene caricatures. As I sat at the desk in my garret, or in my seedy Hibernian local of an evening, or in my office at the polytechnic, I'd fill the pages of my notebook with arcane invocations. In the cryptic alchemical script of Cornelius Agrippa von Nettesheim, I'd address myself to Hermes Trismegistus. *'Don't let me hurt her,'* I'd scribble in 16th century Hermetic. *'Don't let me go cold.'*

'Not Hebrew, is it?' a fat-headed fellow lecturer asked one day, leaning over my shoulder and frowning at the enigmatic glyphs. 'Is it Greek?'

'No,' I growled, irritated as much by his ignorance as by his incursion on my privacy. 'It's Thothic, you might say.'

'Your sinuses sound bunged up, I have some antihistamines in my desk.'

'Not Gothic. Thothic.'

'Er...right,' the mystified moron muttered, edging uneasily away. 'Well, if you want an antihistamine, let me know.'

In the earnestness of my intentions, I was quite prepared to incur such *contretemps*. And yet I'd be disingenuous to deny that, during those early days of our relationship, I was secretly as enamoured of the general situation as I was of Delphine herself. Something similar, I suspect, applied to her. Something similar, I suspect, applies to most lovers in the first heady flush of passion. Something similar applied to Goethe all his life. Like Goethe, Delphine and I began to thrive on the piquancy of our shared condition. And with the arrogant effrontery typical of lovers, we waxed reckless, even brazen, in our defiance of fate and chance and circumstance, of the lacklustre world around us, of all the dingy and mingy mortals who weren't favoured enough to be in love - who pursued their dreary activities, conducted their colourless business, made their tedious decisions in deference to less exalted imperatives. As if our joint enchantment cast a mantle of invisibility over us, we felt mystically protected, absolved of any need for discretion. We wandered and embraced publicly in parks. We dined unabashedly in prominent restaurants.

More so than Delphine, of course, I indulged in flamboyant gestures. As we walked to some friends' premises one evening - the flat of a Scottish novelist and his wife - Delphine, pointing to a garden, remarked on the summer glory of the flowers. Slightly tipsy on calvados, I promptly vaulted the hedge, thrashed through the shrubbery under the lighted window and plundered a nosegay for her, shredding my jacket in the process. On another occasion, having dropped me near my lodgings in Camden, she got trapped at an especially cutthroat junction - no signals or right-of-way lines, no access to the vortex of cars converging at vertiginous speed from every conceivable direction. I stalked out into the middle of the maelstrom, raised my hand like a policeman, brought all traffic to an infuriated halt and, with a cavalier's flourish, waved my lady through. Had I carpet to hand, I'd happily've spread it for her, oblivious to the braying horns.

Still a lowly researcher in those days, she was usually in London only when a particular project justified her presence. This was intermittent enough. She'd often be away for two months at a time, then back for perhaps a fortnight. When she was in town, we'd see each other almost every evening, frequently during the day, occasionally for an entire weekend. With its horde of mongrel vagrants, its incessant bedlamite din and its rancid malodorousness of cat, the squalid menagerie I inhabited was, needless to say, no place for a rendezvous - though Delphine, if only to appease her curiosity, periodically graced it with a visitation. Usually, I'd meet her outside, and we'd drive somewhere in the Lancia - to a restaurant, then to the Holland Park *pied-à-terre* or to premises borrowed from friends, not just in the city, but in Sussex, Oxford or the Cotswolds.

Now and again, her sojourn in London would coincide with school holidays, and she'd be accompanied by her children, as well as by their gorgon of a nanny. On such occasions, Delphine herself would turn impish, displaying a mischievous impudent audacity. We'd dine at one or another establishment around Holland Park or Notting Hill, marking time until eleven. We'd then return to her flat where - after a brief, flamboyantly secretive reconnaissance - she'd dart inside, leaving the door to the lobby on the latch. I'd follow, with all the elaborate furtiveness of a burglar dodging a Clouseau. When the lift reached her floor, we'd unglue ourselves from our embrace and tiptoe into the apartment, sneaking - with much gleeful whispering and antic pretensions to stealth - past the room where the gorgon slumbered. I'd have to be gone by first light, when one or more of the children might burst in upon us and surprise a woozy wastrel in Mummy's bed. At around four, Delphine would therefore telephone for a cab, and we'd pad back down the corridor past the gorgon's lair.

From the very beginning, I dared not let our relationship be sullied by the discrepancy in our respective fiscal circumstances. Delphine had to be kept as insulated as possible from my chronic pecuniary embarrassment. Not that I was ashamed of it. Destitution, after all, had been perfectly respectable for writers and alchemists since the dawn of literary and Hermetic history. But it would've introduced a crass and discordant dimension into our affair – a lopsided dimension, in which I couldn't feasibly reciprocate whatever largesse she might feel disposed to dispense. In consequence, I couldn't tell her I'd squandered virtually all my resources on dinner, had barely enough left for bus fare, certainly not enough for the cab she'd called, its motor now panting under the window like a mechanical dog. After kissing her goodbye at the lift, I'd descend to the nocturnal street, clamber into the taxi and allow it to take me around the corner. I'd then pretend to've forgotten something and order the perplexed cabby to stop. Giving him the few pence I'd clicked up on the metre, I'd dismiss him and start walking in the direction of Notting Hill, until dawn and the first bus of the morning overtook me.

If we were often insouciant, imprudent, even *outré* in braving diverse risks of discovery, we also devised baroque stratagems of concealment. All lovers are, of course, conspirators, and we naturally revelled in the numerous little devices that add tang and spice to subterfuge. There were coded messages, frequently employing Agrippa's alchemical alphabet, which Delphine conscientiously learned. There were letters that opened in a plausibly formal and impersonal fashion – from Dr. Rudolph Aura, for example, expatiating on the depredations of lycanthropy – and shifted abruptly, somewhere around the middle of the third or fourth paragraph, into terms more intimate. There were other letters, inserted into ostensibly anodyne publishing catalogues or brochures for Ulster Television. When I met her at her flat, a repertoire of signals could be deployed to warn me if something unexpected had come up – if her husband had just arrived from Belfast, if the nanny was on the prowl, if the children for some reason were still awake.

We had signals for use on the telephone as well and, when necessary, calls at precisely pre-arranged times. Lest the wrong person answer, I'd seldom ring her – would wait, except in emergencies, for her to contact me. She'd do so, as a rule, every second or third day, between eleven and midnight, when I'd generally just returned from the pub. Keeping the telephone unencumbered inevitably provoked tensions with the house's other occupants; but if Delphine were trying to reach me, I could hardly allow her to be thwarted by lesser beings clogging the line with their quotidia. It took perhaps a month of psychological warfare, threats, bullying and diplomacy before I prevailed. From then on, all outgoing calls were interdicted between eleven and midnight. Incoming calls were brusquely truncated or turned away, and the line was left free, reserved exclusively for Delphine. As a result of her constant absences and our lengthy separations, the telephone became a kind of drip-feed for our relationship; and many of the practises instituted in the early days evolved into established rituals, immutable pillars of policy. For years afterwards - even when I began to live alone and Delphine could ring me at her convenience - eleven to midnight remained, so far as the telephone was concerned, sacrosanct. No friend, no colleague, no associate would dare intrude on what was officially regarded as my lady's hour.

Now and again, of course, there'd be a mishap. Sometimes, for example, her children might enter her room while we were speaking, her husband might pick up an extension. In general, Delphine was deft in dealing with such contingencies. Her voice, in mid-sentence, in mid-word, sometimes even in mid-syllable, would shift an octave, would alter in timbre and inflection, would abruptly become brisk, crisp, businesslike, imperious - the voice of a veteran television professional discussing some technical aspect of a script, a problem in booking or scheduling. I quickly grew attuned to such changes of register and modulation. Adapting my own conversation accordingly, I'd immediately launch myself into whatever *non-sequitur* crossed my mind. Yeats' gyres and a theoretical resurrection of that project. The poetry of Jehan l'Ascuiz. The absence of Hermetic influences on Anglo-Irish relations. The prospect of an undiscovered Templar castle on the coast of Donegal. The evolution of the dreadnought. The rôle of the lap-dog in the lives of 19th century courtesans. Whatever I said, Delphine would pretend to mull it over, thoughtfully repeat a few words, tentatively agree, then declare she'd get back to me on the matter. Only once did things go wrong. On that occasion, hearing the click of the extension being lifted, she suffered an unwonted spasm of panic. Flustered, she hurriedly hung up, leaving me and her husband listening to each other's breathing.

Among the most important external milestones of our relationship was my acquisition of a car - my first London car. In retrospect, I find it astonishing that I survived without one for three years. Astonishing that I'd trudge, despite the surliest of weather, through Camden's desolate nightscape, to friends' flats at Chalk Farm, at Swiss Cottage, on the Holloway Road. Astonishing that, three days a week, I'd embark on the fiendishly complicated safari, by tube, then by bus, then on foot, to the dismal polytechnic in Hendon. Astonishing that, after visiting Snidley or Cassandra or other people in West Hampstead, I'd stand for half an hour on the Finchley Road at three in the morning, braving icy wind and teeming rain, seeking a vagrant cab. Somehow I performed those feats of masochism without even a sense of shame. But my liaison with Delphine soon rendered a car obligatory. This became apparent when she called me a taxi one night as usual, and the driver who turned up proved to be the same man as three nights before.

'Look 'ere, guv'ner,' he drawled, 'I didn't come round at four in the mornin' just to take you round the corner again.'

That pretty much decided the matter. Unfortunately, I allowed myself to be persuaded by the arguments of Selene's consort at the time, who - his own Jaguar notwithstanding - extolled the virtues of smallness, economy, manoeuvrability. I was too desperate by then to debate the issue; I'd even have settled for something as inglorious as a Deux Chevaux. What I ended up with was worse - an experimental, justifiably discontinued German NSU, a dinky phlegm-coloured thing which, in size and shape, resembled a refrigerator on wheels, with the engine of a demented power mower. The ridiculous contraption didn't even sound like a car, more like the electronically amplified buzz of an insect - a mosquito, perhaps, or a gnat, genetically modified to mutant proportions. Although prone to backfire with dyspeptic flatulence, it was handy enough around London - effortless to park, able to nip in and out of traffic like Drake's and Howard's lithe little ships amongst the lumbering galleons of the Armada. On the motorway, however, it was incipiently lethal, becoming virtually airborne at the blast of a passing lorry, the gust of the slightest crosswind. It was also uncomfortable. It was impossible to repair, parts being unobtainable. Its rotary motor baffled British mechanics, who'd take one look at its entrails, then turn away in despair.

Worst of all, it humiliated me on its first outing with Delphine, stalling sanctimoniously, in the middle of an illicit U-turn, opposite the zoo at Regent's Park. Attempts to jump-start it, to kick or cajole it to life, were equally futile, and I had to push it back to Camden while Delphine steered. I never forgave it that mortification. I vented my spleen particularly on Snidley, whose efforts to visualise a sleek 635 coupé into existence for me had gone so ludicrously, so ignominiously, askew. NSU and BMW might both be German companies denoted by initials, but no self-styled *illuminé* could be excused for confusing them - not even Snidley, whose ignorance of cars was awesome in magnitude. Yet for all its fractiousness, the NSU conferred on me - at least until its demise - a mobility I hadn't enjoyed since I'd been in London. And Delphine insisted she liked it, found it somehow endearing. I don't know whether she was trying to soothe my contused pride or expressing some genuine, albeit perverse, feminine compassion for misfits.

Whatever elfin charm Delphine discerned in it, my pseudo-car proved inadequate to the most ambitious of its intended functions - to get me to Wales. Trysts in Northern Ireland were pretty much out of the question. Ulster comprised too small, too incestuous a community, in which everyone knew everyone else, knew what everyone else was doing, watched everyone else with understandably paranoid intentness. As the wife of a prominent civil servant, with numerous acquaintances of her own in the media, Delphine couldn't slink about the province incognito. Every July, therefore, she'd retire for a month, usually with her children, to a house in the vicinity of Snowdonia inherited from her parents. Here, we could hope to find a solitude, a privacy, impossible not just in Belfast, but in London as well.

The first summer of our relationship, the NSU was *hors de combat*, convalescing from some undiagnosed malady contracted apparently during a sudden shower - an allergic reaction, perhaps, to water. I drove out to Wales with two friends, the Scottish novelist and his wife, in their antediluvian Hillman Husky Estate, a vehicle almost as derelict as my own. By the following summer, funds from the auction of my fountain pens - and, Snidley alleged, improved visualisation techniques on his part - had procured me a ten-year-old Triumph saloon, abrasion-red in colour, enervated and sclerotic. In this, I made the journey with another friend, an historian researching Merovingian residues in the *Mabinogion*. When the misnamed

Triumph overheated itself in the Brecon Beacons, we had no orthodox coolant available and topped up the radiator with Pepsi and lemonade. That, of course, did no harm; but on the way home a week later, the car's coughs, gurgles, gasps and sputters graded inexorably into a death-rattle. By dint of rests, pushes, jump-starts, curses and blandishments, we managed to nurse the thing as far as the cottage of a colleague in Gloucestershire, by which time it was moribund. We disassembled the motor, intending to refurbish rings, valves and pistons, but never succeeded in getting the pieces back together. As far as I know, the skeletal remains still lie unshriven, unburied, rusting quietly away, on a peaceful hill in the Cotswolds. It perished nobly, a martyr to love.

Despite this bereavement, the annual Welsh rendezvous became a regular feature of my relationship with Delphine - and my mode of transport to it a barometer of commercial success, if not of literary accomplishment. Thus, in the third summer, I was able to rent a car - a feeble Ford, admittedly, but new, and, for this one pilgrimage at least, reliable. In subsequent summers, I made the trip in an ageing but still nippy 2002 (Polaris silver, according to BMW's colour chart) and then, eventually, at 125 miles per hour, in the new black coupé Snidley'd failed to meditate into existence six years before.

I'd book into an hotel in one of several towns within convenient range of the Snowdonia house. I'd leave my travelling companions, if I had any, to their own devices and my car, while Delphine and I wandered the countryside in hers. Our favourite site, probably, was the majestic gutted grey husk of Harlech Castle, gaunt as the dark towers in the wasteland traversed by Peredur. We poked around the lichened ruins. We plodded up the endless gnawed stone staircases. Like avatars of high romance, we paced the rough, weather-scarred ramparts, gazed west across St. George's Channel, north over the Lleyn Peninsula to the Irish Sea - the barrier which so often separated us, now reduced to a distant diaphanous haze, where a triad of gulls patrolled lazily downwind.

Over dinner one night at an inn near Llandrindod Wells, we devised the project whereby Delphine graduated from researcher to full-fledged producer - a documentary series on mythic heroes, spectres stalking the shadowy frontier between history and legend. In half a dozen popular and highly acclaimed programmes, Delphine explored not just the factual basis, but also the archetypal resonance and significance, of Arthur, for example, and Robin Hood. Nor did she confine herself solely to the obvious. She slipped in lesser known figures as well, such as Thomas the Rhymer, and figures of specifically regional import - Glendower in Wales, Red Hugh O'Neill in Ulster. At present, a follow-up series is in production, extending the format internationally - to Doc Holliday and John Singleton Mosby in the States, Tannhäuser, El Cid, Aleksandr Nevski and (of course) Faust on the continent.

Such were some of the external characteristics of my involvement with Delphine - the logistics, the dodges, the ploys, the techniques of both defiance and guile, bravado and secrecy. Some of our habits, practices and routines were eventually rendered superfluous, and we discarded them. Others we retained, even when they weren't strictly necessary, because they'd become ritual accoutrements, so to speak, of our relationship - the embargo on the telephone, for example, between eleven and midnight. But whatever spice or piquancy we initially derived from subterfuge, from intrigue and furtiveness and craft, it was soon eclipsed for me by the sheer wonder of Delphine herself - her magic, her mystery, her femininity. If at first I was as enamoured of the situation as of her, she quickly came to take precedence over the situation; and the escapade, the dalliance, deepened into a bond.

It'd be unseemly, tasteless, artistically unfashionable and embarrassing to Delphine herself were I to launch into purple prose, wax lyrical about her beauty, her charm, her virtues. Suffice to say that part of what made her unique was a distinctive quality of *being*, a quality which Novalis, Rilke, Broch and some of my other Teutonic mentors (even one as aloof as Mann, as cynical as Musil) might've called '*seelekräftig*' - 'soul-suffused'. In most individuals, the element of *Istigkeit*, of 'is-ness', of 'soul' remains contracted and concentrated, wadded into a tight little ball, circumscribed in circumference, concealed like the kernel of a nut inside its shell - and it's often as dry, as desiccated, as wizened, as shrivelled. In Delphine (as her waterlogged horoscope attested), this element was fluid, constantly circulating through her like a species of spiritual bloodstream. It filled her to her fingertips, as a lake fills its shores. It emanated from her in whatever she said or did. It brimmed over from her eyes, from her voice. It animated her expressions, her movements. It produced - and not just on me, but on most of those who came into contact with her - an effect of luminous effulgence, something akin to radiance. I'd never known a person whose '*Seelekraft*'', whose 'soul-energy' or 'soul-force', was so vibrantly visible, so close to the surface.

In this '*Seelekraft*'' resided, paradoxically, both her vulnerability and her strength. For her very vulnerability protected her, rendered her invincible, irresistible. Instead of coercing circumstances from without, imposing her will on them and bending them to her wishes, she'd allow something of herself to infuse them, imbue them and guide them from within - the traditional dynamic of 'white magic'. Thus she'd disarm antagonism and preconception, prevail over opposition and, with the gentlest of pressure, get her way. And by remaining modest, demure and self-effacing about her powers, by never exploiting or abusing them, she kept them intact, their currency undissipated.

This isn't to suggest, of course, that our liaison was paragon-perfect, wholly devoid of frictions and tensions - or that the idyll of the first few months continued idyllically, immune to reality's corrosive action. As the cliché goes, every relationship entails compromises, and ours was no exception. Contrary to what might be expected, however, the least of those compromises was to conventional and banal jealousy. Certainly I *was* to some extent jealous of Delphine's husband. Certainly I grudged him his access to so much more of her time, so much more of her life, than I had. And I was jealous, too, of her professional colleagues - especially when, as sometimes happened, a particular project took her with them to North America, to regions I considered my stamping-ground, my territory. It chafed me that someone else, a stranger, should introduce her to Boston, to New York, to Chicago, to Montreal, to Vancouver, to other milieux which comprised part of my own past.

But such spasms of jealousy as I did occasionally suffer were tameable, containable, sublimated with relative ease. By the time I became involved with Delphine, I'd acquired, after all, a decade and a half's experience of sharing my women. I'd shared Ilona with JT. I'd shared Nina with Al Hollis. I'd shared at least two paramours on Long Island, including the most important of them, with their husbands. I'd shared Magda with her spouse - as well as the Vancouver muse who'd prompted me to annex Magda as camouflage. I'd thus had abundant training and practice for my present situation; and this had effectively curbed the impulse towards uxoriousness, towards 'ownership' or 'possessiveness' - had accustomed me to the recognition of a beloved woman's independence, her separateness from myself and, if necessary, her conjugal affiliations elsewhere.

Then, too, I'd had enough febrile one-night stands, enough loveless copulations, enough anodyne and innocuous flings to realise how little the sexual act mattered if one's emotions weren't engaged - and how perverse it was to make an extravagant fetish about sole and exclusive access to a few inches of human flesh. If it were genuine, I'd concluded long ago, any intercourse between a man and a woman, whether physical or otherwise, entailed something more than a mere fitting together of bodies - involved some other, some intangible and unquantifiable factor.

To the extent that this factor suffused everything else, including the sexual act, a bond was valid and significant. In the absence of this factor, everything else, including the sexual act, was hollow and meaningless. And it was precisely this factor that invariably got blurred in the murky miasma of jealousy, of uxorious pride. Had Delphine's husband surprised us in bed, he'd've felt outraged, affronted, trespassed upon. He'd've deemed his authority flouted, his rights violated, his prerogatives usurped. He'd've perceived me as a thief and a vandal, who'd 'stolen' something from him, plundered and desecrated his 'property'. With every resource at his disposal, he'd've denied me the nakedness of his wife's body - which, for all its grace and beauty, still conformed to the general design and specifications of most women's. Yet he wouldn't particularly have grudged me the nakedness of her soul - a true treasure, inestimably precious, utterly and consummately unique. Why should nakedness of soul be regarded as less valuable?

But if jealousy on my part posed no serious threat to our relationship, there were other things more difficult to handle, requiring more strenuous adaptation and adjustment. Chief of these, needless to say, was Delphine's schedule and the long partings it entailed, the frustratingly brief meetings. Most couples test the durability and resilience of their bond through cohabitation, through proximity. Delphine and I tested our bond by distance and separation; and the test was made more gruelling because my circumstances differed so radically from hers.

I had no 'regular' job - nine-to-five or otherwise - to preoccupy me, distract me, divert and deflect my energies. I had no professional responsibilities apart from the occasional lecture, no obligations save those to my agent and publisher. My existence, as it became more secure, also became more sedentary, more devoid of external activity, external drama; and in Delphine's absence, I had limited external stimulus, little incentive, to seek any. Thus, for example, not having her either with me or as the goal of a journey, I lost my impetus to travel. Apart from the annual sprint to Wales, the BMW would fester in London, gathering birdshit and treeshit, puttering tamely about town, scarcely seeing the motorways on which it was designed luxuriously to cruise - like a thoroughbred employed to drag domesticated middle-class families in a fake carriage around a theme park. Then, too, Delphine was often inaccessible when I most urgently wanted her - to solace me through moments of depression, to share in moments of triumph. I found myself living largely from rendezvous to rendezvous, with desolate expanses in between filled only by the drudgework of literary composition and its spasmodic euphorias. As my habits became more settled, my reality became increasingly focused on her; and there was nothing to compete with her for supremacy.

Delphine's life, in contrast, was hectic, frazzled, congested, overextended, diffused in a multitude of directions, and I was perforce excluded from extensive tracts of it. Having compelled him to confer full human autonomy on her, she harboured no real antipathy towards her husband. On the contrary, there was an authentic enough attachment between them - not just tolerance or armed truce, but a legitimate companionship and solicitude. She felt impelled - for some years, at any rate - to support him in his career, to aid him in his official functions and duties, to present a 'united front' to the outside world, to serve as his hostess and helpmate, to spare him both public scandal and private humiliation. She was also deeply devoted to her children, with whom she'd contrive to spend as much time as their school schedules allowed. She had other family allegiances in Ulster as well, especially to her uncle; and these became more demanding when, on his retirement, he embarked on his memoirs, conscripting her as everything from stenographer and sounding-board to confidante, advisor and editor. Finally, there were her own professional obligations, the frenetic and erratic schedules imposed on her by the needs of successive television projects.

Tugged to and fro by these commitments, beleaguered by their incessant claims upon her, she teetered constantly on the brink of exhaustion; and the time available for our relationship - if measured in days and hours - was necessarily limited. We still conferred every second day or so on telephone, usually at length, but our actual meetings were exasperatingly sporadic. When they did occur, moreover, they were generally too brief, too hurried, to accommodate everything that'd accumulated during the preceding separation. In the beginning, when we were 'merely' lovers, we could behave as lovers do, using our assignations primarily to make love. As we became more than lovers, our reunions had to encompass more, without any increase in length or frequency.

There was thus an intrinsic imbalance in the situation; and I had to resign myself to occupying, proportionately speaking, less space in Delphine's life than she did in mine. I had the freedom and the leisure to make her, or my relationship with her, the object of a cult. Her existence was too packed, too busy, too fragmented amongst diverse and conflicting priorities to allow her a similar self-indulgence - or a similar burden. For it was, indeed, a burden at times, which conduced to isolation, insulation, spasms of acute loneliness. Simply by my irritability, my impatience, my moroseness, my sarcasm, certain close friends and associates could estimate how long it'd been since I'd last seen Delphine. She herself would suffer bouts of guilt, of concern that she might be depriving me of what she called 'opportunities' - as if such 'opportunities' were commensurate with herself, as if she were interchangeable with the other women I encountered.

'Opportunities for what?' I'd tease her. 'Yoking myself to some docile *Hausfrau* who'll cook dinner for me and sort my socks? Settling into suburban respectability and siring a brood of brats? I can cook frozen dinners as well as anybody. As long as I wear boots, it doesn't matter if my socks don't match. And do you really think the world needs miniaturised replicas of me?'

To outsiders, our liaison would've seemed bizarre, untenable, unhealthy, subject to impossible stresses and pressures. It would only have seemed so, however, according to their own fixed, established, more orthodox habits and patterns. I'd seen enough friends and associates launch themselves precipitously into matrimony, or even just cohabitation, and make the most appalling, most inconceivable concessions to a partner - relinquish independence and self-sufficiency, relinquish the lifestyle, the attitudes and preferences of years, relinquish everything that'd previously mattered to them, everything by which they'd defined themselves. But such acts of self-abdication, because they conformed to familiar and accepted standards, were held to be indicative of 'maturity', of 'growing up'. Insofar as such things can be quantified, I don't think the compromises dictated by my relationship with Delphine were any greater. Probably they were less. But they were radically different in kind; and what would've struck people as their magnitude was in fact only their difference.

'The gauge of a relationship's validity is the degree to which it's not conditioned by questions of what might come of it.' I'd written that more than a decade before, in a fit of neo-Laurentian bravado, iconoclasm and prescience. Delphine vindicated my stylistically gnarled epigram. Indeed, she did more than vindicate it. She also extended it beyond its original *carpe diem* application, into dimensions I'd not suspected when I penned it. In conventional terms, certainly, our relationship had no conceivable future - no imaginable hypothetical point at which we'd begin to live happily ever after, retire to some cosy country cottage and bumble into bucolic senility together, stocking caps on our heads, woollen comforters on our knees.

On the contrary, there was something chronically provisional about our affair, something that had constantly to be affirmed and ratified anew; but this, instead of subverting it, transformed it into a process of continuous creation. The sheer absence of a future projected the bond between us into a species of perpetual present, imparting to each reunion an element of immediacy, of renewal, of rediscovery. Our attachment became disengaged, as it were, from time and time's erosion. We were thus immunised against the staleness which wears smooth the patina, blunts the tang, of more usual romantic partnerships - and against that most withering propensity of all, taking one another for granted. I sometimes wondered whether we hadn't stumbled by accident on some genuine Hermetic secret, some equivalent of an elixir whereby - at the price of certain traditional benefits - an alchemical union could be kept eternally young, incessantly rejuvenated.

None of this, naturally, provided much consolation on gloomy, desolate, womanless winter nights. Most dismal of all, probably, were those just preceding Christmas, when, encased in my solitude, I'd watch couples frolicking with all the ritualised conviviality of the season, trooping boisterously off to parties, trundling trees home to be strung with coloured lights - and then return to my own bleak garret, where there'd be no one to embrace, no one to caress, no one even to speak to save a spectre, a figment, an elusive apparition. At such moments, often lubricated by alcohol and self-pity, I didn't find it unduly difficult to go maudlin, morose or resentful. I'd mentally complain. I'd grouse. I'd tell myself the situation couldn't continue. I'd formulate one or another ultimatum - directed more at myself than at Delphine. I'd consider - at least until AIDS made its début - picking up hookers. I'd snap grouchily at people around me. I'd stalk grimly through the crowds clogging the sidewalks, treading on heels, elbowing brusquely past clots of gabbling pensioners. I'd become particularly bellicose behind the wheel, blaring my horn and cursing at laggardly drivers ahead of me, weaving cyclists, obstructive pedestrians.

And then, abruptly, I'd catch myself up, castigate myself for what I derided as my 'Tonio Kröger Syndrome', subject myself to ruthless interrogation. If I were truly discontent, I had, after all, the power to change things. Did I really want them otherwise? Well, yes - I wanted Delphine with me more frequently. Fair enough. That was a perfectly legitimate desire, but also an attempt to dodge the central issue. What constituted the central issue? Was I prepared to relinquish Delphine for a woman whom I *could* see more frequently, could have with me through the holidays, could call on at other times as well? Was I prepared to relinquish the intensity of each meeting with Delphine - an intensity generated precisely by the separation that'd preceded it? Was I prepared to incur the expectations and demands which any other liaison would've entailed? And could I imagine directing towards anyone else the tenderness I felt for Delphine - a tenderness effectively sealed in a safe deposit box, with her name on it, to which she alone held the key? Such questions, needless to say, had become rhetorical long before I'd finished framing them.

'Why must you leave?' an importunate, presumptuously brazen would-be seductress persisted, on a tedious evening of misunderstanding and confrontation. 'I'd be happy to have you stay the night.'

Having driven her home from a lecture, I'd imprudently accepted her offer of a coffee.

'I'm sorry. I already have a lady.'

'What can she give you that I can't?'

'Herself,' I replied icily. 'What she is. Who she is. Her own unique *Istigkeit*. You can't give me that.'

Nor, of course, could anyone else. What Delphine 'gave' me wasn't an adjunct of anything she did or didn't do, simply of what she was. Ultimately, she didn't have to *do* anything - she had only to *be*. And whatever she 'gave' me thereby couldn't be quantified, couldn't be translated into time, energy or other currencies. Even before she'd entered my existence - as long ago as my affairs with Ilona and Nina - I'd been unable to regard a relationship as a trade agreement, a commercial transaction. *'I'm investing in you an annual sum of 15,000 psychic calories, to be burned off at the rate of 41.09 calories per day thinking about you, dreaming about you, doting on you. I expect this sum to be repaid by regular instalments over the course of the next three years. Naturally, there's an exchange rate, 41.09 of my psychic calories being equivalent to 40.19 of yours, and adjustments will have to be made accordingly. As you're no doubt aware, too, there's the standard interest rate of 19 percent.'*

Were I forced to choose between idiotic extremes, I personally preferred Goethe's lofty and laconic eloquence: *'If I love her, what business is that of hers*?

****

In politics and religion, Delphine defied classification as intractably as I did. If I was aggressively evasive, she was demurely vague, but we were equally difficult to pigeonhole. As a child, she's incurred almost as little religious indoctrination as I had, and it'd been unencumbered by sanctimoniousness, by dogmatism, by musty pieties and hypocrisies. In an Irish context, she might've been considered Protestant, I suppose, only to the extent that she wasn't Catholic. She possessed, certainly, an acutely calibrated sensitivity to the sacred, the ineffable; but this inclined her more towards a healthy, well-adjusted and well-balanced paganism than towards the distortions, the psychic and spiritual mutilations, of Christian theology. Like me, she insisted on the distinction between spirituality and religion, recognising them as quite different from each other, even incipiently inimical to each other. While respecting the validity of true mystery, she had scant sympathy or patience for mystification. If pressed, she could've legitimately invoked my terminology and described herself as an antinomian Hermetic numinist - slightly less antinomian than I was perhaps, but no less Hermetic and, if anything, more numinous.

Her politics were as non-existent as my own. She had, as I did, opinions or attitudes on one or another specific issue, none whatever on a great many. Like most intelligent people, she was lucidly and appropriately cynical, seeing more things to be mistrusted in what passed for politics than to be enthusiastically endorsed. For her, as for me, the deplorable announced itself clearly enough. The laudable - if politics contained anything of the sort - proved trickier to detect.

So far as Northern Ireland was concerned, she shrank from such simplistic labels as 'Unionist' or 'Loyalist'. She felt herself to be as much Irish as British, and would've been more or less sympathetically disposed towards anything that promised a restoration of sanity, a cessation of stupidity, bigotry, mindlessness and self-perpetuating violence. She was obviously quite content to see Ulster remain part of the United Kingdom. At the same time, she had no particularly rabid objection to the alternatives - the province being amalgamated with the South, incorporated in a federation or confederation, rendered subject to joint sovereignty, even established as an independent statelet. Like everyone with a modicum of insight, she recognised that certain of these options were less realistic, less feasible than others - and that any attempt to impose them forcibly could only provoke further conflict. But she could've accommodated herself to any of them - provided, of course, it were implemented constitutionally, conscientiously, responsibly, in an ordered fashion, with the requisite trust and guarantees, the requisite consensus of consent. And without coercion, turmoil, upheaval, internecine strife, loss or infringement of existing freedoms. She wouldn't've cared unduly whether the prevailing laws were promulgated by Dublin, Stormont or Westminster. But she wouldn't've countenanced new laws - prescribed, for example, through Church pressure on government -

which interfered with her personal life, her values or the upbringing of her children.

Yet while she acknowledged no specific tribal allegiances, her very identity, her background, her family, her position, all served to polarise her - in others' eyes, if not in her own. Although she might see herself as non-partisan, as sensibly aloof from political factions, she was still the daughter of an 'old Ascendancy' dynasty; she was married to a British civil servant; she worked for what was, in effect, a branch of the British media; her uncle had enjoyed a distinguished career in the British judicial system. Insofar as she could, Delphine endeavoured to neutralise these factors. In her rôle with Ulster Television, for example, she scrupulously avoided all stories, all features, all subjects pertaining to the current situation in the province, concentrating instead on the arts, on cultural matters, on folklore and mythology, on 'human interest' material and psychology, on international affairs. But that didn't prevent Unionists and Loyalists from perceiving her, if only by default, as one of their own. Neither did it prevent hardline Republicans from perceiving her, or at least her family, as theoretically 'hostile'. This wasn't personal. Her husband maintained a congenial rapport with prominent members of the SDLP, the mainstream, non-violent nationist party. Her uncle was esteemed as much by the North's Catholic community as by everyone else. Yet they were both, even if just symbolically, representatives of an administration 'imposed' by the 'ancient enemy'.

In the early days of our relationship, Delphine and I seldom talked about Northern Ireland and the 'Troubles'. Our absorption in each other precluded almost all interest in such impersonal issues, and she welcomed any distraction from the savagery that maimed the world she inhabited. On rare occasions, she might ask my opinion about one or another recent development - the 'Peace Movement', for instance, of the mid-seventies, in which Conor's parents, as I was later to learn, had been so passionately involved. My replies would derive less from any informed awareness of the circumstances than from my general understanding, such as it was, of human nature, of history, of the dynamics that'd governed such phenomena in the past. If Ulster figured in my consciousness at all, it did so primarily as the incommodious place where Delphine lived - a place separated from me by however many hundred miles and a body of water to boot. If not for the body of water - which precluded non-stop breakneck drives - she might equally well have lived in Wales, in Scotland, in Yorkshire, in Cornwall.

Not that I was wholly oblivious. Like most people on the British mainland, I'd had lurid images of Belfast implanted in me by the media. According to these images, the city was a Celtic equivalent of Beirut, a smoking wasteland of gutted houses, burnt-out cars, bristling barricades, barbed wire, vehicle checkpoints, implacable walls smeared with vitriolic graffiti of hatred - graffiti which Conor, nearly a decade later, would begin converting to an affirmation of love. Here, I'd been led to believe, manic mobs rioted nightly against garish backdrops of apocalyptic conflagration, bombs daily reduced buildings to rubble and people to puddles, while gunmen, police and soldiers engaged in constant murderous fusillades, picking off bystanders by the score as well as each other. I didn't share her sentiments, of course, but my ignorance was almost as gross as that of an idiotic American virago whom I saw interviewed on television, at a demonstration in New York, during the visit of one or another prominent royal personage.

'I think it's awful!' she blithered at the camera in raucous Brooklynese. 'The way the Briddish send in their warplanes, I mean, to bomb Belfast and Dublin...!'

At the same time, however, I was also aware that Delphine drove regularly, and with impunity, through the stricken milieu - drove through it as routinely as one might through any well-behaved English city. Her accounts of her activities implied a setting with no relation whatever to the one purveyed by the media; and as long as she didn't encourage me to do so, I had no pressing incentive to reconcile the discrepancy. I was simply proud of her, regarding her as magnificently brave - and modest about her bravery, as about everything else. Those of my friends who'd met her, or knew of her, had a similar impression.

The impression was accurate enough; but she, of course, had no sense of bravery, no sense of doing anything in any way intrepid. In her own eyes, she was simply doing what she had to do, what daily life, her family and her job required. She'd drive her children to and from school. She's visit friends, colleagues, her uncle and other relatives. She'd attend meetings and conferences, at the television studio and elsewhere. To research a project or speak to an interviewee, she'd travel not just around Belfast, but across the whole of beleaguered Ulster, including the notorious 'Bandit Country' of South Armagh. The conditions which for me, in London, seemed to demand bravery were for her the given conditions of existence. They not only had to be faced, but also taken for granted, if one hoped to survive, to function. The atmosphere of terror had become for her, of necessity, a fact of life, which couldn't be allowed to interfere with 'business as usual'. The only responsible attitude, the only attitude commensurate with her dignity and self-respect, was to ignore it, reduce it to the status of 'white noise'; and Chicago or Mississippi, in my accounts, seemed to her more daunting than her own environment.

Only gradually did I come to understand and appreciate the toll exacted by her imperturbability, her 'stiff upper lip', her determinedly unruffled and unflappable demeanour. It was a toll exacted not just from her, but from Northern Ireland's population as a whole. In order to continue functioning, in order to take the situation for granted and reduce it to the status of 'white noise', she had to absorb it, internalise it. By making it a part of herself, she was able to gain control over it - over such of it, at least, as impinged directly on her life and activities. Thus she subdued it, transformed it into a kind of provisionally neutralised tension, like the contents of a pressurised tin. The effort, however, entailed considerable stress, which many individuals in Ulster lacked the toughness, the resilience, the flexibility of psyche to sustain. Their condition is now dignified as a medically acknowledged syndrome, similar in its dynamics to what used to be called 'shell shock', then, more euphemistically, 'combat fatigue' and now 'post-traumatic stress syndrome'.

Delphine withstood the strain better than most; but even for her, one or another element of the internalised situation would occasionally break loose. It usually manifested itself as exhaustion - an exhaustion verging on debilitation. Sometimes it surfaced in her dreams. Once in a while, it would manage to trick her, slipping in cloaked form through her defences. The disruption, the anxiety, the violence, the terror suffusing her environment might, for example, graft itself, by association, on to some development elsewhere in the world - in the Middle East, in South Africa, in the Soviet imperium, in Latin America. Thus disguised, it would escape the bulwarks and ramparts that generally contained it; and a news story from some remote corner of the globe would suddenly produce an impact more immediate, more jarring and more personal than seemed either warranted or explicable.

As my relationship with Delphine intensified in depth, I came gradually to recognise and fathom such mechanisms. Thus I was prompted to start educating myself about the 'Troubles'. But there was still no reason to do so in anything other than a desultory fashion. I read perhaps half a dozen books. I began paying more attention than before to newspaper reports. I watched television coverage, features and documentaries. In Camden pubs, I sought out Ulstermen of all backgrounds, all political and religious persuasions, and encouraged them to talk - even when, as was sometimes the case, their guttural accents rendered them virtually unintelligible.

Slowly, I began to acquire a kind of layman's acquaintance with the issues - a rough working knowledge which, if nothing else, at least kept me from jamming my foot into my mouth. Northern Ireland came increasingly to resemble for me a snarled ball of yarn - and yarns as well, garbled accounts of both current and historical events which seldom bore much connection to each other. If I couldn't yet disentangle the snagged skeins, I could, at any rate, appreciate the complexity of the muddle. Yet my comprehension remained essentially academic, intellectual, cerebral and, above all, fragmentary. I still required the molten heat of a crucible to fuse the diverse components, then precipitate them out in some coherent pattern, some encompassing vision. My relation to Delphine, and to the domain she inhabited, had yet to pass through their '*Nigredo*', the 'blackening' phase of the alchemical process, the 'dark night of the soul'.

XVIII

The crisis - the first, last and only serious crisis in my bond with Delphine - occurred in the fourth year of our relationship. Ultimately, I suspect, the specific circumstances were incidental. If they hadn't assumed the form they did, the internal logic and rhythm of our liaison would no doubt have chosen, or generated, others against which to prove itself, its durability, tenacity and resilience. Such as they were, however, the circumstances posed a sufficiently gruelling test.

Complications began when Delphine's husband intercepted a letter. He wasn't a deliberate snoop. Civil servant though he might be, he wasn't constitutionally disposed towards skulking, spying or prying. But somehow the envelope I'd addressed to her got shuffled together with his mail; and once launched on his invasion of her privacy, he apparently felt compelled to follow through. Not that the letter, measured by the standards of my usual correspondence, contained anything particularly compromising. Most of it pertained to a television project she'd been contemplating, a survey of the feminine principle in Celtic mythology and, subsequently, in the pre-7th century Celtic Church. But I'd written it in a ruminative romantic mood, saturated with cognac, and my free association had digressed into some affectionate, pseudo-scientific musings on the beauty of her cheekbones; and these musings, insofar as he bothered to pursue them, struck her husband as presumptuously familiar. For some reason, he was even more suspicious of the Hermetic chicken scratches - Agrippa's alchemical alphabet - with which I'd signed off. I've no idea what he thought they were. Some sort of sinister and subversive code? Perhaps they were more magically potent than I'd imagined. Perhaps, in some subliminal fashion, he divined that I'd invoked an ibis-headed Egyptian deity and psychopomp to kiss his wife goodnight for me.

In any case, a row ensued. It was more ritualistic than anything else and quickly defused. He was eager to seize whatever opportunity she gave him to turn a blind eye. But she was forced to dissemble, to prevaricate, to lie outright - to say, when pressed, that I was a sculptor, whose preoccupation with her cheekbones was purely aesthetic, purely clinical and technical. Such flagrant verbal mendacity being incompatible with her nature, she afterwards suffered a bout of guilt.

When we next met, she expressed, for the first time, misgivings, anxiety, a sense of contrition, and hinted we might have to proceed 'on a different basis' - the implication being a mortifying reduction to that nemesis of all passion, *mere* friendship. I, needless to say, was alarmed. Our relationship had by that time undergone a shift in what might be called its 'balance of vulnerability'. In the beginning, Delphine'd been more vulnerable, more insecure, than I had; I could've hurt her more than she me, and she'd often, if implicitly, requested reassurance. I'd assiduously provided such reassurance; and, of course, the more I provided it, the more exposed I'd myself become. By now, I was more vulnerable, more insecure, than she, and the prospect of losing her loomed like an impending amputation.

I was further demoralised when, at the same meeting, she announced her involvement in a new television project - a documentary on Ulster's contribution to Canadian history, the Scots-Irish influence on Canadian culture, the opening of the Canadian West by the Mounties. The project would take her to Vancouver. It would keep her there for nearly five months - from February until the end of June. During that period, she added, she might manage to fly back at intervals to see her children; but she didn't think there'd be much opportunity to rendezvous with me - apart, perhaps, for an occasional brief lunch.

Would her schedule, I wondered, really be so fraught? Or was this further expiation for having fibbed to her husband? Whatever the motive, I felt affronted and snubbed. And there was also, of course, the seemingly endless vista stretching before me, of separation, of deprivation, of Delphineless emptiness, as bleak and depressing as a prison sentence. The thought of her being in Vancouver naturally made things worse - the thought of her discovering the city I loved most in the world, and discovering it in my absence.

I started, half-heartedly, to argue. But what, after all, was there to argue about? I could hardly expect her to stand down from the project. I could hardly expect to accompany her. If I insisted adamantly enough, I could doubtless have bullied her into granting me a tryst on at least one of her returns to Britain; but there wasn't much point in a tryst obtained under duress.

I went morosely silent, stifled by the sickening sensation that always attends romantic rupture. A sense of everything slipping irretrievably away. Of no future save an abyss yawning suddenly at one's feet. Of utter hopelessness - the hopelessness of ever attaining such intimacy again, such euphoria, such exaltation, of even bothering to try. Thus must Sisyphus have felt, panting from his effort at the summit, watching the boulder roll inexorably down the hillside into the valley below. How had I let myself be duped into such vulnerability? Why had I ever renounced black magic, the protective cynicism of *der Geist, der stets verneint*?

She telephoned from Vancouver, almost as regularly as she had from Ulster - usually at bizarre hours, because neither of us could sort out the differences in time zones. Even her calls, however, sounded cooler, mechanical, impersonal, stemming - or so I imagined in my queasiness - less from genuine volition than from habit or duty. And when she returned from British Columbia, she returned not to London, but to Belfast, and remained there for the duration of the summer. Her absence thus extended not over five months, but over eight. During that time, we had three perfunctory lunches in public places which precluded even a cursory embrace. The most painful aspects of our separation for me were, needless to say, the numbed, emotionally dead state of waiting and, above all, the uncertainty. The waiting itself was bitter enough. It became more so as I became less confident of what I was waiting for. Was it indeed time to submit to a necessary amputation? Had our relationship indeed run its course? Or might it eventually resume? And if so, on what basis? Nothing, during the interregnum, offered any reliable indications.

If our former, shorter separations had made me impatient, irascible, testy, the present situation plunged me into chronic gloom, a scowling smouldering black moodiness that cowed everyone around me and seemed constantly a prelude to something worse. My *joie de vivre* seemed to have atrophied. So, too, had my sense of humour. Even attempts to lure me into pranks proved futile. The faithful students in my classes suffered most severely, being mercilessly demolished for the slightest *faux pas*, the slightest breach of aesthetic taste or decorum - and these, needless to say, occurred frequently enough.

Among the most baffled and hapless victims was a tall, willowy and wan-looking housewife, with valium-dulled eyes and the pinched harassed face of a frustrated nun. When she bent her head over her desk, however, her face was invisible, and the shape of her forehead, together with the swirl of her hair, would always remind me poignantly of Delphine. In the past, I'd conferred a sublimated sympathy upon her. Her comments and questions were usually pretty dim, but I'd answer them with unwonted patience - like a gentle giant helping a child leap from rock to rock across a stream. In the process, I'd twist and distort what she'd said to make it sound pertinent, even intelligent. To her own bewilderment, she'd found herself regarded as the most astute of my pupils - a grateful if unwitting beneficiary of Delphine. Now, I savaged her as vitriolically as I did everyone else.

Though genuinely worried about my 'condition', most of my closer friends and confidants maintained an intimidated silence, not presuming to venture an opinion, not daring to cross me or risk my wrath, just keeping discreetly out of my way - and thereby intensifying my isolation and my loneliness. Two people, however, waxed profligate with advice. One of them, inevitably, was Snidley, who'd recently turned his face effulgent orange by supplementing his carrot-rich vitamin supplement with an excess of carrot juice.

In the circumstances that obtained, a person with a modicum of tact might've moistened the tip of his finger with his tongue. Snidley, in those circumstances, jammed both hands and both feet into his mouth simultaneously. Least romantic and most bumptious of individuals, orange-faced Snidley adopted what he fancied to be a pragmatic, no-nonsense, militantly prosaic stance. He urged me, sententiously, to 'write Delphine off' for the moment, if not permanently. Adept at coining clichés, he exhorted me to 'have fun', to 'play the field', to 'explore other possibilities' - to descend from my rarefied plane of lofty passion, relax and enjoy myself. If nothing else, I'd be pleasantly diverted and might even find myself in a new relationship. It might perhaps offer the conventional comforts and amenities which my liaison with Delphine couldn't. If, on Delphine's return, she and I were able to renew our bond, well and good. If we weren't, I'd not have wasted the intervening time moping. At any rate, Snidley stressed in his orangeness, my material circumstances had changed, and it'd be foolish not to turn them to account.

Certainly they'd changed. The gremlin-ridden NSU and the clapped-out Triumph were now but droll memories, and I was dashingly mobile in the polaris silver 2002. It had a tendency, on occasion, to burst its radiator hoses and gush - which, given my rapport with the car, I ascribed to displaced sexual frustration. Apart from that, however, I at last had something both reliable and commensurate with my automotive standards. I'd also moved from the saturnalian premises in Camden - had moved twice, in fact, first to a garden flat in Belsize Park, then to the top floor of the once genteel house in Hampstead where, a few years later, Conor was to catch me laying a carpet in the road for Delphine to park on. My new abode was still squalid, of course, but its squalor was mine alone, not that of other people, their cats and brats. I could revel in spaciousness and privacy, could create my own highly individualised mess, had no need to make concessions to anyone. Thus vehicled and domiciled, I was admirably equipped for a rake's rôle.

Gauche though his promulgation of it might be, Snidley's argument wasn't, therefore, unpersuasive, even if his marmalade pigmentation did somewhat undermine his credibility. Had I been in his position, I'd no doubt've proffered similar advice, albeit more gracefully. It made perfect sense. Its logic - unusually for Snidley - was faultless and unassailable. Its validity was patently apparent. But its validity was also entirely theoretical - the validity of an abstract programme divorced from the situation's emotional facts. In emotional fact, I had no desire, no energy, no volition to translate the programme into practice. Such feeble incentive as I might've exhumed was squelched whenever I visited Cassandra and her consort. On the tape deck in their flat, seeming to have been playing non-stop from one visit to the next, Kristofferson's gravel-voiced drawl would echo my own recognition about Delphine, would succinctly summarise the reality of my dilemma - would remind me, in short, that loving her was easier than anything I'd ever do again. And not only easier. More spontaneous, too. More natural. More essential. Rather like breathing.

'Snidley does for horseshit what Stonehenge does for rocks.'

Thus opined Piers, the historian who'd accompanied me on my second trip to Wales and provided the lemonade to top up the Triumph's radiator. Some twelve years my senior, Piers plumed himself on being as unabashedly a romantic as I was, and even more of an anachronism. In the past, his amorous vicissitudes had roughly paralleled my own. At last, after sundry tribulations, he'd settled with his lady - he used the same terminology as I did - in the Cotswolds.

Brutally, relentlessly, he confronted me with the emotional dimension omitted from Snidley's argument. If I embarked on a spree of bed-hopping, whom, ultimately, would I be deceiving? Did I really think I could thereby 'enjoy myself'? Did I really imagine a facile dalliance, at this point in my life, could fill the void left by Delphine's defection - if, for that matter, she had indeed defected? Could I really pretend that 'equipping' myself with a new woman would be like changing a tyre on the 2002? Hadn't I already invested too much in Delphine not to gamble on another few months? If Snidley's argument made perfect logical sense, the emotional sense of Piers' was equally unimpugnable - even if its logical conclusion might be, for all I knew, a future of monastic celibacy.

As at moments of uncertainty in the past, I identified with Marlowe's Faustus: I imagined a voice badgering at each shoulder, urging diametrically opposed courses of action, and couldn't determine which was celestial, which infernal. My perspective became blurred, as perspectives tend to do when one stares at anything too hard and long, and my decision-making apparatus became paralysed. I fell back on a technique - or, more accurately, a state of mind - I'd employed on previous occasions of crisis, a quasi-Taoist procedure I'd learned during my immersion in Eastern thought as an undergraduate in Boston. It was simple and self-evident enough, though I rarely practised it. In the jargon of the Sixties, it amounted to 'going with the flow'. In more sophisticated terms, it meant avoiding all coercion of circumstance, all artificial imposition of will - neither forcibly actuating nor forcibly precluding possibilities. It consisted of fine-tuning oneself, in a manner of speaking, so as to discern the 'seams' in reality, the pressure points, the soft spots, the avenues or channels of maximum and minimum resistance - the telluric currents of the psyche and its ambience. This didn't imply passivity so much as a certain vigilance - an alert and attentive waiting for the 'ley lines' inherent in a situation to reveal themselves. The governing principle was always to act in the fashion involving least strain - the principle of white magic, in effect, to which Delphine adhered all the time.

Such, I decided, would be my policy, my course of action - or inaction, should inaction prove more appropriate. I'd try to walk a tightrope between Snidley's arguments and Piers'. I'd endeavour to do what 'felt right', what 'came most naturally' - to conduct myself as freely and spontaneously as possible, with as little friction, as little stress. I'd not rush about 'on the make', frantically attempting to shoehorn myself into strange beds. Neither would I subject myself to any abstract code of fidelity, any rigorously imposed monastic regimen. I'd not actively solicit adventures or escapades, but neither, if they presented themselves, would I repudiate them. And if something developed, I'd pursue it as far as effortlessness permitted - as far, that is, as it carried me of its own accord.

As in the days before I met Delphine, there was, at least in theory, no shortage of attractive prospects. There were several eligible women in the circles amid which I moved. There were at least two more in my classes. There was also Winifred, a blonde Tarot reader, psychological counsellor and poster-perfect Nordic beauty, with eyes that dilated to dizzy abysses of pupil and a persona of scatty dithering *Angst* skittering chronically towards hysteria. Most alluring of all, there was Olivia, my literary agent, jet-haired and vivacious, with the lazily sleek sensuousness of a puma and a seductive crystalline laugh. She displayed a bewildering aptitude for shifting, from one meeting to the next, between the brisk efficient femininity of the capable career woman and a pert, exuberantly lilting girlishness. In business negotiations, she was often both devious and tough, adopting a mask of crisp, callous-souled ruthlessness all the more implacable for being relentlessly cheerful. Having induced a fiscal haemorrhage in one or another publisher, she might smile sweetly, solicitously, and proffer a tourniquet. She could indeed be charming - suavely, glossily or winsomely so, as the specific context required. She deployed her charm skilfully, with instinctive finesse and precision - like an artillery officer calibrating range, velocity, trajectory. But beneath her professional charm, there was another charm, deeper, warmer, softer, more ebullient, with an infectious capacity for fun. She was equally comfortable in slick executive milieux and the louche bohemian spheres I frequented. At the time, she was unmarried, a manifestly 'free spirit' with a fiercely defiant sense of independence.

I'd met her some two and a half years before, a year or so after I'd met Delphine. To date, however, our relationship, though relaxed and informal enough, had remained wholly professional. We'd seldom met outside her office; we'd dealt with each other solely on the basis of agent and client, and neither of us knew much about the other's personal life. She, for example, knew only that I was involved with an unidentified woman married to a public figure. I knew nothing more than that she'd had at least one affair with a married man. Whether she was still attached to him, I'd no idea. When our conversation, as sometimes happened, touched on other people's amorous imbroglios, she displayed an impressive self-confidence, an ironic *savoir faire* and maturity which hadn't lapsed into coldness or cynicism. Underlying such conversations, I sensed, or thought I sensed, an erotic current rippling between us. I, certainly, was attracted to her; and I'd like to believe that something of my attraction was reciprocated.

In any case, and whatever its particular components, a rapport had unquestionably developed between us. So flagrant was it that outsiders - who saw us together, who heard one of us speak of the other - promptly pole-vaulted to conclusions and assumed us to be lovers. Thus did an editor in the States, an old university friend, when he met Olivia in New York. Thus did an impertinent and bumbling BBC producer. Thus did my publisher's publicity director. Patiently, ruefully, sardonically, Olivia and I would dispel these misconceptions, then joke about them afterwards. In our laughter, however, there was always an unspoken implication. If so many people apparently deemed us 'right for each other,' might there indeed be more between us than we'd acknowledged?

During the months of Delphine's absence, it was Olivia who figured most prominently in my consciousness. I made, of course, no attempt to woo her. On the contrary, I comported myself scrupulously in accord with the policy I'd resolved to adopt. I saw her as frequently as professional circumstances dictated. I manufactured no spurious excuses for meetings, nor did I shirk those genuinely justified. I tried to take my cue from her, remaining businesslike when that seemed appropriate, shifting to social matters when she encouraged me to do so. And all the while, I endeavoured to keep alert for portents, for omens, for whatever signals, so to speak, the cosmos might deign to vouchsafe me.

In what she thought, or hoped, might be its designs, Selene attempted to aid and abet the cosmos. Somewhere along the line, however, there was a breakdown of communications. Or perhaps a translation got muddled in transmission. But whatever designs the cosmos might've had, it wanted no part of Selene's. Thus, for example, she concocted a party intended to bring Olivia and me together. Olivia readily accepted the invitation, only to be felled by flu on the day. Machinations for a second party were thwarted when the flu pounced on Selene herself, and on her consort, and on me.

Nor was the cosmos content to sabotage just Selene's contrivances. It seemed bent on scuppering any contact with Olivia outside the office, uncontrived though such contact might be. In March, for instance, I flew to Paris for a conference pertaining to a new project. I was due back on a weekend. If there were any significant developments, Olivia'd told me before my departure, I should feel free to drop round her flat in Islington and debrief. There *were*, in fact, significant developments. On the Sunday, therefore, I drove round to Olivia's flat. I didn't get beyond her threshold. Her mother, it transpired, had arrived on an unexpected visitation half an hour before.

And thus things continued. I kept a meticulous tally. On no fewer than six occasions, Olivia and I planned to meet, wanted to meet, should've been able to meet, but were prevented from meeting by unforeseen interventions. Yeats' Thirteenth Cone, which had brought me together with Delphine, was assiduously keeping me apart from Olivia. In order to do so, it was assuming the most banal, the most hackneyed and ignominious forms - was disguising itself as viruses, automotive breakdowns, unsolicited guests, piddling disruptions of schedule, a veritable swarm of gremlins. If the cosmos were indeed sending me signals, they seemed pretty unequivocal. No static. No interference. No crossed lines or faulty connections. Had it announced its judgement through a loud-hailer, the cosmos couldn't've made itself much more explicit - a liaison with Olivia wasn't, in one of Delphine's favourite phrases, 'meant to be'.

Confronted by so seemingly emphatic an interdict, how was I supposed to behave? Presumably by continuing to 'act naturally', neither insisting, persisting nor desisting, whatever that might entail in practice. Eventually, towards the end of May, a routine late-afternoon conference ran overtime, and we went to dinner at a Camden taverna - nothing formal, nothing portentous, nothing pre-arranged, merely a gastronomic extension of our meeting. The occasion proved perfectly anodyne - a ritualised exchange of superficial psychological credentials, a tentative laying on the table of non-professional personalities. It might conceivably, I concluded afterwards, serve as a prelude. No door, at any rate, had closed. If one wasn't altogether open, it seemed at least ajar, or on the latch. And Olivia, disencumbered of her official demeanour, was more attractive than ever.

A fortnight later, I was visited by one of the cyclical afflictions of my existence, the fiscal equivalent perhaps of a monthly period - I ran out of money. Gambling on some hypothetical future solvency, Olivia advanced me funds. In spontaneous token of gratitude, I presented her with a fountain pen. She received it with a girlish enthusiasm that made my own rigidly correct and Prussianised stance wobble. A conversation about fountain pens ensued, and I'm not even sure now which of us offhandedly suggested we should have dinner again. Before I left the office, we'd fixed a specific date, a Wednesday in the first week of July. This time, I was to drive round to her flat and pick her up. I wasn't sure what to expect, nor even what to hope for, if anything. I'd already, by then, begun counting the days until Delphine returned - to Ulster and, shortly thereafter, I anticipated, to London. I wasn't sure what to expect or hope for from her either. So far as both women were concerned, the cosmos had gone ominously inscrutable.

Ten days before my scheduled dinner with Olivia, Delphine arrived back in Belfast. She rang me that evening, sounding jet-lagged and fatigued. It was a slightly stiff, slightly impersonal conversation, as if we both had to fumble our way back to an accustomed frequency. She enthused about Vancouver and recounted some of her experiences there, in more detail than her brief international calls had allowed. While at CTV studios, she told me, she'd exhumed the footage of my feature on the Foundation for Lycanthropic Children. On my asking when she'd be in London, however, she became hesitant, tentative, vague. Probably not until September, she said, and recited a hectic round of obligations - editing sessions on the film, a lavish dinner party to mark her uncle's completion of his memoirs, assorted other claims on her time. And, of course, the opportunity to be with her children for the remainder of the summer holidays.

In itself, it was a familiar enough disappointment, such as I'd felt on numerous occasions in the past. In the wake of her already prolonged absence, however, it was intolerable. When we rang off, I plunged into a vertiginous spin of frustration, exasperation, rage. Not, strictly speaking, with her so much as with the situation - but the distinction was momentarily blurred. Two more bloody fucking months of uncertainty! Two more bloody fucking months of not knowing where I stood! Two more bloody fucking months of living in suspended animation! The hell with it! To avoid recriminations against her, I banished her from my mind - ruthlessly, brutally, as though cauterising a wound - and concentrated instead on my imminent tryst with Olivia. When Delphine rang again two days later, the frostiness of my voice startled me. Never before had I spoken to her in that tone.

On Friday evening, I sat slumped before the television in morose torpor. The film on the screen was a recycled vintage documentary about naval operations during the Second World War - familiar territory to me since my pathologically militaristic boyhood. The narrative, using models and diagrams to compensate for gaps in actual footage, had just got to an episode I'd once found particularly fascinating - the engagement off Norway's North Cape, the last classical slugfest between individual capital ships in maritime history.

The eve of Boxing Day, 26 December, 1943. The lacerating flaying cold of the Arctic Circle. *Scharnhorst* had put to sea, bent on ravaging a Murmansk-bound convoy. No resistance was expected save from light vessels of the escort screen, none of them posing any serious threat to the German battlecruiser. But Hitler, after the loss of *Bismarck*, was paranoid about damage to his surface fleet; and *Scharnhorst* was under orders to avoid any potentially injurious engagements. When her approach to the convoy was intercepted, therefore, she turned and fled, pursued by Admiral Burnett in his light cruiser, H.M.S. *Belfast*, along with accompanying destroyers. The German admiral would've felt confident, knowing he could outrun or outgun his pursuers. But unknown to him, another British contingent, formed around H.M.S. *Duke of York*, was also steaming on interception course - from the southwest, the very direction in which *Scharnhorst* was fleeing. I knew what would happen next. Suddenly, shockingly, without warning, illumined in the bleached white light of a starshell, *Scharnhorst* would find herself confronted by her ultimate and most awesome nemesis - an enemy battleship, more powerful than herself, looming out of the polar night.

As *Duke of York* closed the range, the telephone shrilled. It proved to be Piers. I was surprised to hear his voice, thinking him on the continent at the time. He *was*, in fact, on the continent at the time. He was ringing, he said, from Nancy, in Lorraine.

'Is Delphine all right?'

It seemed a bizarre question. I resented his interruption of the clash off North Cape to ask it.

'Yes, as far as I know. Why shouldn't she be?'

'You've not heard any news?'

'No,' I replied, feeling myself tensing. 'Give me some news.'

'Her uncle was killed. There was a bomb.'

Everything, for an instant - my thoughts, Piers' voice, the action on the screen, the entire world - came to a dead stop. The swirling mist, the mortally cold spume, the freezing blackness of the Barents Sea seemed suddenly to have burst out of the television set, gushing into the room. I waited, sensing Piers had something to add. He sounded reluctant.

'Go on,' I said tightly.

Piers now sounded embarrassed, almost apologetic, as if he personally were somehow responsible:

'Don't know that much. Just heard it on the car radio. A bomb went off during some kind of party at his house. He was killed, Several other people, too. A couple of women. A couple of children. No names given.'

I rang off and immediately dialled Delphine's number in Belfast, not caring whether her husband answered. If he did, I'd improvise. Not surprisingly perhaps, the line was engaged. It remained so for the next twenty minutes - the most hideous twenty minutes I think I've ever passed. I registered no sound from the television set; I saw only vaguely, in grainy black and white, the stunning flash of naval guns through the Arctic darkness. Apart from that, the surface of my mind was numb. Beneath the frozen surface, however, reality spun wildly in a maelstrom, like a film on fast-forward. I felt hope. I felt panic. I felt guilt for my petulance, my coldness of tone in our last conversation. Yawning hugely before me, I saw how utterly empty, how unthinkably destitute, how irreparably shattered my existence would be in Delphine's absence - a great gaping hole torn in the very fabric of creation, through which would pour only the blackness of chaos and the void. Nothing, I knew, could possibly staunch such a gash, except perhaps hatred. If anything'd happened to Delphine, I divined dimly, the rest of my life would be lived in a state of icy dementia - lived solely, obsessively and single-mindedly for vengeance. I felt both humiliatingly helpless and capable of terrifying destruction, even if only of myself.

Eventually, after some twenty minutes, there was a news bulletin. Plastic explosive, apparently, had been attached to the wall of her uncle's house, adjacent to a window. He and six others had perished in the blast, including two women and two children. A dozen or so others had been injured, some critically. They names of the dead were announced. Delphine's wasn't among them. I still had no idea whether she'd been hurt or, if so, how seriously. The Provisional IRA'd claimed responsibility.

Leaving the television on for further bulletins, I spent the rest of the evening pacing, smoking, downing successive brandies, trying repeatedly and fruitlessly to get through to Belfast. At last, shortly after midnight, Delphine rang me. It was the first opportunity she'd had to do so, the telephones until then having been commandeered by police and soldiers, monitoring apparatus being fitted. In consequence, she couldn't speak freely. No, she'd not been hurt. She'd not, in fact, been at the party at all, having felt ill earlier in the afternoon. She's ring again, she said, the following evening. Her voice was almost frighteningly controlled, suffused with a stricken and deathly calm.

It was still calm when she rang some twenty-four hours later. I exhorted her to release and express her anger, to acknowledge the fury she felt - must've felt - towards the bastards who'd murdered her uncle. Using the harshest language I could, I tried to goad her, provoke her. She continued to sound as if she were sleepwalking. Her chief concern, she said, was for the younger people who'd died and for their families - as well as for some of the others, who'd be maimed for life. As for her uncle, he'd probably've wanted to perish in some such fashion as this - dramatically, abruptly, instantaneously, without a demeaning descent into disease, dotage, senility. He'd always bridled at being a burden to others, would've shrunk for the prospect of becoming so through age.

'And maybe,' she concluded wistfully, 'some good may come of it all. Some recognition of the pointlessness of such things, the mindlessness...'

It was, of course, typical of her - to seek some positive aspect in even the grimmest events, to discern some purpose, meaning or coherence, some underlying pattern that justified them. On the whole, I admired and encouraged this tendency. In the present circumstances, however, it seemed to me misplaced, a defensive rationalisation.

Had she been in London, I might've helped her - to weep, to curse, ideally to do both. In the process, I might also have exorcised myself. Denied any such opportunity, I sought refuge, for the duration of the weekend, in generalisation, brooding on masculine and feminine responses to death. Delphine's father'd died two years before, of complications resulting from pneumonia. She'd been constantly at his bedside. She'd waited on him, ministered to him, attended him with a patience, a generosity, a resourcefulness, a tirelessness that were magnificent. Gently, lovingly, responsibly, she'd ushered him, as it were, into death - had smoothed the path, had transformed his death into an effortless transition for him, almost a gift. She'd displayed, throughout the ordeal, a superb largesse and nobility of soul - and then, afterwards, wept. She'd coped with the situation in a way I couldn't've done, faced it with an honesty, a resilience, a serenity I couldn't've mustered or sustained. The present situation, in contrast, seemed to have paralysed her emotionally, caused her to 'seize up'.

In part, of course, it had to do with her capacity, or lack thereof, to express anger. That, however, was only a superficial explanation. Ultimately, something more profound was involved, something more 'universal'. The feminine, it seemed, could confront death as an organic process, just as it confronted birth. Being attuned to natural rhythms, to the pulse of the earth itself, the feminine could acquiesce to death, come to terms with death, accommodate death, face death without squeamishness when death conformed to those rhythms, partook of that pulse. But premeditated cold-blooded murder - death introduced forcibly, deliberately, by a human hand - was violently *unnatural*, a rupture of organic rhythms; and to that extent, it lay beyond the feminine's power to assimilate.

For the masculine, in contrast, death as an organic process engendered a sense of smallness, of insignificance, of helplessness - the shame, the ignominy, the mortification of impotence. Death by natural causes was thus an affront to the fragile and brittle structure of male pride, the male ego. But if it resulted from some human agency, death could be almost reassuring for a man. It fostered the illusion that he could 'do something about it' - could seek vengeance, for example, could produce it himself, and thereby imagine he controlled it.

In the immediate circumstances, of course, such ruminations were incidental, irrelevant, academic. They served merely to pass the empty hours, to occupy my mind, to divert me from more concrete, more distasteful reflections. On Monday, nevertheless, I formulated them in a wild, rambling, multi-paged letter to Delphine, which I knew she couldn't at the moment do justice - if, indeed, it merited any. I tried to project myself into her psychic state, her feelings - remembering how close she'd been to her uncle, how much he'd meant to her, how warmly he'd performed for her a paternal rôle. By the quasi-telepathy that often operated between us, I attempted, insofar as possible, to console her; but I was still too outraged to administer solace, to confer tenderness.

On Tuesday, I tried to ease myself back into my routine, feeling like a convalescent taking his first steps outdoors after a long illness. The nature of my relationship with Delphine remained confused - had become, in fact, more confused than ever. Any resolution of my uncertainty would now not only be postponed, but also in some fashion affected by the weekend's events. In the meantime, I still didn't know what to expect, or hope for, from Olivia, with whom I was scheduled to have dinner the next day. But my dithering between the two women, and the personal crisis I'd laboriously manufactured, now seemed shamefully trivial, even contemptible.

I spent Wednesday morning and early afternoon writing. I then showered, shaved, changed my clothes and - having half an hour to spare - turned on the television for the 5:45 news. The funeral of Delphine's uncle comprised the lead item. I watched the familiar - the sickeningly familiar - spectacle of yet another grim Ulster burial. I watched a bishop in pompously opulent regalia pronouncing the familiar homilies. I watched the cortège file woodenly from the church into a vista of lush greenery, where a grey drizzle needled the air, making the scene seem to flicker like an old film. I saw Delphine, in black, prominent among the bereaved, looking pale but regally composed. I wanted desperately to share her grief, to assume some portion of it and somehow, thereby, to lighten its burden for her. I felt, at very least, that I, too, should be clad in mourning.

My wardrobe, such as it was, contained, of course, nothing even remotely appropriate. Its nearest approximation to anything of the sort was my 'evil suit', the sinister garb I'd used to terrorise my classes on Long Island - black jeans, black shirt, black boots, black leather jacket and wristbands. I changed accordingly into this apparel, knowing I was being ridiculous and not caring. It would constitute my symbolic gesture, however absurd - my expression of sympathy.

While I donned my grotesque costume, I turned to the news again - the BBC's six o'clock version. Coverage of the funeral was more extended; and as I watched it, I slipped imperceptibly into a state of glacial fury. For the second time in my life, I discovered in myself the capacity to kill. Now, however, that capacity had changed.

The first time - when Ilona was drenched with scalding water in Mississippi - I could've killed in a seizure of blind frenzy, of berserk rage. Now the desire was different. Now it was utterly cold. Now I longed to kill slowly, sadistically, fiendishly, with an icy deliberation. The very discovery of this impulse unsettled me, but I made no effort to disown it. I've no doubt whatever that, given the opportunity, I could've acted on it, would've acted on it. Had I, by some fortunate or unfortunate fluke, crossed paths with an IRA 'volunteer' that evening, one of us wouldn't've survived the encounter.

In 'evil suit' and murderous mood, I presented myself, an hour later, on Olivia's doorstep. Not surprisingly perhaps, she gave me a distinctly odd look - as if wondering, albeit briefly, whether this was how I customarily did my courting. For an instant, I think, she was amused by my attire, or at least wanted to be. Then she apparently divined something, or read it in my face, and her smile grew abruptly uncertain, quizzical. When I tried subsequently to visualise the scene, I realised I must've appeared flagrantly demented. Olivia, though, retained her composure and, whatever her initial impressions, brushed them aside.

She suggested, inviting me in, that we not go out to dinner. She'd been feeling slightly ill during the day, preferred not to cope with the noise, fuss and bother of a restaurant; and she may also've wanted to spare my finances a depletion I couldn't afford. In her living room, she said, we could talk more comfortably. She'd prepared some hamburgers, which she'd assumed I, as an American, or ex-American, would like. I followed her through the hall, no more than half-conscious of my surroundings. Whether anything beyond food was being implicitly offered, I was in no condition to assess.

I don't remember when, or even whether, during the three hours or so that followed, I actually ate a hamburger. I only remember Olivia, baffled and no doubt a little uneasy, curled in a corner of the sofa. I made no attempt to approach her - as if, in my present state, I might be radioactive. Certainly I felt myself mantled in malevolent energy. For most of the evening, I faced her, straddling a wooden kitchen chair. At intervals, I got up and paced, stalking manically back and forth along the length of the wall opposite, drinking beer from the can, chain-smoking. As far as I can recall, Olivia said very little, nodded periodic assent, while I sailed off on a sustained soliloquy, a non-stop marathon monologue - not violent, just gloomily smouldering.

I told her about Delphine, the background of the last few months, the trauma of the weekend. I confessed my desire to kill. I described Ilona's ordeal in Mississippi, and how my impulse on that occasion differed from what I felt now. To my own surprise, I found myself stating conclusions I'd never previously thought through, articulating insights into Northern Ireland I hadn't known I possessed - the extent, for example, to which the clash there stemmed from conflicting mythic orientations. Using Olivia as a sounding-board, I began, although I didn't realise it at the time, to evolve some sort of coherent perspective on the 'Troubles', to formulate some sort of context.

While I pursued my harangue, my mind was functioning on another level simultaneously, or in another dimension. When I tried to recall it afterwards, the effect was akin to that of split screen in cinema. I was aware, as I talked, of Olivia's perplexity, then of her despair at establishing any valid communication. She may well've thought I'd gone round the twist. Perhaps, temporarily, I had. For what must've seemed an interminable vigil, she remained patient, sensitive to my need to catharse. Then, gradually, I saw her, as if with peripheral vision, begin to assume the look of a person bored to stupor by the ranting of monomaniacal obsession - saw her eyes grow filmed with ennui, apathy or simple weariness. While I continued to pontificate about Ulster, I vividly sensed a door slamming shut, even imagined I heard it. I knew myself and the evening to've been written off. I felt whatever opportunity there might've been for a liaison slipping irretrievably away. I watched it recede and did nothing to stop it - couldn't do anything to stop it.

In its place, something else began to coalesce. Not a conscious decision. As at certain crucial moments in the past, the decision had already been made within me, made for me, by some aspect of my psyche over which I exercised no control. All I could do was register the process while I continued my diatribe and Olivia went increasingly catatonic.

I recognised, with a sudden startling lucidity, that Delphine needed me at this moment, that I was able to help her in ways no one else could. I recognised, too, that I'd not done giving to her what I had to give. If only for that reason, our relationship wasn't over. It remained 'unfinished'. I hadn't yet completed my contribution to it.

I also recognised that what I still had to give Delphine was something new for me, something I'd never given before, never been required or expected to give. Whatever it was, it would put my resources on trial, would draw on reserves within me I'd never previously tapped - and wouldn't have occasion to tap were I to turn tail, seek refuge elsewhere.

I recognised that an involvement with Olivia might well've been intense, exciting, rewarding, fulfilling and particularly 'fun'. But it would also've been for me, and for her, too, probably, 'more of the same' - a repetition, a replication, yet another cycle, yet another dalliance, yet another escapade that tested us only up to a known point and no further. And in the end, it would've undoubtedly run its course and left one or both of us bereft, hurt, scarred or simply indifferent.

Most important of all, I recognised that a liaison with Olivia would've reduced both her and Delphine to mere figures in a series - a sequence running from my earliest *grands passions,* through Ilona, Nina, my muses on Long Island and in Vancouver. *This can't be allowed to happen,* something within me decreed emphatically. The injunction, the interdict, seemed to print itself in bold letters, like a cosmic telex, across the wall to my left, while my voice, on automatic pilot, pursued its mechanical course through the maze of Ulster's tribal squabbles. Whatever I might still be to Delphine or she to me, *I couldn't allow her to become merely one in a series.* Glimpsed again as with peripheral vision, another sentence seemed to print itself across the wall: *The series stops here – stops with Delphine.*

I'd been confronted, I realised suddenly - and it made me, for an instant, lose the thread of my exegesis on Northern Ireland - with a stark once-in-a-lifetime choice. 'Another adventure'. Or '*The* Adventure'. To embark on a spree, a fling or whatever else it might've proved to be with Olivia would ultimately have constituted 'another adventure' - after which she and I would've moved on to new partners. '*The* Adventure' was - could only be - Delphine.

I couldn't, of course, have stated any of this at the moment. I was simply cognisant of it, with half my mind, so to speak, while the other half remained fixed on the 'Troubles'. It took me some three weeks to conceptualise and verbalise my realisations - to shape them into coherent form, to couch them in communicable language. In the meantime, I only knew I'd relinquished Olivia and wasn't sure whether to be chagrined or relieved. Probably I was both. But I couldn't afterwards remember the end of the evening, couldn't remember the note on which we'd parted, couldn't even remember whether we'd exchanged ritual pecks. I only remembered a sense of gratitude for her tolerance, her patience. I arrived home in a muddle, utterly drained and curiously hungry, trying to recall whether I had indeed eaten a hamburger.

More than a year later, when Olivia had married and my relationship with Delphine had renewed itself, had deepened and carried us into new spheres of intimacy, I began to appreciate how decisive that evening had been. Yes, it had, of course, focused and ratified my bond with Delphine, creating an emotional premise, so to speak, from which I could find my way back to her again. But it also, paradoxically, forged a bond with Olivia as well - a bond more profound, more durable, more fruitful than any we could've achieved as lovers.

By virtue of not becoming lovers, we cleared space, as it were, for a different sort of rapport to develop. We became friends, confidants - almost, in a sense, brother and sister. Almost, but not quite, because we each retained elements of piquant mystery for the other and a current of sexual magnetism continued to flicker intermittently between us. We could allow it to do so, could enjoy the tang it imparted to our interaction, because it posed no threat, would never be acted on - we were both definitively committed elsewhere, and therefore 'safe'.

Stimulated by this current, we could conspire together on business matters, devise stratagems and ploys, play hard and soft policeman as circumstances dictated. We could pool our resources to help mutual associates through their assorted crises. We could rely on each other for personal support. When my father died, for example, both Delphine and Selene happened to be out of the country, and it was to Olivia that I turned - to confront the reality of the situation, to sort out my feelings. When her father died some two months later, she turned to me. In the meantime, inevitably, outsiders persisted in assuming we were involved.

During the course of the next decade, my professional relationship with Olivia evolved in a context, a matrix, of warmth, trust and solicitude. When she was away on holiday, I'd drive round to her flat, check it, patrol the street in a vain attempt to catch and cosh the louts who'd twice burglarised and vandalised the premises. Later, when she and her husband were gone for weekends, I'd occasionally house-sit all night at their new home near Regent's Park, hoping - vainly again - to ambush the malefactor who'd tried repeatedly to break in. During Delphine's absence, Olivia proved a handy and worthy beneficiary of my impulses towards knight-errantry. But such swash as I buckled in the process was an expression of something more profoundly rooted, more genuine. When a mutual friend told me she'd suffered a minor car accident, I was startled by the intensity of my concern.

She, for her part, discharged services for me above and beyond the conventional agent's call of duty. Through her offices, of course, I obtained the BMW which enabled me to chauffeur Delphine about in necessary and appropriate style - rather than conning cab drivers at four in the morning, or being humiliated by the recalcitrance of lesser cars. But she also ministered to diverse practical aspects of my existence, precluding them thereby from intruding on the loftiness of my relation with Delphine. If I was invincibly inept in sundry mundane matters, Olivia was ept enough, and generous enough, to compensate. Almost single-handedly, she assured my economic survival, advancing funds when required, sustaining me through recurrent cycles of fiscal famine, preventing my gas, electricity and telephone from being cut off. When my aged landlady's mercenary son tried to sell my flat from under me, Olivia conscripted a solicitor who negotiated a settlement - a settlement so exorbitant it permitted me to buy a flat of my own. It was Olivia, too, naturally, who procured me a mortgage broker. It was Olivia who guided me through the labyrinthine legalistic *rite de passage* without which, apparently, one isn't qualified for home ownership. I was thus spared the anxiety, the uncertainty, the frazzled nerves and all the other adjuncts of the ordeal usually incurred by novice purchasers.

More heroically still, Olivia would perform for me the rôle I'd so often performed for others - that of 'riding shotgun', acting as 'hired gunslinger'. If I'm subject to any phobia, it consists of dealing with accountants and bank managers. The sheer prospect of such transactions affects me the way mice, snakes or spiders affect other people. Here, too, Olivia would deploy her charm on my behalf, functioning as counsellor, as interpreter, as referee, as guardian angel. Knowing the hopelessness of explaining to me what VAT stood for, much less how it worked, she'd treat with my accountant - and keep him from jilting me when my debt to him surpassed what I owed Inland Revenue. She'd also bewitch my bank into quiescence on my overdraft, pacifying the manager, holding his basilisk of an assistant at bay. In such spheres as these, I'd had least experience, felt least competence. In such spheres, therefore, I allowed Olivia to mother me in a manner I'd never previously allowed a woman to do - and couldn't've allowed her to do, had we been lovers. And, of course, in her capacity as agent, she remains the tutelary genius and protectress of my career - even though she tends to wax primly humourless at some of my practical jokes and still hasn't read Fuentes or García Márquez.

Nor was it solely in external matters that Oliva exercised a steadying influence on my life. She also complemented, or perhaps supplemented, the inspiration I derived from Delphine. When Delphine was in Belfast or abroad, Olivia was usually still in London; and the nature, the quality, of her femininity was sufficiently similar to mitigate my sense of isolation, assuage my loneliness. On sitting down to write in the morning, for example, I'd often need some contact with the feminine principle, some transfusion of feminine energy, to impel me, or propel me, Faust-fashion, *hinan*. I'd accordingly fabricate some spurious, ostensibly professional pretext for telephoning Olivia; and our conversation would sustain me until evening, when Delphine rang. Olivia thus furnished a prop, a support for my psychic and emotional equilibrium, which not only buttressed me personally, but also ensured the stability of my relationship with Delphine.

Such were the consequences of that evening in Olivia's flat. It might've seemed an ignominious failure initially, a clumsily squandered opportunity, a source of subsequent regret. It proved, in fact, the source of something very different. Needless to say, however, the single most important element of that evening was its re-establishment of my perspective and priorities, its restoration of Delphine to her position at the centre of my life.

Only years later did I realise the symbolic significance of the most crucial moment of all - the moment of my recognition that Delphine couldn't be reduced to one in a series, that the series effectively ended, and culminated, with her. In my own private quest for Fausthood, this corresponded to the decisive moment for Goethe's protagonist:

Zum Augenblicke dürft' ich sagen:
Verweile doch! Du bist so schön!
Es kann sie Spur von meinen Erdentagen
Nicht in Äonen untergehn.' -
Im Vorgefühl von solchem hohen Glück
Genieß' ich jetzt den höchsten Augenblick.

And if Mephistopheles should seek to claim whatever might be his due, I had not just one *Ewigweibliche,* but two, to intercede for me.

XIX

Learning results not from study, but from attention - a focusing of the mind analogous to the focusing of the eye. One can gaze at something interminably without seeing it. One can register its presence, be peripherally cognisant of it, and still not see it. And then there occurs an infinitesimal adjustment, a microscopic tensing of the muscle in the eye - and all of a sudden, one focuses, and one *sees*. A more or less parallel process occurs in the mind. One can 'study' a subject exhaustively, 'research' it, read books about it, attend lectures, memorise data, sprain one's brain grappling with its intricacies. And then, prompted by something deeper than consciousness, deeper than the will, something occurs in the psyche similar to the process by which the eye focuses - and through some comprehensive intuitive apprehension, one suddenly understands, understands in a way that no mere plodding intellectual effort can ever make possible. This process had occurred for me perhaps half a dozen times in the past - usually pertaining to literary matters, to aspects of history, to amorous relationships. Following the death of Delphine's uncle, it occurred again. What came into focus now was Northern Ireland.

It occurred one evening, a fortnight or so after my obsessive performance at Olivia's. I'd just prepared my dinner. Having embarked on a half-hearted attempt at culinary competence, I'd undertaken, for the last few weeks, to produce a more or less edible steak. My efforts had yielded things more or less edible, but unlike any steaks I'd ever experienced. They'd emerge from the oven not only desiccated, but also rubberised, as prone to bounce as my cheques at the time. They'd been impervious to standard kitchen cutlery, seemed to demand at least a Bowie knife. Easier not to bother hacking at them - easier simply to hold the chunk of meat in my hand and munch it, as one might an apple. I suspected I was doing something wrong, but it wasn't until some weeks later that Piers would happen by one evening, sniff the air suspiciously, open the oven, peer incredulously inside, then turn to me in amazement and ask: *'Why're you baking your steak?'*

On the evening in question, I was still exercising my jaws on the tenacious resilience of unwittingly baked sirloin. I'd carried the leathery slab of meat into the front room, settled myself before the television for the nine o'clock news and found myself watching coverage of the 'Marching Season' in Ulster - the seemingly interminable sequence of parades during July and August whereby Protestants commemorated the victories of 1689, 1690 and 1691 at the Siege of Derry, the Battles of the Boyne and Aughrim. On the screen, an Orange procession was in progress - staid black bowlers above black suits diagonally crossed by sashes of garish tangerine colour, almost the same hue as Snidley's carrot-glutted face. There followed a cadre of youngsters in scarlet tunics with white facings and epaulettes, apparently modelled on the uniforms of Napoleonic-vintage British infantry. Batons flashed, whirled and spun in the air. Fifes shrilled piercingly, their impudent lilt rhythmically punctuated by the booming detonations, the numbing concussion, of the brass-bound Lambeg drums - a deep bass vibration that made the room seem to shudder, the eardrums pop as on a plane.

The noise of the procession receded, an urbane but sententious voice-over launched into discursive commentary. On the screen, the pageantry of the march gave way to bleak vistas of rubble-strewn streets, desolate tracts of littered waste ground, stumps of gutted buildings jutting from the ground like archaic ruins exhumed by archaeological excavation. The camera shifted from one street, one neighbourhood, to another. In some, the kerbstones were painted red, white and blue, murals depicted 'King Billy' on a chivalric white horse, the Union Jack flew beside another flag, white, with a red cross and, at its centre, the stylised depiction of a severed hand dripping blood. Elsewhere, the flag was the green, white and orange of the Irish tricolour, and the murals portrayed masked or hooded figures poised in assorted combat positions with automatic rifles. Long strips of denuded wall were smeared with venomous graffiti, splashed and stained with an alphabet soup of initials - IRA, INLA, SDLP, DUP, UDA, UVF, UFF.

The graffiti, the murals, the flags, the initials changed from street to street. The jeering raucous-voiced urchins, however, looked the same, regardless of tribal affiliation. So, too, did the paramilitaries caught by the camera - huddled conclaves of hulking figures in combat jackets, with balaclavas over their heads, or face masks surmounted by berets. Like the children, they appeared to be interchangeable. Like the children, they seemed to have found a common denominator in hate.

And suddenly, these glimpses of lunacy made a perverse sense to me. Suddenly, and to my own surprise, I found I could understand them. Suddenly, they comprised part of a larger context, which also included everything I'd articulated to Olivia a fortnight before, robotically assembling the jigsaw in my head as I pontificated to her. Suddenly, I seemed to discern the subterranean currents linking all the diverse phenomena involved in the situation, the force fields surrounding them, the dynamics and dialectics. All at once, I could distinguish each cluster of initials, could recognise each in my mind, instantaneously, without having to pause and think them through. And the vacuous rhetoric and bluster of the politicians, the paramilitary spokesmen, also found a place in the overall design. Instead of a welter of disparate and disconnected fragments, paradoxes and contradictions, I saw the entire thing whole, saw it as a single totality - saw it the way, years before, stoned on acid, having climbed a tower of luminous golden spaghetti stalks, I'd seen the terrestrial globe spinning serenely in space, fissures sealed by the amber epoxy of language. Northern Ireland and the 'Troubles' came together like the multi-coloured elements of a kaleidoscope cohering into pattern.

The following evening, baked steak in hand, I again watched the news. This time I concentrated on the oratory, the pronouncements issued by politicians and paramilitary mouthpieces. The commentator attempted to analyse their words. For me, however, their words had suddenly grown transparent. Nothing, I realised, no statement, no proclamation, could be taken literally, in or of itself. Everything was part of a progression, a stepping-stone to something else, a mask or screen for something else. I sensed I was watching a chessgame being played. Each official utterance constituted a move on the board - a response to an opposing move, a new gambit, a calculated attempt to wrongfoot an adversary. In order to understand any given move, one had to look several moves ahead - or, if the move were a feint, to monitor everything else incipient on the board. This discovery was, in its own unique way, exhilarating - as anything can become exhilarating when one discovers the key to comprehending it, to bringing it into focus and seeing it clearly.

In my exhilaration, I was distracted, for some days afterwards, from more quotidian things. So preoccupied was I, in fact, that I mechanically said 'Thank you' to an automated till as it disgorged the cash I'd requested. When I turned, the woman in the queue behind me backed away in alarm. Seated at my desk, I reached for the cartridge-size cylinder of Chapstick, picked up the similar cylinder of Pritt, applied it to my lips and nearly glued my mouth shut. I also, inadvertently, stabbed my fridge to death with a West German Army bayonet. The bayonet'd been an improbable gift from a friend - a ferocious-looking black thing, made of carbon fibre rather than steel, which rendered it both rustproof and effective as an insulated wire-cutter. In Chicago, there might've been some point in flaunting such a contraption. In London, I couldn't find too many uses for it. I might, I suppose, have used it to slice vulcanised steaks, but I was loth to risk it. For the most part, I employed it to defrost the fridge. I'd hack cheerfully away, dislodging chunks and slabs of encrusted ice, which I could toss from my window at visitors in mid-summer.

On this occasion, however, I was absorbed in contemplation of Ulster, and one of my bayonet thrusts veered off-centre to pierce the freon sac. There was a pop, like that of a punctured balloon, then a prolonged hiss, and I was subjected to a point-blank and sustained squirt of gas, as noxious and foul-smelling as any skunk I'd encountered in the States. When, having fumigated myself, I returned from the loo, I found the fridge quietly and mournfully expiring at the centre of an ever-widening puddle. I was left fridgeless for some ten days, until Piers brought a replacement, a spare he happened to have lying idle around his premises.

Northern Ireland began increasingly to infiltrate itself into my lectures. I added a number of Irish works to my syllabus, regardless of how irrelevant they often were.. Even when discussing books from elsewhere, I'd contrive to slip in allusions, parallels, analogies to Ulster. I'd often dextrously manipulate conversation in classes so that it gravitated towards the subject. When, of their own accord, events led in that direction, I capitalised on them eagerly. I was quite prepared to entertain hostile arguments, provided they issued from an informed position, from some elementary knowledge of the subject. I was impatient, intolerant and merciless, however, about statements promulgated out of ignorance or stupidity. When IRA prisoners embarked on suicidal hunger strikes, for example, one woman in my class - an otherwise intelligent liberal, with whom, on most other topics, I was in accord -- expressed sympathy for the self-styled 'martyrs'.

'Surely,' she suggested, 'there must be some justice in a cause, if men are so prepared to die for it?'

'When,' I snapped back, 'has any cause ever been justified or validated merely through men's readiness to die for it? The SS were fanatically prepared to die for their cause. So were the Kamikaze pilots. Did that make their cause any more legitimate?'

Outside classes, in social situations, I'd often be even more brutal. For visiting Americans, brashly parading their obtuseness, I'd formulated a standard response: '*I sometimes wish I knew as little about the subject as you clearly do. Then I, too, could make crashingly dumb statements like that.*' With this riposte, I alienated an old friend from Long Island, by reducing his girlfriend - a vacuous woman, who extolled the IRA as gallant 'freedom-fighters' - to tears.

I became increasingly conscious of connotations in nomenclature, conscious of the emotive charge in specific words, specific names. Thus, for example, 'Derry', on the one hand, or 'Londonderry' on the other, each proclaimed a tribal and political affiliation; and there was nothing in between, no terminology for implying neutrality. In much the same way, 'Ulster' was unacceptable to Irish Republicans, who referred to the province only as 'the North' or, more frequently, as 'the Six Counties'. If I said 'Londonderry', and continued to say 'Ulster', it reflected an endorsement of the Unionist or Loyalist position less than it did a deliberate repudiation of the IRA and all they represented. And this antipathy wasn't in any sense social or political. It was purely personal. They'd struck at Delphine's family. They'd hurt the woman I loved. They might easily have killed her. I therefore considered myself engaged in a vendetta, and damn whatever politics might incidentally be involved.

For the fourth time in my life, I'd been knocked off my fence of aesthetic detachment, Olympian aloofness. For the fourth time in my life, I'd been polarised, impelled into something more than just an opinion - impelled into a commitment. It'd happened during the Civil Rights Movement in the States, when JT and Ilona'd been busted in Mississippi. It'd happened twice during the conflict in Vietnam - initially when my rabidly zealous Draft Board'd threatened to shanghai me personally, then again when the administration'd declared implicit war on my entire generation and brainwashed people like Gil, the construction worker at the tavern on Long Island, into impugning the literature I taught. The IRA'd now elicited from me a similar determination to do something.

In moments of more extravagant and crackbrained fantasy, I imagined myself catching a flight to Belfast, going 'under cover' in the Falls Road or the Ardoyne, claiming to be an American journalist and playing detective. Or vigilante. The IRA obsequiously deferred to Americans, who, out of ignorance or prejudice, provided them with funds. They certainly wouldn't want to alienate public opinion in the States by interfering with an American citizen. I'd probably be able to move about with impunity. But what then? At this point, fantasy gave way to jaundiced realism. Did I really believe I'd track down those responsible for the death of Delphine's uncle? And even if I could was I going to kill the culprits? How? With what? I'd unquestionably welcome the opportunity, but wouldn't know how to turn it to account. If Delphine herself had been injured, or worse, I might well have attempted something that deranged, feeling I'd nothing left to lose. In the circumstances, however, I retained sufficient lucidity to curb myself.

I longed, wistfully and nostalgically, for the old Musketeer camaraderie – 'One for all and all for one' – that'd I'd enjoyed in North America with Patterson, Radetsky and JT Swift, as well as with a few subsequent associates from Long Island and Vancouver. I was in sporadic contact with Radetzky and JT, more regularly with Patterson. Once or twice a year, often on Bloomsday, one of us would telephone the other. '*What're you drinking*?' he might ask me. '*Hang on*,' he'd say when I replied. '*Let me pour some of my own*.' We'd then settle down to a lengthy and expensive transatlantic conversation, marvelling at how each such dialogue seemed to resume where the last had terminated, with no interval of time or distance. For the crusade on which I was now embarking, however, I could hardly mobilise those allies. And what, in any case, might I've mobilised them to do? Change colour, like Snidley, and join the UVF, the UDA or the Orange Order as mascots?

My preoccupation was temporarily vitiated, if not quite dispelled, when Argentina's military *junta* – one of the more noxious régimes on the planet at the time - impertinently invaded the Falklands. Like most people around me, I followed the ensuing conflict attentively, with an interest I'd never mustered for the muddle in Vietnam. I posted myself at the television for every lugubriously intoned bulletin by the spokesman from the Ministry of Defence, a nerdish mop-haired man with the elocution and charisma of a speaking clock. I watched footage of grey warships slashing through blustery winter seas, of Harriers surging from heaving decks and returning to hover, then descend with the finicky precision of ballet dancers. Argentine aircraft whizzed and swooped like dark meteors, scoring the skies above San Carlos Water. Files of Paras and Royal Marine Commandos, in maroon and green berets, 'yomped' through mud and wind-flayed brush, between scattered boulders, across desolate ridges. And finally, in a nightscape dissected by coloured tracer, an officer unexpectedly ordered his men to cease fire, and announced, almost with surprise, a white flag flying above Port Stanley.

Granted, I regarded the Falklands War as probably the most bizarre and absurd campaign in British history since the War of Jenkins' Ear. I endorsed the pronouncement ascribed to Borges, that it was rather 'like two bald men fighting over a comb'. Granted, too, I found the jingoistic hysteria of the tabloids - like the banner headline *'Gotcha!'* on the sinking of an Argentine cruiser - both tasteless and contemptible. But while I'd deplored American involvement in Southeast Asia fifteen years before, I didn't think Britain had much choice in the South Atlantic. I thought she'd been negligent in allowing the situation to develop in the first place. I thought she'd been grievously lacking in foresight to've scrapped the old *Ark Royal*, the last full-size fleet carrier, the mere existence of which would've deterred Argentine adventurism. I recognised the cynicism with which the British government, like Argentina's, exploited the situation to deflect attention from discontent at home. Despite such reservations, however, I felt Britain'd been obliged to act.

'Of course it's insane,' I stated to one of my classes. 'But by the standards of individual human logic, the logic governing international relations is consistently insane. It's insane for a government to flaunt the name of 'German Democratic Republic' and then build a wall that keeps people imprisoned in a city. Insane that that city should be divided the way it is, half of it belonging to an entirely different country off to the west. Insane to stockpile enough nuclear weapons to blow up the entire globe seventy-two times over. But there's an altogether different sphere - a trans-human and probably inhuman sphere - in which such things make a perverse kind of sense. International relations conform to a logic that has nothing to do with the logic by which we, as individuals, conduct our lives and formulate our values. By the standards governing international logic, Britain doesn't have many alternatives. Not, at any rate, if she hopes to retain any sort of face - which counts for everything in international relations. Not if she expects her voice to carry any weight in the international community. Not if she doesn't want her influence on the world's stage to lapse to the level of, say, Norway's, or Portugal's.'

I was exasperated by the hypocrisy of men I usually admired, like García Márquez, as well as by that of the British left.

'The people who're now complaining,' I said to my class, 'are the same people who, a few weeks ago, were most vociferous and eager to indict Argentina's government. If Britain and other developed Western powers had embarked on some sort of humanitarian crusade against the military junta - against its policies, its brutality, its slaughter of its own citizens - the people in question would've cheered. Because there're other motives behind the war, the people in question whinge - even though the results are the same. The devil with the Falklands as such. If the war can bring about the fall of Galtieri and his mates, it's justified in its result.'

And I capitalised on the slovenly misuse of language, which offended me as a practising wordsmith. It enabled me, at least, to steer back to my theme of Northern Ireland.

'I have no patience for bleatings about "colonialism" and "imperialism". Such bleatings entail an irresponsible use of words. During the early to mid-1950s, anyone who challenged or questioned the proceedings of Joe McCarthy's Committee on Un-American Activities was automatically branded a Communist, even though most were nothing of the sort. During the '60s, anyone who represented or endorsed the so-called "Establishment" was automatically branded a Fascist, even though *they* were they were nothing of the sort. The slapdash bandying about of such emotive labels amounts to sloganeering and crass manipulation. So does a phrase like "foreign army of occupation" used in reference to British troops in Ulster.

Constitutionally, and in international law, Northern Ireland is part of the United Kingdom. How, then, can the British Army be a "foreign" army? Especially when many of them, those in the Ulster Defence Regiment, are Ulstermen – who're no more "foreign" than the National Guard in American cities during times of emergency? And how can a country be in "occupation" of its own territory?'

'I'm not sure I see the connection to the Falklands,' one of my bolder students ventured.

'I'm condemning sloppiness of language. Or sloppy language deliberately used for purposes of emotional manipulation. Whinges about "colonialism" and "imperialism" are illustrations of that. "Colonialism" and "imperialism" imply the establishment of an empire abroad – the imposition of a ruling class from the mother country over an indigenous native population, who're rendered subservient. That's not the case with the Falklands. There's no subservient population, there're no indigenous natives governed by a foreign ruling caste – unless you count penguins. The Falklands are British in the same way that Hawaii's American. If anything, the population of the Falklands is *more* British than the population of Hawaii's American. Whether it's worth sacrificing lives for so meagre a population is, of course, a valid question. But it's a different question. It's a question that has nothing to do with "colonialism" or "imperialism".'

'What's your position on that question?' someone asked.

'I thought I made my position clear. But my position's ultimately irrelevant. It doesn't matter. What matters is precision in language. Which brings us back to the kind of issue we generally discuss in this class. If you call *Madame Bovary* art, and if you also call the graffiti on the Tube art, you have to concoct a new term to distinguish *Madame Bovary* from the graffiti on the Tube. The result is a proliferation of jargon. I prefer to call *Madame Bovary* art and graffiti graffiti.'

As for the war, debate, recrimination and post-mortems were, of course, to continue for some time afterwards, in the media, in Parliament, in a number of other forums. The excitement, however, subsided. Hardly had it done so than the IRA struck again, exploding two bombs on the same day in London – one beside a bandstand in Regent's Park where a military band was performing, one in Hyde Park as a contingent of Household Cavalry rode past. The putative objective, as ever, was to jaundice the British populace, demoralise them, convince them Northern Ireland was no longer worth British lives, bully them to pressure the government into withdrawing troops. But the army, fresh from its triumph in the Falklands, was basking in popular esteem, and the attacks on soldiers, so far as propaganda was concerned, amounted to an own goal. So, too, did the killing of horses. The animal-loving British public was less blasé than usual about the deaths of soldiers. It was galvanised to new octaves of equine outrage by pictures of dead and wounded cavalry mounts.

I'd happened to be at Olivia's office, just opposite Regent's Park, when the bomb exploded there. We heard the hollow thunderous detonation, heard the windows rattle, felt the premises rock and judder. As I learned later, Cassandra'd been in the park at the time, looking after her sister's infant daughter. She and the child were showered with débris from the blast. I felt an eerie sense of some sort of magnetic field at work, some quasi-occult force – as if my hatred of the IRA were drawing me closer to them. Or them to me.

To help steady Cassandra's nerves a few days later, I suggested we stuff Snidley's bedroom with newspaper, the way Radetzky, Nina and I'd stuffed Patterson's in Chicago. It proved an effortless enough task. Cassandra'd contrived to filch Snidley's key for an hour and had a duplicate made. With my car, I was able to collect the requisite newsprint from various people we knew, and transport it to Snidley's lodgings – a squalid domicile in the cinder-strewn, soot-smeared, drearily bleary rear of King's Cross station, a place which made my old Chicago premises appear relatively civilised. Snidley unwittingly abetted us by being absent for most of the working day. By this time, he'd temporarily abandoned his culinary experiments and begun working as part-time bookkeeper for a health food shop. Here, for the moment at least, he'd made himself indispensable, proving more adept at cooking books than he'd ever been at cooking anything edible. Apart from that, his greatest aptitude, probably, was for sleep.

Lugging sheaves of newspaper, we made our way up the vertiginous outdoor stairway, a spidery spiral of rusty wrought iron that resounded clangorously under our feet, evoking memories of Cook County Jail's echoing corridors. En route, we passed the flats of hookers, pimps, pushers, hustlers, derelicts of diverse species. Nursing his own quirky puritanism, Snidley lived serenely amid this *ménage*, oblivious to most of the things and people surrounding him.

The kitchen, through which one passed on entering, resembled an embalmer's studio crossed with the laboratory of a demented alchemist and the den of an undiscriminating packrat. Snidley was messianically frugal, deeming it nothing less than sinful to waste food. In consequence, the table was adorned with blobs of tahini congealed to the consistency of putty. It also sported a scatter of plates with remnants of week-old ex-comestibles glued to them, pans of solidified rice and desiccated former vegetables. In one corner, squadrons of bluebottles circled and sizzled over vile vials, phials and glass bottles filled with murky yellowish liquid, which might've been urine samples but for the light crust of mould floating on their surface. In this array of noxiously malodorous receptacles, Snidley'd been fermenting a species of mushroom juice, his latest remedy and all-purpose cure for everything from piles to water on the brain.

Snidley was a fervent, even fanatical, exponent of fermentation - and, by extension, of decay. He'd experimented with fermentation and decay in a riotous spectrum of forms. Fermentation, he stoutly maintained, was a veritable elixir of life, or of youth, or of immunity against the sundry ills flesh is heir to. Periodic bouts of food poisoning failed to deter his belief in its efficacy. On the contrary, he'd proudly display to visitors platters of rancid muck and gunk cooked a fortnight or so previously, which flaunted mounds of mould in rainbow colours. Sprouts sprouted everywhere, on the windowsill, on every flat surface not already cluttered - bean sprouts, mung sprouts, soy sprouts, alfalfa sprouts, radish sprouts, wheat sprouts. The smell of rancid sprouts competed pungently with the odours of diverse festering fermentations. Out of his repertoire of residues, he'd contrive concoctions which he'd foist on guests, as well as on his adolescent nephew. '*Protein,*' he'd proclaim enthusiastically, placing before the horrified boy a serving of rice inadvertently seasoned with two or three cooked beetles. '*They're a perfectly good source of protein.*' On one occasion, poking about under the compost of moribund vegetables in a particularly foul-tasting stew, Cassandra'd fished out, to her astonished revulsion, a boiled and soggy dishrag.

Every chair, in both rooms of the apartment, was piled high with old socks, stained tea towels, dishcloths in various states of decomposition and pamphlets on such subjects as 'pyramid power', multi-level marketing and meditations guaranteed to make one invisible. In the front room, or bed-sitting room, an ostensible piece of furniture'd been assembled from blocks of foam, which invariably collapsed under anyone gullible enough to mistake it for a settee. Against the far wall, another slab of foam served as mattress, surmounted by an antediluvian fake fur coat exhumed from a charity shop. Above the bed, posters of the Buddha and Janis Joplin vied for supremacy. Assorted paper shapes dangled on discoloured strings from the ceiling - Snidley's efforts to express himself through origami. To one side of the door, a spindly two-shelf bookcase, 'rescued' from a skip, bore testimony to his erudition - *Jonathan Livingston Seagull, Feel Your Way to Power, Full Speed Ahead to the Way Ahead, Giant Steps for Baby Minds, Defeat is Maya* and *I Deserve to Be Rich.*

'This place is disgusting!' Cassandra declared, wrinkling her nose at the rancid redolence.

Our target - the bed-sitting room - was considerably smaller than Patterson's had been in Chicago. It took us no more than an hour, sitting on the floor at the frontier of the kitchen and cheerfully crumpling newsprint, to fill the space before us waist-high. Within another two hours, as I knew from experience, the gradually uncrumpling paper would expand in volume, attaining neck-level or above. I couldn't, unfortunately, wait around for Snidley's return, to monitor, as I'd done Patterson's, his reaction and first words. Cassandra chose to meet him when he emerged from his day of arduous bookkeeping and accompanied him home. She couldn't, apparently, keep a straight face at the crucial moment; and it was therefore at her that Snidley launched his tantrum. As always when he became indignant, he gabbled, gobbled and sputtered, assuming all the pompously monstrous self-importance of a yelling baby. We'd been outrageously irresponsible, he blustered, his sense of humour going frumpishly AWOL. We'd created a fire hazard. We'd put the entire building at risk. And what was more, he seemed to recall having read somewhere, such a concentration of printer's ink might well be toxic.

By the weekend, however, when I next saw him, he'd effectively mollified himself. Stingy and mingy as ever, he'd been reluctant to discard so large a quantity of perfectly good, if rumpled, raw material. Having cleared a few necessary pathways through it, he'd left it in peace while he pondered how to turn it to account - and, ideally, to make some profit from it. He'd initially, I gathered, thought of using it for insulation, which would enable him to economise on heating bills come winter. Inevitably, though, his mind continued to strain in quest of something more mercenary, more lucrative. He'd considered the possibility of using the paper to stuff mattresses, which he'd then market. At last, another solution had occurred to him.

'Bricks!' he announced triumphantly. 'I'll make it into bricks! I'll have to soak it first. Compress it into bundles and soak each one thoroughly. Get each one good and wet. Then compact it flat. Press it really hard, so that it comes out as a solid brick.'

'Which you'd then flog to the construction industry?' I asked. 'To produce literal houses of cards?'

'Not for building,' Snidley protested with weary exasperation. 'For burning. Like blocks of peat. And when you burn them, they go up in smoke and return to what they were. Become trees again. They come from trees, they go back to trees.'

I was tempted to question the logic of the last sentence, but refrained.

'Shouldn't you iron the newspaper first? Place each page on an ironing board, spread a damp sheet over it and smooth out the wrinkles? If you get your timing right, you might even be able to dispense with the damp sheet.'

The issue was soon to prove academic. One afternoon less than a week later, the police found a small IRA bomb factory in the building, on the floor just below Snidley's. They'd been called, apparently, to minister to a 'domestic dispute' - a more vociferous squabble than usual between a hooker, her bullying pimp and a pushy pusher next door, The pusher'd been trundled off with a mashed nose while the cops' noses began twitching to the spoor of bigger game - a noxious reek emanating from the flat two doors away. In the prevailing climate, such reeks were naturally suspicious. It was duly reported, and the beat bobbies, standing guard outside the premises, were shortly thereafter joined by officers from Special Branch and the Anti-Terrorist Squad, armed with warrants. Having forced the door, they found inside a quantity of fertiliser, detonators, timing mechanisms and other relevant components, including some gelignite.

While they waited for the flat's occupants to return, they proceeded to investigate other ratholes in the building, including

Snidley's, which exuded a similar fragrance of *eau de merde.* When he arrived, they rummaged through his premises and subjected him to a brief inquisition. I won't presume to speculate about what sense they made of his concoctions and fermentations. They must've realised fairly quickly that he was nothing worse than a crank, whose most grievous offences were olfactory. In any case, they contented themselves with confiscating a few foul-looking bottles at random and pointing out that the mountain of squashed newspaper was a fire hazard - a vindication of sorts for him. From his window, he watched the bomb-makers from downstairs, who'd just been apprehended, bundled away.

Again, I felt a sense of some occult magnetic force in operation - something drawing my adversaries into my orbit, or drawing me into theirs. That sense was further accentuated a month later by the discovery, in Camden, of another IRA bomb factory. It was found immediately behind my former accommodations, in the shabby depot where taxis came to have moribund batteries rehabilitated. Until nicotine and paraffin fumes rendered my windowpane opaque, I'd've been able to look out and down into the gloomy workshop where explosive devices were being prepared - if they were, in fact, being prepared there when I was in residence.

Shortly afterwards, at the beginning of autumn, a friend in Camden had his vehicle stolen - a wheezy and rackety old Land Rover which hardly seemed worth the bother, but which he perversely cherished as an alleged 'classic'. It turned up in Manchester - outside a house in which an IRA 'Active Service Unit', on the run from a botched robbery, had taken refuge. We saw clips on television of the building surrounded by swarms of patrol cars and personnel from SO19, the armed police detail. Out front was the errant Land Rover. A siege ensued, with the Land Rover caught in a potential crossfire. As at the siege at Balcombe Street a decade or so before, a stalemate imposed itself - until the police threatened to invoke the aid of the SAS. And as at Balcombe Street, the terrorists, daunted by the prospect of confrontation with the 'Hereford Gun Club', promptly surrendered. My friend's Land Rover was hauled off for comprehensive forensic scrutiny, and wasn't returned to him for another fortnight. Why the terrorists had wanted so slow and ungainly a vehicle remained a mystery. Perhaps, thinking of the Land Rovers used by the Army in Ulster, they naïvely imagined armour plate to be standard equipment.

Not long after the advent of the new year, a bomb exploded at Harrods, killing six people and injuring a number of others. It exploded near the door through which Selene had exited less than five minutes before. That galvanised me anew. Despite my antipathy towards the IRA, I'd hitherto remained largely passive, simply waiting and monitoring the magnetic current seemingly at work between them and me. By now, I was tired of waiting; I wanted somehow to force the issue, to take some sort of initiative, though I still had no idea what or how. An opportunity soon afforded itself.

As spring edged tentatively into winter's raw damp, I was invited to give a lecture in Edinburgh. I was booked to spend the night in the city, deliver my talk the following day, then return to London. One of my hosts was a man I'd known cursorily for some years, a journalist who moonlighted as Scottish publicity representative for my publishers. He had his fingers in a veritable patisserie of pies - cultural, political, esoteric, even athletic. I decided to use him to fly a proverbial trial balloon. I knew the Catholic and Protestant enclaves of Glasgow replicated, in miniature, the tensions of Belfast and Londonderry. I also knew that Loyalist paramilitaries in Ulster recruited regularly in Scotland, as the IRA recruited in the Republic to the south; and just as the IRA received supplies, financial aid and other resources from the Republic, so Loyalists received similar support from 'Alba' - once the Celtic Kingdom of the Dál Riata and, before that, alleged home of the 'Cruthin', said to be descended from the legendary Red Branch of Ulster.

In attempting to arrogate a legitimate Celtic pedigree for themselves - a pedigree comparable to that claimed by the so-called 'native Irish' - the UDA had, of late, begun to make a cult of the 'Cruthin', begun to counter Republican Hibernianism by making Cuchulain and the Red Branch their own. I guessed my host, steeped in Scottish lore, might know something of the way it was being conscripted for political and paramilitary purposes. Over dinner at my hotel, therefore, I sounded him out. I played, as usual when dealing with Ulster matters, the typically ignorant American. I said I was talking to my publishers about a book that dealt with the rôle of myth in current affairs - a phenomenon perhaps best exemplified by Northern Ireland. At the same time, I professed befuddlement at the sheer lunacy of the 'Troubles'. And I asked what the 'Cruthin' had to do with anything. Was there someone who could enlighten me?

My host, as I'd hoped, said he might be able to help and excused himself to make a call. When he returned to our table, he told me he'd arranged a meeting for me with someone. At eleven-thirty, he said, I was to take a cab to another hotel, one of the most famous and prominent in Edinburgh, and wait in the lounge. My description had been given to the man I was supposed to meet, and he'd find me. From the few additional things my host vouchsafed, I gathered the man in question was Scottish recruiting officer for one of the Loyalist paramilitary organisations - the UVF, as I subsequently deduced.

At eleven-thirty, I took a cab through a drizzle that slicked the streets shiny as fish skin, rendered them efflorescent with prismatic reflections of streetlamps. At this hour, the more sedate quarters of the city seemed to have gone into hibernation. The hotel lounge in which I found myself - a space of barnlike dimensions, with ornate chandeliers, heavy panelling of burnished wood, carved pillars of Victorian grandiloquence, spindly-legged but plush leather-upholstered chairs and sofas of voluminous amplitude - was deserted, save for one man in a corner, half-hidden behind a thick plaster column. As I approached, he rose from the armchair in which he'd been ensconced and moved forward to meet me, dragging one leg behind him - early forties perhaps, of medium height but robust, barrel-chested, with the physique and swaggering demeanour of a schoolyard bully. Longish sandy hair slicked back, quiffed in front and plastered with pomade. Jeans, cowboy boots, a black leather jacket over an American-style western shirt of faded denim. One might've taken him for an inept Elvis impersonator.

He introduced himself simply as Malcolm, offering no surname. His leg, as I learned subsequently from my host, had been shot away during a 'mission' in the course of 'active service'. The 'mission', apparently, had been an attack on a Republican drinking hall, a known IRA haunt. Malcolm's wound, however, had been incurred during his escape, in a shoot-out with a British Army patrol, a squad of the Black Watch. Malcolm didn't hold it against them. They were, he'd concluded phlegmatically, 'only doing their job.'

'What're ye drinkin'?' he asked, and was pleased when, knowing Jameson to be preferred by Republicans, I ordered a

Bushmills. 'Good man! I can see ye know yer whiskey. Ye're American, are ye?'

I went into my act, trying to look innocent as a new-laid egg, and for the next three and a half hours, we talked. Or, rather, Malcolm talked and I listened, at intervals providing him with dumb questions that served as cues for fresh monologues. From everything I'd previously encountered and known, from everything Delphine'd confided to me, I'd come to think of Ulster Protestants as dour and reticent, trapped within their own muteness. It was a cliché, a truism, that Republicans 'had all the best poems, all the best rhetoric, all the best songs' - and this advantage had certainly been apparent in the propaganda war. Only Paisley at that time provided a mouthpiece for Unionism; and compared to his android-minded bombast, the slithering hypocrisy, equivocation, prevarication, sophistry and casuistry of Gerry Adams passed among the gullible for sanity. But Malcolm wasn't only eager to talk. He was also adept at doing so. Indeed, he demonstrated a degree of eloquence that belied his redneck appearance - eloquence and a measure of realism, a measure of insight. At one point, for example, he addressed himself to the 'Marching Season':

'The anniversaries. The glorious occasions, three hundred years back, when our lot kicked the shit outa their lot, if ye'll pardon my French, an' drove Popery out of Ireland. For a while, anyways. That's what we're supposed to be celebratin'. Basically, though - an' this is just between the two of us here an' everyone else with half a brain - it's an excuse to make a lot of noise, dress up an' play silly-buggers. We don't usually have much opportunity to do that. We've got this Calvinist heritage on our backs, ye see. We're not what yer Americans would call a fun-lovin' people. When we have an excuse to go over the top, we're not slow to take it. But we're not tryin' to rub the other lot's noses in it. At least we weren't, until they started gettin' all sensitive about it. It was just a holiday, pretty much like yer Fourth of July. Don't ye have marches in America then? And would ye stop havin' marches just because a few Brits, there or here, felt uncomfortable about it?'

He paused for a moment, meditated, then beckoned to a waiter for another round.

'Can you see,' I ventured, with studied naïveté, 'why they might find it all provocative?'

'Ay,' he replied. 'I suppose. But so far as we're concerned, they're the ones who're being' provocative. They say they want the Brits out. But we're the Brits. It's us who's the Brits. Oh, we're Irish, too, of course, that goes without sayin'. At least I am. I'm from over the water. Belfast. Me an' my people there, we're Irish, too, but we're still Brits. An' there're times when a kind of shared Irishness takes over. Between us an' the Taigs. That's what we call the Catholics, in case ye don't know. The Taigs an' us, sometimes we understand each other better'n yer average Englishman understands either of us. But yer average Englishman don't understand the Welsh either. Or the Scots. All the same, we're still Brits. It's like you from . . . wherever you're from . . . East Coast somewhere? . . . an' people from yer Midwest. Or from California. Ye don't always see eye to eye. Ye even fought a civil war about it once. But ye're all still Americans.'

'I've read statements like that before - about how both communities over there know each other better than the Brits do either of you. That's why I can't understand why you're at each other's throats.'

Malcolm flashed me a rueful grin, shook his head as if hopelessly, peered down into his whiskey and shrugged.

'We're not always sure of that ourselves. Maybe it's a kinda Cain an' Abel thing. Maybe it's only yer own brother ye can really hate in earnest. Just because ye understand each other so well. Because ye see so clearly in him everything ye hate in yerself. But we don't usually come up with deep answers like that. Don't even ask ourselves deep questions. Ye just accept it from the cradle. They're Taigs. They say it's their country. We say it's ours. As much ours, at least, as theirs. An' there're more of us. Hell, we've been there as long as yer people've been in America. Longer even, by a few years. That gives us some kinda claim. An' if we'd dealt with the so-called "native Irish" the way ye dealt with yer "native Americans", we wouldn't have any "Irish problem" today.'

'You mean the Indians . . . '

'Ay, the Indians. If we'd treated the Taigs the way ye did the Indians, there wouldn't be but a few Taigs left today, an' them on reservations in Connaught. But it ain't really the Taigs we mind all that much. The Taigs - a lot of 'em anyways - can be all right when ye get to know 'em. It's not the Taigs as a whole. It's the IRA.'

For the next half hour or so, he proceeded to scoff at the extravagant mythic claims of the Republican movement, the mystic vapourings of fable, the grandiose accoutrements of a legendary past. The 'nation once again' of song? Never, Malcolm stated with a chuckle of dry cynicism, had Ireland been a single nation - nor would it ever be, as long as he and his colleagues had anything to say about the matter. The 'glorious Army of the Gael'? There'd never been any such army, except in saga and ballad - only ramshackle bands of uncouth barbarians intent on exterminating each other. So much, he concluded, for 'misty Hibernianism'.

'Tell me about the Cruthin,' I invited, after a pause.

'The Cruthin?' Malcolm echoed, allowing himself the trace of a mischievously ironic smirk. 'Ay, there's some of our lot makes a great song an' dance about the Cruthin. Myself, I don't know if there ever was such people. But the name don't matter. What matters is the truth behind the name. The Taigs call themselves the "native Irish". They call us invaders, usurpers, foreigners. But who d'ye think were the real native Irish? We were! Us! We were in Ulster long before the Taigs were. Back in pagan times, Ulster was *our* kingdom. Some of us were driven out, an' crossed the sea to here, an' founded the first kingdom in Scotland. The Kingdom of the Dál Riata. Wasn't until much later - Elizabeth's time, Cromwell's - that we regained a foothold in Ulster. But we weren't strangers. We weren't foreign invaders. We were just returnin' to reclaim our birthright. It's like the Jews returnin' to Israel. D'ye know, there's lotsa fellas in the UDA who wear Stars of David round their necks. Out of sympathy with the Jews. Like us, they know what it's like to be plagued by terrorists.'

'None of this,' I said, 'ever gets across to America. No one in the States ever hears your side of things.'

'Ye know why? I'll tell ye why. It's our own bloody fault. Our own shortcomin'. We don't have a proper voice. That's the problem. We don't have anyone clever with words, any intelligent spokesman to put our case for us. We only have petty politicians, an' thugs, an' clumsy buffoons like the Big Man. It's the Taigs know how to make themselves heard an' listened to. They've got the poets. They've got the storytellers. They've got the writers an' artists an' orators. They know the power of the word, an' they use it. They understand the power of imagination. Us, we tend to be scared of imagination. We don't trust it. We make the mistake of thinkin' it's just laziness an' idleness, whimsy an' fancy. That's our Puritan heritage speakin'. An' so we've muzzled ourselves. We've no one who can express us – to ourselves or to the world. Not even the likes of bloody Gerry Adams.'

'What about you?' I asked, genuinely impressed by his insight and articulateness. 'You're certainly eloquent enough. Why couldn't you provide your people with the voice you say they need? Or at least convince them they need it?'

Malcolm flicked me a sidelong glance, as if to make sure I wasn't mocking him. Reassured, he gave a grateful nod. Then he shook his head, lips pursed in a rueful, even bitter, smirk.

'I thank ye for that. But my eloquence, as ye call it, came a bit too late. It's only since I've been here, in what ye might call retirement, that I've bothered to read. Bothered to meditate. To think about things. To ask myself some basic questions an' try to find answers. Few years ago, ye wouldn't've heard me talkin' like this. Few years ago, ye wouldn't've heard me talkin' at all. Back in those days, I just acted. Didn't talk about my acts. Didn't think about them. Just acted. In ways, sometimes, that don't today make me very proud of myself.'

'But why should it be too late?'

'Can't go back to Belfast, man. Can't risk showin' my face anywhere over the water. Be more'n my life was worth. Too much spilt milk. Spilt blood, too. Too many people hurt, or worse. Too many other people lookin' for me. Brits. RUC. Provos. For all I know, some of my own lot, too, now that the old leadership's gone an' there's new hard men in charge.' He tilted his head towards his false leg, stretched stiffly before him. 'That didn't happen in any industrial accident.'

'You see it continuing over there? Or do you see some sort of solution?'

Malcolm replied with a shrug of bleak resignation.

'We can afford a war of attrition if we have to. There's more of us than there is of them. We kill one of theirs for each one they kill of ours, it's ours'll be left standin' when the dust settles.'

'Does everyone face that prospect as calmly as you seem to?'

Malcolm shrugged, not meeting my eyes for a moment, gazing through me or past me in the general direction of the Irish Sea.

'There's different kinds of calm, man,' he stated in a flat, toneless voice. 'Calm of acceptance. Calm of resignation. Calm of despair. They're all forms of calm. They all look the same from th'outside. But they're not the same at all. An' there's another point, too.' He leaned closer to me, his voice dropping to a mysterious whisper, seeming to be issuing out of some sudden trance. 'I'll tell ye a secret. It's a great secret. A grand secret. A powerful secret. We learned it from the Taigs. Learned to make it our own, as much as it's theirs. Ye see, man, nobody dies over there. Nobody ever dies. What ye see as death here - there it's something different. A fella gets shot, let's say, or blown up - out on a mission, maybe, or maybe just drivin' down a country lane, or just sittin' with his family watchin' the telly. He has his funeral, with the pipes skirlin', an' the mourners round the grave, an' the flag of whatever allegiance on the coffin, along with the gloves. But he's not really died. He's been . . . *changed*. He's passed into some other dimension, ye might say. He's grown more alive in people's minds than ever he was. He's become the stuff of song an' story an' legend. He sits at the table with those who've gone before - all the other heroes an' saints an' martyrs of his tribe. It's a kind of immortality, man. Like the Valhalla of the Vikings. So ye see, man, nobody dies. Not over there. It's only from here that death becomes visible. It's only when ye've been away, and then return, that it all looks small an' piddlin' an' trivial an' ugly an' mad. But at the time, when ye're there, when ye're amidst it - then it's somethin' else entirely. Then ye're a hero. Then ye perform heroic an' glorious deeds, because ye know ye can't die.'

Around us, out in the night beyond the lounge, the city still seethed, but we seemed enclosed in an eerie prism of silence, some species of force field that muted all sounds, held them at a discreet distance. Malcolm drained the last of his beer, wiped his mouth on his sleeve, then looked boyishly abashed at so crass a breach of etiquette.

'Ye'll have to excuse me. I tend to forget myself sometimes. Get carried away. I'm no longer used to civilised company.' Becoming suddenly inhibited, he snorted in self-deprecation. 'Ye must think we're a superstitious lot.'

'Not necessarily.'

'We are, ye know. All of us. The Taigs, too, maybe even more. We live by blessings and curses.'

Malcolm was clearly talked out, and the conversation at this point began to wind down. Shortly thereafter, he took his leave, hobbling off into the night, dragging his artificial leg behind him, and I had the desk clerk call me a cab back to my hotel. En route there, and all through the following day, and during my return flight to London, Malcolm's words continued to haunt me. I rummaged in memory, trying to dredge up what I'd learned long ago of Irish curses. There was, I recalled, a formula - a recipe, in effect, for devising a curse. As if it were some species of occult cuisine, a curse had to be concocted from certain specific ingredients, including 'beauty' and 'terror', mixed in precise proportions. Of even greater importance was the mystical process of '*naming*' - invoking an individual, for example, by his name, enshrining his name in a form sufficiently durable to immortalise him, for good or ill. I remembered tales of poets who, by 'naming' a man, could either bless or curse him, 'unto the seventh generation'. Whether such benefactions or maledictions actually 'worked', of course, was an open question. But the mental soil would be fertile - as fertile as that of the three neo-Nazi Polish youths I'd intimidated in Chicago years before. Here, too, I'd be tapping a reservoir of psychic vulnerability largely engendered by Catholicism.

According to reports in the media, four men were suspected of having participated in the bombing that killed Delphine's uncle. Two of them had apparently remained unidentified. The other two had been arrested and one indicted, tried and sentenced to life imprisonment - which meant, in practice, twenty years, with reduced time for 'good behaviour'. The remaining culprit, one Mickey O'Hagan, escaped jail on a typical 'technicality'. He, I decided, would become the subject of my experiment - or, if I were honest with myself about my own scepticism, of my *jeu d'esprit*.

No slapdash baked steaks this time. With a culinary zeal worthy of Snidley, I proceeded to concoct my prototype Curse Mark I, adhering to all the traditional recipes, adding all the requisite ingredients in appropriate proportions. I plundered occasional images from Yeats, motifs from the Celtic Twilight, purple prose, cadences and rhythms from Pater and the *fin-de-siècle*, Having brought this bouillabesse to a boil, I then *named* Mickey O'Hagan.

XX

MALEDICTION

Under the dripping mossy wall, where the skeleton lies wrapped in mouldered remnants of an abbot's robes, the serpents nesting in the ribcage stair warily. For even here, the reverberations can be felt - a tremor, a convulsion not only of the earth, but of the air as well. Of the air and of something more impalpable than the air, more impalpable even than the ether. A tremor, a convulsion in the grey-gauze fabric of time itself. Or, rather, of the element through which time moves, or in which time hangs suspended.

Even here, in the quartz-veined entrails of the mountain, in this rock-ribbed demesne sealed by the White Stone, which mist veils from all but the visionary eye. Even here, around the serpent-infested skeletons. Even here, amidst ornately carved coffers of jewels and precious metal, the shining untarnished axes and maces and *gae bolga*, the shields preserved against the rust of centuries, the horns of hammered silver, the helms of ruby and gold once worn by princes and kings and magi. Even here, where the bronze cauldron swings from its tripod of pale peeled hazel wands, and the burnished salver beside it echoes the flicker of the flames, and the blond wood of the spear lies crossed on the naked sword. Even here, a shudder troubles the tranced stillness. And in the cauldron, where time's shifting images are mirrored, a chill streak of wind wrinkles and blurs the surface of the water.

She divines the essence of what has happened - the grey-mantled hawk-faced woman seated cross-legged on the stony floor, her grey hair sifting in wisps down her shoulders, down her withered breasts and back. The essence of what has happened. And the messenger, when he arrives, red cap knocked askew by haste, a froth of new milk on his lips, will only furnish specific and ultimately incidental details. But to the grey woman, the essence of the thing is already apparent - that this new outrage, more than any other of late, is not merely political, not transient and ephemeral in the way that politics are, and all that partakes of politics. It is already apparent that this new outrage has transcended such temporal spheres, has rent a jagged gash in some more durable, more perilously inviolable fabric -

the fabric of that dim continuum on which phenomena are printed. In its enormity, this new outrage has already begun to toll with brazen clangour down the vertiginous corridors of eternity; and its shame stains not only the future, but the past as well. In the livid inflamed glare of this transgression, poems have been irreparably tainted, traditions warped and dishonoured, heroic deeds debased and demeaned; and the meaning once informing a soil, a people, a culture, must now be revised.

Peering into the clouded depths of the cauldron, she knows the nature of the transgression. It was more, she knows, than a sin against a man, a state, an institution, a system. It was a sin against a symbol - or, rather, against that which all symbols seek to manifest. A man, she knows, has been murdered wholly as a symbol - not as an enemy, not as an individual, not as a human being. And there is no reprieve, no extenuation, for this act - this act which blurs realities, which diminishes a man to mere symbol, a symbol to mere man. And she knows, too, that symbols cannot be killed. That symbols - though they bleed and their blood corrode history like acid - remain, as does she herself, immortal. And that when one kills a symbolic man, the symbolic part of him, released from its glove of flesh, rises from the ashes of mortality, and circles ever more widely in its ascent, and casts its shadow over unprecedented vistas, and in the end swoops downwards to exact retribution of its murderers. For symbols are indestructible. Symbols are alive. Symbols are both sensitive and implacably powerful. And he who sins by symbols will ultimately be punished by symbols.

She has witnessed it all before - out of there, where the cliffs mix with the sea wind, and grey waves, plumed with scudding foam, charge like spectral horsemen against the strand. She has witnessed it all before, can even now discern it - a pageant of such dramas, frozen in eternal enactment on the misty tapestry of time. A woman, belly distended with child, forced by crass mocking men to race a chariot; and from this blasphemy, this bestial insensitivity, were born the pangs of Ulster. And a man, doomed by self-lacerating pride to slay his son, wielding axe and sword and spear and *gae bolga* at the fords - single-handed, against *her* army and *her* avatar. And holding the fords - holding them with magnificent tenacity. And misplaced tenacity. A blind insentient tenacity, oblivious to the import, the meaning, the consequences of its deeds - a tenacity like an orgasm, with no justification beyond itself. To men's infantile minds, this tenacity would reverberate down the centuries as heroism. And perhaps it was indeed heroic. But if so, it was also catastrophic, not only for her, but for the land as well. In his monstrous appetite for glory, did not that man pervert the very soil, transforming it into a voracious carnivore, a vampire whose insatiable thirst could only be slaked by blood? Because of the blow he'd dealt her - the blow that eroded her sovereignty in these hills and glens and valleys, divorced them from the restorative power of the Feminine, banished her to this bleak mountain cave and heralded a new age of maniacal violence. A uniquely male violence - the violence of men who see only facts or events but not the relations between facts or events, who extol each thing for its own sake alone, who foist their childish games on whole populations and make kingdoms pawns on their board. A violence devoid of the Feminine, and thus devoid of all proportion, all perspective. And without perspective or proportion, without a context or a matrix, a trivial spark struck in petulance becomes a conflagration that consumes entire peoples. And this petulance, too, is lauded in the songs as heroism, as honour and nobility - chimeras of the male psyche, the names with which men disguise their loneliness and their fear.

Yes, she has witnessed it all before - even after her banishment - from the sanctuary of this mountain cave, this sanctuary where even the winds grow old. She witnessed the carnage of Gabhra, where men's madness should have shattered their grandiose illusions, but only furnished fodder for nostalgia and epic vainglory. And she witnessed, too, the coming of the gaunt stranger, his prayers smoking up to a gibbeted god, veiling the sun, freezing the moon to stone. A priest ostensibly, but less a priest in fact than a conqueror, scourge of both men and deities. Of men, and deities, and, so it was said, of serpents - serpents, embodiment of sexuality, of wisdom, of womanhood. No, he did not truly banish the serpents, she reminds herself vindictively, triumphantly, her blazing gaze gloating on the seethe of vipers about her, and the shuttle-swift flicker of their tongues. And yet he did drive them to this refuge, this clandestine subterranean existence, this exile in a womb of stone. And it was then, confronted with popular defection, that her own fine fierce beauty faded, and she began to age. It was then, with no mirror in her people's consciousness, that the Queen shrivelled to the Hag.

And yet even as Hag, she was tolerated. Even then, the old altars - her altars - remained standing, and folk placed offerings on the moss-brocaded stones, and matrons left bowls of milk before their huts. And the priests kept discreet silence when peasants - either in ignorance or cunning - confused her with the mother of their abject emaciated god, or, on occasion, with his consort. And although they could not publicly acknowledge her, there were others who kept faith as well. Gnarled midwives, for example, haggard crones who sneered at the pallid derelict on the cross, and scuttled to the woods when the moon seduced the tides, and adorned her primeval bowers with fresh hazel. And young girls, too, incandescent with lust, smouldering under the strictures imposed upon them and seeking the release only she could provide. And, of course, the bards and poets and seers who, in their songs and visions, kept her memory verdant, and cajoled her, by time-hallowed symbols and invocations, into their dreams. Gradually, like grass thrusting through fissures of ruined palace paving, the ancient ways asserted themselves anew. And the priests acquiesced in the process, secluding themselves, consecrating themselves to study in their bleak rock-hewn temples. And the island prospered, becoming a haven for those fleeing turmoil elsewhere, seeking safety from the continent's incessant strife. Saints, pilgrims, scholars gathered here, forsaking their own flame-wracked lands, and the monasteries shone like beacons to the world. And amid these green velvet valleys, and mist-veiled hills, and brown bog pools, and dim grey haunted shores, beat the glowing heart of Europe.

Until the other priests came, the priests from the south, the grim tight-lipped priests whose doctrine of stern austerity did not preclude resplendent vestments - copes and stoles and chasubles adorned with rich jewels and fringed with silk and ermine. And the hard glittering sense of mission in their eyes was somehow compatible with mitres of gold, and sceptres of silver, and gleaming ciboria encrusted with sapphires and chalcedony. And along with their message of peace, they brought retinues in steel armour, whose swords, forged under dry southern skies, were already reddened with more than the rust of sea winds.

The Celtic Church brings love, people said, while the Roman Church brings law. And it did bring law. Not the law of the god it sought to enthrone here, but the harsher law of men - a law alien to the island and its rhythms, to the sap of the soil itself, to its primordial respiration. A law imposed forcibly, pressed down on the island like a crown of thorns. And then, too, as now, there was talk of unity. Not a unity nurtured in people's hearts and brought organically to blossom. Not a unity rooted in the earth, with the loam of the earth's soul still clinging to it. A cold unity rather, an abstract, ruthless and logical unity - a desiccated rational structure existing solely in the minds of its proponents, a coven of possessed and possessive bigots who promulgated their will with the frigid fervour of archangels. Men for whom salvation entailed setting this isle like an emerald in the tiara of the Bishop of Rome.

Under the dripping mossy wall, the skeleton gleams with a wan, faintly phosphorescent lustre. In the cauldron, the cloudy waters at last grow quiescent, forming a motionless dream-still pool. Peering into their depths, she studies the images mirrored there - images of the days following the Synod of Whitby, when the Church on this island made its final and definitive submission to Rome. Across the leaden-hued waves, in the Kingdom of Austrasia, a pact was broken, a royal dynasty deposed and exterminated. And here, too, there were constant alarums, and cressets trailed red streamers of flame, and fire echoed fire from hill to hill and horizon to horizon, and the tension of taut bowstrings pervaded the High Court of Tara. In the adjacent villages, men in flapping black cassocks congregated and converged like flocks of crows. New tithes, new prerogatives, new mandates were extorted. Guilt and fear sprouted in the furrows with the grain. A bleak grey metallic light benumbed men's minds; and their gaze was coerced heavenwards, away from the feminine mysteries of matter, of nature, of the land. And the land itself fell fallow, congealing in a winter of the spirit, and life ebbed from the groves of hazel, and the chill bogs, and the desolate grey shores where bereft curlews wafted lamentation to the sky.

Now, in the pellucid depths of the cauldron, sacred cistern of all forms, she can once more see the monastery - a jagged rough-hewn monolith hugging the rocky coast, with rooks reeling about it like black snowflakes. And she can see, too, as twilight drives the brethren from the fields, the taper burning in the abbot's cell, transforming the casement to a wedge of luminous amber in the damp stone. Immured within, the abbot himself sits motionless, elbows poised on the arms of his chair, chin resting on his clasped hands - a sallow man with skin like yellowed parchment stretched tautly over cavernous cheekbones, patrician nose, high furrowed brow. But though he himself might be carved from ancient oak, his eyes smoulder with feverish impatience in the taper's flare - a flare that troubles more than it dispels the surrounding shadows.

'It is not,' he declares, his voice rigid with exasperation, 'the most reassuring of prospects.'

From the opposite corner of the cell, there is the swish of a cassock, and a robust, florid-faced priest emerges into the taper's funereal effulgence, the flame imparting a burnished gleam to his tonsure.

'Would that it were, Reverend Sire,' he replies with deference. 'But we no sooner garner a harvest of souls than they lapse back into old idolatries.'

'Even among the hill people?'

'Most particularly among the hill people, Reverend Sire. Indeed, they are the most recalcitrant of all. They still speak of the Sidhe passing in every wind. They will not allow us to baptise the right arms of their sons, that their sons may one day strike stouter blows. And as godfathers of their children, they name the wolves.'

The abbot fidgets in his chair, his mouth stiffening to a tight thin line, like a badly healed wound.

'When you venture to the hills again,' he pronounces at last, 'we shall send four more brethren with you.'

'You may send a score of brethren with me, Reverend Sire,' the priest replies. 'I will be grateful for their companionship. But it will still bid fair to fare ill.'

'A contingent of soldiery then? They would welcome such a sortie. They grow restless here after their campaigns abroad, and slothful for want of activity.'

'I myself, Reverend Sire, might kindle my courage by such company. But the people of the hills would bridle the more against martial persuasion. In my humble opinion, Reverend Sire, we have exhausted the means at our command. In my humble opinion, we must now implore the aid of God. For nothing will further press our suit but a miracle.'

For some moments, the abbot remains silent, his eyes unseeing, but holding eternity in the fixity of their gaze. At last, they focus again, returning as though from some great distance.

'Miracles do not always stem directly from God,' he muses in a slow, silky, meditative voice. 'And there may well be occasions when God enlists the aid of man for His miracles.'

'I do not understand, Reverend Sire.'

'Perhaps it is better so,' the abbot drawls. 'But tell me. Would not an example of some fashion further our purpose? The example, let us say, of a man whom God smote in His august wrath? An esteemed and venerated man, whose name enjoys a certain currency in this isle?'

'What man, Reverend Sire?'

'It hardly matters what man, does it? So long as his status is sufficiently exalted. And his death sufficient to impress itself on the world. But let us say the royal sibling - the brother of the High King of Tara. Is he not widely loved? Were he to fall victim to God's wrath, would this not soften the souls of the populace?'

'Indeed, Reverend Sire. It would. With fear, if not with reverence . . . '

'Is there truly a difference?'

Bewilderment blankens the priest's face, while some faint disquiet imparts a harried tremor to his eyes.

'But why, Reverend Sire, should God smite the brother of the King? He has not opposed God. He has not raised his voice against us. In the past, he has even helped us - years ago, when the Saxon was wont to ravage our shores.'

'But what of his true allegiance? Is it not known where his fidelity finally lies? Where, if not with idolaters? With the remnants of the old Church here - the lax Church of this island, which, for generations, defied the authority of Rome? With those factions, in sum, which menace the unity we seek to impose. Why has he done nothing to abet our cause? To foster that for which we strive?'

'He is an old man now. It is not mete that he embroil himself in public controversy. But he and his people deem it incommensurate with his estate . . . '

'Incommensurate with his estate? Does his estate then exceed that of the Holy Father in Rome?'

'I repeat, Reverend Sire, he has never raised his voice against the Holy Father. Had he done so - had he appealed to the populace - our task would be far more arduous than it is. Forgive me, Reverend Sire. But I cannot understand why God should visit him with divine wrath . . . '

'We need not labour to comprehend God's motives,' the abbot murmurs, in a voice that signifies the audience ended. 'But men must now and again be rendered in tribute to His Most Holy Cause. It is not for us to impugn His justice.'

'Surely, Reverend Sire, you would not wish God to smite the High King's brother...?'

'I do not dictate to God. I serve Him. I am inspired solely by a consuming affection for the flock of Jesus Christ Our Lord. I am inspired by a longing to maintain them in the unity and purity of the faith vested in Rome. And to purge them of all contagion and heretic error. A man may, I grant, himself be innocent of such error. And yet he may unwittingly embody or represent it. Should that be so, I will accommodate myself to his death.'

And again, peering into the pellucid depths of the cauldron, she can see, mirrored in the water, the abbot's cell a week later. Again, the abbot is seated in his magisterial chair. But this time, his parchment-pale face is animated, and a hectic flush tinges his angular cheekbones, and a goblet of wine reposes between his fingers, and the fire of the taper leaps on the silver surface, as though a flame flared in his naked hand. And the figure before him, sculpted by guttering shadows, is not a priest, but a soldier - commander of the contingent from across the sea, brought here to ensure the monastery's protection. From the shirt of woven chainmail rears a ruddy ox-thick neck, with veins like knotted cords. And a bloated, wine-coloured face. And hooded, somnolent, venomous eyes, even the whites of which seem soiled.

'In a month's time, Revered Sire,' he rasps, the words obsequious on his tumid lips, but his rubicund face jutting forward aggressively. 'In a month's time. By the river. With the customary retinue.'

'By river, you say?' the abbot purrs in a suave subdued voice. 'Will he not then pass directly beneath this monastery?'

'He will, Reverend Sire.'

'Very good, Legatus. Now - there is another matter I wish to discuss with you. The fire of the Greeks, as it is called. You are acquainted with it?'

'I am, Reverend Sire.'

'It has never been employed on this isle before? It is not known to the populace?'

'Not to my knowledge, Reverend Sire.'

The abbot pauses, meditating on the goblet in his hand - the molten ruby, kindled by the taper, in its vessel of beaten silver.

'Could you manufacture such fire, Legatus?' he asks at last.

'I believe so, Reverend Sire. I acquired the formula in Gaul. I should require certain ingredients. If the Reverend Sire will undertake to procure them for me...'

'I shall undertake to do so. And you will, of course, construct the requisite catapult?'

'Yes, Reverend Sire. It will not demand much time. My soldiers will profit from such occupation.'

And a month later, when a new moon like a splinter of crystal breasted the eastern sky, the villagers of the region assembled - to witness, in all its ancestral ceremony, the arrival of the royal retinue, the brother of the High King of Tara. Amid the converging shadows of dusk, the sun's roseate reflection bled away into the sea, which merged with the river in ruffles of scrolled silver. And as the cortège of regal curraghs entered the estuary, a vast ball of seething incandescence, streaming billowing banners of fire, hurtled in cataclysmic rush from the rocks above - tearing its terrifying path through the liquid grey-gold of twilight, tracing a blazing arc between the heavens and the waves. A curtain of fiery snowflakes cascaded down upon the populace, who gasped and shrieked and shrank back in horror from the shore, while the wind gusted red, and searing heat withered the willows, and the river erupted in a raging upheaval of flames, and long flaming fingers clawed rapaciously at the sky. And as the conflagration engulfed the boats, as soot and sparks and flying embers and the stench of burning flesh enveloped the strand, the priests among the people extolled the miracle of flames that danced, unextinguished, on the water.

But not all were cowed by the miracle. One among them, the poet Senchán Torpéist, was accustomed to brood on the world's manifold mysteries - on the elemental powers of earth and air, and the hidden virtues of the planets in their courses, and the correspondence between different orders of things, whereby, to the eye of vision, they interpret each other. And as the flames lashed upwards from the river, he turned eyes wild and grey as storm scud to the monastery on the rocks above, and recalled vague rumours of the dreaded fire of the Greeks, and plighted a secret covenant with the deathless love of those who mourned. And as evening freshened towards midnight, he hastened to his lodging, where, in more peaceful days, young poets had gathered to learn from him the mastery of their craft. And here, seated on the floor before the smouldering peat, with his bed of rushes behind him, he proceeded, in accordance with ancient custom, to invoke the Sidhe. To invoke the Sidhe, and the Queen of that dim nation, by the hallowed and consecrated forms - a composition shaped as incantation, embodying the extremes of beauty and terror and compounded, as are all arts, of lawful and lawless things alike. And Senchán Torpéist applied himself to this labour until the rim of the sun seared the horizon, and a pearled light laved the surface of the sea.

In the hollow womb of the mountain, she heard his summons, huddled over her cauldron, caressing the nimble-tongued vipers at her feet. And in the domains of the monastery, the grain wilted in the furrows, and the cattle dropped stillborn calves, and the milk soured in their udders, and red-capped emissaries - invisible save to the visionary eye - poured disquiet, and anguished dreams, and worse, into sleeping blood. A monk went mad, and sought, one sombre rain-streaked evening, to couple with a sow. And as white gusts of winter drove the wolves down from the hills, as the ruts in the roads froze iron-hard beneath drained vitreous skies, the abbot himself succumbed to a feverish restlessness.

At the hour of the first shadows, it was most oppressive. Thus, one night, in the feeble light of an emaciated moon, he peered from the casement of his cell, directing urgent prayers to the heavens. But the heavens remained implacably silent, and cloud-rack masked the moon, as if the very firmament had closed its eye. And in the whole of the stark vista, nothing stirred save the tide furling in a sparkling white frill below, and the dripping gloom of the forest beyond, and a triad of gulls patrolling the estuary, deploying lazily downwind. Impatiently, he turned from his window; and as he stalked the monastery, his footsteps rang with a hollow measured knell of desolation. Until, in the refectory, he happened on a troop of soldiery, hunched in sullen silence over their evening meal. And yet they, too, seemed veiled in a vague unreality, like figures on a tapestry, stirred to a semblance of life by a fitful eddy of wind. Only a bronze tureen impinged on his consciousness, and a silver salver beside it, and a sword in the corner opposite lying crossed upon a spear.

In the corridor outside the refectory, the abbot called for his retainers.

'We have been all day idle,' he announced. 'We will sojourn for the night with our brethren beyond the forest, where the new church is being constructed. A short nocturnal ride in this bracing air will refresh our minds and souls.'

When they clattered forth from the monastery gates, it was a night of misty moonlight after rain, a night of clouds, and frost-bound stillness, and ancient sorceries. A chill wind keened softly through the rushes by the shore, but apart from this, silence hung motionless between the mist and the moon. And the trees winnowed the moonlight into long pallid shafts, which bleached a pathway through the forest.

In the wet wooded darkness, mist rose in druid vapour, making the torches gutter and dim. Enmeshed in the female forest, the trees stood sombre and expectant, as if under an enchantment, and moonlight sifted with wasted whiteness through the shadowed netting of the boughs. The abbot, roused from his torpor, cantered ahead of his retinue, threading his way between gloomy trunks and bogs, moss-bearded logs and roots clutching the soil like the gnarled fingers of malignant old crones. Around him, the mist thickened to a fume of silver, through which, at intervals, stray branches plucked at his robes with dry skeletal claws. From somewhere, the sibilant seethe of a stream was audible; and then, through the latticework of twigs, a ribbon of water revealed itself, shrouded by mist, foaming in white-flecked tumult over its bed of stones. In the sky hung a doleful, half-eaten moon, a fragment blown out of the night by some remote celestial storm.

For half a league, the abbot followed the freshet, which widened and grew more placid and at last flowed calm, embroidered with sinuous shadowy reflections, like a myriad serpents. And then, as he drew rein at a ford, the wisps of mist shaped themselves into the folds of a robe, and a woman stood before him in the water - a grey-cloaked, grey-haired woman with gaunt eager hawk's face and baleful glowering gold-green eyes. Behind her, the mist formed a luminous curtain; and she herself was veiled in mist, mantled in mist, which seemed to emanate from her very body, as if it were but mist incarnate. And as the abbot watched, she arched her back, and bent forward in the stream, and straightened, and bent forward again. She was washing something, he realised - something that glimmered with a livid, blue-white leprous lustre in the suddenly violent white moonlight. And when the mist thinned for a moment, the abbot discerned a corpse beneath her hands, the naked husk of a dead man. And as she prodded it to and fro in the tide, the dead man rolled with the current, and turned a wide-eyed visage upon him, and *impaled him with the sight of his own face.*

At that instant, the moon erupted from the clouds, and clanged like a gong on the wind, and loomed upon him like a glacier in the heartbeat before the world is struck - a blare of ghastly whiteness against which the trees, and the grey woman, and the reeling stars, and the madly rearing horse hung wildly pinioned. Then the surface of the stream shattered like crystal, and a ragged shriek of terror gashed the darkness, and the cattle in the byres of the monastery lifted their heads and lowed; and one of them, a week before her time, dropped her calf. And later, beneath a sky feathered with plumage of manifold greys, they found the abbot's horse, careening riderless in the fields beyond the forest, while hawks floated above on unmoving wings.

In his lodging near the High Court of Tara, the poet Senchán Torpéist slept - slept, as was his wont, until the sun mellowed the dawn and once more coaxed colour into the world. And as he slept, she, from the recess of her cave, wafted him a sign - a token that his curse had been fulfilled. Now, in the depths of the cauldron, she can once more see the portent she vouchsafed him - the uncertainty of dream coalescing to the certainty of vision. Now, in the depths of the cauldron, she can see him as he then, in his sleep, saw himself -

picking his path through hazel thickets, under festoons of apple blossom, into a sylvan glade. Around him, the breeze has subsided to a sigh, four rooks cross the azure overhead and a stillness prevails as at the heart of a lake. And at last, emerging into a clearing, Senchán Torpéist finds himself confronted by her spectral emissary - the Amadán-na-Breena, White Fool of the Sidhe, whose touch smites unbelievers dead or mad.

But Senchán Torpéist is no unbeliever. And thus, in his sleep, he dares approach the wizened wind-pale apparition, which hovers above a pool, and smiles with mournful melancholy, and watches images rise, one after another, and form on the opaline surface - images of lovely women, shaped by the mirror of the water and dissolved again, evanescence seeking incarnation. And Senchán Torpéist watches too, vaguely, until one face arrests his attention. It is the face of a princess or a queen, a gentle soul-suffused face of a pristine haunted saintliness, framed by a cloud of honey-hued hair - pure porcelain skin, exquisitely sculpted cheekbones, long slightly slanted blue-grey eyes to which unusually large pupils impart a wistful depth. And the eyebrows are fine delicate arches, giving the face a certain masklike quality, as if perpetually miming surprise. And perhaps it is a mask, Senchán Torpéist reflects in his sleep. Perhaps the woman behind it must yet be moulded by the elements, while the mask, in the meanwhile, laughs and sighs, rejoices and suffers, at the bidding of beings more or less than man. And yet its beauty is like a species of wisdom, and ages seem prisoned in the troubled gaze, and tempests to wake and perish in the folds of the gown and in the honey-hued hair, and empires to shift their borders as though they were but drifts of leaves.

'You must dream her to life,' Senchán Torpéist, in his vision, commands the White Fool of the Sidhe.

The Wheel has not yet turned sufficiently, the wraith replies, in a voice like the wind among the reeds. *It is not yet time again. And the vessel has not yet been prepared anew - the winged chalice, symbol of her sorrow and her soul.*

As though bereft, Senchán Torpéist meditates once more on the figure mirrored in the pool - the regal stateliness of her bearing, the poignant sweetness of her face, the smouldering scarlet of her gown, the serpent coiled in a cincture round her waist, with its tail between its jaws. And within the crystalline prism of his vision, he understands - that time must spiral back upon itself, that cycles must die and renew themselves, that he and his poems and his world must vanish in the waste of years and the perishing of stars. That an age must wane in the Fish and rise in the Water-Bearer before this woman may tread the earth - this woman who embodies the loneliness of all womanhood, who remains untouched and untouchable, yet is most deeply wounded of all by history. Grieving, Senchán Torpéist turns to the thicket behind him and plucks a wand of hazel - the sacred wood of Aengus, lord of love and poetry, who, in a more gracious era, transformed four of his kisses into birds.

'May she be blessed,' he whispers humbly. 'May Aengus shield and protect her. May the world, when she enters it, be more prepared to receive her than it is now. And let this be her talisman . . . '

And so saying, he twines the hazel wand into a spancel, and presses it briefly to his lips, and casts it into the pool. And the image in the water shudders and ripples and dissolves, like a dream at dawn, or like snowflakes melting into the sea.

****

Now, in the milk-blue dimness of the cave, the grey woman's hawklike visage assumes an imperious maternal majesty. And although four crossing birds mark a grave at Roselawn, she has already gathered the dead into herself, like doves into a dovecote. For some moments longer, she remains brooding over her cauldron, while her serpents slither about her and the troubled echoes from the world beyond subside. At last, she clambers to her feet and beckons to a red-capped servitor, and bids him follow her into the dark recesses of her domain. Here, she pauses before a coffer of antique blackened wood, adorned with ornate, finely-wrought carvings; and though there are crosses in the intricate design, they are not the grisly crosses of pain and renunciation, but crosses enclosed by a circle, contained and tempered by the Feminine. Solemnly, she raises the lid and lifts a chalice from within, a sparkling chalice hewn from diamond-white stone - with an incised serpent coiled round its base and two dove's wings of gold set in its rim.

'You will take this,' she commands, placing the vessel in her servitor's hand. 'You will carry it to where it is awaited. And most deserved.'

As the servitor, clasping the chalice, pales to a film of vapour, she turns again to the coffer before her, and draws from its depths a grey shawl and a mist-grey mantle, and wraps them about her shoulders. For she is aware that she has once again been summoned, invoked according to the hallowed and consecrated forms.

AND YOU, MICHAEL O'HAGAN, YOU AND YOUR COMRADES IN OUTRAGE, WILL NOT DISCERN HER PRESENCE AMONG YOU, EXCEPT PERHAPS, NOW AND THEN, AS A TRANSIENT CHILL. YOU WILL NOT DISCERN THE PORTENTS AND PRESENTIMENTS IMAGED IN THE CLOUDS, NOR THE SCARS OF MAN'S MISDEEDS IN GREATER DAYS THAN THESE. YOU WILL CONTINUE TO BOAST OF YOUR EXPLOITS; AND YOU MAY EVEN KILL AGAIN - FOR 'FREEDOM', FOR 'UNITY' AND THE OTHER NAMES WITH WHICH YOU DISFIGURE HISTORY. AND YOU MAY EVEN KNOW MOMENTS OF TENDERNESS, WITH PARENT, OR CHILD, OR LOVER - FOR A MAN MAY STILL LOVE, IN SOME SENSE, YET REMAIN LESS THAN HUMAN.

BUT ONE EVENING, MICHAEL O'HAGAN, ONE EVENING WHEN WHITE GUSTS OF WINTER WAIL LIKE WOLVES THROUGH THE HILLS, A FEVERISH RESTLESSNESS WILL ASSAIL YOU. AND THOSE AROUND YOU WILL SEEM VEILED IN A VAGUE UNREALITY, LIKE FIGURES ON A TAPESTRY, STIRRED TO A SEMBLANCE OF LIFE BY THE WINGBEATS OF SOME INVISIBLE BIRD. ONLY A BOWL WILL IMPINGE ON YOUR ATTENTION, AND A CRACKED PLATE BESIDE IT, AND AN UMBRELLA PERHAPS, OR A CANE, IN THE CORNER OPPOSITE, LYING CROSSED UPON A BLADE. AND WITHOUT KNOWING WHAT IMPELS YOU, YOU WILL BE SUMMONED INTO THE NIGHT, WHERE SILENCE HANGS BETWEEN MIST AND THE MOON, AND A STREAM, SHROUDED IN A FUME OF SILVER, PURLS, WHITE-FLECKED, BETWEEN BLACK TREES. AND AS YOU NEAR ITS SHORE, THE WISPS OF MIST WILL SHAPE THEMSELVES INTO FOLDS OF A ROBE, AND A WOMAN WILL STAND BEFORE YOU IN THE WATER - A GREY-HAIRED, GREY-

CLOAKED WOMAN, WITH VORACIOUS HAWK'S VISAGE AND BALEFUL GLOWERING EYES...

AND YES, MICHAEL O'HAGAN, YOU WILL SCREAM WHEN YOU SEE WHAT SHE IS WASHING. YOU WILL SCREAM AND, PERHAPS, IN YOUR TERROR, CALL FOR SUCCOUR UPON YOUR SAVIOUR. BUT THE MAN WHO SINS BY SYMBOLS WILL BE PUNISHED BY SYMBOLS; AND EVEN YOUR SAVIOUR, IN SUCH CASES, IS POWERLESS. YOU YOURSELF HAVE RENDERED HIM SO, MICHAEL O'HAGAN. FOR YOUR SIN IS TIMELESS, AND MAIMS NOT ONLY THE FUTURE, BUT THE PAST AS WELL. AND FOR YOU, MICHAEL O'HAGAN, THE EXPLOSION OF A BOMB IN BELFAST HAS ALSO SPLINTERED A STABLE REMOTE IN BOTH MILES AND YEARS – A STABLE WHERE A MAN AND HIS WIFE, NINE MONTHS GATHERED AT HER WAIST, HAVE SOUGHT DOMICILE FOR THE NIGHT, BECAUSE THERE WAS NO SHELTER AT THE INN.

XXI

Having completed my act of execration, I found myself facing a problem I'd not seriously considered before - what precisely to do with the thing. I knew of no literary journal or magazine that might publish it. I couldn't accurately assess its aesthetic quality, though I recognised the turbid turbocharged prose was dated. Even apart from that, it was dauntingly opaque and obscure - the kind of thing that would only make full sense to stodgy scholars or rabid Celtomaniacs. And I recognised that several publications in London, out of either fear or grotesquely misplaced sympathy, shrank from printing anything hostile to the IRA.

In any case, some of the urgency'd drained out of the situation. Perhaps predictably, my composition of the curse had served at least as a partial catharsis. I'd vented my spleen, and the intensity of my hatred'd somewhat dissipated. Had I encountered Mickey O'Hagan in person, I'd still've been capable of violence, but I no longer felt any vehement impetus to seek him out. In retrospect, I wonder whether, in some recess of my psyche, I believed the curse would do that of its own accord. Or perhaps I just wanted to believe it might. I was neither surprised, however, nor unduly disappointed, when, as far as I could gather, nothing happened. Certainly there were no reports of anything untoward in the media.

Although I refrained from sending 'Malediction' out for possible publication, I showed it to a few members of my immediate circle. Delphine was non-committal, simply asking for clarification of certain references and allusions. I didn't expect her to say much more, since she still found it difficult to talk about her uncle's murder. Olivia, too, was non-committal, presumably finding the agglutination of Celtic lore too indigestible. Selene and Cassandra both liked the thing, though I'm not sure on what basis. Snidley, as well as two other people, found it unnerving. Snidley, in fact, was downright queasy -- presumably finding the mood of the piece somewhat dark compared to *Full Speed Ahead to the Way Ahead* and *I Deserve to be Rich.*

'I don't know . . . ,' he mumbled, equivocating energetically. 'I don't know. I'm not sure about this. Are you sure of what you're doing? I mean, like, you're playing with powerful forces here. You might . . . well, you might *unleash* something.'

'Precisely.'

He handed the manuscript hastily back to me, as if he might contract something contagious from it, and waxed querulous:

'It's scary. It's *really* scary. You shouldn't mess around with things like that. You can get bad Karma that way.'

'No more so, I suspect, than by poisoning people with rancid cat-piss juice.'

Snidley bristled with indignation, and I realised, with satisfaction, that I'd tweaked a nerve. There was, I'd learned by this time, a specific purpose behind the malodorous concoctions we'd found in his premises when we'd stuffed them with newspaper. Shortly before, he'd apparently heard about some species of elixir enjoying a vogue in the States, a beverage distilled from mushrooms called *kombucha.* In America -- and also, I discovered subsequently, on the continent -- the stuff was extolled as an ultimate panacea. I was later to find it in the mini-bars of posh European hotel rooms, produced and bottled in Austria, with an ornately heraldic label. It hadn't yet appeared in Britain, however, and Snidley -- extemporising a recipe on the basis of randomly collated data -- was trying to fabricate his own. Here, in short, was yet another get-rich-quick scheme, and one that coincided with his fervour for alternative medicine. To sanitise his Karma by succouring suffering humanity, and, at the same time, to make vast sums of money -- the conflation of these two achievements must've seemed to Snidley the *ne plus ultra* of terrestrial toil, a crowning reward proffered by smiling Destiny, a veritable alembic or even Holy Grail in which all the aspirations of his life congealed.

In theory, I suppose, the endeavour to launch Britain's first home-made *kombucha* was valid enough. But that, surely, required professional production and bottling facilities. Whatever the stuff Snidley'd been decanting in his *ad hoc* laboratory, it was less likely to be therapeutic than toxic. Cassandra refused to taste it, finding its mere appearance 'disgusting'. Another friend, less charitable, described it as 'cat-piss juice', and the appellation, to Snidley's annoyance, had stuck.

A week or so after he whinged about 'Malediction', the overhead light fixture in my bedroom, which must've dated from before the Second World War, peremptorily, and with a languid pop, expired. I'd always had an uneasy relationship with things electrical, and British fixtures, with their bayonet rather than screw fittings, consistently flummoxed me. I suspected a fuse had blown, but guessed there was no point in changing it until the chargrilled fixture'd been repaired. As usual in such contingencies, I telephoned Snidley. Along with his various other self-appointed rôles, Snidley'd increasingly assumed that of all-purpose handyman, ministering to assorted mishaps -- ruptures, lesions, fractures -- in the world of objects. It was probably an adjunct of his image of himself as thaumaturge. Or perhaps the curing of inorganic as well as organic matter was simply a logical extension of his allegedly holistic orientation to medicine. In any case, he'd undertaken -- sometimes with quite genuine generosity of time and effort -- to keep my surroundings in working order.

Whenever anything went wrong, therefore -- when a window broke, when a bookshelf needed an extension, when the kitchen sink became constipated beyond the help of any standard laxative -- I'd call on Snidley, offering him, as I'd tell him on each such occasion, 'another opportunity to justify his existence'. Since he was seldom doing anything constructive during the day anyway, he'd promptly come round, ruefully sustaining my snide remarks. Not, of course, that he always knew what he was doing. More often than not, the work he did for me was dodgy, unreliable, makeshift, scandalously slipshod. The problem he'd undertaken to rectify usually surfaced again within a month. But he provided convenient stop-gap measures in emergencies, giving me time to get the job done properly. I'd reward him by paying for any materials he purchased, then taking him out for a meal to a local restaurant -- a place where the staff were accustomed to seeing me with a bizarre and impressively diverse spectrum of guests, from Delphine all the way down to Snidley. I'd order my customary hamburger. Snidley would munch his rabbit food, employing a diamond-cutter's precision to separate the macrobiotically sanctioned from the macrobiotically profane.

He failed to repair my light fixture, wasting half an hour screwing and unscrewing things, then flicking the switch and eliciting no result. At last, he improvised his own solution. He clamped to the ceiling a new length of white wire, which squirmed its way along like a sidereal tapeworm, running from a free-swinging bulb down the wall to the nearest mains socket. He then installed, dangling from the wire, a separate switch Like most of Snidley's work, the arrangement made little claim to aesthetic finesse. When I said as much, he argued that it made up in function what it lacked in fashion. I wasn't convinced the deficit in fashion had indeed been fully redressed; but the contrivance did, in its eccentric manner, restore visibility to my bedroom. In recompense, I took Snidley out to dinner. As he slurped from a bowl of something that looked like carrot soup, he asked me about Belfast.

'Belfast? Why Belfast?'

'Is it safe?'

'Safe for what?'

'For people.'

'People live there, if that's what you mean.'

'People also die there,' Snidley observed grimly.

'People die in London, too.'

'I mean there's a high death rate there.'

'Only one to a person.'

'Is it your self-appointed mission in life to make me look stupid?'

'Hardly. Any self-respecting mission would entail some element of challenge.'

Snidley exhaled with audible exasperation.

'Let's start all over again,' he grumbled. 'Is Belfast dangerous?

'Depends on what you have in mind, I suppose. If you turn yourself orange again and blunder into certain quarters of the city, yes, it might possibly be dangerous. They might tie you down and feed you pea soup intravenously until you turned green. In other quarters, you'd no doubt be welcomed. Malcolm -- the man I met in Edinburgh -- could probably get you adopted as a mascot for the UVF.'

Snidley, it transpired, had begun to despair of his efforts to produce *kombucha*, which was proving as elusive to him as had, in days of yore, peanut butter. If at first he didn't succeed, however, Snidley would simply redefine 'success'. In accordance with this principle, he'd learned of a macrobiotic couple in Belfast who, on a trip to the States, had acquired a 'secret' and presumably idiot-proof recipe for the mushroom-based concoction. He'd been in touch with them, by letter and telephone. They might be prepared to grant him a franchise to flog their product around London and southeast England. But they took their business rather seriously, it seemed, regarding the dissemination of *kombucha* as a veritable mission, and insisting that it be handled with the requisite responsibility. In consequence, they wanted to vet personally anyone they might accept as their representative, anyone to whom they might entrust their formula. Snidley was torn between the prospect of substantial revenue and the prospect -- which he imagined any visit to Belfast entailed -- of certain death.

'It's a war zone, after all,' he concluded sepulchrally.

'You sound like an American,' I accused, conferring on him a species of ultimate insult, which caused him palpably to wince. 'Americans fancy Belfast to be interchangeable with Beirut. Delphine moves around Belfast every day.'

I'd not, at that time, been to Belfast myself, but I'd formed a vivid and accurate enough image of it -- reinforced, of course, by Delphine's accounts of the city. I therefore spent the next half hour countering Snidley's craven objections. Eventually, he seemed more or less convinced, although, stingy as ever, he bleated about the cost of the odyssey he was contemplating. Two days later, however, my efforts were undone. The media reported another sequence of 'tit-for-tat' shootings, and Snidley panicked, scuttling back into his bunker of preconception.

'No way! A lot of good the recipe'll do me if I get killed!'

'You're suffering from delusions of grandeur. Why should they want to kill you?'

'Innocent people get killed all the time there.'

'That should guarantee *you* a safe conduct.'

Snidley wasn't amused, and all prospects of an odyssey 'over the water' for him were duly shelved. He continued to devise noxious beverages from his repertoire of decaying substances, undeterred even by a bout of food poisoning. I, in the meantime, returned to my accustomed routine -- reading, writing, pubbing, sedating myself with television. To outsiders, my lifestyle -- my relative freedom from external commitments, my licence to maintain the hours I chose -- must've seemed enviable. In fact, it conduced to monotony, ennui and often loneliness, but these were punctuated, vindicated and redeemed by trysts with Delphine. At intervals, our liaison would seem to reach a species of plateau, and I'd begin to wonder, anxiously, whether it might be growing stale. But Delphine, in her mystery, in her demure and gentle charisma, held me captive more surely than any sultry would-be *femme fatale* possibly could. As if endowed with her own internal seismograph or barometer, she'd instinctively, at each threatened moment of stagnation, say or do something, say or do precisely *the right thing* -- revealing anew one or another of her most endearing aspects, provoking in me a fresh eruption of lava-hot tenderness and thereby launching our relationship into yet another cycle of renewal.

In June, I received an invitation for the autumn. My publisher wanted to arrange a tour for me, which entailed a sequence of book-signings, radio interviews and public lectures in Ireland, on both sides of the border. I was to be flown to Belfast, where I'd be met by my publisher's representative, a journalist named Stuart Reeve. He'd take me round my appointed itinerary and then, early in the evening, chauffeur me down to Dublin. After spending a night at the culturally historic Shelbourne Hotel, I'd complete the southern half of my tour with a talk the following day. I looked forward to the trip. I even fantasised that somehow, by some as yet indeterminate occult process, I might pick up something of Mickey O'Hagan's spoor -- though what I might do then remained unresolved.

To avoid thinking too obsessively about such possibilities, I suggested to Snidley that he accompany me. If he were squeamish about visiting Belfast alone, I told him, I'd hold his hand -- metaphorically, of course. Stuart Reeve could direct him to the address of the macrobiotic couple with the secret mushroom recipe. We might even get Reeve to shunt him around, thereby saving him transport costs around the city. He'd only have to pay his air fare, which, by the regular shuttle, would be modest enough. In the evening, he could catch the shuttle back to London while I proceeded south to Dublin.

Snidley at first quailed queasily and querulously at my suggestion; but there were two full months in which to circumvent his equivocation, blunt his prevarication and wear down his cringing resolve. I'm not altogether sure why all of us -- Cassandra, Selene, several other friends -- colluded in urging him to make the journey. Perhaps it was just the surreal appeal of the prospect, the image of Snidley at large in Belfast. He continued to resist, until Delphine joined our chorus in egging him Ulsterwards. Not even Snidley's rabidly hyperdeveloped sense of self-preservation was proof against her charm. Once he'd purchased a ticket, of course, I performed a rapid *volte face* and traumatised him with gruesome scenarios.

'They're probably already waiting for you.'

'Who?'

'Everybody. They wouldn't just kneecap you, you know. They'd do it with a Black and Decker drill.'

'Who would?' Snidley quavered.

'Anyone. Doesn't really matter, does it?'

If he hadn't already invested *money* -- actual *money*! -- in a ticket, he undoubtedly would've withdrawn at that point. His stinginess, however, would never've exonerated such wastage. As summer mounted towards its ascendancy, he assumed increasingly the resigned fatalistic demeanour of a man sentenced to a firing squad.

I would've liked, of course, to rendezvous with Delphine in Belfast, but the old prohibitions continued to prevail. It was a small, incestuous city; and perhaps even more than before, everyone knew everyone else, everyone watched everyone else. Undercover personnel of the security services were everywhere. So, too, were scouts and spies for the paramilitaries. As an influential television producer, Delphine'd become a prominent figure in Northern Ireland, and her network of contacts had grown proportionately, In consequence, she'd be less likely than ever to escape scrutiny. At the airport, at the radio and television studios, at restaurants around the city centre, she was bound to encounter friends, acquaintances, colleagues. We might still, I suppose, have contrived an ostensibly innocent lunch -- for it would, after all, have been plausible enough for her to meet, in her professional capacity, with a visiting author. But on several occasions in the past, she'd had dealings with Stuart Reeve. I wouldn't be able to shake him; and the strain of dissembling in his presence, for both Delphine and myself, would've vitiated the pleasure of our tryst. In the circumstances, it would've been more frustrating than anything else. And as things transpired, Delphine was due at a conference in London on the same day that I'd be in Belfast. Her flight was scheduled to leave Ulster at eight in the morning, two hours before mine arrived.

I passed the remainder of my summer in a mood of intensifying eagerness and expectation. Snidley passed the remainder of his in a state of revivified anxiety -- 'nerving on a vergous breakdown', as he confided one day to Cassandra, tripping even more clumsily than usual over his tongue. On the evening before our departure, he telephoned me, frazzled, to ask whether the rain forecast for the morrow might ground flights -- and whether there'd be more than the customary security checks, and whether the sample bottles of his own mushroom juice might be confiscated, and whether pen knives were allowed to be carried into Northern Ireland. It was clear that he fervently wished for a hurricane to scupper the journey. I didn't think it wholly beyond him to bring a sword-sized knife along, hoping it would get him turned back at the airport.

Cheerfully, I outlined our arrangements. Since he shrank from squandering money on taxis, he could report to my flat in the morning, where the car and driver sent by my publisher would pick me up. We could travel in chauffeured luxury to Heathrow, then proceed to Belfast, where Stuart Reeve would meet us at the airport. Snidley could then sally forth in quest of his magical elixir while I performed my own antics with the media. When I asked him, for safety's sake, to repeat the details to me, Snidley responded lugubriously. My explanation of our arrangements must've sounded like a sentence to the gibbet being pronounced by a merciless judge.

'And may God have mercy on your soul,' I concluded, to reinforce that impression.

The car sent to collect me arrived duly at seven-thirty. Snidley, by then, hadn't yet appeared. I waited as long as was feasible. At last, I capitulated, realising that any further delay would cause me to miss my flight, and told the driver to start. I assumed Snidley'd panicked anew at the last minute and imagined him hiding under his bed, fearing someone might come to drag him out and transport him forcibly to Ulster. En route to the airport, I vowed to exact retribution for such cowardice, vowed to keep him stigmatised for at least another few years.

In fact, as I learned later, he'd simply overslept -- not an unusual practice for him, sleep being perhaps his most dynamic form of creative expression. On waking belatedly, he'd been forced to get to the airport by himself -- forced, in other words, *to spend money*! Taking a taxi was, of course, unthinkable, a taboo never to be violated. Lugging his backpack with its samples of catpiss juice, he'd resigned himself stoically to the press and crush and swelter of the tube. In the process, he'd got his pocket picked, but the culprit, it transpired, hadn't obtained anything save a new recipe for nut cutlets and a geometrical diagram with instructions for building a replica of the Great Pyramid. By the time he got to Heathrow, my flight'd already departed, and he'd had to wait for the next one, an hour later.

The plane descended on Belfast through thick cloud, which precluded any coherent panorama of the city. As I emerged into the terminal of Aldergrove Airport, a placard with my name on it was brandished in my face. Stuart Reeve proved to be a short stocky man with a fastidiously pruned beard and sleekly coiffed hair. As we shook hands, I mentioned that a friend from London was supposed to've accompanied me. In all likelihood, I explained, he'd bottled out; but there *was* a remote possibility that he'd been late and simply missed the flight. Reeve suggested we leave instructions for Snidley at the desk -- have him paged with a message when the next flight from London arrived, telling him to meet us at a prominent hotel around, say, one o'clock.

From the windows of Reeve's pedestrian Sierra, I surveyed my surroundings with a vague sense of dislocation, of unreality -- the sensation one often experiences on entering a place which figures prominently in one's personal mythology, a place long familiar from pictures and films, but never before visited. Over the rooftops, etched black against the sky, was the stark L-shape of 'Goliath', the gargantuan crane at the Harland and Wolff shipyard. Beyond, the city looked tilted askew -- brooding humped mountains in the background, stepped tiers of terraced houses slanting up the lower slopes. Most prominent was Ligoniel Hill, with the spired, turreted, grey-brown bulk of Belfast Castle at its foot. From a distance, the vista suggested a monotonous, even stultifying, uniformity that reminded me very much of Leeds, where I'd given a lecture some two years before. In film dramas, as I subsequently learned, Leeds was often used as a stand-in for Belfast. It enabled directors to do their shooting in relative peace, uninterupted by shooting of other kinds.

Switching on to auto-pilot, I embarked on my programme for the morning -- an intervew at a garish chrome-and-plastic radio studio in Newtonards, another at the informal offices of a newspaper on the Antrim Road, in what appeared to be a private house. There was then a book- signing at a shop within sight of Queen's University. An interview with a second newspaper was cancelled, the interviewer apparently having been taken ill. This left Reeve and me with an hour and a half or so of free time. I asked him if he could take me on a cursory tour of the city.

We'd already passed Stormont -- a long straight approach, almost a ceremonial boulevard, leading in undulations up a gentle, punctiliously manicured green eminence, flat-topped, in the manner of a prehistoric burial mound.. A massive, garishly white classical frontage crowned the summit with all the majesty of a palace, all the solemnity of an ancient temple -- an immense colonnaded portico, surmounted by a ponderous pediment. Delphine'd once said she found the edifice disproportionate to the province it represented, too pompous and portentous, too boastfully grandiloquent -- a cumbrous presence pressing oppressively down on the entire island, like an unwieldy paperweight on an unstable desk. I now saw her point. If one judged by façade alone, Buckingham Palace and the White House would've seemed quaint, even puny, by comparison. Ultimately, however, Stormont was little more than façade -- and, with direct rule being exercised from Westminster, hollow inside.

At intervals, I'd see a police station, banked with sandbags, swathed in films of silvery-grey wire mesh, like an immense cocoon -- a defence against mortar and rocket attack. Apart from such precautionary measures, most of the streets through which we passed bore little resemblance to those depicted on television. They might've been the streets of any urban suburb on the British mainland. Even the city centre looked placid and normal enough, except for the conspicuous absence of parked vehicles -- a prohibition introduced to preclude car bombs. Here and there, I noticed checkpoints, but they weren't active. Only at one did I see a few soldiers lounging casually, wearing the khaki berets of a Guards regiment. The occasional armoured Land Rover rumbled by. There were also pairs of RUC officers on patrol in their dark green tunics, revolvers tugging down the belts at their hips. On the whole, however, I saw fewer police in Belfast than I would on an ordinary day in Hampstead. It was obviously a quiet time.

Still having nearly an hour to spare, I asked Reeve to drive me through some of the city's more notorious sections -- the Falls, for example, and the Shankill. Somewhere, in this labyrinthine warren of alleys and passageways, lived a man I hated, a man whose death I'd tried by occult means to orchestrate. I picked up, of course, no spoor of him, no indication of where precisely he might be found. But here, at last, I *did* see the blight familar from the television screen -- gutted buildings, boarded up houses, stretches of littered waste ground aglitter with splintered glass, murals depicting masked gunmen or

King Billy on his white horse, kerbstones daubed lurid red, white and blue. There were, of course, copious graffiti. On one wall in the Falls, some presumably youthful amorist or practical joker had painted two letters in front of a clichéd slogan, transforming '*IRA RULES*' to '*MOIRA RULES*'. On the whole however, derelict though these quarters of Belfast appeared, they were no more so than vast tracts of American inner cities -- much of the Bronx, for example, or of Harlem, much of Roxbury and Dorchester in Boston, many of the neighbourhoods I'd inhabited and frequented in Chicago. Snidley's paranoia would've had little on which to feed -- though he, naturally, would've found some means of sustaining it.

Thus reminded of Snidley, I checked my watch, saw it was nearly one o'clock and suggested to Reeve that we head for the hotel. I doubted Snidley'd be there, still imagining him cowering in London. In fact, however, he *was* there. He was standing outside, along with forty or fifty other people evacuated from the premises, held back from the entrance by a cordon of green-tunicked RUC. The entrance was thronged with soldiers, some standing as sentries, others huddled in conference. The adjacent roads were sealed off by barricades of armoured Land Rovers. As Reeve and I pushed forward through the press, I saw Snidley, gesticulating frenetically, engaged in some sort of altercation with a police officer. Before I got close enough to hear what he was saying, the crowd fell silent, and everyone's eyes turned to the hotel entrance.

While two soldiers held open the glass doors, a metal contraption appeared, a robot resembling a sort of stylised steel dachshund -- caterpillar tracks, a pair of stiff rods for arms which ended in claws, a cylindrical ground-hugging belly comprising a container, a canister of some kind. It was moving forward mechanically, emitting a shrill, tensile, high-pitched hum, a whirring electronic whine. Tentatively, it came to a halt, then shuddered into movement again, swivelled jerkily and proceeded on its motorised way towards the weirdly empty car park.

'Bomb disposal,' Reeve said into my ear. 'Controlled explosion.'

At that moment, Snidley, having seen us, broke off his disputation and shouldered his way to my side, looking distraught. As he did so, there was a loud but dull *CRUMP*! from the car park, like the sound of a mortar, and the electric dachshund juddered.

'*My kombucha*!' Snidley yelped, spinning round.

Soldiers and police began to wave people away, official voices announcing everything to be all over. As the throng dispersed, Snidley stared, stricken, at the car park, then poured forth his lamentations. Having arrived at Aldergrove an hour late, he'd been paged and given my instructions at the enquiries desk. On reaching the hotel, he'd left his bags in the lobby and wandered off to the loo. He'd emerged to find the premises swarming with soldiery and police, who'd shunted him outside along with everyone else, before he'd had a chance to rescue his precious elixir. To his horror, both bag and elixir had then been gulped down the gullet of the robotic dachshund

'I was only gone for five minutes,' Snidley snivelled..

'You left an untended bag in the lobby of this hotel?'

'It was only five minutes!'

'In *this* hotel?'

'Only five minutes!'

I turned to Reeve ironically.

'How many times has this place been bombed?'

'Not sure exactly,' Reeve replied with a diffident shrug. 'Thirty-eight? Maybe thirty-nine.'

Snidley's mouth dropped open on its hinges and his eyes bulged behind his spectacles. Aghast, he stared at me, then at Reeve, then at me again.

'Oh . . . !' he moaned softly. 'That was my *kombucha* . . . '

As we filed into the now *kombucha*-purged lobby, Reeve asked what the stuff was that'd been blown up. Not wanting to sit through another of Snidley's exegeses on the virtues of his noxious potion, I made for the bar to order drinks. When I returned to our seats, Snidley was expostulating volubly, and I saw pretty much the expression I expected on Reeve's face -- a mixture of befuddlement, bemusement and courteously concealed scepticism. It transpired, however, that he knew the road on which the microbiotic couple lived. The place wasn't far, and he offered to run Snidley round to their address. It was in Reeve's departing car that I caught my last glimpse of Snidley in Belfast.

Reeve reappeared within half an hour, obviously convinced Snidley was a certified crank, but too polite to say so. I was conducted to another interview, then to a brief talk in a second bookshop. Towards four o'clock, Reeve drove me southwards, through the notorious

'Bandit Country' of South Armagh, of Newry and Warrenpoint, to Dublin. At the Shelbourne, I was met by my publisher's Irish distributor, who regaled me with a lavish dinner. After my lecture the following afternoon, I returned to London; but not until a day later did I learn of Snidley's epic tribulations.

He himself didn't understand what'd happened, and wasn't to do so for another week or two. To me, however, it was obvious enough. Primly prudish and puriticanical as he was, Snidley prided himself on never having polluted with drugs his allegedly finely-tuned metabolism. He shunned antibiotics. He boycotted standard over-the-counter remedies, such as aspirin. He'd never even tried tobacco, still less anything with psychotropic effects. And the beverage he'd guzzled as a sample in Belfast had, it transpired, been distilled not from the common toadstools he probably used in his own version, but from so-called 'magic mushrooms', the active ingredient of which was psilocybin. Such mushrooms, I knew, grew wild all over Wales and Ireland. They weren't as potent as the capsules of concentrated pscilocybin we'd ingested in the States. Delphine, who'd tried them, reported them to be no more so than some of the stronger varieties of cannabis. They were conducive to fits of giggles, to euphoria or perhaps mild paranoia, to a typically stoned sense of dislocation, of being situated slightly outside oneself, as if one'd become one's own astral double. But Snidley, unaccustomed to such psychic adventures and explorations—and, moreover, not expecting or suspecting anything of the sort—had been rampantly unsprocketed. For a person who'd come to kindergarten Taoism by way of *Jonathan Livingston Seagull*, the altered state of consciousness was disorienting.

The Belfast *kombucha* had tasted plausible enough—better, he'd ruefully acknowledged, than his own -- and he'd come to some sort of provisional agreement with its bootleggers. It was only after he'd boarded his flight back to London that the drug began to scramble his internal wiring, render his neurons soggy; and he'd soon attained an altitude well above that of the plane. What solecisms he might've committed during the course of the journey, he declined to say. But when he touched down at Heathrow, he couldn't determine where he was, and had trouble finding a telephone to ring Cassandra in a state of panic, addled and raddled. Being unnecessarily merciful, she'd gamely trekked out to the airport to collect him, and found him curled up, foetal-fashion, on a bench in one of the lounges, mumbling something about marketing rice cakes between earth and the moon.

En route home in the cab (for which, of course, she had to pay), he'd slumped back in a reasonable simulation of catalepsy. Assuming him to be merely tired, Cassandra'd tried to engage him in mundane conversation. Her queries about his quest failed to extricate him from his slough of torpor. Guessing his journey to've been in vain, she changed topics, mentioning their thirteen-year-old nephew, Clive, who'd come down from the wilds of Shropshire to spend a week with her. A few days before, the boy'd apparently gashed his arm in a fall from a bicycle. Now, he kept complaining that the scab itched, and she'd been trying to deter him from scratching it.

'Let him scratch it,' Snidley'd intoned in an oracular mumble.

'Let him scratch it? Don't be ridiculous. That's the worst thing he could do.'

'No,' Snidley'd uttered somnambulistically. 'Dogs scratch their scabs. We should learn from dogs. Dogs are wise.'

On reaching his premises, he'd skittered into another, equally bizarre, mood. Muttering something about orange and green and the need to transcend 'conflicts of colour', he'd suddenly announced the intention of dyeing all his clothes purple. Before he could attempt to implement this design, sleep summarily felled him. Cassandra'd stopped by to check on him the following morning. At some point during the night, he'd apparently wakened and undressed properly for bed. Before doing so, however, he'd placed his jeans, for some unknown reason, in the refrigerator -- which left them, of course, too cold and stiff to be worn comfortably. For whatever paranoid purpose, he'd also, it seemed, filled half a dozen socks with metal objects -- coins, nails and screws, rivets, anything else he could find -- and thereby transformed them into coshes, which were scattered at strategic points around his bedroom.

****

Some six weeks later, I'd rendezvoused with Delphine for lunch at a restaurant we both liked near Marylebone. As it often did at some point during our trysts, conversation veered towards the constantly mutating and evolving situation in Northern Ireland. From there, proceeding by association, Delphine reminisced briefly about a holiday she'd once spent with her uncle and his family in Donegal. Suddenly, she fell pensively silent.

'And the man who killed him,' she murmured softly after a moment, 'is still walking around Belfast, boasting about it.'

Her tone pierced me. It wasn't manifestly bitter. It was more wistful, wondering, slightly incredulous -- and hurt. I was aware, however, of the bitterness it concealed. And this was the first time I'd heard her even come near to expressing bitterness at what'd happened. In the television business, she'd naturally encountered the inevitable quota of twits, prats, gits, fools, dunderheads, incompetents of diverse species and sub-species. She'd learned to feel ennui, exasperation, impatience, irritation. Yet more than anyone I'd ever known, she was constitutionally incapable of genuinely wishing a person ill. She'd probably never come closer than now to wishing it on Mickey O'Hagan.

I felt a new access of protective tenderness and also a painful impotence, a helplessness to console her. Then, perverse and unjustified though it might be, I felt guilty. I suddenly regretted not having made an effort of some kind when I was in Belfast two months before. Effort to do what? I wasn't sure. In fact, I had no idea. Yet I might at least have tried to find O'Hagan's name in the directory, even though it was hardly likely to be listed. What I might've done if I'd found him, of course, remained, still, an unanswered question. Perhaps some species of psychological warfare conducted on the telephone? Something that would work in a fashion akin to voodoo? Telephone terrorism? In any case, I felt I'd been shamefully lax, inexcusably remiss.

On my way home, I stopped at the local library and checked Directory Enquiries for Belfast. There were upwards of eight or nine O'Hagans in the city, but none with M for a first initial. That effectively ruled out terror by telephone. Once back in my flat, however, I thought of 'Malediction'. Granted, it might not've worked as a curse. Not, at any rate, when read only by my immediate circle. But it might at least have an unsettling effect on O'Hagan. There remained, of course, the question of how I could possibly get it to him, not having any idea of his address.

Ordinarily, when I had a problem requiring research of this kind, I farmed it out to Snidley. In the present circumstances, however, Snidley proved consummately useless. The least idiotic of his suggestions was that I telephone MI5 or Special Branch and ask them.

'Of course! Why didn't I think of that? Just ring MI5 and tell them I'd like O'Hagan's address because I want to send him a curse. Maybe if I drop some psilocybin, I'll also be visited by trenchant inspirations.'

The resources to which Delphine had access might, perhaps, be more helpful, but I could hardly solicit her aid. If she'd known what I had in mind, she would've felt obliged to disapprove, whatever her antipathy to O'Hagan. And telephone enquiries of any sort beyond my immediate circle would very likely be hampered by the surveillance of the security forces. Lines to and from Ulster were routinely bugged. At GCHQ in Cheltenham, there was high-tech equipment programmed to record all conversations containing certain 'buzz words'. O'Hagan's name was almost certainly one such word; and any attempt to ask about him from, say, Sinn Féin's offices in Belfast would no doubt subject me to the unwelcome scrutiny of Special Branch or MI5. I had nothing to hide from them, but I couldn't expect them to sanction my meddling.

I toyed with the possibility of posting the manuscript to O'Hagan in care of Sinn Féin's offices, which I could probably locate without too much difficulty. That remained an option, but it wasn't altogether satisfactory. The narrative might well be read by other people, and might not even be passed on to its target.

I thought suddenly of Malcolm, the UVF recruiter I'd met in Edinburgh. Granted, he was on the opposite side from O'Hagan, but that might make him even more disposed to help me in my vendetta. He wouldn't, of course, have O'Hagan's address to hand, but he could almost certainly, through his network, obtain it. Whatever their reciprocal hostility, the paramilitaries in Northern Ireland still knew each other intimately -- knew each other's identities, each other's movements, each other's whereabouts, each other's most personal details. And Malcolm would perhaps understand better than anyone else. He, after all, had enunciated for me the importance of superstition, the rôle it played in the minds of the gunmen and the bombers.

I rang my contact in Edinburgh, the man who'd arranged my meeting with Malcolm. Keeping my explanation as vague and succinct as possible, I said I wanted to get in touch with Malcolm again -- preferably, if possible, by telephone.

'No telephone lines to where he is now,' my contact replied. 'Not any I know of, at least. Malcolm was shot dead. Must be three months ago or more. No one claimed responsibility, but my sources tell me it was most likely the Provies. Old scores bein' settled from over the water.'

During the month or so that followed, I tried other avenues. I thought, for example, that my intended target, even if he were ex-directory now, might've been listed in an older book, pre-dating his notoriety. I thought of trying to locate him through his family, assuming I could locate them. I thought of currying favour with any of half a dozen journalists who covered Ulster. I even thought of returning to Belfast myself, and posing as an American reporter desirous of an interview. In one way or another, for one reason or another, circumstance or better judgement thwarted all my attempts.

I concluded, eventually, that I'd have no recourse other than Sinn Féin's offices in Belfast. But if 'Malediction' were posted not from London, but from the States, ostensibly from some fervent supporter there, it would, I suspected, have a better chance of being passed on. A Boston postmark would've been most plausible, given the city's considerable Irish-American population. Most of my contacts in Boston, however, had long since migrated elsewhere; and I wasn't sufficiently close with who remained to enlist them in my scheme. I would've had to explain too much, and they would've been hesitant or sceptical. That night, accordingly, I rang Patterson in Montana, explained something of my design and solicited his collusion. I sounded, no doubt, as bonkers as Snidley; but Patterson and I were accustomed to indulging each other's idiosyncrasies, and he already knew, from previous conversations and letters, of my self-declared feud with the IRA.

I typed a brief cover note to O'Hagan, saying I was enclosing something I'd written to commemorate his deeds. Resisting the temptation to use some cryptically allusive name, I signed the first anodyne Irish-sounding appellation that came to mind, Sean Hanrahan. I typed an additional cover note, addressed this time to whomever at Sinn Féin's offices might open the package; I professed admiration for O'Hagan and requested that my manuscript be forwarded to him. If a stranger -- or, for that matter, O'Hagan himself -- skipped to the last page, there was, I realised, some risk. Too much might be given away. I was hoping, however, that any interloper reading it would start at the beginning, and find the thing too opaque to warrant further attention. The next morning, I posted my curse and its accompanying cover notes to Montana.

A week or so later, I received a postcard from Patterson, which, he said, had been dispatched at the same time as the manuscript. I could therefore assume my curse would reach Sinn Féin's offices within a day, if it hadn't already done so. Being nominally 'realistic' about such things, I didn't seriously expect anything to happen. Nevertheless, I couldn't keep from toying with tantalising possibilities. '*What if . . . ?*' After another week, however, I began to forget about the matter.

Another fortnight passed. On a Wednesday morning, Delphine, after a week in town, was due back in Belfast for a conference. Her London car having been stricken with some species of automotive embolism, I'd driven her out to Heathrow. I returned to my flat shortly before noon, walked up the hill into Hampstead and picked up cigarettes and newspapers at the tobacconist's, a sandwich at the delicatessen whose staff I'd trained to appease my tastes. Back at my flat again, I spread a newspaper open on my desk and skimmed through it while addressing myself to the sandwich.

I noticed the report only by chance. I might well've missed it, had Snidley not rung at the crucial moment to bleat about an argument he'd had with his nephew. While I pretended to listen to his inventory of grievances, my eye strayed over the page of newsprint open before me. A single succinct and neutral-sounding paragraph announced that Mickey O'Hagan, a known IRA 'volunteer' exonerated for the assassination of a distinguished jurist the year before, had died in what RUC officers called a freakish accident. He'd been changing a tyre on his car, without, apparently, having pulled the handbrake. The jack had apparently collapsed. The vehicle had rolled downhill, crushing O'Hagan beneath it in its momentum.

To this day, I don't know whether Mickey O'Hagan ever received the curse I sent him. But that night, I dreamed of a desolate derelict urban moonscape, with waste ground and lightless stumps of buildings to either side. It might, I suppose, have been Belfast, but the atmosphere it conveyed was of Chicago. I was walking through it, and someone, somewhere behind me, was whistling. I couldn't identify the tune, if there was one, but it felt disturbingly ominous, a sinister trill of menace arrowing through the dark. Perhaps as a kind of protective mantra, I muttered something to myself in German: '*Alles Vergängliche / Ist nur ein Gleichnis; / Das Unzulängliche, / Hier wirds Ereignis; / Das Unbeschreibliche, / Hier ist's getan . . .*'

At this incantation, I sensed a presence materialising beside me, keeping pace with me -- a spectral feminine figure, seemingly shaped from shifting wisps of mist which coiled and sifted like serpents around her. With a seething sibilance, she was whispering into my ear, but I couldn't decipher her words -- no more than I could discern her face through the skeins and scarves and veils of vapour mantling her. And then, abruptly, I was in my bed, dreaming in my dream that I was dreaming. '*She has been dreamed to life,*' a voice murmured, softly as wind through reeds.

Again, I sensed a presence beside me -- the same presence that'd accompanied me on my nocturnal walk, or perhaps an avatar of that one, now more substantially incarnate. In my dream, I was suddenly aware of breathing at my shoulder, the gentle serene breathing of sleep, like a silvery thread on the very threshold of sound. When I looked round at her, the beauty of Delphine's sleeping face tipped out through the darkness a soft spill of radiance.

www.ingramcontent.com/pod-product-compliance
Lightning Source LLC
Chambersburg PA
CBHW020918020726
47495CB00002B/248
9780615159379